PENGUIN BOOKS

SOVEREIGN

After a career as an attorney, C. J. Sansom now writes full time. This is his third Matthew Shardlake mystery. He is also the author of *Winter in Madrid*, a thrilling mystery and love story set amid the aftermath of Spain's bloody Civil War. He lives in Brighton, England.

Praise for *Sovereign*

"Even if heart-pounding suspense and stomach-tightening tension were all Sansom's writing brought to the table, few would feel short-changed. Added to these gifts is a superb approximation of the crucible of fear, treachery and mistrust that was Tudor England. . . . A parchment-turner, and a regal one at that."　　　　　　　　　　—*The Sunday Times* (London)

"*Sovereign*, following *Dissolution* and *Dark Fire*, is the best so far. . . . Sansom has the perfect mixture of novelistic passion and historical detail."
　　　　　　　　　　　　　—Antonia Fraser, *Sunday Telegraph* (London)

"Here is a world where life is short and brutal. Crows pick at the rotting corpses of felons left to dangle from gibbets as a warning to others. Religious persecution and political conspiracy are everywhere and trust in anyone is a dangerous assumption. The foul-smelling, festering ulcer on the leg of the now grossly obese king, in Sansom's melancholy vision, is an emblem of the larger cancer eating into the body of the politic of England."　　　　　　　—Desmond Ryan, *The Philadelphia Inquirer*

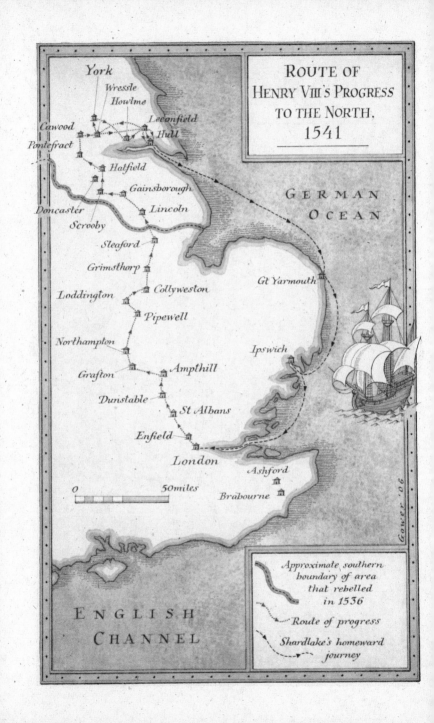

ROUTE OF
HENRY VIII'S PROGRESS
TO THE NORTH,
1541

York
Wressle
Howlme
Cawood
Leconfield
Hull
Pontefract
Hatfield
Gainsborough
Doncaster
Lincoln
Scrooby
Sleaford
Grimsthorp
GERMAN
OCEAN
Collyweston
Gt Yarmouth
Loddington
Pipewell
Northampton
Ipswich
Grafton
Ampthill
Dunstable
St Albans
Enfield
London
Ashford
Brabourne

0   50 miles

ENGLISH
CHANNEL

Gower '06

Approximate southern
boundary of area
that rebelled
in 1536
Route of progress
Shardlake's homeward
journey

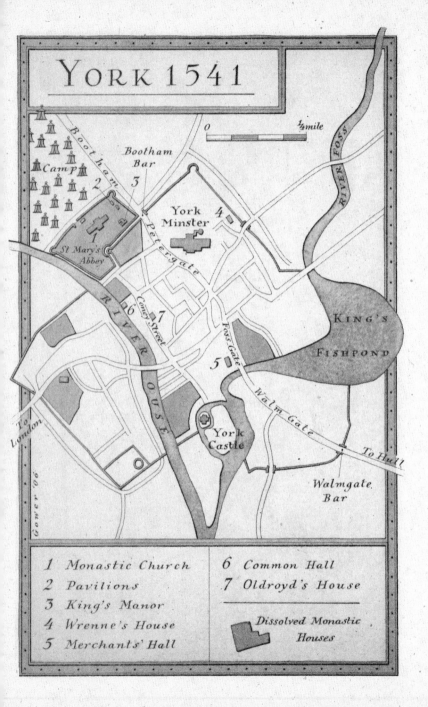

YORK 1541

0 ¼ mile

Camp

Bootham Bar

2

3

York Minster

4

St Mary's Abbey

Peter gate

RIVER FOSS

KING'S FISHPOND

6

Coney Street

7

Foss Gate

5

York Castle

RIVER OUSE

Walm Gate

To Hull

To London

Gower '06

Walmgate Bar

Bootham

1 Monastic Church
2 Pavilions
3 King's Manor
4 Wrenne's House
5 Merchants' Hall

6 Common Hall
7 Oldroyd's House

Dissolved Monastic Houses

C. J. SANSOM

Sovereign

PENGUIN BOOKS

PENGUIN BOOKS

Published by the Penguin Group

Penguin Group (USA) Inc., 375 Hudson Street, New York, New York 10014, U.S.A.
Penguin Group (Canada), 90 Eglinton Avenue East, Suite 700, Toronto,
Ontario, Canada M4P 2Y3 (a division of Pearson Penguin Canada Inc.)
Penguin Books Ltd, 80 Strand, London WC2R 0RL, England
Penguin Ireland, 25 St Stephen's Green, Dublin 2, Ireland (a division of Penguin Books Ltd)
Penguin Group (Australia), 250 Camberwell Road, Camberwell,
Victoria 3124, Australia (a division of Pearson Australia Group Pty Ltd)
Penguin Books India Pvt Ltd, 11 Community Centre,
Panchsheel Park, New Delhi – 110 017, India
Penguin Group (NZ), 67 Apollo Drive, Rosedale, North Shore 0632,
New Zealand (a division of Pearson New Zealand Ltd)
Penguin Books (South Africa) (Pty) Ltd, 24 Sturdee Avenue,
Rosebank, Johannesburg 2196, South Africa

Penguin Books Ltd, Registered Offices:
80 Strand, London WC2R 0RL, England

First published in Great Britain by Macmillan,
an imprint of Pan Macmillan Ltd 2006
First published in the United States of America by Viking Penguin,
a member of Penguin Group (USA) Inc. 2007
Published in Penguin Books 2008

5 7 9 10 8 6

PUBLISHER'S NOTE
This is a work of fiction. Names, characters, places, and incidents are either the product
of the author's imagination or are used fictitiously, and any resemblance to actual persons,
living or dead, business establishments, events, or locales is entirely coincidental.

ISBN 978-0-670-03831-2 (hc.)
ISBN 978-0-14-311317-1 (pbk.)
CIP data available

Printed in the United States of America

To P. D. James

Chapter One

IT WAS DARK UNDER the trees, only a little moonlight penetrating the half-bare branches. The ground was thick with fallen leaves; the horses' hooves made little sound and it was hard to tell whether we were still on the road. A wretched track, Barak had called it earlier, grumbling yet again about the wildness of this barbarian land I had brought him to. I had not replied for I was bone-tired, my poor back sore and my legs in their heavy riding boots as stiff as boards. I was worried, too, for the strange mission that now lay close ahead was weighing on my mind. I lifted a hand from the reins and felt in my coat pocket for the Archbishop's seal, fingering it like a talisman and remembering Cranmer's promise: 'This will be safe enough, there will be no danger.'

I had left much care behind me as well, for six days before, I had buried my father in Lichfield. Barak and I had had five days' hard riding northwards since then, the roads in a bad state after that wet summer of 1541. We rode into wild country where many villages still consisted of the old longhouses, people and cattle crammed together in hovels of thatch and sod. We left the Great North Road that afternoon at Flaxby. Barak wanted to rest the night at an inn, but I insisted we ride on, even if it took all night. I reminded him we were late, tomorrow would be the twelfth of September and we must reach our destination well before the King arrived.

The road, though, had soon turned to mud, and as night fell we had left it for a drier track that veered to the northeast, through thick woodland and bare fields where pigs rooted among the patches of yellow stubble.

The woodland turned to forest and for hours now we had been picking our way through it. We lost the main track once and it was the Devil's own job to find it again in the dark. All was silent save for the whisper of fallen leaves and an occasional clatter of brushwood as a boar or wildcat fled from us. The horses, laden with panniers containing our clothes and other necessities, were as exhausted as Barak and I. I could feel Genesis' tiredness and Sukey, Barak's normally energetic mare, was content to follow his slow pace.

'We're lost,' he grumbled.

'They said at the inn to follow the main path south through the forest. Anyway, it must be daylight soon,' I said. 'Then we'll see where we are.'

Barak grunted wearily. 'Feels like we've ridden to Scotland. I wouldn't be surprised if we get taken for ransom.' I did not reply, tired at his complaining, and we plodded on silently.

My mind went back to my father's funeral the week before. The little group of people round the grave, the coffin lowered into the earth. My cousin Bess, who had found him dead in his bed when she brought him a parcel of food.

'I wish I had known how ill he was,' I told her when we returned to the farm afterwards. 'It should have been me that looked after him.'

She shook her head wearily. 'You were far away in London and we'd not seen you for over a year.' Her eyes had an accusing look.

'I have had difficult times of my own, Bess. But I would have come.'

She sighed. 'It was old William Poer dying last autumn undid him. They'd wrestled to get a profit from the farm these last few years and he seemed to give up.' She paused. 'I said he should contact you, but he wouldn't. God sends us hard trials. The droughts last summer, now the floods this year. I think he was ashamed of the money troubles he'd got into. Then the fever took him.'

I nodded. It had been a shock to learn that the farm where I had grown up, and which now was mine, was deep in debt. My father had been near seventy, his steward William not much younger. Their care of the land had not been all it should and the last few harvests had been poor. To get by he had taken a mortgage on the farm with a rich landowner in Lichfield. The first I knew of it was when the mortgagee wrote to me, immediately after Father's death, to say he doubted the value of the land would clear the debt. Like many gentry in those days he was seeking to increase his acreage for sheep, and granting mortgages to elderly farmers at exorbitant interest was one way of doing it.

'That bloodsucker Sir Henry,' I said bitterly to Bess.

'What will you do? Let the estate go insolvent?'

'No,' I said. 'I won't disgrace Father's name. I'll pay it.' I thought, God knows I owe him that.

'That is good.'

I came to with a start at the sound of a protesting whicker behind me. Barak had pulled on Sukey's reins, bringing her to a stop. I halted too and turned uncomfortably in the saddle. His outline and that of the trees were sharper now, it was beginning to get light. He pointed in front of him. 'Look there!'

Ahead the trees were thinning. In the distance I saw a red point of light, low in the sky.

'There!' I said triumphantly. 'The lamp we were told to look out for, that's set atop a church steeple to guide travellers. This is the Galtres Forest, like I said!'

We rode out of the trees. A cold wind blew up from the river as the sky lightened. We wrapped our coats tighter round us and rode down, towards York.

✝

THE MAIN ROAD into the city was already filled with packhorses and carts loaded with food of every kind. There were enormous forester's carts too, whole tree-trunks dangling dangerously over their tails. Ahead the high city walls came into view, black with the smoke of hundreds of years, and beyond were the steeples of innumerable churches, all dominated by the soaring twin towers of York Minster. 'It's busy as Cheapside on a market-day,' I observed.

'All for the King's great retinue.'

We rode slowly on, the throng so dense we scarce managed a walking pace. I cast sidelong glances at my companion. It was over a year now since I had taken Jack Barak on as assistant in my barrister's practice after his old master's execution. A former child of the London streets who had ended up working on dubious missions for Thomas Cromwell, he was an unlikely choice, even though he was clever and had the good fortune to be literate. Yet I had not regretted it. He had adjusted well to working for me, doggedly learning the law. No one was better at keeping witnesses to the point while preparing affidavits, or ferreting out obscure facts, and his cynical, slantwise view of the system was a useful corrective to my own enthusiasm.

These last few months, however, Barak had often seemed downcast, and sometimes would forget his place and become as oafish and mocking as when I had first met him. I feared he might be getting bored, and thought bringing him to York might rouse him out of himself. He was, though, full of a Londoner's prejudices against the north and northerners, and had complained and griped almost the whole way. Now he was looking dubiously around him, suspicious of everything.

Houses appeared straggling along the road and then, to our right, a high old crenellated wall over which an enormous steeple was visible. Soldiers patrolled the top of the wall, wearing iron helmets and the white tunics with a red cross of royal longbowmen. Instead of bows and arrows, though, they carried swords and fearsome pikes, and some even bore long matchlock guns. A great sound of banging and hammering came from within.

'That must be the old St Mary's Abbey, where we'll be staying,' I said. 'Sounds like there's a lot of work going on to make it ready for the King.'

'Shall we go there now, leave our bags?'

'No, we should see Brother Wrenne first, then go to the castle.'

'To see the prisoner?' he asked quietly.

'Ay.'

Barak looked up at the walls. 'St Mary's is guarded well.'

'The King will be none too sure of his welcome, after all that's happened up here.'

I had spoken softly, but the man in front of us, walking beside a packhorse laden with grain, turned and gave us a sharp look. Barak raised his eyebrows and he looked away. I wondered if he was one of the Council of the North's informers; they would be working overtime in York now.

'Perhaps you should put on your lawyer's robe,' Barak suggested, nodding ahead. The carts and packmen were turning into the abbey through a large gate in the wall. Just past the gate the abbey wall met the city wall at right angles, hard by a fortress-like gatehouse decorated with the York coat of arms, five white lions against a red background. More guards were posted there, holding pikes and wearing steel helmets and breastplates. Beyond the wall, the Minster towers were huge now against the grey sky.

'I'm not fetching it out of my pack, I'm too tired.' I patted my coat pocket. 'I've got the Chamberlain's authority here.' Archbishop Cranmer's seal was there too; but that was only to be shown to one person. I stared ahead, at something I had been told to expect yet which still made me shudder: four heads fixed to tall poles, boiled and black and half eaten by crows. I knew that twelve of the rebel conspirators arrested that spring had been executed in York, their heads and quarters set on all the city gates as a warning to others.

We halted at the end of a little queue, the horses' heads drooping with tiredness. The guards had stopped a poorly dressed man and were questioning him roughly about his business in the city.

'I wish he'd hurry up,' Barak whispered. 'I'm starving.'

'I know. Come on, it's us next.'

One of the guards grabbed Genesis' reins while another asked my business. He had a southern accent and a hard, lined face. I showed him my letter of authority. 'King's lawyer?' he asked.

'Ay. And my assistant. Here to help with the pleas before His Majesty.'

'It's a firm hand they need up here,' he said. He rolled the paper up and waved us on. As we rode under the barbican I recoiled from the sight of a great hank of flesh nailed to the gate, buzzing with flies.

'Rebel's meat,' Barak said with a grimace.

'Ay.' I shook my head at the tangles of fate. But for the conspiracy that spring I should not be here, and nor would the King be making his Progress to the North, the largest and most splendid ever seen in England. We rode under the gate, the horses' hooves making a sudden clatter inside the enclosed barbican, and through into the city.

✝

BEYOND THE GATE was a narrow street of three-storey houses with overhanging eaves, full of shops with stalls set out in front, the traders sitting on their wooden blocks calling their wares. York struck me as a poor place. Some of the houses were in serious disrepair, black timbers showing through where plaster had fallen off, and the street was little more than a muddy lane. The jostling crowds made riding difficult, but I knew Master Wrenne, like all the city's senior lawyers, lived in the Minster Close and it was easy to find, for the Minster dominated the whole city.

'I'm hungry,' Barak observed. 'Let's get some breakfast.'

Another high wall appeared ahead of us; York seemed a city of walls. Behind it the Minster loomed. Ahead was a large open space crowded with market stalls under brightly striped awnings that flapped in the cool damp breeze. Heavy-skirted goodwives argued with stallholders while artisans in the bright livery of their guilds looked down their noses at the stalls' contents, and dogs and ragged children dived for scraps. I saw most of the people had patched clothes and worn-looking clogs. Watchmen in livery bearing the city arms stood about, observing the crowds.

A group of tall, yellow-haired men with dogs led a flock of odd-looking sheep with black faces round the edge of the market. I looked curiously at their weather-beaten faces and heavy woollen coats; these must be the legendary Dalesmen who had formed the backbone of the rebellion five years before. In contrast, black-robed clerics and chantry priests in their brown hoods were passing in and out of a gate in the wall that led into the Minster precinct.

Barak had ridden to a pie-stall a few paces off. He leaned from his horse and asked how much for two mutton pies. The stallholder stared at him, not understanding his London accent.

'Southrons?' he grunted.

'Ay. We're hungry. How much – for – two – mutton pies?' Barak spoke loudly and slowly, as though to an idiot.

The stallholder glared at him. 'Is't my blame tha gabblest like a duck?' he asked.

''Tis you that grates your words like a knife scrating a pan.'

Two big Dalesmen passing along the stalls paused and looked round. 'This southron dog giving thee trouble?' one asked the trader. The other reached out a big horny hand to Sukey's reins.

'Let go, churl,' Barak said threateningly.

I was surprised by the anger that came into the man's face. 'Cocky southron knave. Tha thinkest since fat Harry is coming tha can insult us as tha likest.'

'Kiss my arse,' Barak said, looking at the man steadily.

The Dalesman reached a hand to his sword; Barak's hand darted to his own scabbard. I forced a way through the crowd.

'Excuse us, sir,' I said soothingly, though my heart beat fast. 'My man meant no harm. We've had a hard ride—'

The man gave me a look of disgust. 'A crookback lord, eh? Come here on tha fine hoss to cozen us out of what little money we have left up here?' He began to draw his sword, then stopped as a pike was jabbed into his chest. Two of the city guards, scenting trouble, had hurried over.

'Swords away!' one snapped, his pike held over the Dalesman's heart, while the other did the same to Barak. A crowd began to gather.

'What's this hubbleshoo?' the guard snapped.

'That southron insulted the stallholder,' someone called.

The guard nodded. He was stocky, middle-aged, with sharp eyes. 'They've no manners, the southrons,' he said loudly. 'Got to expect that, maister.' There was a laugh from the crowd; a bystander clapped.

'We only want a couple of bleeding pies,' Barak said.

The guard nodded at the stallholder. 'Gi'e him two pies.'

The man handed two mutton pies up to Barak. 'A tanner,' he said.

'A what?'

The stallholder raised his eyes to heaven. 'Sixpence.'

'For two pies?' Barak asked incredulously.

'Pay him,' the guard snapped. Barak hesitated and I hastily passed over the coins. The stallholder bit them ostentatiously before slipping them in his purse. The guard leaned close to me. 'Now, sir, shift. And tell thy man to watch his manners. Tha doesn't want trouble for't King's visit, hey?' He raised his eyebrows, and watched as Barak and I rode back to the gates to the precinct. We dismounted stiffly at a bench set against the wall, tied up the horses and sat down.

'God's nails, my legs are sore,' Barak said.

'Mine too.' They felt as though they did not belong to me, and my back ached horribly.

Barak bit into the pie. 'This is good,' he said in tones of surprise.

I lowered my voice. 'You must watch what you say. You know they don't like us up here.'

'The feeling's mutual. Arseholes.' He glared threateningly in the direction of the stallholder.

'Listen,' I said quietly. 'They're trying to keep everything calm. If you treat people like you did those folk you don't just risk a sword in the guts for both of us, but trouble for the Progress. Is that what you want?'

He did not reply, frowning at his feet.

'What's the matter with you these days?' I asked. 'You've been Tom Touchy for weeks. You used to be able to keep that sharp tongue of yours in check. You got me in trouble last month, calling Judge Jackson a blear-eyed old caterpillar within his hearing.'

He gave me one of his sudden wicked grins. 'You know he is.'

I was not to be laughed off. 'What's amiss, Jack?'

He shrugged. 'Nothing. I just don't like being up here among these barbarian wantwits.' He looked at me directly. 'I'm sorry I made trouble. I'll take care.'

Apologies did not come easily to Barak, and I nodded in acknowledgement. But there was more to his mood than dislike of the north, I was sure. I turned thoughtfully to my pie. Barak looked over the marketplace with his sharp dark eyes. 'They're a poor-looking lot,' he observed.

'Trade's been bad here for years. And the dissolution of the monasteries has made things worse. There was a lot of monkish property here. Three or four years ago there would have been many monks' and friars' robes among that crowd.'

'Well, that's all done with.' Barak finished his pie, rubbing a hand across his mouth.

I rose stiffly. 'Let's find Wrenne. Get our instructions.'

'D'you think we'll get to see the King when he comes?' Barak asked. 'Close to?'

'It's possible.'

He blew out his cheeks. I was glad to see I was not the only one intimidated by that prospect. 'And there is an old enemy in his train,' I added, 'that we'd better avoid.'

He turned sharply. 'Who?'

'Sir Richard Rich. He'll be arriving with the King and the Privy

Council. Cranmer told me. So like I said, take care. Don't draw attention to us. We should try to escape notice, so far as we can.'

We untied the horses and led them to the gate, where another guard with a pike barred our way. I produced my letter again, and he raised the weapon to let us pass through. The great Minster reared up before us.

Chapter Two

'IT'S BIG ENOUGH,' Barak said.

We were in a wide paved enclosure with buildings round the edges, all overshadowed by the Minster. 'The greatest building in the north. It must be near as big as St Paul's.' I looked at the giant entrance doors under the intricately decorated Gothic arch, where men of business stood talking. Below them, on the stairs, a crowd of beggars sat with their alms bowls. I was tempted to look inside but turned away, for we should have been at Wrenne's house yesterday. I remembered the directions I had been given, and noted a building with the royal arms above the door. 'It's just past there,' I said. We led the horses across the courtyard, careful not to slip on the leaves that had fallen from the trees planted round the close.

'D'you know what manner of man this Wrenne is?' Barak asked.

'Only that he's a well-known barrister in York and has done much official work. He's well stricken in years, I believe.'

'Let's hope he's not some old nid-nod that's beyond the work.'

'He must be competent to be organizing the pleas to the King. Trusted, too.'

We walked the horses into a street of old houses packed closely together. I had been told to seek the corner house on the right, and this proved to be a tall building, very ancient-looking. I knocked. Shuffling footsteps sounded within and the door was opened by an aged dame with a round wrinkled face framed by a white coif. She looked at me sourly.

'Ay?'

'Master Wrenne's house?'

'Ar't gentlemen from London?'

I raised my eyebrows a little at her lack of deference. 'Yes. I am Matthew Shardlake. This is my assistant, Master Barak.'

'We expected thee yesterday. Poor maister's been fretting.'

'We got lost in Galtres Forest.'

'Tha's not t'first to do that.'

I nodded at the horses. 'We and our mounts are tired.'

'Bone-weary,' Barak added pointedly.

'Tha'd best come in then. I'll get the boy to stable thy horses and wash them down.'

'I should be grateful.'

'Maister Wrenne's out on business, but he'll be back soon. I suppose tha'd like some food.'

'Thank you.' The pie had merely taken the edge from my hunger.

The old woman turned and, shuffling slowly, led us into a high central hall built in the old style with a hearth in the centre of the floor. A fire of coppice-wood was lit and smoke ascended lazily to the chimney-hole high in the black rafters. Good silver plate was displayed on the buffet, but the curtain behind the table that stood on a dais at the head of the room looked dusty. A peregrine falcon with magnificent grey plumage stood on a perch near the fire. It turned huge predatory eyes on us as I stared at the piles of books that lay everywhere, on chairs, on the oak chest and set against the walls, in stacks that looked ready to topple over. I had never seen so many books in one place outside a library.

'Your master is fond of books,' I observed.

'That he is,' the old woman answered. 'I'll get tha some pottage.' She shuffled away.

'Some beer would be welcome as well,' I called after her. Barak plumped down on a settle covered with a thick sheepskin rug and cushions. I picked up a large old volume bound in calfskin. I opened it, then raised my eyebrows. 'God's nails. This is one of the old hand-illustrated books the monks made.' I flicked through the pages.

It was a copy of Bede's *History*, with beautiful calligraphy and illustrations.

'I thought they'd all gone to the fire,' Barak observed. 'He should be careful.'

'Yes, he should. Not a reformer, then.' I replaced the book, coughing as a little cloud of dust rose up. 'Jesu, that housekeeper skimps her labours.'

'Looks like she's past it to me. But maybe she's more than a housekeeper, if he's old too. Don't think much of his taste if she is.' Barak settled himself on the cushions and closed his eyes. I sat down in an armchair and tried to arrange my stiff legs comfortably. I felt my own eyes closing, coming to with a start as the old woman reappeared, bearing two bowls of steaming pease pottage and two flagons of beer on a tray. We set to eagerly. The pottage was tasteless and unspiced, but filling. Afterwards Barak closed his eyes again. I thought of nudging him awake, for it was ill-mannered to go to sleep in our host's hall, but I knew how tired he was. It was peaceful there, the noise from the close muffled by the windows of mullioned glass, the fire crackling gently. I closed my eyes too. My hand brushed the pocket where Archbishop Cranmer's seal lay, and I found myself thinking back a couple of weeks, to when the trail of events that had led me here began.

☩

THE LAST YEAR HAD BEEN a difficult time for me. Since Thomas Cromwell's fall, those associated with him could be dangerous to know, and a number of clients had withdrawn their work. And I had gone against convention by representing the London Guildhall in a case against a fellow barrister of Lincoln's Inn. Stephen Bealknap may have been one of the greatest rogues God ever set on earth, but I had still offended against professional solidarity in acting against him, and some fellow barristers who might once have put cases my way now avoided me. Things were not made easier by the fact that

Bealknap had one of the most powerful patrons in the land behind him: Sir Richard Rich, Chancellor of the Court of Augmentations. Then, at the beginning of September, had come the news of my father's death. I was still in a state of shock and grief when, going into chambers one morning a few days later, I found Barak waiting for me, a worried expression on his face.

'Sir, I must speak with you.' He glanced at my clerk Skelly, who sat copying, his glasses glinting in the light from the window, then jerked his head towards my office. I nodded.

'A messenger came while you were out,' he said when the door was closed behind us. 'From Lambeth Palace. Archbishop Cranmer himself wants to see you there at eight tonight.'

I sat down heavily. 'I thought I was done with visits to great men.' I looked at Barak sharply, for our assignment for Cromwell the year before had made us some powerful enemies. 'Could it mean danger for us? Have you heard any gossip?' I knew he still had contacts in the underside of the King's court.

He shook his head. 'Nothing since I was told we were safe.'

I sighed deeply. 'Well then, I shall have to see.'

That day it was hard to keep my mind on my work. I left early, to go home for dinner. As I walked towards the gate I saw, coming in, a tall, thin figure in a fine silk robe, blond curls peeping out from under his cap. Stephen Bealknap. The most crooked and covetous lawyer I ever met. He bowed to me.

'Brother Bealknap,' I said politely, as the conventions of the inn demanded.

'Brother Shardlake. I hear there is no date for the hearing of our case in Chancery. They are so slow.' He shook his head, though I knew he welcomed the delay. The case involved a little dissolved friary he had bought near the Cripplegate. He had converted it into tumbledown tenements without proper sewage arrangements, causing great nuisance to his neighbours. The case turned on whether he was entitled to rely on the monastery's exemption from City Council regulations. He was backed by Richard Rich, as Chancellor of the

Court of Augmentations that handled the property of the dissolved monasteries, because if he lost the case, the sale value of those properties would fall.

'The Six Clerks' Office seems unable to explain the delays,' I told Bealknap. I had sent Barak, who could be intimidating when he chose, to harangue them several times, but without result. 'Perhaps your friend Richard Rich may know.' I immediately wished I had not said that, for I was effectively accusing the Chancellor of Augmentations of corruption. The slip showed the strain I was under.

Bealknap shook his head. 'You are a naughty fellow, Brother Shardlake, to allege such things. What would the Inn Treasurer say?'

I bit my lip. 'I am sorry. I withdraw.'

Bealknap grinned broadly, showing nasty yellow teeth. 'I forgive you, brother. When one has poor prospects in a case, sometimes the worry of it makes you forget what you say.' He bowed and walked on. I looked after him, wishing I could have planted a foot in his bony arse.

✝

AFTER DINNER I DONNED my lawyer's robe and took a wherry across the river and down to Lambeth Palace. London was quiet, as it had been all summer, for the King and his court were in the north of England. In the spring news had come of a fresh rebellion nipped in the bud in Yorkshire, and the King had decided to take a great progress up to awe the northmen. They said he and his councillors had been sore alarmed. As well they might be; five years before the whole north of England had risen in rebellion against the religious changes and the Pilgrimage of Grace, as the rebel army had called itself, had raised thirty thousand men. The King had gulled them into disbanding with false promises, then raised an army to strike them down. But all feared the north might rise again.

Throughout June the King's purveyors had roamed all London, clearing shops and warehouses of food and other supplies, for they said three thousand people would be going north. It was hard to

comprehend such numbers, the population of a small town. When
they left at the end of June it was said the carts stretched along the
road for over a mile, and London had been strangely quiet all
through that wet summer.

The boatman pulled past the Lollards' Tower at the north end
of Lambeth Palace and in the failing daylight I saw a light shining
from the window of the prison atop the tower, where heretics in the
Archbishop's custody were held. Cranmer's eye on London, some
called it. We pulled up at the Great Stairs. A guard admitted me
and led me across the courtyard to the Great Hall, where he left
me alone.

I stood staring up at the magnificent hammerbeam roof. A black-
robed clerk approached, soft footed. 'The Archbishop will see you
now,' he said quietly. He led me into a warren of dim corridors, his
footsteps pattering lightly on the rush matting.

I was taken to a small, low-ceilinged study. Thomas Cranmer
sat behind a desk, reading papers by the light of a sconce of candles
set beside him. A fire burned energetically in the grate. I bowed
deeply before the great Archbishop who had renounced the Pope's
authority, married the King to Anne Boleyn, and been Thomas
Cromwell's friend and confederate in every reforming scheme. When
Cromwell fell many had expected Cranmer to go to the block too,
but he had survived, despite the halt to reform. Henry had placed
him in charge in London while he was away. It was said the King
trusted him as no other.

In a deep, quiet voice he bade me sit. I had only seen him at a
distance before, preaching. He wore a white clerical robe with a fur
stole but had cast off his cap, revealing a shock of greying black hair.
I noticed the pallor of his broad, oval face, the lines around the full
mouth, but above all his eyes. They were large, dark blue. As he
studied me I read anxiety there, and conflict and passion.

'So you are Matthew Shardlake,' he said. He smiled pleasantly,
seeking to put me at ease.

'My lord Archbishop.'

I took a hard chair facing him. A large pectoral cross, solid silver, glinted on his chest.

'How goes trade at Lincoln's Inn?' he asked.

I hesitated. 'It has been better.'

'Times are hard for those who worked for Earl Cromwell.'

'Yes, my lord,' I said cautiously.

'I wish they would take his head from London Bridge. I see it each time I cross. What the gulls have left.'

'It is a sad thing to see.'

'I visited him, you know, in the Tower. I confessed him. He told me of that last matter he engaged you in.'

My eyes widened and I felt a chill despite the heat from the fire. So Cranmer knew about that.

'I told the King about the Dark Fire quest. Some months ago.' I caught my breath, but Cranmer smiled and raised a beringed hand. 'I waited until his anger against Lord Cromwell over the Cleves marriage faded, and he'd begun to miss his counsel. Those responsible for what happened walk on eggshells now; though they denied they were behind it, they dissembled and lied.'

A chilling thought came to me. 'My lord — does the King know of my involvement?'

He shook his head reassuringly. 'Lord Cromwell asked me not to tell the King; he knew you had served him as well as you could, and that you preferred to stay a private man.'

So he had thought of me kindly at the end, that harsh great man facing a savage death. I felt sudden tears prick at the corners of my eyes.

'He had many fine qualities, Master Shardlake, for all his hard measures. I told the King only that servants of Lord Cromwell's had been involved. His Majesty left matters there, though he was angry with those who had deceived him. He told the Duke of Norfolk not long ago he wished he had Lord Cromwell back, said he'd been tricked into executing the greatest servant he ever had. As he was.' Cranmer looked at me seriously. 'Lord Cromwell said you were a man of rare discretion, good at keeping even the greatest matters secret.'

'That is part of my trade.'

He smiled. 'In that hotbed of gossip, the Inns of Court? No, the Earl said your discretion was of rare quality.'

Then I realized with a jolt that Cromwell, in the Tower, had been telling Cranmer about people who might be of use to him.

'I was sorry to hear your father died,' the Archbishop said.

My eyes widened. How had he known that? He caught my look and smiled sadly. 'I asked the Inn Treasurer if you were in London, and he told me. I wished to speak to you, you see. May God rest your father's soul.'

'Amen, my lord.'

'He lived in Lichfield, I believe?'

'Yes. I must leave for there in two days, for the funeral.'

'The King is well north of there now. At Hatfield. The Great Progress has had a hard time of it, with all the rains in July. The post-riders were delayed; often ascertaining the King's wishes was not easy.' He shook his head, a strained expression crossing his features. They said Cranmer was no skilful politician.

'It has been a poor summer,' I observed. 'As wet as last year's was dry.'

'Thank God it has lately improved. It made the Queen ill.'

'People say she is pregnant,' I ventured.

The Archbishop frowned. 'Rumours,' he said. He paused a moment as though gathering his thoughts, then continued. 'As you may know, there are several lawyers with the royal train. This is the greatest Progress ever seen in England, and lawyers are needed so that disputes that arise within the royal court, and with suppliers along the way, may be resolved.' He took a deep breath. 'Also, the King has promised the northmen his justice. At every town he invites petitioners with complaints against the local officialdom, and lawyers are needed to sort through them, weed out the petty and the foolish, arbitrate where they can and send the rest to the Council of the

North. One of the King's lawyers has died, poor fellow, he took pneumonia. The Chamberlain's office sent a message asking the Council to send a replacement to meet the Progress at York, for there will be much business there. I remembered you.'

'Oh.' This was not what I had expected; this was a favour.

'And if you are going halfway there already, so much the better. You'd return with the Progress next month, and bring back fifty pounds for your work. You'd only be allowed one servant; best to take your assistant rather than a bodyservant.'

That was generous, even for the high rewards royal service brought. Yet I hesitated, for I had no wish to go anywhere near the King's court again. I took a deep breath.

'My lord, I hear Sir Richard Rich is with the Progress.'

'Ah, yes. You made an enemy of Rich over the Dark Fire matter.'

'And I am still involved in a case in which he has an interest. Rich would do me any ill turn he could.'

The Archbishop shook his head. 'You need have no dealings with Rich or any royal councillor. He is there in his role as Chancellor of the Court of Augmentations, to advise the King on the disposition of lands seized in Yorkshire from the rebels. Neither the councillors nor the King have any real involvement with the petitions – the lawyers deal with everything.'

I hesitated. This would solve my financial worries, ensure I could discharge my responsibility to my father. Moreover, something stirred in me at the prospect of seeing this great spectacle; it would be the journey of a lifetime. And it might distract me from my sorrow.

The Archbishop inclined his head. 'Be quick, Master Shardlake. I have little time.'

'I will go, my lord,' I said. 'Thank you.'

The Archbishop nodded. 'Good.' Then he leaned forward, the heavy sleeves of his tunic rustling as they brushed the papers on his desk. 'I also have a small private mission,' he said. 'Something I would like you to do for me in York.'

I caught my breath. I had let him spring a trap. He was a good politician after all.

The Archbishop saw my expression and shook his head. 'Do not worry, sir. There is no scurrying after danger in this, and the mission itself is a virtuous one. It requires only a certain authority of manner, and above all –' he looked at me sharply – 'discretion.'

I set my lips. Cranmer made a steeple of his fingers and looked at me.

'You know the purpose of the Great Progress to the North?' he asked.

'To show the King's power in those rebellious parts, establish his authority.'

'They say the north is the last place God made,' Cranmer said with sudden anger. 'They are a barbarous people there, still mired in papist heresy.'

I nodded but said nothing, waiting for him to show his hand.

'Lord Cromwell established forceful government in the north after the rebellion five years ago. The new Council of the North employs many spies, and it is as well they do, for the new conspiracy they discovered last spring was serious.' He stared at me with those passionate eyes. 'Last time they called only for the King to rid himself of reformist advisers.'

Like you, I thought; they would have had Cranmer in the fire.

'This time they called him tyrant, they wanted to overthrow him. And they planned an alliance with the Scotch, though the northmen have always hated them as even worse barbarians than themselves. But the Scotch, like them, are papists. Had their plan not been exposed, Jesu knows what might have followed.'

I took a deep breath. He was telling me secrets I did not wish to hear. Secrets that would bind me to him.

'Not all the conspirators were caught. Many escaped to the wild mountains up there. There is still much we have to learn about their plans. There is a certain conspirator of York, recently taken prisoner there, who is to be brought back to London by boat. Sir Edward

Broderick.' Cranmer set his lips tight, and for a moment I saw fear in his face.

'There is an aspect of the conspirators' plans that is not generally known. Only a few of the conspirators knew, and we believe Broderick was one. It is better you do not know about it. No one does except the King, and a few trusted councillors in London and York. Broderick will not talk. The King sent questioners to York but they got nowhere, he is obstinate as Satan. He is to be brought from York to Hull in a sealed wagon when the Progress moves on there, then sent back to London by boat, guarded by the most loyal and trusted men. The King wants to be in London when he is questioned, and it is safe to question him only in the Tower, where we can trust the interrogators and be sure their skill will extract the truth from him.'

I knew what that meant. Torture. I took a deep breath. 'How does this involve me, my lord?'

His reply surprised me. 'I want you to ensure he is alive and in good health when he arrives.'

'But – will he not be in the King's care?'

'The Duke of Suffolk is in charge of arrangements for the Progress, and he chose Broderick's gaoler. A man who can be trusted, although even he has not been told what we suspect of Broderick. He is in charge of Broderick in the prison at York Castle. His name is Fulke Radwinter.'

'I do not know that name, my lord.'

'The appointment was made hurriedly, and I have been – concerned.' The Archbishop pursed his lips, fiddling with a brass seal on his desk. 'Radwinter has experience of guarding and of – questioning – heretics. He is a man of true and honest faith, and can be trusted to keep Broderick under close guard.' He took a deep breath. 'Yet Radwinter can be too severe. A prisoner once – died.' He frowned. 'I want someone else present, to keep an eye on Broderick's welfare till he can be brought to the Tower.'

'I see.'

'I have already written to the Duke of Suffolk, obtained his agreement. He understands my point, I think.' He picked up the seal and laid it flat on the desk before me. A big oval lozenge, Cranmer's name and office traced in Latin round the edge, a portrayal of the scourging of Christ in the centre. 'I want you to take this, as your authority. You will have overall charge of Broderick's welfare, in York and then on to London. You will not talk to him beyond asking after his welfare, ensuring he comes to no harm. Radwinter knows I am sending someone, he will respect my authority.' The Archbishop smiled again, that sad smile of his. 'He is my own employee; he guards the prisoners under my jurisdiction, in the Lollards' Tower.'

'I understand,' I said neutrally.

'If the prisoner be bound uncomfortably, make the fetters looser though no less certain. If he is hungry, give him food. If he is ill, ensure he has medical care.' Cranmer smiled. 'There, that is a charitable commission, is it not?'

I took a deep breath. 'My lord,' I said. 'I undertook to go to York only on a matter of pleas before the King. My past service on matters of state has cost me much in peace of mind. Now I wish to remain, as Lord Cromwell said, a private man. I have seen men die most horribly—'

'Then ensure for me that a man lives,' Cranmer said quietly, 'and in decent conditions. That is all I want, and I think you are the man for it. I was a private man once, Master Shardlake, a Cambridge don. Until the King plucked me out to advise on the Great Divorce. Sometimes God calls us to hard duty. Then –' his look was hard again – 'then we must find the stomach for it.'

I looked at him. If I refused I would no doubt lose my place on the Progress, and might be unable to redeem the mortgage on the farm. And I had made enemies at court, I dared not alienate the Archbishop too. I was trapped. I took a deep breath.

'Very well, my lord.'

He smiled. 'I will have your commission sent to your house

tomorrow. To act as counsel on the Progress.' He picked up the seal
and set it in my hand. It was heavy. 'And that is my authority to
show Radwinter. No papers.'

'May I tell my assistant? Barak?'

Cranmer nodded. 'Yes. I know Lord Cromwell trusted him.
Though he said neither of you had real zeal for reform.' He gave me
a sudden questing look. 'Though you did, once.'

'I served my apprenticeship.'

The Archbishop nodded. 'I know. You are one of those who
worked in the early days to bring England to religious truth.' He
gave me a keen look. 'The truth that the right head of the Church
in England is not the Bishop of Rome, but the King, set by God
above his people as Supreme Head, to guide them. When the King's
conscience is moved it is God who speaks through him.'

'Yes, my lord,' I said, though I had never believed that.

'These conspirators are dangerous and wicked men. Harsh
measures have been needed. I do not like them, but they have been
forced upon us. To protect what we have achieved. Though there is
much more to be done if we are to build the Christian common-
wealth in England.'

'There is indeed, my lord.'

He smiled, taking my words for agreement. 'Then go, Master
Shardlake, and may God guide your enterprise.' He rose in dismissal.
I bowed my way out of the chamber. As I walked away, I thought,
this is no charitable mission. I am keeping a man safe for the torturers
in the Tower. And what had this Broderick done, to bring that look
of fear to Cranmer's eyes?

✝

MY MUSINGS WERE interrupted by voices outside the room. I
nudged Barak awake with my foot, and we stood up hurriedly,
wincing, for our legs were still stiff. The door opened and a man in
a rather threadbare lawyer's robe came in. Master Wrenne was a
square-built man, very tall, overtopping Barak by a head. I was

relieved to see that although he was indeed elderly, his square face deeply lined, he walked steady and straight and the blue eyes under the faded reddish-gold hair were keen. He gripped my hand.

'Master Shardlake,' he said in a clear voice with a strong touch of the local accent. 'Or Brother Shardlake I should say, my brother in the law. Giles Wrenne. It is good to see you. Why, we feared you had met with an accident on the road.'

I noticed that as he studied me his eyes did not linger over my bent back, as most people's do. A man of sensitivity. 'I fear I got us lost. May I introduce my assistant, Jack Barak.'

Barak bowed, then shook Wrenne's extended hand.

'By Jesu,' the old man said. 'That's a champion grip for a law-clerk.' He clapped him on the shoulder. 'Good to see, our young men take too little exercise now. So many clerks these days have a pasty look.' Wrenne looked at the empty plates. 'I see my good Madge has fed you. Excellent.' He moved over to the fire. The falcon turned to him, a little bell tied to its foot jingling, and let him stroke its neck. 'There, my old Octavia, hast tha kept warm?' He turned to us with a smile. 'This bird and I have hunted around York through many a winter, but we are both too old now. Please, be seated again. I am sorry I cannot accommodate you while you are in the city.' He eased himself into a chair, and looked ruefully at the dusty furniture and books. 'I fear since my poor wife died three years ago I have not kept up her standards of housekeeping. A man alone. I only keep Madge and a boy, and Madge is getting old, she could not cater for three. But she was my wife's maid.'

So much for Barak's theory about Madge, I thought. 'We have accommodation at St Mary's, but thank you.'

'Yes.' Wrenne smiled and rubbed his hands together. 'And there will be much of interest to see there, the Progress in all its glory when it arrives. You will want to rest now. I suggest you both come here at ten tomorrow morning, and we can spend the day working through the petitions.'

'Very well. There seems to be much work going on at St Mary's,' I added.

The old man nodded. 'They say any number of wondrous buildings are being erected. And that Lucas Hourenbout is there, supervising it all.'

'Hourenbout? The King's Dutch artist?'

Wrenne nodded, smiling. 'They say the greatest designer in the land, after Holbein.'

'So he is. I did not know he was here.'

'It seems the place is being prepared for some great ceremony. I have not seen it, only those with business are allowed into St Mary's. Some say the Queen is pregnant, and is to be crowned here. But no one knows.' He paused. 'Have you heard anything?'

'Only the same gossip.' I remembered Cranmer's annoyance when I had mentioned that rumour.

'Ah well. We Yorkers will be told when it is good for us to know.'

I looked at Wrenne sharply, detecting a note of bitterness under the bluffness. 'Perhaps Queen Catherine will be crowned,' I said. 'After all, she's lasted over a year now.' I made the remark deliberately; I wanted to establish that I was not one of those stiff-necked people in the royal employ that would talk of the King only with formal reverence.

Wrenne smiled and nodded, getting the point. 'Well, we shall have much work to do on the petitions. I am glad of your assistance. We have to weed out the silly fratches, like the man disputing with the Council of the North over an inch of land, whose papers I read yesterday.' He laughed. 'But you will be familiar with such nonsense, brother.'

'Indeed I am. Property law is my specialism.'

'Ah! You will regret telling me that, sir.' He winked at Barak. 'For now I shall pass all the property cases to you. I shall keep the debts and the feuds with the lesser officials.'

'Are they all such matters?' I asked.

'For the most part.' He raised his eyebrows. 'I have been told the point is that the King must be seen to care for his northern subjects. The small matters will be arbitrated by us under the King's authority, the larger remitted to the King's Council.'

'How shall our arbitration be conducted?'

'At informal hearings under delegated powers. I will be in charge, with you and a representative of the Council of the North sitting with me. Have you done arbitration work before?'

'Yes, I have. So the King will have no personal involvement with the small matters?'

'None.' He paused. 'But we may meet him nonetheless.'

Barak and I both sat up. 'How, sir?'

Wrenne inclined his head. 'All the way from Lincoln, at the towns and other places along the road, the King has received the local gentry and city councillors in supplication, those who were with the rebels five years ago on their knees, begging his pardon. He seeks to bind them anew with oaths of loyalty. Interestingly, the orders have been that not too many supplicants were to gather together at once. They are still afraid, you see. There are a thousand soldiers with the Progress, and the royal artillery has been sent by boat to Hull.'

'But there has been no trouble?'

Wrenne shook his head. 'None. But the emphasis is on the most abject forms of surrender. The supplication here at York is to be the greatest spectacle of all. The city councillors are to meet the King and Queen outside the city on Friday, dressed in humble robes, and make submission and apology for allowing the rebels to take over York as their capital in 1536. The citizenry will not be there, because it would be bad for the common folk to see their city's leaders thus humbled –' Wrenne raised his heavy eyebrows – 'and in case they might be angered against the King. The councillors are to hand presents to Their Majesties, great goblets filled with coin. There has been a collection among the citizenry.' He smiled sardonically. 'With some cajoling.' He took a deep breath. 'And they are talking of us going too, the King's lawyers, to present him formally with the petitions.'

'So we'll be thrust into the heart of it.' Despite Cranmer's promise, I thought.

'We could be. Tankerd, the city Recorder, is in a great lather about the speech he must make. The city officials are sending constantly to the Duke of Suffolk to make sure everything is done just as the King would wish.' He smiled. 'I confess I have a great curiosity to see the King. He sets out from Hull tomorrow, I believe. The Progress spent much longer than planned at Pontefract, then went to Hull before York. And apparently the King is going back to Hull afterwards; he wants to reorganize their fortifications.' And that, I thought, is where we put the prisoner in a boat.

'When will that be?' I asked.

'Early next week, I should think. The King will only be here a few days.' Wrenne gave me another of his keen looks. 'Perhaps you will have seen the King before, being from London.'

'I saw him at the procession when Nan Boleyn was crowned. But only from a distance.' I sighed. 'Well, if we are to be present at this ceremony, it is as well I packed my best robe and new cap.'

Wrenne nodded. 'Ay.' He stood up, with a slowness that revealed his age. 'Well, sir, you must be tired after your long journey – you should find your lodgings and have a good rest.'

'Yes. We are tired, 'tis true.'

'By the way, you will hear many strange words here. Perhaps the most important thing you should know is that a street is called a gate, while a gate is called a bar.'

Barak scratched his head. 'I see.'

Wrenne smiled. 'I will have your horses fetched.'

We took farewell of the old man, and rode again to the gate leading from the Minster Close.

'Well,' I said to Barak, 'Master Wrenne seems a good old fellow.'

'Ay. Merry for a lawyer.' He looked at me. 'Where next?'

I took a deep breath. 'We cannot tarry any longer. We must go to the prison.'

Chapter Three

WE PAUSED OUTSIDE the gates, wondering which way to take to York Castle. I hailed a yellow-haired urchin and offered him a farthing to direct us. He looked up at us suspiciously.

'Show me thy farthing, maister.'

'Here!' I held up the coin. 'Now, lad, the castle.'

He pointed down the road. 'Go down through Shambles. Tha'll know it by smell. Cross the square beyond and tha'll see Castle Tower.'

I handed him the farthing. He waited till we had passed, then called 'Southron heretics!' after us before disappearing into a lane. Some of the passers-by smiled.

'Not popular, are we?' Barak said.

'No. I think anyone from the south is identified with the new religion.'

'All still stiff in papistry, then?' he remarked.

'Ay. They don't appreciate this happy time of the gospel,' I answered sardonically. Barak raised his eyebrows. He never spoke of his religious opinions, but I had long suspected he thought as I did, that neither the evangelical nor the papist sides had much to commend them. I knew he still mourned Thomas Cromwell, but his loyalty to his old master had been personal, not religious.

We picked our way through the crowds. Barak's clothes, like mine, were covered in dust, his hard comely face under the flat black cap tanned from our days riding.

'Old Wrenne was curious about whether the Queen is pregnant,' he said.

'Like everybody else. The King has only one son, the dynasty hangs on a single life.'

'One of my old mates at court said the King nearly died in the spring, some trouble with an ulcer in his leg. They had to push him round Whitehall Palace in a little chair on wheels.'

'I looked at Barak curiously. He heard some interesting nuggets of news from his old cronies among the spies and troubleshooters in royal service. 'A Howard prince would strengthen the papist faction at court. Their head the Duke of Norfolk being the Queen's uncle.'

Barak shook his head. 'They say the Queen has no interest in religion. She's only eighteen, just a giddy girl.' He smiled lubriciously. 'The King's a lucky old dog.'

'Cranmer indicated Norfolk is less in favour now.'

'Maybe he will lose his head then,' he replied, bitterness entering his voice. 'Who can ever tell with this King?'

'We should keep our voices down,' I said. I felt uncomfortable in York. There were no broad central avenues as in London, everywhere one felt hemmed in by the passers-by. It was too crowded for riding and I resolved that we should walk from now on. Although the streets were thronged and much trading was going on in anticipation of the arrival of the Progress, there was little of the cheerful bustle of London. We attracted more hostile looks as we rode slowly on.

The boy had been right about the Shambles, the smell of ripe meat assailed us when we were still twenty yards away. We rode into another narrow street where joints were set out on stalls, buzzing with flies. I was glad we were mounted now for the road was thick with discarded offal. Barak wrinkled his nose as he watched the shoppers waving flies from the meat, women holding the ends of their skirts above the mess as they haggled with the shopkeepers. When we were through the disgusting place I patted Genesis and spoke soothing words, for the smells had frightened him. At the end of another quieter street we could see, ahead, the city wall and another barbican patrolled by guards. Beyond, a high green mound was visible, with a round stone keep on top.

'York Castle,' I said.

A girl was advancing towards us. I noticed her because a servant with the King's badge prominent on his doublet was walking behind her. The wench wore a fine yellow dress and was exceptionally pretty, with soft features, a full-lipped mouth and healthy white skin. Fine blonde hair was visible below her white coif. She caught my eye, then looked at Barak and, as we passed, smiled boldly up at him. Barak doffed his cap from the saddle, showing his fine white teeth in a smile. The girl lowered her eyes and walked on.

'That's a bold hussy,' I said.

Barak laughed. 'A girl may smile at a fine fellow, may she not?'

'You don't want any dalliances here. She's a Yorker, she may eat you.'

'That I wouldn't mind.'

We reached the barbican. Here too a crop of heads was fixed to poles, and a man's severed leg was nailed above the gate. I brought forth my letter of authority, and we were allowed to pass through. We rode alongside the castle wall, beside a shallow moat full of mud. Looking up at the high round keep I saw it was in a ruinous state, the white walls covered with lichen and a great crack running down the middle. Ahead two towers flanked a gate where an ancient drawbridge crossed the moat. People were going in and out across it, and the sight of black-robed lawyers reminded me the York courts were housed within the castle bailey. As our horses clattered across the drawbridge two guards in King's livery stepped forward, crossing their pikes to bar our way. A third took Genesis' reins, looking at me closely.

'What's your business?' His accent showed him to be another man of the southern shires.

'We are from London. We have business with Master Radwinter, the Archbishop's gaoler.'

The guard gave me a keen look. 'Go to the south tower, the other side of the bailey.' As we went under the gate I turned and saw him staring after us.

'This city's nothing but walls and gates,' Barak said as we came out into the bailey. Like the rest of the place it had seen far better days; a number of imposing buildings had been built against the interior of the high castle walls but like the keep many were streaked with lichen, gaps in the plaster. Even the courthouse, where more lawyers stood arguing on the steps, looked tumbledown. No wonder the King had chosen to stay at St Mary's Abbey.

I saw something dangling from the high keep. A white skeleton, wrapped in heavy chains.

'Another rebel,' Barak said. 'They like to drive the point home.'

'No, that's been there a long time, the bones are picked quite clean. I'd guess that's Robert Aske, who led the Pilgrimage of Grace five years ago.' I had heard he was hanged in chains. I shuddered, for that was a dreadful death, and pulled at Genesis' reins. 'Come, let's find the gaoler.'

Another pair of towers flanked the opposite gateway. We rode across and dismounted. I was still stiff and tired despite the brief rest, though Barak seemed to have recovered his energy. I must do my back exercises tonight, I thought.

A guard approached, a fellow of my own age with a hard square face. I told him we had come from Archbishop Cranmer, to see Master Radwinter.

'He was expecting you yesterday.'

'So was everyone. We were delayed. Could you stable our horses? And give them some feed, they are sore tired and hungry.'

He called a second guard. I nodded to Barak. 'Go with them. I think I'd best see him alone, this first time.'

Barak looked disappointed, but went off with the horses. The first guard led me to a door in the tower, unlocked it, and led me up a narrow spiral staircase lit by tiny arrow-slit windows. We climbed perhaps halfway up the tower, and I was panting by the time he halted before a stout wooden door. He knocked, and a voice called, 'Come in.' The guard opened the door, standing aside to let me enter, then closed it behind me. I heard his footsteps descending again.

The chamber was gloomy, more arrow-slit windows looking out across the city. The stone walls were bare, though scented rushes were scattered on the flagstones. A neatly made truckle bed stood against one wall, a table covered with papers against another. Beside it a man sat in a cushioned chair reading a book, a candle set on a little table beside him to augment the dim light. I had expected a gaoler's slovenly dress but he wore a clean brown doublet and good woollen hose. He shut his book and rose with a smile, smoothly as a cat.

He was about forty. There was a pair of deep furrows in his cheeks; otherwise his features were regular, framed by a short beard, black like his hair but greying around the corners of his mouth. He was short, slim but strong-looking.

'Master Shardlake,' he said in a melodious voice with a slight Londoner's burr, extending a hand. 'Fulke Radwinter. I had expected you yesterday.' He smiled, showing small white teeth, but his light-blue eyes were hard and sharp as ice. The hand that took mine was clean and dry, the nails filed. This was indeed no common gaoler.

'Did the stairs tire you?' he asked solicitously. 'You seem to breathe a little heavily.'

'We had to ride through the night, Master Radwinter.' I spoke firmly, I needed to establish my authority. I felt inside my coat pocket. 'I should show you the Archbishop's seal.' I passed it to him. He studied it a moment, then handed it back.

'All in order,' he said with another smile.

'So, then. My lord Archbishop has written to you, told you I am to have oversight of the welfare of Sir Edward Broderick?'

'Indeed.' He shook his head. 'Though really, there was no need. The Archbishop is a great and godly man, yet he can become — overanxious.'

'Sir Edward is in good health, then?'

Radwinter inclined his head. 'He had some rough treatment from the King's interrogators when he was first taken. Before certain matters came to light, and it was decided to hale him to London. Most secret matters.' He raised his eyebrows. He must know that the nature of those matters had been kept from me as it had from him; Cranmer would have told him in his letter.

'So, then, he was tortured before you came.'

The gaoler nodded. 'He is in some discomfort, but nothing can be done about that. Otherwise he keeps well enough. He will be in London soon. Then he will be in far greater discomfort. The King wants him questioned as soon as possible, but it is more important that it is done by the most skilled people, and they are in London.'

I had tried not to think of what must await the prisoner at the end of his journey. I suppressed a shudder.

'Well, sir,' Radwinter said cheerily. 'Will you have some beer?'

'Not now, thank you. I ought to see Sir Edward.'

He inclined his head again. 'Of course. Let me get the keys.' He went over to a chest and opened it. I glanced at the papers on his desk. Warrants and what looked like a sheet of notes in a small, round hand. His book, I saw, was a copy of Tyndale's *The Obedience of a Christian Man*, a reformist text. The desk was set beside one of the narrow windows, giving a good view across the city. Glancing out, I saw many steeples and one larger church that had no roof, another dissolved monastery no doubt. Beyond lay marshland and then a lake. Looking directly down, I saw the moat ran broader on this side of the castle, a wide channel fringed thickly with reeds. People were moving about there, women with large baskets on their backs.

'They are picking reeds to make rushlights.' I started at Radwinter's soft voice beside me. 'And see there?' He pointed down to where one woman was pulling at something on her leg. I heard, very faintly, a little cry of pain. Radwinter smiled. 'They're gathering the leeches that bite them, for the apothecaries.'

'It must be a miserable occupation, standing deep in mud waiting for those things to bite.'

'Their legs must be covered in little scars.' He turned to me, his eyes looking into mine. 'As the body of England is covered in the scars left by the great leech of Rome. Well, let us see our friend Broderick.' He turned and crossed to the door. I took the candle from beside his chair before following him out.

✝

RADWINTER CLATTERED RAPIDLY up the stairs to the next floor, halting before a stout door with a little barred window. He looked in, then unlocked the door and went inside. I followed.

The cell was small, and dim for there was but one tiny window, barred and unglassed, the open shutters letting in a cold breeze. The chill air smelled of damp and ordure, and the rushes beneath my shoes felt slimy. The clank of a chain made me turn to a corner of the room. A thin figure in a dirty white shirt lay on a wooden pallet.

'A visitor for you, Broderick,' Radwinter said. 'From London.' His voice kept its smooth, even tone.

The man sat up, his chains rattling, in a slow and painful way that made me think he must be old, but as I approached I saw the face beneath its coating of grime was young, a man in his twenties. He had thick, matted fair hair and an untidy growth of beard framing a long, narrow face that would have been handsome in normal circumstances. I thought he did not look dangerous, but as he studied me I started at the anger in his bloodshot eyes. I saw that a long length of chain, looped through manacles on both his wrists, was bolted into the wall beside the bed.

'From London?' The hoarse voice was that of a gentleman. 'Are there to be more gropings with the poker, then?'

'No,' I replied quietly. 'I am here to ensure you get there safe and well.'

The anger in his gaze did not change. 'The King's torturers prefer a whole body to work on, hey?' His voice broke and he coughed. 'For Jesu's sake, Master Radwinter, may I not have something to drink?'

'Not till you can repeat the verses I set you yesterday.'

I stared at him. 'What is this?'

Radwinter smiled. 'I have set Broderick to learn ten verses of the Bible each day, in the hope that God's pure word in English may yet amend his papist soul. Yesterday he was obdurate. I told him he would have no more drink till he could say his verses.'

'Get him some now, please,' I said sharply. 'You are here to care for his body, not his soul.' I held the candle up to Radwinter's face. For a moment his lips pressed hard together. Then he smiled again. 'Of course. Perhaps he has been too long without. I will call a guard to fetch some.'

'No, you go. It will be quicker. And I will be safe, he is well chained.'

Radwinter hesitated, then strode from the room without another word. I heard the key turn in the lock, shutting me in. I stood and looked at the prisoner, who had bowed his head.

'Is there anything else you need?' I asked. 'I promise, I am not here to harm you. I know nothing of what you are accused, my commission from the Archbishop is only to see you safe to London.'

He looked up at me then, and gave a grimace of a smile. 'Cranmer worries his man may make sport with my body?'

'Has he?' I asked.

'No. He likes to grope at my mind, but I am proof against that.' Broderick gave me a long, hard look, then stretched out again on his pallet. As he did so the open neck of his shirt revealed the livid mark of a burn on his chest.

'Let me see that,' I said sharply. 'Open your shirt.'

He shrugged, then sat up and untied the strings. I winced. Someone had drawn a hot poker across his body, several times. One mark on his chest was red and inflamed, oozing pus that glinted in the candlelight. He stared at me fiercely, I could almost feel his rage. I thought, if Radwinter is ice, this man is fire.

'Where did you get those?' I asked.

'Here, in the castle, from the King's men when they took me a fortnight ago. They could not break me. That is why I am being sent to London, to be worked on by men of real skill. But you know that.'

I said nothing.

He looked at me curiously. 'What manner of man are you then, that my marks seem to offend you, yet you work with Radwinter.'

'I am a lawyer. And I told you, I am here to ensure you are well cared for.'

His eyes burned again. 'You think that will suffice, in God's eyes, for what you do here?'

'What do you mean?'

'You keep me safe and well for the torturers in London, that they may have longer sport. I would rather die here.'

'You could just give them the information they want,' I said. 'They will have it from you in the end.'

He smiled, a ghastly rictus. 'Ah, a soft persuader. But I will never talk, no matter what they do.'

'There are few who go to the Tower who do not talk in the end. But I am not here to persuade you of anything. You should have a physician, however.'

'I ask nothing from you, crookback.' He lay down again, looking across at the window. There was silence for a moment, then he asked suddenly, 'Did you see where Robert Aske still hangs in chains from Clifford's Tower?'

'That is Aske then? Yes.'

'My chain is just long enough to allow me to stand at the window. I look out, and remember. When Robert was convicted of treason, the King promised he should be spared the pains of disembowelling at his execution, that he would hang till he was dead. He did not realize the King meant he was to be dangled alive in chains till he died from thirst and hunger.' He coughed. 'Poor Robert that trusted Henry the Cruel.'

'Have a care, Sir Edward.'

He turned and looked at me. 'Robert Aske was my best friend.'

A key grated in the lock and Radwinter returned, bearing a pitcher of weak beer. He handed it to Broderick, who sat up and took a deep draught. I motioned Radwinter into the corner.

'Has he spoken?' the gaoler snapped.

'Only to tell me he knew Robert Aske. But I have seen the burns on his body; I do not like the look of them. One is inflamed, he should have a physician.'

'Very well.' Radwinter nodded. 'A man dead of fever will be no use to the Archbishop, after all.'

'Please arrange it. I will call tomorrow to see how he does. And he should have fresh rushes.'

'Scented perhaps, with sweet herbs?' Radwinter still smiled, but there was cold anger in his voice. 'Well, Broderick,' he continued. 'You have been telling Master Shardlake about Aske. I am told that in the first winter after he died, when all his flesh had been eaten by the ravens and little bones began falling to the ground, they had to set a guard, for people were taking away the bones. Bones from his hands and feet are hidden by papists all over York. Usually in the dunghills, for that is the safest place to keep relics safe from a search. It is also where Aske's bones belong—'

Broderick jumped up, with a sound between a groan and a snarl. There was a rattle of chains as he sprang at Radwinter. The gaoler had been watching for the move. He stepped quickly back and the chains holding Broderick's arms tautened, jerking him back on the bed. He slumped with a groan.

Radwinter laughed softly. 'Watch him, Master Shardlake. You see, he is not as weakly as he looks. Well, Broderick, I shall ignore your violence, and comfort myself with the knowledge of what awaits you in London. As 'tis well said, there is truth in pain.' He stepped past me and opened the door. I followed, with a last glance back at the prisoner. Broderick was staring at me again.

'You are a lawyer?' he asked quietly.

'I said so.'

He laughed bitterly. 'So was Robert Aske. When you see him again, think on what even lawyers may come to.'

'Words, Sir Edward, words,' Radwinter said as I went out past him. The gaoler locked the door and I followed him back downstairs. In his room the gaoler stood and faced me, his eyes cold and his expression serious.

'I wanted you to see that he is dangerous, for all he may look helpless.'

'Then why provoke him?'

'To show you. But I will have the physician fetched.'

'Please do. Whatever he has done, that man is to be treated as well as safety allows. And you should call him Sir Edward – he is still entitled to the courtesy.'

'Safety means he should be kept in no doubt who is master. You do not know what he is capable of.'

'Very little, chained to a wall.'

Radwinter's mouth set in a line as hard as a knife-blade. He stepped forward so his face was close to mine. His eyes seemed to bore into me.

'I saw your sympathy for him,' he said. 'The softness in your face. That worries me, with a man as dangerous as that.'

I took a deep breath, for it was true that there was something about people being kept in cells that revolted me.

'I have struck a nerve, I see.' Radwinter smiled softly. 'Then let me strike another. I distrust that sympathy in you, sir. Perhaps those who seem outcasts resonate in your soul. Perhaps because of the condition of your back.'

My mouth tightened at the insult, at the same time as my stomach lurched in recognition that, again, he spoke true.

He nodded. 'I am the one responsible for keeping Broderick secure, and for getting him back to London. There are those in this city who know he is here and would free him if they could, so I must study and scrutinize all those I meet, look as far as I can into their souls. Even yours, sir.'

I stared into those cold eyes. 'Get him his physician,' I said curtly. 'I will come again tomorrow to see how he progresses.'

He stared back a moment longer, then gave that little incline of his head. 'At what time?'

'When I choose,' I answered, then turned and left the room.

✝

OUTSIDE, BARAK WAS sitting on a bench watching the comings and goings at the courthouse. A chill autumnal wind had risen, bringing more leaves tumbling from the trees. He looked at me curiously.

'Are you all right?' he asked. I must have looked as drained as I felt.

I shook my head. 'I don't know which man is the worse,' I said. 'It seemed the gaoler, yet – I don't know. ' I looked to where Aske's skeleton dangled. The breeze made it swing a little to and fro, as though the dead white bones were struggling to be free.

Chapter Four

A GUARD TOLD US THAT to reach St Mary's Abbey we should follow a street called Coneygate. This was another narrow lane full of busy shops, and again we proceeded at a snail's pace. I noted a number of even narrower alleyways leading off, perhaps to squares and courts behind. I felt hemmed in by the city.

As we passed a large inn I saw a group of young men in colourful slashed doublets standing in the doorway, flanked by watchful servants, looking out over the crowd as they drank wine from leather bottles. One, a tall handsome young fellow with a dark beard, was pointing out members of the citizenry and laughing at their poor clothes. The evil looks he received made him laugh all the louder. The advance guard of the Great Progress, I thought; these gentlemen should take better care.

I thought about Radwinter and Broderick. Gaoler and prisoner, ice and fire. It was clear Radwinter visited whatever petty torments he could on Broderick, to keep him down and probably for his own enjoyment too. Such treatment could be dangerous; Sir Edward might be young but he was a gentleman, unused to privation. That burn on his chest could turn bad; I hoped there were good medical men in York. I wished my old friend Guy was with me. But Guy was far away, working as an apothecary in London.

I could not help being troubled anew by Sir Edward's accusation that I was keeping him safe for the torturers. He was right. And yet, for all his brave defiant words, Sir Edward had begged Radwinter for something to drink. And I had been able to order it brought.

I remembered, too, Radwinter's remark about my condition

making me sympathetic to poor outcasts. How he could see into a man. Did he use such skills to delve into the minds of the heretics in Cranmer's gaol at the top of the Lollards' Tower? But he was right; sympathy for Broderick could cloud my judgement. I recalled the prisoner's sudden furious lunge at the gaoler, and thought again, what has he done that he must be kept sealed away like a plague-carrier?

Outside a candlemaker's shop I saw a plump, choleric-looking man in a red robe and broad-brimmed red hat, a gold chain of office round his neck, inspecting a box of candles. The mayor, I thought. The candlemaker, his apron spotted with grease, looked on anxiously as the mayor lifted a fat yellow candle from the box and inspected it closely. Three black-robed officials stood by, one carrying a gold mace.

'It'll do, I suppose,' the mayor said. 'Make sure only the finest beeswax goes to St Mary's.' He nodded and the group passed on to the next shop.

'Doing his rounds.' I said to Barak. 'Making sure everything is in order for when the Progress arrives. And—' I broke off with a start at the sound of a scream.

A young woman, standing at the mouth of one of the narrow alleys, was clutching a large basket, struggling to keep it from the grip of a ragged youth with a large wart on his nose who was trying to pull it from her. I saw it was the girl who had winked at Barak earlier. Another churl, a fair-haired boy with a broken nose, held her round the waist. Barak threw me Sukey's reins and leaped from his horse, drawing his sword. A couple of passers-by stepped back hastily.

'Leave her, you arseholes!' Barak shouted. The two youths at once let go, turned and ran pell-mell up the alley. Barak made to follow, but the girl seized his arm.

'No, sir, no! Stay with me, please, these are for Queen Catherine.'

Barak sheathed his sword, smiling at her. 'You're all right now, mistress.'

I dismounted carefully, keeping hold of both horses' reins. Genesis shifted his hooves uneasily.

'What happened?' I asked her. 'What do you mean, your basket is for the Queen?'

She turned to me, her cornflower-blue eyes wide. 'I am a servant in the Queen's privy kitchen, sir. I was sent to buy some of the things the Queen likes.' I looked in the basket. There were sticks of cinnamon, almonds and pieces of root ginger. The girl gave a little curtsey. 'My name is Tamasin, sir. Tamasin Reedbourne.' I noted she had a London accent and it struck me her fustian dress was expensive wear for a kitchenmaid.

'Are you all right, mistress?' Barak asked. 'Those knaves looked as though they'd pull your pretty arms from their sockets.'

She smiled, showing white teeth and a pair of pretty dimples. 'I wouldn't let go. When the Queen arrives her lodgings are to be filled with her favourite doucets, all made from ingredients bought here in York.' She looked between us. 'Are you here to meet the Progress, sirs?'

'Ay.' I gave a little bow. 'I am a lawyer, Master Shardlake. This is my assistant, Jack Barak.'

Barak doffed his cap and the girl smiled at him again, a little coquettishly now. 'You are brave, sir. I noticed you earlier, did I not?'

'You know you gave me a pretty smile.'

'You had a bodyservant in King's livery with you then,' I said.

'Ay, sir. But Master Tanner wished to buy a piece of cloth and I gave him leave to go into that shop.' She shook her head. 'It was foolish, sir, was it not? I forgot what a barbarous place this is.'

'Is that him?' I asked, pointing to a thin-faced young man wearing the King's badge who had just left a shop on the other side of the road. I recognized him from that morning. He crossed to where we stood, hand on his sword-hilt.

'Mistress Reedbourne?' he asked nervously. 'What is the matter?'

'Well may you ask, Tanner! While you were choosing cloth for your new doublet, two youths tried to steal the Queen's dainties. This man rescued me.' She smiled again at Barak.

Master Tanner cast his eyes to the ground. Genesis pulled at the reins.

'We must go,' I said. 'We are due at St Mary's. Come, Barak, they will be waiting like everyone else to tell us we were expected yesterday.' I settled matters by bowing to Mistress Reedbourne. She curtsied again.

'I am lodged at St Mary's too,' she said sweetly. 'Perhaps I shall see you again.'

'I hope so.' Barak replaced his cap, then winked, making the girl turn scarlet. We rode off.

'That was a bit of excitement,' he said cheerfully. 'Not that there was any danger, they were just ragamuffin lads. Must have thought there was something valuable in that basket.'

'You did well.' I smiled sardonically. 'Rescuing the Queen's doucets.'

'The girl's a little doucet herself. I'd not mind a game of hot-cockles with her.'

✝

AT THE TOP OF Coneygate we passed into another road that ran alongside the high walls of the abbey. The King's guards patrolled the top of the walls, and beyond them I saw the high steeple we had seen on our way in, almost as high as the Minster. The monasteries had all had enclosing walls, though I had never seen any so high as this; St Mary's must have been an enormous site. Such a wall would greatly help security and I wondered whether this was why the abbey had been chosen for the King's base in York.

Once again we passed under the barbican at Bootham Bar, this time turning left to join a queue of riders and pedestrians waiting to go into the abbey. My commission was scrutinized with care before we were allowed to pass. Inside, we dismounted. Barak took the panniers containing our belongings from the horses' backs and slung them over his shoulders, then joined me in staring at the scene before us.

Directly ahead was a large manor house that must once have been the abbot's residence. It was splendid even by the standards the abbots of the large monasteries allowed themselves, a three-storey building in red brick with high narrow chimneys. Beds of small white roses lined the walls. There had once been a lawn too but it had been turned to muddy earth by the passage of innumerable feet and cartwheels. Some men were excavating what turf was left, replacing it with flagstones, while a little way off others were digging up what must have been the monks' graveyard, hauling up the gravestones and manhandling them onto carts. Above the main door of the manor the royal arms had been hung on a large shield.

Beyond the manor house stood an enormous monastic church of Norman design, one of the largest I had seen, its square tower topped by an enormous stone steeple, the façade decorated with ornate buttresses and carved pillars. The manor house and the church made two sides of a great courtyard, an area perhaps a furlong in length. There an amazing spectacle was taking shape. Outbuildings had been demolished, leaving trenches where foundations had once stood. Dozens of tents had been planted on the space, and hundreds of men were labouring in the open, working on the final stages of the construction of two enormous pavilions. Forty feet high, they had been built to resemble castles, complete with turrets and barbican gates; all in wood but painted and designed to resemble stone. Workmen on ladders swarmed over the extraordinary buildings, fixing plaster images of heraldic beasts, painting the walls in bright colours, glazing the windows. As I watched, I thought there was something familiar about the designs of the pavilions.

Trestle tables stood everywhere in the yard, carpenters hewing and planing huge lengths of wood. A pile of perhaps fifty trunks of young oak was stacked against the abbey wall, and sawdust lay everywhere. Other workmen were carving ornamental cornices in complex designs, the colours bright in the dull afternoon.

Barak whistled. 'God's wounds. What are they planning here?'

'Some spectacle the like of which I've never imagined.'

We stood a moment longer watching the extraordinary scene, then I touched Barak's arm. 'Come. We have to find the man in charge of the accommodation. Simon Craike.' I smiled. 'I knew him, a long time ago.'

Barak shifted the weight of the panniers on his shoulders. 'Did you?'

'He was a fellow student at Lincoln's Inn. I haven't seen him since, though. He never practised, he went into the royal adminis-tration.'

'Why'd he do that? The pay?'

'Ay. He had an uncle in royal service who got him a post.'

'What's he like?'

I smiled again. 'You'll see. I wonder if he's changed.'

We led the horses over to the manor house, which seemed to be the centre of all the great bustle; people were running in and out, officials standing on the steps giving orders, arguing and looking over plans. We asked a guard where Master Craike might be found, and he told us to wait, calling a groom to take the horses. As we stood there a high officer of state in a green velvet robe waved us out of the way, then another barged between us, as though we were dogs in his path.

'Arseholes,' Barak muttered.

'Come, let us get out of their way.'

We walked to the corner of the manor house, near to where two women were arguing with an official who held a floorplan of some sort. He was bowing and scraping almost to the ground, risking his plan falling in the mud, as the more richly dressed of the two ladies berated him loudly. She was in her thirties, with brown hair under a French hood set with pearls, and a high-collared robe of red silk. A woman of status. Her square plain face was red with ill-temper.

'Is it too much for the Queen to know how she may leave her lodgings in the event of a fire?' I heard her say in a deep, sharp voice. 'I ask again, which is the nearest door and who has the key?'

'I am not sure, my lady.' The official turned his plan round. 'The privy kitchen may be nearest—'

'I'm not interested in may be.'

The other woman saw us looking and raised her eyebrows in an affronted stare. She was slim, with a face that might have been attractive but for its cold, haughty expression. The brown curly hair beneath her plain hood was unbound, signalling unmarried status, though she too was in her thirties. She wore an expensive-looking engagement ring, however: a diamond set in gold. She frowned again and I nudged Barak out of hearing. Then I smiled at the sight of a man in a brown robe who had come out of the manor house and stood on the steps, staring round him. A little portable writing desk was tied round his neck with blue cord. An inkpot and a quill were set there, and a thick sheaf of papers was pinned to it.

I remembered Simon Craike by his anxious, harried air. But for that I might not have recognized him, for the years had changed my old fellow student greatly. The good fare of court had given him a plump face and wide girth, while the shock of fair hair I remembered was mostly gone, leaving only a yellow fringe. As he turned at my call, though, his careworn features lit up. Barak and I doffed our caps as he crossed to us, one hand on the little desk to keep it steady. He shook my hand with the other.

'Master Shardlake! I recognized you at once. The years have dealt kindly with you, sir. Why, you still have your hair. Not even grey.'

I laughed. ''Tis a wonder, given some of the affairs I have had to deal with.'

'By Our Lady, it must be near twenty years.' Craike smiled sadly. 'The world has seen many changes since then.'

'Truly it has.' I thought: a revolution in religion, the end of the monasteries and a great rebellion. And my father now dead, I remembered with a sudden stab. 'So,' I said. 'I hear you are in charge of accommodating the gentlemen in York.'

'Ay. I have never had such a task as this Progress. Everywhere I have been going ahead to work with the harbingers to ensure everyone has accommodation at each stop. The problems with the rains, the King ever changing his plans.'

'You have been with the Great Progress from the start?'

'Ay. There has never been one anything like so large.' He shook his head. 'The problems, you cannot imagine. Dealing with the waste has been the worst thing. Everywhere we stop vast pits have to be dug. With three thousand people, five thousand great horses, you may imagine?'

'Cannot the local people use the dung for manure?'

'There was far more than they need. And the stink, you can imagine . . .'

'I can.'

'Even with the pits, all the road from London to Hull is littered with rubbish. It has been a nightmare, sir, a nightmare.' He shook his head. 'And my poor wife left behind in London.'

'You are married?'

'Ay. Seven children we have.' He smiled with pride. 'And you, sir?'

'No, I have never married. This, by the way, is my assistant. Master Barak.'

Craike studied Barak solemnly with his pale blue eyes. 'You will need him, all the work there is here. As for me, I am surrounded by incompetents. So much to be got ready. Indeed I fear I cannot spare much time now, though I am glad to see you again. But I will show you your quarters.'

I nodded at the manor house. 'That is a fine building.'

'Ay. It was the abbot's house. The King will be staying there when he arrives – it has been renamed King's Manor in his honour.'

'Perhaps we may have an opportunity to meet later, discuss old times.'

'I should like that, sir. I will if I can—' He broke off, as the two women came round the corner, and a hunted look came into his face. 'God's death,' he muttered, 'not Lady Rochford again.'

I started, for that was a name whose mention could send a

shudder through any group. The three of us bowed hastily. As we rose I looked more closely at the square-faced woman. Her high-coloured features were still set in an angry frown, and I noticed she seemed strung tight with nervous tension. Her companion, who was holding the plan the official had been showing them, saw me studying her mistress and gave me another disapproving look.

'Master Craike!' Lady Rochford snapped. 'Your churl of a planmaster cannot answer the simplest question. I want to know, sir, is there a privy way out of this house on this side that the Queen might take? She is terrified of fire, when she was a girl in Horsham the house near burned down—'

'I am sorry, my lady—'

'Pox on sorry! Jennet, the plan! Hurry, woman!'

Her companion held it up. Craike laid it out on his desk, studied it a moment and then pointed out a door. 'There. The privy kitchen is nearest.'

'Is it guarded?'

'No, madam.'

'Then I will need a set of keys. Arrange it. Jennet, come on, do not stand there like a lost sheep!' And with that, Lady Rochford snatched the plan and the two women left, holding their skirts up above the muddy ground.

Craike wiped his brow. 'By heaven, that woman's an ogre.'

'Ay. I know her history. Who is her sour-faced companion?'

'Mistress Jennet Marlin, a maid in waiting. She has cause to look sour. Her fiancé is in the Tower, accused of a part in the conspiracy.'

'She's local, then?'

'Ay, she was picked to come to York for her local knowledge. There's no taint of disloyalty against her, her family are reformers.' Craike made a little moue of distaste, faint but enough to show me where he stood in matters of religion. 'Come, I'll take you to your accommodation. It's not the best, I fear, but in a few days there will be thousands here. Thousands.' He shook his head.

'Four days now until they come, is it not?'

'Ay. I have to send my officers to the inns today, to check all is
ready. Something can always go wrong. By Our Lady, the trouble
we had during the rains in July. The number of carts broken and
stuck in the mud, they nearly called the whole thing off.'

'I am sure all will be well,' I said with a smile. I had a sudden
memory of Craike as a student in the Lincoln's Inn library, working
late on his exercises — surrounded by papers, his hands stained with
ink, determined everything should be exactly right.

'I hope so,' he answered with a sigh. 'The itinerary has been
constantly changed, it has driven me half mad. The King was
supposed to be in Pontefract two days and stayed near two weeks,
and now he's diverted to Hull.'

'Perhaps to allow time to finish all this work going on in the
forecourt, those pavilions. What is it all for?'

Craike looked uncomfortable. 'I am sorry, I may not say. It will
be announced when the Progress arrives.' He stepped away, leading
us to the monastic church. 'But the work — it is a nightmare, a
nightmare!'

Barak grinned at his back. He seemed to be in a better mood
since meeting the girl. 'Was he always like this?' he whispered.

'He was the most conscientious student I ever met. Everything
had to be done just right.'

'That's a recipe for a seizure.'

I laughed. 'Come, or he'll leave us behind.'

As we reached the church I saw that many of the stained glass
windows had been removed, while others were broken. A dark
haired, middle aged man stood on a ladder some distance off,
carefully removing a pane. At the foot of the ladder an enormous
black horse stood grazing beside a high sided wagon.

'The glass is all going, then,' I observed to Craike. 'It'll make
the church look bleak when the King comes.'

'That glazier is trying to get as many windows as possible out before the Progress arrives, for the King will want to see it has been put beyond use.'

At the sound of our voices, the glazier stopped working and looked down. He had a thin, careworn face and sharp, watchful eyes.

Craike called up to him. 'How goes it, Master Oldroyd?'

'Well enough, maister, thank you.'

'Will you have all the windows out before the King comes?'

'Ay, sir. I'll be here at first light every day till 'tis done.'

Craike led us up the worn steps of the church. The great door stood half open, a trail of muddy footprints leading in; evidently the church had become a thoroughfare.

It had been a magnificent place once. Great decorated arches and pillars rose to dizzying heights, richly painted in green and ochre; the floor was of decorated tiles in many designs. Lit with candles, it would have been an awesome sight. Now, though, the many empty windows cast a cold dim light on side-chapels stripped of furniture and empty niches where statues had stood, some now lying in pieces on the floor. A trail of mud and broken tiles marked a shortcut leading to another half-open door at the south end of the nave. As we walked down the gutted church, our footsteps echoed eerily in a silence that contrasted strangely with the bustle outside. I shivered.

'Ay, 'tis cold,' Master Craike said. 'We're near the river here, 'tis a damp and foggy place.'

I saw that a considerable number of wooden stalls had been erected along the walls. Some horses already stood there though many were empty. Piles of straw spilled out on to the aisle.

Barak pointed at a stall. 'There's Sukey and Genesis.'

'They're using this place as a stable?' I asked incredulously.

'The horses of the courtiers and the senior servants will all be stabled here. 'Tis a sensible use of the space, though it seems sacrilegious, even if the church has been deconsecrated.'

We stepped out of the south door into a second large courtyard, just as bustling. More buildings were set along the walls, and there was an imposing gatehouse and another smaller church. This was still in one piece, the parish church perhaps. In the yard all manner of produce was being unloaded from carts: apples and pears by the sackful, heaps of charcoal and bundles of faggots, armfuls of candles of every size, and bale after bale of hay. Servants were carrying the goods to the buildings and to a series of temporary huts. Rows of stockades had been erected, accommodating a whole flock of sheep, numerous cows and even some deer. In one enclosure hundreds of fowls, jumbled together, were pecking the ground bare. I saw hens and ducks, turkeys and even a pair of great bustard, their giant wings docked. Nearby a gang of men was laying pipes in a trench that ran down to the south wall of the monastery. There, through an open gate, I glimpsed mudflats and a wide grey river. I shook my head. 'I've never seen such labour.'

'They'll be feeding three thousand on Friday. But come, we go this way.' Craike led us past the animal enclosures towards a large two-storey building. 'This was the monks' hospital,' he said apologetically. 'We have partitioned it into rooms. It is the best we can do. Most of the law officers are here. The servants have only poor tents.'

A little group of officials stood talking at the door, some holding the red staffs of office of the porters who watched the royal palaces for intruders. A big, burly man in a lawyer's robe, who overtopped the others by a head, was questioning them. Craike lowered his voice. 'That is Sir William Maleverer. He's a lawyer, a member of the Council of the North. He has overall charge of legal matters and security.'

Craike approached the big man, coughing to attract his attention, and he turned irritably. He was in his forties, with hard, heavy features and a black beard cut in a straight line at the bottom, the fashionable 'spade-beard'. Cold dark eyes studied us.

'Well, Master Craike, whom have you and your little clerk's desk brought me now?' Maleverer's voice was very deep, with a northern accent. I remembered the Council of the North was staffed by local loyalists.

'Brother Matthew Shardlake, Sir William, from London, with his assistant.'

'You're dealing with the King's pleas, aren't you?' Maleverer looked me over, his expression contemptuous, as though he had achieved his high stature and straight back by some great virtue. 'You're late.'

'I am sorry. We had a hard ride.'

'You'll need to prepare for Friday. With Brother Wrenne.'

'We have seen him already.'

Maleverer grunted. 'He's an old woman. But I'll have to leave it between you, I've other issues to deal with. Just make sure a summary of those petitions is prepared for the Chamberlain's office by Thursday morning.'

'I am sure we can put all in order.'

He looked at me dubiously again. 'You'll be in the King's presence on Friday. I hope you've better clothes than that mud-spattered coat.'

'In our baggage, sir.' I indicated the panniers, which Barak shifted again on his shoulders.

Maleverer nodded brusquely and turned back to his companions. Barak pulled a face at me as we passed into the building. The interior was gloomy, with small arched windows, a fire of kindling set in the centre of the stone floor. The religious scenes with which the walls had once been painted had been scraped off, giving the place an unkempt look. The hall had been divided into cubicles by wooden partitions. There seemed to be no one else there – all out at work, probably.

'A stern fellow, Sir William,' I observed quietly.

'A harsh man, like all those on the Council of the North,' Craike replied. 'I am grateful I have little to do with him. Now, sir,' he looked at me apologetically, 'I have taken the liberty of giving you and your assistant adjoining cubicles. Otherwise Master Barak would have to go into the servants' tents. With so many people of such varying ranks, it is hard to give everyone an appropriate place.'

'I do not mind,' I said with a smile. Craike looked relieved. He scrabbled on his little desk, found a piece of paper and led us past the row of stalls. The doors were numbered.

'Eighteen, nineteen – yes, those are yours.' He made a mark on the paper, then smiled. 'Well, sir, it has been good to see you again, but I must leave you now.'

'Of course, sir. But I hope we may meet for that cup of ale while we are here.'

'If time allows, I would be pleased. But all this –' he waved a hand towards the courtyard – 'a nightmare.' He gave a quick bow and then, with another glance at his list, he was gone.

'Well, let's see what we've got,' I said to Barak. There was a key in the lock of the cubicle door and I turned it. Inside, apart from a small chest for storage, a truckle bed was the only furniture. I eased off my riding boots and lay down with a groan of relief. After a few minutes there was a knock and Barak came in, barefoot and carrying my pannier. I sat up.

'God's wounds,' I said. 'Your feet stink. But I dare say mine do too.'

'They do.'

I noted the tiredness in his voice. 'Let us take the chance to rest this afternoon,' I said. 'We can sleep till dinner-time.'

'Ay.' He shook his head. 'What a scurry. I've never seen so many goods and animals in one place. And whatever secret pageantry they are planning out there to be catered for.'

I clicked my fingers. 'Those pavilions reminded me of something,' I said. 'I've just realized it. The Field of the Cloth of Gold.'

'When the King went to Calais to meet the French King?'

'Ay. Twenty years since. There's a painting of the pageant in the Guildhall. They built huge pavilions of just those designs, and giant tents all gilded with cloth of gold, which gave the occasion its name. Of course, Lucas Hourenbout is using those designs as a precedent.'

'For what?'

'I don't know. Some very great celebration. But perhaps we should restrain our curiosity, just get on with our business.'

'Dun's the mouse.'

'Exactly.'

'And Lady Rochford's here. God's death, she's one to avoid.'

I looked at him seriously. 'Ay. She was part of your old master's darkest scheme.'

Barak shifted uncomfortably. Jane Rochford had been one of those used by Thomas Cromwell to discredit Queen Anne Boleyn through accusations of sexual misconduct five years before. Lady Rochford's evidence had been the most terrible: that George Boleyn, her own husband and Queen Anne's brother, had had incestuous relations with the Queen. I had reason to know for certain what most people believed, that the charges against Queen Anne had been fabricated for political reasons.

'She has made herself a byword for the worst treachery,' I continued. 'And was well rewarded for it. Made Lady of the Privy Chamber to Jane Seymour, then Anne of Cleves and now Catherine Howard.'

'Didn't look very happy on it, though, did she?'

'No, she didn't. There was something underneath her angry bluster. Well, it cannot be much fun knowing the whole world hates you. Let's hope we don't have to see her again.'

'But you've to meet the King.'

'So it seems.' I shook my head. 'Somehow I cannot quite take that in.'

'And you have to be involved with the prisoner at the castle. No choice there.'

'No. But again, I'm going to ask as few questions as I can.' I told Barak the details of what had passed at York Castle, Radwinter's cruelty and Broderick's sudden lunge at him, though I left out what the gaoler had said about my having sympathy for the prisoner. At the end he looked thoughtful.

'Those skilled in dealing with dangerous prisoners, guarding and watching them, are rare. Earl Cromwell prized such men greatly.' He looked at me seriously. 'I think you're right. Don't get involved with either of them any more than you have to.'

He left me, saying he would call me in time for dinner. I heard a creak and a sigh as he lay down on the bed next door. I closed my eyes and was soon asleep. I dreamed I heard my father calling to me from outside the room, his voice clear and vivid, but that when I rose from the little bed to join him the cubicle door had been replaced by one as thick and heavy as the one in Broderick's cell, and it was locked.

✟

BARAK HAD THE ENVIABLE gift of being able to tell himself, before he went to sleep, when he wanted to wake, and he seldom failed to do so at his allotted time. His knock at my cubicle brought me from my troubled dreams. The room was gloomy, and glancing from the window I saw the sun was low in the sky. I joined him in the hall. There were other people there now, clerks and two lawyers in black robes, young fellows. One of them, a small thin man who stood warming his hands by the fire, caught my eye and bowed.

'You have newly joined us, sir?' he asked, studying us with large curious eyes.

'Yes. Brother Shardlake of Lincoln's Inn and my assistant Barak. We are here to assist with the petitions to the King.'

'Ah.' He looked impressed, and smiled ingratiatingly. 'Paul Kimber, sir. I am also from Lincoln's Inn.' He bowed again.

'What work are you doing with the Progress?'

'Supervising the drawing up of contracts with suppliers along the way, in the Purveyor's office. Well, helping to. I have come all the way with the Progress, and hard work it has been negotiating with these northern barbarians.' He laughed contemptuously.

'Do you know where we might find some dinner?' I asked.

'At the common dining hall. We have to eat all hugger-mugger with the clerks and carpenters. You'll need a docket, though, to show you are entitled to bouche of court.'

'Where do we get those?'

'At the Office of the Great Hall.' He wrinkled his nose. 'Not sure where that is now. They were moving it today, to bigger premises, in anticipation of the Progress arriving.'

'Well, we will find it, I dare say.'

We stepped outside, into an autumnal smell of woodsmoke. I shivered a little, for the damp feel of the air was more pronounced now. A little way off, brown-smocked servants were feeding the crowds of animals in their makeshift paddocks.

'Let's go through the church again,' I said. 'It'll be somewhere round the manor house.'

Again we trod with echoing footsteps through the monastic church, cold and full of deep shadows as the light faded, the only sound the horses stirring in their stalls. We walked out through the main door and stood looking out over the front courtyard. The workmen were busy as ever sawing and painting. I had never seen so many work so fast. Two servants were unloading lamps containing fat white candles from a cart and carrying them over to the men. Many of the tents were already lit by a glow from within.

'Do they plan to work into the night then?' Barak asked.

'Looks like it. Let's hope for their sakes it doesn't rain.'

I turned at a clinking sound. The glazier Oldroyd whom we had seen earlier walked slowly by, leading his enormous horse. It was one of those black Midland giants, the largest and strongest in the land, and it pulled a high-sided cart, full of glass.

'A good day's labour, fellow?' I asked.

'A busy day, maister, ay,' he said in a quiet voice. He touched his cap and I saw his hand was criss-crossed with tiny scars; from a lifetime's cuts, no doubt. 'They let me keep the glass and lead as payment for my services.'

'What do you do with it?'

'It goes to gentlemen's houses. A mythical beast or a ploughman at his toil makes a pretty centre-pane for a window, and cheaper than staining new glass.' He paused. 'But I am commanded to melt down the figures of monks and saints. It is sad, they are often beautiful.' He stopped suddenly and gave me an anxious look; such comments could be construed as criticism of the King's policy. I smiled to show I took no exception to his words. For a moment I thought he might say something more, but he lowered his head again and led his mighty horse off towards the gate.

I looked round the tents, wondering if I might spot Lucas Hourenbout. Barak asked a couple of officials if they knew where the Office of the Great Hall might be as they scurried past, but they only shook their heads; everyone was still in a great hurry. He sighed, and nodded in the direction of the little sentry box by the gate where the soldier who checked the papers of those coming in and out was posted.

'Let's ask him.'

We walked over to the gate. A young sergeant in the scarlet livery of the King's yeomen was checking a carter's papers. He was in his twenties, tall and flaxen-haired, with a handsome, open face. Glancing into his booth, I saw a Testament open upon a shelf under the window, one of those with notes to explain the words for those with little reading.

'All in order,' he said, handing the carter's papers back, and the man led his horse in.

'Know where the Office of the Great Hall is?' Barak asked. 'We've just arrived, we're hungry.'

'Sorry, sirs,' he said. 'I don't know. I heard it's moved.'

'So everyone says.'

'His pies aren't bad.' The young soldier nodded to where a pieman was touting his wares among the carpenters. He was doing a good trade.

'Fancy another pie?' Barak asked me.

'Better than wandering among all these folk all evening.'

Barak went over to the pieman. The fellow gave him a deferential little bow; he was on royal territory now.

'Thank you,' I said to the soldier.

'No trouble, sir. Everything is bustle and confusion tonight.'

'Where are you from, sergeant?' I asked, noting he had a southern accent.

'Kent, sir.'

'Ah, yes, I thought I recognized those tones. I had a job of work down there a few years ago.'

'Most of us recruited for the Progress are from Kent. There's six hundred Kentish archers arriving with the King on Friday. He knows we're the best in the country, and the most loyal.'

I nodded at his book. 'You are improving your knowledge?'

He blushed. 'Our chaplain says all should learn to read well.'

'That is true. Well, good evening, sergeant.' I went out and joined Barak. We stood eating our pies, watching the craftsmen. It was an extraordinary scene, men calling, hundreds of lamps shining, while, above, the guards patrolled the high walls with their pikes and guns. I looked at the huge silent bulk of the church outlined against the darkening sky.

'I could do with going back to bed,' Barak said.

'Ay, me too. We had no sleep last night.'

We returned to the lodging house. Our quarters were full of lawyers and officials now. We were too tired to do more than nod greetings to them as we headed for our stalls. I fell asleep at once.

✝

I WOKE VERY EARLY, surfeited at last with sleep. It was barely dawn, and all around came the snores and grunts of slumber. It was rare for me to wake before Barak. I rose and dressed silently, rubbing my hand over stubbly cheeks; I must get a shave.

I stepped quietly outside into a misty half-light, white and still. I realized that for the first time since our arrival there was silence at St

Mary's, no calling or sawing, no tramping feet. The animals stood quietly in their byres, their breath steaming. I crossed the courtyard towards the church, my feet silent on the grass. It was very wet; it must have rained in the night. The roof was hidden in the mist. I reflected that only two or three years ago the monks would have been at service now, their chants rising and falling.

I decided to walk through the church and see what was happening in the main courtyard. A dim light came through the windows, but all round the side-chapels, where once candles would have been lit before saints' images, stood empty and dim. I went over to the horses and spoke a few words to Genesis and Sukey, then walked on. Halfway down I was puzzled to hear a scraping, chinking noise, repeated over and over. Turning, I saw above me the shape of Master Oldroyd, already at work hacking at the lead round a stained-glass window.

I came out into the main courtyard. All was silent here too, the huge pavilions ghostly shapes in the mist. The gate on to Bootham was closed, a guard leaning on his pike and yawning sleepily. Lights flickered, however, at the window of the abbot's house, and a few officials were already standing around the doorway, stamping their feet and coughing.

'Master Shardlake. Sir!' I turned at the sound of a woman's voice. The girl Tamasin, wearing a fine hooded coat of demi-worsted, was walking towards me. I halted.

'Mistress Reedbourne.'

'Good morning, sir,' she said with a curtsy. 'I am glad we are met. I would like to thank you properly for your help yesterday.' She looked around through the fog. 'Is Master Barak with you?'

'He is abed yet,' I said. 'And you, Mistress Reedbourne, is it not early for you to be abroad?' I thought again of yesterday's adventure. It was convenient for her the assault should have happened just as we rode past.

She smiled at me. 'I am to meet my mistress, Jennet Marlin, and go over to the cooks. Lady Rochford is unhappy with the arrangements for the Queen's privy kitchen. My mistress has a busy day ahead and wished to start early.'

I eyed her narrowly. So she worked for Jennet Marlin, the sour-looking woman who had been with Lady Rochford yesterday.

'I fear Mistress Marlin is still abed too,' the girl said, drawing her coat round her. 'But I have to wait for her here.'

I nodded. 'Well, I must be on my way,' I said.

'Perhaps I may see Master Barak again,' she continued, unabashed by my cool manner. 'And thank him.'

'We shall be very busy. I doubt our paths will cross.'

'They may, if we are all lodged here—'

She broke off suddenly, and we both jerked round as a great scream sounded through the fog from the direction of the church: it was a terrible, animal sound, inhumanly loud, and it made the hairs on the back of my neck stand up. An official in a red robe walking towards the works stopped dead, his mouth falling open.

'What in Jesu's name . . .' the girl breathed.

The dreadful sound came again, closer, and suddenly a huge blurry shape appeared, charging through the mist. It hit the red-robed official, knocking him aside like a skittle, then charged on, straight to where Tamasin and I stood.

Chapter Five

IT WAS AN ENORMOUS HORSE, the glazier's; I recognized it in the same moment that I grabbed the girl and jumped back, just in time for I felt the wind of its passing and caught the stink of its sweat. I almost fell, but Tamasin, reacting quickly, put her hand on my back and managed to steady me. I hate being touched there but for the moment scarcely registered it. We stared at the great horse. It had run up to the wall of the manor and stood there at bay, trembling, its eyes rolling wildly and its mouth flecked with foam.

I turned to the girl. 'Are you all right?'

'Yes, sir.' She looked at me oddly. 'You saved me.'

'We'd only have been knocked over,' I said brusquely. 'See, yonder fellow is getting up.' I pointed to the official the horse had set spinning; he was rising painfully to his feet, his red robe covered in mud. People were running out of the abbot's house, fetched by the din, including a couple of guards with drawn swords. They approached the horse; with another shrill scream it reared up on its hind legs and kicked out, causing them to jump back hastily, for those gigantic hairy hooves could have smashed their skulls. I stared at the animal that had passed me so peacefully the night before. What had happened to drive it near-mad?

'Leave it!' someone called. 'Leave it and it'll calm.' The crowd stood back, forming a semicircle round the horse. It stood still, shivering, rolling terrified eyes at the crowd.

'God's teeth, what has happened? Are you all right, Master Shardlake?' I turned at a voice at my elbow. Master Craike had appeared and was staring open-mouthed at the scene.

'Ay. It's the glazier's horse, something has terrified it.'

'Goodman Oldroyd?' Craike looked around. 'Where is he?'

'I can't see him.'

He stared at the terrified horse. 'That animal is usually the quietest of beasts. It didn't even need tying up. Master Oldroyd would leave it to graze beside his cart.'

I looked at him. 'Will you come with me, sir, to see what has happened?'

The crowd was growing, servants from the house and half-dressed workmen from the tents milling around. I saw the sergeant I had spoken with the evening before hurrying over with a little group of soldiers.

'Ay, sir,' Craike said. 'I will come.' He looked at Tamasin, still standing beside me. 'I am surprised you are about so early, girl, and alone.'

'I am waiting for Mistress Marlin.'

'I think you should go indoors,' I said firmly. She hesitated a moment, then curtsied low and walked away. Craike went over to the sergeant and I followed. I saw Tamasin had stopped on the edge of the crowd and was still looking on. I remembered her hand on my back and I must have glared at her, for she turned then and walked back to the house.

Craike addressed the sergeant. Like some habitually anxious men, when a real crisis came he was quite cool. 'That horse belongs to the man who has been taking the windows from the church. I fear something has happened to him. Will you bring another man, and come with us?'

'Ay, sir.'

'The other soldiers had best stay here. To watch the horse and get this crowd back to their duties. And send someone to inform Sir William Maleverer. What is your name?'

'George Leacon, sir.' The sergeant spoke quickly to his men, selected another fellow as tall and broadly built as himself, then took a firm hold of his pike and led the way towards the side of the church.

The mist was still thick. We tramped carefully along wet duckboards that had been laid to the right of the church. I wished Barak were with us. Then I heard a sound ahead of us, a rusty creak. I turned to Craike. 'Did you hear that?'

'No.'

'It sounded like a door closing.'

'What's that ahead?' He pointed at a large brown shape that appeared ahead of us through the mist. As we approached we saw it was the glazier's cart, his ladder leaning against it.

'Where is he?' Craike asked, puzzled. 'You can see nothing for this damned fog. Master Oldroyd!' he called loudly. The soldiers followed suit, their voices muffled by the mist. There was no reply, no sound at all.

'He must have let the horse loose to graze. But what terrified it so?'

The soldiers called out again. I studied the cart. The ladder was propped against it at an odd angle, the end leaning right over the cart. Struck with a sudden foreboding, I touched Leacon's arm.

'Can you give me a lift up, sergeant? I want to look inside there.'

The young man nodded and bent to make a stirrup of his hands. I grasped the top of the cart and felt myself levered up. I heard my robe rip, caught in a sliver of glass embedded in the wood. Then, the sergeant still holding my foot, I looked over the top, at one of the most terrible sights I have ever seen.

The cart was three-quarters full of shattered pieces of stained glass. Master Oldroyd lay on his back on top of the glass, his body pierced in several places by sharp fragments. A big piece, sharp as a pointed sword and covered with blood, had gone right through the centre of his body and protruded from his stomach. Oldroyd's face, directly below mine, was white, his eyes closed. Blood covered the glass beneath his body.

I swallowed hard. 'He's in here!' I called. 'He's dead!'

'Help me up,' I heard Craike order someone, and a moment later his round face appeared on the other side of the cart. He blenched.

'Dear Jesu. He must have fallen from the ladder.' He turned to where a little crowd was gathering, and called out, 'Here! Four of you climb up, stand on others' shoulders. We must pull the body out!'

There was more scrabbling, and the heads and shoulders of four stout workmen appeared. They all looked shocked at the scene in the cart, but hesitantly reached out. They grasped Oldroyd's feet and hands and pulled at them. The body slid up that terrible spike of glass, a great gout of blood pouring from the wound. Then I nearly fell from the cart as the glazier's eyes opened wide. 'He's alive!' I cried, startling the workmen. They dropped him back onto the broken glass with a tinkling crash.

Oldroyd stared at up me. He tried feebly to lift an arm and his mouth worked in an attempt to speak. I leaned over, as far as I dared. He reached up and gripped my robe with his scarred bloody hand. I held the side of the cart convulsively; terrified I might fall in with him, face-first onto that broken glass.

'The Ki— The King!' he said in a trembling whisper.

'What about him? What is it?' I heard my own voice shake, for my heart was juddering mightily in my chest.

'No child of Henry and—' He gasped and coughed up a dribble of blood. 'Of Henry and Catherine Howard – can ever – be true heir!'

'What? What is this?'

'*She* knows.' He gave a convulsive shudder. 'Blaybourne,' he whispered frantically, his blue eyes staring into mine as though by doing so he could hold onto life. 'Blay-bourne—' The word ended in a rattling gasp, Oldroyd's grip slackened, and his head fell back. He was dead; being lifted up had opened his wounds and the last of his blood was even now spilling out over the spikes and needles of glass.

I hauled myself upright, my arms trembling. The workmen were looking at me, aghast. 'What did he say, sir?' Craike asked.

'Nothing,' I answered quickly. 'Nothing. Take him out.' I called over my shoulder to Sergeant Leacon: 'Help me down.' He did so, and I steadied myself against the cart, just as Barak ran up to us. 'Where in God's name have you been?' I snapped, quite unfairly.

'Looking for you,' he answered truculently. 'The whole place is abuzz. God's nails, what's going on?'

'The glazier fell off his ladder into his cart, it sent his horse running off in terror.'

The tall figure of Sir William Maleverer appeared, his black robe flapping round his long legs. The crowd parted hastily before him. He watched, frowning, as Oldroyd's bloody corpse was dragged to the top of the cart and fell with a sickening flop to the earth.

'What's going on here?' Maleverer snapped. 'Craike, and you, brother lawyer, what's happened?'

'The glazier fell in his cart,' Craike answered.

Maleverer gave the body a look of distaste. 'Wantwit fool. As if we haven't enough to do. I'll have to trouble the King's coroner now.' He looked round the crowd. 'Who found him?'

I stepped forward. 'I did.'

Maleverer grunted, then turned to face the crowd. 'Get your mangy arses back to work!' he shouted. 'You as well, Craike. And you, soldier,' he said to Leacon. 'Take that carcass to the manor. And see that mad horse gets an axe to the head!'

Such was the force of Maleverer's presence that the crowd dissolved at once, excited mutters floating back through the mist. Leacon and the other soldier lifted Oldroyd's body between them and walked away, followed by a frowning Maleverer. Barak made to follow, but I held him back. 'No, Jack,' I said quickly. 'There's something I must tell you. My head's awhirl.'

We stood there, in the shadow of the cart, and I told him Oldroyd's last words.

'Jesu,' he said. 'The man spoke treason. Was he some sympathizer with the conspirators? Shouting his defiance when he knew he was about to die?'

I frowned. 'He seemed to be trying desperately to tell me something.'

'Why you? You only spoke to him for a minute yesterday.'

'He was dying, there was no one else to tell.'

'Who is this Blaybourne?'

'I don't know. Maybe the man who killed him.' I shook my head.

'But it was an accident, surely. He fell from his ladder.'

'I'm not so sure.' I took a deep breath. 'I think he could have been pushed. He was a glazier, they're not people to fall off ladders.' I looked down the length of the church, past the cart. 'And as I was walking down to the church I heard something, a creak. It sounded like a door closing.'

Barak's face became sharp. 'Someone who'd killed the glazier, and heard you coming?'

'Possibly. And escaped into the church.'

'Then let's go and look.' The old eagerness for combat was back in his eyes. I hesitated.

'I don't want to get involved, Barak. That's why I said nothing about Oldroyd's last words. No one heard them but me. No one needs to know.'

'But if he spoke against the King and Queen, you must tell.' His face was full of anxiety. 'There were people this spring hanged for knowing something was afoot and saying nothing. What if there's something else abroad here, and Oldroyd knew? The King's due here in two days. Tell Maleverer what you heard, for Jesu's sake!'

I nodded slowly. He was right.

'And we can try to find that door you heard creak. See if there's anybody in the church. Come along, if we heard something in the church Maleverer would expect us to look.' Barak fingered the hilt of his sword, which he had buckled on as usual.

I looked at him. For more than a year I had been the one in charge, showing him the ways of the law, but suddenly he was Lord Cromwell's man of action again, keen and alert. I nodded reluctantly and felt for my dagger. 'Come on then.'

Barak led the way along the wall. The mist was thinning now, a pale sun showing through. Sure enough, a short way beyond the cart a little door was set in the wall. It had a big keyhole and I wondered if it was locked, but when Barak pushed the door it opened with the same rusty creak I had heard earlier. Drawing his sword, he pushed the door wide. We stepped in.

'Look,' he breathed. He pointed down at a fresh set of foot/prints. The damp smudges went from the door across the church. I strained to look, twisting my head, for a large pillar blocked our view.

'I can't see anything,' I whispered.

'Let's just follow the footprints. They're very recent – whoever made them was in the damp grass for a good while.'

'So there *was* someone.'

Barak nodded. 'Dodged into the church when he heard you coming, and ran. He's probably gone out one of the main doors now.'

I shook my head. 'If I was him, knowing there was about to be a great hue and cry, I'd have hidden in the church until the crowds were gone. Jesu knows there are enough dark spaces.'

Barak took a firm grip of his sword. 'Let's follow those prints.'

The marks on the tiled floor were faint but visible. They crossed the breadth of the church, intersecting with the trail of mud and dung left by those taking the shortcut along the length of the nave, then continued, fainter, on the other side to where a large internal doorway stood, its arch decorated with scenes from the life of Christ. The door was open a little, and the wet smudges ended there.

Barak smiled. 'Got him,' he whispered. 'This'll be a feather in our caps.' He stepped back, then kicked the door wide, the crash echoing and re/echoing around the great abandoned church. We looked in. An elaborately decorated vestibule lay ahead, with a low vaulted ceiling supported by wide carved pillars. Ahead, another archway led to a large inner room, lit by a big stained/glass window that had survived and through which daylight filtered dimly; prob/

ably the chapterhouse. We stepped inside, watching the pillars carefully lest our quarry had concealed himself behind one.

'Come on!' Barak called out. 'We've got you! Give yourself up!'

'Stay by the door,' I suggested. 'I'll go and find those soldiers.'

'No, I fancy taking this one myself.'

'Barak!' I said. 'Be sensible!' But he was already moving round the room, sword held out before him. I pulled out my dagger, peering into the corners. The anteroom was ill-lit, it was difficult to see. Then Barak let out a sudden yell.

'Jesu Christ!'

I ran across to where he stood in the doorway to the inner room. It was empty, all the furniture removed, but round the walls stood two tiers of men, dressed in brightly coloured robes. I saw white hair, long beards, pink faces and glinting eyes. I stood with my mouth open for a second, then laughed.

'They're statues, Barak. The prophets and apostles.' They were so lifelike in the dim light that his astonishment was understandable. 'Look, that's Moses in the blue robe. Jesu, even his lips are painted to look real—'

We both whirled round at a patter of footsteps, just in time to glimpse the hem of a dark robe disappearing through the door before it slammed shut with a bang. As we raced up to it we heard the sound of a key turning. Barak grasped the handle frantically.

'Shit!' he cried. 'He's locked us in!' He tugged again, but it was no good.

I set my lips. 'Then it's us who are trapped now, while he gets away.'

We walked back into the chapterhouse, where there was more light. Barak's face was red with embarrassment.

'I'm sorry,' he said. 'That was my fault. Charging in here without a thought like an arsehole, then crying out at those statues, pox on them. He must have been hiding in one of those corners, you'd have seen him but for my foolishness.' There was real distress in his face.

'Well, it's done now,' I said.

'I'm not the man I was,' he said with sudden, bitter anger.

'What do you mean?'

'I'd never have made a mistake like that a couple of years ago. I've had too much soft living at Lincoln's Inn.' He set his teeth. 'How are we going to get out of here?'

I looked up at the stained-glass window. 'There's only one way. You'll have to climb up those statues, break the window and call for help. Use your sword-hilt.'

He set his lips. 'They'll be laughing at us from one end of St Mary's to the other.'

'I doubt Maleverer will be laughing. We need to see him as soon as possible.'

'Better get on with it, then.' Barak took a deep breath, then climbed up the statue of Moses. Balanced on his stone head, he shinned up the figure of St Mark above him. He had not, at any rate, lost his agility. Balanced on the stone head of the apostle, he put one arm round a decorated pillar and then, with the hilt of his sword, leaned over and dealt the nearest pane of glass a heavy blow. It shattered, the noise echoing round the chapterhouse. I winced. He smashed the one next to it, then leaned out of the window and shouted 'Help!' in a great bellow that echoed round the chapterhouse. I winced again. He yelled twice more, then called down to me. 'They've seen us. People are coming.'

✝

AN HOUR LATER we stood before Maleverer's desk in his office at the King's Manor. On the way in we had seen a crowd of people standing round Oldroyd's horse lying still on the ground. I recoiled at the sight of a wide stream of blood running across the yard; Maleverer's orders had been carried out. Inside the manor, there was a smell of wood shavings. The sound of sawing came from outside Maleverer's office, for elaborate works of decoration were going on in the manor house too, making it fit for the King. I told Maleverer our story. He listened with that hard, angry expression that seemed fixed on his face. A big hairy hand toyed with an inkwell as though he would crush it in his palm. A tall thin man in a silk lawyer's robe and the coif of a serjeant at law at his elbow; he had been called in and introduced to me as Archbold, the King's coroner, with jurisdiction to investigate all deaths on royal property.

Maleverer was silent a moment after I finished, running a finger along the flat edge of his beard. 'So the man spoke against the King and Queen. Well, that's common enough up here. There should have been more hanged last spring. You should hear some of the things our informers tell us.'

'Yet I felt, sir, that the glazier was trying to tell me something important. And there must have been some reason he was killed.'

'*If* he was,' Maleverer said. 'What if this person in the church was just someone passing through, who was frightened by that oaf running in his with sword?' He gave Barak a look of disfavour.

'I don't think so, Sir William.' This was not the reaction I had anticipated. 'The footprints led from the door near the cart to the chapterhouse. I suspect the person had a key to both, and planned to go into the church from the beginning, so he would not be seen. And that is another thing. Who would have keys to the church?'

Maleverer grunted. 'The monks probably took copies before they left, so they could come back and steal.' He studied me. 'So, then. Are you one of those lawyers who likes ferreting about after puzzles and mysteries? You have the pinched look of such a funny-ossity.' His Yorkshire accent strengthened as he used a dialect term I did not understand but could guess was uncomplimentary. I did not answer.

'You haven't done very well, have you, letting him get away? Did you see nothing of what he looked like?'

'Only the hem of a dark robe.'

Maleverer turned to the coroner. 'Have you ever heard that name the glazier mentioned? Blaybourne?'

'No, sir.' He looked at me with sharp blue eyes. 'Mayhap it was the man who pushed the glazier into the cart, if anyone did. Some fellow guildsman he quarrelled with.'

Maleverer nodded. 'More than likely.' He leaned across the desk. 'Brother Shardlake, the King and his Progress will be here in three days. Every official here is working all hours to get everything ready for His Majesty, to ensure all goes smoothly. Especially the submission of the town councillors and the local gentry. What we do *not* have time for is a lot of fuss about some stupid workman who fell, or was pushed, into his cart of glass. Understand?'

'Yes, sir.' I felt disappointment, but also relief. I had discharged my duty and it was up to Maleverer to decide what if anything was to be done. But his next words made my heart sink.

'Since you like mysteries, you can investigate the glazier's death on the coroner's behalf.'

Archbold smiled and nodded. 'An excellent idea, sir. I've no one else to spare.'

'Go to the man's house, talk to his friends, find if he had any enemies.' Maleverer turned to the coroner again. 'There *will* have to be a formal investigation, won't there?'

Archbold nodded. 'I fear so, Sir William. We can't just leave it, though if it wasn't an accident it's probably some quarrel among the guildsmen, like I say. But we have to be seen doing something. We don't want the city made even more hostile.'

'There we are then. Brother Shardlake and his assistant can deal with it.' Maleverer delved into his robe, produced a large iron key and laid it on the table. I picked it up reluctantly. 'That's all he had on him, apart from a purse with a few groats. His house key, probably. Bring the results of your enquiries to me. And it would be good if the evidence supported death by misadventure, you understand?' He smiled then, showing big yellow teeth. 'I'll report to the Duke of Suffolk, tell him it will be settled quietly.'

'But Sir William,' I said. 'I am a witness. It would not be proper—'

'Pox on what's proper. I want this out of the way. We can empanel a jury from among the workmen here.'

'I have to prepare the petitions for the King,' I ventured.

'Then you'll have to work round the clock like the rest of us,' Maleverer answered bluntly. He turned to Archbold. 'Master coroner, will you leave us a moment? Take him –' he waved at Barak – 'with you.' They bowed and went outside, leaving Maleverer staring coldly at me. I sensed his dislike, and I wondered whether it was the contempt big hearty fellows will sometimes have for deformity. His eyes narrowed.

'You have another task as well, don't you?' he asked. 'At the castle? Don't gawk at me like a new-landed fish. I sit on the Council of the North, I know everything. You know how delicate the political position is. You will obey me to the letter in this matter of the glazier, do you understand? Get it out of the way quick.'

'Yes, sir,' I answered heavily. So Maleverer was one of the trusted men on the Council of the North, whom Cranmer had told me of. I wondered if he knew what Broderick was accused of.

He gave his harsh smile again. 'As for your other task, it is probably a good idea for someone to keep an eye on Master Radwinter from what I hear of him. How is Broderick, have you seen him?'

'Yesterday. He has an infected burn, I ordered a physician fetched.'

'Good. But one thing, Brother Shardlake.' He pointed a big square finger at me. 'Apart from watching for Broderick's welfare, you keep that long nose of yours out of that matter. Right out.' He stared hard at me again. 'I don't like long noses. I cut them off sometimes, and the heads as well.'

Chapter Six

I FOUND BARAK STANDING ON the steps of the manor house, looking across the courtyard. The day's work had begun and was continuing at the same breakneck pace. Visible progress had been made on the two pavilions; through the open doors I could see workmen finishing the interior decorations. Nearby, frames were being erected for three enormous tents, carts loaded with huge canvases standing by. The mist had cleared, leaving a grey sky.

'They took the horse away.' Barak nodded over to the wall, where a man with a brush and pail was washing away the blood.

'Killing the poor beast was unnecessary,' I said. I told him of Maleverer's orders. 'I wish I'd kept my mouth shut after all. Now I'm landed with this task, and if I find evidence Oldroyd *was* murdered I'll be less popular than ever.'

'Where do we start?'

'At the Guildhall, I suppose. I should liaise with the city coroner. And if poor Oldroyd was a master glazier they'll be able to put us in touch with his guild, and perhaps tell us where he lived.'

Barak nodded. He still had a gloomy look, I saw, and I remembered his sudden outburst in the church. I must talk to him later on. 'Let's get started, then,' I said with a sigh.

'We're due to meet old Wrenne at ten.'

'Damn it, so we are. I'll send a message to say we'll be late. I must visit the prison as well, to see if Radwinter's brought a doctor to Broderick.'

'Master Shardlake!' I turned at the sound of a familiar voice, and saw Tamasin Reedbourne approaching from the direction of the church. She was accompanied by the sour-looking woman who had been with Lady Rochford the day before. I set my teeth; was there no avoiding this importunate girl? She came up to us.

'There is no time to stand talking, Tamasin,' her companion said disapprovingly.

'But these are the gentlemen who saved the Queen's doucets yesterday. And Master Shardlake came to my aid today, when the horse ran at us.'

The older woman looked at me curiously. 'You are the lawyer that found that man's body?'

'I am, madam.' I bowed. 'Matthew Shardlake. And you are Mistress Marlin, I believe.'

I was surprised by the angry look that came into her large brown eyes. 'And how, sir, do you know that?'

'Master Craike mentioned your name after we saw you yesterday.'

'Did he?' Again that cynical, humourless smile. 'Yes, I am Jennet Marlin, I attend on Lady Rochford as you saw yesterday.' She looked at me. 'They say you got yourself locked in the chapterhouse afterwards and had to call for help.'

I looked at her evenly. 'Indeed we did.'

'How did that come about?'

'I am not at liberty to say,' I answered coldly.

'A man of mystery,' she said, turning away. 'Come, Tamasin, we must see what they are about in the Queen's kitchen.'

Tamasin smiled at us, her smile lingering on Barak. 'The King and Queen are having their own privy kitchens installed in the abbot's house,' she said proudly. 'We are helping with the arrangements, as I told you earlier.'

'Come on!' Mistress Marlin walked away with a swish of skirts. There was an odd stiffness about her gait, as though her body was held tight with tension. If she had a fiancé in the Tower she would have much to worry about. Tamasin spoke quickly to Barak. 'Will you be dining in the hall tonight?'

'I don't know, mistress. We haven't even had time for breakfast yet.'

'But you will be entitled to bouche of court. Do you not have dockets?'

'Not yet,' I said.

'I will get some for you.'

'We will not be dining till late,' I said. 'We have a busy day.'

'Say six, then?'

'That will be fine,' Barak said. 'Six o'clock.'

Tamasin curtsied quickly and went to join her mistress. They disappeared into the house. I shook my head. 'That girl is the most pert creature I have ever come across.'

'Her mistress is a rude bitch.'

'Yes, she is. These royal women-servants seem to think they can take any liberty. And that young Tamasin has set her sights on you.'

Barak smiled. 'Can't say I mind. Not short of spirit, is she?'

'Come,' I said. 'Let's see if there's anywhere in this great warren where we can arrange for messages to be sent.'

A guard directed us to a tent where boys were running in and out, carrying papers. A whole system for sending messages around the city had been set up. The man in charge seemed reluctant to get word to Wrenne, but mention of Maleverer's name worked wonders, and a lad was despatched with a scribbled note.

We fetched our outdoor clothes and made our way to the gate to Bootham. People were scurrying in and out under the barbican and one of the King's soldiers was arguing with a dusty-looking couple who had stepped down from a poor wagon covered with sacks. Both wore baggy smocks of strange design, green squares of different sizes intersecting across a russet background.

'We heard they were crying out for all the produce as they can get for the King's visit!' the man said in the accent of a Scotchman.

'No Scotch in the city while the King's here, no vagabonds,' the guard said implacably.

'But we've driven from Jedburgh. We've the year's oat harvest here.'

'Then serve it to thy border reivers that steal our cattle. Turn round and be off. No Scotch!'

The couple remounted their wagon wearily. The guard winked at us as we approached. 'Keep the barbarians out, eh?' A Yorkman by his accent, he looked pleased with himself. I reflected that yesterday Brother Kimber had used the same word about the northern English.

We walked back into the city. The Guildhall was only a few streets away, in a square next to another abandoned monastery, the roof gone. How full this city must have been of monks and friars. The Guildhall was busy as the King's Manor, a scurry of people going in and out. It was an imposing building, though far smaller than its counterpart in London. I asked the guard at the door where I might find the city coroner.

'He's not here, maister.' The man looked at us curiously. 'But Recorder Tankerd is within.' He let us pass, into a big hall with a splendid hammerbeam roof where merchants and officials stood talking as officials bustled in and out of side-rooms. I asked a passing clerk where I could find the Recorder; the title of the city's chief legal officer was the same as in London.

'He's with t'mayor. I doubt he can see you, sir.'

'I come from Sir William Maleverer.'

Once again that name brought results. 'Oh. Then come with me, sir.'

We followed the clerk to a large room with a fine view across the river, where two men stood at a table poring over gold coins, counted into piles. I recognized the plump figure of the mayor in his bright red robes from the day before. 'With all the people we've canvassed,' he was saying crossly, 'they'll say we should have collected more.'

'It was hard enough getting this much. And the gold cup is a good one.' The other man was younger, with a thin, serious face, wearing a lawyer's robe.

'This won't fill it.' The mayor looked up angrily at our entrance. 'Jesu's blood, Oswaldkirke, what is it now?'

The clerk bowed almost to the floor. 'Maister Mayor, this gentleman has come from Sir William Maleverer.'

The mayor sighed, waving the clerk out, and turned protuberant eyes to me. 'Well, sir, how can I help Sir William *now*?' He pointed irritably at the piles of coins. 'The Recorder and I are preparing the city's present to the King for Friday.'

I introduced myself and explained my mission to investigate the glazier's death. 'I have been asked to deal with the matter,' I said, 'but wished to inform the York coroner, as a courtesy. Perhaps he may be able to give me some aid,' I added hopefully.

The mayor frowned. 'I knew Peter Oldroyd, he was chairman of the glaziers' guild two years ago. The city should investigate this.'

'If the death took place on royal property, the King's coroner has jurisdiction,' said the thin-faced man. He extended a hand. 'William Tankerd, the city Recorder.' He smiled, but eyed me curiously.

'Matthew Shardlake, of London.'

'God's death,' the mayor snapped pettishly. 'Am I to have no authority left in my own city?' He sighed and waved a hand at the Recorder. 'Take them outside, Tankerd, they shouldn't be in here with all this gold. Tell him what he needs to know, but don't be long.'

Tankerd led us outside. 'Forgive Mayor Hall,' he said. 'We have much to do before Friday. People are still throwing rubbish in the streets and they won't clear their middens, no matter how we threaten them.'

'I am sorry to trouble you, sir. If you could tell me where I may find the coroner . . .'

He shook his head. 'I fear Maister Sykes is out of town today, holding an inquest over at the Ainsty.'

'Then may I ask where Master Oldroyd lived? His family should be told.' That was an aspect of my task I was not looking forward to.

'All the glaziers live in Stonegate. It is almost opposite here, up the road from St Helen's church. Oldroyd lived just beyond the churchyard, I believe.'

'Thank you, sir. Then I will go there.'

He nodded, then gave me a sharp look. 'Take care, sir. With the monasteries going down, the glaziers have lost much of their work. They are not friendly to southrons.'

✝

ALMOST OPPOSITE THE SQUARE from the Guildhall stood an old church with fine glasswork, and a passer-by confirmed the narrow street running alongside it was Stonegate. It was bounded on one side by the ancient churchyard and the buildings were tall and narrow, overhanging eaves cutting out much of the light from the grey sky. As we walked down it we saw some houses had signs outside showing glazed windows, and I could hear tinkling and hammering from workshops behind. Halfway down Stonegate the churchyard ended. 'Round here somewhere,' Barak said.

I stopped a passer-by, a middle-aged man with a square face and black hair under a wide cap, and asked if he knew which was Master Oldroyd's house.

'Who wants t'know?' he replied, looking at me keenly. I noticed his hands were covered in scars as Oldroyd's had been.

'We come from St Mary's,' I said. 'I am afraid he has met with an accident.'

'An accident? Peter?' His face filled with concern.

'Did you know him, sir?'

'Of course I did, he is in my guild and a friend too. What happened, maister lawyer?'

'He fell from his ladder early this morning while working on the monastery church. I fear he is dead.'

The man frowned. 'Fell from his ladder?'

'The circumstances are uncertain. We have been appointed to investigate by the King's coroner,' I said. 'If you knew him, Master . . .'

'Ralph Dike. I'm a master glazier, as Peter was. He was a good man.'

'Perhaps you could tell us about Master Oldroyd. Does he have a family.'

'His wife and three bairns all died in the plague in '38.' The glazier crossed himself. 'He had only an apprentice.'

No family then, I thought with relief. Master Dike pointed to a house two doors down. 'Peter lived there.' He gave us a long look, then took a step away. 'I have business now,' he said. 'I must tell the guild of this.' He turned and walked hastily off.

'He didn't want to talk, did he?' Barak asked.

'I think he was suspicious of us, southerners from St Mary's. Let's see his house.'

The property Master Dike had pointed out needed plastering, and the paint on the front door was cracked and flaking. I knocked, but there was no reply so I took the key and turned it in the lock. As I did so Barak nudged me, nodding at a window in the house opposite. A woman's face was quickly withdrawn. I pushed the door open.

The house was built round a central hall, like Master Wrenne's but smaller, with a hearth in the middle and a smoke-hole in the black-raftered ceiling. The ashes of last night's fire lay in the little grate. I noticed the plate displayed on the buffet was mostly pewter, the furnishings clean but cheap.

'Hullo!' I called out. 'Anyone at home?' There was no reply.

'That's odd,' Barak said. 'You'd expect a servant to be around, or the apprentice.'

I walked over to an inner door. It gave on to a hallway doors, and a wooden staircase leading to an upper floor. Opening the first door I found myself in the kitchen. I went to the oven; it was warm. Someone had been baking recently. Apart from faint sounds from the street, the house was silent. I crossed to the other door, which led to an enclosed yard with a gate and a furnace in an open shed in one corner. Windows of stained and painted glass, mostly with two broken, were stacked in piles against the walls. I shuddered, remembering that blood-soaked cart. I saw Oldroyd had been separating out some of the small painted panes for reuse. He had laid them on a cloth, representations of birds and animals and mythic beasts. None had religious themes. 'It's like he told us,' Barak said. 'He's been taking the glass to reuse.' I bent and looked down at the figures; some of them were beautiful, hundreds of years old. I wondered if they had come from St Mary's.

Barak had gone over to the furnace. A large bucket full of pieces of glass showing monks at prayer stood beside it, for melting down no doubt. Barak touched the side of the furnace. 'It's cold,' he said.

'Let's try upstairs.'

We went back in and climbed up to a little hallway with two more doors. I opened one; it gave on to a bedroom, empty save for a truckle bed with a straw mattress and an open trunk containing clothes and a blue cloak.

'The apprentice's room, perhaps,' I said.

'Lucky to have his own room.'

'Poor Oldroyd may have had no other use for the room if his family all died of plague.' I opened the other door, which led into a master bedroom. A wall-cloth in green and yellow stripes went round the whole room, leaving a gap only for the window. There was a good bed with a feather mattress and a couple of big solid trunks, carved and painted. Opening them I found a stock of clothes, neatly folded.

'Wonder where he kept his papers,' I said, then turned as Barak laid a hand on my arm. He held a finger to his lips for silence and nodded over his shoulder. 'There's someone on the stairs,' he mouthed. 'I heard the boards creak.' Motioning me to stay where I was, he crept to the door, listened a moment, then threw it open. There was a shrill cry and he stepped back in, his arm round the neck of a plump lad in his early teens with a shock of red hair and an apprentice's blue coat.

'Listening at the keyhole,' Barak said. 'Tried to bite me when I grabbed him, the little weasel.' He released the boy, giving him a shove that sent him spinning against the opposite wall, then stood with his back to the door. The lad stared between us, his eyes wide.

'Are you Master Oldroyd's apprentice?' I asked.

He gulped. 'Ay, maister.'

'We are King's officials.' The words made the boy open his terrified eyes even wider. 'We come from St Mary's Abbey. What is your name?'

'P-Paul Green, maister.'

'You live here?'

'Ay, sir, with Maister Oldroyd.'

'Have you been with your master long?' I asked more gently.

'Two years. I were 'prenticed at fourteen.' He took a deep breath. 'I meant no harm, maister. I came back from fetching the charcoals and heard voices in Maister Oldroyd's bedroom.' I saw the boy's eyes flicker to a spot low down on the wall, just for a moment. 'I thought it might be robbers, sir.'

'There's a sack of charcoal at the foot of the stairs,' Barak confirmed.

'Are there no other servants here?' I asked.

'Only the cook, sir. She's gone to try and find some fowl for maister's supper. There's a shortage, everything in t'city's being bought up by King's purveyors. Maister told me to set up furnace to melt down the monkish glass, but I had to go and get the coals.' He stared at me, his eyes still full of fear.

'I have bad news, Green,' I said gently. 'I fear your master is dead. He fell from his ladder at St Mary's into his cart, early this morning.'

The boy went white. He sat on the bed with a thump, his mouth open.

'Master Oldroyd was good to you?'

'Ay,' he whispered. 'He was. Poor maister.' He crossed himself.

'We have been asked by the King's coroner to investigate his death.'

The boy's eyes narrowed. 'Was it not an accident?'

'That is what we have to find out.' I looked at him. 'Had your master any quarrels with anyone, that you know of?'

'No, maister.' But there was a hesitation in the boy's voice, and I saw his eyes start to move to the spot on the wall again, though this time he checked himself.

'Did you know the names of all your master's friends and family?'

'His friends are mostly guildsmen, and them he did business with. He had no family, maister, they all died in the plague. His old apprentice died too, he took me on afterwards.'

'So you know of none who might have wished him harm?'

'No, sir.' Again that slight hesitation.

'Are you sure?'

'Yes, sir. I—'

But before the boy could answer there was a bang at the front door, not a knock but a loud crash. We all started, and the boy let out a squeak of fear. Heavy footsteps sounded, some going into the downstairs rooms and the yard and others thundering upstairs. Barak jumped away from the door just before it was thrown open and two guards in the King's uniform stormed in, swords held at the ready. Barak stood in the centre of the room, his hands raised. The apprentice moaned in terror. The nearest guard looked at us, then smiled wolfishly. 'Don't move, any of you,' he said threateningly, then called downstairs. 'Sir! There's three up here, in the bedroom!'

'What is going on?' I asked. 'We are—'

'Shut up!' He smiled evilly again. 'You're in the shit, you are.'

A moment later Maleverer strode into the room.

Chapter Seven

S IR WILLIAM GLARED FROM me to Barak and then at the terrified apprentice. 'What's going on?' he barked.

I managed to keep my voice calm. 'We are investigating the glazier's death for the coroner, Sir William, as you instructed. We just arrived; I was questioning the apprentice—'

'Oh. Yes.' To my surprise, he seemed to have forgotten his own instructions. 'Why up here?'

'He was listening at the door,' Barak said, nodding at young Green.

Maleverer leaned over and grasped the apprentice by the ear, yanking him to his feet. He stood, plump limbs trembling, as Maleverer glared into his terrified face before turning to me. 'Well, what have you got out of him?'

'He says Master Oldroyd had no enemies he knew of.'

'Does he?' Maleverer turned back to the boy. 'What do you know of your master's affairs, eh? What have you heard listening at doors?'

'Only about his business, sir, only his business.'

Maleverer grunted, released the boy's ear and drew a deep breath. 'I've talked with the Duke of Suffolk,' he said. 'His instructions are that I should investigate this personally. It seems Oldroyd was crooked in his business dealings with us. It needs looking into.'

'No, sir,' the boy said. 'Not maister—'

He broke off as Maleverer landed him a terrific clout across the face. He fell back across the bed, blood pouring from his mouth and from his cheek where a ring Maleverer wore had cut a gash. Sir

William looked at me. 'I'll take this little squealing pig back to St Mary's and see what some questioning can get out of him. Are there any other servants?'

'A housekeeper, I believe, who is out shopping.'

'We'll have her in too.' He turned to the nearer guard. 'Get two men and take the boy back to St Mary's. The rest of you can help me search this place.' A guard hauled young Green to his feet. He gagged, spat a tooth into his hand, then started weeping in terror and shock. The guard manhandled him out of the room, still bleeding profusely. Sir William turned brusquely to the other guard. 'Now go down and get that search organized.'

'What are we looking for, Sir William?'

'I'll know when I see it.' Maleverer watched him go, then glared at me. 'This matter is out of your hands. Forget about it, understand?'

'Yes. We—'

'Out of your hands. And those words you heard Oldroyd say this morning, about the King and about that name —' he lowered his voice — 'Blaybourne. You say nothing of that to anybody, do you understand? Have you mentioned it to anyone?'

'No, Sir William.'

'Then leave, both of you. Go about your business—'

He was interrupted by the sound of a commotion outside. He turned to the window. Two soldiers could be seen hauling the apprentice up the street. The boy's legs had given way and they were dragging him along the earth by the arms. He was howling with fear, begging to be let go. The doors of all the neighbouring houses had opened and there was a babble of voices as a crowd, mostly women, came to their doors. Someone called 'For shame!' after the soldiers. 'Southron dogs!' another shouted. Maleverer set his lips.

'God's death, I'll have them all in gaol!' He marched furiously out, and a moment later I heard him bawling at the crowd. 'Be about your business, unless you want taking in for a whipping!'

Barak nudged me. 'I think we should get out while we can. Let's go the back way.'

I hesitated, glancing at the spot on the wall the apprentice had looked at, then nodded and followed him downstairs. Another two soldiers were guarding the back gate. I explained we had been there on official business, but had to show my commission before they would let us out. We found ourselves in one of the narrow side-lanes and followed it out to the main street. We walked slowly back towards the Guildhall, both a little shocked by what had happened.

'Can we get some lunch?' Barak asked. 'My stomach feels my throat's been cut.'

'Ay.' I realized I was hungry too; we had had no breakfast. We found a busy inn where we ordered some bread and pottage and sat at a vacant table.

'What was all that about?' Barak asked, quietly so our neighbours would not hear.

'Jesu knows.'

'Why's the Duke of Suffolk involved? He's in charge of the Progress, isn't he?'

'Yes. He's the senior official, close to the King.'

'What was Oldroyd up to? They wouldn't send a troop of soldiers if he'd been overcharging for taking out the glass. That's balls.'

'No. I think that was the first thing that came into Maleverer's head when he saw us.' I lowered my voice. 'It's something political, it has to be.'

'Something to do with the conspiracy?' Barak whistled softly. 'I remember Oldroyd sounded like he might be a papist, mourning the stained glass.'

I nodded, then frowned. 'God knows what they'll do to that apprentice.'

'Poor little arsehole.' Barak gave me a hard look. 'Still, apprentices often learn things through listening at doors and with a callow lad like that scaring it out of him is the quickest way to the truth.'

'That's what Lord Cromwell would have done?'

He shrugged. 'If the boy has any sense he'll tell them all he knows.'

'And he did know something,' I said thoughtfully. 'He kept glancing at a spot on the wall, as though there were something hidden behind that hanging.'

'Did he? I missed that.'

'I was going to tell Maleverer about it, but he stormed out.'

'Maybe we should go back and tell him now.'

I shook my head. 'You saw he wanted us out of there quick. I'll speak to him later.'

'Anyway, we're off the case. Can't say I'm sorry.'

'No. Yet . . .' I hesitated. 'I cannot but wonder what it is all about. I'll never forget that desperate look in Oldroyd's eyes. What he said about the King and Queen and that name, Blaybourne. It was obviously important after all.'

'Seems so.'

'I'd guess that when Maleverer told the Duke of Suffolk about Oldroyd's words they meant something to him. He'd know secrets of state Maleverer wouldn't.'

'Your curiosity is piqued, then?' Barak grinned. 'We'll have to watch out now; you will be wanting to investigate the glazier's death after all.'

'No, I have enough to deal with.' I pushed my bowl away. 'We should go,' I said. 'There is another delightful gentleman I should see today. Master Radwinter. As we are in the city, let's get it out the way before we go to Master Wrenne's.'

✝

IT WAS EASIER TO negotiate the narrow crowded streets on foot than on horseback, and within half an hour we had crossed the city. York was far smaller than London, and we were beginning to recognize the landmarks. It was raining again by the time we reached the castle, a mizzling rain that seemed to sink into one. The leaves and mud of the inner bailey were slimy underfoot. I looked up at Aske's skeleton.

''Tis not healthy to stare too long at these displays,' Barak said quietly.

'Broderick told me that sight should be a reminder of what lawyers may come to.' I looked up at the tower, the little window at the top that marked Broderick's cell. 'Well, I had better go in.'

'Do you want me to come with you this time?' Barak asked.

'No.' I smiled. 'I know you're curious, I would be in your shoes. But I feel I have to meet Radwinter man to man. If I took someone with me he'd take it as a sign of weakness.'

He nodded, and I led the way to the guardroom, where the hard-faced fellow from the day before agreed Barak could sit by his fire. He took me again to the tower, unlocking the outer door.

'May I leave you to go up by yourself, sir?'

'Very well.' I passed inside. He turned the key behind me. I climbed the stone steps again. All was silent apart from the drip of water somewhere, and I guessed Radwinter and Broderick were the only people in the tower. Broderick was secure indeed, I thought; between him and the outside world stood the guards at the castle drawbridge, those in the guardroom, then the locked door to the tower and another to his cell.

I paused on the landing outside Radwinter's door to catch my breath, so that he should not see me out of wind again. But he had the hearing of a cat, for I had only stopped a few moments when the heavy door jerked open. Radwinter stood in the doorway, his face set hard and holding a sharp-looking sword. When he saw it was me, he laughed.

'Master Shardlake!'

I reddened, expecting some sardonic remark, but he beckoned me in. 'I fear you startled me, I heard someone outside.' He put down his sword. 'You are wet, sir, come and stand by the fire.'

I was glad to go and stand by a charcoal brazier in the centre of the room. 'The year tumbles to its end, does it not?' Radwinter said in the same friendly tone, smoothing down his already tidy hair. 'We must hope for dry weather on Friday when the Progress arrives. Though in this damp demesne of York nothing is guaranteed.'

'No indeed.' Why was he being friendly now, I wondered.

'You will have a glass of wine today?' he asked. I hesitated, then nodded. He passed me a goblet. 'There, sir. The doctor has been and dressed Sir Edward's burns. He gave him a poultice for the one that was weeping fluid. He will come again tomorrow.'

'Good.'

'I fear we made a bad start yesterday. You must forgive me, I am alone in this tower with only my prisoner and those churls of guards for company. Such isolation causes the black humours to rise.' He smiled at me, yet his eyes still held that icy glitter.

'Consider it forgotten,' I said mildly. I hoped this might mean I had won, that there would be no more challenges to my authority. Radwinter nodded, then stepped to one of the windows and beckoned me over. Through the rain-spattered pane I saw a view of the broad river, some houses and, beyond the city wall, a bleak flat countryside of woods and heath. Radwinter pointed to a road leading out of the city.

'That is the Walmgate. The Progress will enter there on Friday.'

'I wonder how those thousands will get across the city to St Mary's.'

'The royal household has been organizing progresses time out of mind. Though never one like this.' He pointed to the horizon. 'Over there is Fulford Cross, which marks the boundary of the city. The city fathers will make their submission there.'

'I am to be there,' I said.

He turned to me. 'Indeed?'

'I am involved with the preparation of the petitions to the King. I will be at the presentation to him.'

'You do not sound as though it is a task you relish.'

I hesitated. 'It is a little daunting.'

'I have seen the King, you know.'

'Have you?'

Radwinter nodded proudly. 'Do you remember the trial of John Lambert three years ago?'

I did. The King, as Supreme Head of the Church, had presided over the heresy trial of Lambert, a radical reformer. It was the first sign he felt reform had gone far enough.

'Ay,' I answered slowly. 'He was burned.'

'As he deserved. Lambert was under my care while he was held in the Lollards' Tower; I accompanied him to the trial. The King was —' a smile played round the corners of his mouth — 'splendid. Magnificent. Dressed all in white, the colour of purity. When Lambert tried to air his heretical interpretations of the scriptures, he shouted him down, reduced him to a cringing dog. I saw Lambert burned too, he made a great shouting.' Radwinter looked at me; I sensed that he guessed how distasteful I would find this. He was playing with me again after all. I did not reply.

'And he will be magnificent again, with the Yorkers. He has been clever, forcing the gentry to take personal oaths to him. He forgives their trespasses and at the same time makes it clear that if those oaths are broken they can expect no mercy. Carrot and stick, that is how one deals with donkeys like these. So,' he added, 'your journey to York is concerned with more than Broderick.'

'The Archbishop offered me the legal position first. I was only given this second mission once I had agreed.'

Radwinter laughed softly. 'Yes, he can be a fox. But it will pay well.'

'Well enough,' I said stiffly.

'Enough to buy a new robe, I hope, especially if you are to see the King. The one you wear is torn. I only mention it in case you had not seen.'

'I have another. This one was torn this morning. On a glazier's cart.'

'Really? A strange mishap.'

'Yes.' I told him the story of finding Oldroyd's body, though only the parts that were public knowledge. The gaoler smiled again. 'It seems a lawyer's work is never done,' he said. He put down his goblet. 'Well, I expect you would like to see Sir Edward.'

'Please.'

Once again I followed as he ascended with his quick, light steps. I thought about what he had said about Lambert's trial and burning, and remembered Cranmer's description of Radwinter as a man of true and honest faith. That meant following the orthodoxy that the last word on religious matters belonged to the King, as Supreme Head. Such a man might well approve of burning a heretic, but his light and jesting tone had repelled me. Were his professions of faith merely a cover for enjoyment of cruelty? I stared at his back as he turned the key in the door to Broderick's cell.

Sir Edward was lying on his dirty pallet. Fresh rushes had been laid on the floor as I had ordered, though, and the cell stank less. I saw his shirt was open, a poultice strapped to his chest. He was emaciated, all his ribs visible under dead white skin. He stared at me coldly again.

'Well, Sir Edward,' I asked, 'how are you today?'

'They've poulticed my burn. It stings.'

'That can be a sign it is having effect.' I turned to the gaoler. 'He is very thin, Master Radwinter. What does he have to eat?'

'Pottage from the castle kitchens, the same the guards get. Not too much, certainly. A weakened man is less likely to make trouble. You saw yesterday how he can spring at one.'

'And how well he is chained. And he has been ill; a sick man may waste away without food.'

Radwinter's eye glinted. 'Would you like me to order thrushes in a pie from the King's kitchen, then, perhaps a plate of marchpanes?'

'No,' I answered, 'but I would like him put on the same rations as the guards.' Radwinter set his lips. 'See to it, please,' I said quietly.

Broderick laughed hoarsely. 'Does it not occur to you, sir, I would *rather* be weak when I get to London? So weak the torturers' first attentions kill me.'

'They would take care not to do that, Master Broderick,' Radwinter said softly. 'When you are brought to them they will study you carefully. They know how to bring each man to a degree of pain that will make him talk, yet keep him conscious and alive. But certainly a weaker man is likely to be able to endure less, to talk more quickly.' He smiled at me. 'So you see, the better you treat him, the more pain he will endure.'

'No,' I said sharply. 'He is to be fed properly.'

'And I will eat, for I am hungry. Even though I know what awaits me.' Broderick gave me a look full of pain as well as anger. 'How we hold on to life, eh, lawyer? We struggle to survive, even when there is no sense in it.' He looked towards the window. 'I came to see poor Robert every day while he hung out there, so he might see a friendly face. Each day I hoped to find him dead, yet each day he moved still, trying to ease his pains as he dangled, making weak groans. Yes, how we hold on to life.'

'Only the innocent deserve a quick death,' Radwinter said. 'Well, Master Shardlake, I will arrange for the extra rations for Sir Edward. Is there anything else?'

I looked at Broderick; he was staring at the ceiling again. There was a moment's silence, the only sound the patter of rain at the window. 'Not for now. I will come again, tomorrow probably.'

Once again Radwinter led me outside, locking the heavy door. I could tell by the set of his shoulders that he was angry, yet I was surprised by the ferocity of his look when he turned to me. His face was red, he almost scowled. Now I saw he nourished fire under that ice. In a way it was a relief.

'You undermine me before that treacherous, filthy rogue, sir.' His voice was thick with anger. 'If you wanted to change his rations, could you not have waited till we were outside to tell me?'

I looked at him steadily. 'I want him to see that I am in charge of his welfare.'

'I told you before, you do not know what manner of man you are dealing with. You may regret this softness.'

'I will obey my orders.' I took a deep breath. 'I think your judgement is clouded, sir. Not by zeal as the Archbishop told me, but by delight in cruelty.' The look he gave me was chilling, but anger drove me on. 'But you will not indulge yourself at the expense of the Archbishop's orders. He will hear what manner of man you are.'

To my surprise Radwinter laughed in my face, a mocking laugh that echoed round the dank corridor.

'You think the Archbishop does not know me? He knows me well, sir, and knows that England needs such as me to keep it safe from heretics!' He stepped closer to me. 'And we all serve a just and angry God. You should not forget it.'

Chapter Eight

WE HEADED BACK TO the Minster, walking quickly for we were very late for Master Wrenne.

'Perhaps I should take a message to Maleverer at St Mary's now,' Barak suggested. 'About the boy looking at the spot on the wall.'

I hesitated. 'No, I need you to help with the petitions, the summaries must be ready for tomorrow morning. We will leave as soon as we can, go straight back to St Mary's. Besides, they've probably scared whatever he knows out of that unfortunate boy.'

Arriving at the Minster, I showed my papers again at the gate and we passed inside once more.

Just then a shaft of sunlight pierced the clouds that were gathering, shining on the huge windows of the great church and making a riot of colour.

'Why is York Minster allowed to keep its stained glass,' Barak asked, 'while the monasteries have it all torn out as idolatrous?'

'There are reformers who would pull the coloured glass from all churches, have only plain windows. But the King's limited himself to the monasteries. For now.'

'It makes no sense.'

'It's part of the compromise with the traditional party. You can't expect politics to make sense.'

'You're right there.'

The old housekeeper answered Wrenne's door, her look as cheerless as ever. The old man sat reading in the candlelit hall, where a good fire blazed in the central hearth. I saw an effort at cleaning had been made since the day before, for the books had been tidied and the green and yellow floor-tiles shone. The peregrine falcon still stood on its perch by the fire; the bell on its leg tinkled as it turned to stare at us. A fine cloth with a design of white roses had been put on the table, where three large stacks of paper stood. Master Wrenne rose slowly to his feet, laying down his book.

'Brother Shardlake. And young Barak, good.'

'I am sorry we are late,' I said. 'You had my note?'

'Yes. Some urgent business, you said?'

Again I told the story of the glazier falling into his cart, leaving out the subsequent events. Wrenne frowned thoughtfully.

'Peter Oldroyd. Yes, I knew him; I have done legal work for the glaziers' guild, he was chairman one year. A quiet, respectable fellow; lost his family in the plague in '38. It is sad.' Wrenne was silent for a long moment, then said, 'You catch me at my books. Sir Thomas More, his history of Richard III. A man of rare invective, was he not?'

'Yes, he was not the gentle saint some people paint him.'

'But he had a good turn of phrase. I have been reading what he said about the Wars between the Roses last century. "These matters be Kings' games, as it were stage plays, and for the most part played upon scaffolds."'

'So they were. Upon bloody fields of battle too.'

'Indeed. But sit; take some wine before we begin. You look as though it has been a hard morning.'

'Thank you.' As I took a cup my eye strayed to the piles of books. 'You have a most rare collection, sir.'

'Yes, I have many old monkish books. They are not theological works, that would have me under surveillance from the Council of the North, but I have saved some valuable works of history and philosophy. For their interest, and their beauty too. I am something of an antiquarian, you see. It has been an interest all my life.'

'That is a worthy task, sir. There was much wrong with the monasteries, but so much learning and beauty has gone to the fire. I have seen pages written with care hundreds of years ago used to wipe down horses.'

Wrenne nodded. 'I thought we would be of like mind, brother. I can tell a scholar. There has been a great cull of monastic libraries in York these last three years. St Clement's, Holy Trinity, above all St Mary's.' He smiled. 'The antiquarian John Leland was here in the spring. He was most interested in the library I have collected upstairs. Even a little jealous, I think.'

'Perhaps I may see it some time.'

'Indeed.' Wrenne nodded his leonine head. 'But I fear we must study some lesser documents today. The petitions to the King.' He smiled ruefully. 'Where do you practise, Brother Shardlake?'

'Lincoln's Inn. I am lucky, I have a house hard by in Chancery Lane.'

'I studied at Gray's Inn. Many years ago.' Wrenne smiled. 'It was 1486 when I came to London. The King's father had not been on the throne a year.'

I did a quick calculation in my head: fifty-five years ago, he must be well over seventy. 'But you returned to practise in York?' I asked.

'Ay, I was never at ease in the south.' He hesitated, then said, 'I have a nephew at Gray's Inn, the son of my late wife's sister. He went down there and stayed. Perhaps you may have heard of him.' He looked at me keenly. 'Martin Dakin. He would be near your age now, a little older. Just past forty.'

'No, I do not know him. But there are hundreds of barristers in London.'

Wrenne looked uncomfortable. 'There was a bad fratch, a family quarrel, and we lost touch.' He sighed. 'I would like to see him again before I die. He is my only family now, you see. His parents died in the plague three years ago.'

'Many seem to have died then.'

He shook his head. 'York has had a terrible time these last five years. The rebellion in 1536, then in 1538 the plague. It returned in 1539 and again last year, though mercifully this year we have been spared.' He smiled wryly. 'Otherwise the King would not have come. His harbingers have been around the hospitals all summer, making sure there have been no cases. Instead this year we have had the new conspiracy. Troubled times.'

'Well, let us hope for a better future now. And I would gladly take a message to your nephew in London, sir. If you wished.'

'Thank you.' Wrenne nodded slowly. 'I will think on that. I had a son, who I dreamed would follow me in the law, but he died when he was five, poor nobbin.' Wrenne looked into the fire, then shrugged and smiled. 'Forgive an old man's gloomy talk. I am the last of my line and some days it weighs on me.'

I felt a catch at my throat, for his words made me think of my father; I too was the last of my line.

'We have noticed, sir,' Barak said, 'that security in the city seems very great. We saw some Scotch turned away at Bootham Bar.'

'Yes, and all the stout vagabonds are being cleared from the city. The beggars will be gone from the Minster tomorrow. Poor caitiffs. Security is tight.' Wrenne hesitated, then added, 'You must know, sir, the King is not popular up here. Not among the gentry, though now they bow and scrape, and even less among the common people.'

I remembered Cranmer's scathing words about northern papists. 'Because of the religious changes, that caused the rebellion?'

'Ay.' Wrenne clasped his hands round his goblet. 'I remember the rebellion. The King's agents were closing the small monasteries and assessing church property. Then suddenly the commons erupted all over Yorkshire. It was like a wildfire.' He waved a large, square hand where a fine emerald ring glinted. 'They elected Robert Aske leader and within a week he had marched into York at the head of five thousand men. The City Council and the Minster authorities were terrified. This was an explosive crowd of rough peasants who had turned themselves into an army. So they agreed to obey Aske; the church authorities held a celebratory Mass for him in the Minster.' He nodded at the window. 'I watched the rebels processing into the Mass from there; thousands of them, all with swords and pikes.'

I nodded reflectively. 'And they thought they could make the King agree to reverse the religious changes.'

'Robert Aske was a naïve man for a lawyer. But if the King had not tricked them into disbanding his army I believe they could have taken the whole country.' He looked at me seriously. 'The discontent in the north goes back a very long way. To the Striving between the Two Roses last century. The north was loyal to King Richard III and the Tudors have never been popular. The rebellion was about more than religion, too. The Dalesmen sent round tracts by a "Captain Poverty" full of complaints about high rents and tithes. When the religious changes came –' he spread his big hands – 'it was the straw that broke the camel's back.'

'King Richard?' Barak asked. 'Yet he seized the throne, and murdered the rightful heirs. The Princes in the Tower.'

'There are those who say it was the King's father that killed them.' He paused. 'I was a boy when King Richard processed through York after his coronation. You should have seen the city then. People hung their best carpets from the windows all along the way, petals were showered on him as he rode by. It is different today. The common folk are reluctant even to lay gravel before their doors to smooth King Henry's way, for all the council have ordered it.'

'But the quarrels of the Two Roses can hardly have meaning today,' I said. 'The Tudors have been on the throne near sixty years.'

'No?' Wrenne inclined his head. 'They say after the conspiracy was uncovered this spring, the old Countess of Salisbury and her son were executed in the Tower.'

I recalled the story of the aged countess's dreadful death; it had circulated in London that summer. Imprisoned without charge, she had been led to the block where an inexperienced boy had hacked at her head and shoulders; the King's executioner had been busy in York, despatching the conspirators.

'She was the last Yorkist heir,' Wrenne said quietly. 'Was that not done because the King still fears the name Plantagenet?'

I sat back. 'But surely the conspiracy this year was mainly about religion, like the Pilgrimage of Grace?'

'Old loyalties played their part too. The King killed the countess and her son to make sure.' He raised his eyebrows. 'And they say *his* young children have disappeared into the Tower?'

'No one knows.'

'More Princes in the Tower.'

I nodded slowly. I remembered Cranmer saying, 'This time they called him tyrant; many meant to overthrow him.'

'I see more clearly now why there is such tight security for this visit,' I said. 'And yet, the house of Tudor has brought safety and security to England. No one can deny that.'

'Very true.' Wrenne leaned back in his chair with a sigh. 'And for the King to come and set his stamp on the north is an intelligent plan. I only say, sir, do not underestimate the currents that run here.'

I looked at the old man, wondering where his sympathies lay. I guessed that like many an aged student of the world's affairs, he was past feeling any great passion. I changed the subject.

'It seems we will be present at the King's reception on Friday. Sir William Maleverer confirmed it to me yesterday at St Mary's. We are to hand over the petitions.'

'Yes, I have had a message. We are to take the petitions to the Office of the Great Chamberlain tomorrow. He will see us at nine and take us through our paces for the meeting with the King. He wants me to bring the petitions and the summary half an hour early so he can go through them. So I will start early for St Mary's, and see you there at nine.'

'I hope we will be properly rehearsed.'

'I am sure we will. The Council will want everything to go with perfect smoothness.' Wrenne smiled and shook his head. 'By Jesu, to see the King at my age. That will be a strange thing.'

'I confess I am not looking forward to it.'

'We have only to perform our little duty. The King will barely notice us. But to see him. And that wondrous train of waggons a mile long. They've been bringing in hay to feed the horses from as far as Carlisle.'

'It is very well organized. They even have a girl going round the town buying sweet doucets for the Queen.' I told him of our encounter with Tamasin Reedbourne. Wrenne winked at Barak.

'Pretty, was she?'

'Fine enough, sir.'

Something struck me then. I remembered the girl had told me she had given her servant leave to choose some cloth for a new doublet from a shop. Yet he had come back empty-handed. I put the thought aside.

'Well,' Wrenne said, 'we should begin work. The summaries need only be brief. We can start now and go on till we finish.'

'Yes. I would not like to annoy the Chamberlain's office. Nor Sir William Maleverer.'

Wrenne frowned. 'Maleverer is a boor, for all he comes of an old Yorkshire family. He is like many of those appointed to the Council of the North since the Pilgrimage of Grace. Gentry who did not join the rebellion and now proclaim their loyalty to reform, but have no real religion beyond their own advancement. Ruthless and ambitious men. But tell me, sir, what did you see of the building at St Mary's?'

'It is extraordinary. Hundreds of carpenters and artists, building great pavilions. By the way, when was the monastery put down?'

'Two years since. Abbot Thornton wrote to Cromwell asking for the monastery to be saved, or if it could not that he be granted lands and a pension. Which he was.' The old man laughed cynically.

'The abbots of the large houses were corrupt and greedy men.'

'And now St Mary's is the King's, the abbot's house renamed King's Manor.' Wrenne rubbed his hand across his cheek thoughtfully. 'Perhaps we shall have an announcement the Queen is with child.'

'The King would certainly welcome a second son.'

'The royal succession.' He smiled. 'The bloodline of God's anointed rolling down the ages. The head and soul of the realm, the peak of the chain of degree that binds man to man and keeps all safe.'

'And where we lawyers hang somewhere in the middle, hoping to rise and fearing to fall.'

'Ay.' Wrenne laughed and waved a hand round the room. 'See my table on its dais, nearest the fire, so that when the household servants lay their own table to dine they are lower down and further from the heat. All part of the great chain of earthly rank, this world's great theatre. Well, so it must be, or we should have chaos.' He winked conspiratorially. 'Though I allow Madge to sit close to the fire, that she may warm her old bones.'

✝

WE SPENT THE REST OF the day going through the petitions, breaking only for a dish of old Madge's bland pottage. Some petitions were in elegant calligraphy, impressed with heavy wax seals, others mere scrawls on poor scraps of paper. Barak prepared brief summaries of the points at issue in each case at dictation from myself and Wrenne. The old man proved quick and decisive, ruthlessly separating the wheat from the chaff. Most were relatively trifling complaints against minor officials. We worked companionably, candles lit against the dull afternoon; the only sounds the falcon's bell as it stirred on its perch and the occasional boom of the Minster bells.

Late in the afternoon Wrenne handed me a paper filled with a laboured scrawl. 'This is interesting,' he said.

The petition was from a farmer in the parish of Towton, outside the city. He had changed the use of his land from pasture to growing vegetables for the city, and his ploughmen kept digging up human bones which the church authorities commanded he deliver to the local churchyard for burial. He asked for the cost of his travelling to and fro, and time lost, to be defrayed.

'Towton,' I said. 'There was a battle there, was there not?'

'The greatest battle of the Wars between the Roses. 1461. There were thirty thousand dead in that bloody meadow. And now this farmer goes to law to be paid for delivering their bones for burial. What do you think we should do with the farmer's claim?'

'It is surely outside our jurisdiction. It is a church matter, it should go to the Minster dean.'

'But the church is hardly likely to rule against its own interest and pay the man, is it?' Barak interjected. 'He should at least have representation.'

Wrenne took the petition back, smiling ruefully. 'Yet Brother Shardlake is right, as a matter of canon law it falls outside the remit of petitions to the King. Church jurisdiction is a sensitive issue these days. The King would not wish to raise a storm on such a trifling issue. No, we must refer the farmer to the dean.'

'I agree,' I said.

Wrenne gave his wry smile again. 'We must all be politicians now. And recognize the law has its limits. You must not expect too much of it, Master Barak.'

✝

BY FIVE O'CLOCK we had all the petitions briefly summarized. It was getting dark, and I heard rain pattering on the windows. Wrenne looked over the summaries. 'Yes,' he said. 'I think that is all clear.'

'Good. And now, we must get back. We have some business at King's Manor.'

Wrenne looked out of the window. 'Let me lend you a coat, it is raining hard, pewling down as we say. Wait there a moment.' He left us in the hall. We went and stood again by the fire.

'He is a good old fellow,' Barak said.

'Ay.' I stretched out my hands to warm them. 'Lonely, I would guess. No one in the world but his old housekeeper and that bird.' I nodded at the falcon, which had gone to sleep on its perch. Wrenne returned, bearing a coat, good and heavy but far too large for me, the hem nearly scraping the floor. I promised to return it on the morrow. We set off into the rain, to find out if poor young Green had said anything about a hiding place in Oldroyd's wall.

Chapter Nine

W E WALKED THROUGH dark empty streets, tired again. The air was full of autumnal smells of woodsmoke and the dank odour of fallen leaves.

'So you'll see the King?' Barak shook his head in wonder.

'You never saw him when you worked for Cromwell?'

He laughed. 'No, it was the back ways for the likes of me.'

'Would you like to see him?'

'Ay.' He smiled thoughtfully. 'Something to tell my children one day.'

I looked at him. He had never spoken of having children before; always he had seemed one who lived from day to day.

'Perhaps we could help Master Wrenne find this nephew of his,' I said. 'You could ask around the Inns for me.'

'Might be best to leave well alone. Might find this nephew doesn't want to see him.' A hard note crept into Barak's voice, and I remembered he had cut himself off from his mother when she remarried, with much bitterness.

'Perhaps. But we could try. It was sad his only child died.'

'Ay.' He paused. 'Master Wrenne runs on a bit. All that talk of kings and the old wars.'

'I remember a talk I had with Guy, just before we left.'

'How is the old Moor?'

'Well enough. I was talking of the King's Progress, and he told me the story of the last king of his country, Granada. When he was a boy it was still a Moorish kingdom, independent from Spain. The last ruler, King Boabdil the Small—'

'There's a name! '

'Listen, will you. Guy saw him as a child carried through Granada in a litter, everyone bowing and showering him with flowers, as Brother Wrenne said the Yorkers did for King Richard. But Boabdil lost his kingdom to Spain, and had to flee in exile to the land of the Moors.'

'What became of him?'

'Guy said it was rumoured he died in a battle in Africa. The point is, no one knows. His power and glory were gone.'

As we walked up the street called Petergate, we heard a commotion of cries and shouts. Turning to look, we saw four ragged-looking beggars running towards us, holding up their arms to ward off blows aimed at their shoulders by three men in official-looking robes carrying stout birching-rods. They passed us and were driven on towards the river that divided the city. 'Clearing the beggars from the city,' I observed.

Barak watched as the ragged men were driven on to a large stone bridge. 'And how are they supposed to live outside?' he asked. 'Beg alms from the trees and bushes?'

We were silent as we walked under the barbican at Bootham Bar. I saw that the heads on their poles, and the disgusting hank of flesh, had been removed. 'No beggars, no rebels' carrion,' Barak observed. 'The city's to look its best for the King.'

I wondered if they would take Aske's remains down from the castle. But probably the King would not visit that decayed and doleful spot.

✝

DESPITE THE RAIN and darkness at St Mary's, the workmen were still labouring away. Sounds of sawing and hammering came from the pavilions, while beside them men were working at putting up the gigantic tents, smoothing canvas and tautening ropes. I remembered seeing enormous tents in pictures of the Field of the Cloth of Gold.

The courtyard was a sea of mud. I had never seen men work in such conditions before. Evidently there was a problem with drainage, for a group of labourers, caked in mud, had excavated a trench around the second pavilion and were extending it into a long channel, with much shouting and cursing. Officials stood arguing over plans in the doorway of the manor house; we squeezed through them and told the guard we needed to see Sir William Maleverer.

'He's not here, sir,' the man said. 'He's ridden off to meet the Progress. At Leconfield, I believe.'

'How far is that?'

'Thirty miles off. He had an urgent summons. But he'll be back tomorrow morning.'

I thought a moment. 'Is the King's coroner here? Master Archbold?'

'He's gone with him.'

I bit my lip. 'There was an apprentice boy taken in the town by Sir William this morning, held for questioning. Perhaps a female servant too. Do you know what happened to them?'

He looked at me suspiciously. 'Why do you ask?'

'We were there when the apprentice was taken. I need to speak to Sir William about it.'

'The boy's been locked up, with strict orders he is to be held close till Sir William returns. The woman-servant was sent home; Sir William had just finished questioning her and was about to start on the boy when the summons came.'

'Can I get a message to Sir William?'

'In this weather it would take hours even for a fast messenger to reach the Progress and find him, sir. It would be just as well to wait until tomorrow morning. He is setting off first thing, I believe.'

I thought a moment. 'All right. We'll wait. Could you have a message left for Sir William, that Master Shardlake needs to see him, in connection with that boy? I shall be here tomorrow morning.'

There was nothing left to do but return to our lodgings. We

walked along the side of the church — I was not going to take any
shortcuts through that church again, even if it got us out of the rain.
I saw the glazier's cart had been removed.

'I said I should have come back and given Maleverer a message,'
Barak said.

'Thank you for reminding me,' I answered drily. 'I'll probably
get into trouble now. Why has he gone to meet the Progress? God's
wounds, is this matter important enough for him to need to consult
the Privy Council?'

'Richard Rich is on the Privy Council, isn't he?'

'Don't remind me.' I sighed deeply. 'God's death, I wish I'd
never got entangled in this!' I kicked out in anger at a discarded
piece of wood on the duckboards, then reddened with embarrassment
as I saw the stout figure of Master Craike approaching through the
gloom. He was walking carefully along the slippery duckboards,
swathed in a fur-lined coat with a hood up against the rain. He
smiled, affecting not to notice my outbreak of temper.

'Foul weather,' he said.

'Ay, it is. I see the glazier's cart has gone.'

He nodded. 'It was ordered to be searched, Jesu knows why. But
are you all right, I heard you got locked in the chapterhouse?' His
eyes were alive with curiosity.

'A foolish accident. I must thank you, sir, for your help this
morning.'

'It was nothing. But the glazier's death seems to have caused a
great stir. I was brought before Sir William earlier. He made me tell
him everything that happened. Something is going on, sir,' he said
portentously.

'Yes,' I said. 'There seems to be. Tell me, Master Craike, how
well did you know Oldroyd?'

He gave me a sharp look. 'Not well,' he answered quickly.
'When he came to start work last week he asked if there was a place
he could keep his horse and cart overnight, and I had to tell him he
must leave the cart in the open, and take the horse home each night.

There is so little room, you see. Afterwards, if I was passing I would exchange a few words with him. He seemed a pleasant enough fellow, and I was curious to talk to a Yorker. I have scarcely been into the town,' he added; it seemed to me a little too quickly.

'He seemed to regret the passing of the old ways.' I looked keenly at Craike.

'Perhaps. I did not discuss that with him. I have little time for talk, the amount of work there is. The Knight Harbinger has arrived, to see all is ready for the King. I am on my way to meet him.' He wiped a drip of water from his hood. 'In fact, I must be off.'

'Ah well, no doubt I shall see you later. We must have that drink.'

'We must,' he said hastily. He stepped off the duckboards to walk round us, his feet squelching in the grass, and was gone.

'He was keen to leave,' Barak observed.

I watched his big form disappearing in the rain. 'Yes. I suspect he's a sympathizer with the old religion – he and Oldroyd probably shared opinions together. I hope that's all.' We resumed our way, passing the door we had gone through that morning.

'He couldn't have had anything to do with Oldroyd's death,' Barak said. 'He was with us when we heard that door creak open in the church.'

'True. But he was abroad very early, he came up to me right after that horse charged into the courtyard. There could have been more than one person involved. You've seen how secure this place is, Barak. Whoever killed the glazier was already at St Mary's. It was a resident.'

'But there are hundreds here.'

'There are.'

We walked on to our lodgings. The cattle and sheep stood dripping in their pens; the fowls were huddled up against the walls, seeking some protection from the rain. Inside the building a group of clerks was standing talking round the fire, which was blazing merrily, and passing round a big leather pouch of wine. The young lawyer we had met earlier, Master Kimber, stood a little apart from them, warming his hands.

'Good evening, sir,' he greeted us. 'You have been caught in the rain?'

'Ay, we have been in the city. And you fellows, have you finished work?'

'Yes, sir. The clerks here and I have been sorting through the bills for all the food that has been bought.' He pointed to a young man. 'Master Barrow here made an entry for fifty pigs where he should have put five hundred this afternoon. The cofferer threatens to send him back to London. Have you any need of a clerk for your counting house?'

Master Barrow scowled at him. I laughed. 'No, thank you.'

'Someone was asking for you a little while ago.' Kimber turned and called out, 'Hey, Tom Cowfold, are you there?' A round-faced man, young but already balding, put his head out of a nearby cubicle. 'Here is Master Shardlake,' Kimber said importantly.

'Ah, yes, sir.' The clerk approached us. ''Tis about the rehearsal tomorrow, for the presentation to the King—'

'Come to my room,' I said, aware the clerks were listening with interest. I led him into my cubicle, Barak following.

'Now, sir.' Master Cowfold looked at me self-importantly. 'You are asked to come to my master's office at nine, for the rehearsal for the presentation. Sir James Fealty, of the steward's office. Master Wrenne is to be there too, with the petitions. My master will take you through the manner in which they are to be offered to the King.'

'Who is actually to make the presentation?'

'Master Wrenne.' I was relieved to hear that. 'Er, and you should be in the clothes you will wear at the presentation.' The clerk was looking at my ill-fitting, voluminous coat.

'Very well.'

'Until tomorrow then, sir.' He bowed and left.

'Let's change,' I said to Barak, 'and get some supper. That

Mistress Reedbourne said she'd meet you at the hall at six, it's near that now.'

'All right. I'll go and ask those lads where it is.' He stepped outside. A moment later I heard Cowfold greet him. 'Here's the crookback lawyer's clerk.'

My heart lurched with anger; the churl might have lowered his voice.

'Shut up, you arsehole,' I heard Barak say quickly. There was a moment's silence, then the conversation continued more soberly. I changed my wet hose, took a deep breath and stepped out, self-conscious now in Wrenne's big coat. I wished God had not made the old man so tall. The clerks had dispersed, and Barak was standing alone by the fire. He gave me an uneasy look; he knew that overheard insults did not improve my temper.

'Where is the dining hall, then?' I asked curtly.

'The clerks say it is set up in the old monks' refectory. Everyone's together apart from the high officials at the abbot's house.'

'Come on, then.'

☩

OUTSIDE A NUMBER OF people were heading for the long row of claustral buildings running alongside the church. A large door stood open. We followed a group of carpenters, covered in wet sawdust, towards it. Standing in the archway, in the expensive-looking yellow dress we had first seen her in and a blue French hood that set off her eyes, was Tamasin. To my surprise Jennet Marlin stood beside her, wearing the slight frown that seemed to be her habitual look. Tamasin greeted us with a curtsy, though Mistress Marlin merely nodded coldly. Tamasin passed us two strips of paper. Mine had my name and the words 'Lawyer for the King's petitions', stamped by the Chamberlain's office.

'Thank you, Mistress Reedbourne,' Barak said. 'You've saved us a wait in a draughty tent.'

'Yes. Thank you,' I added. I disapproved of the girl's forward-ness, but she had gone to trouble for us. I determined to make myself pleasant, though I did not feel much like it. 'We are hungry,' I said. 'You must be, too. No doubt the Queen's servants have their own dining place.'

'Oh no, sir,' Tamasin said. 'We have to eat in the common hall too.'

'With the rabble,' Mistress Marlin added in her sharp voice. 'Thank the Lord the Queen's dining quarters will be set up tomorrow, we can eat in peace.' She gave Barak a sour look. 'Tonight I thought I would accompany Tamasin, she should not be dining alone.'

I could think of nothing to say to that, so I bowed for the women to precede us inside. We mounted a wide staircase, the cornices ornamented with beautifully carved angels. Waiters were running up and down the stairs bearing trays and leather pitchers of wine. We entered the monks' old refectory. Rows of trestle tables were set out, packed together so closely there was scarcely enough room for the waiters to pass. I estimated there were places for two hundred people. Most seats were occupied by tired-looking workmen and carpenters. I saw the clerks sitting together in a little group some distance off. At the next table a little group of women sat together. One of them looked at Mistress Marlin, then nudged her fellows. They looked at her and giggled. Jennet Marlin's face reddened. I felt for her.

A man in the black robe of an usher bustled over to us. We handed him our dockets and he led us to a table with four vacant spaces. I was glad it was some distance away from those clerks. Mistress Marlin wrinkled her nose as we sat down, for the tablecloth and napkins were stained. A waiter dumped down a flagon of ale and hurried off. I poured for the others.

'At least the bowls and cups at this table are pewter,' Mistress Marlin said. Glancing round, I saw the carpenters were drinking from wooden cups.

'So some of the proprieties are being observed,' I said. Another waiter appeared, bearing a big bowl of pottage. He set it down hurriedly, spilling a little on the cloth. Mistress Marlin sighed, but Tamasin laughed, passing the bowl down to her.

'We must bear with it, mistress,' she said, and to my surprise Jennet Marlin gave her a quick, affectionate smile.

'How came you to be in the Queen's service?' Barak asked Tamasin when we were all served.

'My mother served in the royal kitchens before me. I have been there two years, working for the Queen's confectioner. They asked me to accompany the Progress for my experience with sweetmeats,' she added proudly. 'I was sent ahead with Lady Rochford and Mistress Marlin to help prepare for the Queen and her household, and ensure she may have the pretty comfits she likes so much. Expensive doucets of marzipan and almonds and ginger.'

I turned to Jennet Marlin. 'And you, mistress, have you served Lady Rochford long?'

She gave me her haughty look. 'No, sir. I served Lady Edge-combe when the Lady Anne of Cleves was Queen. I moved to Lady Rochford's service last summer.'

'And you are from the north?'

'Originally I come from Ripon. But I was sent to court at sixteen.'

'And you have come all the way with the Progress?'

'Yes,' she said with a sigh. 'Through cold and rain in July, everything more filthy than you could believe. It was so wet all the roads turned to mud. The household officials said we should return but the King and his councillors insisted the Progress must go on.'

I nodded. 'Because its political importance is so great.'

'Yes. Then after the weather improved the King delayed at Hatfield and Pontefract, none knew why. Then we were sent to York while the King diverted to Hull. We have been here near a week.'

'How long is the King to stay in York?'

'They say three days, but always there seem to be delays.'

'It must be frustrating.' I hesitated. 'Do you know what the great celebration is to be, that they are all preparing for?'

She shrugged her shoulders. 'No. There are all sorts of rumours.' She changed the subject. 'You are a barrister, sir?'

'I am. At Lincoln's Inn.'

'My fiancé is a barrister at Gray's Inn.'

The same as Wrenne's nephew, I thought.

'You will doubtless have been told,' she continued, 'he is in the Tower on suspicion of involvement in the conspiracy. It is a subject of great gossip.'

'I had heard,' I replied uncomfortably.

'You may have met him. Bernard Locke.' Her full mouth, which she seemed to hold perpetually in a tight line, softened a little.

'No. I'm afraid not,' I said. It was the second time today I had been asked if I knew a Gray's Inn barrister.

'He is from Ripon too, we have known each other since we were children.' She looked at me with sudden intensity. 'His arrest was a terrible mistake. He will be freed. Many have been arrested who were guilty of nothing. They had to cast the net wide, but they will realize Bernard is innocent and release him.'

'Let us hope so, mistress.' I was surprised at her discussing the matter so freely. I hoped she was right; but I knew that those suspected of political offences could languish in the Tower for years.

'I will never abandon hope,' she said with fierceness.

'Your loyalty does you credit, madam.'

At that she gave me one of her contemptuous looks. 'I owe him all.'

A waiter came up, laying a big mutton pie on the table. Barak cut it for us; as Jennet Marlin reached to take her share, I saw the hand holding her knife was trembling slightly. Despite her rudeness I could not help feeling sorry for her. If she wore her heart on her sleeve like this all the time, I could imagine the other women in the household mocking her; women can be crueller even than men.

'I heard the Queen has been ill on the journey north,' I said. 'I hope she is better now.'

Again she gave that mirthless smile. 'She had a summer cold, that was all. She made much of it, as young girls will.'

'I am glad it is nothing worse.'

'She got my mistress Lady Rochford fussing over her, calling her poor baby and bringing her cushions.' She spoke with distaste. I remembered how rudely Lady Rochford had addressed her the day before. It struck me Jennet Marlin was a very angry woman. She reminded me of someone, though I could not remember whom it was.

'There are rumours the Queen is pregnant,' I said.

She stared at me coldly. 'I know nothing of that. You fish for gossip, sir.'

'I am sorry,' I said stiffly. Mistress Marlin bent her head to her plate. Evidently she had had enough of conversation with me.

Around us the talk grew louder as the wine loosened tongues. Barak was telling Tamasin an edited tale of how he came to be my assistant. 'Before last year I worked for Lord Cromwell. Master Shardlake also had his patronage, and when my master fell he took me on as clerk.'

'You worked for Lord Cromwell,' she said, her eyes wide. 'Did you know him?'

'Ay.' Barak looked sad for a moment.

'Tell me how you came to be locked in the monks' chapterhouse,' she said with a smile. 'I am sure it was not mere foolishness.'

'It was,' Barak said. He smiled wryly. 'I am but a wantwit, a foolish jester.'

She laughed. 'I think you are a man of many parts.'

'Many parts I have.' They both laughed. Mistress Marlin gave Tamasin a severe look. I thought again, who is it she reminds me of? I worried at the matter while next to me Barak and Tamasin's conversation grew more flirtatious. At length, Mistress Marlin stood up.

'Tamasin, we should leave now. Lady Rochford will be finished her meal now, she may wish some task of me. And you should not walk back alone.'

'We can accompany you back to the abbot's house, madam,' I offered.

'Thank you,' she said quickly, 'but no. Come, Tamasin.' Barak and I stood and bowed as the ladies left, Tamasin drawing one or two admiring glances along the tables. We sat down again.

'You two got on well,' I said to Barak.

'Ay, she's a fine girl. She says the day after tomorrow some of the townsfolk are rehearsing a musical display to be put on before the King when he arrives. I asked her to accompany me there. If that is all right,' he added.

'So long as some new demand on us does not arise.' I looked at him. 'Are most of the women you dally with so forward?' I meant the words in jest, but they came out sharp. He shrugged.

'Perhaps she is forward. But in these strange circumstances for all of us, why should we not snatch a little pleasure where we can?' There was a slight truculence in his tone. 'Do you disapprove of her?'

'I think she has something scheming about her, for all her merry airs.' I wondered whether to tell him I believed there was something odd about the incident the day before, but held my tongue.

'Mistress Marlin is a strange woman,' he said. 'How old is she, I wonder?'

'About thirty. Same age as you.'

'She might be attractive if she did not always look as though she were sucking on a bad tooth.'

'Yes. Her fiancé is in the Tower. She said she had known him since childhood.'

'A long engagement, if she's thirty.'

'Yes, it is.'

He smiled. 'I can ask Mistress Tamasin about it tomorrow, if you like.'

'I confess she piques my curiosity. I have a feeling she dislikes me, I wish I knew why.'

'I think she dislikes everybody.'

'Perhaps. But now we are done, I have been waiting for a chance to speak with you about this morning. What you said in the chapterhouse, that you'd never have made a mistake like that when you worked for Cromwell. Is that what has been on your mind these last weeks?'

He hesitated, then said quietly. 'These days I feel neither fish nor fowl.' I nodded, encouraging him to continue. He reddened. 'When I first came to work for you it was something new, it was interesting. But now I realize . . .'

'Go on.'

'I am too rough and crude ever to fit in with the world of the courts. You do not know how many times I have sat taking notes in court, or greeted other barristers in your chambers, and have wanted to call them all pompous arseholes and tweak their noses.'

'That is mere childishness.'

'No, it is not. You know what my life was before I met you. A rough life among rough people, Lord Cromwell prized me for my contacts among such folk. But now he is gone, if I were to leave the law without a trade, I should soon sink to being a man of the streets, end up where I was as a child.' He sighed and rubbed his hand across his forehead.

'The law may be a dull life sometimes. But, Jack, look ahead ten years. Would you rather be a trickster on the streets then, your joints stiffer each winter, or secure in your post at Lincoln's Inn?'

He looked me in the eye. 'I am torn. Part of me wants to stay, settle down, yet part of me enjoyed the excitement this morning.'

'I saw.' I took a deep breath. 'I would be sorrier than I can say to lose you. You have brightened up life in chambers no end. But it is your life, you must decide.'

He smiled sadly. 'I have been an unruly clerk these last weeks, have I not?'

'That you have.'

'I am sorry.' He bit his lip. 'I will decide, one way or the other, before we return to London. I promise.'

'If you want to talk more with me, I shall be ready.'

'Thank you.'

I drew a deep breath. 'One more thing,' I said. 'I have decided. I think we should get up very early tomorrow, visit the glazier's house again before this rehearsal of the presentation to King. I am worried Maleverer will say we should have sent a messenger after him. I want to go and check whether the searchers found anything in that room. If there are signs they did, there is less to worry about.'

'And if they did not?'

'Then we shall have to look ourselves.' I spoke with trepidation. Barak's eyes, though, had lit up at the prospect.

Chapter Ten

BY THE TIME WE left the refectory the rain had stopped. It was dark now, but in the courtyard the men laboured on. Three enormous tents now stood beside the pavilions, and men were taking furniture inside — ornate chairs, big carved wooden buffets and boxes that probably contained gold plate, for soldiers accompanied them. And all of this, I thought, must have been carried from London.

Back in our lodgings the clerks had brought a small trestle table up to the fire and sat playing cards. Kimber and a couple of other young men in lawyers' robes were with them and I reflected on the odd, temporary egalitarianism the Progress seemed to have brought to its employees. Kimber asked if we would join them and I told Barak to do so if he wished, but I would go to my cubicle. The words 'crookback lawyer's clerk' still rankled. A little to my disappointment, he said he would. I left him and went to repair my robe as best I could with my little sewing kit, then lay down on my bed.

It was too early to sleep, though, and as I lay there listening to the whoops and groans from the card players as their fortunes changed, I found myself prey to a succession of worrying thoughts. I thought about Maleverer's sudden dash to visit the Privy Council, and my failure to tell him there might be something concealed at Oldroyd's house. My decision to go there early on the morrow had been an impulsive one, but on reflection it was the safest thing to do to avoid possible trouble. If there was a hiding place in the wall and it had been discovered, nothing was lost, but if it had not and I discovered it, that could only be to my credit. I did not hide from myself that Maleverer frightened me; he was a man as ruthless and brutal as my old master Cromwell had been, yet without his sophistication, and without, I guessed, any principles beyond ambition and a naked love of exercising power. A brute and a bully, a dangerous man.

And then there was Broderick. I recalled his cold assertion that I was feeding him up for the torturers in the Tower. And yet I must not forget that Broderick had been part of a plot which, had it succeeded, would have plunged the realm into untold bloodshed. I wondered again what secret it was he knew, a secret that even Cranmer was afraid of, then told myself that it was safer not to know.

Eventually the card players trailed off to their cubicles. Through the wall I heard Barak come in next door, and the chinking sound of coins laid on his chest; evidently he had had a successful evening. I undressed and got into bed, but still my thoughts turned in my head, worrying at me. I thought of that strange grim woman Jennet Marlin, with her angry grievance against, apparently, the whole world. And then it came to me whom she reminded me of, with a clarity that made me catch my breath.

My disability had marked me out from my earliest days. I had never been at ease among the boys from the local farms who gathered together and played and hunted rabbits in the woods. I had never been welcomed by them; it was as though in some way I threatened their rough physicality. And hunchbacks are known to bring bad luck.

For some years my only companion at play had been a little girl of my own age. Her name was Suzanne, and she was the daughter of the owner of the farm next to my father's. The father was a widower, a big rough cheerful man with a brood of five hulking boys. Suzanne was the only girl and after his wife died the farmer did not seem to know what to do with her. One day she had appeared in our yard where I was sailing paper boats in a large puddle. She watched me for a while; I was too shy to talk to her.

'What are you doing?' she asked at length.

'Playing at boats.' I looked up at her. She wore a dirty dress too small for her and her fair hair stuck out like straw. She looked more like the child of a vagabond than a respectable farmer.

'I'd like to play too.' She frowned slightly as she spoke, as though anticipating being told to go away. But I often longed for playmates, and decided even a girl would do. 'All right.'

'What's your name?'

'Matthew.'

'I'm Suzanne. How old're you?'

'Eight.'

'So'm I.'

She knelt beside me and pointed to a boat. 'That one's lopsided. You ain't folded the paper very well.'

And so, for the next few years, Suzanne became my playmate. Not all the time – sometimes months would pass when I hardly saw her and perhaps her father had told her she should not be playing with me, but sooner or later she would return and, without explanation for her absence, join in my solitary games. She would cajole me into playing at houses in a corner of her barn, serving water from puddles to her collection of raggedy dolls. She could be bossy but she was company and I felt sorry for her; I think I realized then that she was more of an outcast than I was, an outcast in her own home.

Our friendship, if it could be called that, ended abruptly when we were thirteen. I had not seen her for some months, except at church on Sunday, and then from a distance as her family had a pew on the other side of the church. Walking home after the service one summer's day, I saw a little group of girls and boys walking ahead of me in the lane. The girls wore coifs tied under their chins and smart, full-length adult dresses, the boys proper little doublets and caps. The girls were jostling for places next to Gilbert Baldwin, a handsome lad of fourteen who had always been the leader in the boys' games. Trailing behind the group, alone, holding a long hazel twig with which she was beating the long grasses at the side of the road, was Suzanne. I caught up with her.

'Ho, Suzanne,' I said.

She turned on me a face that would have been pretty had it not been red and distorted with anger. I noticed that her dress was shabby and had a tear at the hem, her hair wildly uncombed. 'Go away!' she hissed furiously.

I stepped back. 'Why, Suzanne, what have I done?'

She turned round, facing me. 'It's all your fault!'

'Why – why, what is?'

'They won't let me walk with them! They say my clothes smell, I'm dirty, I've no more manners than a tinker! And it's all because I spent my time playing with you instead of learning girlish things! Gilly Baldwin tells me I should make eyes at my hunchback friend!' Her voice rose, became tearful; her mouth was like a great angry 'O' in her scarlet face.

I looked up the lane. The troop of lads and girls had come to a halt and were watching the scene. The boys looked uneasy but there was a ripple of nasty laughter from the girls. 'Suzy's rowing with her swain,' one called.

Suzanne rounded on them. 'Don't,' she screamed. 'He's not! Don't! Stop it!' As the laughter redoubled she turned and ran off into a field, still howling, striking out at the ears of young wheat with her branch like one possessed. I looked after her for a while, then turned and walked back the way I had come. I would resume my way home once the boys and girls had gone. I had long ago learned that keeping silent and walking away was the best way to avoid mockery. Yet despite Suzanne's own cruelty to me, despite knowing that it was her family, not me, that had made her an outcast, whenever I saw her afterwards, always alone, always giving me vicious looks when she acknowledged me at all – I felt guilty, as though I was indeed partly responsible for her fate. I left for London a few years later and never saw her again, though I heard that she had never married and in later years had become a fierce reformer, denouncing neighbours for popery. And Jennet Marlin, though she came from a different class, had that same air of being consumed by anger against a world that had done her wrong. And with her, too, I had the same odd urge to appease. I sighed and lay back on my pillow, reflecting on how strange were the ways of the mind. And then, at last, I slept.

✝

BARAK HAD SET HIMSELF to wake at six and shortly after that he knocked softly at my door. I felt unrefreshed by such sleep as I had had, but rose and dressed in the chill damp air. I put on Wrenne's coat again rather than my own; it would remind me to return it to him when we met at the rehearsal. We slipped out quietly so as not to wake the men sleeping all round us. Outside dawn was only just breaking and everything was deep in shadow. We took the path alongside the church, where we had found poor Oldroyd the morning before, and made our way to the gate, where young Sergeant Leacon was on duty again.

'Up again early, sir?' he asked me.

'Ay, we have to go into town. You have been on night duty again?'

'Ay, and for another two days until the King comes.' He shook his head. 'That was a strange business yesterday, sir, with the glazier. Sir William Maleverer questioned me about it afterwards.'

Him too, I thought. 'Yes,' I said. 'You are right, it was a strange matter. When that horse charged out of the mist I did not know for a second what it was – something from hell perhaps.'

'They say it was an accident, sir. Do you know?'

I could see from his sharp look that he doubted that, perhaps thinking Maleverer was taking a lot of trouble over an accidental death. 'That is what they say.' I changed the subject. 'I expect you have seen a few strange things have happened on the way from London.'

'None as strange as that. Until I was sent here from Pontefract it was all walking and riding alongside the Progress, through thick mud when it rained and great clouds of dust when it didn't.' He smiled. 'Though there was great to-do near Hatfield, when a monkey one of the Queen's ladies had brought escaped and made its way to a local village.'

'Oh, yes?'

'The poor heathen folk there thought it was a devil, fled to the church and called the priest to go and send it back to Hell. I was sent with some men to take it. It was sitting in a cottager's outhouse, happily working its way through his store of fruit.'

Barak laughed. 'That must have been a sight!'

'It was. Sitting there in the little doublet its mistress dressed it in, its tail sticking out behind. Those villagers were all papists, I'd swear they thought the King's Progress had its own legion of devils in attendance.' He paused and shook his head.

'Well, we must be on our way, we have business.'

We passed through the gate and walked to Bootham Bar. 'Sharp young fellow, that,' I observed.

Barak grunted. 'Soldiers should ask no questions.'

'Some people cannot help asking questions.'

He gave me a sidelong look. 'Don't I know it?'

We arrived at the gate. It was shut, the curfew not yet lifted, and the guard was unwilling to let us through. I felt in my pocket for my commission, then cursed as I realized I had left it in my cubicle.

'Can't let tha in without it, sir,' the guard said firmly.

I asked Barak to go back to Sergeant Leacon and see if he could send someone to vouch for us. He returned in a few minutes with another big Kentishman, who peremptorily ordered the guard to let us through. Grumbling, the man opened the huge wooden gates and we slipped out.

We walked to Stonegate as the sun rose and the city came to life, keeping under the eaves as people opened their windows and threw the night's piss into the streets. The shopkeepers appeared in their doorways and the noise of their shutters banging open accompanied our passage.

'You are quiet this morning,' I said to Barak. I wondered if he had been thinking about our conversation.

'You too.'

'I did not sleep well.' I hesitated. 'I was thinking about Broderick, among other matters.'

'Ay?'

'You know my instructions are to make sure he is safe and well when he is delivered to London?'

'Is the gaoler making that difficult?'

'He likes to visit Broderick with pinpricks, but I think I can stop that. No, it is Broderick himself. He says I am keeping him healthy so the torturers can have a better time with him.'

'It is harder to break a fit man.'

'He says nothing will make him talk. He will die under the torture.'

Barak turned to me, his face impassive. 'Lord Cromwell said most men talk in the end. He was right.'

'I know, but this Broderick is not most men.'

'A lot may happen between now and the Tower. He may decide to talk, or some new information may appear that makes his interrogation less important. Who knows? He may yet be grateful for your attentions.'

I shook my head. 'No. Cranmer stressed his great importance. He will be tortured, and if he does break in the end it will be after much agony.'

Barak gave me the impatient look that came over his face sometimes. 'Didn't you think of that at the start?' he asked.

'Yes, but I was much preoccupied with my father then, and his estate. I will profit from this,' I added heavily.

'You're stuck with it now.'

'I know. By God,' I said forcefully, 'I will be glad to see London again.'

'Me too.'

As we passed along Petergate we heard an altercation and saw, a little way ahead, two beggarmasters with their staves urging half a dozen ragged lads along. As we came close I stopped, for among them I recognized the lad with the big wen on his nose who had grabbed Tamasin Reedbourne's basket two days before. His companion was there too. I saw from Barak's face he recognized him too. I stepped quickly over to the beggarmasters.

'Excuse me, sirs. Are you taking those lads from the city?'

'Ay, maister.' The beggarmaster who replied was an older man, with a thin hard mouth. 'No beggars or Scotch in the city for the King's visit.'

I pointed to the boy with the warty nose. 'I would like a quick word with him.'

'Is he known to thee? He hasn't robbed tha, has he?' The boy was looking anxiously at Barak and me, obviously recognizing us.

'No, but he may be able to answer a question on a matter I am concerned with.' I raised a hand with a sixpence in it.

The beggarmaster eyed it greedily. 'I don't mind letting you have him for a few moments. The City doesn't pay us much, do they, Ralph?'

'No,' his companion agreed. With a sigh, I produced another sixpence for him, nodding to Barak to take the boy's collar. The lad looked frightened as we led him to the side of the street, out of earshot of the beggarmasters and their wretched charges, who stood looking on.

'I want to ask you about two days ago.' I looked into the boy's dirty face. He stank mightily. He was even younger than I had thought, no more than thirteen or so. 'Just information, you are not accused of anything. It could be useful to me.' I produced another sixpence from my purse.

'What is this about?' Barak asked, puzzled. 'He tried to rob Tamasin.'

'What is your name, lad?' I asked, ignoring Barak.

'Steven Hawkcliffe, maister.' The boy's accent was so thick it was hard to understand him. 'It weren't a real robbery,' he said. 'She asked us to pretend to steal her basket.'

'The girl?'

'Ay, ay. My friend John and I were begging in the streets, trying to get what we could before we were thrown out of t'city. The girl came up to us and asked us to pretend to rob her. Her bodyservant that was with her, he wasn't happy but she made him go to a shop and pretend to buy something. It weren't robbery, maister.'

Barak jerked the boy round to face him. 'You'd better tell the truth, or I'll chop you smaller than herbs for the pot. Why would the girl do that?'

'She said she wanted to attract the attention of a man who would be passing soon. 'Tis true, maister,' he added, suddenly tearful. 'She bade us wait in the mouth of the ginnel till she called. She did, and I pretended to try and take her bag, but I didn't pull it hard. Then you came rushing over with your sword. That scared us and we ran.'

Barak frowned mightily. He could see the boy was telling the truth.

'Where are you from, lad?' I asked.

'Northallerton, maister. There's no work there, my mate John and I came to York but ended by begging.'

'Where are the beggarmasters taking you?'

'We're being put on the road. We've to be ten miles from York by Friday. The infirm are hidden away at Merchant Taylors Hall but all who can walk are to go out. And not even any houses of religion left where we can claim doles.' He looked at me, dark blue eyes wide in his grimy face. I sighed, but replaced the sixpence and brought out a shilling, making sure my back was to the beggar-masters. 'Here. Don't let them see.'

'Thanks, maister,' the boy muttered. I waved the beggarmaster across and handed the boy over.

'What the fuck was Tamasin playing at?' Barak asked after they had gone. His face was furious.

'I don't know. I felt something was not right, but held my

tongue.' I looked at him. 'Now, though, I will have to ask her. In case this was a ploy to get to know me.'

Barak looked surprised. 'You? But it is me she has been after.'

'It is me who is responsible for the welfare of an important prisoner. I have to discover what this is all about, Barak.'

He nodded. 'May I ask one thing? Don't report her to that Marlin woman. Not yet. Question her yourself—'

'I intend to. Mistress Marlin herself has connections to a suspected conspirator.'

'Shit. You don't think . . .'

'I don't know what to think. But I must find out. Now come, let us see what has happened at Oldroyd's house before too many people are abroad.' I fingered the key in my pocket, glad Maleverer had not asked for it back.

✝

THE SHOPS WERE OPENING as we walked down Stonegate. The shopkeepers glanced at us coldly and I felt eyes following us down the street. I wondered if a guard might have been left at the house but there was no one outside. Shutters had been drawn across the windows. The door was locked; Maleverer must have found another key inside the property. I unlocked it.

With the shutters closed it was dim inside. Barak stepped across the room and threw them open wide. Then we both jumped convulsively at a loud yell of distress from behind us.

In the light we saw the room was in chaos. The buffet had been pulled away from the wall, chairs and settles and table lay overturned. In the midst of all, in a truckle bed before the hearth, a plump middle-aged woman in a white nightcap and nightgown sat up. She screamed again, fit to shake the rafters.

I made a soothing gesture. 'Madam, please. We mean no harm! We did not know anyone was here.' But she went on yelling, her eyes wide with fear, until Barak stepped forward and gave her a slap across the face. She stopped, put her hand to her cheek, then burst out crying.

'God's mercy,' Barak said. 'You'll wake the dead. We told you, we mean no harm.'

The woman's sobs subsided and she pulled the thin blanket up around her neck. I felt sorry for her. She looked utterly helpless sitting there, a red mark now on her cheek. I noticed her clothes were folded by the bed. 'Are you Master Oldroyd's housekeeper?' I asked.

'Ay, maister,' she answered tremulously. 'Kat Byland. Art tha King's men?'

'Yes. Please, compose yourself. Barak, let us step into the passage a moment, allow this good woman to dress.'

We went and stood in the hall. From within came a creak, then a muted sobbing as the housekeeper sought her clothes. 'I'm sorry I had to slap her,' Barak muttered. 'It was the only way to silence her before she roused the neighbourhood.'

I nodded. After a minute the housekeeper opened the door. Her face was unutterably weary. 'We wish to cause you no more trouble, madam,' I said. 'We need merely to look upstairs for something.'

She sat on the bed again. 'I can't tell you any more than I told Sir William yesterday. I knew nothing of poor Maister Oldroyd's affairs, God rest his gentle soul.' She made the sign of the cross, then looked miserably around the wreckage. 'See what they did to his house, they turned the yard inside out too. And poor young Paul taken and locked up, that never hurt a fly. I don't understand any of it.'

'If you know nothing, you will come to no harm.'

She raised an arm, then let it fall in a helpless gesture. 'I ought to set all this to rights. But for who?' She gave a despairing laugh. 'There's no one left.'

We left her and mounted the stairs. The doors to both bedrooms were open and both, like the hall, had been turned upside down. We stepped into Oldroyd's room. The bed had been overturned and the chests up-ended, Oldroyd's clothes strewn around. The wall-hanging had been torn down and lay in a heap. The wall behind was of painted wooden panels.

'No sign of anything there,' Barak said. 'What were you hoping for, an alcove?'

'*Something*, at least.' I stepped to the area the boy's eyes had gone to yesterday and tried tapping the wall. It sounded solid enough, it was a supporting wall between Oldroyd's house and the next one. Barak joined me, bending down and tapping the panels.

'Aha, what's this?' he said.

I knelt beside him. He tapped again at a panel by the floor. It sounded different, hollow. I felt the edges with my fingers. There were a series of recesses cut into the wood of the joist, just big enough to slip fingernails into. I pulled gently, and the panel came out of little grooves that held it into the wood and fell on the floor, exposing a hollow space behind. It was skilfully done; but then, I reflected, poor Oldroyd had been a craftsman.

We looked inside. A space, perhaps eighteen inches square. And, almost filling it, a box. I pulled it out. It was a foot square, strongly made from some dark wood, the lid beautifully painted with a scene of Diana the huntress, her bow and arrow raised at a stag. It was the sort of box a wealthy woman might keep her jewels in. I noted the paint was faded; the huntress's dress and indeed the whole design of the box were in the fashion of a hundred years ago, before the Wars between the Two Roses. Barak whistled.

'You were right. We've got something.'

'It's very light,' I said. 'But I think there's something inside.' I grasped the lid, but it would not budge and I saw there was a strong lock. I shook the box, but heard no sound.

'Let's smash it open,' Barak said.

I hesitated. 'No. This should be opened in the presence of Maleverer.' I stared at the box.

'That apprentice must have known it was here, whether by spying through his master's keyhole or some other means.'

'He can't have told them at St Mary's or they'd have been after it. I can understand the searchers missing it yesterday, it is well hidden.'

'But why hasn't the apprentice told them? You saw him, he was terrified.'

'Maleverer left before he could question him. Come, the sooner this goes back to St Mary's the better.'

Barak frowned. 'What's that noise?' He stood and went to the window. A loud murmuring was audible from outside. I joined him. Goodwife Byland was standing there, weeping on the shoulder of another woman. Three or four other women stood around, with half a dozen men, shopkeepers by the look of them. I saw three blue-coated apprentices join the group.

'Damn it,' I breathed. 'The housekeeper's roused the neighbours.'

'Let's get out the back way.'

I tucked the box under Master Wrenne's coat, glad now of its voluminous folds, and followed Barak down the stairs. But there was no escape. The housekeeper had left the door open and as soon as we reached the bottom of the staircase we were visible to the crowd. An apprentice pointed at us. 'Look, that's them.'

'Come on,' I said. 'Put on a bold face.' I stepped out, remembering with sinking heart that I did not have my commission with me. 'What is this commotion?' I asked, adopting a stern tone.

A shopkeeper in a leather apron stepped forward. He had the scarred hands of a glazier and carried a wooden stave in his hand. 'Who art tha? What business hast tha in that house?' he asked angrily. 'My friend Peter Oldroyd is dead and the King's men take licence to knock his house and servants about. Poor Goodwife Byland is scared out of her wits.'

'I am a lawyer sent from St Mary's. We merely wished to check the house was in order.' It sounded lame even to me.

'Crawling hunchback,' an apprentice called out, to murmurs of approval. Barak laid a hand on his sword, but I shook my head. If this crowd turned violent we could be in trouble. I looked up and down the street, hoping to see one of the guards or constables, but there was none in sight.

I raised a hand. 'Listen, please. I am sorry for the damage that has been done here. I have had no part of it. I am sorry if we frightened the good woman there. But there are enquiries into Master Oldroyd's affairs—'

'What enquiries?' the glazier said. 'Peter was a good man, he did none wrong.'

'I cannot say more. And now, please let us pass.'

The glazier tightened his hold on his club. 'Where's thy papers? Come on, tha awd scrat! King's men all have papers!'

'Mebbe they're thieves!' someone called out.

I glanced over the hostile crowd, looking for Master Dike, the glazier I had met yesterday. He could at least vouch I had made enquiries on behalf of the King. But he was not there.

I took a deep breath. 'Let us pass,' I said curtly, taking a step forward. Neither the glazier nor the rest of the crowd budged an inch. That meant we were in real trouble. Then a stone, thrown by someone at the back of the crowd, struck me painfully on the arm that held the box under my coat. My arm jerked and the box dropped to the pavement with a clatter.

'Thieves!' someone called out. 'They *are* thieves!' Another stone struck Barak on the shoulder, and the crowd surged forward, pressing us against the wall of the house. The glazier raised his stave, and I braced myself for the blow.

Chapter Eleven

'STOP!'

A fierce shout, in a deep voice I recognized. The glazier lowered his stave. Looking past him I saw Giles Wrenne's tall head as he shouldered his way though the crowd.

'Sir!' I called out. 'I have never been so glad to see anybody!'

The old man stepped in front of us, placing himself between us and the crowd. He looked impressive in a robe with a fur trim, his best no doubt, and a black cap with a red feather. 'What is happening here?' he asked the glazier sharply. 'Master Pickering, what are you doing?'

'These men were in Peter Oldroyd's house, maister! The hunchback says he's a lawyer, but I say they're thieves.' He pointed to the painted box lying at my feet. 'He had that hidden under his robe.'

Wrenne looked at the box with a puzzled frown, then sharply at me.

'We were on King's business, sir,' I said. I felt myself reddening.

Wrenne then raised himself to his full impressive height and addressed the crowd. 'You all know me here in Stonegate! I can vouch for this man. He is a lawyer sent to work with me on the petitions to the King. I will deal with this!'

The crowd muttered, but the heat had gone out of them. Faces began to look worried as it sank in that they had been about to assault an officer of the crown. The apprentices who had thrown the stones sidled away. Barak glared at them, rubbing his shoulder. 'Arseholes,' he muttered.

Wrenne put his hand on Pickering's shoulder. 'Come now, sir. Leave this to me. Return to thy shop, you will be losing business.'

'What business that is left for us with all the religious houses gone,' the glazier answered, casting me a bitter look. 'Peter Oldroyd is well out of it, God rest him.'

'Ay, ay.'

'The people here are angry, Maister Wrenne. Half their trade gone, then Peter dead while working for the King and all they can do is send soldiers to wreck his house and scarify his servants.' He glanced at where Goodwife Byland was looking on with a haggard, tear-stained face. 'And young Green that's nowt but a good-natured lump of a lad, hauled off and locked up at St Mary's.'

'I heard. I came this way to find out what was happening. But none of this is Master Shardlake's fault. Come now, let us pass. Pick up that box, young Barak.'

Much to my relief, the crowd parted to let us through. Wrenne went over to where a young lad stood staring wide-eyed at the scene. He held the reins of a donkey weighed down with heavy panniers; the petitions, no doubt.

'Come, Adam,' Wrenne said. The boy patted the donkey on the rump to set it going. As we walked away he gave Wrenne a questioning look. 'You did well to stay calm, lad,' Wrenne said to him. He turned to us. 'My kitchen-boy. He's been pestering me to let him see the preparations at King's Manor.'

I nodded. I felt a score of eyes on our backs and breathed more easily as we passed the church and the Guildhall came into view across the square at the top of Stonegate. 'I thank you with all my heart, sir,' I said. 'If you had not come by I fear what might have happened to us.'

'Ay,' Barak agreed. 'They had started throwing stones. I have seen what can happen when a London crowd start doing that to some foreigner.'

Wrenne looked at him seriously. 'Which is much how they see

you, I fear. Feeling in Stonegate has been much stirred by what happened yesterday. It has become the talk of the town. That is why I took this way round to St Mary's this morning, to see what was going on.'

'The blame was Maleverer's,' I observed. 'And he is a York, shireman.'

'He is on the Council of the North, and so far as the Yorkers are concerned that means he is a King's man.' He shook his head. 'He is too rough in his ways.'

I sighed. 'I have to see him later.'

'In connection with that?' He nodded at the box, which Barak held clasped to his chest. 'You found that at Oldroyd's house?'

'Yes. Yes, we did.'

'What is it, if I might ask?'

'We do not know. We are taking it back to Sir William.'

He looked at me sharply. 'Something the poor apprentice told them about, at St Mary's?'

'I may not say, sir. And we do not know what is inside, it is locked.'

Wrenne looked at the box again, but said no more. We walked on to St Mary's. Master Wrenne walked slowly, remarkable though he otherwise seemed for his age. Young Sergeant Leacon was still at his post at the gate, and I asked him whether Sir William had returned, noticing as I did so that Wrenne gave him a curious look.

'Not yet, sir,' he answered. 'He's expected any time. There's many that want to see him and are having to wait. Master Dereham has arrived, the Queen's new secretary, and he is making a mighty stink.'

Wrenne glanced at a little clock that had been set on the table in the sergeant's cubby hole. It stood at twenty to nine.

'We are due at Master Fealty's office,' Wrenne reminded us.

'Barak and I still have half an hour. And first we must make sure this box is kept somewhere safe until Maleverer comes.' I thought a moment, then turned to the sergeant, who was looking curiously at the casket in Barak's arms. 'Do you know where Master Craike might be found?'

'He should be at his office in the manor house.'

'Thank you.' I turned to Barak and Wrenne. 'We will ask him where the box may be kept safely, then change and go to the rehearsal.'

Wrenne turned to look over his shoulder at Sergeant Leacon, who was still watching us curiously. 'That young fellow has a look of my father,' he said in a voice tinged with sadness. 'The same height and broad build, and my father's hair was yellow and curly like that into his old age. He brought him back to mind.' He turned round, then stopped and stared at his first clear view of the courtyard. Young Adam, too, was staring open-mouthed at the pavilions and the three huge tents. Men were still moving in furniture under the watchful eyes of red-coated soldiers. Through the door of one tent I saw a gigantic tapestry, bright with rich colours, being hung.

'Jesu,' Wrenne said again. 'I have never seen anything like this.'

'We still do not know what is planned. The senior officials do but may not say.'

Wrenne's eyes turned to the monastery church. He looked sadly at the empty windows, the trail of mud by the door. A packman was leading a train of donkeys inside. 'I expect the interior has been gutted,' he said quietly.

'Completely destroyed. It is being used to stable the horses.'

'Sad,' he murmured. 'I visited it many times in the old days. Well, we had better get to the manor house. Sir James Fealty will be there as well as your Master Craike. Master Barak, could you carry the petitions? They are rather heavy.'

Barak took the heavy panniers from the donkey, which a guard allowed us to tie to a post. We left the boy with it, though he obviously hoped to come inside, and mounted the steps. We entered the large central hall. Here too the carpenters were finishing work, and I saw the hall had been hung from floor to ceiling with their the most splendid tapestries I had ever seen, interwoven with gold leaf that glinted among the bright colours. Looking up I saw the roof too had been painted in the most intricate and colourful designs.

Several officials stood around in earnest discussion and I saw Lady Rochford in a corner, speaking in a low voice to a bearded young man in a silken doublet with slashed sleeves, the colours gaudy. It was the man we had seen in the inn doorway the day we arrived, mocking the locals. Both their faces were tight with anger. Jennet Marlin stood a little way off. She looked curiously at Barak, the heavy panniers over his shoulders and holding the brightly painted box in his hands. Catching my eye, she made the briefest nod. Lady Rochford and the young man, catching her look, followed her gaze; Lady Rochford raised her eyes haughtily.

'What's the matter with them?' I muttered.

'Your coat's all white down the back,' Barak said. I twisted to look at it and saw it was smeared with white plaster dust where I had backed against Oldroyd's wall. I heard a guffaw from the gaudily dressed young man.

'Your coat, Master Wrenne,' I said apologetically.

'No matter. It will rub off. Come, sir, we must go.'

We walked on. We asked a guard where Craike's office was located and he directed us up two flights of stairs to a suite of rooms behind the hall. Wrenne left us to find Sir James Fealty's office, and we promised we would see him there shortly. I gave him his coat, apologizing again for its state.

There was a great bustle on the top floor, servants in King's livery heaving trunks and boxes out of the rooms. Craike stood in a little office floored with rush matting, watching anxiously as papers and books were loaded into a chest. 'Have a care,' he said fussily. 'Don't get those papers out of order.' He looked up in surprise as we entered. 'Brother Shardlake!'

'Good day, Brother Craike. Might we speak with you in confidence?'

He gave me a puzzled frown, but ordered the servants out. They took the chest with them, leaving the room bare save for a table on which Craike's portable desk stood, a thick wad of papers pinned to it. I closed the door.

'We are being shifted to the monks' dormitory,' he said. 'It is a nightmare.'

'I understand. But something has come into my possession, sir, that belonged to the dead glazier.' I indicated the casket under Barak's arm. 'It is vital it be kept secure till Sir William returns. Do you know where I might leave it? I have to attend Sir James Fealty shortly.'

Craike ran a hand through his scanty hair. 'The whole house is being turned upside down. You could leave it here, I suppose. I have been told to lock this room when I leave, but I do not have to surrender the key till six.'

I looked round dubiously. 'Will this room be secure enough?'

'The door is solid,' Barak said, 'and we are two floors up.'

Craike ran his hands through his hair again, then gave me a sudden apologetic smile. 'Oh, Master Shardlake, you must think me an unhelpful churl. Only, with so much to do . . .' He delved in his pocket, and handed me a key. 'Here, take this. When you are done perhaps you could find me and return it.'

'I will, sir. And thank you for your help at this busy time.'

'Then I will see you later.' Craike picked up his little desk, slung it round his shoulders and hurried from the room. Barak placed the box on the table.

'It is light.' He shook it. 'There's something inside. Cloth, perhaps?' He gave the lid another experimental tug but it stayed fast.

'Empty or no, it is safe now. Come, we must get changed.' We left the room, but I cast a last anxious look at the casket before I locked the door behind us.

✝

BARAK AND I SOON found Sir James Fealty's office, a large room on the ground floor of the manor. We were in our best clothes, I in my best robe and my new cap, which I had bought in London. It was expensive, black velvet decorated with tiny garnets and a blue feather on the side. I disliked the gaudy thing. The feather had come a little loose in its clasp and the tip drifted in and out of my vision like a circling insect.

Sir James was a thin old fellow in a brown doublet, an embroidered collar to his shirt and a long wispy white beard that came to a point halfway down his chest. He was sitting at a large desk, reading the petitions and frowning. The clerk Cowfold who had insulted me behind my back the night before was standing at his shoulder, his face expressionless. His demeanour did not change as I gave him a hard look. Wrenne stood a little way off.

After a minute Sir James deigned to look up. 'So you're the lawyer,' he said in a reedy voice. 'Well, I suppose your clothes will do, though that feather in your cap needs straightening.' He pointed his quill at Barak. 'Who is that?'

'My assistant, sir.'

He made a flicking motion with the quill. 'You won't be there. Outside.'

Barak gave him a nasty look, but left the room. Sir James turned back to the petitions and our summary. He studied them for another ten minutes, ignoring Wrenne and me completely. I had met self-important officials in my time, but Fealty was something new. I glanced at Wrenne, who winked at me.

After a while my back started to hurt, and I shifted my weight from one foot to the other. 'You'd better not bob around like that on Friday,' Sir James said without looking up. 'You stand stock-still when you're in the presence of the King.' He tossed the summary aside. 'Well, those will do I suppose.' He heaved himself up from his desk. 'Now listen carefully. This is what will happen on Friday.'

He took us through the planned event step by step. Early in the morning we would journey to Fulford Cross with the deputation from York sent to abase themselves before the King and present him with gifts from the city. We would all wait until the Progress arrived. All would kneel, as Henry had decreed everyone must do at his approach. There would be various ceremonies, during which Recorder Tankerd and I would wait, kneeling, at the front of the York delegation. Then the King and Queen would step forward and Tankerd would make his speech from his knees. Afterwards, Wrenne and I could rise to our feet, to present the petitions.

'You will hand the petitions to the King's pages, who will be standing by; they in turn will hand them to the King. Having thus formally accepted the documents, the King will pass them to another official. Later they will be given back to you to deal with from then on.'

'Round in a circle like the maypole,' Wrenne said with a smile. He seemed not at all intimidated by Sir James, who gave him an offended stare.

'His Majesty will have graciously consented to deal with them,' he rasped. 'That is the point.'

'Of course, Sir James,' Wrenne answered mildly.

'One thing more. The King may choose to address some words to you, some pleasantries. If he does you may look him in the face and reply, *briefly*, and thank him for addressing you. And you address him as Your Majesty, not Your Grace – he prefers that term now. Is that understood?'

'It would be a great honour,' Wrenne murmured.

Sir James grunted. 'But unless he addresses you – ' Sir James leaned forward threateningly – 'do *not* look the King in the eye. Keep your heads bowed. It is a fact that many of the common sort who are brought into His Majesty's presence never actually see his countenance. People *will* try to risk an upward glance, from vulgar curiosity. If the King sees that – well, he has a harsh tongue, and if he is in ill-humour, from the pain he suffers in his leg or some other cause, he is good at thinking up nasty punishments for those who offend him.' He smiled tightly at us.

A picture of Aske's skeleton, hanging in its chains, came into my head. 'We will be careful on Friday, Sir James,' I said.

'You had better be. This is not a game. It is to show these barbarian papists the power and glory of their king.' He motioned to Cowfold who replaced the petitions in the panniers and handed them to me.

'That is all. Present yourselves in the hall of King's Manor at eight on Friday. And you, master lawyer, make sure you get a shave before then. Barbers are being laid on.' He motioned us away with his pen.

We left and rejoined Barak, who was waiting outside. I blew out my cheeks.

'He was a pompous old arsehole,' Barak said.

'I am glad that's over, though I confess I am looking forward to Friday even less now.' I took a deep breath. 'Let us see whether Maleverer is back yet. Brother Wrenne, I shall see you on Friday morning. Can I give you the petitions to keep?'

'Ay. I will take them back to my house.'

I shook his hand. 'Thank you again for what you did this morning. You saved us a nasty beating, or worse.'

'I am glad to have helped. Well, good luck with Sir William.'

'Thank you. Until Friday then.'

'Until Friday. The great day.' He raised his eyebrows, then turned and left us.

✝

MALEVERER, THOUGH, was not yet back. We waited for a while in the hall of the manor, where quite a little group had gathered with matters requiring his attention on his return. Lady Rochford and Jennet Marlin were still there, and the bearded young man, talking intently to Lady Rochford.

'Is he going to be all day?' Barak asked.

'I am reluctant to leave that box all this time.'

'Then let's wait with it,' Barak said. 'We might as well be there as here.'

I considered. 'Yes, why not. We can see from the window when he returns.' I looked at him. 'You don't think I'm being too anxious.'

'Not where Maleverer's concerned, no.'

'All right.'

He leaned close. 'And perhaps we could take a look inside.'

I looked at him irritably. 'It's locked. I am not going to break it open.'

'Don't need to.' Barak gave a sly smile. 'You forget my skills at picking locks. A box like that would be child's play.' He glanced at my cap, which I had removed and was holding carefully. 'Give me the pin keeping that feather in your cap and I could easily unlock it, see what is inside. Then we can lock it up again. No one need know if we didn't want them to.'

I hesitated. Barak had that eager light in his eyes again. 'We'll see,' I said.

We walked up to Craike's office. My heart was beating fast, for I had an irrational fear the wretched casket might be gone. The corridor was silent and empty, the work of moving the officials out evidently complete. I unlocked Craike's door and sighed with relief at the sight of the box sitting where we had left it on the table.

We locked the door again. Barak looked at me questioningly. Curiosity fought the fear of getting ever deeper into this grim business. But we were in deep as it was, and I knew how good a lockpick Barak was – I had seen him in action before. 'Do it,' I said abruptly. 'But for Jesu's sake, be careful.' I removed the pin from my cap and handed it to him

He inserted it into the little lock, twisting it gently to and fro. I looked again at the scene painted on the box, Diana the huntress.

The paint was lined with hairline cracks through age, but the picture was very well done; this box must have been very expensive once.

'Shit,' Barak said suddenly. He stood holding up half the pin. It had broken off, leaving the other half stuck in the lock. I could just see a tiny sliver of metal protruding. He tried to grasp it but it was not sticking out far enough.

'You dolt!' I cried 'So much for your brag! If that pin's stuck the box will have to be smashed open. Maleverer will see it's been tampered with.'

'The damned pin was too thin.'

'Excuses won't help.'

'We could say we found it like that.'

'I do not fancy lying to him. Do you?'

He frowned. 'If I could lay hold of a pair of thin pliers I could have that pin out of the lock. Those workmen are bound to have pliers.'

I took a deep breath. 'Well, go and find some, for Jesu's sake. I knew I should not have agreed to this.'

He looked, for once, crestfallen. 'I'll be back as soon as I can,' he said, and made for the door. He turned the key to let himself out. I heard his footsteps moving away down the corridor and sighed, looking anxiously at the box. I gently touched the broken end of the pin, wondering if my thinner fingers might get it out, but it was impossible.

Then I heard a faint click. I stared at the casket. Had my fiddling moved the tumblers? Hesitantly, I grasped the lid. It opened. Very tentatively, I pulled it fully up. A musty smell assailed my nostrils. I bent my head and slowly, carefully, looked inside.

The box was half full of papers. I picked out the top one, unfolded it carefully, then stared in puzzlement. It was a chart of the royal family tree such as one sees in ornamental genealogies, but written crudely in ink. It went back a century to Yorkist times, though some minor members of the family who had died without issue were missing. I studied it carefully, quite bemused. There was nothing secret here – it was the familiar royal line such as one saw displayed in many official buildings. If someone had made an abbreviated family tree of the royal house for a pastime, why on earth hide it?

I looked in the box again. Underneath the family tree was a scrappy piece of paper on which a rude text had been written. 'This is the prophecy of the great magician Merlin,' it began. 'Revealed in the days of King Arthur, his prophecy of the Kings that will follow John . . .' There was stuff about monarchs who would be called the Goat, the Lion and the Ass, before it concluded with, 'The eighth Henry, that shall be called the Mouldwarp, who shall be cursed by God for his actions. His kingdom shall be divided into three, and none of his heirs shall inherit.'

I laid the scrawl down. It looked like one of the scurrilous prophecies that had been hawked around London at the time of the Pilgrimage of Grace. The penalty for distributing such things had been death.

The next document was not a paper but a parchment, quite a large one, folded over several times. I opened it out. To my astonishment it had the seal of Parliament at the bottom: this was an Act of Parliament, though not one I recognized. '*Titulus Regulus*,' I read. '*An Act for the Settlement of the Crown upon the King and his Issue . . .*' Which King? I hastily scanned the thick, beautifully inscribed black lettering. '*Our Soveraign Lord the King Richard the Thirde . . .*' I read. I frowned again. I had never heard of this Act. I laid it carefully aside and turned to the box. The rest of the pages seemed to be a series of handwritten scrawls on cheap paper. The top one was larger than the rest. I took it out and laid it on the table.

This is the true confession of me, Edward Blaybourne, that I make in contemplation of death, that the world may know of my great sin . . .

Then something struck me on the side of the head, a heavy blow that made me gasp. My vision went misty, but I saw a big red drop fall on to Blaybourne's confession. As I realized that it was my own blood, I felt another blow on the back of my neck. My legs buckled beneath me, and I fell into a great darkness.

Chapter Twelve

MY FIRST SENSATION WHEN I woke was of unaccustomed warmth. I luxuriated in it for a second, realizing how used I had become in York to feeling cold and damp. But why was I in York? Then I remembered everything in a rush. I tried to sit up but a throbbing pain banged at the back of my neck. Hands grasped me and eased me back to a lying position. 'He's awake!' I heard Master Craike call out. 'Bring the hippocras! Careful there, sir, you have had a bad blow to the head.'

I opened my eyes: I was lying on a nest of cushions on a rush-matting floor. Master Craike stood above me, his plump hands clasped anxiously. Barak appeared behind him, bearing a jug and a glass. 'Have some of this, sir,' he said. 'Not too much.'

I drank some of the warm wine. The sweetness revived me. I endeavoured again to sit up but the back of my neck hurt and there was another pain at the side of my head. I felt it and my hand came away sticky with blood.

'It's not as bad as it looks,' Barak said. 'That one was a glancing blow.'

I stared groggily around the room, which seemed familiar, and realized I was in Maleverer's office at the King's Manor. The warmth came from a firepan, one of the charcoal-burning braziers used to heat rooms in wealthy houses. A red-coated soldier with a pike stood by the door, watching us, and I realized we were under guard.

'How long have I been unconscious?' I asked.

'Over an hour,' Barak answered. 'I was worried.' And indeed his face was as anxious as Craike's.

'Do you remember what happened, sir?' Craike asked.

'Something hit me. The box clicked open when I touched the lock, there were papers inside. I was looking at them – Barak, the box! Where is it?'

'The box is safe enough.' He nodded at the table, where the casket stood, the lid open. 'It's empty,' he said heavily.

'Papers,' I said. 'It was full of papers.'

His face set. 'We're in the shit,' he said. 'I came back with some pliers, perhaps half an hour after I left you. I found you lying on the floor of Master Craike's office, with him bending over you.' He looked suspiciously at Craike, who frowned back at him.

'The steward's office asked me for the key,' the plump official said. 'They had told me it wasn't required till this evening but they changed their minds.' He gave Barak a haughty look. 'You may check with them. I looked for you but could not find you. In the end I came to the office. As I turned the corner I heard footsteps, someone going down the back stairs. The office door was open and you were lying on the floor. Then this fellow came in.'

I felt my head carefully. It was a wonder I had not been killed. Oldroyd had been, I thought, and felt a stab of terror lance through me. I looked at Craike. 'You must have interrupted the person who assaulted me. You may have saved my life. Did you hear or see anything of the person running?'

'No. Only those footsteps.'

I sighed deeply. 'So the papers are gone.' I looked at Barak. If his lockpicking had not come to grief this would not have happened. I tried to marshal my thoughts. 'If whoever attacked me heard Master Craike coming they could have grabbed the papers and fled. The box would be more difficult to hide.' I looked at the wretched thing that I had tried to guard with such care. 'With the papers gone it has no value.'

Barak stepped in front of Craike and bent to refill my glass. 'Yes. Anyone could hide the papers in their clothes.' He inclined his head slightly at Craike, still suspicious of him.

I glanced again at the guard. 'Why are we being held here?'

'Sir William returned just after I found you,' Barak said. 'He ordered us all to be brought here. He has gone to make some enquiries.' He reddened. 'He is in a mighty rage with us for opening the box. I had hoped it had been empty. What were the papers?'

'They were – they made no sense.'

The guard stirred himself. 'I should send word you have recovered.' He opened the door, spoke to someone outside, then returned to his post, gripping his pike. A few moments later we heard heavy footsteps outside, and I braced myself as the door banged open and Maleverer came in.

He was still in riding clothes, heavy boots and a riding coat spattered with mud. He stared at me coldly. 'So you are awake,' he said unceremoniously. 'Well, would you care to tell me what in Christ's name has been going on? I come back to find you attacked right here in King's Manor, with His Majesty due in two days.' His Yorkshire accent strengthened as his voice rose with anger. He threw off his coat, revealing a black velvet jerkin over a silk shirt. A thick gold chain of office gleamed on his broad chest. He stood, hands on hips, glaring down at me.

I struggled to sit up properly. 'In the box, Sir William. We found it at Oldroyd's house. There were some papers in it—'

His eyes widened and he leaned forward. 'What papers? Quick, what were they? Who saw them?'

'Only I. When I was attacked, they were taken—'

'You had them and let them be stolen. You—' He checked himself and turned to the guard. 'Wait outside, this is a privy matter. You too, Master Craike. No, wait. You were the one who found the lawyer?'

'Yes. I told you—'

'You came upstairs,' I said, my mind beginning to work again. 'To the top floor, and as you reached the hallway you heard someone going down the back stairs?'

'Yes.'

'So you say,' Maleverer interjected brutally. 'And just afterwards this Barak found you bending over his body.'

'That is right,' Barak confirmed.

Craike's lips set. 'I see. I am under suspicion.'

Maleverer turned to Barak. 'You have been with Master Craike since you found him?'

'Yes, Sir William. We went together to tell the guards—'

Maleverer turned back to Craike. 'So if you had some implement you used to try to brain the lawyer here, it'll be about your person still. And now we have these papers missing too. Take off your robe, let's see if there's anything under there besides your fat carcass.'

'I have nothing to hide, sir.' Craike removed his long robe. I was relieved to see, underneath, only a doublet whose buttons strained at his plump stomach. Maleverer called the guard in. 'Search him. See there's nothing concealed in his upper hose.' He turned to me. 'These papers, how many were there?'

'The box was half full. A thick packet.'

Maleverer nodded to the guard. 'See if they're there.'

The guard came over and patted Craike from neck to feet. Craike began to sweat. The guard turned to Maleverer with a shake of his head. 'Nothing, sir.'

Maleverer gave a grimace of disappointment. He nodded at Barak. 'Now him, just to be sure.' He watched as Barak submitted to the same treatment, then looked balefully at Craike. 'Right, you can go. For now. But I find it hard to credit that someone heard you coming upstairs in time to run off without being seen. You *are* under suspicion, sir. You have long been known for papist leanings.'

Craike's eyes were wide with fear as he turned and left the room. Maleverer turned his gaze to Barak. 'You can stay. You were Lord Cromwell's trusted man once, were you not?'

'You are well informed, sir,' Barak said quietly.

'Yes. I am.'

I struggled to get up. Barak helped me to a chair. Maleverer studied me. 'Are you all right?' he asked.

'Yes. A little dizzy, and my head and neck are sore.'

He grunted. 'Your head sits oddly enough on your body to start with.' He crossed the room and sat on a corner of his desk, thrusting a booted foot out in front of him and folding his arms. He looked at me, his dark eyes hard and probing. 'What were these papers you saw?'

'I looked at the top four. There were more underneath I did not see. The first was a royal family tree. Hand drawn.'

'Where did it start? Think a moment, get this right.'

'With Richard Duke of York, father of Edward IV. And his wife, Duchess Cecily Neville.'

Maleverer sighed, a sigh that turned into a bitter laugh. 'Oh yes. Everything starts with Cecily Neville.' I noticed a look of strain about his face. 'Do you think you could draw that tree?'

'Yes. I think so.'

He nodded. 'Ay. Lawyers ever had good memories for papers, that they may quote them to ordinary men to puzzle them. Do that today, but in secret, and get Barak there to bring it to me.'

'I will, sir.'

'And the others?'

'There was a scribbled paper that claimed to tell of a legend from the days of Merlin, that our present King would rouse God's enmity and be driven from the realm.' I hesitated. 'It called him the Mouldwarp.'

Maleverer smiled cynically. 'The Mouldwarp legend. Those fake prophecies were circulated by the hundred during the Pilgrimage of Grace. Sounds like this box may have been full of rubbish. What else?'

'The third document was written on parchment. It was an official copy of an Act of Parliament. But one I have never heard of. It was called the *Titulus Regulus*.'

Maleverer's head jerked forward. 'What?' He hesitated, then asked, very quietly, 'Did you read it?'

'No. Only the title page. It was from the reign of Richard III.'

Maleverer was silent a moment, running a finger along the edge of his black beard. 'That was not a real Act of Parliament,' he said at length. 'It was a fake.'

'But the seal—'

'God's body, did you not near me! It was a forgery.' He leaned forward. 'Produced by the followers of Lambert Simnel, who pretended to be one of the Princes in the Tower and challenged the King's father.'

It was clear he was lying – mention of that Act had shaken Maleverer to the core.

'And the fourth document?' he asked.

'Different again. An old scrawled paper. It claimed to be a confession. By a man named Edward Blaybourne. It said it was made in contemplation of death, that the world might know of his great sin.'

Maleverer seemed to have stopped breathing for a moment. 'And that great sin,' he said very quietly. 'Did he say what it was?'

'I had got no further when I was struck down.'

'Are you sure?' His voice was scarce above a whisper. I looked back at him steadily.

'Yes.'

He considered a moment. 'You said the paper was old. There was no date on it?'

'Not at the head of the paper, at least.' I hesitated. 'Blaybourne, that was the name Master Oldroyd mentioned.'

He nodded. 'Yes, it was. That glazier was not what he seemed, he was part of the conspiracy to topple the King from his throne this spring.' He gave me a long hard look. 'Do you swear you read no more than you have told me, that you do not know what Blaybourne's sin was? Think before you answer. If you lie you make yourself liable to great penalties.'

'I will swear on the Bible, sir.'

He stared at me a long moment, then looked away. For a moment he seemed distracted. Then he glared at us again. 'You fools. If only you had left that box alone, got those papers to me.' He clenched his big fists. 'Right, the boy.'

'The apprentice?'

'Ay. Barak said you saw him looking at a spot on his master's bedroom wall, it was there you found that casket. I'd no time to question him yesterday, I was summoned to the Privy Council.' He nodded to the guard. 'Let's have him brought up.'

The guard left. Maleverer sat behind his desk. He picked up a quill and began writing rapidly, pausing occasionally to ask me to confirm a point about the papers I had seen. He was making notes of what I had said. I looked uneasily at Barak, glad I had spoken only the truth.

'Sir,' I ventured. 'May I ask whom these notes are for?'

'The Privy Council,' he answered bluntly, without raising his head.

There was a knock at the door. The guard, helped by another, dragged the red-headed apprentice into the room. He was in a terrible state, his cheek and lip both thick and bloodied where Maleverer had struck him. He was dressed only in his shirt, and the long tail, which barely covered his arse, was streaked with faeces, as were the backs of his fat legs. The stink from him was enough to make me recoil.

'He shit himself on the way,' the guard said.

Maleverer laughed. 'Better than doing it in here. Let him go.' The guards released the apprentice, who staggered a moment then stood looking at Sir William, his protuberant eyes almost starting from his head.

'Well, boy,' he said. 'Ready to talk?'

'Maister!' The boy wrung his hands together. 'Maister, I bain't done nowt. For mercy.'

'Stop whining!' Maleverer raised a big fist. 'Unless you want some more teeth out.' The boy gulped and fell into a tremulous silence. 'Now then, remember these gentlemen were talking to you yesterday, before I came?'

Green cast a fearful look at us. 'Yes, sir.'

'The lawyer said he saw you looking at a spot on the wall in Master Oldroyd's bedroom. Today he went back and found a hole

concealed in the wall, with' – he pointed to the casket – '*that* inside.'
The boy's gaze swivelled round to the casket, and paled with fear.

'I see you recognize it,' he said sharply. 'Tell me what you know
about it.'

Green gulped several times before he could speak. 'Maister had
visitors sometimes, that he would take to his bedroom to talk in
secret. Once I – I – looked through the keyhole, out of curiosity – I
know it was a wicked thing, t'devil made me do it. I saw them
sitting on the bed, reading a whole lot of papers. I saw the hole in
the wall, and the box. I heard one of them say these would be
enough to do for the – the King . . .'

'Did they say the King?' Maleverer asked, catching the hesitation.

'No, maister. They said – they said the old Mouldwarp.' Green
shrank back in fear, but Maleverer only nodded.

'After that I were afeard, I didn't want to hear no more, I went
away.'

'When was this?'

'At the start of the year. January, there was snow on the ground.'

'You should have come to the Council of the North, if you had
heard words against the King,' Maleverer said threateningly.

'I – I were afeard, sir.'

Maleverer sat looking at Green for a long moment, then spoke
quietly. 'Now, boy, I want you to tell me who those men were. If
you lie, you can expect a good taste of the thumbscrews and the rack
in York gaol. Do you understand?'

Green had turned pale and started to tremble. 'I – I'd never seen
them before. They came many times, from the back end of last year
till the conspiracy was discovered in the spring. They weren't from
the town, I'd have known them. They always came after dark, when
business was done.'

'Describe them.'

'One was tall and fair and had a harelip.'

'How old?'

'Thirty-five or so, maister. He had a gentleman's voice, sir, though he dressed poorly. T'was that I found strange, it made me curious.'

'Hm. And the other?'

'He was a gentleman too, though he had a strange accent, as though he'd lived in the south. He sounded a little like him.' He pointed to me with a trembling finger.

'What was he like?'

'The same age, mayhap a bit older. He had brown hair and a thin face. I – I am sorry, maister, that is all I know, if I knew more I would tell you, I swear.' And then he sank to his knees with a thud and wrung his hands together, raising them to Maleverer in supplication. 'Oh, maister, have mercy, don't send me to t'gaol, I can't tell you more than I know.'

'All right. I'm letting you go, but breathe a word of this and you'll be in irons before you can turn round. Understand?'

'Yes, maister. I—'

'Guards!' Maleverer called. The two soldiers entered. 'Take this snivelling wretch and put him out of doors.'

'Shall we give him clean clothes and a wash?'

'Nay.' Maleverer gave a bark of laughter. 'Put him out on the road as he is, bare-arsed and shitty-legged. He can make his way through the town like that, it'll be a lesson to him not to meddle with things he shouldn't.' They dragged the apprentice out. A minute later he appeared in the courtyard outside. We watched from the window, Maleverer grinning broadly, as he ran for the gate, trying at the same time to pull his shirt down to cover himself as people laughed at the sight. Maleverer turned to us.

'I'll have him followed and watched,' he said. He took a deep breath. 'The fair man that Green described was the clothier Thomas Tattershall. He was executed in June, damn it, he can't tell us any more. Who the other man might be I have no idea. The conspirators were careful – they organized themselves in cells, each man knew only two or three others and only some elements of the conspiracy, not all. But this matter of those papers went right to the top.' He gave me a sudden evil look. 'To have found those papers, and then lost them. If you'd left matters alone I'd have got the information out of the boy, then had the box fetched.'

'I am sorry, Sir William.'

He looked out of the window again. 'It seems whoever killed Oldroyd attacked you, and would have killed you if Craike hadn't appeared – unless it *was* Craike. But, if not Craike, who?'

'Someone who wants those papers, whom Oldroyd perhaps refused to give them to.' I hesitated. 'Someone who has the run of King's Manor. They got the keys to the chapterhouse from somewhere.'

Maleverer turned and looked at me, for the first time, without contempt. 'Ay. A good point. That could all incriminate Craike.' He began pacing up and down, his big feet in their heavy boots making the floorboards creak. 'When I reported Oldroyd's death to the Duke of Suffolk, and mentioned the name Blaybourne, all hell broke loose. I was ordered by the Privy Council itself to take over the investigation. And keep it secret. Who or what Blaybourne is I know not, except that there is some connection to the prisoner Broderick.'

'Does Radwinter know anything?'

'No. Only the Privy Council, and Cranmer in London. Better Oldroyd had not mentioned that name, Master Shardlake, he threw you into a hornets' nest. When the Privy Council hear you have been responsible for losing those papers, you may hear sharp words from them, be warned.' He shook his head, his jaw twitching as he clenched his teeth in anger and frustration.

'We are sorry,' I said again.

'Pox on sorry. Sorry does not help.' He came up to us and stood looking down at me, so I had to bend my neck painfully to meet his gaze. I caught the ripe stink of a man who has ridden hard. 'Did you tell *anyone* the glazier's words? Of his words about the King and Queen, of that name Blaybourne?'

'No, sir.'

He went over and picked up the box, turning it over in his big hairy hands. 'This is old, a hundred years at least. And very finely made, valuable. Odd thing to choose as a strongbox. He frowned thoughtfully. 'Who could have known you were here with the box? Who saw you?'

'A hundred people in the courtyard could have seen it. But people that we knew? Master Craike, of course, whom we asked for the key. Lady Rochford and her lady Mistress Marlin in the hall. They were with a bearded young man who laughed at some plaster I had on my coat.'

He grunted. 'That'll be Francis Dereham, Queen Catherine's secretary. A young fool.'

'Then there was the young guard at the gate, Sergeant Leacon. Master Wrenne, too, and his boy.' I hesitated, for mention of Mistress Marlin had brought the girl Tamasin to mind.

'What?' Maleverer asked sharply. 'What else?'

I looked at Barak, then took a deep breath. 'There was something we discovered this morning, sir.' I looked quickly at Barak again. 'I think we must tell you. It involves one of the Queen's servants, a Mistress Reedbourne.' Barak set his lips as I told Maleverer what we had learned about the staged robbery.

'We'll resolve that one now,' Maleverer said firmly. He opened the door and spoke to the guard. Barak gave me an accusing look. I could see he was wondering, as I was, whether Tamasin might be subjected to the same treatment Maleverer had meted out to Green. The fact she was a woman would mean nothing to Maleverer. 'We mustn't hold anything back from him now,' I whispered intently. 'Nothing. Don't you see the danger we're in?'

Maleverer returned. 'She's being fetched. And that Marlin woman too.' We waited in tense silence for a minute, then footsteps were audible outside, there was a knock, and two guards thrust a terrified-looking Tamasin Reedbourne, an apron over a working dress, into the room. Behind her Jennet Marlin followed. She cast Maleverer a look of such hatred my eyes widened in surprise. Maleverer met her look with an unpleasant smile. Tamasin stared in horror at the caked blood on the side of my head.

Maleverer went over to them. He glanced at Tamasin briefly, then looked at the older woman. 'Mistress Marlin, I think.'

'Yes, sir,' Mistress Marlin replied coldly. 'Why have we been brought here? Lady Rochford would expect—'

'Piss Lady Rochford.' He turned back to the white-faced Tama-sin, and stood over her, his arms folded. 'Now then, Mistress Reedbourne. You know who I am?'

'Yes, sir.' She gulped. 'Sir William Maleverer.'

'And you and Mistress Marlin were sent with Lady Rochford to York, to ensure the arrangements at King's Manor for the Queen were satisfactory. You are a kitchenmaid?'

'A confectioner, sir,' she ventured.

'A scullion. You are under Mistress Marlin's orders?'

'Yes, she is,' Jennet Marlin said. 'And I am under Lady Rochford's.'

'Shut your gob, I didn't ask you.' He turned back to Tamasin. 'Now then, these gentlemen bring me a strange tale.' I saw Barak look at Tamasin with an anguished expression as Maleverer towered over the girl, intimidating her with his height. 'They say you faked a robbery to make their acquaintance. They have evidence. Now, Master Shardlake here is involved in important matters of state. He may not look like it but he is. So, you will tell me, now, why you played this game, and whether your mistress is involved.'

Tamasin stood silent a moment, then seemed to compose herself; her breathing steadied and the colour came back to her cheeks.

'It was not Master Shardlake whose acquaintance I sought to make,' she said clearly. 'But Master Barak. I saw him ride by in the city, I liked his looks so well. Then I saw him pass by again, and thought to make him stop. The city was full of beggar lads, I knew they'd do it for a shilling.' She glanced at Barak, her face quite red now, then back at Maleverer. 'It was worth a shilling,' she said, a note of defiance in her voice.

Maleverer slapped her hard across the face. Barak took a step forward. I gripped his arm, the sudden movement making my head throb. Tamasin put a hand to her cheek but did not cry out, only looked at the floor, trembling.

'Don't speak to me like that, you malapert creature,' Maleverer snapped. 'That was all there was to it, then – you hatched this plan because you liked the look of that churl?'

'That was all, sir. I swear.'

Maleverer took hold of her chin and lifted her head roughly to look her in the eye.

'You are a wilful, saucy, unbroken wench. Mistress Marlin, you will see this girl's behaviour is reported to Lady Rochford. It will serve you right if you are set back on the road to London. That is where you are from, by your tones?'

'Yes, sir.'

'Then get out, back to your fellow scullions. And you, Mistress Marlin, keep a better eye on your servants instead of going around whining about how hard done by your fiancé is and making everyone laugh at you.'

Mistress Marlin reddened. 'So this is why we were brought here? You feared I had involved Tamasin in some plot? That I am not loyal?' Her voice rose. 'I am made a victim again as poor Bernard has been.' Maleverer stepped over to her but she did not quail, looking him hard in the eye. I had to admire her courage.

'Do you want a slap too, you prune-faced baggage? Don't think I wouldn't give you one.'

'I do not doubt it, sir.'

'Oh get out, both of you. You're wasting my time.' He turned away and the women left the room, Tamasin scarlet-faced.

Maleverer gave Barak a look of distaste. 'So that was all it was. God's nails, the things the royal servants get up to on this Progress. They could both do with a whipping.' He turned to me. 'You said that Marlin creature saw you bring the box into the hall? You know her?'

'I have spoken with her briefly,' I said. 'She told me of her fiancé in the Tower.'

'She talks of nothing else. For all her local knowledge, she should not have been allowed to come on the Progress – she is fixated on the innocence of that papist Bernard Locke. She has been after him since she was a girl. It took her until she was thirty and his first wife dead before she cozened him into proposing. And then he gets snatched away to the Tower.' He gave a bark of laughter. 'Right. Go and make a copy of that family tree. And be careful, the eyes of the Privy Council will be looking at it. I shall have Master Wrenne in here to question.' He must have seen my face fall, for he added, 'You do not wish that?'

'It is only – he seems a harmless old fellow.'

'Harmless?' Maleverer gave another bark of humourless laughter. 'How do you know who is harmless and who is not in this place?'

✝

OUTSIDE, THEY WERE MAKING the final arrangements for the Progress. Great drapes of cloth of gold were being set in layers over the tents. A queue of carts stretched from the gate to the church, loaded with bales of hay: the bedding and fodder for all the horses that would soon arrive. It was cold, with a raw wind, the sky grey. I took a deep breath, and felt giddy for a moment. Barak took my arm.

'Are you all right?'

'Yes.' I looked at him. 'I am sorry about Mistress Reedbourne, but I had to tell him what I knew.'

He shrugged. 'Well, it's done now.'

'Come, I must do that family tree. God's death, Maleverer is a brute. I hope he is not rough with Master Wrenne.'

'I think that the old fellow can look after himself.'

'By God, I hope so.'

Barak looked back at the house. 'We've got off lightly.'

'Don't be too sure,' I said. 'I doubt Maleverer has finished with us yet. Nor the people he was writing those notes for.'

Chapter Thirteen

AT OUR LODGINGS EVERYONE was out at work; the building empty, the fire low. Barak fetched a bench and lugged it into my cubicle. He brought my cap too, which he must have retrieved from Craike's office when he found me. He had fixed the feather back crudely with what was left of the pin.

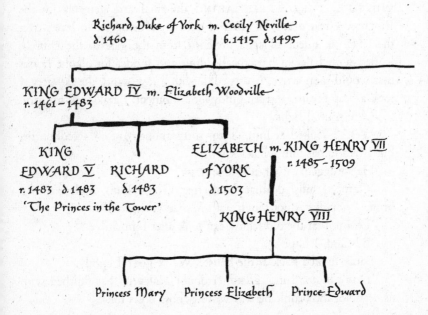

I locked the door, then brought out a big sheet of paper from my knapsack and laid it on the bed while he sharpened a goose-feather quill for me.

'You sure you can remember how the family tree looked?'

'Ay.' I shifted my position on the bench, trying to get my neck comfortable. 'My head still feels woolly, but Maleverer's backhanded compliment was right, lawyers are good at remembering what is in documents. Let me see what I can recall.' I dipped the pen in the inkpot. I was relieved that Barak did not seem angry with me over Tamasin. He sat subdued, watching as I sketched out the tree. I recalled that the line of descent leading to the present King had been inscribed in bolder ink, and pressed the pen down more heavily there. In a little time a scrawled version of what I had seen lay before us.

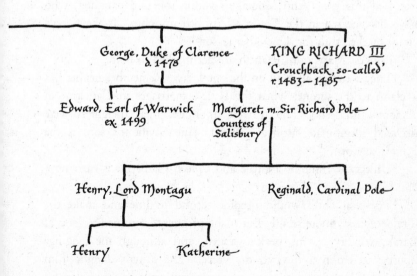

'I saw a lot of these genealogies round Whitehall Palace when I worked for Lord Cromwell,' Barak said. 'This looks different somehow.'

'Yes. They have missed out a number of children, like Richard III's son, who died young.'

'And the King's two sisters.'

'Yes.' I frowned. 'Every genealogy tells a story. Its purpose is always to prove someone's legitimacy to a title through descent. It is because the Tudor claim was originally so weak that they have put family trees showing the marriages that strengthened it everywhere in official buildings.'

Barak studied the tree. 'Our King's descent from Edward IV is marked in bold.' He looked at me. 'So this tree *supports* the King's claim.'

'Yet it includes the family of the Duke of Clarence, which most omit. See there, his daughter Margaret Countess of Salisbury and her son Lord Montagu, whom we spoke of with Master Wrenne. Both executed this year. And Montagu's young son and daughter, who have disappeared in the Tower.' I rubbed my chin. 'Is the King's claim marked thus for some other reason?'

'Princess Mary and Elizabeth are not marked in bold.'

'They were not in bold on the one I saw. Remember neither has a claim to the throne; when the King's marriages to Catherine of Aragon and Anne Boleyn were annulled, their daughters were declared illegitimate. Prince Edward, Jane Seymour's son, is the King's sole heir.'

'Unless the rumours are true and Queen Catherine is carrying a child.'

'Yes, that child would become second in line and make the Tudor dynasty more secure. But *is* she pregnant?' I turned to look at Barak, wincing as my neck twanged, and although the lodging-house was empty I lowered my voice. 'The King's divorce from Anne of Cleves last year cited non-consummation; he said he found her so repulsive he could not mount her. Yet when the Act of

Annulment was discussed at Lincoln's Inn, some said quietly that perhaps the King, ill as he often is now, had become impotent. That he married pretty young Catherine Howard in the hope she could stir his jellied loins.'

'People said the same in the taverns. But quietly, as you say.'

'Perhaps we shall find out if Queen Catherine is expecting when the King arrives. Perhaps it will be announced from those pavilions.' I turned back to the family tree. 'In any event, this is all quite orthodox.'

Barak pointed at the name that headed the list. 'Who was Richard Duke of York? I confess I get lost among those competing claims during the Striving between the Roses.'

'It all goes back to the deposition of Richard II as a tyrant in 1399. He had no children, and there were competing claims among his cousins. Eventually it came to war, and in 1461 the Lancastrian Henry VI was deposed and the rival house of York took the throne in the person of Edward IV. Edward's father, Richard Duke of York, would have become King but he died in battle the year before.'

Barak traced his finger down the line. 'And Edward IV was our present King's grandfather.'

'Yes. Through the King's mother, Elizabeth of York. It is said the King greatly resembles him.'

'What about our King's father's claim? King Henry VII?'

'His claim was weak, but he joined his bloodline to that of Edward IV by marrying his daughter. It is that which makes King Henry's position dynastically secure.'

Barak's finger followed the line back up the paper. 'When Edward IV died his son inherited briefly as Edward V, did he not? But he and his brother were killed when the throne was usurped by King Edward's brother Richard.'

'That is right. The Princes in the Tower.' I took a deep breath. 'Something interesting there. Richard III is named as "Crouchback, so-called".' Barak looked uncomfortable, and I smiled sadly. 'Oh, let us not beat about the bush. It was said Richard III was a hunchback, though others say that is a lie invented by the Tudors. Because hunchbacks are said to be unlucky, and our outward shape a sign of inward degeneracy. The fact the writer says "so-called" indicates he did not believe the stories about King Richard. In any case, Richard III's seizure of the throne angered the country, so that when the King's father rose against him he got much support. Then he made his heirs secure by marrying Elizabeth of York.'

'And the Duke of Clarence, Edward IV's other brother, he died before him?'

'He was executed for treason – he had tried to seize the throne as well.'

'Jesu, what a family. The mother of those three, Cecily Neville. Maleverer mentioned her. He said it all starts with her.'

'Yes. And there was a bitterness in his tone.' I frowned. 'I wonder why. All those shown here are her descendants, but they are Richard of York's too and the line of descent runs through him.'

Barak thought a moment. 'If the conspirators had overthrown the King this spring, little Prince Edward would be the rightful heir.'

'Yes, but a child king. That is a recipe for strife among the nobles. No, if the conspirators were going to replace the King, Margaret of Salisbury would have been their choice.'

'Yes.'

'And the conspirators would have wanted them for one reason above all others. The family are all papists, like the conspirators. Montagu's brother Reginald Pole is a cardinal in Rome.'

'Jesu.'

'And the royal bloodline now gives the King not only the right to the throne but to headship of the Church in place of the Pope. As Cranmer said to me, when the King's conscience is moved it is God who speaks through him, giving him the right to make or break religious policy.' I raised my eyebrows. 'Anyone who took the throne would take the title Defender of the Faith as well.'

'God speaking through the King's voice.' Barak shook his head.

'That has always seemed to me as stupid an idea as that he speaks though the Pope's. Though it gives the King great power.'

It was the first time he had spoken so frankly of his beliefs. I nodded slowly. 'I agree. But to talk thus is treason.'

''Tis what many think.'

'Ay, it is. But come, we are straying into dangerous waters.' I sanded the paper carefully. 'Here, take this to Maleverer. Make sure it is placed in his hands only.'

He hesitated. 'I wonder if it might be prudent to take a copy.'

'No. No more hostages to fortune. Besides, I have a copy already.' I tapped my bruised head. 'In here.'

☦

AFTER BARAK LEFT I lay down on my cot. I fell asleep at once, and did not wake till Barak shook my shoulder some hours later. 'What time is it?' I asked.

'Near five. You've slept the afternoon.' He seemed more cheerful.

I sat up. My head felt clearer, but I winced at a jab from my neck. 'Did you take the family tree to Maleverer?'

'Yes, and got a growl for thanks.' He hesitated. 'Then I went to find Mistress Tamasin.'

'What?'

'I tipped a guard to fetch her, saying I had news of a relative.' He gave me one of his hard direct looks. 'I understand why you felt you had to tell Maleverer what Tamasin did, but I wanted to tell her it was not my decision.'

'I see.'

'She forgave me readily enough. And admitted her own fault in deceiving us, though she said she didn't regret it. By Jesu, she has spirit.'

I grunted. 'You've told me more than once you like a woman who keeps her place.'

'I don't like bossy women. But Tamasin is not like that. In fact –' he smiled – 'I have never met anyone quite like her before.'

'Women with strength of spirit may come to rule their men.'

'Oh come,' he said hotly. 'You know you do not believe that. How often have you told me you admire women with minds of their own? Like Lady Honor.'

'The less I am reminded of Lady Honor Bryanston, the better I like it.' I heard the bitterness in my own voice at the memory of my ill-fated dalliance the year before. 'And do not mistake reckless improvidence for an independent mind.'

'Well, I am meeting her tomorrow evening at the singing, as we arranged.'

'Is that wise? Maleverer was not happy about what she did.'

'He's not one to care what dalliances men and women may have so long as there are no political implications.' He looked at me hard again. 'Do *you* disapprove?'

''Tis not for me to approve or disapprove,' I replied defensively. I still had doubts about the girl, but I realized too that I was jealous, not of Barak for having a pretty girl chase him, but of her for taking the attention of one of the few real friends I had. I changed the subject, asking Barak if he had seen Master Wrenne.

'In the courtyard when I went in to Maleverer. Only in the distance – he was making for the gate and did not see me.'

'Did he look all right?'

'Yes. He was walking towards the gate. I thought I caught a slight smile on his face.'

'Thank God. I feared Maleverer might take him in for rough questioning.'

'I told you he could look after himself.'

'Ay.' I got up. 'Well, I shall go for a walk, I think. I need some air.'

'Want some company?'

I smiled. 'All right.'

✝

OUTSIDE A WIND HAD GOT up, and I smelled rain in the air. 'Autumn is well on here,' I observed. My head felt clearer, but with the clarity came apprehension. I watched the people passing to and fro and thought, somebody here, one of these people, attacked me. Will they try again? I was glad of Barak's company.

We walked past the animal enclosures. Two big metal cages had been set up to one side; in each a huge brown bear crouched, staring out through little red eyes full of fear and anger.

'There's to be bear-baiting among the public entertainments for the King,' Barak said. 'I dare say you'll steer clear of that.' He smiled slightly, for he found my squeamishness about such things odd.

'Yes,' I replied shortly.

'A whole lot of fighting cocks were being brought in when I was in the courtyard earlier. Games for the soldiers and workmen. They're not allowed in the city in case they fight with the Yorkers. They've put the birds in the chapterhouse, I was told.'

I shook my head. 'How the world is everywhere turned upside down.'

We walked down the side of the church to the main courtyard. Men on ladders were fixing pennants to the pavilions now, in the green and white Tudor colours, the red-on-white cross of England and, I saw to my astonishment, blue flags with a slantwise white cross. I pointed. 'Look! Isn't that the Scotch flag? Jesu, King James must be coming here! That is what all this is for!'

Barak whistled. 'A meeting of kings.'

'So King Henry has come to make his terms with the Scots as well as the Yorkmen. He's after a peace treaty.' I shook my head. 'King James would be mad to abandon his alliance with the French, it's all that's ever stopped us overrunning them.'

'Maybe he's offering James a choice between peace terms and invasion.'

'If this is what it is all about, perhaps Queen Catherine is not pregnant after all.'

I looked round the courtyard, less crowded now the building work was finished. Men were loading surplus building material on to carts, while more flagstones were being laid near the manor house, covering the earth so the King – the Kings – should not get their robes muddy. I shivered, feeling tired again. 'Come, let us go back through the church. We can see how the horses are doing.'

The monastic church was also full of workmen. Row upon row of wooden stalls had been set up along the nave now for the horses, and men were piling up bales of hay for fodder and setting straw in the stalls. The banging down of the bales, the swish of the straw being laid, echoed round the place. As we walked down the church another sound became audible, an angry crowing from the chapter-house. There must be hundreds of fighting cocks, I realized, and wondered what they made of the holy statues, whether they took them for real men as Barak had. I looked around. For all the great vaulting arches this was the corpse of a church, a corpse set out to be mocked and desecrated as they said Richard III's was after the Battle of Bosworth. I felt suddenly giddy, and went over to a bench that someone had left in the middle of the nave. 'I must rest a moment,' I said.

Barak joined me. We sat in silence for a minute, then I turned to him, wincing at a spasm in my neck.

'I wonder if I am safe now,' I said.

'You mean your assailant would have killed you had Craike not interrupted him?'

'I'm not sure Craike *did* interrupt him.'

'You mean he was the attacker?'

'No. Otherwise the cudgel, or whatever else he used, would have been found on him when he was searched. And those damned papers. No, I mean my assailant had already left the room when Craike arrived in the corridor. Think about it. That is a long corridor, whoever attacked me would have heard Craike's footsteps as he arrived at the far end. He could not have left the room and run down the other staircase without Craike seeing him. And Craike said he heard footsteps *descending*, not running.'

'So the attacker thought he had killed you.'

'Unless he did not mean to kill me, just knock me out. Say he entered the room just as I lifted that confession by Blaybourne from the box, and hit me before I could read it.'

'If it's that important, surely he'd kill you to make sure.'

I sighed. 'Yes, unless he thought I was already dead. If so, he showed carelessness. And when he sees I am alive, he may try again.'

'But the damage has been done. You've told Maleverer everything you saw.'

'The attacker may not know that.'

'Then we'll have to keep watch,' Barak said.

'Thank you for the *we*. I wonder what those papers signify. An orthodox-seeming family tree, a copy of the Mouldwarp legend, an Act of Parliament Maleverer says is a fake and a confession by someone called Blaybourne whose name appears to strike terror into the hearts of the mighty. There were other papers too, quite a few, they looked like statements of some sort. And who was the thief? A conspirator, trying to keep the papers out of the King's hands? But if so, why did Oldroyd not give them to him — I am assuming that was why he was killed.'

'I don't know. Jesu, I wish we could go home.'

'So do I.' I shivered in a cold wind that came through an empty window-arch. I looked through it at the grey sky, just beginning to darken. Oldroyd would have removed that glass. I wondered what would happen to his house and business; he was another who had died without heirs.

'What are you thinking of?' Barak asked.

'How since we got here my mind has run on genealogies. Those like the King's that have heirs and those like Wrenne's and Oldroyd's that have run out. And mine, perhaps.' I smiled sadly. 'Your tree I suppose will go back to Abraham, through your father's Jewish blood.'

He shrugged. 'And we all go back to Adam, the first sinner. I am my father's only child too. I would like the line to go on.' He smiled mirthlessly. 'The secret line of Jewish blood.' He turned back to me. 'You could still marry. You are not yet forty.'

'I will be next year. Then people will start to think of me as an old man.'

'Ten years younger than the King.'

I sighed. 'After Lady Honor, last year—' I changed the subject. 'So, you have made up with Tamasin?'

'Yes.' He smiled, then looked at me seriously. 'She was frightened at being hauled up before Maleverer, I think, though she tried to hide it. She said Mistress Marlin was sharp with her, but has promised she will not tell Lady Rochford.'

I nodded. 'That is in her own interest. Lady Rochford might blame Mistress Marlin for not keeping proper control of the girl. Mistress Marlin is a strange creature. What does young Tamasin think of her?'

'That she is mostly a kind mistress, oddly enough. It was she who chose Tamasin to come to York. I think Tamasin feels sorry for her, because the other ladies mock her. Tamasin has a kind heart.'

'Well, that is a virtuous thing in a woman.' I massaged my neck again. 'Jesu, I am tired. I should go to the prison tonight, but I cannot face trailing through York again in the dark.'

'Hardly surprising, after being knocked out. You should rest tonight.'

'I shall go tomorrow, and call on Master Wrenne as well. I grow fond of that old man.' I was quiet for a moment then said, 'He is alone. That reminds me of my father, and then I feel guilty for not visiting him for a year before he died.'

The events of the day seemed to have put us in a rare mood for confidences, there in the huge desecrated vault of the church, the swish of straw and crowing of fighting cocks echoing in the background. 'I dream of my father sometimes,' Barak said. 'When I was small he always wanted to hold me and I would squirm away because I could not stand the smell of his trade. The emptying of cesspits. I often dream he comes to me with arms outstretched, but I catch the smell of him and draw back as I did then, I cannot help myself. Then I wake with that smell in my nostrils. I thought of it when they brought that apprentice into Maleverer.' He fingered his breast, where I knew he carried the ancient mezuzah his father had bequeathed him. 'Perhaps such dreams are sent to punish us,' he concluded softly. 'To remind us of our sins.'

'You are a Job's comforter.'

'Ay.' He rose. ''Tis this grim place.'

'I wonder what will happen to that boy.'

'Young Green?'

'That was a cruel humiliation Maleverer visited on him, sending him bare-arsed into the town.'

Barak suppressed a laugh. 'Sorry,' he said, 'but it did look funny. The Yorkers will probably sympathize. He'll find another place. Come, shall we get some supper before you retire?'

'Yes.' I rose and we walked to the far door.

He turned to me. 'I am sorry for causing you to lose the papers, more than I can say.'

I clapped him on the shoulder. 'Come, no recriminations. There is no point.'

We went to look at the horses, complimenting the stable boy on how well they were cared for, then went and ate companionably in the refectory. As we walked we were both on the alert, looking into shadowed corners. The refectory was busier and noisier than the night before. The carpenters, their work done, were in boisterous mood. If they were allowed into the town tonight there would be revelry and probably bloody noses too. I was tired again, glad to return to my cot. Barak said he was going into the town, 'to see what I can see'.

'No adventures.'

'No, I'll save those for Tamasin tomorrow. Shall I wake you at six in the morning?'

'Ay.' He left me then, and I sank into a deep and thankfully dreamless sleep, disturbed only when the lawyers and clerks returned late and went to bed. Yet it was not Barak who woke me next morning but a soldier, a hand shaking me roughly awake. It was still dark, he carried a lamp. I stared at him. It was young Sergeant Leacon. His face was serious. My heart leaped in terror, and I feared for a second that Maleverer might have put me under arrest.

'What is it?'

'I have been sent to escort you to York Castle, sir, at once,' he said. 'The prisoner Broderick, he has been poisoned.'

Chapter Fourteen

IT WAS STILL ONLY five in the morning as we marched through a dark and silent York. Barak had been woken when Leacon roused me and I asked him to accompany us; whatever awaited us at the castle, I wanted another pair of eyes to see. The town constables, roused by our footsteps, shone their lamps at us but retreated again at the sight of Leacon's red uniform. I shivered and drew my coat round me, for a cold gusting wind had risen.

'Who brought you the news?' I asked the young sergeant.

'A messenger sent by the captain of the castle guard. He said the prisoner had been poisoned and seemed like to die, and you were asked for at once. I thought it best to come myself as we must cross the city. The constables would stop you otherwise.'

'Thank you.' By the light of his lamp I could see a worried expression on Leacon's boyish face. 'I put you to much trouble, I fear.'

'I was called to Sir William yesterday, asked for the details of your arrival at St Mary's with that box. He questioned me closely.' He hesitated, looking at the bruise on my head. 'He told me you were attacked. The guards at St Mary's have been warned to be triply attentive. The King arrives tomorrow.'

The castle tower reared up on its hill, outlined against a sky which was just beginning to lighten. We hurried on to where torches burned brightly on the drawbridge; we were expected and quickly gained admittance. I thanked the sergeant and told him to go back to St Mary's. Barak watched him return across the drawbridge.

'He must think trouble surrounds us everywhere we go.'

We hurried across the bailey to the guardroom. The door was open, light spilling into the yard. The hard-looking fellow who had met me on my previous visits was standing in the doorway, looking worried.

'I'll take you up, sir,' he said at once.

'What happened?'

'Master Radwinter came into the guardroom not an hour ago, said the prisoner was taken ill. He suspected poison, said to send for you and the physician. The physician's just gone up.'

So Radwinter had summoned me. To protect his back, perhaps, share the blame if Broderick died. I set my lips tight as we followed the guard up the damp spiral staircase. The door to Broderick's cell was open. Inside, by the light of a lamp set on the floor, a stout man in a black fur-trimmed robe and close-fitting cap was bent over the bed. The sour stink of vomit filled the room. Radwinter stood looking on, holding another lamp high. He turned as we came in. His face was pale against his black beard. He had dressed hurriedly; he looked far from his usual dapper self and his eyes had a look of fear and anger. He stared at Barak, who met his gaze unflinchingly. 'Who's that?' he snapped.

'My assistant, Barak. He is privy to everything, by the Archbishop's authority. How is Sir Edward?'

It was the physician who answered, rising and turning to me. He was in his fifties, the hair under his cap grey, and I was glad to see his broad face seemed intelligent. 'This man has undoubtedly been poisoned. Master Radwinter tells me he heard the prisoner fall heavily from his bed, from his own room underneath, about an hour ago.'

'You are the physician who examined the prisoner two days ago?'

'I am, sir.' He bowed. 'Dr Jibson, of Lop Lane.'

I leaned round him to get a view of Broderick. He lay on his pallet, the long chains slack across his body. His beard was wet with vomit, his face a ghastly white.

'Will he live?'

'I hope so. Whatever he was given, he seems to have vomited it all up.' The physician glanced at a half-full pail on the floor. A cup and a wooden bowl, both empty, lay there as well. 'Are those for his food?'

'Yes,' Radwinter said. 'He had his supper late last night.'

Dr Jibson frowned. 'Then I would have expected him to vomit before now. But different poisons act in different ways.' He peered into the stinking pail with professional interest.

'It must have been in his food,' Radwinter said. 'There's no other way. I have been in my room constantly, Broderick's cell has been locked as always and a mouse could not get past my room without me hearing. And the guards say no strangers have been anywhere near this end of the bailey all day.'

Dr Jibson nodded. 'The food seems most likely.'

'His pottage comes from the common cooking pot,' Radwinter said. 'I fetch it myself from the guards' quarters, 'tis a menial task but I can ensure against anything being concealed in the food, like messages.' His face set hard, and he turned to me. 'What the doctor says confirms what I thought. I already have the answer to this. The guards' cook. He used to cook for the monks at St Mary's Abbey, and he has a shifty air about him. I have had him confined in the guardhouse.'

The physician looked between us, then spoke seriously. 'I must warn you, this man is not out of danger. Some poison could still be in his system. He was weak enough before, from his treatment –' he made a grimace of distaste – 'and the poor rations he seems to have had, and confinement in this doleful place.' He looked round the cell. Looking out of the barred windows, I saw dawn had come, the castle keep grey against the lightening sky. Something white moved there, Aske's skeleton turning in the wind that moaned louder now against the tower.

'It would help if Sir Edward were moved,' Dr Jibson added. 'Laid in comfort somewhere.'

'He is too dangerous,' Radwinter answered firmly. 'He must be kept secure and chained.'

The physician looked at me. I hesitated. 'He does need to be kept secure. But he should be given more blankets, and perhaps a little brazier put here to heat the room.'

The physician nodded. 'That would help.'

'Very well,' Radwinter agreed. He gave me a nasty, sidelong look. Jibson's comment on the prisoner's poor diet would not have pleased him.

Broderick stirred, and I realized he was conscious. How long had he been listening? He looked at me and smiled bitterly. 'Still careful of my welfare, master lawyer?' he croaked. 'Someone was less careful. They sought to end my pain.' He sighed deeply. I looked into his eyes; the fire had gone out of them, I saw only a terrible exhaustion.

'Do you know how this was done, Broderick?'

'It was the King poisoned me,' he said, breathing heavily.

'You will tell us,' Radwinter said threateningly.

'Come, Master Radwinter,' I said. 'We should talk. Dr Jibson, will you call again later?'

'Certainly, this afternoon.' He smiled, and I reflected that on the King's work he would get a handsome fee.

We left the cell, Radwinter locking it carefully. 'Wait in my room, please,' he said curtly. 'I will see Dr Jibson out and lock the lower door.'

Barak and I descended the stairs to the gaoler's quarters. The clothes from his bed had been thrown hurriedly to the floor but otherwise it presented its usual tidy aspect. I massaged my neck, which had begun to ache.

'So that's Radwinter,' Barak said. 'Professional inquisitor, by the look of him.' He took up *The Obedience of a Christian Man*, which lay open on the chair. 'A twopenny-book man too.'

'Fancies himself an agent of the Lord.'

'There's enough of them these days. He doesn't seem that frightening. Looked a bit scared himself up there.'

'Wait till he starts trying to ferret into your mind. But you're right, this has rattled him.' I paced the room restlessly. 'All these precautions are to prevent anyone trying to rescue Broderick; we couldn't expect someone would try to kill him. Could this be tied to Oldroyd's death, to those papers? Maleverer said there was some connection between Broderick and that name Blaybourne.'

'Perhaps we should warn Radwinter.'

'No. That's Maleverer's job, this will have to go to him.'

We broke off at the sound of light footsteps on the stairs. Radwinter entered. He closed the door and studied Barak. Then he smiled humourlessly at me, showing his little white teeth. 'Do you feel you need a man to protect you when you meet with me?' he asked.

Even now he was trying to undermine me. 'Master Radwinter,' I said, 'I have no time for games. This is a serious business.'

'I have ordered the blankets and brazier to be brought,' he said curtly. 'I will not have that man die under my watch,' he added angrily. 'By the throat of God, I won't!' He turned to us. 'I want you to come with me. I am going to question that cook.'

'But surely if it was the cook who provided it he would have fled the scene after adding the poison to his meal,' Barak observed. 'He'd be the obvious suspect, he wouldn't hang around.'

Radwinter gave him an evil look, then turned to me. 'You allow your servants to speak on your business?'

'Barak talks sense,' I answered flatly.

'Does he?' Radwinter's eyes went to the bruise on my head. 'Have you been angering someone else with your caustic manners?'

'I told you before, there is no time for games. Let us see this suspect.'

'Very well.' Radwinter grasped his bunch of keys tightly. 'By Jesu, I'll have the truth from him.' He waved us out of his room with an angry gesture.

✝

THE COOK SAT ON a stool in the guardhouse, a soldier either side of him. He was a fat fellow, as good cooks are, with a bald, egg-shaped head. Yet there was a sharpness in his face and in his frightened eyes; Radwinter was right, the man had something shifty about him. The gaoler walked over to the prisoner and stared into his face, smiling grimly. There was a brazier in the room, with a poker sticking out of the charcoal. Radwinter turned quickly, pulled it out and held it up. The cook started, then gulped as Radwinter showed him the glowing tip. It was red-hot, I could feel its warmth faintly from where I stood. The soldiers looked at each other uneasily. Radwinter stroked his neat little beard thoughtfully with his free hand, then said to the cook, softly, 'Your name?'

'D-David Youhill, sir.'

He nodded. 'And you used to work for the monks at St Mary's.'

Youhill's eyes went to the poker, widening in fear. 'Yes, sir.'

'Look at me when you answer, churl. How long for?'

'Over ten years, sir. I was third cook to the monks.'

'An abbey-lubber then. Soft living and easy work. Must have been a shock when you were put out on the road when that papist den closed.'

'I got work here, sir.'

'And now you have used your post to poison a man the King wants kept alive. You know the punishment for a cook who tries to kill by poisoning the food he cooks? It is to be boiled alive. By order of the King.' Youhill gulped again; he was sweating now. Radwinter nodded seriously, fixing the man with his merciless eyes. 'That's a painful death, I'll warrant. Though I've not seen it done. Yet.'

'But – but I didn't do anything, sir.' Youhill broke down suddenly, words tumbling out of him, his eyes staring wildly at the poker. 'I only made the leek pottage for the guards same as always, with ingredients I bought in town. The prisoner's food was taken from the common pot, the last of it's still in the kitchen. If there was poison in there everyone would have had it.' He turned to the soldiers. 'Giles, Peter, you'd swear to that.'

The guards nodded. 'That is true, sir,' one said. Radwinter frowned at him.

'I can only tell what I saw, sir,' he said. 'The cook had no chance to interfere with the prisoner's food.'

'And you brought his bowl and cup, maister,' Youhill said. 'And his beer was poured from the common barrel as you saw.'

'Who cleans his bowl and cup?' I asked.

'I do that.' Radwinter stroked his black beard, then lowered the poker slowly towards the cook's nose. I decided if it came too near his skin I would intervene. Youhill squirmed in his chair, making little mewling sounds of fear.

'I don't know how you did it, yet, master cook. But no one else could have. I'll get it out of you, never fear. You see, I know you servants from the monasteries. You took in the papist ideas that infested those places, then when you were turned out it went to resentment against His Majesty, and if a chance to do ill comes you'll take it. I've had abbey-lubbers brought to me in the Lollards' Tower. Mostly they're like you, fat and soft; they break after a little pain.'

'But I *hated* the monks!' Youhill burst out. Radwinter halted the poker, six inches from his nose.

'What?'

'I *hated* them! Hated the way they lived soft and easy while I slept on sacks. I always knew their ceremonies were aimed at nothing more than getting money from gullible folk. I was one of Lord Cromwell's informers!'

Radwinter's eyes narrowed. 'What nonsense is this?'

The cook twisted his face desperately away from the heat. 'It is true,' he cried, 'by God's holy blood! When Lord Cromwell's commissioners came in '35 they questioned all the servants; they found I'd been in trouble for drunkenness, though a man may surely take a drink in the town. They asked if I'd pass any snippets of gossip to Lord Cromwell's office, promised me a good job if the place closed. And they kept their promise, they got me work at the castle. I'm as loyal to the King as any man in England!'

Radwinter studied Youhill, then shook his head slowly. 'That is too easy a tale, master cook. I see by your face you are a crafty and devious man. But you poisoned my prisoner, and I will have the truth. I'll have you brought up to my room. Then we shall have another conversation – there is a brazier there as well.' He thrust the poker back into the coals. 'Bring him,' Radwinter ordered the guards. He looked into my disapproving face. 'Master Shardlake, you will not be needed.'

Youhill gripped the arms of his chair convulsively. The soldiers looked at each other. Then, to my surprise, Barak stepped forward and addressed the cook. 'I used to work for Lord Cromwell,' he said. 'I did some work with monastery informers back in '36, learned how the system worked.'

The relief that came into the cook's face showed that what he had said was true. 'Then help me, sir!'

'You would have had to send letters. Can you write?'

'My brother can. I told him what to put.'

'To whom did the letters go?'

'The office of Master Bywater, at the office of the Vicar-General at Westminster,' he said eagerly. 'For the attention of Master Wells.'

Barak turned to us. 'He speaks true. He worked for Lord Cromwell all right.'

'He could have turned his coat,' Radwinter said.

Barak shrugged. 'True, but he looks too scared to me.'

'And there's no evidence,' I added. 'Also, Master Radwinter, you have no legal authority to torture this man. He may be kept close for now, but he is not to be harmed. I will report to Sir William Maleverer, but I cannot see how this man can have poisoned Broderick.'

'Perhaps the poison wasn't in his food at all,' Barak added.

'Ay. Consider what other ways there might have been, Master Radwinter, and I shall too. I will return once I have seen Sir William.'

☩

OUTSIDE THE WIND was fiercer, whipping more rain in our faces and sending leaves whirling across the bailey. Radwinter followed us out, his face dark with fury, and grasped my arm.

'You will not interfere with my enquiries, sir! Your duty is limited to the welfare of the prisoner!'

'You have no authority to make any enquiries! This must go before Sir William.'

He gripped my arm harder, eyes blazing with anger.

Barak put a hand on his shoulder. 'Enough, sir,' he said quietly.

Radwinter paused, then released me with a laugh. 'It is as I said, you fear to face me without protection.' He looked at my assistant. 'Barak, is that your name? A Jewish name, is it not? From the Old Testament.'

Barak smiled. 'I said you were a twopenny-book man.'

Radwinter pointed to the tower. 'See yonder, where Aske hangs. I'm told there was a wooden tower there before, and one night hundreds of years ago the citizens of York, bled dry by the Jews, chased them all in there and burned the lot alive. Best thing for cheating heathens!' He turned and walked away. Barak's face was white and it was my turn to grasp his arm and hold him.

'Arsehole!'

'He is. And he's out of his depth, this has driven him frantic with worry. He is not capable of solving this, he only knows how to guard men and torment them. His control is starting to break.' I shook my head. 'As well it might. How in God's name could anyone get poison in there, if Radwinter attends to everything?' I took a deep breath. 'Come, this belongs on Maleverer's plate.'

Chapter Fifteen

THIS TIME MALEVERER SAW US at once. He sat in his office behind a paper-strewn desk, his big dark head thrust back.

'God's body,' he said heavily. 'You pair bring nothing but trouble. For Jesu's sake do not tell me Broderick is going to die.'

I started telling him all that had passed at the castle. There was a big lump of red sealing wax on Maleverer's desk and he turned it over, squeezing its hard surface with his broad hairy fingers. When I finished he ran his other hand along the edge of his beard, as though trimming it with invisible scissors. 'If what Radwinter told you is true, how in God's name could anyone have got to Broderick? Is the physician sure it was poison?'

'He believed so. He is to conduct some tests and return later.'

'Tests!' Maleverer screwed up his face with impatience. 'Could anyone have got past Radwinter yesterday? Could he have fallen asleep in his room?'

'I think not, Sir William. He is utterly dedicated to his task.'

He grunted. 'That was my impression when I met him.'

'And a poisoner would have had to get past the guardhouse first. Then open two locked doors, then administer the poison.'

Maleverer looked at Barak. 'You can vouch for what the cook said about being one of Lord Cromwell's informers?'

'I recognized the names, Sir William.'

Maleverer looked at the wax, squeezing it as though he could squash the truth from it. 'How was it done, then?' He gave me an interrogative stare. 'Well, lawyer, you're the investigator of mysteries?'

'I do not know, sir. But no one could have got to his cell without Radwinter knowing.'

'Then Radwinter himself must be under suspicion,' Maleverer said, setting his lips.

I hesitated. 'He is no friend to me, sir, but I believe he is loyal to Archbishop Cranmer and reform. He would do nothing to help the conspirators.'

Maleverer frowned and bit at a long yellowish fingernail. 'I will have Broderick and Radwinter brought to St Mary's,' he said. 'Kept under my eye. I'll have Broderick in the cell where Green was put, see it is guarded twenty-four hours a day. I'll put young Leacon in charge of security, he seems a good man. Broderick himself has said nothing of how this happened?'

'No. I believe he knows but will not say. He talks nonsense about the King's poisoning him. Perhaps he means he has been driven to the extremity of taking poison because of what the authorities have in store for him. In London.'

Maleverer looked at me sharply, then grunted. 'Very well. The cook can go in Broderick's old cell at the castle for now while I check that story of how he got that job. And I'll write to the Archbishop about Radwinter.' He looked at me. 'You told Radwinter nothing about the missing papers?'

'No.'

'You've said nothing to anyone else?'

'Not a word. As you commanded.'

He grunted. 'I will have to take this news to the Privy Council. The Progress is on the way here from Leconfield, it won't take me long to reach them. I must get instructions.' He leaned back in his chair and looked out of the window, still pressing and squeezing the unyielding wax, then threw it impatiently on the table to land with a bang among his papers. 'What in Christ's name is going on?' he burst out fiercely. 'It is as though we were dealing with some spirit of the air that can roam freely about St Mary's and York Castle too, slip through locked doors and murder at will. And the King will be lodging here tomorrow. And the Scotch King coming too. That's official now, by the way, that's what the tents and pavilions are for, though nobody seems to know when he'll arrive.' He looked at me. 'I've increased security. The King must be told there is a problem. God's body, he will be angry.'

'The figure we encountered in the chapterhouse was real enough, Sir William. I do not understand how Broderick was reached in the castle, but events here show the attacker has the run of the site, including King's Manor. Strangers are not allowed to enter St Mary's without authority. We are dealing with someone people would be expecting to see walking round both the house and grounds, someone whose presence would not be remarked.'

'Then that means danger for the King.'

'But if someone had secreted themselves at the manor with the aim of harming the King, would they then advertise their presence by attacking or killing people at St Mary's?'

Maleverer nodded, stroking his black beard again, then gave a little grunt of laughter. 'You have some brains, lawyer. I'll give you that. Though after losing those papers your name will be mud among those who rule us. There may yet be repercussions for you.' He smiled coldly. 'You would probably rather go back to London, I imagine.'

'Yes,' I replied.

'Afraid whoever knocked you out may try again, perhaps. Well, too bad, you'll stay here unless I am told differently. And you'll stay in charge of Broderick.' There was a spatter of rain at the window and Maleverer looked out irritably. 'The King will not wish to ride in this, he and the Queen will be in their litters, it will slow everything down. Ellerton!' He shouted for a clerk, so loudly I jumped, and ordered the man to have his horse made ready. 'You,' he addressed us, 'tell Leacon to arrange a guard of men to bring Broderick over. They're to take a cart, tie him inside and cover it. I don't want him seen in the city. You two can accompany him, see him to the cell. And as few as possible are to know he has been brought here.'

✝

WE LEFT, DESCENDING THE staircase to the Great Hall. Here, amid the glowing tapestries, painted ceilings and buffets shining with gold plate, cleaners were at work. With brushes and pans they cleared the last wood shavings and dust away, making sure the place was spotless. I saw Master Craike standing by the wall, shuffling papers piled on his portable desk. I could not help reflecting that if there was anyone whose wanderings about the precincts of St Mary's would attract no notice, it was him. And no one would have easier access to keys, to the monastic church or anywhere else.

'Good day, sir,' I called to him. 'All is ready?'

'Ah, Master Shardlake, and young Barak.' He looked at us a little uneasily, I thought. 'Jesu, sir, you have a great bruise there.'

'Ay, tho' 'tis my neck that hurts.'

'I am sorry for that, sir. Do they know who did it?'

'Not yet. How does your work proceed?'

He sighed. 'It is all a nightmare. I have been up since three finalizing all that must be done before tomorrow. Master Dereham, the Queen's secretary, says he has been allotted a place at York's best inn.' He pulled a document from the desk and held it up. 'It turns out not. There will be a great brabble about it.'

'Master Dereham? A tall young popinjay in gaudy clothes? We saw him yesterday.'

'He is a ruffian, but an old friend of the Queen's from her youth in Horsham. She wanted him as her secretary. And what the Queen wants, she gets.'

'You sound disapproving, sir.'

He shrugged. 'Queen Catherine is a giddy girl. Too young and silly for the high office she has been called to, in my opinion. Kindly enough, but concerned with naught beyond clothes and jewels. The King though, he is besotted.'

'You have met her?' I asked.

'No. Only seen her.'

'They say the conservative party in religion hoped much from her marriage to the King, and are disappointed now.'

Craike nodded. 'She is no Jane Seymour to whisper in the King's ear how much better the old ways were. So they say, at least,' he concluded, perhaps deciding he had said too much.

✟

'DO YOU TRUST HIM?' Barak asked as we crossed the hall.

'I do not feel I can trust anyone here now.'

In the doorway a blast of rain-laden wind hit us. In the courtyard, there was pandemonium. One of the three tents had blown over. Heaps of magnificent gold-leaf tenting billowed in the wind, the fine damask curtains and carpets inside now exposed to the elements. Workmen tried frantically to lift the tenting, as a young man who must be the King's designer Lucas Hourenbout stood looking on, shouting, then almost dancing in frustration as a man stepped on a piece of priceless tapestry, leaving a muddy footprint on it.

✟

WE FOUND SERGEANT LEACON at his lodge. I was impressed again by the young officer's efficiency as he ordered soldiers to be rounded up and a cart fetched. While he went off to supervise matters, Barak and I waited in the gatehouse, watching the labourers collecting the materials from the tents and carry them off for cleaning.

'I worry about Maleverer,' Barak said. 'He dislikes us. He is ruthless and has much power behind him. He's the sort who will blame us if he can for anything that goes wrong.'

'Yes. You are right.' I broke off, for Sergeant Leacon had returned. He ran a hand through curly blond hair which the rain had plastered over his forehead. 'Everything is being fetched round.

Sir, could Master Barak help with the cart? It is very muddy down by the storehouses.'

Barak nodded. The sergeant gave him directions and he went out into the rain cheerfully enough. I smiled at Leacon. 'Well, sergeant, it seems service to Sir William keeps throwing us together. You are to be in charge of Broderick's security.'

'It will make a change from guard duties, sir.'

'Where in Kent are you from?' I asked to make conversation.

'Waltham. But my family came from the Leacon, some miles off.'

'Hence Leacon, eh? I have read that many people moved to new places after the Great Pestilence, but kept the names of their old homes.'

'That is so.'

'I know Kent a little. A few years ago I was engaged on a complex dispute involving the boundaries of some properties near Ashford. Different conveyances had contradictory maps attached, details of landownership locally were in a terrible muddle.'

Leacon shook his head. 'Strange work lawyers do, sir. I have some experience of it, I fear.'

'Have you?' I looked at him curiously.

'Ay. Perhaps you might even advise me,' he added diffidently.

'If I can.'

'There is a dispute regarding my parents' farm. My family have owned the land for generations, it was gifted them by the local priory more than a hundred years ago. But since the priory was dissolved the new owner claims the land is his, that the priory's gift was defective in some way.'

I nodded sympathetically. 'There have been many such claims since the dissolution. Sometimes the smaller monastic houses were not good with their documentation. But after such long usage – though I could not advise without seeing the papers.'

'You would think these landowners would be content to get so much of the monks' lands cheap.'

'People who covet land are never content. Have your parents taken legal advice?'

'They cannot afford it. My uncle is helping them – he can read, which they cannot. It is a worry to be posted so far away.'

'Yes. I can see you would help them all you could.' I remembered the extortionate mortgage on my father's farm that he had not even felt able to tell me about, and bit my lip. 'I wish you good luck.' Then a thought struck me, and I took a sharp breath.

'Have you thought of something?' he asked eagerly.

'No,' I replied hastily. 'My neck hurts a little, that is all.' But it was not that. Our talk of names, and my time in Kent, had brought back the name of one of the districts I had been concerned with. Braybourne. Or perhaps, corrupted as a man's name, Blaybourne.

✝

A SMALL, HIGH-SIDED cart with a big cloth cover had been provided, drawn by a pair of horses, and Barak and I and the sergeant walked alongside with half a dozen soldiers with pikes, who shoved a way though the crowds. Despite the wind and rain, the city was busier than ever with the Great Progress's arrival imminent.

I had expected argument when I told Radwinter of Maleverer's plans, but though his eyes gleamed bitterness he merely nodded. At Leacon's direction he unlocked the long chains binding Broderick to the wall, though his wrists were kept manacled. He groaned into wakefulness; he still looked weak. When he saw the helmeted soldiers standing over him I noticed terror spark in his eyes.

'You're to be taken to St Mary's,' I told him quietly. 'For your own safety.' He gave me a bitter smile but said nothing.

On the way down the steps to the cart, Broderick's legs trembled mightily, his steps uncertain, and I guessed it had been long since he had walked more than a few yards. I was surprised to see that he was a small man, shorter than me. When we reached the open air he paused for a moment, bracing himself against the wind and rain, and looked up at the clouds scudding across the sky in various shades of dirty grey. He took in a deep lungful of air that almost made him faint.

'Take care,' I said, as a soldier steadied his arm. Broderick stared for a moment at his friend Robert Aske's skeleton, swinging to and fro in the breeze, then gave me that twist of a smile again.

'Who poisoned you?' I asked him quietly. 'Do you know?'

He laughed weakly. 'King Henry did.'

I sighed. 'Get him in the cart. He'll catch an ague standing out here.' Broderick had gone very pale, and was only half conscious as the soldiers raised him and laid him gently in the bottom of the cart, where someone had thought to lay some cushions. The cart smelled of apples, oddly domestic in the grim context of our business. The soldiers covered him and so we drove back, to all appearances soldiers escorting some goods of value to the abbey. I watched the rainswept crowds and wondered how many, had they known Broderick lay there, might have rushed to rescue him.

Chapter Sixteen

I WALKED WITH BARAK along the Fossgate, one of the main city roads, among a crowd heading for the public rehearsal for the musical entertainment that would be given before the King tomorrow evening. As night fell the wind and rain had ceased, though the street was miry, strewn with leaves and small branches, and the doorsteps and shopfronts glinted wetly in the moonlight. It was a merry crowd, the most cheerful I had seen in York, that made its way towards the Merchant Adventurers' Hall.

I had decided to accompany Barak to the rehearsal rather than sit alone in the lodging-house with anxious thoughts for company, listening for more nasty comments from the clerks. Barak was dressed in his best green doublet and, above it, a pretty shirt-collar decorated with lacework. Both our faces were smooth, cleared of nearly a week's growth of beard, for that afternoon the barbers from the Progress had ridden into St Mary's. There had been a mass shaving, so all the gentlemen should look their best when the King arrived. I had put on my best robe but donned my old cap. I had had trouble fixing the feather back properly on the new one and did not want it coming unstuck again tonight. Tomorrow I would doff it to the King. My stomach gave a strange lurch at the thought.

We passed the Minster; it was brightly lit from within, the huge stained-glass windows a shout of colour against the dark sky.

'Look at that,' I said to Barak.

He gave it a glance. 'Ay. All ready for the King.'

I jerked my robe aside as a couple of apprentices ran past, splashing us as they ran whooping through a puddle.

Barak smiled sardonically. 'I heard in the taverns last night that the latest instructions about clearing the middens have caused prob- lems because people have been forbidden from dumping anything in the river — they want it smelling sweet for the King. So people without proper cesspits are having to keep everything in their back- yards, which will stink to heaven at the same time they're being told to prettify the housefronts.'

'There is discontent, then.'

He nodded. 'Most Yorkers don't want the King here at all.'

'You kept out of trouble, then, last night?'

'Ay. I attached myself to a group of carpenters. Most of the workmen came up from London but there were Yorkmen too. Paid well, so quite happy with His Majesty. We steered clear of the taverns where they don't like southrons.' He looked at me. 'I saw one interesting thing though.'

'What was that?'

'We were passing through a poor part of town, past some alehouses the carpenters said we should avoid, and who do you think I saw down an alley, going through the door of a mean-looking little place?'

'Go on.'

'Master Craike. He had on a dark cloak and a cap, but I recognized that fat face of his in the moonlight. It had an odd, set look.'

'Did he see you?'

'No, I'm sure he didn't.'

'Craike,' I said thoughtfully. 'He's the last person I'd have expected to be visiting disreputable alehouses at night. What was he up to?'

'Maybe someone should ask him.'

I nodded as we turned into the square that housed the Merchant Adventurers' Hall. It was an impressive old building, wide and three-storied, with a cobbled space before it that was already crowded. A stage had been erected in front, covered by curtains, torches blazing around it. Guildsmen in their robes stood in little groups among the crowd, and I saw a number of richly dressed men surrounded by retainers: the advance guard of the Progress. The open space was lined with constables in York livery, and I glimpsed little groups of soldiers in the doorways, breastplates glinting in the torchlight. I remembered what Maleverer had said about increased security.

A serious-faced young man in a lawyer's robe came across to us and bowed. 'Brother Shardlake.'

'Brother Tankerd.' I recognized the city Recorder, who had been at the Guildhall two days before. 'How is it all going?'

'I think all is ready at last. We have been waiting so long, I cannot believe the King will actually be here tomorrow.' He laughed nervously. 'And that I shall be making a speech to him. I gather Sir James Fealty is happy with the petitions.'

'Yes.'

'I confess I am somewhat nervous.'

'I think everyone is.'

'It will be a wondrous thing to see the King. They say in his youth he was the most magnificent prince in Christendom, tall and strong and fair of face.'

'That was over thirty years ago.'

He studied my face. 'You have a nasty bruise there, sir.'

'Yes.' I adjusted my cap. 'I shall have to try and hide it tomorrow.'

He looked at me curiously. 'And your enquiries about Master Oldroyd, how are they proceeding?'

'Sir William Maleverer has taken it into his own hands.'

Someone hailed Tankerd, and he excused himself. I turned to Barak, who was craning his neck to look over the crowd.

'Where is she?' he muttered.

'Mistress Reedbourne? Over there.' I pointed to a group of courtiers some way off. I recognized Lady Rochford, her face alight as she retailed some story to a little group of ladies. As always there was something hectic, overexcited, in her expression. Jennet Marlin stood a few paces off, Tamasin beside her. Mistress Marlin was looking disapprovingly at the stage, but Tamasin was glancing around eagerly.

Then I drew in my breath, for I recognized a small, neat man with sharp, delicate features and a rich fur robe who stood near to Lady Rochford. He was talking to Dereham, the Queen's young secretary. Sir Richard Rich, Chancellor of the Court of Augmenta/ tions, whom I had made an enemy of the year before, and who had backed my opponent Bealknap in my Chancery case. I had known I might encounter Rich here, but now I shrank away.

Barak had seen him too. 'That arsehole,' he murmured.

'I don't want to meet him unless I have to.'

'Then I'll leave you if I may, go over and see Tamasin. Rich won't remember a common fellow like me.'

'All right.'

'Take care for cutpurses,' he warned, then threaded his way through the crowd towards Tamasin. Alone, I felt suddenly vulner/ able. Cutpurses, yes. And assassins.

Musicians had appeared in the hall doorway, carrying sackbuts and lutes. A man in a chorister's robe shepherded a group of chattering boys on to the stage. They disappeared behind the curtain.

'That's my bairn Oswald!' a woman behind me called out excitedly. I shifted my position, wishing I could sit down for my neck hurt again. I thought about what I had remembered earlier, the name Blaybourne and the place in Kent. Should I tell Maleverer? If there was a connection between this Blaybourne and Kent he should perhaps know, for York was already full of Kentish soldiers and hundreds more would be arriving tomorrow. Yet I sensed Maleverer would not be pleased to find that I had not put that name out of my mind.

'Brother Shardlake.' I started at a deep voice at my elbow, then smiled as I turned.

'Brother Wrenne. How are you, sir?'

The old lawyer wore his cap and thick coat and, I saw, carried a cane that he seemed to lean on heavily.

'A little stiff this evening. But what of you? Maleverer told me you were attacked after I left you yesterday, and that old casket you found at Oldroyd's stolen.'

'I am all right, I was only knocked out.'

'Is that a bruise you have? It looks painful.'

'It is nothing. I was sorry to learn Sir William questioned you.'

He smiled wryly. 'Oh, Maleverer does not frighten me. I answered his questions and left.'

'He did a cruel thing to Oldroyd's young apprentice.'

'Madge told me. That news is all over York. But the glazier's guild are looking for another place for Master Green.'

'I am glad.'

'I remember Sir William when he was but another younger son of an old family, twisting and bullying his way towards power in the aftermath of the rebellion. He is a man of great ambition. As men often are when they have the taint of bastardy.'

'He is illegitimate?'

'So 'tis said. Not a true sprig of the old Maleverer family. His mother and father were part of the train that accompanied Margaret Tudor to Scotland when she married the Scotch King's father forty years ago. His mother had a dalliance up there, they say.'

'Really?'

'William Maleverer is a man driven to prove himself. But he will overreach himself one day, for he lacks subtlety.' Wrenne waved his free hand, dismissing Maleverer, his big emerald ring catching the torchlight. 'I thought I would come out and see the performance. I asked Madge to accompany me, but she says it will be a heathen thing.'

''Tis but a musical entertainment.'

'Ay, but they are using the musicians and some of the equipment from the Mystery Plays. She does not approve. She is another York traditionalist in religious matters.' He smiled gently, the lights from the stage emphasizing the deep lines in his face.

The curtains began to move. The excited voices of the crowd

faded to whispers as a beautifully decorated stage was revealed. Backcloth curtains had been painted to resemble a sylvan glade, with blue sky and a bright rainbow just visible behind painted mountains beyond. Paper clouds suspended by invisible wires from the canopy slid back and forth. The musicians had gathered in a semicircle round the choirboys. 'Those are the city waits,' Wrenne told me. He smiled sadly. 'I have loved the York Mystery Plays since I was a child. Yet there are reformers who would have them banned as yet another superstitious ceremony.'

'Yes,' I agreed. 'It is sad.'

'What better way to reveal the stories of the Bible, of their Saviour, to the unlettered?' I realized that Wrenne was something I could hardly call myself these days, a man of faith.

The musicians tuned their instruments. The whispering ceased and in the sudden silence I heard Lady Rochford's voice, on a high, excited note. ''Tis true! Anne of Cleves was so innocent she thought a mere kiss—' I turned, as others did, and saw her redden and bite her lip. What a loud-mouthed foolish creature she was. I saw that Barak was in animated talk with Tamasin. Then I saw Sir Richard Rich's eyes upon me, his expression speculative. I turned away as the music began.

The players were skilful, producing a selection of merry tunes. Then the boys began to sing:

> Welcome to York, Great Sov'reign King,
> Fair glades and dark mountains welcome you,
> Justice and mercy do you bring,
> Forgiveness for our grievous sins;
> And light to banish dark and rain,
> Prosperity to come again.

Moved by their wires, the paper clouds parted and a bright yellow sun was revealed as the rainbow lifted higher and higher.

'Let's hope they're not playing this in another downpour tomorrow,' Wrenne whispered.

Other songs followed, all extolling Yorkshire's loyalty, its regret for its past sins and its delight the King had come to bring justice and prosperity. I glanced round the crowd. Many stood watching eagerly, enjoying the spectacle, but others, especially the big Dalesmen, stood with folded arms and cynical smiles. After half an hour there was an interval, the curtain descended and pie sellers appeared, carrying their wares on trays that made me think of Craike's little desk. I turned to find Wrenne looking at me seriously.

'Brother Shardlake, do you know how long the King is to be here? They have announced the Scotch King is coming to York, yet no one has heard of any party leaving Scotland.'

'I do not know.'

He nodded. 'Perhaps some days then. I wished to know because I have arrangements to make.' He took a deep breath, then looked at me seriously. 'May I confide in you, sir?'

'Of course.'

'You see, I plan to return to London with the Progress. To visit the Inns of Court, see if I can find my nephew, Martin Dakin.'

I looked at him in surprise. 'Might it not be better to write first? If there was a family quarrel?'

He shook his head vigorously. 'No. This may be my last opportunity. Already I am too old to travel to London alone. I have done many favours for people in York over the years. Including friend Maleverer, in his less exalted days. I think I may work a place for myself on the Progress.'

'Even so. After a family quarrel . . .'

'No! I must see him.'

I was startled by the sudden passion in Wrenne's voice, normally so evenly modulated. He winced, his strong face racked by a sudden grimace. I took his arm. 'Brother! Are you all right?'

He gave me a serious look, then to my surprise grasped my hand. 'Here,' he said. 'Press my belly. On the side, there.' Astonished by his request, I let him put my hand to his lower stomach. I felt something strange there, a little hard lump. He let my hand go.

'There. I have a growth inside me; it gets bigger every week and now it starts to give me pain. My father had the same thing and in a year he died of the wasting sickness such lumps can bring.'

'A physician—'

He waved a hand impatiently. 'I have seen physicians. They know nothing, they can do nothing. But I remember how it passed with my father. I shall never see another spring Mystery Play.'

I looked at him, aghast. 'Brother Wrenne, I am sorry.'

'No one knows, only Madge. But . . .' He sighed deeply, then resumed in his usual even tone. 'You see why I do not feel I can travel to London on my own. If I could go with the Progress to Hull, then on to London by easy stages or even by boat, it would be easier. And if you would accompany me, help me should I fall ill, it would be a great comfort.' He looked at me pleadingly. 'It is much to ask, sir, but I had a feeling you might be willing to help me.'

'Brother Wrenne,' I said warmly, 'I will aid you in any way I can.'

'And perhaps in London, you could guide me to Gray's Inn, smooth my path. I have not been there in fifty years and they say London is far bigger now. Forgive me telling you this, sir, but –' he smiled at me sadly – 'I fear the time has come when I must ask for help.'

'It will be done. I am so sorry.'

'No!' he said fiercely. 'No pity, I cannot bear that. I have lived far beyond the age of most men. Though it is always better not to see your end walking down the road towards you. I would like to see Martin again, make up with him. It is the one important thing I have left undone.'

'Of course.'

In front of us the singing rose to a new crescendo, but I had no ears for it now. Wrenne sighed as the voices descended the scale again. 'My father was a farmer, out towards Holderness. He had great hopes for me, worked hard so he could send me to law.'

'Mine was a farmer too. In Lichfield. I buried him just before we came to York. I – I did not take good care of him in his old days.'

'I cannot believe you were not a good son.'

'I left him to die alone.'

Wrenne's eyes became unfocused for a moment, as though looking deep within himself, then his face set in firm resolve. 'When my son died and no more children came, for a time I was not easy to live with and perhaps that was why I quarrelled with my poor wife's family. I want to make it up with Martin; he is the only family I have left.'

I took his arm. 'We will find him, sir. Barak can find anyone in London.'

He smiled. 'I did not know you were a farmer's son. Perhaps that is why we seem to rub along so well,' he added awkwardly.

'Perhaps it is.'

'I am sorry to throw my troubles at your head.'

'I am humbled you have confided in me.'

'Thank you. From now on, please call me Giles. As a friend.'

'Matthew,' I said. I extended my hand, and he took it. His grip was so strong that I thought, perhaps he will not die, perhaps it is a mistake. He patted my arm, then turned back to watch as the curtains parted again and a choirboy, rouged and dressed as a noblewoman, began to sing plaintively of love.

☦

I WALKED BACK TO St Mary's alone, for after what Giles had told me, I had no wish for company, whatever danger I might be in. I thought of poor Wrenne's family quarrel. I had a sense it had been serious. What had his dead wife's feelings been about it, I wondered?

'Fine singing, eh?' I jerked round to find Barak at my elbow. He was in a cheery mood, young Tamasin walking by his side. I saw her look up at him, her pretty face flushed. Yes, I thought, you've got what you wanted, as a pretty girl often will. Jennet Marlin walked on her other side, looking as though she was chewing sour cheese, the brown curls bobbing on her forehead making her look oddly childlike at the same time. Yes, she reminded me of my childhood friend Suzanne.

''Twas well enough,' I acknowledged.

Tamasin smiled. 'The King will be happy to see it, I am sure. Perhaps they will perform it at St Mary's too for the Scotch King. Though 'tis a pity the preparations turn out to be for him. We had thought the Queen pregnant, that there might be an announcement and perhaps a coronation for her. She is very pretty, sir.'

'Is she?'

'Very much. I have seen her several times, though of course I have never spoken to her.' Tamasin was trying to ingratiate herself with me. Barak looked at me then, no doubt gauging my mood, then nudged her arm. 'Come,' he said. 'We block the way standing four abreast.' He steered her in front of me, leaving me with Mistress Marlin, who gave me a smile that contained no warmth at all.

'Well, mistress,' I asked, 'did you enjoy the performance?'

'Not really,' she answered. She fixed me with her large dark eyes. 'I must speak with you.' She nodded ahead, at Tamasin and Barak's backs. 'I am disturbed your man is still courting Mistress Reedbourne. She is my responsibility in York. And after being brought before Sir William like that.'

'It was Mistress Reedbourne's behaviour that caused the trouble, not Barak's.'

'He is a man, he is the one with the authority.'

'Mistress Reedbourne strikes me as well able to look after herself. You know her, Mistress Marlin, you must see that. She dresses very well,' I added, looking at her fine green dress.

Her disapproving look intensified. 'I do not think their association wise. And your man looks to me like a lecherous monkey. Tamasin is still young, with no one to protect her in the world. Her mother is dead. It is my duty to look after her.' She looked at me fixedly. 'From those who might seek to use association with her to find a way into court employment. As for her clothes, her grandmother who was her guardian left her a little money. She is not extravagant, merely likes to turn out well.'

'You do my assistant an injustice,' I said abruptly.

'Do I? Royal servants are a great catch, they earn so much.' Again that pursing of the mouth as though a bad tooth stabbed at her.

'I doubt Barak has given that a thought. He earns a good enough wage with me,' I added.

'I see much greed about the court, sir.'

'No doubt. But we have nothing to do with the court. We are London lawyers.'

She gave me a sharp look. 'But you have contacts in the court as well, I believe. They say you will go before the King tomorrow.'

'With the petitions, yes.' I wished she had not reminded me.

'And I hear you have been working directly for Sir William Maleverer.'

I frowned. 'Where did you hear that?'

She shrugged. 'The world of the royal servants is a small one.'

'Legal matters,' I said brusquely. 'And what has that to do with Barak and Mistress Reedbourne?' Ahead of us Barak leaned close and said something to Tamasin, making her trill with laughter. Mistress Marlin watched them, then turned and gave me a look that had something like hate in it. It took me back over twenty years, to Suzanne standing in that country lane – it was the same look of ferocious, unreasoning anger.

'You are one of those have spent your life climbing towards profit in the service of the state,' Mistress Marlin said viciously. 'And like master, like servant.'

'How dare you!' I replied hotly, angry now. We had almost slowed to a halt, people were barging past us. She faced me.

'I believe you are one of those who has used reform as a ladder for ambition. Like Maleverer.'

'By my oath, lady. You have an accusing tongue for a stranger. What do you know or care of my life?'

She did not quail, merely looked me hard in the eye. 'I have heard Tamasin and your man talking of your history. How you were a reformer in the old days, how Lord Cromwell was your patron. But you have no zeal left in you now, anyone may see that. Like so many, you care only to guard your wealth.'

Yorkers passing turned to look at us. One called, 'Slap thy scolding wench, maister!'

'Do you know why my poor Bernard lies in the Tower?' Mistress Marlin went on regardless. 'Because people in London would like him convicted of conspiracy and papacy, so that they may have his lands! His lands!' Her voice was almost hysterical.

'Then I am sorry for you, mistress,' I said evenly. 'But that has nothing to do with me. Do not dare to assume you know my mind or history. That is an insolence and I will not have it. I will not be your scapegoat!' And with that I turned and walked away, leaving her standing alone in the street.

✝

I RETURNED TO ST MARY'S half an hour later. The tent was up again, workmen brushing it down by candlelight to remove every speck of mud. I went into the manor house. It was very quiet there now, everything standing ready for the King's arrival, the few servants and courtiers walking with an air of quiet reverence, practising the demeanour they must use when the King was in residence. A guard took me up to Maleverer's office. He was still working, his big black-bearded face white in the candlelight. He looked up angrily.

'What now?'

'I thought of something, sir.'

'Well?'

I told him of my work in Ashford, my recollection of the name Blaybourne. 'I thought you should know, sir. With so many Kentishmen among the guard.'

He grunted. 'So he was from Kent, was he? Well, that fits with what we know. Interesting.' His mouth twisted into a sardonic smile.

'But not useful. Edward Blaybourne died long before you or I were born, Master Shardlake. I have been with the Privy Council this afternoon. I have learned much about him.' He shot me a hard look. 'Secret matters.'

'Then I am sorry to disturb you.'

'Someone from the Privy Council has been deputed to see you tomorrow. To go over what you know, remind you to keep silence, twist your tail for your foolishness.' He seemed to have recovered his confidence; no doubt he had been able to convince the Privy Council that everything was my fault.

'You still have charge of Broderick. Visit him before you go to bed. I want you to see him at least once every day, check on his welfare. Get one of the guards to take you to his cell.'

'Yes, Sir William.'

'And I have had words with Master Radwinter, told him to make no more mistakes.' He waved a hand in dismissal and gave me a look of amusement, a cruel look.

✝

A GUARD LED ME deep into the complex of monastic buildings grouped round the church. Here the monks of St Mary's had lived and worked; now the rooms were mostly empty and stripped of furniture, though some had been fitted out with beds to accommodate the host who would be coming tomorrow. The guard led me down a narrow, stone-flagged corridor at the heart of the warren, stopping at the end where a wisp of candlelight came though a barred window in a stout door. Two of Sergeant Leacon's men, who had accompanied us to the castle earlier, stood guard.

'How does he fare?' I asked.

'Just lays there quietly, sir. The physician has been again, says he is improved.'

'Thank Jesu for that. Where is Radwinter?'

'With him now, sir. Shall I let you in?'

I nodded. He unlocked the door. Broderick lay on his blankets, asleep. Radwinter sat on his haunches beside him, looking into the prisoner's sleeping face, his expression one of concentrated, malevolent anger. He looked round when I entered, then rose to his feet with a suppleness I envied.

'I hear he is better,' I said quietly.

'He sleeps. And I have to sleep with him. I must even share his pisspot. 'Tis Sir William's way of showing his discontent.'

'Has he said anything?'

'No. He was conscious earlier. I asked him what happened, but he only repeated his nonsense about the King having poisoned him. If only I had a free hand, I would have the truth out of him, I'd have him humbled.'

'If it was that easy, they would not be taking him to London.'

He gave me that icy, glittering-eyed look of his. 'There is a way to scare and humble every man, Master Shardlake. It is merely a question of finding it.'

✝

I MADE MY WAY BACK to our lodgings. Again a few clerks sat playing cards. I nodded at them curtly, then knocked at the door of Barak's cubicle.

'Ay?'

''Tis I. I would talk.' I went into my cubicle and sat down on the bed, suddenly exhausted. Barak entered. He had a jaunty air about him.

'You're back, then,' I said. 'I thought you might have found a quiet spot with Mistress Reedbourne.'

'Not with Mistress Marlin guarding her. She had a fierce look after you left her. I wondered where you had gone, so suddenly.'

'I have been to see the prisoner while you have been dallying.'

'How is he?'

'Radwinter stands guard over him like the midwife of Hell. As for Mistress Jennet Marlin, she thinks you are after Tamasin to find a position as a court servant.'

He laughed. 'A murrain on her. She fears to lose Tamasin.'

'Why does she value the girl so?' I asked. 'They seem unlikely friends.'

'I asked Tamasin about that. Mistress Jennet likes Tamasin's merry ways, it seems. Says they take her mind from her troubles. Her swain in the Tower.' He shrugged impatiently. 'Who can fathom the hearts of women?'

'I had the pleasure of her company on the way back. She seems to dislike me very much. Thinks I am one of those who would do anything for office and profit. She was so fierce, I am not sure she is not a little brainsick.'

'I asked Tamasin about Lady Rochford,' Barak said. 'Apparently the women are all afraid of her, she does nothing but gossip maliciously about everyone. They say she was paid to bring gossip to Lord Cromwell about the wives she served as lady's maid. Jane Seymour, then Anne of Cleves.'

'And Catherine Howard?'

'Apparently she and Queen Catherine have become close, but Tamasin says the Queen should not trust her one inch. Mistress Marlin does not like Lady Rochford either. Says she has no morals.'

'Who does, in that court? Our self-righteous Mistress Marlin is a naïve woman, I think.' I sighed. 'Well, what will you do while I am greeting the Progress tomorrow? See Tamasin again?'

'She will be busy preparing for the Queen's arrival. I might walk into town, see the Progress enter.' He looked at me. 'Tamasin thought you were a little sharp with her, when we were talking about the Queen.'

'I cannot forget her trickery. But also, I had had bad news.' I told him of Giles Wrenne's illness, his request that I help him find his nephew.

'Poor old arsehole.' Barak shivered. 'That's hard.'

'I said you would help him too, when we get back to London.'

'Ay. All right. I wish we were there now.'

'Me too.' I paused. 'When Mistress Marlin was talking about Tamasin, she mentioned the girl had no one in the world. She said her mother was dead, but made no mention of her father. She has a little money, apparently, from her grandmother.'

'Tamasin does not know who her father was. Her mother would never tell her. Someone around the court, though, for that was the only world her mother knew, working in the Queen's sewery. She has some ideas, but does not know.'

'Oh?'

He looked uncomfortable. 'Girlish fancies.'

I smiled. 'Fancies she is a nobleman's daughter, perhaps?' He shrugged, and I saw I had hit the mark. 'Will you see more of Tamasin, when we are all back home?' I asked with deliberate casualness.

'Perhaps.'

I think you will, I thought. I think you are smitten, perhaps for the first time in your roisterous life. I wondered if this meant he would stay with me.

'Tamasin has seen the Queen, you know,' he said.

'Yes, she told me.'

'Says she is more like a girl than a woman. There is some trouble because she has given her old friend Dereham a job and now he has come here trying to give Lady Rochford orders about the arrange-ments. Tamasin says it has put the old witch in a fine temper.'

I shrugged. I was not interested in the gossip that went on in the royal household.

Barak was silent a moment, then said in more serious tones, 'I have been thinking about Master Craike, wondering what he was up to last night.'

I nodded slowly. 'Yes. If anyone has a free run of St Mary's it is him. And he was up and about when Oldroyd was killed. And in his post he could get keys easily. Like the keys to the chapterhouse.'

'Yet as you said, nothing was found when he was searched.'

'What if he had an accomplice? What if they spoke to Oldroyd and he refused to give up the papers? They kill him. Then I turn up with them at King's Manor.'

'And the accomplice hit you and got away, while Craike stayed there. But why not kill you, knowing you'd seen some of the papers at least?'

'I don't know,' I said heavily. 'And somehow I can't see Craike involved in the conspiracy. I can't see him having the nerve for dangerous work. And what's the connection to Broderick? Is it the same people trying to poison him?'

'Why? If they're on the same side, the side of the conspirators?'

'Perhaps he asked for poison to be brought,' I said slowly. 'At the moment he is speaking in riddles. If he was given a way to kill himself, that would stop him ever talking. But how was it done?' I sat frowning a moment. 'These damned papers, I think they hold something of value to the conspirators. They must do, to have the Privy Council involved. People involved in the conspiracy, seeking the papers and also trying to put Broderick out of the way so he can't tell what he knows.'

'If they were conspirators, why did Oldroyd not give up the papers to them?'

'Perhaps he was unsure of them. Jesu, they gave him a dreadful death. And yet spared me. By accident or design. By God, I hope they meant to spare me.' I took a deep breath. 'Someone from the Privy Council is to interview me tomorrow, no doubt after the presentation to the King. That I am not looking forward to.'

'They might send us home,' Barak said.

I smiled wryly. 'That's what I hope. I'd not mind that, even if it's in disgrace. I want no more of this matter. A pox on Cranmer for involving me with Broderick.' I stretched my arms above my head. 'Dear God, Barak,' I said passionately. 'I wish tomorrow was over.'

Chapter Seventeen

I was wakened by cocks crowing. Not one or two but dozens, a tremendous cacophony. I lay puzzled for a moment, then realized it was the fighting cocks in the monastery church. All round the cubicles people coughed and groaned and cursed the birds.

The sun was rising in a sky of unrelieved blue and when I opened the window I felt warm air for the first time in York. As the song had promised, the King had banished rain. So superstitious folk would say. I looked up at the great bulk of the church, realizing it was the first morning the huge spire had not been wreathed in mist. It pointed to the sky like a huge dead finger.

I dressed in my best robe, adjusting the fur trim, then put on my coif and above that my new cap, for which I had hunted out a new pin. Arranging it carefully, the brim leaning to the left to hide my bruise, I left the cubicle.

All around the clerks were smoothing clothes and checking their faces in steel mirrors. There was none of the usual bantering conversation today; everyone was preoccupied, serious, preparing mentally for their allotted role. Barak, dressed in a red doublet, stood leaning on the door of his cubicle, watching the clerks with a sardonic smile.

'What are you doing?' I asked.

'Watching these fellows. Thought I'd wait for you, see if you wanted to take breakfast in the refectory. You should have something to eat, you do not know when you may get lunch.'

'Ay, let's eat,' I said, touched by his concern. 'How do I look?'

'Dressy. Doesn't suit you. But that bruise is well hidden.'

We walked across to the refectory, which was full of clerks and minor officials, likewise snatching a meal while they could. The carpenters were no doubt all abed, their work done at last. Here too there was an air of tension, and little talk. Everyone jumped and looked round when a groom dropped a plate of cold meat and it clattered on the floor. 'God's body!' he yelled. 'There's grease all over my damned tunic now!'

Barak grinned. 'It's getting too much for some folk.'

'All right for you,' I murmured. 'Don't tire yourself out walking round the town,' I added sardonically, as we parted on the refectory steps. He gave me a mock salute and I turned, joining a steady stream of the well-dressed heading for the manor house. I felt as though I were on a ship, leaving for a voyage to a far, unfamiliar shore.

✝

IN THE COURTYARD the rising sun was reflected in flashing streaks from the gold leaf woven into the fabric of the tents and from the polished breastplates of the soldiers standing before the pavilions, pikes raised and bright plumes in their helmets. The pennants with the Scotch and English flags waved in a warm breeze. Grooms were leading horses out of the church, saddling them and tying them up to await their masters, each with a number round its neck. I looked for Genesis but could not see him.

By the manor house dozens of men in colourful doublets, coats and robes stood talking in groups. There was an occasional burst of nervous laughter. I went inside.

Within, soldiers lined the walls of the Great Hall, standing rigidly to attention. At each of the two staircases a group of servants was struggling to haul up pieces of a large bed to where the King and Queen's privy chambers would be. Lady Rochford and the Queen's secretary, Dereham, were berating two men as they tried to manoeuvre an enormous, richly decorated wooden headboard into the narrow staircase on the Queen's side. Lady Rochford wore a red brocade dress decorated with a fleur-de-lys design, a jewelled pomander dangling from her waist, and her face was painted thick with white ceruse, hiding her high complexion.

'Churl! Churl!' she shouted excitedly. 'You'll chip that edge! Master Dereham, you must watch them, I have to make ready!'

'I am a secretary, not a steward,' Dereham growled. On closer inspection I did not like his mien. He looked well enough in his short coat lined with beaver, an enormous gold codpiece underneath, but his narrow handsome face was shifty.

'Then fetch the Queen's Chamberlain!' Lady Rochford snapped over her shoulder as she swept past me. I looked at the other staircase, where a group of men were struggling with the largest mattress I had ever seen, so wide and thick it threatened to fall back and suffocate them.

I felt a sharp poke in the ribs. I jumped and whirled round to find Sir James Fealty in an ankle-length robe of fine brocade with puffed shoulders and a wide fur trim, frowning at me. Recorder Tankerd stood by him, like me in a good black robe, fiddling nervously with the buttons. A knapsack with gold edges hung over his shoulder, no doubt containing his speech. Fealty's servant Cowfold stood holding the petitions, bound together with red tape and sealed with wax.

'Why are you standing around?' Sir James snapped at me pettishly. 'I need everyone together! Where is Brother Wrenne?'

'I have not seen him yet.'

'Come outside. You should be with your horses. And Brother Tankerd, stop messing with your buttons, you will have them off. And as for your employers, I am angry to hear their news. I hope they know what they are doing!'

'The city councillors are adamant they will not change clothes till they are beyond the city.'

Fealty gave a snort, then marched to the door. I gave the city Recorder a look of commiseration as we followed. Fealty's face brightened a little as he descended the steps, though, for Giles Wrenne was at the bottom, and a groom stood at a respectful distance holding three horses by the reins. One was Genesis, who whickered with pleasure at seeing me.

'Good morning, Matthew,' the old man said cheerfully. Looking at him today one would not have guessed he was ill. He looked well set up in his best robe; his jewelled cap was in the old high-crowned style, a touch of individuality.

Sir James fussed about getting the petitions placed in the saddlebags on Wrenne's big horse, his long wispy beard blowing from side to side in the light breeze. When all was settled and we were mounted he pointed to the gate. 'The city delegation is outside, you will ride to Fulford with them at the guards' signal.' He raked us with his eyes for a moment. 'Remember all I told you, do not disgrace me.' We waited while a little group of courtiers passed us and rode through the gate; among them I saw Lady Rochford and Rich. As we made to follow them I heard someone call 'Good luck, Master Shardlake!' and turned to see Tamasin Reedbourne standing on the steps, looking on. She wore yet another fine dress, a blue and orange one today. I briefly raised a hand to her. I wondered how much was left of her grandmother's inheritance.

✝

ON THE OTHER SIDE of the gates, the Bootham was crowded with men on horseback, all in their best finery. I estimated there must be near two hundred of them. I recognized the mayor at the front, his face almost as red as his robes. We pulled to a halt beside them and waited. A little way up the road a crowd of thirty mounted soldiers waited, their horses resplendent in rich cloths.

I studied Wrenne. He was looking round at everything, and had an air of suppressed excitement about him. 'What a crowd,' I said. 'Who are they all?'

'The city council and guild officials. And the local gentry from the Ainsty. We should set off soon.'

'What is the problem with the councillors getting changed?' I asked Tankerd.

'They have been asked to meet the King dressed in dull and sombre clothes, to show their humility for their part in the rebellion five years ago. But they were adamant they would not change till they were outside the city, lest the common folk see them and mock. Sir James is worried they may mess up their robes while they are changing, as it is to be done in the fields. Mayor Hall has been in a great floughter, caught between the council and yon Fealty.'

Something flickered in front of my vision, and I realized the wretched feather had come loose in my cap again. I pulled it off and fiddled with the pin, careful not to break the delicate feather vane. Then the guard captain called 'Fall to! Fall to!' and I had to jam it back on my head as everyone began to move forward. We followed the procession of councillors as they rode under Bootham Bar, the soldiers clattering behind us.

We rode through a deserted city. Every window was crammed with faces, though, as the Yorkers watched us pass. In the night the streets had been covered with sand and ashes that dulled the clatter of hooves, and as we rode by men with rakes darted out behind us to smooth them again. In some streets garlands of white roses had been hung across the way, and here and there a gaily coloured carpet or cloth flew from a window, but these were few. I remembered Giles telling me how gay and colourful the Yorkers had made their city for King Richard III, and turned to look at him.

'How is the investigation of Master Oldroyd's death going?' he asked me.

'The King's coroner is investigating now.'

'He was a skilful man, it was strange he should fall in his cart. Some in the city say he must have been pushed from his ladder, but surely that cannot be?'

'I do not know,' I answered uncomfortably.

'There has been quite a chapter of accidents at St Mary's, has there not? Maleverer must be concerned.'

'He is.'

'Are you still involved?' he asked.

'No. Not any more.'

We were passing towards another gate now, Fulford Gate it must be, festooned with garlands. I wondered, would they nail the heads and bits of men's bodies back afterwards?

Beyond the gate there was a straggle of houses but after a few minutes we found ourselves in flat open country, green pastures and brown ploughed fields dotted with patches of water after yesterday's rain. The road had been put in good order, potholes filled up.

A little way ahead a number of carts was drawn up beside the road, watched by servants and half a dozen soldiers. Here the city officials dismounted. In uncomfortable silence they removed their finery and put on long robes of a dark, saddle-tawny colour that they took from the cart. It was strange watching Mayor Hall undress, his red face frowning, then thrust stringy white arms into the plain robe. The servants packed the finery carefully into boxes in the cart, and the councillors' caps too; evidently they were to go bareheaded. I glanced over the fields; in the distance a husbandman could be seen leading a team of oxen in the first winter ploughing. I thought suddenly of my father.

The captain carefully pulled a little portable clock from his pouch. 'Fall to!' he called again. The councillors mounted and we rode on a little further, to where a big white stone cross stood by the road. Here fences had been knocked down to create an open space extending into the pastureland on either side. The captain dismounted and went to stand on the plinth of the cross. In a loud clear voice he ordered all to dismount and stand in ranks of twenty, councillors in front, officials like Giles and I to one side, the others behind. Giles handed me the petitions from his knapsack.

'Here, you must keep these till the King comes. Remember, you hand them to me then.' I nodded and grasped them to my chest, wishing they were less heavy. Tankerd, with a nervous twitch of his eyebrows, hitched the gold-edged knapsack over his shoulder and went off to join the councillors. The grooms collected the horses and led them into the pasture. The captain surveyed us then went to stand in front of us, looking down the Fulford Road. 'Now we wait,' Giles said quietly. I stretched my neck, for it ached again, then winced as it gave a painful click.

We stood in silence, all that great concourse, watching the road ahead. At first nothing could be heard but the gentle *tick-tick* as leaves fell from the trees beside the road. The horses had been led some way into the field, near a long, low wooden structure draped with brown cloth. I wondered what it was for. A group of servants were manhandling long wooden planks behind the cloth. The planks had round, head sized holes cut in them at long intervals, putting me in mind of an enormous row of stocks. I looked at Giles, who shrugged. I shifted the heavy petitions in my arms.

It was hot now and I caught the stink of sweat as men began perspiring in their robes. I touched my cap to make sure the wretched feather was still fixed properly, feeling sorry for the councillors standing bareheaded in the sun. Mayor Hall passed a hand over his bald crown.

✝

WE HEARD THE PROGRESS before we saw it, a sound like distant thunder. The rumble grew louder and I realized it was the sound of thousands of hooves. Then I saw an enormous brown patch appear over a slight rise in the distance. It spread slowly up the road towards us like a giant stain, filling the wide road from side to side. It rolled on and on, no sign of an end. The rumbling and thunder of hooves filled the air, startling the birds from the trees, and I made out the shapes of hundreds of high-sided carts, pulled by teams of enormous draught horses. Red-coated soldiers rode alongside, knee to knee in two rows. And at the head a shimmering mix of bright colours that resolved itself into a crowd of gorgeously robed people on horses dressed almost as richly as their riders. I strained my eyes to see if I could make out the King, but just then a blast of trumpets sounded from the throng, making us all start, and the whole giant concourse stopped dead a quarter of a mile in front of us. The hoofbeats died away, to be replaced with a murmur of voices that rose and fell like the sea, with occasional shouted instructions audible to us as, under the soldiers' eyes, we waited in expectant silence. I sensed the nerves of all around me were strained to breaking point. Even Giles seemed tense, his blue eyes alight with curiosity. He caught my eye and smiled. 'Well,' he whispered, 'here it is.'

Lady Rochford, Rich and the other courtiers detached themselves from the Yorkers and rode over to the Progress, disappearing into the brightly arrayed throng at the front. There was silence for a few seconds more. Then things began to happen. The soldiers accompanying us rode ahead to form a line on each side of the road, between us and the Progress. Then figures began to detach themselves from the gorgeously robed crowd ahead and approach slowly on foot. First, half a dozen heralds, red tunics emblazoned with the leopards and lilies of the King's arms, came to stand with the soldiers, holding aloft long trumpets from which bright pennants hung. Then two grooms wearing particoloured jackets in Tudor green and white led a pair of horses up, halting before us and a little to one side. Long coats, richly embroidered, hung over the animals' backs almost to the ground, and the gold fringes and tassels on their black velvet harnesses glinted in the sun. One horse, a grey mare, was large enough but the other was gigantic, a huge charger. The King and Queen's horses of state, I realized.

They kept coming, these harbingers of the King, in ones and twos, building the tension to breaking point. I felt my collar slick with sweat. The Chamberlain, an old man bearing a huge golden-handled sword of state, came and stood facing us, holding the sword up by the hilt. Nobles and ladies in scarlet and gold took places behind him. Among them I noticed a very big, barrel-chested man with a broad face framed by a brown spade-beard like Maleverer's. From his appearance I knew this must be Charles Brandon, Duke of Suffolk, the peer who had organized the Progress. He was on the Privy Council, he would know about Oldroyd, Blaybourne, my loss of those papers. And I thought, with a sudden tremor, does the King know too?

A group of small boys, the children of honour in yellow and green tunics and caps, now rode up and halted before us. A whole crowd of courtiers faced us now, their clothes swirls of gorgeous colour, caps and robes gleaming with jewels, their faces expressionless. It is a strange thing, but even the greatest tension can only be held for so long, and my mind drifted back to the ploughman I had seen earlier. I thought of how many hundreds of times my father must have walked behind the plough. If he could see me now, about to meet the King, would he be proud?

My attention was jerked back, not by a noise but by a new silence. The low rumble of murmurs and shufflings from the procession ahead fell away. Then the heralds raised their trumpets and blew long notes in unison. At once, behind us, there was a rustling sound as the York councillors fell to their knees. Recorder Tankerd stepped forward, then he too fell to his knees. Giles and I took off our caps and followed. The grass was damp under my knees.

Two figures then stepped forth. I had a quick glimpse of an enormous man, a small girl dressed all in silver by his side. I pulled off my cap and bowed my head deeply as the King and Queen approached, their footsteps audible in the sudden, total silence. I heard a faint creak and remembered it was said the King wore corsets now to hide his girth.

They stopped perhaps six feet away. On my knees, with my head bowed, I could see only the hem of the Queen's dress, intricately sewn with tiny jewels of every colour, and the King's white netherhose and square-toed white shoes, buckled with gold. His legs were thick as a bull's. I saw he carried a jewelled walking stick that he pressed heavily into the cinders of the road as he approached. My heart pounded as I knelt there, gripping the petitions tightly, my cap held crushed against the papers.

'Men of York, I will hear your submission!' The voice that came from that enormous figure was oddly high-pitched, almost squeaky. Looking sidelong, I saw Recorder Tankerd, crouched on his knees, unroll a long parchment. He looked up at the King and took a long, shuddering breath. He opened his mouth but for a long, terrible second, no sound came. That moment's silence was utterly terrifying. Then his wits returned and he began declaiming, a loud clear lawyer's address.

'Most mighty and victorious Prince –'

It was a long speech, the tone one of utter abasement.

'We your humble subjects, who have grievously and traitorously offended Your Most Royal Majesty in the most odious offence of traitorous rebellion, promise and vow in the words of faith and truth to love and dread Your Majesty Royal to the utter effusion of our hearts' blood . . .'

I dared not raise my head, though my neck was hurting again and my back too after so long kneeling, still holding the wretched petitions. I looked sideways at Giles. His big head was bowed almost to the ground; I could not see his expression. Tankerd concluded at last.

'In token of our submission, Gracious Sovereign, we give you our address, sworn to by all here.'

He bowed low and handed the big parchment to one of the children of honour who came forward to take it.

Next the mayor stepped up, bearing the two ornate cups I had seen at the Guildhall. He knelt and with more words of abasement begged the King to accept the city's gift. He was, I saw, sweating like a pig. He tumbled his words nervously and I could not catch all he said. My attention wandered again for a moment. Then a sudden fierce whisper in my ear from Giles. 'Quick! It is us now!' I felt my bowels lurch as I rose and turned to follow Giles, keeping my head bent. It was foolish, I that had once had Thomas Cromwell for a friend and confronted Richard Rich and the Duke of Norfolk, reduced to such a jelly. Yet this was not an official or nobleman I was approaching now. This was God's anointed on earth, Head of

His Church, guardian of the souls of three million subjects, more than human in his glory. In those few seconds I believed it all.

We halted beside Recorder Tankerd. Amidst that kneeling crowd I felt horribly exposed. The King was so close now that with my eyes cast down I could see the thick fur on his coat stirring slightly in the breeze, the huge rubies set in gold on his doublet. Still looking down, I saw his left calf was thicker than his right, and made out the criss-cross shape of bandages beneath the white hose. I noticed a slight yellow stain there. And then a puff of wind carried a foul smell to my nostrils: like a blocked drain, the sharp rancid smell of pus.

Giles began speaking in his loud clear voice. 'I come to you, dread Majesty, as representative of the citizens of York, in prayer that you might hear the petitions for justice of the people.'

'I will,' the King replied. Giles turned to me and I placed the petitions in his hands, keeping my head still bent. And then I dropped my cap. The feather came off as it hit the ground. I dared not pick it up and stood looking down at it, cursing inwardly. Giles handed the petitions on to the children of honour in two bundles and they put them into the King's hands — delicate white hands, each long finger adorned with a jewelled ring. I heard an official step forward; the King handed the petitions on to him.

Then I heard him laugh.

'By Jesu, sir,' he said to Giles in his high voice. 'You are a fine-looking old fellow. Are they all so big in the north?' I raised my head slightly, daring to glance at Wrenne's face though not the King's. He was smiling up at the monarch, quite composed. 'I am not so tall as Your Majesty,' he said. 'But who may rise so high?'

The King laughed again, heartily, a rich booming sound. 'Let all hear,' he called loudly, 'that I say this good old man shows the north breeds fine fellows. See the other lawyer by his side, the one that dropped his cap! I know he is a southron, see what a poor bent bottled spider he appears by his side!'

Then, as the Yorkers around me broke into sycophantic laughter,

I looked up. I must, now the King had spoken. He was so tall I had to lift my head to see his face beneath its thickly jewelled cap. I saw a red, jowly face, a fringe of reddish-grey beard, a pursed little mouth under a commanding beak of a nose. The King was looking straight at me, from small deep-set eyes that were mirrors of Radwinter's: blue, icy, glinting, cruel. I realized that he knew who I was, he knew about the lost papers, he had marked me. He gave me a barely perceptible nod, twisting his tiny mouth into a little smile, then turned and limped away to his horse, pressing heavily on his stick. Then I saw Queen Catherine looking at me. She had a plump countenance, bonny rather than pretty. She was frowning a little, but sadly, as though sorry for the King's cruelty. Abruptly she turned away and walked to her own horse. Behind me there was a collective flutter of movement as the Yorkers rose to their feet.

I bent and retrieved my cap and the feather. For a second I stood rooted to the spot, my mind blank with shock and pain, then I felt my bowels lurch again, painfully. I glanced round for Giles, but he had gone; I saw his tall form walking away into the Yorker crowd. Many of them were staring at me, grinning or laughing. Recorder Tankerd still stood hard by, looking embarrassed. I grabbed his arm.

'Brother Tankerd!' I whispered. 'I need the jakes, now. Where can I go?'

For answer he pointed across the meadow to where the large board stood. 'Behind there.' Now I understood the significance of those planks with holes in them. 'But you must hurry,' he said. 'Half the council is ahead of you.' And indeed men were peeling off from the Yorker crowd, brown-robed figures limping and stumbling across the meadow. I followed them at a run, pursued by a fresh burst of laughter; my ears burned. Ahead of me an agonized moan from a staggering councillor told me that for one, at least, it was too late.

☩

I RODE BACK TO TOWN with the Yorkers, behind the royal party and the soldiers and ahead of the vast rumbling procession that I felt looming at my back like the great behemoth in the Book of Job. The King's words had left me crushed; it was hard to ignore the sidelong looks of amusement people gave me.

We passed under Fulford Gate and so back into York. The streets were lined with people now, held back by soldiers; I heard cheers ahead as the King rode by, but they sounded ragged. I looked out for Barak and Tamasin but could not see them. I knew the next ceremony would be for the King to receive those who had been actively involved in the 1536 rebellion but had escaped execution because they were needed politically. I had heard they were to crawl to the King on their bellies in front of the Minster; then he would take Mass and the formal ceremonies would be over.

I wanted only to get away, and took the opportunity of a gap in the soldiery to slip down a side-street and make for St Mary's. I thought, the story of the King's mockery will get back to Lincoln's Inn; lawyers' gossip could reach as far as the moon. This day would haunt me for the rest of my life. As for any danger I might be in, wandering around alone, I was past caring.

✝

I LEFT GENESIS WITH a groom at the church, without even a farewell pat, and marched away. I frowned at the thought that Giles had deserted me; he might have stayed, said something supportive to dull my shame a little. I halted, irresolute, for I did not want to take my bitter thoughts back to my lodgings; I felt they might overcome me. I decide to go and see how Broderick fared; the prison would suit my mood.

I acknowledged the guard's salute with a curt nod. Radwinter was sitting on a chair outside the cell door, reading his *The Obedience of a Christian Man*, that lauded the King's role as God's anointed. The gaoler looked as neat and self-contained as ever, his hair and little beard trimmed by the barber.

'How went the reception for the King?' he asked. I shivered. His eyes and the King's were so alike in their cruel glitter. He was looking at me keenly, the wretch could see I was upset.

'Well enough,' I said brusquely.

'Your cap feather is askew.'

I took my cap off, crushing it in my hand. Radwinter looked at me with interest. 'Did it go badly?'

'All went according to plan.'

'Was the King merry, or sombre?'

'He was in most merry mood. How is Broderick?'

'He sleeps. He ate a little earlier. Food I watched the King's privy cook prepare himself in His Majesty's privy kitchen. I brought it to Broderick, watched him eat.'

'I had better see him.'

'Very well.' Radwinter rose and took the keys from his belt. He looked at me speculatively again.

'Did the King speak to you?'

'A word only.'

''Tis a great honour.'

'Ay.'

He smiled. 'Did he comment on your bruise?'

'No. He did not.' I felt anger starting to boil within me.

'What then?' Radwinter smiled. 'I see I have hit a mark. Ah, did he remark your bent back? I know he dislikes those with deformities, for all his fool Will Somers is a crookback. He is said to be superstitious. Perhaps the sight of you—'

I threw myself at Radwinter, as I had done at no man since my student days. I grabbed him by the throat and slammed him against the stone wall. But he was stronger than I, he reached up, twisted my arm away and sent me flying back against the wall. The soldiers rushed forward, but Radwinter raised a hand.

'It is all right,' he said smoothly. 'Master Shardlake is in quarrelsome mood, but I have him. No need to report this for now.' The soldiers looked at me doubtfully. I leaned against the stone wall, breathing heavily. Radwinter was smiling, gloating.

'Do you not know the penalty for fighting in the precincts of the King's court? The loss of your right hand. By the King's special order. And for a man responsible for an important prisoner to assault his guard?' He shook his head, then gave me a triumphant look. 'I have you now if I want you, sir,' he said quietly. 'Mark that. The soldiers saw.' He laughed. 'I knew the way to break you was your hatred of what you are, a scrabbling bitter hunchback.'

'And you are Death,' I answered savagely. 'You are the Bane, the antithesis of everything good and alive under the sun.'

Radwinter laughed again, merrily. Suddenly my anger left me. It was no use against this man; one might as well rage against a rabid dog. 'Let me in the cell,' I said.

He opened the door, bowing me in with a mocking flourish. I actually entered the dank hole with relief. Broderick lay on a pallet, looking up at me. He was filthy, smelling still of vomit. I decided I would order him washed. His eyes were full of speculative interest. He would have heard every word of what had passed outside.

'I have come to see how you fare,' I said tonelessly.

He looked at me, then beckoned with a thin arm. 'Come, kneel by me,' he said, 'and I will talk. *He* will not be able to hear, that man outside who as you say is Death. It will anger him.'

I hesitated, then knelt down carefully, my knees cracking protestingly. He looked at my crushed cap that I still held.

'So the King was cruel to you?' he said quietly.

I did not reply.

'Yes, he is a cruel man, he strikes as harshly as he can for pleasure, like Radwinter. Poor Robert Aske's fate testifies to that.'

'I say nothing against the King.'

'He is the Mouldwarp.'

'Not that old legend,' I answered wearily.

'No legend,' Broderick said firmly. 'A prophecy. They all knew it at the Pilgrimage of Grace. Merlin prophesied the Mouldwarp, the tyrant who would be driven from his realm with all his line. No

child of his should succeed.' I looked at him keenly. Oldroyd had
said something very similar as he was dying.

Broderick reached out and gripped my arm with sudden strength,
then whispered softly but fiercely: '*Forth shall come a worm, an Aske
with one eye; He shall gather of chivalry a full fair flock, The chicken shall
the capon slay.*' His eyes burned into me. 'You have seen him. The
creature that claims to represent Christ's will on earth, to be our just
ruler. Can you deny he is the Mouldwarp?'

'Let go my arm, Sir Edward.'

'Aske's coming was prophesied. Robert had only one eye, he lost
the other in an accident.'

'But it was Aske who was overthrown, not the King.'

'He sowed the seed that will flourish. The Mouldwarp will be
thrown down yet.'

I shook my arm free. 'This is nonsense.'

'The prophecy is true,' Broderick said. He spoke calmly now,
with certainty. 'The King *will* fall. Soon, though probably not before
I am dead.'

I met his gaze. 'What you say is treason, for all that it is silly
nonsense.'

He sighed. 'Go then. Only – I thought you had seen the truth
about the King.'

I got up painfully. It gave me some satisfaction to see Radwinter
looking frowningly through the bars. He opened the door for me.

'What did he say?' he asked sharply. 'What were you whispering
about?'

'Nothing important,' I answered. I looked at my cap. It was
crumpled, the feather broken, the little garnets hanging loose. I turned
my back on him and walked away. I felt the soldiers' eyes following
me. They would tell Leacon about my assault on the gaoler.

I reached the lodging house, and in my cubicle I threw my cap
on the floor and kicked at the damned thing until it was a shapeless
wreck. Then I sat down heavily upon the bed.

I sat in silence. I thought how, for years, as Thomas Cromwell rose steadily in the service of the state, I had had a tiny share of reflected glory as my one-time friend rose nearer and nearer to the ultimate source of that light, the throne. The King, Head of the Church, fount of law and justice; to meet with him was the greatest glory an Englishman could dream of. Now I had met him. I felt for a second that he shown me what I was, an unworthy creature, a beetle crawling on the earth. Then anger came again. I had not deserved that dreadful humiliation. I thought, perhaps Broderick is right, perhaps Henry VIII is indeed the Mouldwarp, whose rule of terror – for such I had seen it grow into these last few years – would be overthrown. And perhaps should be, I thought.

Chapter Eighteen

I LAY THERE FOR HOURS in a half-stupor of misery, until I heard footsteps and voices as the clerks and lawyers bustled in, their business with the Progress over. They were in a state of high excitement, jabbering excitedly round the fire.

'D'ye see that fat old merchant dressed in sackcloth, crawling across the cobbles? I thought his eyes would pop from his head!' Evidently they had witnessed the former rebels abasing themselves before the King at the Minster.

'Ay. He had to lift his stomach up lest it scrape the cobbles.'

'D'you know what it all reminded me of? The old creeping to the Cross ceremony, at Easter!'

'Hey, Rafe, be careful where you say that, creeping to the Cross ain't allowed now—'

'I was only saying—'

I lay, half listening as they prattled on. I did not want to go out and face them. Then I heard a familiar voice: it was Cowfold.

'Hear about what the King said to the hunchback lawyer at Fulford?'

'Ay, one of the city clerks told me.' I recognized the voice of Kimber, the young lawyer who had greeted me that first evening. 'Said he was a bent bottled spider beside the old Yorker lawyer he was with. The clerk said Shardlake's face went like chalk. He looked at the Queen with a sort of desperate appeal, then staggered away.'

'T'was cruel,' someone observed.

'Cruel nothing!' Cowfold said. 'Fealty and the court should have known better, putting someone who shames the south up before the

King, a hunchback. My mother was touched by a hunchback beggar once, nothing went right with her after that—'

I could take no more. I got up, opened the cubicle door and went out. Silence instantly fell among the group standing round the fire. I stared at Cowfold. 'When was your mother touched by the hunchback?' I asked in a loud clear voice. 'Before she conceived you, I'll warrant, if nothing went right with her after. By the look of you it set her to copulating with pigs.'

Some of the men laughed nervously; Cowfold glowered and I knew that but for my rank he would have launched himself at me. I turned to go, leaving a dead silence behind me. Outside I felt pain in my hands and realized I had clenched my fists together so hard my fingernails had almost broken the skin of my palms.

I cursed myself for my crude outburst; it would only make things worse. Cowfold would be furious and would mock me behind my back at every opportunity now. First I had lost control with Radwinter, now this. I must pull myself together. I stood under a tree, taking deep breaths, watching as a fresh batch of the local black-faced sheep were led into an empty pen. No doubt the previous occupants had all been taken for slaughter, to feed the thousands that had now arrived.

A big, rough-looking fellow in a smock appeared, carrying a heavy stick and a bag from which blood dripped, and approached the bears' cages. The great shaggy creatures, which had been lying curled up, rose and sniffed the air as the man laid his package on the ground, pulled out chunks of meat and began throwing them through the iron bars, taking care to keep a safe distance. The bears seized the meat in their long muzzles, displaying yellow fangs. One piece of meat fell short and the bear reached an arm through the bars and scrabbled for it with long greyish claws. The man shouted and hit the arm with the stick; the creature roared and drew its arm back between the bars as the keeper used the stick to flick the meat inside. 'You stay back there, Master Bruin!' the man called, as the creature stared at him with its tiny red eyes.

I walked down the side of the church to the main courtyard. It was late in the afternoon but fortunately the day was still warm, for in my haste I had come out without robe or coat. It had turned into one of those golden autumn afternoons when everything is still and full of colour, a slight misty quality in the air. The pleasantness of the day seemed only to point up my black mood.

The courtyard was a hive of activity. There were many soldiers outside King's Manor and I wondered if the King and Queen were in there now. Servants were rushing to and fro and I almost collided with a fellow carrying a huge carved chair to the pavilions. I went to lean against the wall, out of the way, watching the scurrying figures as they weaved to and fro.

I heard a bray of cultivated laughter. A little group of courtiers appeared. I recognized Lady Rochford, who had changed now into a yellow silk dress. Beside her Jennet Marlin clutched a little flop-eared dog to her chest. Some other ladies I did not recognize were with them, all richly dressed, with painted faces and necks, waxy in the sunlight. Their wide skirts swished on the paving stones as they walked towards me.

The women were jesting with a group of young men, among whom I recognized the Queen's secretary, Francis Dereham. He wore a discontented scowl, perhaps because the ladies seemed to be giving most of their attention to an athletic-looking young man with a pretty, sculpted face and curled brown hair, resplendent in a purple doublet with slashed yellow sleeves and a curved golden codpiece. He turned his head, a jewel in his ear flashing in the sun. His features had a weakness to them, a lubricious smoothness.

'You should take your dog, Lady Rochford,' the young popinjay said. 'I think it heats up Mistress Marlin's bosom too much, she is quite flushed.' He gave a teasing smile at Jennet, who was indeed pink. She gave him a vicious look in return.

'Perhaps I should, Master Culpeper,' Lady Rochford replied. 'Here, Jennet, let me have him.'

Mistress Marlin handed over the dog, which struggled as Lady

Rochford clasped it to her chest. 'There, to hold a dog thus is wholesome for a weak stomach. Is it not, my Rex?'

'I know better things to comfort a woman's stomach,' Culpeper said, bringing a titter from the group. Lady Rochford, to my surprise, gave him a look of girlish coquettishness. 'Come, sir, fie,' she said with a laugh.

'No shame in bringing comfort to a fine lady,' he answered, touching the dog. It growled and struggled again, its tan coat marked with flecks of whitelead from Lady Rochford's neck. The group was level with me now and I turned away, but not before Jennet Marlin caught my eye; she frowned at me. They passed on and I followed them with my eyes. Lady Rochford, Mistress Marlin and that glowering young secretary, Dereham. Three who had seen me enter King's Manor with the box the day I was struck down.

I left the wall and wandered back to the lodging house. Where was Barak, I wondered? Somewhere with young Tamasin, probably. I was about to go in when a voice called my name. I turned and saw Master Craike heading towards me.

'Brother Shardlake,' he said with a smile. 'How are you?'

His manner was friendly. I wondered if he had heard what had happened to me at Fulford, and guessed not. 'Well enough,' I answered. 'And you, sir?'

He sighed. 'There are endless complaints about the accommodation. People seem to think I can conjure the lice from the beds at all the inns in York.'

'What of those thousands of people?' I asked. 'Where have they all been put?'

'I have a minute,' he said. 'Would you like me to show you where they all are?'

I raised my eyebrows. 'All? In one minute?'

He smiled. 'All the servants and carriers, at least. Over two thousand of them.'

'Very well. I could do with a distraction.'

'So could I, sir. This nightmare – but, come.'

To my surprise, Craike led me to the church. We stepped inside, into a tumult of noise. Most of the stalls were occupied now with riding horses. Grooms were carrying great bundles of hay to the animals, who ate lustily as more grooms washed them down. There was an overwhelming stink of dung. I saw that in some of the empty side-chapels blacksmiths' forges were being erected; one or two fires had already been lit and the smiths were working hard, mending shoes that had been damaged on the journey. Five thousand horses on the Progress, I thought. Twenty thousand shoes.

I followed Master Craike's example as he lifted the hem of his robe above the straw and dung that littered the nave. He stopped at a door in the centre of the nave, under the great steeple, where two soldiers stood guard. They saluted him.

'Anyone up there now, soldier?' Craike asked.

'No, sir, not at present.'

Craike turned to me. 'Come, sir,' he said. 'Are you fit to climb some steps?'

'I think so.' For a moment I hesitated; was this wise, allowing myself to be led away, alone, by the man who might have been my assailant? But I thought, to hell with it. I will not cower away in that damned lodging house.

We passed through the door and up a long winding staircase. We climbed very high, and were both out of breath by the time Craike opened another door and we stepped into what had once been the belltower, though the bells themselves were long gone for melting down. Over the railings that had once enclosed them we could see down into the nave. Far below us another blacksmith's forge flared redly into life, the effect unearthly against the pillared walls. I suddenly remembered the fight to the death I had had in another belltower, at Scarnsea four years before; then I had nearly gone to my death. I did feel afraid then, and jumped as Master Craike touched my arm.

'Do heights trouble you, sir? I do not like them either. But this sight makes it worthwhile.' He beckoned me over to a window. 'Down there, look.'

I joined him, my eyes widening at what I saw. Behind the monastery, several fields had been enclosed with wicker fencing, forming a gigantic campsite. Conical soldiers' tents were pitched in hundreds around an open grassy space where cauldrons and gigantic spits were being set up over wood fires from which smoke was beginning to drift into the late afternoon sky. In the next field hundreds upon hundreds of wagons were drawn up, guarded by soldiers, while the big carrying horses had been stockaded in more fields beyond and stood cropping the grass, hundreds upon hundreds of them. In a nearer field I saw the latrine-men digging. What seemed like a city full of men sat around in front of the tents, or diced or ran at football games. Laughter and cheers drifted up from a makeshift ring where a cockfight was taking place.

'Jesu,' I said.

'The Progress at camp. It was my idea to make this belltower a watching place, the officials and captains can come up here from time to time to see what is going on. Though thank God I am responsible only for the courtiers' and gentlemen's accommodation, not all this.'

'Such organization,' I said quietly. 'It is a marvel. Somehow terrifying.'

He nodded slowly, the sun catching the wrinkles in his plump face. 'The Royal household has been organizing progresses for years, of course. Armies too, for this is an army as well. But to have done all this in weeks! It cost much effort. And money,' he added, raising his eyebrows. 'You have no idea how much money.'

I looked at the rows and rows of carts. 'It astounded me this morning, how much was being carried.'

'Oh, yes. All the tents, for there have been country places along the way where even privy councillors have had to make do with canvas. And a thousand other things, from stores of food and fodder to the Privy Council records and the King's greyhounds for when he goes hunting.' He looked at me gravely. 'And extra weapons, in case there was trouble in the north and the carriers and drivers had to be pressed as soldiers.'

I pointed to a row of gaily coloured tents a little distance apart from the others, where a straggling queue was waiting. 'What is happening there?'

Craike flushed and cleared his throat. 'Those are the – er – followers.'

'The what?'

'The whores.'

'Ah.'

'Only single men have come on the Progress, apart from the noblewomen and the Queen's household. We could not let the men run amuck in the towns along the way. So necessity meant –' He shrugged. 'It is not pleasant. Most of these queans were picked in London and carefully examined, for we did not want to spread the French pox across the land. You can imagine what a state some of them are in by now.'

'Ah well, men have their needs.'

'Yes, they do. But I am not used to dealing with such a rabble as the Royal Household's servants. You should see them on the road: insulting the villagers, getting drunk, shitting wherever they list in the fields; they would have stolen everything in the carts if we did not have the soldiers. And their insolence – they blow their foul breath on the courtiers, claw their cods in front of you.' He shook his head. 'The new learning has made common men arrogant.' He turned to me, the sharpness back in his eyes. 'But perhaps you have a different view? I heard you became a supporter of reform.'

'In the early days,' I said. 'I am nobody's partisan now.'

Craike sighed. 'Do you remember our student days, before Nan Boleyn turned the country upside down? Peaceful times, season following season at Lincoln's Inn, the future as certain as the past.'

'One may view those times through rose-coloured spectacles,' I said.

He inclined his head. 'Perhaps. Yet they were better days. When I first went to work at court the old nobility still ruled. But now — these commoners, these new men. Cromwell has gone but there are so many others.'

'Yes.' I nodded. 'I saw Richard Rich earlier.'

I was surprised at his reaction to that name. He jerked away and stared at me with a scared, angry look. 'You know Rich?'

'As an adversary in the law. I have a case in London where he is backing my opponent.'

'He is a serpent,' Craike said with passion.

'That he is.' I waited for him to say more, but he changed the subject. 'I meant to ask, is any more known of the person who attacked you in the manor?'

'No.' I looked at him keenly. 'But he will be found.'

'You may not know, security has been greatly increased since the attack on you. And people say poor Oldroyd's death was not a natural one. That for some reason he was murdered.'

'Do they?' I asked.

'Yes. Those in charge of security are worried. On every progress checks are kept to weed out those who batten on to the household, pretend to be servants so they can steal food and other trifles. But tonight I am told every man's papers are being checked thoroughly, and anyone who is not authorized to be in camp is questioned, not merely turned out.' He looked at me. 'What is going on, sir?'

Is he fishing for information, I wondered. Yet he seemed genuinely puzzled. 'I know nothing, Master Craike.'

'It was frightening, being searched by Maleverer the day I found you.'

'But you have nothing to fear. He let you go. Or have you been questioned again?'

'No. Only — I did speak with Oldroyd, probably more than

anyone else at St Mary's.' He sighed. 'I confess when I was sent ahead of the Progress to York, to arrange the accommodation, I was a little afraid of what the Yorkers would be like, we had heard such stories of them as savage rebels. And indeed they were very guarded with me, not friendly. But Master Oldroyd seemed happy to talk. He was a friendly face, that was all.' He took a deep breath. 'But I fear some may try to make more of it. Master Shardlake, you must have seen, beneath the pomp everyone here, everyone, Yorkers and southrons, walks on eggshells. It makes one nervous.'

You are keeping something back, I thought, I smell it. I remembered Barak's story of him going to a tavern in a poor part of town late at night.

'I can understand it must have been lonely for you when you first came,' I said.

'It was. Master Oldroyd was someone to talk to.'

'You will be glad when all this is over, I'll warrant. To get back to your family in London. Seven children, eh?'

'Ay. All alive and well by God's grace. And their mother. My Jane.' To my surprise, his face clouded. 'Ah, she did not want me to come on the Progress.' He fiddled nervously with the buttons on his robe. 'We have been away longer than was expected, and no one seems to know when we will be leaving York. I fear I will have a mighty tongue-lashing when I return. Held four months in reserve.' He laughed nervously. I realized the picture I had formed of his contented family life was perhaps wrong. I wondered whether to tackle him directly about his visit to the tavern, then thought, no, that will put him on his guard. I will go there with Barak.

'Well, sir,' I said. 'It is growing dark. We should go back down while we can still see. Thank you, Master Craike, for showing me the camp. I think I shall go and look at it.'

'A pleasure, sir.' He smiled, and led the way down.

☦

I WALKED THROUGH to the far end of the church. I saw a stream of people passing through the side-gate beside the church, which I had heard was called St Olave's; like me no doubt going to look at the great camp. I felt reluctant to face the crowds, some among them must have been at Fulford. A little way off I saw a big copper beech, the grass underneath thick with dark purple leaves. There was a bench set against the trunk and I went over and sat down. The sun was setting now and it was a dim, shadowed spot. I watched the people passing in and out of the gate, listening to the ticking sound of the leaves falling around me.

My thoughts returned to Fulford. They had been circling round it all afternoon and now they went back to the scene as a dog will return to its vomit. Had I really gone chalk-white, had I really given the Queen a look of desperate appeal? I wondered what it must be like for that girl, married to that gross old man with his stinking leg. I remembered the King's eyes, cruel as Radwinter's. And that was the King of England, the man Cranmer believed had been appointed by God himself as guardian of our souls. We had all learned, from childhood, to see the monarch as no ordinary mortal man, and in recent years as a sort of demigod. I had never believed that; but nor had I believed that the cloak of majesty covered such physical and moral ugliness. Surely others must see it too; or were they dizzied by the panoply, his power? I wondered what Giles had made of the meeting, Giles whom the King had called a fine fellow in contrast to me. I thought again that I would have expected him to wait, give me some comfort. I had not thought he was one to disappear and avoid embarrassment.

'There you are. Thank heaven.'

I looked up to see Barak standing in front of me.

'Yes, here I am. I fear I have been thinking treasonous thoughts.'

'Is it safe to be out alone?'

'I have been in no mood to care. Did you hear what happened at Fulford?'

'Ay. That fellow Cowfold was in the lodging house when I went there just now, making a great joke of it.'

'I gave him a few choice words earlier. Probably a mistake.'

'I told him if he didn't shut his mouth I'd bang his head against the wall till it was soft as a baked apple. I think I've shut him up.'

I smiled then. 'Thank you.' I noticed Barak's face was anxious. 'Is something the matter?'

'Ay, it is. I have been looking all over this damned place for you. Maleverer wants to see us both, at King's Manor.'

'Oh.' Suddenly my head was clear, my self-indulgent gloom chased away.

'A representative of the Privy Council is there. He wants to talk to us about the missing papers. Now.'

Chapter Nineteen

W E STOOD AGAIN BEFORE Maleverer's desk. A pair of guards had escorted us through King's Manor, where richly dressed servants and officials walked in decorous silence. The King and Queen would be upstairs now, in the royal apartments. I remembered the men that morning, labouring to get the King's giant mattress upstairs.

Maleverer sat behind his desk, dressed in a red silk doublet, a chain of office round his neck. He motioned Barak and me to stand before his desk and sat surveying us.

'Well, sir lawyer, I told you the Privy Council would be sending someone to talk to you.' He smiled evilly as footsteps were audible outside. 'You will be interested to see whom they have sent.'

I did not reply. There was a peremptory knock at the door. Maleverer stood up and in the instant before he bowed deeply his expression was transformed from hulking bully to fawning courtier as Sir Richard Rich, swathed in a magnificent beaver-lined robe of dark-green velvet, walked in.

'Sir Richard. This is an honour. Please take my chair.'

'Thank you, Sir William,' Rich replied smoothly. He sat down, Maleverer taking up a respectful position beside him. Rich looked at me, his pale features puckering into an acid smile.

'Master Shardlake, my brother in the law. I saw you in York the other night. I know Master Shardlake, Sir William.'

'He is a great nuisance,' Maleverer said.

'I know that well.' Rich's cold grey eyes scanned my face. 'We had several — encounters — last year, and have another pending in Chancery.'

'Indeed?'

'But did you know, Sir William, the King did Brother Shardlake the honour of speaking to him this afternoon. Or at least, speaking *of* him.'

'I gathered something had happened.'

'It is the talk of all the law clerks. Brother Shardlake was appointed to present the gripes and whines of the York petitioners to His Majesty at Fulford Cross, together with a Yorker lawyer—'

'Old Wrenne.'

'Is that his name? You should have seen Brother Shardlake and this Wrenne standing before the King. Wrenne is a very tall and straight old fellow, and from a distance they looked like some proud old pensioner out with his bent crone of a wife.' Rich laughed. 'The King remarked they breed fine fellows in the north, finer than some of the creatures the south can produce.'

Maleverer looked at me, then smiled. 'His Majesty ever knew the value of a timely jest. That will have gone down well with the Yorkers.'

'So it did. They stood there cackling with laughter.'

Maleverer gave me an evil grin. 'You see, Master Shardlake, you have helped the King a little in bending the north to his will.'

I fought to keep my voice under control. 'Then I am happier for it.'

Maleverer laughed. 'Well answered, eh, Sir Richard?'

Rich grunted. 'Sarcastically answered, if I know the mind of our friend.' He made a steeple of his fingers and leaned forward. 'But now, there are other matters on hand. Master Shardlake, you had possession of a cache of papers — very important papers, more than you can know. And you let them be stolen. Sir William has told me what happened, but I want the story from your own lips.'

'Very well, Sir Richard.'

I told him of our visit to Oldroyd's house, the discovery of the secret panel in the wall and the papers, and how I had been struck down. Rich frowned mightily when I told him how Barak had tried to open the box.

'You had no right to open that casket. Your duty was to leave it till Sir William returned.'

'I am sorry, Sir Richard.'

'And I,' Barak said.

Rich snorted, then turned his gaze to Barak. 'You seem to think you can still take liberties, you churl, as though Lord Cromwell were still alive. Well, he is not. You are a pair of meddling fools.' He frowned thoughtfully for a moment. 'Who saw you bring the casket to King's Manor?'

'When we came into the house, Lady Rochford and her lady Mistress Marlin were with secretary Dereham. They looked over at us. My coat was dusty.'

Rich's eyes widened. 'How come you to have acquaintances in that quarter?'

'Not acquaintances, Sir Richard. But – er . . .' I looked at Barak.

'There was some dalliance between this Barak and a kitchenmaid under Mistress Marlin's authority,' Maleverer said.

'Who else?' Rich snapped.

'Only Master Craike, who let us leave the casket in his office. And Master Wrenne whom we met on the way, and the sergeant at the gate.'

'I've questioned all three,' Maleverer said. 'And the girl. And Oldroyd's apprentice, but he said nothing useful either.'

'Many others that we do not know must have seen us,' I said.

Rich sat considering. 'Have you questioned Lady Rochford about the casket?' he asked.

'No, sir. I questioned Jennet Marlin. I did not think I could interfere with members of the Queen's household.'

Rich nodded. 'No, Lady Rochford and Dereham can't be questioned by the likes of you, but the Queen's Chamberlain could put some careful questions to them. As for that Mistress Marlin, she has a fiancé in the Tower. Suspected of being part of a Gray's Inn link to the spring conspiracy.'

'She was investigated and declared safe to come on the Progress,' Maleverer said.

'I will arrange to have some questions asked of Lady Rochford and Dereham. And you can question the Marlin woman again. We shall see if that throws anything up.' Rich turned and pointed a long finger at me, then Barak. 'And you had better keep your curiosity to yourself, Brother Shardlake. You know too much as it is. Some on the Privy Council think that is reason to send you back to London, but I think I would rather have you under my eye. Besides, the Archbishop wants you to look after Broderick. Not that you've done well there, either. I hear someone tried to poison him.'

'Yes, Sir Richard.'

'And he won't say whom?'

'No. I have wondered . . .'

'Well?'

'Whether he is party to the plot to poison him. I know he wishes to die.'

Rich looked at Maleverer. 'Is that possible?'

'It could be. He's an unusual one. He was well groped in York Castle, but said not a word. The torturers there feared he'd die if they went on much longer.'

'What instruments do they have there?'

'The rack, pokers, the usual. But the men are not skilled.'

'And the locals cannot be trusted with what Broderick might know. Hence the King's order he be taken to the Tower, where the real professionals will work on him.' He shook his head. 'Yet time passes.'

'Hopefully he will be on a boat in a few days,' Maleverer said.

'We must hope for a fair wind. We could send him by road, but that's not safe and the roads are still in a mess from the rains and the passage of the Progress.' Rich turned to me. 'What is his state of health now?'

'Weak still from the poisoning.' I hesitated. 'I saw him earlier today. He was talking about the Mouldwarp legend. He seems to believe in it.'

Rich looked at Maleverer. 'There were papers about that legend in the box.'

'It was a common currency among the rebels in the commotion time. It is of a piece with Broderick's fanaticism.'

Rich cast sharp eyes at me. 'Why should Broderick relate the Mouldwarp legend to *you*? He can hardly have thought you would credit it. Can he?'

'He overheard me talking to Radwinter.' I took a deep breath. 'Radwinter wormed out of me that the King mocked me at the Progress today. Broderick overheard our conversation and related the Mouldwarp nonsense. But I swear I said no word against the King.'

Rich leaned back, giving me a sidelong look. 'You had better not, or you will be in the hottest of hot water. You are in bad enough odour with the Privy Council. My advice to you, Master Shardlake, is to follow the natural inclination of your bent body and keep your head down.'

'Yes, Sir Richard.'

'A low profile. That is the best course for you from now on.' He spoke slowly and carefully, fixing me with his eyes, grey and lifeless as those of a corpse. He leaned forward. 'It might help your reputation a little if you were to advise the London Guildhall to drop the Bealknap case.'

I met his gaze. I realized Rich had probably volunteered to be the Privy Councillor who would question me; it was a chance to put some pressure on. I did not reply. He inclined his head slightly.

'In any event it will do no good to keep on with that matter. I have found the judge I want, the case has been assigned to him.'

'Who?' I asked.

'The case has not been *formally* set down yet. You will find out if you continue. You would be better to take my word for it, advise the Guildhall to drop the case now, and save costs.'

Take Rich's word was one thing I would never do. I saw Barak look at me anxiously. Rich saw too. 'Perhaps you can advise your master to see sense,' he snapped. 'Otherwise, I do not know what will become of him. All right, that will be all. You can go.'

Maleverer leaned over to Rich and spoke quietly but eagerly. 'May we take the opportunity, Sir Richard, of discussing the property of Aske's family? If the disbursements can be agreed—'

'Not now.' Rich frowned and looked at me. 'I told you to go,' he said. 'Send for that Marlin woman.' He waved a hand at us and we left the room. Outside, a guard was waiting to lead us downstairs.

'Some corrupt business between those two,' I murmured to Barak.

✝

It was almost dark now.

'Shit,' Barak said. 'Shit, shit, shit.'

'Couldn't have put it better myself,' I said bitterly.

'What are you going to do about the Bealknap case?'

'I don't believe Rich has managed to bribe a judge. If he had he'd have given the name. No, he was just using the opportunity to intimidate me.'

'Intimidate you?' Barak came to a halt. He looked angry, and as worried as I had ever seen him. 'Intimidate you?' he repeated. 'Have you any idea just how much pressure he can put on you if he wants? On a man who has the disapproval of the Privy Council? What he could do to you now if he really wanted?'

'I have Cranmer's protection.'

'And Cranmer's here, is he? I can't see any archbishop's robes among this lot. And Cranmer can't stand against Rich, not if Rich has the Privy Council behind him.'

'Cranmer—'

'Would only risk so much for someone as lowly as you. Or me. I'm in trouble too — it was me decided to try and open that fucking box!'

'I will not be pressured or blackmailed into giving up a case!'

'You've said yourself you didn't think you could win.'

'I won't be blackmailed!' I realized I was shouting.

'Obstinacy,' Barak said. 'Obstinacy and pride. It'll be the death of you — of both of us.' He opened his mouth to say more, then closed it again and walked away.

I ran a hand across my brow. 'Shit!' I said. A passing official looked at me curiously. I turned, walked down the side of the church and made my way to the bench under the copper beech. I sat down heavily under the branches. People were still going to and fro through the gate that led to the encampment. I shivered, for there was a chill in the air now.

Barak's outburst had surprised me. When I first met him a year ago he had been defiance itself, ready to treat the highest with disrespect. But then he had been under Lord Cromwell's patronage and, as Rich had taken pleasure in reminding us, Cromwell was dead. And now, as Barak had said, part of him at least wanted a quiet life. But it had been strange to hear him accuse me of obstinacy and recklessness. I felt a warm flush of self-righteousness. I was protecting my clients, as every honest lawyer must. My integrity in the often corrupt world of the law was my badge, my identity. Was even that to be taken from me by these mocking courtiers?

But as I sat under the tree a while a calmer humour settled on me. I knew I was clinging on to my reputation for integrity because, after the battering I had taken during that long day, it was all I felt I had left. And I had no right to involve Barak in any unwise defiance of Rich. Yet I could not abandon my clients if, as I thought, we had a chance of winning. Barak should surely know that.

I jerked upright at the sound of approaching footsteps. I remembered that I could still be in danger. A dim figure was approaching across the grass; I was relieved to see it was a woman, her dress rustling as she stepped into the carpet of fallen leaves under the tree. As she came close I saw to my surprise that it was Tamasin, in her yellow dress and wearing a fine silver necklace.

'Mistress Reedbourne?'

She curtsied, then stood uncertainly before me. She seemed nervous, not at all her usual pert self.

'I wondered, sir, if I might speak with you,' she asked hesitantly. 'I saw you sitting there.'

'What about?'

'It is important, sir. Important to me.'

'Very well.' I gestured to the bench and she sat beside me. She did not speak for a moment, she seemed to be considering what to say. I studied her. With her high cheekbones, full mouth and determined chin she was indeed a very pretty girl. Yet so young; little more than a child it seemed to me.

'Mistress Marlin has been taken to Sir William for questioning,' she said at length.

'Yes. Barak and I have just been with him. And Sir Richard Rich.'

'Mistress Marlin looked angry. She dislikes Sir William greatly.'

'Yes. I saw that when you were brought in for questioning on Wednesday.'

She reddened at the reminder of her deception.

'You would have been better to have left Barak and me alone,' I said. 'I am involved in some very confidential matters.'

'Yes, sir.'

'We have had words. He will have told you. He is an impertinent fellow, Master Jack.'

'He is anxious, sir.'

'Usually it is me who is the anxious one.' I hesitated. 'But perhaps this time he is right.' I looked at her, wondering how much of our business he had told her. The less the better, for her sake. 'Do you know where he is now?'

'He has just left to look at the camp. I have been wanting to say, sir . . .' she added, then hesitated again.

'Yes?' I said encouragingly. It cannot have been easy for her to come and seek me out; Barak's cross-grained old employer as she probably thought of me.

'I am sorry for the trick I played that day you first came to York.'

I nodded. 'It was foolish. And unbecoming for a woman. Maleverer was right there. Yet he should not have struck you.'

She shook her head. 'I care little for that.' She looked at me steadily now. 'I have had a strange life, Master Shardlake. I have had to make my own way. My mother was a servant at court.'

'Yes, Barak told me.'

'She sewed the Queens' bodyservants' clothes in the sewery. In Catherine of Aragon's time, then Anne Boleyn's.'

'Did she?'

'Yes. Then she died, in the plague in London seven years ago.'

'I am sorry,' I said gently. 'So many were lost then. I lost someone too.'

'I was but twelve, with no one but my grandmother to care for me, or rather me for her as she was old and ailing.'

'I see.'

'I never knew who my father was. But I believe he was of good blood.' She seemed to straighten a little with pride. 'My mother told me he was a professional man.'

'Did she?'

'Yes. He might have been a senior courtier.'

Or a tailor. I felt sorry for her. Her mother had probably told her the tale to comfort her, to ease the girl's shame at her origins.

'I see you doubt me, sir. But I believe it. I take pride in myself, whatever cruel people may say about my birth.'

'That is good. You should not listen to what cruel people say.' I thought, but if it is the King?

'My granddam told me to take advantage of the dearth of servants caused by the plague to seek the place my mother held,' the girl went on. 'And I did, sir. I told them in the chamberlain's office I was a skilled seamstress, though I knew nothing of the work.'

'It seems you have a talent for deception.'

She frowned then. 'I worked, sir, I worked day and night to learn until I made myself a competent seamstress, learning from the other girls, who helped me for my mother's sake. And poor folk must make shift for themselves. I had my granddam and myself to feed, and the Queen's sewery offers good wages. And protection from the world outside,' she added.

'Yes. I can see that.'

'I learned to live by my wits, sir.'

'As Barak did.'

'When I saw him that day in the town, something stirred in me, as it has seldom done before, and I thought – why not manufacture a meeting?'

I smiled reluctantly. 'In truth you are clever, mistress, as well as bold.' I looked at her directly. 'And now you hope to hook your fish, eh?'

Her face was serious. 'We are becoming fast friends, sir. I wanted only to ask you not to stand in our way. And please, where is the boldness in asking that?'

I studied her a long moment. 'I think you are an unusual woman, Mistress Reedbourne,' I said. 'I had thought you of a frolic disposition but I see I was wrong.'

'Jack is sorry for his words earlier,' she said.

'He used to be very bold. But I think part of him wants to settle down. Though part does not,' I added.

'I hope he would settle down,' she said. 'Stay working for you, give proper value to the opportunities you have given him.'

I smiled wryly. 'So that is it, Mistress Tamasin,' I said. 'You have come to offer me an alliance.'

'We have an aim in common. Jack admires you greatly, sir, he says you have known troubles and have sympathy for poor folk and the necessities of their lives.'

'Does he truly say that?' I asked. I was touched, as no doubt she meant me to be.

'He does, sir. And he feels it was his fault that casket was lost. I think he is angry with himself more than anyone. Do not be too hard on him.'

I took a deep breath. 'I will think on what you have said, mistress.'

'That is all I ask for, sir.'

'Well, I see you care for him. And he perhaps for you?'

'I hope when this wretched Progress is done, Jack and I may meet again in London. But it will be as he wishes.'

I nodded. 'Tell me, how did you get from the sewery to working for Mistress Marlin and Lady Rochford?'

'After Jane Seymour died her household was broken up. I obtained a post with Mrs Cornwallis, the Queen's confectioner. She trained me in the art of making comfits and sweets.'

'You made her your friend too, eh?'

'She is a good old body.'

'You have a talent for making the right friends. But as you say, poor folk must shift as they can.'

'When the King married Queen Catherine last year I was taken into her household, since she too is fond of comfits, and placed under Mistress Marlin. She has been kind to me.'

'Mistress Marlin is a strange woman.'

'She is good to me. The other women mock her.'

And you are naturally kind, I thought. Yes, I think you are. 'And Lady Rochford?' I asked. 'What is she like?'

'I have little to do with her. All fear her, they say she is dangerous.'

'And is she?'

'I think so. She likes nothing better than to dig up juicy gossip and take it where it may do most harm.' She frowned. 'She is not a stupid woman, I think. Yet she behaves stupidly.'

'Dangerously.'

'Yes. It is what she has always done. Yet she has attached herself to the Queen, they are fast friends.'

'I saw the Queen today.'

She hesitated. 'At Fulford?'

'At Fulford. Jack told you what happened to me there?'

She cast her eyes down. 'It was a cruel thing.'

'Well, as you say, the sooner we are all out of York the better.'

She rose. 'I should go, sir. I must see how Mistress Marlin fares.'

'Does Barak know you are having this conversation with me?'

'No, sir. It was my idea.'

'Well, Tamasin, you have charmed me, as I guess you have charmed many. Would you like me to accompany you back to your lodgings?'

She smiled. 'Thank you, sir, but no. As I said, I am used to making my own way.'

'Goodnight, then.'

She bowed, then turned and walked confidently away, to be lost in the crowd. I watched her go. I had been wrong about her, she was a girl of mettle. Perhaps Barak had met his match.

Chapter Twenty

Tamasin's courage in approaching me with her confidences made me feel rather abashed; after all, I had been less than civil to her these last few days. I rose from the bench, for I was getting chilled, and decided to visit the camp across the road and see if I could find Barak. I went through the door in the precinct wall by St Olave's church and crossed the lane to where guards stood at a gate in the wicker wall. I showed my papers and was allowed through. My nostrils were at once assailed by a harsh smell of woodsmoke, unwashed bodies and excrement. As I entered the field, where grass was already turning to mud under the pressure of feet and hooves, someone blew a horn nearby. Men began walking to the nearest cooking-fire, carrying wooden bowls and mugs. It was late for dinner, they would be hungry.

I stood and watched as a large group gathered round the fire, a huge blaze of wood set in a rectangular pit under a huge spit, six feet high and a dozen long, an enormous metal construction on which a whole ox turned. Scullions ran up with more wood while others turned the immense handles under the supervision of a sweating cook. The spit was an amazingly complex piece of equipment. Underneath chickens turned on smaller irons, and gallapins darted in and out, pulling out the cooked birds and slicing them deftly on big platters, fat dripping on them from the ox. Wearing leather aprons and neckerchiefs over their faces against the spitting fat, the little kitchen boys moved with extraordinary speed and skill to fill the plates held out by the hungry men. There was joking and catcalling but the men were well behaved; all looked tired for they would have started travelling at dawn, waited during the spectacle at Fulford and then come on here to set up the camp.

Watching the little scullions darting among the flames and hot fat, I reflected that Craike was incorrect. The organization of the Progress was an extraordinary thing, but to sneer at the workmen was wrong; without the discipline and skill of these men, the drivers and cooks and carriers, nothing would have been accomplished at all.

I heard a cough, and turned to find Barak at my elbow. 'Oh, you're here,' I said roughly. 'Quite something, isn't it?' We were silent a moment, watching as the men crouched on their haunches by the fire, eating hungrily.

'There's hundreds of great Suffolk horses in the far fields,' Barak said. 'I've never seen so many.'

'I saw. Master Craike took me to the belltower. The officials have an eyrie there to watch the camp. In case the men make trouble.'

He grinned. 'A nightmare, eh?'

'Ay, a nightmare!' I laughed.

'I'm sorry for losing my temper earlier. Being with those arseholes Maleverer and Rich unnerved me.'

'You had a point. But I do not feel I can abandon this case, not when it seems there may be even a slim chance of winning. Can you understand that?'

'Yes, I suppose so.' He was silent a moment, then changed the subject. 'I was talking to one of the clerks earlier, who was at Fulford.'

I looked at him sharply. 'Oh, yes?'

'He said Master Wrenne was taken ill, just after he met the King.'

'What?'

'He collapsed in the midst of the city councillors, had to be taken home in a cart.'

'So that was why he disappeared. I thought he'd run out on me. How is he?'

'I only know he was taken home to rest. He can't have been too bad, or they'd have fetched a physician.'

'I will visit him tomorrow. Did you and Tamasin see the King when he entered York?'

'Ay. Jesu, he's a big fellow. The Queen looked tiny next to him, a mouse beside a lion. He smiled and waved merrily, but there were hostile faces in the crowd, and a line of soldiers between him and them.'

'Yes.' The cooking-fire was blazing now. I wondered how the four sweating men who turned the handles of the spit could bear the heat. 'Let's walk on,' I said, 'before we roast like that ox.'

✝

WE WANDERED ROUND the camp. It was quite dark now, though the many cooking-fires and lamps set before the tents gave enough light to see by. A cool breeze had risen, sending smoke drifting into our faces and making us cough.

'I should tell you,' I said. 'I had a fight with Radwinter this afternoon.'

'A *fight*? You?' Barak looked at me incredulously.

I told him what had happened. He whistled. 'I wanted to fly at him myself after what he said about the York Jews. Jesu, he knows how to provoke.' He gave me a shrewd look. 'Do you think that was what he was after, making you lose control?'

'I'm sure of it. He means to hold it over me. No word among the clerks on the Scotch King's arrival, I suppose?'

'No. I've been talking to some of the men in the camp. They're happy to sit it out here for a few days so long as it doesn't rain and the countryside can bring in enough supplies. They ran out at Pontefract they were there so long, and were put on short rations.'

'It's harvest-time. I imagine the farmers will be making money out of the Progress.'

'They get paid over the purveyance rate, I hear. Part of the plan to win the Yorkers over.'

I looked at the men walking to and fro or sitting by their tents with their bowls, waiting as more cooking-fires were lit around the camp.

'They're tired,' Barak said. 'They've had near three months on the road.' I nodded, envying the ease with which Barak could strike up conversation with common folk.

We had arrived at a cockfighting ring. Men stood cheering as two black cocks, feathers slick with blood, circled in a clear space next to the fire, slashing at each other with the fierce hooks fixed to their claws.

'Your bird is losing again,' I heard a cultivated drawl. 'You may strive till you stink, Master Dereham, but you will never beat me in a cockfight wager.' Looking round, I saw the louche handsome face of the courtier Lady Rochford had referred to as Culpeper. A little group of male courtiers stood at the front of the crowd. The rest of the audience, out of respect, had left space around them. Culpeper's face was lit redly by the flames, as was that of secretary Dereham who stood next to him, a saturnine smile on his face.

'No, sir,' Dereham replied. 'I took a wager on your bird as well as mine. For two marks.'

Culpeper looked puzzled. 'But then . . .' He still looked puzzled as Dereham laughed in his face. For all his charm with the ladies, young Culpeper had little intelligence.

Then Dereham saw me. He frowned and stepped forward with a bullying swagger. 'Hey, you!' he said sharply. 'You're Lawyer Shardlake, ain't you?'

'I am, sir.'

'I've had Sir William Maleverer asking me questions about seeing you carrying some decorated casket at King's Manor a few days ago. What have you been bandying my name about for, you stinking knave?'

'I have not, sir,' I said evenly. 'Sir William wished to enquire of everyone who had seen me with the casket, and I remembered you and Lady Rochford looked over at me. I had some plaster on my cloak,' I added.

'What's so important about the box, hey?' Dereham demanded. 'Maleverer wouldn't say, only that it had been stolen.'

I looked around uneasily; several people had turned at the sound of Dereham's loud braying voice. Maleverer would be furious if he knew Dereham was broadcasting the news like this.

'It was lost, sir,' I said quietly. 'Sir William has the matter in hand.'

'Don't answer me back, you baseborn slug.' Dereham's face reddened. 'Do you know who I am?'

'You are Master Dereham, the Queen's secretary.'

'Then have respect.' Dereham frowned, then smiled cruelly. 'You're the hunchback the King made mock of, aren't you?'

'I am,' I said wearily. With one of Dereham's rank, as with Rich and Maleverer, there was nothing one could do but take it.

'It's all round the town.' He laughed and turned away.

Barak took my arm and walked me off. 'Parasites,' he said. 'Tamasin says that Culpeper made a pass at her, he tries it on with every woman he likes the look of. He's one of the King's body-servants, he can do as he likes.'

'I am going to have to develop the hide of a crocodile.'

'It'll be a two days' wonder. There's to be a big bear-baiting at the manor tomorrow, all the York gentry invited, and half the camp will straggle along to watch. That'll be the talk tomorrow night.'

I nodded. 'Will you take Tamasin?'

'She doesn't like the bear-baiting. Another one with a weak stomach.'

I smiled. 'When we return to London, will you see her there? Or is she just another of your dalliances?'

'I thought you didn't like her?'

'Maybe I was too harsh. Anyway, 'tis your business.'

'Well,' he said. 'We'll have to see.' He smiled enigmatically. 'I can't think that far ahead. I feel like we've been here for ever.'

'So do I. Come, this walking is making me hungry. Are they serving food in the refectory?'

'Should be.'

We started walking back to St Mary's. I saw young Leacon standing with a group of soldiers by the tents; he bowed to me and I nodded in reply. Then I espied another figure, standing with arms folded at the edge of a crowd, cheering on a bloody dogfight between two great mastiffs. He nodded approvingly as one dog tore open the other's stomach, spilling a mess of guts and blood.

'Radwinter,' I said. 'Come, this way, I don't want to see him.' The wretch, though, had seen me. He smiled at me sardonically as we slipped away into the darkness.

'What's he doing here?' Barak said. 'I thought he was guarding Broderick.'

'I suppose Maleverer must allow him time to exercise. Damn him. Beware, it's muddy here.'

We had come to the edge of the camp, beyond the tents, where the ground sloped down to some trees. Beyond I saw the Ouse gleaming in the moonlight. We turned and walked back.

'Saturday tomorrow,' I said. 'You can have a free day. I will go and see Master Wrenne, see how he is. And what the arrangements are for hearing the petitioners. I may have to do it myself if he is indisposed.'

'The bear-baiting is in the morning,' Barak said. 'But some of the clerks are going hawking, I thought I might accompany them.' He hesitated. 'Tamasin would like to go.'

'Good idea. Get some fresh air. How does the old rhyme go? A Greyfalcon for a King . . .'

'A Merlin for a Lady,' Barak continued cheerfully.

'A Goshawk for a Yeoman, a Sparrowhawk for a Priest—'

'A Kestrel for a Knave. I'm hoping someone might lend me a kestrel.' He laughed.

'Tamasin was telling me about her father,' I said.

'Oh?' He looked surprised. 'When did you see her?'

'We happened to meet. Had a little talk. Perhaps I have been a little hard on the girl.'

'I'm glad you see that.'

'She believes her father was a professional man.'

'I think that's probably a story her mother told to comfort the girl. Nobody likes the taint of bastardy.'

'That's what I thought.' I was reminded of Maleverer. He too had that taint. His way of dealing with it was more brutal.

Barak shook his head. 'Tammy is so practical in many ways. But she has this notion about her father fixed in her head.' He sighed. 'Women need things to comfort them, and she sets no great store by religion. At the court she has seen something of the politics and greed that have brought the religious changes.'

'You will see eye to eye with her on that, I think. As do I.'

Barak nodded. 'I thought I might write to a contact of mine in the household office. I did him a favour in the old days, when I worked for Lord Cromwell. If someone is illegitimate, there is always a trail of gossip.'

'Might be better not to find out the truth.'

'If her father turns out to have been in charge of putting stray dogs out of the kitchens or something, I needn't tell her.'

'No.'

We heard voices. It was dark here, on the fringe of the camp, but I saw, a little way ahead, the light of a small fire, a group of men and boys gathered round it. A pit had been dug and filled with faggots. A group of gallapins had unloaded the pieces of another giant spit from a cart and were labouring to set it up, thrusting the great spiked central rods through the centre of the apparatus.

'Don't put the turning-handles on yet, Danny,' a stout cook in an apron called out.

'All right, Father,' a boy's high voice replied from the far end of the spit. The spit was so long that I could only make out his dim shape at the end.

'Where's that damned ox?'

252 C. J. Sansom

'Owen has gone to look.'

'Keep your voice down. We don't want the men from yonder tents shouting for food before the beast's even skewered. Who's that?' the cook demanded sharply as he heard our footsteps, then doffed his cap at the sight of my robe. 'Ah, sir, I'm sorry, only we don't want people here till the cooking's under way.'

'We were just walking by.' I stepped away from the end of the spit, where the sharp points waved to and fro as the little gallapin at the other end adjusted them. 'That is a mighty spit,' I said. 'Are you cooking a whole ox on there?'

'Ay, and chickens and ducks underneath. We must feed a hundred tonight.'

'Have you been doing this every night since London?' It was a relief to talk to someone who would neither know nor care about what had happened at Fulford.

'Ay. In worse conditions than this too. In fields turned to seas of mud in July. One day the rains put out the fire and the men looked set to riot – the soldiers had to be brought in.' The cook shook his head. 'I will never complain about the cold in the Hampton Court kitchens again—'

He broke off, as a cry sounded from the gallapin at the other end of the spit. I heard a sudden grating noise. Then Barak grabbed me and threw me to the ground.

'What in Hell—' I shouted as I thudded heavily into the rough grass. Then I stared up in horror at the great metal spike that had been thrust through the centre of the spit and now quivered in the air three feet above my head. If Barak had not pushed me it would have skewered me through. Barak and the cook were running to the other end of the spit, then there was another loud cry, in the cook's voice: 'Murder!'

I got to my feet, wincing at the renewed pain in my neck, and ran to where Barak and the cook were crouched over a small figure lying on the ground. 'Someone knocked the gallapin on the head,'

Barak called out to me. 'Then he pushed that spike at you, he was trying to kill you!'

'Danny!' the cook was crying. 'Danny!'

'That boy,' I breathed. 'Is he . . .'

'Let's see.'

The cook was crouched on the ground, the boy's head in his lap. To my relief the small figure was moving.

'Careful with him,' Barak said. 'Watch his head.'

The cook gave him an angry stare. 'Do you think I don't know that? He is my son!'

'I am sorry.' I bent down. 'Where is he hurt?'

'There's blood on the back of his head,' the cook said. I felt the lad's skull carefully. 'I think it's just a scalp wound. Someone hit him on the back of the head.'

The boy groaned. 'Father! I can't see properly,' he said. The boy was no more than twelve or so. I felt a sudden rage at the brute who had struck him down.

'Hold him still,' I said. 'See if his vision settles down.'

The cook was looking at me. 'This was meant to kill you, sir.'

'I can see better now, Father.' The boy tried to lift himself up, then groaned and leaned back. 'I'm dizzy.'

'Listen, fellow,' I said. 'Your lad has a concussion. Let him lie and rest, cover him with a blanket. If he is no better tomorrow, come to me and I will pay for a doctor. What is your name?'

'Goodrich, sir.'

'Ask for Master Shardlake, at the lawyers' lodging house.'

'All right.' The cook looked fearfully at the spit, then at the darkness beyond. 'What if he should come back?'

'We'll see to that,' Barak said grimly. He ran back and lit a stick of wood from the fire. I followed him as he walked into the darkness, but we could see nothing, only the river flowing strongly and behind us the lights of the camp. Barak looked back.

'He'll have gone back to the camp. Shit.'

'Ay,' I said quietly. 'Come on, let's get back ourselves.' We returned to where the cook still crouched by his son. I saw a group of men approaching, a cart laden with an ox carcass. I touched the cook's arm. 'Remember my name, Master Shardlake. Let me know how he does.'

'This should be reported!'

'I'll deal with that. Don't forget. Come and see me, at the lawyers' lodgings.'

We walked away, back to the relative safety of the lit areas, and stood looking over the crowd. Some of the men who had finished eating were sitting around their tents playing music, the sound of shawms and bagpipes wafting through the air.

'So,' I said quietly. 'I *am* in danger. I have been careless today, grumbling about on my own.'

'Why haven't they tried before this?'

'Perhaps this was the first opportunity. Someone who saw us come into the camp.'

'There must be hundreds here from King's Manor. If Maleverer would tell you what those damned papers were, why they were so important, you might know where to start looking.'

'He won't do that. I'll tell him what's happened, but even if he cared enough he wouldn't be able to protect me, not among these hundreds of people.'

'He's an arsehole.'

'And he's up to some corrupt business with Rich. No, I doubt I can look for aid from that quarter. Rich would probably be glad to have me out of the way.'

Barak whistled. 'You don't think . . .'

'I don't know. Except that whoever tried to kill me tonight is likely to try again.'

'We could ask to go home. As you're in danger.'

'They seem to want me here. Besides, even if we did go back to London, what's to stop whoever it is following us there? And there are supposed to be conspirators at the Inns of Court too.' I looked out again over the milling crowds. It was not the first time in my life that I had walked in fear of an assassin, though never had I felt so helpless. I looked at Barak. 'Thank you, Jack,' I said quietly. 'You saved my life there. You reacted quickly.'

'I turned when I heard the metal grating, saw it moving. By Jesu, though, it was a matter of a split second.'

I was silent a moment, then took a deep breath. 'I have resolved something. Now I know someone is after my life I am going to try and track *them* down. I have had enough, I will *not* allow myself to be beaten down into a mere hunted quarry. And other lives may be at risk too, since this enemy thinks nothing of knocking children on the head.' I looked at him. 'Perhaps yours too. Will you help me? I have no right to ask, I have been a boorish churl with you over the girl Tamasin.'

He nodded. 'I'm with you all the way. I'd prefer action to sitting around like a target.' He extended a hand, and I took it. 'Like last time,' he said.

Chapter Twenty-one

SATURDAY DAWNED CHILL, a light rain falling through a grey mist that hid the St Mary's steeple. I had tried to see Maleverer the night before, but was told he could not be disturbed. Barak and I rose early, both having slept very little, and went outside. I locked the door behind me; since the first attack on me at King's Manor I had always locked myself into my cubicle.

A little way off the two bears lay asleep in their big iron cages. Today they would be set to fight with great mastiffs for the King's entertainment. We made our way over to King's Manor again. I noticed the trees were becoming bare; autumn was further on up here. Squirrels ran to and fro along the branches, blurs of red movement. I looked up at the walls where the soldiers patrolled with their guns and swords, the only people allowed to carry weapons in the royal precincts. The household officials had sharp eyes out for weapons, particularly given what had happened at St Mary's. Barak and I had sat up late talking, and agreed I was probably safe from a sword-thrust. Our assailant, whoever he was, would be concerned not to be recognized by anyone. It looked as though someone in the darkness of the camp had seen us and followed at a distance, waiting for an opportunity to strike unseen and seizing it boldly when it came.

'Are you sure you don't want me to stay with you today?' Barak asked.

'No — after I've seen Maleverer I'll walk over and see Wrenne, then come back to the lodging house. I'm safe enough in daylight if I keep to public areas. No, you have your day's hunting.'

'Thanks. One of the clerks is lending me a goshawk. 'Tis newly trained, only a few weeks since its eyes were sewn closed to tame it, but it will be better than nothing.'

'Then take care.'

He walked off and I went across to the manor, a phalanx of soldiers now guarding the steps. I looked up at the windows of the upper rooms where the King slept. They were shuttered. I wondered if he had taken the Queen to his bed with him. I remembered the smell of his huge leg, and shuddered.

I gained admittance and was led again to Maleverer's office. He was up already, working at his papers. He looked tired, there were dark rings under his fierce eyes. He was not afraid of hard work, I had to grant him that.

'What now?' he grunted, looking at me balefully. 'I'm surprised at you showing your face again.'

'I was attacked last night, Sir William. I thought you should know.'

That got his interest. He listened attentively as I told him what had happened. He frowned thoughtfully, then gave me a hard look.

'Are you sure it was no accident? Servants can be cunning as cats. Perhaps the gallapin was never struck, only made it up to excuse carelessness with the spit. Did you think of that?'

'His head was bloody. And that spit was pushed at me with more force than a child could command.' I remembered the sharp tip, quivering in the air.

Maleverer was silent for a moment. When he spoke again it was in a quiet voice. 'We thought whoever took the papers had fled. There are escaped conspirators among the fells, others in Scotland, and some in London too. That would have been the sensible thing to do. Yet no one has been reported as leaving the Progress unexpectedly. Perhaps they passed the papers on to an associate and came back here. To finish you off, as the only one who had seen inside that box. Or so at least they think.' He frowned. 'Perhaps they believe you have kept the knowledge to yourself and not told me.'

'That is possible.'

'I shall have to report this to the Privy Council.'

I hesitated. 'I wondered whether it might be better for me to leave the Progress now, go back to London?'

He smiled coldly. 'No. No, Master Shardlake. You can be our stalking horse. Perhaps you will lead our killer into the open.'

'Perhaps he will kill me,' I said.

Maleverer shrugged. 'Then you must take care. This can be your penance for losing the casket in the first place. No, I forbid you to leave the Progress.' And he smiled at me for a long moment, running a thick hairy finger along the edge of his beard, the yellow nail standing out against the black hairs.

'As you command, Sir William.' I kept my voice neutral, professional. 'I plan to go to see Master Wrenne now. I gather he has been taken ill. Other arrangements may need to be made if he cannot attend the hearings on the petitions.'

Maleverer grunted. 'I said he was too old for this. Send a message to me if he is unable to do it. We'll have to find someone else. You can't do it, we need someone with presence and a reputation up here.' He smiled at me again.

I bowed and left. As I descended the staircase I thought, so, it is up to me to save myself. From now on I would wear a dagger at my belt, for all it was forbidden to carry weapons at King's Manor.

✝

As I walked down a misty Petergate towards the Minster I saw men in city livery raking the sand and ashes back into place on the roads; no doubt the King would be returning to the city for more ceremonies and entertainments. I looked at the little houses along Petergate and thought again of the rule preventing citizens from casting sewage in the streets or in the river while the Progress was here. It would be piling up in their backyards. It was symbolic of the King's visit: all glitter and show in front, a pile of turds behind.

I gained entry to the Minster precinct and knocked at Master

Wrenne's door. The old housekeeper answered. Her face was drawn with anxiety. 'Good morning, Madge,' I said. 'How is Master Wrenne? I heard he was ill.'

She sighed. 'Maister can attend to no work today. He's happed up in bed. His physician is with him.'

'I came only to see how he was.'

She hesitated. 'Come in then, maister. I will see if he can receive thee.'

She left me in the solar. The fire was unlit; the greyfalcon asleep on its perch, head tucked under its wing. It made me think of Barak, out hunting with Tamasin at his side. I had not wanted to stay at St Mary's alone, I knew I would feel safe at Wrenne's.

I looked around the stacked piles of books. It had occurred to me that if I could find a map of Kent somewhere I could confirm where Blaybourne village was. I did not know where that would get me but it was something and my determination to discover what was happening had grown. It was a counterweight to the shame and anger I felt over what had passed at Fulford Cross.

Madge returned and said Master Wrenne would see me. I followed her up to a small but well-appointed bedroom. Giles lay on a good feather bed. I was shocked at the change in him: his strong square face was white and it seemed to me some of the flesh had fallen away from it since yesterday. To my surprise, Dr Jibson was there talking to him. He smiled at my entrance.

'Master Shardlake, good morning.'

Giles reached out a hand. 'Dr Jibson tells me you are acquainted. He will not say how, professional discretion. But I hope you are not ill too?'

I took his hand, glad the old man's voice at least seemed strong and clear as ever. His grip, too, remained firm. 'No,' I said. 'But you . . .'

'Oh, I had a bad moment, but I am recovering. I shall be ready for work on Monday. We have to hear the first petitions then, down at the castle.'

'I will leave you now, sir,' Dr Jibson said. 'I will instruct your housekeeper how to make up that powder.'

The physician left. 'Draw up a chair, Matthew,' Giles said. I brought a stool to the bed. He looked at me seriously, then sighed. 'What the King said yesterday must have caused you grievous hurt. And for me to have been made part of his evil jest gives me sorrow.'

''Tis not the first such jest I have had to endure, though never from a King nor in front of such a concourse. But what of you, sir, I heard you were taken ill just after?'

'Ay. That was the worst attack I have had so far. I was quite composed until the King looked into my eyes and spoke to me. Then—' He broke off with a visible shudder.

'What?'

'You will think me an old fool.'

'No.'

'I felt a sudden horror, that is all I can call it. For a second I did not know where or who I was. When the King turned away I stumbled away into the crowd and almost fell. Fortunately I know the townsmen and they helped me back to York without anyone seeing my piteous state.' He reached for a mug by his bed and took a draught. I caught the spicy smell of an ale posset. He shook his head. 'When I looked at the King's eyes it was as though all the power drained out of me.'

'His eyes are cruel.'

Giles gave a sudden bark of laughter, yet I caught fear in the sound. 'It made me think of that old legend of the commotion time.'

'That the King is the Mouldwarp?'

'Ay.' He raised his eyebrows. 'You know of it?'

'I have heard.'

He shook his head. 'It is dangerous to speak of such things, such foolish superstitions. I had been working too hard, the strain was too much. But still – well, I have often wondered what the King was really like. Now I know.' He shook his head. 'And the Queen, she is so young.'

'I feel sorry for her.'

'A buxom little thing. Yet not regal.'

'She has Howard blood.'

'The Howards. Their lineage is not as old as they make out.' He sighed. 'Perhaps all those trappings of power, all we are told of the ordained power of royalty, perhaps they addle the mind so that when we see the reality it is a shock.'

'The reality. Ugly and sordid.'

Giles looked at me. 'Yet we must have royalty, it is the peak of the social order, without it everything would collapse into chaos.'

'It has already done that in York, has it not? Five years ago, and nearly this spring too?'

'Ay, there is a great grudge here. Tell me, how did the city receive the King?'

'Barak said the cheers were ragged.'

'How different it was for Richard III.'

'Richard Crouchback,' I said softly. 'I remember . . .'

'Yes?'

'Once when I was small, I was playing in the parlour. My father and some of his friends were talking round the table. Someone mentioned something that had happened in Richard's time. Richard Crouchback's time was what they said, forgetting I was there. My father looked at me. I can still see the look on his face. Pity. Disappointment.'

'You had a hard time of it,' Giles said gently.

I shrugged. 'Mayhap.'

He sighed. 'That was propaganda, anyway. You forget I saw King Richard. His back was straight. He had a hard face, serious. But not cruel.' He leaned back on his pillows. 'I was a boy then, so long ago.' He looked up at me. 'Matthew, I had hoped to keep my strength a little longer. But this attack of pain and weakness has been bad. If it goes with me as with my father, there will be spells of better health but more of these attacks. I may not be an easy companion on the road back to London.'

'Do not fear. You will have any aid that Barak and I can give.'

'You are kind.' He looked at me, and I saw his eyes were wet with tears in the second before he turned away, that I might not see them.

I thought, all my life I never saw tears in my father's eyes, even when my mother died. There was silence in the room for a moment. Then I said, lightly, 'I came to ask a small favour as well as to see you.'

'Of course. Anything.'

'I need to check something on a map of southern England. In connection with a matter I have on in London. Are there any maps in your collection?'

His eyes lit up with interest. 'Why yes, I have some. They are mostly old monkish things but you are welcome to look. Most are of the north but I have one or two of the southern counties, I think. I wanted to show you my collection, it is in two rooms at the back of the house. Tell Madge to give you the keys. The maps and plans are on the third shelf on the south wall in the first room. I must stay in bed, I fear.'

'Of course.' I rose, for I could see he was tired. 'I shall send word tomorrow, see how you are. If you are still poorly I will speak to Maleverer about getting someone else to deal with the petitions. Maleverer will not allow me to chair the arbitrations.'

He smiled and shook his head vigorously. 'I will be better by tomorrow.' He hesitated, then said, 'Do not take what the King said too hard, Matthew. It was part of a political game. It was not personal.'

'A chance to praise a Yorker at my expense. That point has been made. No, the worst thing was that I could see the King enjoyed what he did.'

Giles looked at me seriously. 'Politics is a hard and cruel game.'

'I know.'

I left him and descended the stairs. In the hall Dr Jibson was talking to Madge. 'Master Wrenne says I may check something in his archive,' I told her.

She hesitated a moment, then said, 'I will get the keys.'

She left me with the doctor. 'How is he?' I asked.

Jibson shook his head. 'He has a wasting sickness.'

'He told me his father died of the same thing. Is there nothing to be done?'

'No. These cruel growths eat away at a man. One can only pray for a miracle.'

'And without a miracle? How long does he have?'

'It is hard to say. I have felt that lump in his stomach, it is not too large yet, but it will grow. A few months at most, I would guess. He says he plans to go to London. I must say I think that foolish.'

'Perhaps. But it is important to him. I have said I will take care of him.'

'That may not be easy.'

'Then I will deal with that.' I paused. 'Have you seen Broderick again?'

'Ay. He has thrown off the effects of whatever poisoned him. He is young and strong, for all his ill-treatment.'

I nodded, frustrated the physician never had anything definite to say. Madge reappeared with the keys, and I bade him farewell. I followed the housekeeper back upstairs, to a passage beyond Wrenne's bedroom.

'Maister doesn't let many in here,' she said, looking at me dubiously. 'Tha won't disturb his books and papers, will tha? He likes them kept in order.'

'I promise.'

She unlocked a stout door and ushered me into a room that smelt of dust and mice. It was big, the master bedroom in fact, and half a wall had been knocked through to another room beyond. The walls of both were covered from floor to ceiling with shelves filled to bursting with books and papers, rolled parchments and piles of manuscript. I looked round in astonishment.

'I had no idea the collection was so big,' I said. 'There must be hundreds of books alone.'

'Ay. Maister has been collecting near fifty years.' The old woman looked round the library and shook her head, as though Wrenne's occupation was beyond reason.

'Is there an index?'

'Nay, it is all in his head, he says.'

I saw that a little picture of the points of the compass had been set on the wall. The third shelf by the south wall was full of rolled-up papers, as he had said.

'I will leave you, sir,' Madge said. 'I must prepare the powder the physician prescribed, to ease maister's pain.'

'He suffers, then?'

'Much of the time.'

'He conceals it well.'

'Ay, that he does.' She curtsied and went out.

Left alone, I stood looking round the shelves. I went to investigate the maps, and my wonder grew. The collection Wrenne had rescued was astonishing, and fascinating. I unrolled ancient painted maps of the Yorkshire coast and countryside, illuminated by monkish scribes with pictures of pilgrim shrines and places where miracles had been wrought. There were maps of other counties, too, and among them I found a large one of Kent, perhaps two hundred years old. It was none too accurately drawn, but full of place-names.

There was a desk by the window, giving a view of the Minster. I sat and studied the map. I located Ashford, and then, to the southwest, saw the name Braybourne. To the west I saw the Leacon, where the young sergeant hailed from. I stroked my chin. So, a man called Blaybourne or Braybourne might have come from Kent some time last century, and left a confession in York that was of concern to kings. But where did that get me? I realized I had been hoping for some further clue, some lead, from the map, but there was just the name – a village off the main routes.

I returned the map to its place and walked along the shelves, wondering at the variety and the age of the books and papers. There were biographies, histories, books on medicine and horticulture and the decorative arts, books in English and Latin and Norman French. It struck me I had seen no books on law, but when I walked into the other room there were whole shelves of them, classic works like Bracton, old casebooks and yearbooks and volumes of Acts of Parliament. Some of them, I saw with excitement, had dates that were missing from Lincoln's Inn library, for there were many gaps in the records of law cases there.

I took some of the yearbooks and went back to the desk. These were indeed lost casebooks. I sat reading the old cases, becoming lost to time. Since I was a child, whenever I was troubled I had always been able to escape into the world of books, and as I delved through Wrenne's collection I felt my mind and body settling, relaxing. By the time I came to myself again with the thought that Lincoln's Inn would pay well to have copies of some of these casebooks, I realized that hours had passed. I went downstairs to the kitchen, feeling a little embarrassed. Madge sat there sewing. I coughed.

'I am sorry, Madge, I lost myself in the books up there.'

She smiled, the first smile I had had from her, a surprisingly sweet one. ''Tis good to see someone take an interest in maister's collection. Few do. People now say we must forget the past and the old ways, bury them.'

'It is a remarkable library.'

'Maister is sleeping.' She looked out of the window, where the rain still fell through the mist. 'It's still mizzling. Would tha like something to eat?'

'Ay, thank you.' I realized I was hungry.

'I can bring it to the library if you wish. And a candle.'

I thought, why not. 'Yes,' I said. 'I think I will stay. Thank you.'

I went back upstairs, where Madge soon brought me some bread and beer, more of her tasteless but filling pottage, and a big beeswax candle which she set upon the desk. As I ate I looked round the library. It was an oddly Spartan place: no furniture apart from the desk, the floorboards bare, not even any rushes laid. How many years had Giles laboured here alone, I wondered? And what would happen to his collection when he died?

A thought struck me, and I went to the shelves where the books of Acts of Parliament stood. It was a long shot, but just as some of the yearbooks were unique, so some of the collections of Acts might be. I looked along the shelves until I found a volume that covered the latter third of the preceding century. A big book with a brown leather cover and the Minster's coat of arms on the front. I took it to the desk. I was glad of the candle, for the sky was starting to darken.

I turned the heavy parchment pages. And there it was, among the Acts for the year 1484. The Act I had glimpsed in Oldroyd's box, the same heading: *Titulus Regulus.* The title of the King. 'An Act for the Settlement of the Crown upon the King and his Issue . . .' My heart began to pound. I examined the binding, studied the seal of Parliament at the foot, compared it with the Acts before and after. This was an authentic copy, bound here half a century ago. I thought, this Act is no forgery. Maleverer lied. But I had never heard of it; at some point this Act had been expunged from the Parliamentary record, quietly suppressed.

Now I read it through. It was short, only five pages. It was couched as an address to King Richard III, stating why the Lords and Commons wished him to take the throne. After much flowery language about the decay of the country, it turned to the marriage of King Edward IV. This was a story I vaguely remembered. King Edward, our King's grandfather, had married a commoner, Elizabeth Woodville, though it had been alleged he had already had a contract of marriage, that he had been, as the Act said, in *truth plight to Dame Eleanor Butler ... the said King Edward during his life, and the said Elizabeth, lived together sinfully and damnably in adultery ... it followeth, that all th'issue and Children of the said King Edward, been bastards, and unable to claim any thing by Inheritance.*

The Act related that since the next heir, the Duke of Clarence and his line, had been disbarred for treason, the next in line was the Duke of Gloucester – *Richard III,*

the undoubted Son and heir of Richard late Duke of York ... ye be born within this land; by reason whereof you may have more certain knowledge of your birth and filiation.

I sat back in my chair. No wonder Maleverer had wanted knowledge of this Act kept hidden. My mind went back to the family tree. King Henry's principal claim to the throne came through his mother, the daughter of Edward IV. If she was illegitimate, Henry VIII had no real claim to the throne. And that meant the issue of George Duke of Clarence were the true heirs, which explained why Margaret of Salisbury and her son had been butchered in the Tower. I got up abruptly and walked agitatedly around the room.

But my lawyer's instincts reasserted themselves. I had heard the story of King Edward's precontract before, it was not a secret. And precontracts were slippery things, difficult to prove. Any man who wished to nullify his marriage could say he had promised to marry another before he and his wife were betrothed; I had heard of husbands who had paid women to swear falsely they had a precontract, to escape an unwanted marriage. And King Edward, his queen Elizabeth Woodville and this Dame Eleanor Butler had all been dead half a century, nothing could be proved now – unless there was a written contract, and there could not have been, for such conclusive evidence would have been referred to in the *Titulus*. No, the whole thing read of a cobbling together of whatever reasons could be found to justify Richard's seizure of the throne after the fact; he had already been king a year when this Act was passed in 1484. Revelation of the *Titulus* now would be an embarrassment, but not a real threat.

I read it through again, carefully. One passage puzzled me, that description of Richard as '*the undoubted Son and heir of Richard late Duke of York*'. Had someone suggested Richard was a bastard? The child of Cecily Neville and *someone else*? I remembered the strange comment Maleverer had bitten off when I told him about the family tree. 'Oh yes,' he had said. 'Everything starts with Cecily Neville.' Yet that made no sense either. If Richard III was illegitimate, the Tudors would not have hidden the fact – they would have shouted it from the rooftops as another justification for their usurpation of his throne.

I read through the Act again, but could gain no further illumination about what that passage meant. I sat looking out at the Minster, its beautiful windows alight with colour now for the sun was sinking. Had I really been here all day?

I replaced the book then stepped out, closed the door and went back to Madge. She was in the solar, feeding the greyfalcon with a plate of chopped meat.

'I am sorry to have been so long. The time ran away with me.'

She put down the tray and wiped her hands on her apron.

'Thank you, Madge, for your hospitality.'

'Maister still sleeps. Sir,' she added suddenly, 'if he goes to London, you – you will take care of him?'

'As though he were my own father.'

'How is he, maister? That physician won't say, thinks I'm just a poor silly servant.'

'Not well.'

She nodded. 'Ay, Maister says he will never get better. I shall miss him, he has been good to me, as his wife was before him, Jesu rest her.' She crossed herself. 'He is a good man, for all the bad feeling there was when he quarrelled with his wife's family. And now he seeks to make matters right, by finding young Martin.'

'I will help him there.'

'It was but a quarrel over politics. Maister was wrong to cut Martin off. I think he knows that.'

'Is that what it was about?'

She bit her lip. 'You did not know? I thought he had told you.'

'I won't say anything, Madge. And with God's aid I will deliver him safe back to you.'

She nodded, her eyes full of tears but too proud to cry before me. She let me out and I walked away.

✝

OUTSIDE, THE RAIN had stopped, but there was a cold and biting wind. I remembered the night Master Wrenne had quoted from Thomas More's writing about the Striving between the Roses. 'These matters be Kings' games, as it were stage plays, and for the most part played upon scaffolds.' I shivered again and began walking back to St Mary's, keeping to the centre of the streets, on the lookout for shadows in doorways, a hand on the hilt of the dagger beneath my coat. It would be like this, I thought, from now on.

St Mary's was quiet. I passed by the looming bulk of the church and made my way to the lodging house. I paused at the door, for I could hear merry voices within. I must face the law clerks again. I pushed the door open. A group of them sat before the fire playing cards, the central hall hot and fuggy with smoke. All turned to look at me, their faces full of curiosity, except for Master Cowfold, whose head Barak had threatened to smash against the wall, who looked hastily away.

'Good evening,' I said. 'Is Master Barak about?'

'He's out, sir,' young Kimber said.

'With a pretty wench,' another added, and several laughed. I nodded and went to my cubicle. I felt their eyes on my back until, with relief, I closed the door behind me, locked it and lay down on my bed.

After a while I heard the clerks leave the lodging house, making their way over to the refectory for dinner. I was hungry again but could not face all those staring eyes, and I confess I was nervous at the thought of walking to the dining hall alone. I closed my eyes, and at once fell asleep.

When I woke it was very late; the clerks had come back and gone to bed for I could hear their snores and mumbles. I went outside to the hall. The fire was low but still burning.

I decided to take a little walk outside to clear my head. No one would be about at this hour. I opened the door carefully, for it had a creak and I did not want to wake anyone. I stepped out. The clouds had passed and a moon had risen. I looked round carefully, eye out for anyone hidden in doorways, then walked round the corner of the building, where an arch led through to a path to the river.

I jumped, and my hand went to my dagger, as I heard a sound. There was a figure, two figures, crouching by the arch. 'Who's there!' I called out.

Barak and Tamasin stepped out of the arch, hand in hand. I laughed with relief, thinking I had caught them kissing against the wall. Then I saw their faces. Tamasin's eyes were wide with terror, and Barak's face was stiff with shock.

'What's the matter? What in God's name has happened?'

'Quiet, for Jesu's sake.' Barak grabbed my arm and pulled me into the shadow of the arch. 'We mustn't be seen!' he hissed.

'But why? What—'

He took a deep breath. 'Tamasin and I have been out,' he whispered. 'Tamasin shouldn't be out so late.'

'That's not so serious. Who—'

'We saw something, sir,' Tamasin said. 'Something we weren't meant to.'

'I know now what Oldroyd's words meant,' Barak breathed. '"No child of Henry and Catherine Howard can ever be true heir, *she knows*." Oldroyd knew, Jesu knows how but he knew.'

'Knew what? Listen, I found something at Wrenne's house today. A copy of that Act of Parliament—'

'Forget that!' Barak shook his head, his eyes wide with impatience. 'What Oldroyd knew was nothing to do with old papers. It's here and now. And we are all three of us deeper in the shit than we could have thought possible.'

Chapter Twenty-two

I STARED AT THE TWO of them, dumbfounded. Barak leaned his head out, eyes raking the darkness in front of the lodging house.

'Anyone there?' Tamasin whispered.

'No. Jesu knows where *he's* gone!'

'Who?' I demanded.

Barak turned to me. 'Listen, we must find somewhere we can talk.'

'The refectory is open round the clock,' Tamasin said. 'So the soldiers may take their breaks there.'

'The soldiery?' Barak said dubiously.

'Yes, but it will be almost empty. We could find a quiet table.'

'What time is it?' I asked, realizing I had no idea.

'Near two.' Barak nodded at Tamasin. 'All right, let us go there.'

'What in God's name is this about?' I asked, almost as rattled as they were by now.

Tamasin looked at me. 'If we tell him he's in danger too.'

'He's in danger already. Come on.' Barak stepped out and began walking rapidly to the refectory. We followed.

The door was open, the big dining hall lit dimly by candles on the tables. The place was empty apart from a group of soldiers drinking quietly at a table near the door. The men had cast off their breastplates and plumed helmets and sat slumped heavily over their drinks, tired after standing long hours at their posts. Barak led the way to a table in the farthest corner of the room. 'We'd best buy some ale.' He walked off to where a bored-looking servant sat at a table next to a large barrel. Tamasin and I sat down. She bent her head and put a hand to her brow, messing her long blonde hair. Her hand, I saw, was trembling slightly. Something had shaken the girl to the core.

Barak reappeared, set three mugs down on the table and sat next to Tamasin. His place gave him a good view of the door. He leaned forward, took a deep breath, then began speaking quietly.

'You know we went out hawking today, while the bear-baiting was on. Me and Tamasin and a party of the law clerks.'

'Ay.'

Tamasin shook her head. 'What a carefree day it was. I cannot believe it now.'

'We had good hunting, then went to a village when it started raining hard. We did not get back till nightfall. We went to the lodging house, but you were fast asleep and we didn't want to wake you. We had something to eat here. Then we went—'

'Jack.' Tamasin looked at me and reddened.

'He has to know the whole story, Tammy. One of the clerks has a key to a room in the monastery complex, an office with a fire. We went—'

'All right,' I said. 'I can guess the rest. But what happened to scare you so?'

'We left the room an hour ago. Tamasin should have been back at King's Manor long before, she sleeps in the servants' quarters. We wondered how she would get back in, for the doors are guarded and we thought the soldiers would make a jest of us. Then we saw a door with no one outside. By the kitchen on the Queen's side. We went down the side of the manor to see if it was unlocked. That was where we saw them.'

'Who?'

Barak looked around the refectory, then at Tamasin. It seemed he could hardly bring himself to speak. Then he said, 'Remember that popinjay Thomas Culpeper, that was at the cockfighting yesterday with Dereham?'

'Ay. You said he was one of the King's bodyservants.'

'Bodyservant. He's that all right.' Barak gave a bark of nervous laughter. 'He was standing just inside the doorway. Taking his leave of the Queen.'

'The *Queen*?'

'Queen Catherine herself. I didn't recognize her, but Tammy knows her well enough by sight.'

Tamasin nodded. 'It was her, sir. And Lady Rochford standing beside her.'

I stared at them in horror. 'Do you realize what you are saying?'

'Oh, yes.' Barak gave that hoarse croak of a laugh again. 'I'm saying the Queen was showing the most notorious rake at court out of her privy chamber at past one in the morning.'

'Jesu.' I remembered that first morning at King's Manor, Lady Rochford pestering Craike about doors and locks in case the Queen needed to escape a fire.

'You haven't heard the worst,' Tamasin said heavily. 'They saw us.'

'What!'

'Culpeper saw us first,' Barak said. 'He turned and looked at us and stood rooted to the spot. Then Lady Rochford leaned out and stared at us; Jesu did she look angry. And frightened. She pulled the Queen in – she gave a startled little cry – and slammed the door. Young Culpeper just stood there like a ninny, he'd no idea what to do. Then he doffed his cap and turned and walked away.' He gave that strange harsh laugh again. 'Doffed his cap.'

I reached and took a swig of ale, for my mouth had gone dry. I thought a moment, then turned to Tamasin. 'How was the Queen dressed?'

She saw what I was aiming at. 'Fully. In a yellow dress, one of her finest. Her face was made up and she wore a necklace and earrings.'

'No evidence they'd been romping, then. In fact, if she was fully dressed, and her face painted, that's evidence they hadn't.'

Barak shook his head. 'It doesn't matter. Culpeper had been in her rooms at one in the morning. That alone is enough to lose him his head.'

'And the Queen hers. She'd not be the first. Lady Rochford too. Jesu, why would that woman risk her life by getting involved in this?'

'Heaven knows, sir,' Tamasin said wearily. 'Perhaps it is as some say, she is half crazed.'

I frowned. 'Are you sure Culpeper was leaving? Could he not have just called for some reason? He knocks and they answer the door?'

Barak shook his head impatiently. 'If someone knocks at the kitchen door at one in the morning, are the Queen and her principal lady in waiting going to come down and answer?'

'No, they're not. It looks bad, I agree.'

'There have been rumours among the ladies,' Tamasin said. 'That Master Culpeper and the Queen had some affection before she married the King. And that she and her secretary, Master Dereham, had a dalliance when the Queen was a girl. Dereham and Culpeper dislike each other. But no one suspected she would—'

'She must be *mad*,' Barak said, clenching his hands.

'Jesu,' I said. 'If the Queen announces she is pregnant, the child may be Culpeper's.' I bit my lip, breathing hard. 'That fits exactly what Oldroyd said. 'No child of Henry and Catherine can ever be true heir. She knows.' He meant the Queen.'

'Exactly,' Barak said. 'This could have been going on for months, what if somehow the northern conspirators got to hear of it? Jesu.' He shook his head in amazement. 'Has Culpeper been foolish enough to tup the old man's ewe?'

I nodded slowly. 'If there were an announcement the Queen was pregnant and this came out, imagine how it would weaken the King. Remember when we brought that box in — Lady Rochford and Dereham saw it. What you saw casts a new light on that fact.'

'Perhaps that confession you saw was written by someone who saw them together, like us,' Barak said.

'No.' I shook my head, frowning. 'Blaybourne's confession was years old. And the *Titulus* dates from 1484.'

'You said there were other papers, that you never saw.'

I nodded slowly. 'Yes. There were.'

'Perhaps about the Queen and Culpeper.'

'Sir,' Tamasin ventured. 'I do not understand what is this *Titulus*, nor this Blaybourne.'

I looked at her. I was so shocked by what they had told me that I had mentioned the contents of the casket without thinking. I had put her in even more danger than she was in already. All three of us were in danger now; we had to pool our resources. I took a deep breath.

'Jack and I found a box of papers, that was stolen later. In the glazier Oldroyd's house.'

'I know. That was when Jennet and I were questioned.'

'Someone killed him because he had it. And is now, I think, trying to kill me because I saw what was inside. Saw only a small part, though they will not know that.' I told her about the attacks on me at King's Manor and at the camp, about Blaybourne's confession and the *Titulus*, adding that I had found another copy in Wrenne's library. Her eyes widened.

'Jesu,' she said quietly. 'What have you got into?'

'The biggest pile of shit you ever saw,' Barak answered starkly.

I looked round at a noise from the far end of the refectory. The soldiers had risen wearily to their feet and were making their way to the door, leaving us alone but for the servant. He had fallen asleep on his table, head pillowed in his arms. I turned back to Barak and Tamasin. The strained expressions on their faces made both look years older.

'What do we do now?' Barak asked. 'Report this to Maleverer?'

'Not just yet,' I said. 'There is only your word for this. They'll deny it. You'll just get into trouble, perhaps serious trouble, for nothing.'

Barak leaned forward. 'But if there's a connection between the Queen and Culpeper and the papers in that casket, Lady Rochford could be behind these attempts on your life. She will redouble her efforts now.'

'No.' Tamasin spoke quietly. 'The Queen would never involve herself in murder. Of that I am sure. She is a kind, generous woman – no, girl. In some ways she is very innocent.'

'She's part of the vipers' nest that is the court,' Barak said.

'But that's just it, she isn't. She's a silly innocent girl, everyone says so. She's at sea, she must be, or she wouldn't be as foolish as she has been.'

'But Lady Rochford looks capable of anything,' Barak replied. 'Look at her history.'

'And yet I cannot see her being behind these attacks,' I said thoughtfully. 'She does not strike me as a careful organizer.' I considered a moment. 'Tamasin, what do you think Lady Rochford will do now? About what you and Jack saw?'

'The Queen would decide, surely,' Barak said.

Tamasin shook her head. 'The Queen will take Lady Rochford's advice, I think.' She looked at me. 'If I were her, I think I would try and scare us into silence, or buy it.'

I nodded. 'I think you are right. I think we wait and see if she approaches you. What we do after that can depend on what is said. If we are *not* approached, and especially if anything more is attempted against us, we go to Maleverer. On Monday. And meanwhile we stick to safe places.'

'I think we should go to Maleverer now,' Barak said.

'No. Not without evidence. Not when you and I are in trouble already. Can you imagine how the King would react if this story were brought to him, and turned out to be untrue? It would be our heads in danger then.'

I turned to Tamasin. 'We'll walk you back to the manor. Will the soldiers let you in at this hour?'

'Ay. There's more than one girl sneaks out at night.'

I smiled wryly. 'The morals of the court.' I turned to Barak. He still looked dubious. Then he saw something behind us; his eyes widened and his lips set.

'Too late,' he said.

I turned quickly. Another troop of soldiers had come in, Sergeant Leacon at their head. We stared as he left his men and marched up to us, his pike grasped firmly. He looked at the three of us in puzzlement.

'What's amiss? You all look startled as dogs cast out of a window.'

'Nothing, sergeant, we—'

'You are supping late.'

'We got to talking. We should go to bed.'

'There is something I must mention to you, sir. In confidence.' The sergeant inclined his head. I got up and followed him. His soldiers, I saw, were crowding round the servant, who had woken up and was serving them beer. I realized they had all just come off duty; they had not been sent to arrest us after all.

Leacon looked at me seriously. Always when we had met before he had been open and friendly, but now I sensed something wary, almost hostile, in his manner.

'One of my men reported there had been some trouble outside Broderick's cell,' he said. 'Between you and gaoler Radwinter.'

'Ah,' I said. 'That.'

'I should report it to Sir William Maleverer. But my man said that Radwinter provoked you.'

'Yes, sergeant, he did. But I should not have let him.'

'I will say nothing for now. I do not want trouble with Radwinter, and Sir William has enough to occupy him. But I must have your assurance nothing like that will happen again.'

'It will not.'

He nodded.

'How does Broderick fare? I should have visited him today.'

'The same.' He gave me another measured look, then made a

little bow and went off to rejoin his men. I went back to Tamasin and Barak.

'What was that about?' Barak asked.

'My fight with Radwinter. He says he won't report me if I don't let Radwinter provoke me again. Well, I have other things to think on now.'

We walked Tamasin back to King's Manor. All was dark and silent; a gold half-angel ensured Tamasin was admitted by the guards. Barak and I walked back to the lodging house. I went to bed, but it was long before I slept.

†

SUNDAY MORNING dawned fine. I was dressing in my cubicle when Barak knocked at my door.

'That cook's outside, Master Goodrich.'

I finished dressing hurriedly and stepped out. He was standing by the door.

'How is your son?' I asked.

'Better, sir, but he's a nasty gash on his head. I've told him not to work again today.'

'Thank God it was no worse.'

'True. But, sir . . .'

He looked at me. I wondered if he was going to ask for money, and slipped my hand to my purse. The cook shook his head.

'I only wanted to ask – who would do such a thing? Is my boy safe?'

'I am sure he is, Master Goodrich. The person who struck your boy down was after me. Rest assured, we will find who is responsible.'

'It ought to be reported, sir. With the King himself here . . .' He cast a look of mingled awe and fear in the direction of King's Manor.

'Leave it with me. And my good wishes to your boy.'

I watched as the cook walked off towards the camp. Barak joined me. 'Is he all right?'

'Ay. Come, let us get some breakfast.'

We began walking to the refectory. Outside, among the animal pens, I saw that one pair of bears' cages was being taken to pieces by some workmen under the bearward's supervision. I stopped and looked.

'He killed six dogs before the King and was left standing,' the bearward said to me. 'But then he died most honourably.' He gave a satisfied smile. The other cage was still occupied; the surviving bear was awake, lying curled up in a corner on the floor, its back to us. The creature shifted its position and gave a low, whimpering groan. Its coat was slashed and stiff with blood in several places.

'Will that one fight again?' Barak asked.

He studied the bear professionally. 'Ay, he's fit for another bout. They're strong brutes.'

I walked away, suppressing a shudder.

✝

IN THE REFECTORY we ate in silence, among courtiers and servants breakfasting before church. I thought of the day before. Those quiet hours in Wrenne's library seemed far off now.

'I don't like leaving Tamasin alone at the manor,' Barak said at length. 'It worries me.'

'I believe this way is best, Jack, we mustn't act precipitately.'

He shook his head. 'I can't think straight after last night. Are you going to church? They're doing Mass in shifts at St Olave's.'

'No. I can't face it.'

'I don't want to sit cooped up here all day.'

'I know somewhere we can sit and watch what goes on.'

I led him to the bench where Tamasin and I had talked two nights before. Crowds of people were going in to the first service at St Olave's. The whole atmosphere at St Mary's had changed now the King was here: people moved and talked quietly, sedately.

A little group of courtiers appeared, and I recognized some of the young men who had been at the camp two nights before. Dereham was among them; he flicked me a contemptuous glare as he passed. Culpeper, I saw, was not with the group.

'I wonder where the King and Queen will be hearing Mass,' Barak said.

'Privately at King's Manor, I should think.'

'For security? Keeping safe from the Yorkers?'

'Maybe.' I sighed. 'I don't wonder they rebelled.'

Barak looked at me askance. 'You're not turning papist, are you?'

'No. I mean, the way they've been treated for years. Like second-rate Englishmen.' I saw Master Craike passing with a group of richly robed officials, and raised a hand in a wave. He hesitated, then came over to us.

'Are you going into church, Master Shardlake?'

'Perhaps a later service.'

He smiled. 'We have just been up the belltower. Priests are holding open-air Masses all over the camp, 'tis quite a spectacle. Well, I must go, or I shall be late.' He bowed and hurried off.

'That man has an uneasy air for all his pleasant words,' Barak observed.

'Ay, he does.'

'We should find out what goes on at this tavern I saw him at.'

I nodded. 'Ay. Let's do that. There's something Tamasin might find out, too.'

He looked at me askance. 'I'll not have her in danger.'

'It might be useful if we could find out Master Culpeper's antecedents. Who his friends and family are. Does he have northern connections, I wonder.'

'I'll see.' He frowned. 'I feel responsible for Tamasin. Involving her in this.'

I nodded. It was the first time Barak had ever seemed really to care for a girl. 'I fear she is involved anyhow.'

'I pray this may all be a mare's nest and Oldroyd's words meant something different.' He put his hand inside his shirt, fingering his father's old mezuzah. 'If this *is* about an affair between these two, do you think Maleverer and the King's men even suspect it?'

'I don't know.'

'Is the King impotent, I wonder?' Barak pondered. 'All know he has been ill with his leg for years.'

'God knows.'

'Perhaps his seed is thin and weak, old and ill as he is, while Culpeper's flows thick and strong.'

I shuddered slightly. 'I'd rather not think too much on that.'

'Talking of illness, how is old Wrenne?'

'Not good. He was in bed, though he insists he'll be fit to hear the petitions tomorrow. I said I would go and see him again today. Come with me, at least his house is a place of safety.'

'All right. Here. Look who is coming now.'

Latecomers were still heading for the church, and among them I saw Jennet Marlin, walking with a couple of ladies I did not recognize.

'Where's Tammy?' Barak asked anxiously. 'Mistress Marlin likes to keep her round her.' He bit his lip. 'Could you ask her? My rank forbids it.'

I stood up and bowed. Mistress Marlin, in a grey damask dress, the tails of an old-fashioned box hood streaming behind her head, signalled to the other ladies to walk on. She halted and, to my surprise, smiled at me a little nervously.

'Master Shardlake. Are you on your way to church?'

'Ah – no. But I wondered if I might trouble you with a query. Mistress Reedbourne is not with you?'

'No. She is a little ill and has kept to her room.' She gave that uncertain smile again, then took a deep breath. 'I spoke harshly to you the other night, sir,' she said. 'I wish to apologize. Only, Tamasin has been a good companion to me. But –' she looked at Barak – 'I think perhaps she and your man do care for each other, and one should not stand in the way of love, should one?'

'No,' I said, a little taken aback. This was a change of mind indeed, yet not that dissimilar from my own. Perhaps Tamasin had appealed to her too, charmed her, for all that Mistress Marlin did not seem a woman susceptible to charm. She looked at me seriously with her large brown eyes. 'I spoke bitterly to you, sir, only because my own fiancé is unjustly in the Tower.'

'I understand.'

'Have you heard any news, sir, of how long the King may be in York?' She grasped her engagement ring, turning it round and round on her finger.

'No, mistress. No one seems to know. I imagine it all depends on the Scotch King.'

She shook her head. 'There is no word of him even being on the road. And there was talk at the manor last night of new raids by the border reivers.' She looked around her. 'Oh, I wish I were gone from here.'

'I too.'

'Bernard has still been neither accused nor released. Sir, you are a lawyer, how long can they hold him in the Tower?'

'On the King's authority, indefinitely. But representations can be made. What contacts do you have in London?'

'Only Bernard's lawyer friends. And some of them fear to get involved.'

'Your constant spirit may save him,' I said.

She looked at me again with those large, intense eyes. 'I was sorry to hear how the King treated you on Friday.'

I shifted uncomfortably. 'Thank you.'

'I know what it is like to be mocked without just cause. The other women mock what you call my constancy.'

'That too is cruel.'

'I am sorry I associated you with Sir William Maleverer. He is known throughout Yorkshire as a dangerous, covetous man.'

'He is no friend or patron to me.'

'No. But may I ask, how did you come to be with the Progress?'

'At the request of Archbishop Cranmer.'

'Ah, they say he is a good man. He is your patron?'

'In a sense.'

'I – I am sorry I misjudged you.' With that, she curtsied swiftly and walked away to the church, where the warden stood at the door, looking impatient. The door closed behind her. I returned to Barak.

'What was all that about?' he asked.

'She apologized for her behaviour the other evening. She seems to have lost her opposition to your seeing Tamasin.' I shook my head. 'She is a strange woman. Under great strain, that much is clear.'

'Did she say where Tamasin is?'

'Tamasin told her she was ill and wished to stay in her room. Probably keeping out of the way.' I looked at the closed door of the church. 'If what you saw last night comes out, Jennet Marlin will be in a difficult position. Lady Rochford is her employer, Tamasin her servant.'

'Nothing to the trouble we'll be in.'

I nodded. 'Let us go to Master Wrenne's. Get us out of this damned place.'

We set off for the gate watchfully, past the empty pavilions with their guards, our eyes alert for danger.

Chapter Twenty-three

As we passed the front of King's Manor I saw a man in a grey furred robe with a heavy gold chain round his neck descending the steps, accompanied by a little group of clerks. It was Sir Richard Rich. He caught my eye. My heart sank as he dismissed the clerks and strode rapidly over. I bowed deeply.

'Master Shardlake.' Rich smiled coldly. 'And young Barak again. He is your clerk now?'

'Yes, Sir Richard.'

Rich flicked Barak an amused look. 'Has he enough learning?' He smoothed his robe with his slim hands, and smiled. 'I have been with the King,' he said cheerfully. 'When the spring conspirators were attainted, their lands passed to my department. We have been discussing how they might be best disposed of.'

'Indeed, Sir Richard.'

'The King will be generous to those who have been loyal in Yorkshire. Although with the constant dangers of foreign invasion he needs his lands to bring in all the revenue they can.' He smiled thinly. 'Which brings me to the other matter. Have you passed on what I told you about the Bealknap case to the Common Council?'

I took a deep breath. 'That you think the right judge has been chosen? I have told them those who say they have a good hand early in the game are usually bluffing.' It was a lie; I had not yet written, though I planned to. I wondered how Rich would react; to speak thus to the Chancellor of Augmentations would normally be impertinence, but we were talking now as lawyer to lawyer. Rich gave me an uneasy look. His eyes narrowed, and I saw that I had guessed correctly, he did not have a judge yet.

'Come over here,' he said sharply. He grasped my arm and led me out of earshot of Barak. He gave me a hard, fixed look. 'You know I have been having dealings with your master here, Sir William Maleverer.' His thin face was tense with anger now. 'He is interested in buying more lands up here, and Augmentations has lands to sell. Do not forget, *Brother* Shardlake, that Sir William has many powers here, and that you are alone in York but for your boorish servant. And not liked by the King, it appears. Tread carefully.' He paused significantly. 'And do not send that letter about the Bealknap case to London; I know you have not sent it already.' I looked surprised, and he laughed. 'Do you think, sir, with the political trouble there has been up here, that the posts from the Progress go unwatched?' He looked at me with those cold grey eyes. 'Mark well what I say, and do not trifle with me.' He turned and walked away with sharp, rapid steps.

Barak came over to me. 'What did he want?'

I told him what Rich had said. 'He always threatens much,' I said. 'He did last year.' Yet I felt uneasy. More threats, more danger.

'We need to get home,' Barak said emphatically. 'We and Tamasin.'

'We can none of us go till we are ordered. For now we are trapped here like flies in jam.'

'In shit, more like,' Barak muttered as we headed for the gate.

✝

WE WENT THROUGH TO the Minster precinct and down to Giles's house. He answered the door himself. He looked much better; there was colour in his cheeks again. He welcomed us into the solar where Madge sat by the fire ticking at some plain beads. Madge rose and bowed, then went to fetch some wine for us. Master Wrenne urged us to sit. The greyfalcon on its perch inclined its head at us.

'You look much better, sir,' I said.

He smiled. 'Thank you. My rest did me much good. And Dr Jibson's prescription eases my pain. How do you fare, Master Barak, did you see the King yesterday?' His manner was easy, he mentioned the King's name in a light tone.

'Yes, sir. When he entered the city. He is a man of great presence.' Barak looked at Giles a little uneasily; I guessed he had never encountered a man who was dying slowly before. But if Giles noticed he did not show it.

'Let none doubt the King has presence,' he agreed, nodding wisely.

Madge brought in the wine and a plate of little cakes. She seemed to avoid my eye, I wondered why. Giles took an appreciative swig from his goblet. 'Ah, good French wine, nothing better on a fine morning. And jumble cakes, help yourselves.' He smiled at us. 'Now, I have had a list from the steward's office of the petitioners who will present themselves at the castle tomorrow. It will be the first of two hearings.'

'You are sure you feel well enough to preside?' I asked him.

'Quite sure.' He nodded emphatically. 'They are mostly simple enough matters.'

'What if the parties refuse to accept our arbitration?'

He smiled. 'Then they may try their luck in the London courts. I doubt many will want to do that.'

'Then we must be sure we do justice.'

'Indeed. I have left the list in my little study next door, together with the knapsacks containing the petitions. I wonder if Master Barak might be set to marrying up the papers with the names, and our summary, then we can have a quick look through them together.'

'A good idea. Do that, would you, Barak?'

'And take your wine,' Giles added. 'Do not go dry to your task.'

When the door was closed Giles turned and gave me a wry smile. 'Madge tells me she committed a small indiscretion when you were here yesterday. She told you a little of my quarrel with my nephew.'

'Only that it was a quarrel over politics.'

'She felt she had to tell me.' He smiled sadly. 'Well, Matthew, if you are to help me in London, you should know. Only – it was a little difficult for me to speak of.'

'I understand. But – Giles, are you sure you are well enough to travel? After Fulford—'

He waved a large hand, his emerald ring catching the light. 'I am going,' he said with sudden sharpness. 'That is decided. But let me tell you about my nephew.'

'If you wish.'

Giles began. 'It was a great sorrow to me that my wife and I had no children that lived. My wife had a sister, Elizabeth, and she married a man called Dakin. A law-clerk, a mousy little fellow without ambition. I always thought him a poor creature, and – well, if I am honest, I was jealous they had a son who grew up tall and strong, never had a day's illness. He went to read for the bar at Gray's Inn when he grew to manhood. With a letter of recommendation from me.' He smiled tightly. 'An affection for the boy had grown in me by then. Martin was clever, he liked to think for himself and I admired that. It is an uncommon quality. You have it,' he added, pointing at me with his goblet.

I laughed. 'Thank you.'

'And yet that quality can be carried too far, it can take one into dangerous waters.'

'It can,' I agreed.

'Martin would return to York to visit his parents every year.' He looked at the table on its dais. 'We had some merry evenings here, Martin and his parents, me and my wife. All dead now, apart from Martin and me.' His mouth hardened. 'And yet he never spoke to me of something that must have been working secretly in his mind for a long time. Not till he came home in the summer of 1532, nine years ago. The King was still married to Catherine of Aragon then, though he had been trying to get a divorce out of the Pope for years so he could marry Anne Boleyn. He was coming to the end of that

road, soon he would break with Rome, appoint Cranmer Archbishop of Canterbury and get him to declare his first marriage
invalid.'

'I remember it well.'

'Virtually everyone in the north viewed the prospect of a break
with Rome with horror. We knew Anne Boleyn was a reformer, we
feared this would mean heretics like Cromwell coming to power, as
indeed it did.'

'I was a reformer then, Giles,' I said quickly. 'I knew Cromwell
well in the days before he came into his great power.'

Giles gave me an interrogative look. His eyes could be very sharp.
'From what you have said, I think you are no longer an enthusiast?'

'I am not. For neither side.'

Giles nodded. 'Martin was. He was as much of an enthusiast as
it was possible to be.'

'For reform?'

'No. For the Pope. For Queen Catherine. That was the problem.
Oh, it was – and is – easy to be sentimental about the King's first
wife. How she had been married to him for twenty years, always
been loyal, how wicked the King was to cast her aside for Anne
Boleyn. Yet there was more to it than that, as we both know. Queen
Catherine was in her forties, past child-bearing, and she had not
given the King a male heir. Unless he could marry a younger woman
who might provide an heir, the Tudor dynasty would die with him.'

'All that is true.'

'And there were many of us who thought the only way to
preserve true religion in England was for Queen Catherine to do
what the Pope himself had suggested to her: go into a nunnery, allow
the King to marry again.' He shook his head. 'Foolish, obstinate
woman. By insisting God intended her to be married to the King
until death, she brought about the very revolution in religion she
hated and feared.'

I nodded. 'It is a paradox.'

'A paradox Martin could not see. He stood stiff in the view that the King must stay married to Catherine of Aragon. So he told us over the dinner-table that day, in no uncertain terms.' Giles looked over at the table. 'It made me wroth, furious. I saw, if he did not, that unless Catherine of Aragon agreed to a divorce, or to go to a nunnery, the King would break with Rome. As in the end he did. It may seem strange, now both Catherine of Aragon and Anne Boleyn are dead, to think we argued so fiercely, but we who supported the old religion were split: the realists like me, and those like Martin who urged Queen Catherine should not give an inch. I was angry, Matthew.' He shook his leonine head. 'Angry too to hear Martin's parents support him, and realize he must have discussed his beliefs with them, though not with me that had done everything to smooth and aid his path into the law.' A heavy bitterness came into Giles's voice.

'Perhaps he had not told them. His parents might only have felt they must stand in their child's corner in argument.'

Giles sighed. 'Perhaps. And perhaps the old sourness at my childless state was part of my anger, especially when my wife began to argue Martin's side too. She should not have, that was disloyal of her. Anyway, in the end I ordered Martin Dakin and his parents from my table.'

I looked at Giles in surprise. It was hard to imagine him full of such fierceness. But before his illness he must have been formidable.

'I never spoke with Martin or his parents again. My wife was sore upset when I forbade her sister our table. She never really forgave me.' He shook his head sadly. 'My poor Sarah, her sister's family forbidden the house. And then three years ago the plague came to York and they all died, my wife, and both Martin's parents, a few weeks later. Martin came up and arranged his parents' funerals, but I could not bring myself to contact him, or attend. I do not even know whether he is married now; he was single at the time we quarrelled.' I saw shame on his lined face.

'That is a story to pity a man's heart, Giles. Yet one that has been all too common these last few years, families split apart over religious differences.'

'Pride and obstinacy are great sins,' he said. 'I see that now. I would be reconciled with Martin if I can.' He laughed mirth-lessly. 'In the end we both lost, and Cromwell and the reformers won.'

'You should know, Giles,' I said, 'I may have become disil-lusioned with the reformers but I hold the old regime to be no better. No less ruthless, no less fanatical.' I paused. 'No less cruel.'

'For all I may have grown sadder and mellower these last few years, at the end I cleave to my faith.' He looked at me. 'As all men must at the end. They say the King himself is disillusioned with reform,' he added. 'Yet I am not so sure. Cranmer is still in charge of the church.'

I shrugged. 'The King plays one faction off against the other. He trusts neither now.'

'So with him it is all politics?'

'Perhaps he believes every twist and turn he makes inspired by God himself working in his mind.'

He grunted. 'I think we are agreed at least that the notion God works the King's mind for him is nonsense.'

'We old reformers never sought to put the King in the Pope's place.' I looked at him. I was not surprised he was a religious conservative, I had gathered as much. Yet the obstinate bitterness he had shown towards his family had shown me a new side to his character. But we all have darker sides to our natures, I thought.

'Well,' he said with a sigh. 'Let us leave these sad topics. We should go and see how young Barak is doing.'

I hesitated, then said, 'Giles. Before we do, there is something I ought to tell you in my turn.'

He looked at me curiously. 'What is that?'

'Yesterday, when I was in your library, looking at your maps—'

'Ah, yes. Did you find what you wanted? Madge said you stayed a long time.'

'I did, and thank you. Your collection is truly remarkable.'

He smiled with pleasure. 'It has been my pastime for fifty years.'

'Did you know you have some lawbooks there that I think no one else has, that have been lost?'

He gave a childlike smile of pleasure. 'Really?'

'Lincoln's Inn would pay well for copies. But I found something else.' I took a deep breath. 'An Act of Parliament, that I think has been excised from the records. Called the *Titulus Regulus*.'

He sat very still then, looked at me from narrowed eyes. 'Ah,' he said.

'I wondered if you knew you had it.'

'Yes, I did. You read it? What did you think?'

I shrugged. 'It repeats the old rumours that King Edward IV's marriage to Elizabeth Woodville was invalid because of a precontract. Impossible to prove one way or the other now. It seemed to me King Richard was cobbling together all the arguments he could to justify his seizure of power.'

He nodded judiciously. 'Perhaps.'

'Yet if it came to light now, it could cause trouble.'

To my surprise he smiled. 'Matthew, for those of us past seventy, especially lawyers, the suppression of the *Titulus* is an old story. I was a student at Gray's Inn when it was published for all the world to see, and also when next year the new King's men came to the Inns to seize all copies. There is nothing new there.'

'Forgive me speaking bluntly, Giles, but there will be few left alive now who remember. And that Act could cause embarrassment if it came to light.'

He continued to smile. 'I found the *Titulus* ten years ago, when they were clearing old lawbooks from the Minster library. I kept it. But few have any interest in my collection. Martin used to go and look at the books, he was interested, and occasionally one of my fellow lawyers, but I think you are the first person other than me to have spent much time up there in years. And the Act is well hidden in its way, unmarked among the dusty shelves, for I keep the index in my head. And you would not tell Maleverer.'

'Of course not. But you should know, there is a hunt on for subversive documents at King's Manor—'

'A hunt? What documents?' He looked at me with interest.

'I cannot say more. But believe me when I say you should get rid of the *Titulus*.'

He pondered a moment. 'You speak true, Matthew?'

'Yes. I care little for any embarrassment disclosure of the *Titulus* might cause the King. But I would not have you, or anyone, in danger because of that wretched Act. This is not a good time to have a copy in your possession.'

He looked into the fire, considering, then sighed. 'Perhaps you are right. I have been too vain of my collection. Pride, again.'

'I hope you have no other dangerous materials in those rooms.'

'No. Only the *Titulus*. When I am gone, if the *Titulus* were found I suppose it could be a problem for my executors.'

'Yes,' I said uncomfortably. 'It could. Madge could end up being questioned too.'

'Danger to Madge. By Jesu, what has England come to, eh? Very well. Wait here, Matthew.' He rose slowly from his chair, holding the arm a moment when he stood to get his balance.

'Do you need help?' I asked, getting up.

'No, I am a little wembly after being in bed so long, that is all.' He walked steadily enough to the door, and left the room. I stood looking into the fire. I wondered if he had made a will, who the library would go to. His nephew, perhaps. And then I thought, if Martin Dakin was a strong political conservative and a lawyer at Gray's Inn, he was a prime candidate to have been involved with Robert Aske's group of conservative lawyers there in 1536. And a man likely to be a suspect in the present rebellion; for all I knew Martin Dakin could be in the Tower, like Jennet Marlin's fiancé, that other Gray's Inn lawyer.

Giles reappeared. To my surprise he was carrying the book containing the *Titulus*, together with a sharp knife. He smiled at me sadly. 'Here, Matthew,' he said. 'See how I trust you.' He laid the book on the table and, taking the knife, carefully cut out the pages of the *Titulus*. He lifted them with a sigh. 'There, I have never done such a thing with one of my books before.' He walked over to the fire and, with a steady hand, laid the pages on the flames. We watched as the thick old parchment flared and blackened. The greyfalcon turned on its perch to watch, the dancing flames reflected in its eyes.

'That must have been hard to do,' I said.

'Well, you are right, we live in dangerous times. Come, look out of the window.' He beckoned me over and pointed at a small stout man who was walking confidently down the street towards the Minster, clerical robes flapping round him. 'I saw him from the library. Do you know who he is?'

'No.'

'Dr Legh. The Minster Dean. Formerly Cromwell's most feared commissioner. The hammer of the monasteries.'

I looked at Giles. 'They made him Dean?'

'To keep an eye on the Archbishop of York. You are right, Matthew, even mere scholars must keep watch these days.'

I turned back to the window. The figure of a woman had caught my eye, half-running down the narrow street towards the house, skirts lifted above her ankles and blonde hair flying out behind her. It was Tamasin.

Chapter Twenty-four

T HERE WAS A LOUD KNOCK at the front door, and a moment later Madge ushered Tamasin into the room. The girl was flushed and anxious-looking, and gave us the briefest of curtsies. 'Sir,' she said. 'I have come from the King's Manor. The guard on the gate said you had gone into the city and I guessed you might be here. We are ordered to return there now. Is Jack here?'

I nodded. Madge went to summon him. Giles smiled and looked admiringly at her clothes, her green dress and her blonde hair beneath her French hood. 'By heaven,' he said. 'They employ pretty messengers at the court these days.'

'I fear we must leave without looking at the petitions,' I said.

'Well, they are simple enough and we have seen them already. Come to the castle at nine and we can take an hour then.' He looked at me curiously. 'Is something amiss? Does Maleverer require you?'

'I was half expecting a summons,' I said evasively.

Giles nodded, then went back to studying Tamasin with frank appreciation; she coloured a little.

'And where are you from, mistress?' he asked.

'London, sir.'

'Like Master Barak.'

Barak appeared in the doorway. He gave Tamasin an anxious look.

'Well,' Giles said. 'I will see you both tomorrow morning.'

I apologized again for our hasty departure, and we left the house.

✝

'WHAT'S HAPPENED?' Barak asked as Tamasin led a rapid pace down the street.

'It is as I thought would happen,' she replied a little breathlessly. 'I was in my room and Lady Rochford herself came in, looking grim as an ogre. She told me to fetch you, Jack. We are to meet her in one of the pavilions. I ran almost all the way.'

'Looks like you were both right,' Barak told me. 'She wants to talk to us, not kill us.'

I took a deep breath. 'We shall see.'

Tamasin looked at me earnestly. 'The summons was for me and Jack alone.'

'I want to see what she says for myself,' I said firmly. 'And perhaps she will be less bullying with a lawyer present.'

'You do not know Lady Rochford, sir,' Tamasin answered uncertainly.

We walked rapidly to King's Manor and headed for the pavilions, which had stood guarded but empty over the weekend. ''Tis the nearer one,' Tamasin said, leading the way across to the fantastic structure. The towers on either side of the entrance arch, which seemed so like brick till you came right up and saw the grain of wood through the paint, had guards posted in front of them. They crossed their pikes to bar our way. I glanced at Tamasin, who nodded.

'We are due to meet Lady Rochford here,' I told him.

The guard looked us over. 'Her ladyship said a young man and woman only.'

'The instructions have changed.'

As the guard looked me over I was uncomfortably aware that I was carrying a dagger, against all the rules. But he nodded, deciding I was not dangerous. 'Second door on the left,' he said. He and his colleague raised their weapons and we passed through. I felt suddenly afraid. What if Lady Rochford was behind everything, and had associates ready to kill us? But that was ridiculous; the soldiers had seen us come in and knew she was here, how could she ever escape discovery?

Beyond the arch a whole inner courtyard had been laid in marble, which the walls had also been painted to resemble. All smelled sweetly of new-cut wood. A number of doorways led off, each with its own guard. I whispered to Tamasin, 'Won't the guards think it odd, Lady Rochford meeting us in here?'

'Lady Rochford's oddity is well known. And they will see no harm in it — the pavilions will stand empty till the Scotch King comes. Their concern is to prevent servants entering to steal the tapestries and furnishings.'

We walked on to the door the guard had indicated, passing one that stood open, leading into a reception room decorated with brilliant tapestries. I glimpsed a buffet laden with gold plate, servants strewing scented rushes on the floor. Two great chairs of state with purple cushions had been set there. So this was where the kings would meet.

The guard at the next door opened it as we approached. We entered a chamber that was smaller than the one we had seen, unfurnished but with a magnificent series of tapestries showing the life of John the Baptist on the walls. Lady Rochford stood at the far end. She wore a bright red dress, low-cut to show her upper bosom, which like her face and neck was white with ceruse; her dark brown hair was drawn back tightly under a French hood lined with pearls. She had composed her features into a haughty frown, which intensified as she looked at me.

'Why have you brought this lawyer?' Her rich voice rose. 'God's death, Mistress Reedbourne, if you try to set a lawyer on me I shall set something far worse on you.'

I bowed, then looked her in the eye. I was intimidated, but I must not show it. 'My name is Matthew Shardlake, my lady. I am the employer of Master Barak here. He and Mistress Reedbourne sought my protection, after their encounter last night.'

Lady Rochford stepped forward to Tamasin. I feared she might strike her. 'Who else have you told?' she hissed. 'Who else?' And I saw that she, too, was sorely frightened.

'No one, my lady,' Tamasin answered in a small voice.

Lady Rochford looked at me again, uncertainly, then turned to Barak. 'That's an odd name you have,' she said. 'Are you English?'

'Through and through, my lady.'

Lady Rochford turned her stare back to Tamasin: she would concentrate her fire on her, I thought, a junior servant in her direct power. 'And just what did you and this rude lump of a clerk see, or think you saw, last night?'

Tamasin answered clearly, though a tremble underlay her voice. 'Master Culpeper outside the kitchen door, the Queen in the doorway, and you behind, my lady. The Queen seemed to be taking leave of Master Culpeper.'

Lady Rochford gave a forced, hollow laugh. 'Stupid children! Master Culpeper had called late to see me, it was I that took leave of him. The Queen heard us and came down to see. Culpeper is always playing jests on me, he is a naughty fellow.'

It was such palpable nonsense that Tamasin did not reply.

'It was innocent,' Lady Rochford went on. Her voice rose. 'All innocent. Anyone who says differently will face the King's wrath, I warn you.'

I spoke up. 'If the King heard his Queen was seen in a doorway with the sauciest rake in the court, I think he would be wrathful indeed. However innocent, that meeting must have broken every rule of conduct there is.'

Lady Rochford's white bosom heaved, her eyes flashing. 'You are the crookback the King jested over at Fulford. What is this, lawyer – do you seek revenge on your monarch because he mocked your bent back?'

'No, my lady. I seek only to protect these young people.'

Her eyes narrowed. 'Lawyers ever speak with coloured doubleness. Is it money you want, to buy your silence and theirs?'

'No, my lady. Only their safety. And mine.'

She frowned angrily. 'What do you mean? Why should any of you be unsafe?'

'People who learn naughty secrets by mistake often are. I work with Sir William Maleverer in connection with certain matters of security here, so I know that well.'

Lady Rochford's eyes narrowed at the mention of Maleverer's name. She made herself smile. 'There is no secret, sir,' she said in a tone of forced lightness. 'None. The Queen merely enjoys the company of the friends of her young days. It has been hard for her, this Progress, all the formal receptions, the endless journeys along the miry ways, hard for a young girl. The King would not mind her meeting old friends, but people will ever gossip, so she meets them in secret sometimes. Were that to be known it would be an – embarrassment.'

'Then all is well,' I answered smoothly. It was interesting that she had changed her story. 'We have no interest in gossip, all three of us wish only to return to London as quickly as possible and forget all about this tiresome Progress.'

'Then you will say nothing?' Lady Rochford said, a touch of her old imperiousness returning. 'Say nothing and all will be well, I promise you.'

'That is our intention,' Barak replied, and Tamasin nodded.

Lady Rochford looked at our serious faces. 'Just as well,' she said, her voice taking on a bullying tone again. 'After all, one might ask what you young people were doing abroad at past one in the morning. You, Mistress Reedbourne, should have been long abed. Mistress Marlin is too lax with you. I could easily have you both dismissed from the King's service, remember that.'

'She will,' I said. 'By the way, my lady, does Mistress Marlin know anything of what happened last night?'

Lady Rochford laughed incredulously. 'That sour prig? Of course not. No one else knows, or *will* know.'

'Then as you say, all will be well. Though I should tell you, as a lawyer, that I must take precautions.'

Lady Rochford looked scared again. 'What do you mean? You said you had told nobody!'

'We have not. But certain writings may be left, should I die suddenly.'

'No! You must not do that. If they came to light – you fool, do you think I would harm you? Think! Even if the Queen would permit that, which she would not, do you think I would want to draw attention to any of you?' She paused, then her voice rose to a shout. 'I want you quiet, quiet!' Her body began to tremble slightly.

'My lady, unless you are quieter yourself the guard will know your business; he is probably listening at the door as it is.'

She put a hand to her mouth. 'Yes,' she said distractedly. 'Yes.' She looked at the door then back at me, so frightened I felt sorry for the beldame.

'Quiet we shall be,' I said.

Lady Rochford gave me a hard look. 'It seems I must trust you.'

'Then we will take our leave.' I waited to see if she had more to say, but she only nodded, though she looked at me savagely. Barak and I bowed, Tamasin curtsied, and we left the room.

I glanced at the guard outside, who stood poker-faced. But we said no more till we were clear of the pavilions, in the open space between them and the manor. Then I leaned against a cart and wiped my brow with my handkerchief.

'Thank you, sir,' Tamasin said. 'But for you I would have collapsed with fear.'

'Ay,' Barak added. 'That was well done. You kept your composure.'

'Years of dealing with bad-tempered judges teaches you that. But it wasn't easy. Jesu, my heart is thumping now.' I felt a little giddy.

'Are you all right, sir?' Tamasin asked. 'You are very pale.'

'Give me a moment.' I sighed and shook my head. 'These days I feel as though I were adrift in a boat in a storm, wave after wave crashing over me as the wind drives me God knows where.'

'Hopefully soon we will be on a real boat,' Barak said. 'And away from here.'

'Ay. By God, Lady Rochford is terrified of what we might say. *Is* there something between the Queen and Culpeper? Or is she afraid for her own position?'

'Jesu knows,' Tamasin said. 'All I know is that the servants say there is bad blood between Culpeper and Francis Dereham.'

'Yes, Dereham,' I said thoughtfully. 'Another old friend of the Queen's.'

'Are Culpeper and the Queen and Lady Rochford all *mad*?' Barak asked.

'Lady Rochford seems – well, not quite normal. And Culpeper seemed a wantwit.'

'A lecherous preening creature.' Tamasin shuddered and I remembered Barak saying he had tried subjecting her to his attentions. 'And Queen Catherine is a giddy girl,' she added. 'But not so giddy surely that she would lie with Culpeper.'

'What now?' Barak asked me. 'Do we keep quiet, or tell Maleverer?'

'We keep quiet. I do not think Lady Rochford can be involved with the stolen papers, or even know what they are.'

'I asked some questions of the servants,' Tamasin said, 'about Culpeper's background. He has been at the court four years. He returns to his family home occasionally. It is in Goudhurst, in Kent.'

'Thank you, Tamasin.' I spoke neutrally, but this was interesting news.

'I must go now. Mistress Marlin will be wondering where I am.' She curtsied and walked away, steadily enough.

'She did well,' I said to Barak.

'Ay. Though all this has upset her. Do you know what she said yesterday? She said if only she could find who her father was, if he was a high official, he could protect us. I told her even if he was you can't go higher than the King. She loses her sense over that topic.'

I nodded. 'And as we have said, it could be anyone. It was interesting what she said about Culpeper being from Kent. I wonder if Goudhurst is near to Blaybourne village, whether someone called Blaybourne has links to the rebels.'

''Tis far from Kent to York,' Barak said. He looked behind me. 'But here comes one who has made that journey.'

I turned. Sergeant Leacon was walking rapidly towards us, his face set. 'God's death,' I muttered. 'What now?'

The sergeant came up and saluted. As at the refectory, his manner was cold, formal. 'I have been looking everywhere for you, Master Shardlake,' he said. 'Sir William Maleverer wants you right away. He is with Sir Edward Broderick, at his cell.'

'Broderick?' In the press of events since last night I had forgotten him.

'There has been another attempt on his life.'

Chapter Twenty-five

TELLING BARAK TO WAIT for me at the lodging house, I followed Leacon as he marched rapidly into the complex of monastic buildings. 'What happened?' I asked.

The young sergeant did not break his stride. 'Radwinter took one of the exercise breaks Sir William allows him. He had just watched the prisoner eat. Ten minutes later the soldiers guarding Broderick heard a retching sound and found him lying on the floor, gasping and vomiting. The man who found him called me and I ordered some beer and salt fetched. I mixed them and forced him to drink, then sent a man to fetch Dr Jibson. He is there now, with Sir William. Sir William is in no good temper.'

'You did well.'

He did not reply; again I sensed that for some reason Sergeant Leacon had become hostile to me. We walked down the corridor, our footsteps ringing on the stone flags. The door of Broderick's cell was open. It was crowded, although like the cell at the castle it was now filled with the stink of vomit. Two soldiers were holding Broderick in a sitting position on the bed. He seemed half conscious. One of the soldiers held his jaw open while Dr Jibson poured a flagon of liquid down his throat. Radwinter stood looking on, his eyes full of fury; and something else. Puzzlement? Maleverer stood next to him, arms folded, frowning mightily. He turned to me angrily.

'Where have you been?' he snapped.

'I – I have been at Master Wrenne's, Sir William.'

'Come outside. No, you stay there,' he barked at Radwinter as he made to follow. He led me back out of the cell. He folded his arms again and looked at me.

'It's happened again,' he said.

'Poison?'

'Radwinter oversaw the preparation of his food in the King's kitchen as usual today, brought it here and watched Broderick eat. Ten minutes later Broderick is writhing on the floor. Radwinter swears his food could not have been interfered with. He prepared it himself. Sergeant Leacon bears out what Radwinter says. And in that case –' he set his lips hard – 'I cannot see how anyone but Radwinter can have poisoned him.'

'But if he did, Sir William, why incriminate himself so obviously?'

'I don't know,' he replied in angry perplexity.

'And if not him, then who? Who knows Broderick is here?'

Maleverer shook his head angrily. 'Quite a few, by now. Word has got around.'

'Sergeant Leacon said Radwinter left right after feeding the prisoner,' I said. 'He went for some exercise. Could someone have got to him then?'

'Past the soldiers? And forced him to take poison?' he snapped. 'Where else could the poison have been but in his food?'

'Perhaps he was not forced to take it,' I said. 'Perhaps he wanted to.'

Maleverer turned at a commotion in the doorway. The soldiers were dragging Broderick outside now, the heavy chains securing his ankles clanking. They brought Radwinter's chair and sat him on it. Dr Jibson followed. The physician was in his shirtsleeves, his cuffs stained and his plump face red. 'I can't see properly in there,' he explained.

I looked at Broderick. His face was ghastly and he breathed in ragged gasps. His eyes flashed at me angrily for a moment. Radwinter stepped out, and Maleverer called him over.

'I have been telling Master Shardlake,' he snapped. 'I can see no answer to this but that *you* poisoned this man.'

Radwinter gave me a look of sheer evil. 'He will say nothing to disabuse you of that.'

'Master Shardlake does not agree with me.'

Radwinter looked taken aback. He eyed me. 'I swear I did not poison him,' he said. 'God's death, why would I place myself in such a position of suspicion?'

'Don't chop word for word with me, you bag of shit!' Maleverer stepped forward, looming over the gaoler. Radwinter stepped back and for the first time I saw him look afraid.

'I know nothing, Sir William, I swear.'

I looked over his shoulder. The physician had forced yet more beer down Broderick's throat and he retched again, a thin trail of yellow liquid spilling from his mouth.

'Is it all out?' Maleverer asked the physician.

'I think so. It was good that soldier thought of making him sick at once.'

'May I look in the cell?' I asked Maleverer.

'What for?'

'I do not know. Only – if Master Radwinter had left the cell ten minutes before Broderick fell on the floor, what if Broderick took something himself?'

'There is nothing in that cell!' Radwinter snapped. 'It is searched daily. Where would he get poison?'

'Oh, look if you must,' Maleverer said wearily.

I went into the empty cell. I stared at the stoneflagged floor, stained with patches of vomit. I wrinkled my nose against the smell as I paced to and fro, looking for something, anything unusual, Maleverer and Radwinter watching me from the door like two black crows.

There was nothing on the floor apart from Broderick's wooden bowl, spoon and cup, all empty. Dr Jibson could take those away and examine them anew, for all the good that might do. The only furniture was a stool, the bed and an empty chamberpot. I pulled the stained blankets from the bed and felt the straw mattress.

Then I saw something white, wedged between the bed and the wall. I reached and pulled it out.

'What's that?' Maleverer asked sharply.

'A handkerchief,' I said. To my astonishment it was a lady's handkerchief, light and lacy and folded into a square.

'Is that all?'

It felt unpleasant, stiff, had dark stains on it. I took out my own handkerchief, laid it on the bed, then put the folded handkerchief on top. 'Let me take a closer look outside,' I said quietly. I carried it carefully to the door, picking up the stool on my way. Broderick was sprawled in the chair now, apparently insensible, Dr Jibson standing over him. I walked a little way down the corridor, placed my handkerchief on the stool and unfolded it. The three of us bent to look at the smaller one within.

'So,' Maleverer growled impatiently. 'He got a kerchief as a keepsake from some lady—'

'He had no handkerchief,' Radwinter said, his brow creased in puzzlement. 'He was searched when he was taken to the castle, and again when he was brought here. He has never had a handkerchief. And no visitors who could have brought it to him, and certainly no lady.'

I bent closer and looked at the stains. 'You say he was searched when he was brought here from the castle?' I asked Radwinter.

'Yes. Stripped naked and his clothes searched.'

'That left one place where he could conceal this.' I pointed to the dark stains. There was a moment's silence, then Maleverer laughed incredulously.

'Are you telling me this man has been walking around with a lady's kerchief stuffed up his arse?'

I looked at him. 'Yes, he used a lady's because it is smaller, lighter. So a woman need not have been involved at all.'

'But why would he do that?'

'To carry something.' I was reluctant to touch the thing again, but I took a corner and unfolded it carefully. To my disappointment there was nothing within. I bent again. There was a faint smell, not faeces but something else, nasty and rotten. I frowned. It was familiar — I had encountered it before, recently. I jerked upright as I remembered. It was the smell I had caught, briefly, from the King's bloated leg as I stood with head bent before him at Fulford Cross.

'What is it?' Maleverer asked sharply. 'What have you got hold of, lawyer?'

'I am not sure, Sir William. May we have Dr Jibson here?'

Maleverer called to the physician and he came over. I told him where I suspected the handkerchief had been hidden and that something had been inside it. Reluctantly, Jibson bent and placed his nose close.

'What is that smell, sir?' I asked. 'Some poison?'

He laughed bitterly. 'God knows, it is a familiar smell for me. Rot and decay. Something nasty.'

'The poison,' Maleverer said.

'If it is, 'tis none I recognize.'

Maleverer's eyes glinted. 'He kept it in that safest of places until he had leisure to use it. Poisoned himself to escape what lies before him in London.' I looked over to where Broderick still slouched half conscious on the chair. 'God's wounds,' he continued, 'he must have been desperate.'

'But he had no visitors,' Radwinter said. 'None were allowed, in all the time he was at the castle.'

'Did he have a priest to confess him?'

'No, it was ordered from London he was to be kept away from everyone. That has been the rule since he was first put in the castle last month. And he was taken from his house at night, bundled to the castle in a nightshirt. Clothes and other things were brought from his house later. A kerchief full of poison would have been noticed.'

I shook my head. 'Then it must have reached him in the castle. He tried to poison himself there once and failed. Then he brought what was left of the poison here in that extraordinary way, and tried again. I guess he was taken ill so quickly this time, he had no time to hide the kerchief in its usual place, he just shoved it between the bed and the wall.'

'And failed a second time,' Dr Jibson said. 'When the sergeant made him vomit.'

Maleverer looked over to where Broderick sprawled gasping between the soldiers. 'So there was no poisoner here after all.'

'No,' I said quietly. 'I don't think there was.'

'Only the person who brought the poison.' Maleverer looked at Radwinter. 'And got it past you, or maybe even gave it to you.'

Radwinter quailed. 'I swear not.'

'I am relieving you of your duties till this is resolved.' Maleverer said. 'Sergeant Leacon!' he shouted, and the young Kentishman stepped round the partition. 'I am placing you in charge of the prisoner. You will stay here and watch him, all the time. Gaoler, give him the keys.'

Radwinter hesitated, then unhooked the keys from his doublet and handed them to Leacon. Broderick was coming to himself a little, he groaned and sat up. Leacon looked doubtfully at Maleverer. 'Sir, I have no experience—'

'Master Shardlake here can instruct you in your duties. Dr Jibson, take that handkerchief and examine it. I want to know what that stuff is.' He turned to Radwinter. 'You, gaoler, come with me. Two of you soldiers come too. You will stay under guard, Master Radwinter, until further notice.'

Radwinter glared at me. His lips parted and I thought he would say something but a soldier took a place on either side of him and he turned away, following Maleverer. I took a deep breath and turned to Leacon.

'I think you should get him back inside, sergeant.'

Leacon told the soldiers to lift Broderick. The prisoner looked at me.

'So,' I said. 'You poisoned yourself.'

'Do not tell me it was a great sin,' he croaked. 'I was only anticipating a more painful death. Which I will have now.'

'Who brought the poison?' I asked.

'The Mouldwarp brought it.' He bent over, seized by a fit of retching and coughing, and I motioned the soldiers to return him to his cell. I stood in the cell, then started a little as the sergeant coughed at my elbow.

'What should I do, sir?' he asked stiffly. 'What is his routine?'

I explained how Broderick was to be watched constantly, how Leacon would have to oversee the making of his food and watch him eating it. 'I suggest you seek further instructions from Sir William when he has more leisure. Oh, and you are not to encourage him to talk. That is to be left until he gets to London.'

Leacon nodded, then looked at me. 'Did the gaoler poison him?'

'I don't think so. But I don't know.'

'I have heard tales of the torturers in the Tower. I can see why Broderick would wish himself out of the world.'

'Then I must close the way if I can.' I sighed. 'But what else could I do? I had to investigate.'

'Investigations can cause more trouble than they solve.' Something harsh came into Leacon's voice.

'What do you mean?' I asked.

He hesitated, then sighed deeply. 'Do you remember I spoke of my parents' land case, at Waltham?'

'Ay.'

'I had a letter a few days ago. You remember their case hinges on whether certain old woods were truly in the gift of the local priory? It seems they were.'

'Then surely that is good news?'

He shook his head. 'It would be, save for a matter of boundaries. A boundary settled between the old priory lands and those of the lord, four years ago. My parents' farm is on the wrong side, they owe service to the lord after all. The matter was settled by arbitration by a lawyer.' He took another deep breath. 'It was you, sir, the records in Ashford show it. My uncle, who can read, looked at them for my parents.'

I stared at him. 'Oh,' I said. 'That work I did—'

'The lands whose boundaries you settled belonged in part to my parents' lord. You may have settled it fairly between him and the man who bought the abbey lands, but it has left them penniless.'

I was speechless. The sergeant turned away. 'Ay, well, poor folk are never considered,' he said with quiet bitterness. 'I had best go and care for my ward.'

✝

HALF AN HOUR LATER, Barak and I sat on the bench under the copper beech. It was a safe spot, with a good view all around. It was late afternoon now; a cold wind had risen and we sat muffled in our coats. Leaves pattered down around us, adding to the thick carpet under the tree.

'Autumn's well and truly here,' Barak said. 'Looks like the King's visit was the last fine day.'

'Yes.' I stared at the tower of St Olave's church, frowning hard.

'Still wondering how the poison got to Broderick?' he asked. I had told him of the events at the gaol.

'Yes, I want to go to the castle tomorrow, look at his cell again.'

'That cook was put there.'

'He'll be released now. Now we know the poison wasn't in his food.'

'You did well there,' Barak said. 'Maleverer should be grateful.'

I laughed. 'That's not in his nature.' I sat up. 'Barak, I have been trying to think, draw all the threads together.'

'So have I. Till my head aches.'

'Try this,' I said. 'Assume Broderick's poisoning has no direct connection with the other events – the murder of Oldroyd, the attack on me when that box was stolen and again the other night.'

'Is that what you think?'

'It's possible. Let's assume so for now.'

'Well – all right.'

'Look at those other matters. Oldroyd's death first. Who was about that early morning when he was killed? Craike, to begin with.'

He looked at me and laughed uneasily. 'Tamasin was about, for that matter.'

'She said she had been asked to meet Jennet Marlin.' I looked at him meaningfully. 'Who apparently was not at the place they had arranged to meet. Mark that for the moment.'

'It was a foggy morning, anyone from St Mary's could have gone down to where Oldroyd was working and tipped over his ladder.'

'Yes, they could. Craike, Lady Rochford, even young Leacon who came running up afterwards.'

'Who in God's name *was* it we disturbed in the chapterhouse?' he asked, kicking at the leaves in frustration.

'I caught only the glimpse of a black coat, or robe, as they ran out. Someone fleet of foot.'

'Everyone is fleet of foot when their life's at stake.'

'Let us move on to when I was attacked and the casket stolen.'

'That again could have been anyone with freedom to wander about King's Manor unnoticed.'

'And who saw us bring the box in. Craike again. Jennet Marlin again.'

'Lady Rochford. Leacon again. And half a hundred people we don't know, who could have seen us come in.'

'Yes. Leacon, for instance, always seems to be around, but we notice him because we know him. There could have been a dozen soldiers around when we brought the box in, whom we haven't noticed because to us they're just another red uniform.' I sighed.

'By the same token Craike is the only official we know. And you've missed one person who saw us with that box.'

'Who?'

'Master Wrenne.'

I frowned. 'Giles? But he was not at King's Manor when Oldroyd was killed.'

'How do we know? He has authority to be here. Who would notice another black-robed lawyer? He could have come in early that morning and killed Oldroyd. Sir, I know you have become good

friends with that old man, and I do not blame you for there are few
enough friendly faces here. But if you are looking for someone who
has links to the town, who knew Oldroyd and has access to St
Mary's, he does.'

'But is he a main capable of killing? And consider his state of
health. He is dying. He cares about nothing except reconciling with
his nephew before he dies.'

'Yes, you are right.'

'You are right too, though in principle we should exclude
nobody.' I frowned, remembering my uneasy thought that Martin
Dakin could be linked to the conspiracy. 'Do you remember the
Pilgrimage of Grace?' I asked.

'Ay. Lord Cromwell set me and some others to listening around
London, to see how much support the rebels had.' He looked at me
seriously. 'More than he thought.'

'And there was gossip among the lawyers that some from Gray's
Inn were involved. Many from the northern counties practise there;
like Robert Aske.'

'No one was prosecuted.'

'No. But I am reminded that Jennet Marlin's fiancé practised
there, as does Giles's nephew. I hope he is safe.' I sighed. 'I am sorry,
I digress. Let us move forward, to the attack at the camp.'

Barak gave a hollow laugh. 'Jesu, there were hundreds there.
Dereham and Culpeper, for example. Young Dereham saw us and
he's a fierce brute.'

'Yes, he is. Could he have a connection to the spring conspiracy?
The Queen's secretary? He was in York when Oldroyd was killed.
Remember we saw him at the inn? He was part of the advance party.
Yes, we should consider him.'

'Leacon was there,' Barak added. 'Radwinter, too; he has it in
for you.'

'No. He's loyal to Cranmer, I am sure. Anything he knew about
the conspiracy would go straight to Maleverer or the Archbishop.' I
rubbed my chin. 'Craike was not at the camp but I had just seen

him and I told him I was going there. Let us go tonight and visit this inn where he went.'

'I might be better going alone.'

'No, I'll come. I need to be doing something. I am still in the dark. There was another thought I had. What if the attack on me at the camp happened for a different reason than the first one?'

'What do you mean?'

'Rich's threat. I was attacked once, if I was attacked again it would be assumed it was connected to the stolen box.' I shook my head. 'Yet would Rich go to the trouble and risk of employing some rough to kill me, just because I have been tenacious on the Bealknap case?'

'Too tenacious.' Barak looked at me seriously. 'Rich is capable of putting someone out of the way if they cause him trouble. But I doubt he'd do it just to get a troublesome lawyer off his back, especially when given time he can find the right judge.'

I sighed. 'You are right. But Jesu, what a tangle. 'Tis hard to be the hunted rather than the hunter.'

'That *Titulus* you found did not help?'

'No. Though there are things in it that puzzle me. And we are left with this dangerous knowledge about the Queen. I still think we should tell Maleverer.'

'But if we do, and Lady Rochford and the Queen and Culpeper deny it, as they will, what proof have we? We will be punished as troublemakers. And I do not want to place myself in Maleverer's hands. He lied, you know, when he said the *Titulus* was a forgery. Couldn't you write to Cranmer, tell him all that's happened, let him deal with it?'

'A letter wouldn't get out of here unread. And it would take ten days for a reply to get back.' I looked at him. 'No, we're stuck here. And I can't trust anyone. Except you.'

Barak sighed. 'Well, I said I would see Tamasin. I ought to go, if I may.'

'Of course.'

'She is afraid.'

'I know.'

'I'll walk you back to the lodging house?'

We returned and arranged that Barak would be back at nine and we would visit the tavern. I went into my cubicle and locked the door. It was starting to get dark. I sighed. I seemed to be making trouble for everyone: Barak, young Leacon over that arbitration, and Broderick, whose life I had saved for the torturer. I saw again in my mind's eye the King's face as he smiled cruelly at me at Fulford. I shook my head. How that image kept haunting me, biting into my guts, somehow at the centre of everything that had happened. The Mouldwarp.

Chapter Twenty-six

THE BELLS OF THE Minster sounded loudly as Barak and I passed it, booming through the damp night air. It was dark, and we stumbled on the unpaved streets as we headed down the Fossgate towards the corner from which Barak had seen Master Craike emerge.

'This is the way,' Barak said.

He pointed down a narrow lane, the sky almost hidden by the overhanging top storeys of the tumbledown houses. Doors and shutters were closed, only strips of yellow light showing through warped timbers. A white board creaked and flapped in the wind at the far end of the lane. 'That's the alehouse sign,' he said. 'The White Hart.'

I studied it. 'Seems a mean place. You're right, Craike wouldn't put folk from the Progress up there.' I wrinkled my nose at the strong stench of piss from the alley.

'Sure you want to come?' Barak asked. 'This is a rough spot.'

'I want to find out what he was up to.' I followed him into the lane, hand at my dagger. At his suggestion I had donned my cheapest-looking clothes. I looked at the doorways we passed; I had a sense of eyes watching. But no one had followed us from St Mary's; we had watched and listened carefully.

Barak pushed open the door of the alehouse. It was the sort of poor place I expected, merely a room set with benches and tables and a hatch through which a slatternly looking woman passed home-brewed beer to the men in ragged clothes who sat on the benches lining the walls. The floor was bare and the room cold, without a fire. A dog, belonging to a pair of young Dalesmen in sheepskin coats who sat together by the wall, growled at us then barked loudly.

'Down, Crag.' The dog's master laid a big hand on its back. 'Look, Davey, here's gentlemen come to't White Hart.'

Barak went up to the bar and asked the landlady for two mugs of beer. She did not understand him at first and he had to repeat his request. 'Southrons,' the man with the dog said loudly to his friend. 'Crag caught their stink.'

Barak turned to them. 'We've just come for a drink, my friend,' he said. 'We want no trouble.'

I looked around uneasily. There were a dozen Yorkers there, all glaring at us with hostile expressions. The Dalesmen, from their looks, had been drinking for some time.

The woman handed two wooden mugs through the hatch. All the benches were taken; we could have found spaces if some of the customers had moved up but they sat where they were. We stood awkwardly. The Dalesman called Davey laughed.

'Can thee not find a bink, maisters?' He turned to his friend. 'Tha should make a seat for the southron gentlemen, Alan. They must be gentlemen, they don't allow the soldiers and servants into York. We should mebbe stand in their presence.'

'I say we're all made by one workman, of like mire,' Alan replied.

'I agree,' Barak replied cheerfully. 'From London to Carlisle, we are all one.'

'Nay, maister. Not in riches, when all our rents go down to London.'

'We've done well enough out of them today,' his friend said. 'Selling those poor nawtes of sheep to the purveyors for five nobles.'

'Ay, but when the Progress leaves prices will fall again. Our folk can't pay the money southrons can.' He looked at us belligerently, hunting for an argument. I took a sip of the foul-tasting beer.

'Has tha come on business, maisters?' one of the men on the benches asked, and to my surprise some of the others laughed.

'Business?' I repeated.

'Ay, tha'll not have come for our company.' There was more laughter.

Just then a door opened and a tall stringy fellow in an apron appeared. He frowned at the Dalesmen then came over to us.

'Can I help thee, maisters?' he asked quietly.

I exchanged a look with Barak. Something more than the selling of ale was going on here.

'I don't know,' he replied. 'Can you?'

The man inclined his head towards the door, and we were glad enough to follow him into a narrow passageway beyond, that stank of old beer. A candle burned in a lamp on the staircase. He closed the door. 'I'm sorry about that, maisters. Southrons aren't popular here.'

'Never mind,' I said. 'Now then, how can you help us?'

'Depends on your wants.' He scanned our faces with narrow, calculating eyes.

'A friend of mine was here a week or so ago. An official from the Progress. A large fellow with a fringe of fair hair.'

'Ay.' His face relaxed into a leer. 'I remember him. Tell you what we have here, did he?'

'That's right.'

'Well.' He smiled confidingly. 'Tell me what your pleasure is. Sharp little nips from a girl with a dagger, or a belt-thrashing from an old carrion-whore, like your friend enjoys?' He leered again. 'I can arrange to indulge the most *sinful* lusts.'

I was taken aback. Whatever I had expected, it was not this. Barak stepped in. 'You provide girls who cater for special tastes, hey?'

He nodded eagerly. 'Tastes the ordinary houses don't cater for. Boys, too, if you like. Got a good network in York, going back to the days of the monks. Sinful, some of those fellows were.'

'Tell you what,' Barak said quickly. 'We're making enquiries on behalf of one of the senior officials at St Mary's, who doesn't care to be seen here himself. I think you have what he wants. We'll talk to him and come back. He wouldn't want to be seen here, perhaps some private room?'

'Ay, sir, that can be arranged.'

'Here's two shillings for your trouble in the meantime.' Barak produced the coins and handed them over. The man looked at them.

'He'd pay well, then? This official?'

'Handsomely.'

The pimp's eyes narrowed. 'What's his name, maister?'

'Now, you know better than that. Just wait for our return.'

'Come in the morning, before we open. You won't be bothered by the customers then.'

'We will. And talking of that, is there a back way out of here?'

He nodded and led us to another door that gave on to the stinking alley. We walked quickly away, and did not relax till we reached the Fossgate again. Then Barak laughed loudly.

'So that's it. That pompous old fellow Craike likes to be whacked about by some old doxy. Wonder if he thinks about that as he shuffles his papers on that little desk of his.'

I looked at him. 'You handled that very smoothly. As though you knew what you were doing.'

He shrugged again. 'Lord Cromwell had contacts among the London whoremasters, especially fellows like that who deal with those who have outlandish tastes. Often the whoremasters could come up with the name of someone at court, and then they were in my master's power.'

'Blackmail?'

'If you like.'

'And you were involved?'

'I was Lord Cromwell's contact with some of the whoremasters, ay.' Barak frowned at me. 'You know well my duties were more than running errands. I didn't like it much, if you have to know.' He shrugged. 'But if men of rank choose to delve in the stews, they take a risk.'

'They do if there are spies about.' I snapped my fingers. 'I'll wager that's why he got to know Oldroyd. To find out if there were places like this in York.'

'Only one way to find out. Ask him.'

I was reluctant to shame Craike, but realized there was no alternative. 'I'll see him tomorrow,' I said. We walked on in silence for a time, then I asked, 'Does Tamasin know about your work for Cromwell?'

'Not the details.' He looked at me sharply. 'She doesn't need to know those. After all, you have never enquired too closely before.'

'I suppose I haven't.'

'It's just as well I was able to work out what was going on there as quick as I did. Or we might have found ourselves presented with some salty old whores with birch-rods ready to beat hell out of us, and a little report going to someone at King's Manor.'

I laughed. We walked on, our steps echoing on the cobbles. As Bootham Bar came into sight I asked him, 'Have you thought any more about what we talked about? Your future?'

'All I want now is to get safe back to London. And be sure I have one,' he added grimly.

✝

WE RETURNED LATE TO St Mary's. It was eleven o'clock by the time the guard let us through the gate; everyone had retired to bed. A big, yellowish harvest moon had risen and in its dim light the helmeted soldiers continued their endless walks along the walls, more standing guard outside the tents and pavilions and the doors of King's Manor, all its windows dark. I had heard the King was going hunting on the morrow; there was no word yet of the Scotch King's arrival.

'I've a meeting with Tamasin,' Barak said. 'I'll come to the lodging house with you first.'

'At this hour? Ah, in your secret love-nest?' I did not mean the words to come out in the supercilious way they did. He gave me a sharp look.

'Ay. She feels safe with me.'

'She will get in trouble if she is found out.'

'She won't. After three months of the Progress half the servants in the Queen's household have a dalliance with someone. And the Queen is hardly one to keep her ladies on a tight moral rein.' He stepped ahead of me and walked briskly to the church. I realized I had annoyed him. One of the guards by the pavilions sneezed, making me jump. But I was glad of those armed men nearby. Always now at night my senses were alert for danger, for an assassin.

The monastic church was inhabited by a number of grooms who slept on blankets in the straw near the horses, their forms illuminated by candles burning in big iron sconces, five feet high. The gentlemen's horses – over a hundred of them – stood quietly in their stalls, each stall with a paper pinned to the door with the name of the owner. It was a good system, enabling the horses owned by individuals to be readily available, while the huge herd of carthorses was left to browse in the fields. We walked down until I came to Genesis and Sukey's stalls, side by side.

'Let's see how the horses are,' I said.

'All right.'

A young groom, rolled in his blanket on a pile of hay in the nave, sat up sleepily. He was a round-faced fellow in his teens, his smock covered with pieces of straw.

'Who is it?' He looked dubiously at our poor clothes.

'We are the owners of these horses. We just came to see how they do.'

'They are all well, sir.'

'Good. Go back to sleep, fellow, we will only be a moment.' We went over and spoke with the horses a little, stroking them. Genesis seemed happy enough in his stall but Barak's Sukey was restless and pulled away from his hand.

'Are you bored, here, Sukey?' he asked. 'Nothing to do? Well, hopefully we will soon be on our way. It all depends on the King of the Scotch.'

'We walk them up and down the nave.' The groom had got up.
'We can't take them out. There's so much going on in the courtyard,
we're not allowed.'

'I understand.'

'When do you think King James will come, sir?' he asked. 'We
are all anxious to move on again.'

'I wish I knew,' I said with a smile. 'Well, we must to bed.
Goodnight.'

We walked on to the open north door of the church that led to
the courtyard where the lodging house and the animal pens were.
Barak looked left, along to the claustral buildings at the other end of
the courtyard.

'Waiting for you there, is she?'

'Ay.'

'Go on. I can walk to the lodging house alone." I felt guilty for
annoying him earlier.

'Sure?'

'Ay. Off you go. No one's followed us through the church, I
was looking out.'

He left me, and I turned along the path to the lodging house.
Beside a pen full of black-faced sheep I saw the bear standing upright
in its cage, resting its clawed arms on the iron bars of its cage. As I
walked past it made a whimpering sound. I stopped and looked.
Poor bruin, it must be in pain from its wounds. I stopped a few feet
from the cage and studied it. It made a low, angry growling sound
and shifted its stance. Its little eyes glinted at me. I caught a rank
smell from the thick fur.

I thought of how it would have been captured in some far-off
German forest, brought over to England in a boat, suffered taunts
and beatings to keep it savage, then let loose in an arena full of dogs.
The King would have relished that spectacle, I thought.

I heard a creak, metal against metal. I stared round wildly for at
once I thought of the spit at the camp. But no one and nothing was
near. I looked back at the cage. Something was different. Then I

realized the door was opening. I saw a rope was fixed to the top, it was being pulled upwards from the back of the cage. The bear stepped back, its eyes still fixed on me. There was a clang as the door suddenly crashed back on the cage roof.

The beast stepped out and stood for a moment on the path, looking straight at me. There was a frantic bleating from the sheep-pen. The bear let out a hoarse roar and waved its big forelegs at me, the moonlight glinting on its long curved claws.

I stepped backwards. My hand went to my dagger, but it would be useless against a charge by this creature. The bear dropped to all fours and began walking towards me, growling horribly. It dragged one of its hind legs, which must have been injured in the baiting before the King; otherwise it would have been upon me in seconds. Even so it moved fast, its big claws scraping on the path. I turned and ran, back to the open door of the church, and raced inside; fearing every moment to feel those claws raking my back, the terrible weight of the huge creature felling me to the earth.

Inside the church I grabbed the big door to pull it shut, but it had stood open a long time now and rain had warped the wood. It would not shift.

'Help!' I cried out. 'The bear's loose!' I heard startled voices behind me. The bear must have halted somewhere outside, I could not see it. Perhaps the noise would drive it away.

The groom I had spoken to earlier ran up to me with a couple of others. 'What's happening?'

'The bear, it's got out, it's out there! Help me close the door. And someone run to find some soldiers! Hurry!' I had remembered that weapons were forbidden at King's Manor. The grooms, still half asleep, stared at me stupidly. 'God's blood,' I cried. 'Will you help me with this door!'

One of the men stepped forward. 'But what – oh, fuck!' He broke off as the bear appeared in the doorway. It was a huge animal. It shambled inside, turning its massive head to look at us, its nose twitching. Everyone jumped back. The horses, catching its smell, began neighing loudly, banging against the sides of their stalls. The sudden cacophony seemed to startle the bear. It stood where it was, looking from side to side with its small deep-set eyes, saliva dripping from the corner of its mouth. It stood again on its hind legs and opened its mouth, showing us a pair of enormous canines. I saw that a long wound on its hind leg had opened, blood was dripping on to the floor. After its recent experiences the creature must be confused, frightened, in pain. That only made it more dangerous.

I joined the grooms as they retreated, step by step, everyone terrified of a sudden charge by the bear, and looking round desperately for somewhere to escape to. But there was nowhere in the stripped, empty church, nothing to climb on. The terrified horses were making an enormous din now, some of them rearing up and battering the sides of their stalls with their hooves, splintering the wood. I hoped the noise would drive the bear out but the creature dropped back on all fours again and began advancing, turning its head and looking between me and the half-dozen grooms as we retreated, its terrible human enemies now exposed in all their puny weakness. As its head swayed on its powerful neck, looking from one to the other of us, it seemed it fixed its attention particularly on me: the first man it had encountered after its release.

It seemed like an eternity, but it can only have been for a minute or so that we retreated down the church, eyes on the bear, terrified to turn and run lest we provoke a charge. Then I slipped on some dirty straw on the floor of the nave and went over backwards. I cried out, then hauled myself frantically to my feet. The grooms had retreated farther, leaving me closest to the bear, which was staring at me from ten feet away. I saw the trail of blood from its leg ran all the way to the door. The noise from the horses as they cried out and battered at their stalls was indescribable.

The bear walked slowly forward, never taking its eyes off me. I heard the distant footsteps of the grooms, running away fast now; they had abandoned me. The bear quickened its pace. I saw, just beside me, one of the big sconces of candles, and I seized it in both hands and hurled it at the huge animal. The sconce crashed against its side and the bear jumped away with a roar, striking out at the sconce, which fell on to a little pile of straw. At once it caught light, flaring yellow. The bear stepped back, then fixed its angry pain-filled eyes on me. It rose to its hind legs again and charged. I cried out as I braced myself for the tearing claws.

Then I saw something flash by me. There was a dull thud and the bear jumped back. I looked, dizzily, at an arrow poking from its chest, the feathered end quivering. Another whistled by and buried itself in the bear's fur, then another. It cried and thrashed the air with its claws until a fourth arrow landed in its chest, and must have pierced its heart, for with a dull grunt it crashed over sideways, landing in the pile of burning straw. It lay there, its pelt beginning to smoulder, beyond suffering at last.

I leaned against a pillar, shaking from head to foot, as a voice I recognized cried, 'Get that fire out before it spreads! Water!' The grooms dashed forward, together with two soldiers, beating at the fire with brooms until buckets were brought up and the flames extinguished. I stared foolishly at the red-coated soldiers, at the bows slung over their shoulders. A figure stepped before me: Sergeant Leacon.

'Sergeant,' I said. 'How – what happened?'

'We heard the commotion from Broderick's cell, it's just behind the church wall. I brought my men through here. Fortunately they had their bows with them.' He looked at me grimly. 'You've cause to be thankful Kentish archers know how to shoot straight.'

I took a deep breath. 'You saved my life.'

'How in God's name did that bear get inside the church?'

'Someone let it out of its cage.'

'What?'

'It chased me into the church, then I slipped.' I looked past Leacon to the grooms, who were checking the fire was out. One met my eye and looked away, shamefaced. The bear's carcass lay smoking amid the burnt straw.

More voices sounded, it seemed the noise from the church had wakened half the camp. Servants and soldiers appeared, milling about and staring at the dead bear. 'It went for the crookback lawyer,' someone said. 'You remember, from Fulford?' Sergeant Leacon looked from me to the bear and back again, his broad handsome face creased with a frown.

'Are you saying someone let that bear out deliberately?' he asked.

'Yes.' I took a deep breath. 'Someone knew I was coming that way and waited for me.' But who? And how did they know?

Chapter Twenty-seven

Sergeant Leacon ordered a soldier to accompany me to the manor. The soldier explained our business to one of the guards on the door and an official led me into the house, ordering me to walk quietly and talk in whispers for the King and Queen were abed upstairs. All was silent within, the soldiers lining the walls looking half asleep, the gorgeous tapestries and furniture dimly lit by a few sconces of candles.

Again I was led upstairs. The official knocked on the door of Maleverer's office and his deep voice called 'Enter!' To my surprise Sir Richard Rich was with him; the two of them were sitting at his desk poring over some land deeds. As I entered with the soldier I saw the name 'Robert Aske of Aughton' in large bold letters heading a conveyance just before Maleverer hastily rolled up the document.

'What do you want at this time of night?' he barked.

'You should know, Sir William, there has been another attempt on my life.'

'What?'

I told him about the bear, and the events in the church. When I had finished, Rich laughed softly.

'Brother Shardlake, perhaps when the bear saw your bent form in the dark it thought you were a little female bear.' As he spoke, looking me hard in the eye, he was rolling up more conveyances from Maleverer's desk. I thought, he is trying to distract me, he does not want me to see.

'Someone opened the cage deliberately.'

Maleverer called in the official, who was waiting outside. 'Fetch the bearward,' he snapped. 'Have him brought here.'

The soldier bowed and left. Maleverer looked at me keenly. 'I spoke to that cook from the camp, Goodrich. I couldn't make up my mind whether what happened with that spit was an accident and they were trying to cover it up, or whether someone did attack that boy and try to kill you. This might throw a different light on matters. We'll see what the bearward says.'

'No more news on the missing papers?' Sir Richard asked. He glanced at me again. 'The ones this fool lost?'

'Nothing. They are long gone to the rebels.'

'But someone has stayed behind, to give Broderick poison and attack Shardlake here. I think there is something to be said for groping Broderick again, at the castle. Prick out what he knows.'

Maleverer shook his head. 'The Duke of Suffolk says no, and the King agrees. They talked of getting an expert up from the Tower dungeons but by the time he gets up here we'll be well on our way back if we go by boat. Hopefully.'

'If the Scotch King ever arrives.' Rich's mouth twisted in amusement.

'If James doesn't show his mangy arse in York soon the Scotch will smart for this.'

There was a knock at the door and the soldier led the bearward into the room. The big man cringed. Rich waved a hand in front of his nose. 'God's bones, you stink!'

'I'm sorry, my lord,' the fellow quavered. 'Only I've just been getting the bruin's carcass out of the church—'

'How did it get out of its cage?' Maleverer asked. 'Were you careless with the latch?'

'No, sir, I swear. It doesn't open on a latch. The door is pulled upward from behind. There is a rope from the top of the door. For safety, you see. Someone stood behind the cage, raised the door and tied the end to the back of the cage. Then they ran, leaving the bear to get out.'

'Anyone could do that?' Maleverer asked, frowning. 'Is the door not secured in any way?'

'No, sir. Who – who would want to let a wild bear out?'

'Someone who knew I would be walking along that path, late at night,' I said. 'I see what happened now. When I came into St Mary's with Barak someone was in the yard and saw me. They ran down the side of the church, went behind the bear's cage, then when I left the church they let it out. To kill me.'

'Where was Barak?' Maleverer snapped.

I hesitated. 'I gave him permission to visit someone.'

'That girl, eh?'

I did not reply. Rich gathered up his papers. 'Well, Sir William, I cannot stand this stink another moment. If you will excuse me.' He bowed to Maleverer and left the room. Maleverer glared at the bearward.

'You should have taken greater care of that animal. What if it had got out when the King was abroad?'

'But I—'

'Shut your gob. Now listen, you say nothing about someone opening the cage. Say you forgot to secure the door properly. I don't want rumours getting about. Understand?'

'Yes, Sir William. I promise.'

'You'd better. Now get out. Are there more bear-baitings planned?'

'Yes, there's one to entertain the camp on Tuesday. They're bringing in new bears tomorrow.'

'Well, keep them somewhere else, outside the manor. Any more escapes and I'll have you put you in the ring with the bears instead of the dogs. Understand?'

'Yes, Sir William.'

'Right. Get out.'

The man left, still cringing. Maleverer sighed, then turned to me. 'From now on you keep that Barak with you, you don't go wandering anywhere alone. I'm surprised you did tonight, after nearly being spitted at the camp.'

I sighed. 'That was careless of me.'

'Who is doing this?' he growled savagely. 'It's like dealing with a spirit of the air.' He sighed, then waved a hand. 'All right. Go.' He gave me a sidelong look. 'You've another enemy in Richard Rich, by the way. You'd be better off advising the London Council to drop their case. Better for your business, your reputation, everything.'

I did not reply. Maleverer frowned. 'Obstinate, aren't you? You'd do better to calculate where your own interests lie.'

As I descended the steps with my guard, I thought of Maleverer's advice. You certainly protect your own interests, I thought. Getting hold of Aske's lands that were forfeited to the King and passed to the Court of Augmentations. I wondered what Rich was getting in return.

✝

BARAK RETURNED TO THE lodging house in the small hours. I called him into my cubicle and told him what had happened. I said Maleverer had ordered he must accompany me everywhere.

'If it must be, it must,' he said. He looked at me.

'He guessed you were with Tamasin. You'd better arrange your trysts for when I am safe indoors.'

'Why does he not just send us back? The petitions are almost done with.'

'I'm not sure.' I looked out of the little window of my cubicle. 'I think I may be bait. To draw out the assassin.'

'Who the hell is it?' Barak asked.

'As I said to Maleverer: someone who watches and waits in the dark for an opportunity. Someone was hidden in the courtyard when we came back from the inn, waiting for an opportunity. They ran round the church and behind the bear's pen. They probably planned to let the bear loose on me anyway, and by going up to the pen I gave them a wonderful opportunity. This is someone very persistent, waiting for the chance of an ambush like a cat.'

'One person?'

'I think so.'

'A professional?'

I looked at him. 'What do you think?'

He shook his head. 'No, this is an opportunist. A professional would have come up behind you and knifed you in the guts. This is someone from the manor, afraid of being seen and recognized. With me with you all the time, you should be safer. And when you're alone here, he wouldn't dare risk coming in and letting the clerks see him.'

I laughed bitterly. 'Those people, my protectors?' I walked over to the window. 'Such persistence, such determination. And all because they think I know more about those papers than I do, unless there is something I am missing. If only I *could* find out more about them. I have turned the contents of that *Titulus* over in my mind a hundred times. It is so ambiguously worded in places.'

I looked out of the window. I remembered the dream I had had our first day here, that it was like Broderick's cell in the castle. Then I thought of something, and drew in my breath sharply.

'What is it?' Barak was suddenly alert. 'Someone outside?'

'No. No, I have thought of something. That poison Broderick used. He had it in his cell at York Castle, but could not have brought it in and no one can have brought it to him. How did he get it?'

'It's a riddle.'

'There must be an answer.'

'Have you thought of one?'

'Possibly. When we go to the castle to hear the petitions tomorrow, I want to take another look at that cell.'

♰

NEXT MORNING WE SET OUT early for the castle. Another high wind had risen overnight, full of gusty rain. Aske's skeleton still hung from the tower; the sight of it made me shudder. I looked at the tower where Broderick had been held; as soon as we had a break I intended to visit his old cell.

We entered the courthouse; the benches in the outer hall were filled with people, mostly tradesmen and poor farmers though a few men in more expensive clothes sat stiffly among them. All looked at me apprehensively as I entered in my lawyer's robes.

Giles sat in a courtroom with dark panelled walls, at a table drawn up beneath the royal arms and covered with a green cloth. He seemed fully restored to health, and with his broad craggy face looked impressively judicial. Beside him sat a thin, dark-haired fellow in his thirties, wearing a dark robe with the badge of the Council of the North.

Giles greeted us cheerfully. 'Matthew. And Barak, would you sit at the end here and take notes. There is ink and a quill sharpened for you.' He waved to the man beside him. 'Master Ralph Waters, representative of the Council of the North.'

I bowed. Master Waters looked amiable enough, a junior official by the look of him. 'Master Waters is here to represent the council's interests, for some of the cases this morning involve complaints against it. The compulsory purchase of a piece of land here, a requirement to provide food at low prices there. Master Waters has been instructed to be – accommodating.'

The official smiled. 'Ay, so the King's justice can be seen to be merciful. No try-ons, mind,' he added, raising a finger. 'I won't have try-ons.'

'Nor will we,' Giles agreed heartily. 'Eh, Brother Shardlake? We'll send false petitioners out with their tails between their legs.' He seemed to be enjoying the prospect of the day's work. 'Now then, let us make ready, look over the cases then have the petitioners in.'

✝

WE WERE THERE all morning, listening to disputes and adjudicating. After the horrors of the night before it felt strange to be sitting there, surrounded by the trappings of power. I managed to forget what had happened, for a few hours at least, for adjudicating was a role I enjoyed.

Most of the cases were petty enough matters, some of the parties' anger with each other far out of proportion to the matter in dispute. Those we dealt with sharply. Where the council was the party petitioned against, Master Waters was a model of reasonableness, but it struck me from the cases that the council had often been high-handed in its dealings with the Yorkers.

We adjourned for a break at twelve, a servant bringing in some cold meat and bread. I ate quickly, then nodded at Barak.

'I wonder if we might leave you for a short while, gentlemen,' I said. 'We will be back within the half hour.' Master Waters nodded; Giles looked at us curiously.

We went out into the courtyard; the rain had stopped but the wind was higher than ever, making my robe billow around me. 'My wrist hurts,' Barak said. 'All those notes. Well, what is this mystery in the tower?'

I led the way across the courtyard to the guardroom, where the hard-featured guard I had met before agreed to take us up to Broderick's cell.

The cell had not been cleaned since the cook left it; messy rushes still lay on the floor, the truckle bed under the window still had a dirty sheet on it. Broderick's chains were still fixed to their bolt on the wall, the chains themselves lying in a pile of links on the bed.

'Well?' Barak asked.

I walked to the bed and picked up the manacles at the end of the chain, which had been fixed to Broderick's wrists. I walked away from the bed, drawing out the chain to its fullest length. Standing up, Broderick could have walked perhaps eight feet. I walked round the cell in a half-circle, looking inwards. Barak and the guard looked on in surprise.

'What are you doing?' Barak asked.

'I'm tracing the limits Broderick could have walked. Seeing if there is anything odd on the floor, the walls.'

'I can't see anything.'

'No – ah.' I stopped at the window. 'Yes, he can walk this far.

SOVEREIGN

I thought so; he told me he used to stare at Aske's bones.' I looked out. I could see the opposite tower, the shape of the skeleton swinging in its chains in the cold wind that whipped rain into my face, along with something else: a smell I recalled from the handkerchief in Broderick's cell at St Mary's, and from Fulford when I bowed and looked at the King's leg – rot and decay. I studied a long leaden pipe that ran down the wall and broke off to one side of the window, where a crack in the wall ran jaggedly along beside it. From the end of the pipe a white, slimy-looking deposit hung, water sweating from it into the crack. And something else: a couple of brown stems, broken off from the fungus that had grown in this filth.

'That looks like a lightning strike,' I said to the guard.

'Ay, maybe.' He sounded puzzled by my interest.

'Where does the pipe come from?'

'It's an overflow pipe, from the guards' little kitchen at the top of the tower. Some of the guards sleep there usually, though they were turned out when Broderick came.'

'So the pipe will be full of the nastiest stuff you could imagine. Bits of bad meat, rotten vegetables.' I took off my robe, took out a clean handkerchief and then, with some difficulty, reached my hand through the bars and broke off a chunk of the white slimy deposit. As I touched it I felt my stomach turn. I sniffed at it, then showed it to Barak. He bent his head, then recoiled.

'Ugh. It's like shit, only worse.'

I reached out again, and plucked a couple of the little mushrooms. I held them in my palm.

'This is Broderick's poison,' I said quietly. 'And the smell in his handkerchief was the stuff from the pipe. This is where he got it. He then ate the fungus, hoping it would poison him.'

'Jesu!' The guard's face wrinkled in disgust. 'What manner of man could do such a thing?'

'A man of great desperation. And courage. He was in a state when he would try anything.'

'He wouldn't know what the mushrooms would do,' Barak observed

'No, but he knew it would be nothing good. That perhaps it could kill him.'

'And he kept it in a handkerchief stuffed up his arse,' Barak added, making the guard cringe even more.

'As I said, desperate. What courage it must have taken to make that plan, collect that stuff and actually force oneself to swallow it, stomach heaving, hoping but not knowing if it would poison you to death. Well, that is one mystery solved. No one else was involved in his poisoning.'

'How did you know?' Barak asked.

'I didn't. But I knew he had to get it from somewhere and I thought, what if he got it from outside the window. It was the only possible place left.' I smiled. 'There is as always an answer if you look hard enough.'

We left the cell and returned to the courtyard. I watched the leaves skittering over the courtyard in the wind. 'I'll tell Maleverer,' I said. 'This will let Radwinter off the hook.' I laughed softly. 'I wonder if he'll be grateful?'

'I should think he'll hate you worse than ever.'

'Poor Broderick. I suppose he thought anything was better than what he faces in the Tower.' I shook my head. 'Well, I have ensured he is safe for that now.'

'He would never have died. That filth was so strong his body just rejected it at once.' Barak looked at me. 'You sound as though you admire him.'

'In a way I do. Jesu, that stink reminds me of the smell that came from the King's leg.' I laughed. 'Mould from the Mouldwarp.'

✝

THE AFTERNOON WITH ITS succession of petitioners passed much like the morning. There was one case, though, which troubled me, and brought me as close as I had come to a disagreement with Giles.

It was a petition from a supplier of wood to St Mary's, which had gone into the building of the pavilions. He had provided the materials months ago and according to the terms of his contract with the Council of the North he should have been paid long before. He invoked the King's justice in seeking payment now.

'This is a difficult one,' Master Waters said uncomfortably as we studied the papers before the petitioner was admitted.

'Why?' Giles asked. 'It seems clear enough Master Segwike's payment is overdue. I know him, his business is small, he cannot afford to continue unpaid.'

The young official shifted uncomfortably in his seat. 'The problem is, if his petition is granted, the council will be deluged with demands for payment. Our clerks have had some difficulties in managing the – er – flow of cash.'

'You mean they've made a mullock of things, ordering more than they can pay for?'

'Sir Robert Holgate is in discussions with the King's treasury.' Waters looked between us. 'I have been generous on other matters concerning the council. I am instructed to continue to be: provided this petition is dismissed. Master Segwike *will* be paid, and the others, but we need time.'

Giles nodded and smiled softly. He looked at me.

'We are here to do justice,' I said. 'We should not be subject to pressure from a member of our panel on individual cases.'

'When was justice ever divorced from politics?' Giles asked quietly.

'Under the constitution of England, the answer to that is "always".' I knew it sounded priggish, but I would not let this go by unchallenged.

'Then I will be less accommodating with other petitioners,' Master Waters said. 'I'm sorry, but those are my instructions.'

'We are stuck with this, Matthew,' Giles said. I shrugged angrily, but said no more. Justice for this one man would mean less justice for others. The woodsman was called in. An elderly fellow, nervous to be before us, stated his case haltingly.

'But you cannot doubt the Council of the North will meet its debt,' Giles said when he had finished. 'They are the King's representatives.'

'But *when*, sir?' the old man asked. 'I have debts to meet myself.'

Giles raised his eyebrows at Waters, passing the problem over to him.

'Soon, fellow,' he said reassuringly. 'It is in hand.'

'But my creditors—'

'Must wait a little too,' Giles said in a grave voice. 'Then all will balance out. You can tell them this tribunal has confirmed payment will be made —' he paused — 'soon.'

The woodsman was dismissed. I watched him go, his shoulders slumped in dejection. Giles took a deep breath and looked at Waters. 'I hope it *will* be soon, sir,' he said.

'It will be. We can't afford to have York full of discontented traders for too long. Not with the mood as it is.'

I looked at Giles. 'You overawed the poor fellow.'

He shrugged. 'Lawyers must ever be good actors and play their part boldly for the greater good.' Yet he frowned, and was sharp with the petitioners who followed. The cases came and went, while outside the wind had risen to a gale. We heard shutters banging around the castle keep.

'Well, that is done,' Giles said when the last petitioner had gone. He looked at Waters. 'Another day should finish matters.'

'You have proceeded with admirable dispatch, sir,' Waters said. 'If we meet at noon tomorrow, that should be enough time to finish the business.'

I found myself thinking sadly of my arbitration of the Kent land disputes, and the injustice that had been done to Sergeant Leacon's family as a result. 'Barak will draw up the orders for us,' I said. 'Shall we send you copies, Master Waters?'

'Ay.' He stretched out his legs. 'How goes it at King's Manor? I hear Sir William Maleverer is in charge of the King's security.'

'Yes. Do you know him?'

'No, I work in the administration. But he is known as a fierce fellow. All fear his swaggering ambition.' He smiled maliciously. 'But men are often like that where there's a taint of bastardy.'

'I heard that story.'

''Tis said he has decided not to marry till he has accumulated so much land people will not care about his origins. They say he was much in love with a Neville girl when he was young, but she would not have him. With their Yorkist blood they are a proud old family. She turned him down because of that whiff of bastardy.'

'Really?' It reminded me of Maleverer's comment when I had mentioned Cecily Neville's name on that family tree. 'Everything starts with Cecily Neville,' he had said.

'That would make him bitter,' I observed.

Waters nodded. He looked at me. 'Sir William's mother and father — well, his supposed father — went as part of the train that accompanied Queen Margaret to Scotland, when she married the Scotch King's father forty years ago. Sir Martin Maleverer had to return early. His wife came back with the ladies many months later with a baby, and he doubted it was his. Not even born in this country.'

I sat up, for Waters' words had rung a bell. What the *Titulus* had said about Richard III: 'Ye be born within this land; by reason whereof you may have more certain knowledge of your birth and filiation.' I drew a sharp breath. That must mean one of his siblings was not. Someone had a taint of bastardy. I tried to remember how the lineage ran.

'Brother Shardlake?' Waters asked. 'Are you all right?'

'Er, yes.'

'You were in a brown study,' Giles said with a laugh.

'I am sorry—' I broke off at the sound of a great shout from outside, the sound of running feet. 'What on earth?'

Giles and Waters looked at each other in surprise, then rose and went out. Barak and I also exchanged a glance. I shuddered. The commotion had brought back the cries and yells in the church the night before.

'Shall we see?' Barak asked.

We descended the steps to the castle bailey. There servants and clerks were standing around, heedless of the rain, watching as soldiers spilled from the guardhouse. They ran up the mound to where the castle keep stood. At the bottom of the keep I saw a pile of chains and bones strewn across the grass. Master Waters crossed himself. 'Jesu. Aske's skeleton. The wind has brought it down.' I watched as the guards ran to the white bones and began picking them up, making them safe from relic hunters.

'That this should happen while the King is here.' Wrenne laughed softly, then raised his eyebrows at me. 'People in York will take this as an omen.'

Chapter Twenty-eight

MALEVERER STARED WHEN, an hour later, I explained how Broderick had worked his own poisoning. Then he shook his head and gave a bark of laughter. He looked at me across his desk, a smile playing at the corner of his lips as he ran his finger along the edge of his beard, as he liked to do.

'By Jesu, you're a clever fellow. So Broderick outwitted Radwinter.' He laughed again. 'God's body, that gaoler's reputation will never be the same when this gets out. I told him to keep to his room. Well, now we know nobody else was involved I suppose he can go back on duty. You have rescued him from suspicion, Brother Shardlake.'

'I would not have anyone under false suspicion. Even Radwinter.'

Maleverer's smile turned into a cruel smirk. 'Jesu, sir, you are a righteous prig. I wish I could afford your scruples.'

I said nothing. He turned and stared out of the window, to where workmen were tying thick ropes across the royal tents to secure them against the wind. I studied his heavy dark face, wondering if it was angry shame at the taint of bastardy that drove this relentless, cruel man. Strange to think that he too knew mockery and heard the laughter behind his back.

'Those tents can't stand there for ever,' he said. 'Damn the Scotch King.'

'Still no word of his arrival, sir?'

'That's not your business.' He changed the subject. 'I'll tell Radwinter he can go back to work. And you're still to keep an eye on Broderick. Visit him at least once a day, without fail. He might try something else.' He looked at me speculatively. 'If Broderick's poisoning was all his own doing, that means it's only you someone is trying to kill.'

'It seems so.'

'Make sure you do as I ordered, keep your randy clerk with you. That's all.' He waved a quill dismissively, and I bowed and left. As I walked away I felt more determined than ever to say nothing to Maleverer about what had happened with the Queen and Culpeper; I could not trust him a single inch. He disliked me strongly; he would do me ill if he could.

✝

OUTSIDE THE WIND WAS dropping, though still blowing hard. Barak was waiting for me. As we walked past the pavilions I saw a familiar plump figure going into the church: Master Craike, his robe billowing round his ankles.

'Here's the chance to resolve another mystery,' I said.

The church was a hive of activity. Grooms went to and fro, straw and dung lay everywhere, and forges flared red in every side-chapel. In the daylight I saw the walls were smeared with dirt and graffiti, crude drawings of bare-breasted women and men with gigantic penises.

'Where is he?' Barak asked.

'He's probably gone to the belltower.' I paused and looked at a charred heap of straw that had been piled against the wall; the bear's body was long gone.

Craike had disappeared by the time I reached the door to the belltower, but the guard confirmed he had gone up. We found him sitting on a stool, a picnic meal on his knee, staring out of the window. He looked up at me in surprise. 'Why, Master Shardlake, what brings you up here?' His greeting was cheerful but his eyes, again, were watchful. He smiled at the bread and cold meat spread on a cloth on his lap. 'I have had a busy day, I thought to escape up here and have some food. I never tire of looking out over the camp. It is a strange thing to watch it from up here, like a bird on the wing.'

I looked from the window, screwing my eyes up against the wind that whistled round the belltower. I saw again, in the fading light, the hundreds of men sitting before the tents, playing cards or watching cockfights. Campfires were lit, the wind blowing the smoke in all directions. A large group of workmen were digging fresh latrines near the ranks of carts. Craike came and joined me.

'They are having problems with the sewage,' he said. 'You can imagine, with more than two thousand in the camp it becomes disgusting if they stay in one place more than a few days. There's fields along the route so choked with filth they'll not be able to use them for years. They're worried about it all getting into the river, killing the fish. Filth will seep out, you see. It seeps out.'

I looked at his plump, bland face, then took a deep breath. 'Master Craike, there is something I must discuss with you.'

'Indeed. You sound serious, sir.' He looked from me to Barak and laughed nervously.

'It is serious.'

He went and sat back down on his stool.

'You remember that box?' I asked. 'That was stolen from me, in your old office?'

'I am hardly likely to forget, sir.'

'You know it was important.'

'I know I was roughly searched by Maleverer's men. He told me to say no more about the matter, and I have not.'

'Barak saw you a few nights ago, going into an inn in York. To the White Hart.'

He looked at Barak and I caught a flicker of fear in his eyes.

'What has that to do with the hunt for that wretched box?' There was a tremor in his voice.

'We were there last night. And I learned the innkeeper there can arrange to provide — well, certain women . . .'

A shudder ran through Craike's body then, and his face turned scarlet.

'Is that why you went there?'

He did not reply, but buried his face in his hands.

'Come,' I said sharply. 'Answer me.'

His voice was a shaky whisper. 'I am ashamed. Ashamed to show you my face.'

'I have no wish to shame you, Master Craike. Look at me.'

With a great sigh, he lifted his face to me. He looked suddenly old, his red face haggard, tears in the corners of his pale blue eyes.

'That inn is a hateful place,' he said. 'But Jesu knows I have seen enough like it in London. Oh, I may seem like a fellow who has succeeded in life, I know.' He laughed bitterly, then began talking rapidly, words tumbling over each other. 'I have a wife, children, a good position, respect. But – but you do not know me, I am a bad unworthy man, a sinful man. The priests who taught me as a child knew that, they mocked me and – and hurt me. And I need to be hurt, 'tis only then I feel safe.' He laughed then, with such hollow bitterness it made me shudder.

What he said should have disgusted me but I only felt sorry for him, caught as he was in some trap of the mind I could barely comprehend.

'How did you find it?' I asked. 'Was it through the glazier Oldroyd?'

'No. I sounded him out about the brothels in the town, said I was asking on behalf of the officials who would be coming, but he knew nothing. He was a respectable man. No, I asked others in the city and they led me to the White Hart.'

'Well, if that is all,' I said, 'it is no business of mine.'

'If that is all.' He sighed again, as though he would wrench out his heart. His expression changed, seemed to shift from his private hell to the real world again. 'It is not all. There is a house I frequent in Southwark. The madam there is a paid spy of Sir Richard Rich.'

'Rich,' I said slowly. 'I know that Cromwell used such methods.' I glanced again at Barak.

'And when he was executed Rich took over his networks. Paid

those in charge of certain houses to give him names. Oh, I was of no interest to Lord Cromwell, I was too lowly. But Rich is a different matter. You know my work, I allocate accommodation to courtiers in the King's London palaces as I do here.'

'Yes.'

'And Sir Richard Rich hungers for property like no man in England. And if I certify to the Chamberlain that this or that London house that belonged to some monastery is unfit to accommodate courtiers, then it will be sold cheaply. And Richard Rich will be ready to snap it up.'

'He is blackmailing you?'

'If I do not cooperate with him he will tell my wife. She is a fierce woman, sir. She would leave me, tell the world of my sins and I would never see my children again.' The tears began flowing down his cheeks. Then, suddenly, he brushed them aside and looked at me defiantly. 'Well, that is the truth. Nothing to do with your stolen box or the attack on you. If you tell, you will incur Sir Richard's wrath, I warn you, and that is no light thing. And ruin me.'

'Is he putting pressure on you now?'

'Yes. Maleverer wants a London house. There is a property near Smithfield that is in royal ownership. He and Rich will share the difference between the price I set for the London house and its true value.'

'I see,' I said. 'Maleverer is trying to get hold of land up here too, I think.'

'I know nothing of that. I beg you, sir,' Craike said. 'Keep my secret.'

'I will say nothing, Master Craike. None of this is any concern of mine.'

'Truly?' I saw hope rise in his face.

'I swear. I would help you if I could. It seems to me Rich is the greater rogue in this.'

He sagged with relief. 'Thank you. Thank you. And . . .'

'Yes?'

'You do not even mock me,' he said wonderingly. 'Most men would.'

I looked into Craike's haggard face, and wondered at the strange darkness that lay behind it. But then darkness lies behind so many faces.

'I know mockery too well,' I answered.

☦

I HAD TO VISIT BRODERICK before I went to my next task, which was to ponder on that royal family tree, and what the *Titulus* had said about Richard III's being born in England. I felt buoyed by my successes at the castle, and by my conversation with Craike.

Sergeant Leacon was standing guard with one of his men outside Broderick's cell. He nodded to us stiffly.

'All well?' I asked.

'Ay. He's just lain on his pallet all day. Won't talk to the man I have posted with him.'

'I have solved the mystery of how the poison reached him.' I told the sergeant of my discovery at the castle. 'I think Radwinter will be back soon.'

He shrugged. 'I hoped we had seen the last of him.'

'I fear not.' I took a deep breath. 'Sergeant, I have to thank you and your men. For shooting the bear last night. I fear if you had not arrived when you did, it would have had me.'

'We were just doing our duty,' he said stiffly. 'Though I wondered if it was a ruse to distract me and free the prisoner; I wondered whether it was safe for us to lock Broderick up and go to the church.'

'Thank Jesu you did. I shudder to think what might have happened had you not been so close.'

He nodded, but his look was still cold.

'Sergeant,' I said, 'I have been thinking on your parents' troubles. That it seems I helped land them in. It struck me: I made that arbitration without knowledge of any underleases or copyholds. Do your parents have any documents about their tenancy?'

He shook his head. 'No. The manor court records were destroyed in a fire years ago. But they always thought they were tenants of the monks.'

'I did not have that evidence before me. It might have made a difference, especially if any records could be found.'

'My parents can barely read or write,' he said awkwardly. 'They rely on my uncle, and he is no great reader either. And they are not people who can afford a lawyer.'

'How long before they have to be out?'

'Six months. Spring quarter-day.'

'Listen, sergeant, I feel some responsibility for this. When we get back to London, if you wish, I could try to help.'

'I told you, my parents have no money for a lawyer.'

'I would do it for nothing. *Pro bono*, as we say.'

His face lightened a little. 'Would you, sir? If you could help . . .'

'I cannot guarantee anything. But if I can, I will.'

'Thank you.' He looked at me. 'I confess I cursed you hard when I learned of your involvement.'

'Then undo the curse. I have had enough of those recently.'

He smiled. 'Right readily, if you will aid us.'

'Well,' I said, a little embarrassed, 'I must see how Broderick fares.'

Leacon shook his head as he reached for his keys. 'Why do folk bring themselves to such a dreadful place as he is in? Is there not enough trouble in the world?'

✝

BRODERICK LOOKED PATHETIC when I entered his cell, lying pale and drawn on his pallet. I stood looking down at him. A candle had been lit against the gathering dusk and it made deep shadows of the premature lines in his young face. He looked up wearily.

'You have something to drink?' I asked.

He nodded at a pitcher on the floor. 'Ay.'

'I know how you did it, Sir Edward,' I said quietly. 'The poison. You took those horrible toadstools from the drainpipe, didn't you?'

He looked at me for a long moment, then let his eyes fall. ''Tis all one now,' he said apathetically. 'I failed. And now you have moved me there will be no more chances.'

'Your very being must have cringed when you forced those things into your mouth.'

'It did. I forced them down with water, held my nose to avoid that smell.'

'Yes. The smell.'

'But it did no good. My body voided them.' His face twisted in a spasm of anger.

'Listen,' I said. 'Why not talk now, give them what they want? They will torture it out of you in the end. There is no virtue in pain. You may be able to negotiate a pardon if you talk; it has been done before.'

He laughed then, a harsh croaking sound. 'You think I would believe their promises? Robert Aske did, and consider how they served him.'

'His skeleton fell from the castle tower today. The wind blew it down.'

He smiled slowly. 'An omen. An omen the Mouldwarp should take note of.'

'For an educated man, sir, you talk much nonsense.' I studied him, wondering how many of the answers I sought might lie within his scarred breast – the connection between the Queen's secret and the conspirators, the contents of that box of papers. But I was forbidden to probe his secrets.

'If King Henry is the Mouldwarp,' I asked him suddenly, 'who then is the rightful King? Some say the Countess of Salisbury's family.'

He gave me a crooked smile. 'Some say many things.'

'Prince Edward is the rightful heir, is he not, the King's son?' I paused. 'And any son Queen Catherine may have after him. There have been rumours she is pregnant.'

'Have there?' No flicker in his eyes, only an expression of amused contempt. He laughed coldly. 'Are you turned interrogator, sir?'

'I was merely making conversation.'

'I think you do not *merely* do anything. But you know what I would like?'

'What?'

'To have you with me in that room in the Tower, while they work me. I would have you watch what your good custodianship will bring me too.'

'You should talk now while your body is still whole.'

'Go away.' Broderick's voice was full of contempt.

I sighed, and knocked on the door for the guard. As I stepped outside, I saw with a sinking heart that Radwinter was there. His eyes looked tired, the skin around them dark. His arrest had told on this man who loved his authority. He stood glaring at Barak, who leaned against the wall, a picture of studied nonchalance.

'So,' Radwinter was saying. 'I hear your master found out how Broderick poisoned himself.'

'Yes. Broderick did it cleverly.'

'He will get no further chance. I am restored to my duties.' He turned to me. 'Maleverer says I have you to thank for that.'

I shrugged.

'And you will enjoy the thought I am beholden to you,' he said bitterly.

'I do not care,' I said. 'I have other matters to think about.'

'I put you down once,' Radwinter said. 'And I will again.' He shouldered his way past me, almost knocking me into Barak, and called sharply to the soldier to surrender the keys to the prisoner's cell back to him.

Chapter Twenty-nine

B ARAK AND I SAT IN my cubicle at the lodging house. Between us on the bed was the piece of paper on which I had copied out again, from memory, the family tree I had found in the box. A lamp set precariously on the bed cast a dim yellow light over the royal names.

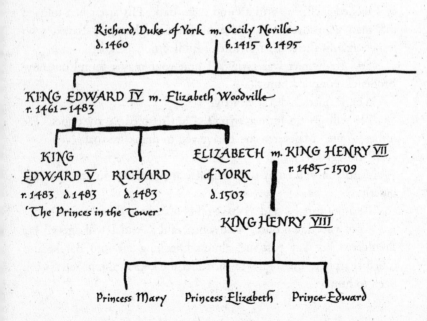

Richard, Duke of York m. Cecily Neville
d. 1460   b. 1415 d. 1495

KING EDWARD IV m. Elizabeth Woodville
r. 1461 – 1483

KING   ELIZABETH m. KING HENRY VII
EDWARD V   RICHARD   of YORK   r. 1485 – 1509
r. 1483 d. 1483   d. 1483   d. 1503
'The Princes in the Tower'

                                    KING HENRY VIII

Princess Mary   Princess Elizabeth   Prince Edward

'How can this lead us to who attacked you?' Barak asked wearily.

'The answer is always in the detail,' I said, frowning at it. 'Bear with me,' I continued. 'Now, the *Titulus* stressed that Richard III was born in England, which gave "*more certain knowledge of your birth and filiation*". I have been thinking. I think they were saying between the lines that one of Richard's brothers was a bastard.'

'You said yourself the *Titulus* seemed to be scraping together everything, no matter how shaky, to justify Richard usurping the throne. Where is the evidence?'

I looked at him. 'Perhaps in that jewel casket?' I pointed at Cecily Neville's name at the head of the tree. 'If one of her children was a bastard that would explain Maleverer's remark when the box went missing. "Cecily Neville. It all goes back to her."'

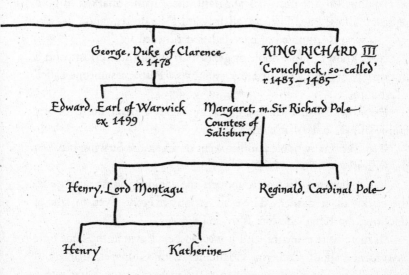

Barak stroked his chin. 'There are two sons beside Richard III.'

'Yes. George Duke of Clarence who was the father of Margaret of Salisbury, who was executed this year, and Edward IV. The grandfather of the present king.'

'If the Clarence line were being called into question, that would be useful for the King. He'd want to make it public.'

'And the conspirators would not. They'd have destroyed any evidence, not kept it hidden and protected. So the allegation must have been aimed at Edward IV, the King's grandfather. Whom it is said he much resembles.'

Barak looked at me with a horrified expression. 'If Edward IV was not the son of the Duke of York—'

'The one through whom the royal bloodline runs — in that case the King's claim to the throne becomes very weak, far weaker than the Countess of Salisbury's line. It rests on his father's claim alone, Henry Tudor.'

'Who had but little royal blood.'

I pointed to the tree. 'If I am right, those names marked in bold represent a false line. They are all Edward IV's descendants.'

'So who is supposed to have fathered Edward IV?'

'Jesu knows. Some noble or gentleman about the Yorkist court a hundred years ago.' I raised my eyebrows. 'Perhaps someone called Blaybourne.'

Barak whistled, then thought a moment. 'I never heard of any family of note with that name.'

'No. But many noble families went down in the Striving between the Roses.'

Barak lowered his voice, though the lodging house was quiet, the clerks all at dinner. 'These are serious matters. Even to talk of doubting the King's descent is treason.'

'If there were evidence, and it were to be released at the same time as evidence about Catherine's dalliance with Culpeper, that could truly rock the throne. It would turn the majesty of the King into a complete mockery.' I laughed incredulously.

'It's no laughing matter.' Barak was looking at me narrowly.

'I know. Only – great Henry, nothing more than the descendant of a cuckoo in the royal nest. If I am right,' I continued seriously, 'the information the conspirators had was the most potent brew imaginable, challenging both the King's own legitimacy and that of any children Catherine Howard may have. I imagine it was planned to reveal it when the rebellion got under way. Only it never did, the conspirators were betrayed before it could start.'

'Betrayed? Don't you mean discovered? The informer did the country a service.'

'Discovered, then. And the papers were spirited away, hidden in Oldroyd's bedroom.' I looked at him. 'Until the time was ripe to try again. Broderick told me once the King would fall soon. Perhaps he meant, when all this comes out.'

'You think another rebellion is brewing? But York is sewn up tight. There's never been such a well-guarded city.'

'It's quiet now, but when the Progress leaves the soldiers will go too. Then York will be left to the local constables, and who is to say where their sympathies lie? And the people here have hardly welcomed the King. Remember what Master Waters said about the Council of the North not being able to afford to have a city full of discontented traders. Cranmer himself admitted they hadn't got to the bottom of the conspiracy. Many leaders escaped and the authorities are still after information from those locked up on suspicion, like Jennet Marlin's fiancé.'

'And Broderick. But it's all supposition. Dangerous supposition too,' Barak added.

'Is it? It explains the wording of the *Titulus Regulus*, and the way that family tree is set out. And Maleverer's remarks about Cecily Neville.'

'It doesn't help us towards guessing who is trying to kill you.'

'No. But it shows why someone connected to the conspiracy would want me dead if they thought I had read what was in those papers. Perhaps they know my links to Cranmer and think I am waiting to get back to London and tell him the story, leaving Maleverer out of the picture.' I got up, opened the lamp and set the scribbled family tree alight.

'Is that necessary?' Barak asked.

'Oh, I think so.' It burned quickly; I dropped the remains on the floor and stamped on them. I stood thinking a moment, then turned to Barak. 'What would you do, if you were a member of the conspiracy who had escaped arrest? Perhaps hiding out in some refuge with that cache of papers?'

He considered. 'I'd wait till the Progress and all the soldiers were safely back in London. Then I'd try and revive my networks in the north, being very careful about informers this time.'

'And keep your networks in the south going too. At Gray's Inn perhaps.'

'Then I'd raise my standard when the time was ripe. And make any proof I had about Henry's ancestry, and Queen Catherine, public. I'd probably wait till the spring. A winter campaign would be hard, with men to feed and clothe.'

'That's what I'd do too. And if Catherine Howard was pregnant by then, so much the better when her dalliance with Culpeper was exposed.'

'What about all the oaths the local gentlemen have taken to the King? If there was evidence the King was not the true King, would those oaths still be valid?'

'No. No, that would overturn everything.'

Barak shook his head. 'So Maleverer could end with *his* head above the gates of York?'

'Possibly.' I sat down again. 'And part of me thinks, would that not be a sort of justice, seeing how sore oppressed the people are here?'

Barak frowned. 'Those conspirators would have the Pope back, and they'd have allied with a foreign power. The Scotch, and where you find the Scotch, the French are never far behind.'

'A sea of blood could be spilled,' I said.

Barak scratched his head. 'Do you think . . .'

'What?'

'That the King knows the Blaybourne story? Knows he may not be the legitimate heir. He must do. Maleverer took the name to the Duke of Suffolk, and that was when the hue and cry started. If the Duke knows, the King knows.'

'So he knows he may not be the true King, but carries on anyway?'

'Wouldn't you?'

'I suppose I would,' I answered. 'But he doesn't know about Catherine and Culpeper. He can't. And I am not going to Maleverer with the story. If he got wind I'd worked out what the *Titulus* meant, our lives might be worth little.'

'Dead men tell no tales, eh?'

'I wouldn't put it past him. The King can't stay here for ever. And we have passage booked on a fast boat from Hull.'

You should tell Cranmer when we get back,' he said.

'We'll see.'

'Tamasin will have to return with the Progress. That could take weeks. She doesn't show it but she is frightened after Lady Rochford's interrogation.' He looked at me and in that moment I saw how much she had come to mean to him. 'Is there any chance you could get her a place on the boat?'

'That may be difficult. There is no official reason for her to return early.'

'We could make up some story about a sick relative.'

'I'll do what I can,' I said. 'But let's wait till we get to Hull.'

'Thank you.' Barak looked relieved. 'Why is the King going back to Hull, anyway? He's already been there once.'

'He has plans for strengthening the town's defences.'

'It's a long way to drag the Progress.'

'He's the King. He can do what he likes. And I must get Giles a place on the boat too. I feel a responsibility for that old man. It is as though he had taken the place of my father.'

'Poor old devil. You wouldn't think he was so ill to look at him. And he was sharp enough at the hearing today.'

'Yes, he was. But Dr Jibson says there is no hope for him,' I answered heavily.

'You didn't agree with him about turning away that woodsman's claim?'

'No. But he knows the political realities up here.'

'Will we be able to finish with the petitioners tomorrow afternoon?'

'Ay. Then our work will be done.'

'Perhaps we could go to town in the morning. Get a break from this place.' He reddened. 'Tamasin said she and Mistress Marlin are going shopping tomorrow. For some sewing materials to repair the Queen's linen. I said I might be at St Helen's Square around ten thirty. I haven't seen her today. But I'm supposed to stay with you.'

'I'll have to come too then. Be your chaperone. It's all right. I could do with getting out of here too.'

✝

NEXT MORNING DAWNED fine and sunny, but with a chill wind. The King, they said, had gone hunting again. We set off into the city. It was market day and York was busy; we passed officials from St Mary's arguing with some merchants, evidently buying up more stores.

Tamasin had told Barak she and Mistress Marlin would be visiting a shop in Coneygate that sold fine fabrics. We arrived in St Helen's Square shortly after ten. I glanced down Stonegate towards Oldroyd's house, remembering the day the glaziers had surrounded us there. We might have come to grief if Master Wrenne had not happened along then. On the other side of the square people were going in and out of the Guildhall.

Barak nodded at St Helen's church on the corner. Where the churchyard faced the street, a bench had been set under a tree.

'Let's sit there for a bit,' I said.

'You've taken a fondness for sitting under trees.'

'Your back is safe against the bark,' I said quietly. 'And you can see who's coming.'

'They have to pass this way to return to St Mary's,' Barak said. 'It'll look as if we've just stopped for a rest.'

We entered the churchyard and sat on the bench. The graves were covered with fallen leaves, red and yellow and gold. It was a restful spot.

Barak nudged me. 'There's the Recorder waving at us,' he said.

I looked up. Recorder Tankerd had come out of the Guildhall. Seeing him reminded me of Fulford. I waved back and he came over to us.

'Taking a rest, sir?' he asked. His look at me was curious, appraising. Perhaps he wanted to report back to his colleagues about how I looked after being mocked by the King. Well, no doubt I looked tired and strained, though there were other reasons for that.

'Ay. We have a morning's leisure before tackling the rest of the petitions this afternoon.'

'Have the hearings gone smoothly?'

'Very well. Brother Wrenne knows what he is doing.'

'No lawyer in York is more respected. But he is taking on no new work, I hear. Perhaps he is retiring at last.'

'He is ripe in years,' I answered evasively.

'And has begun to look his age recently.'

I did not reply, and Tankerd smiled uncertainly. 'Well, I must be off. The council has been asked to press the Ainsty farms to deliver all their produce to St Mary's, even the seed corn. But they are offering a good price. It looks like it may be a while before the Scotch King comes. Well, good day.' He paused a moment, then said quietly, 'What the King said to you was shameful, sir. I am not the only one who thinks so.'

I looked up in surprise. 'Thank you.' I paused. 'They do not all laugh, then, at the Guildhall?'

'By no means, sir. It was a cruel jest, it has not improved the King's reputation.'

'Thank you, Brother Tankerd. That is good to know.'

He bowed and left us. I sat watching him go.

Barak nudged me. 'Here they come.' I looked up to where Mistress Marlin and Tamasin were walking slowly up the street. Behind them an armed servant carried a large box, full of sewing materials no doubt.

'Good morning!' I called.

The sun was behind us, and Jennet Marlin squinted frowningly for a moment before recognizing us. She hesitated.

'May we rest here a moment, mistress?' Tamasin asked sweetly. 'I have been standing all morning, I would be glad to sit down.' She certainly had skills in diplomacy.

Mistress Marlin looked at us, perhaps guessing this meeting was no accident. She hesitated, then nodded. 'Yes. Let us rest a few minutes.'

I stood up and bowed her to sit there.

'There is not room for all of us,' Tamasin said. 'Come, Master Barak, let us sit under that tree. I will show you the fine stuff we have bought.'

'Eh? Oh, yes.' Barak followed Tamasin as she led the way to a secluded spot under an oak. I was left with Jennet Marlin. The servant went and sat down on the grass at a respectful distance. I smiled at her uncertainly. 'Well, Mistress Marlin. How do you fare?' She looked tired and preoccupied, her large eyes unhappy. Untidy brown curls had escaped from her hood and she brushed them from her forehead. 'Have you any news from London?'

'No. And still no word of when we may leave this wretched city.'

'The Recorder says they are buying up still more provisions.'

'The men will be getting restless in camp, breaking out at night as they did at Pontefract.' She sighed deeply. 'By our Lady, I wish I had never been persuaded to come on this enterprise.' She looked at me seriously. 'Bernard, my fiancé, was supposed to accompany us.'

She hesitated. 'In fact, he was to have the job you have now. Working on the petitions.'

'Ah. I did not know.'

'First Bernard was arrested, then his first replacement died. Yours is an unlucky post.'

No wonder she had been so hostile at first. She seemed to have accepted me now, though, even to see me as a confidant. That pleased me; in an odd way it was as though little Suzanne and I had made friends again. I thought, I must stop seeing people as substitutes. Mistress Marlin for Suzanne, Giles Wrenne for my father.

'It was one of his friends persuaded me to come away,' she said. 'Another lawyer of Lincoln's Inn. When Bernard was taken to the Tower in April I visited him every day. But his friends said I might attract suspicion to myself, it might be better if I came away on the Progress. And Lady Rochford was very insistent. She is used to me dealing with her clothes for her.'

'I can see it must have been hard leaving London.'

'If there are any developments, I have leave to return to London. But nothing has happened for almost three months. Forgive me, sir,' she said suddenly, 'I must bore you with my talk.'

'No, no. I sympathize, madam.' I looked at her. 'How does your fiancé fare in the Tower? His friends will visit him?'

She twisted at her engagement ring. 'Yes, they bring him food and clothes, and he has a cell that is less miserable than most, above ground. We had to pay the gaolers well for that,' she added bitterly.

'I can imagine.'

'And yet I fear for his health in there. Winter draws near.'

'Perhaps he will be freed ere winter.'

She only sighed.

'His friends,' I asked. 'They are all from Gray's Inn?'

She looked at me sharply then. 'Why do you ask?'

'I wondered if he might know the nephew of a friend of mine.

Another Gray's Inn lawyer from the north.' I told her of Giles's determination to find his nephew, my offer to help.

She considered. ''Tis true the northern lawyers at Gray's Inn tend to stick together. Most of them are traditionalists in religion.'

'I believe this man is. Martin Dakin.'

'I do not know the name.'

'Have any other Gray's Inn lawyers been arrested? There was suspicion of them in 1536.'

'Not that I know of.'

'That is reassuring. Thank you. What chambers did your fiancé practise in at Lincoln's Inn?'

'Not *did*, sir, *does*. He will be free. The name of his chambers is Garden Court.'

'I am sorry. Thank you.'

She was silent a moment, then turned those large sorrowful eyes on me again. 'Do you know what my Bernard is accused of?'

'No, mistress.'

Her look was penetrating. 'I thought you might have heard, since it is common gossip.'

'No.'

'Of knowing two Yorkshire gentlemen who were part of the conspiracy. But they were both old friends, of course he knew them.'

'Did they say he was involved?'

'No, though they were tortured. They are dead now, their remains were on the Fulford Gate till it was cleaned up for the King.' She clenched her hands into tight little fists in her lap.

'Then there is no evidence.'

She looked at me. 'There was a letter that one of them sent to Bernard at Gray's Inn, at the end of last year. They say it speaks of better times coming this year. But Bernard told me it meant only hope for a better harvest after last year's drought.'

'If that is all, it seems paltry.'

'It takes little to condemn a man these days. Especially if he is fond of the old ways in religion. Oh, he is no papist, far from it, and I believe I was persuading him of the truth of Bible religion – so far as any woman can influence a man. But he was known as a traditionalist and that is enough to condemn him. If poison is whispered in the right ears.' She looked at me, her eyes sharp and focused now.

'Whose ears?' I sensed she had wanted me to ask.

'Bernard bought the land of a small dissolved abbey up here,' she said. 'It was next to his family lands.' Her mouth set tight and hard again. 'But a certain other family, whose lands it abuts on the other side, wanted it for themselves. It would suit their purposes if he were attainted for treason. So that his lands would go to the King, and could be bought cheap.' She paused. 'The family's name is Maleverer.'

I remembered the look of hatred she had cast at him at King's Manor when Tamasin was brought in for questioning.

'By heaven,' she said. 'He is hungry for land.'

'I know he is bidding for some of Robert Aske's estates and – and I believe he also seeks a property in London.'

'It is because he is a bastard.' Jennet Marlin almost spat the word. 'He believes if he can get enough land he can outrun it.' She looked at me. 'People will do any evil thing for money these days, there was never so much greed in the land.'

'There I agree with you, mistress.'

'But Maleverer will not win.' She clenched her fists more tightly. 'Bernard and I are destined to be together. It is meant.' She spoke quietly. 'People laugh at me, say I am determined to marry before I am too old—'

'Mistress,' I murmured, embarrassed at her frankness, but she continued.

'They do not understand what there is between Bernard and me. He was my childhood friend. My parents died when I was small and I was brought up in his household. He was three years older, he was father and brother to me.' She was silent a moment, then looked at me again. 'Tell me, sir, do you believe two people can be destined to be together, that God may set their path before they are born?'

I shifted uncomfortably. Her words sounded as though they came from some flowery poem of courtly love. 'I am not sure I do, mistress,' I answered. 'People fall in and out of love, or do not speak until it is too late. As I did once, to my sorrow.'

She looked at me, then shook her head. 'You do not understand. Even when Bernard married another, I knew that was not the end. And then his wife died, and he proposed to me. So you see, it is as it was meant.' She stared at me with a sudden fierceness that was unnerving. 'I would do anything for him. Anything.'

'I am sorry for your trouble,' I said quietly.

She stood abruptly. 'We should be going on.' She looked over to where Tamasin was showing a bored-looking Barak some richly dyed cloth. 'Tamasin,' she called. 'We should be on our way.'

Tamasin packed up the cloth, brushed some fallen leaves from her dress and walked across to us, Barak following. Mistress Marlin curtsied to me. 'Good morning, sir.' The women turned and walked out of the churchyard, the servant following. Barak shook his head.

'By Jesu, Tammy can be a tease. She made me look at those damned cloths, told me all about what they were. She knew it bored me, but I was a captive audience.'

'She'll domesticate you if you're not careful.'

'Never,' Barak said; emphatically, but with a smile. 'Sorry to leave you with Mistress Marlin.'

'Oh, it seems we are becoming friends.'

'Rather you than me.'

'She told me more about her fiancé. And I learned more about our good Sir William.' I told him what she had said about Maleverer and about Bernard Locke. 'Mistress Marlin seems to have given her whole life over to that man. Her heart and her soul.'

'Is that not a creditable thing in a woman?'

'What if something should happen to him? She would be quite undone.'

'Maybe you could step into his shoes,' Barak said with a grin.

I laughed. 'I do not think anyone could do that. Besides, Mistress Marlin's intensity would be hard to live with.' I looked down the road the women had followed. 'For her sake I hope they find nothing against Master Locke.'

Chapter Thirty

THAT AFTERNOON WE RETURNED to the castle to deal with the last of the petitions. Aske's bones had gone from the grass below the keep; there was nothing to show they had hung there save a thin red streak at the top of the tower. It looked like blood. Then I realized the chains must have rusted through.

I thought Giles uncharacteristically sharp with the petitioners, and I intervened a couple of times when he became impatient with some stumbling complainant. We finished around five, and Master Waters collected up his papers and bowed to us. 'Well, gentlemen,' he said. 'I bid you well on your journey to Hull.'

'Thank you,' I replied. 'Though Heaven alone knows when we get there.'

'Yes, the King appears seems set for a long stay.'

Waters left the room, and I turned to Master Wrenne. He looked pale and tired, and when he stood up his big body stooped. He had brought his walking stick today and now he leaned on it heavily, in a way that reminded me for a moment, oddly, of the King.

'Are you in pain, Giles?' I asked.

He nodded. 'Ay. Would tha walk home with me, give me your arm?'

'Of course,' I said, touched by the way he had slipped into the old Yorkshire usage. I helped him down the stairs and out to the street, Barak following on. Giles shivered in the cold wind.

'How long is the King going to let James keep him waiting?' he said anxiously. 'He's not coming!'

'We do not know what messages may be passing between here and the Scotch court.'

'He's not coming!' Wrenne repeated forcefully. 'Jesu, would you come into a foreign land and place yourself at the mercy of someone like Henry?'

Barak looked around him anxiously; fortunately no one was within hearing distance. 'Keep your voice down, Giles,' I urged him.

He spoke in lower tones. 'I speak the truth, as tha know'st. Oh, God,' he said with uncharacteristic vehemence. 'I want to make it to London.'

We left him with Madge and returned to King's Manor. I prayed for him to be given enough strength to make his last journey of reconciliation. We had arranged to meet Tamasin for dinner. There was a casual air in the refectory as we entered, people talking and joking and eating sloppily as they had before the King came; they were used to his presence now. Tamasin was sitting at the table we had made our own, at the back with a good view of the door. She wore a fetching blue dress, her bright gold hair unbound below a small coif and tumbling to her shoulders.

'Have you had a busy afternoon, mistress?' Barak asked her fondly.

'Quiet enough, the King and Queen have been away hunting for the day again. Good evening, sir,' she said to me, smiling.

'Good evening, Tamasin.' I sat next to Barak, feeling like a gooseberry. 'I will spend the evening in the lodging house tonight, I think,' I said. 'I have some papers to go over.' I did not, but it would allow them some time together. Tamasin, realizing my purpose, gave me a grateful smile.

'I had an interesting talk with Mistress Marlin today,' I told her. 'She told me more about her fiancé.'

'Poor Mistress Marlin. She tells everyone who will listen. She should take care her accusations do not get back to Sir William.'

'I doubt she cares. She seems to think of nothing but Master Locke's imprisonment.'

'Is that not understandable?' Tamasin asked. 'With the man she

has loved all her life in the Tower? Some of the maids make cruel
remarks, and cruel remarks can hurt—'

'I know that well.'

'Yet she has never burst out in anger, always held herself under
control. I could have wept for her sometimes.'

'She told me she thinks it is destiny that she and Master Locke
should be married. I am not sure that such a degree of devotion is a
healthy state of mind.'

Tamasin smiled, a smile that had something of steel in it. 'I
admire her determination.'

There was an uncomfortable silence for a few moments. Then
Barak leaned forward. 'There is something we should tell you,
Tammy. Master Shardlake was attacked again last night.'

'What?' She looked up at me and now I saw the strain in her
face and the shadows under her eyes. Barak told her about the bear.
When he had finished she took a long shuddering breath.

'So, but for the soldiers coming, you might have been killed?'

'Ay,' Barak answered on my behalf. 'If they had not been near,
guarding the prisoner.'

'The man Broderick?' she asked.

I looked at her sharply. 'How do you know about Broderick?
His presence here has been kept quiet.' I turned to Barak. 'Did you
tell her? The less she knows, the safer she is.'

He looked uncomfortable. 'Yes. But quite a few know.'

'We must be careful about what we say.'

Tamasin gave me look of unexpected hardness. 'I am always
careful, sir. Life has taught me that.'

'Tammy says Lady Rochford is watching her carefully,' Barak said.

'That she is.' As Tamasin helped herself to pottage from the
common bowl, I saw her hands were shaking, and realized again
the strain she had been under since that encounter with Culpeper.
She was good at hiding it but tonight it showed.

✝

A DAY PASSED, then another and another, and still there was no word of the Scotch King. The guards still stood before the pavilions and the tents, the surfaces of which were cleaned with fine brushes every day. One day, as Barak and I were walking in the courtyard, I saw Sir Richard Rich standing in the doorway of one of the pavilions. He was studying me coldly. We turned away.

'Any developments on the Bealknap case?' said Barak.

'No. I wrote to London, telling the council we should proceed, that I had hopes of the matter now. I doubt it will have got there; Rich will have ordered letters from me be intercepted before they leave with the postboy.'

'Then why write it?'

'So he could see my resolve stays firm.'

Barak raised his eyebrows, but said no more. I risked a backward glance. Rich had gone from the doorway.

✝

THE WEATHER STAYED FINE but grew colder; the leaves continued to fall in the courtyard and were burned in big smoking piles. I went to visit Giles again the next day. He had rallied but I could see his square cheeks had fallen in a little more. I dined alone with him, and he told me stories of the cases he had dealt with in York over the past fifty years; lawyer's tales, some funny and others tragic. Yet I sensed he had things on his mind.

'Giles?' I asked him at one point. 'Have you thought of writing to your nephew? You could send a letter by fast messenger.'

He shook his head firmly. 'No. Our quarrel was bitter, Matthew. He might ignore a letter. I need to see him face to face. Besides, I do not have his address.' He looked at me keenly. 'You think I am not up to the journey.'

'You know best, Giles.' I hesitated. 'By the way, what chambers did Martin Dakin practise in, before your quarrel?'

He looked at me. 'Garden Court. Why?'

'It will help us find him. He is probably still there.' I thought, the same chambers as Bernard Locke. That was a damned mis-chance. Or was it just a coincidence; there were not that many chambers at Gray's Inn, and I knew the northern lawyers tended to stick together. But I would not tell him, would not worry him unnecessarily.

At ten Barak called as arranged to accompany me home. As Giles saw me to the door he laid his hand on my arm.

'Thank you for your care,' he said. 'You watch over me like a son.'

'No, no,' I said. 'Only as a friend should. Thank you for a pleasant evening, Giles. It has taken my mind from my troubles.'

'Is your father's estate settled yet?'

'Soon. I have written to the mortgagee, told him I will have the balance of the funds when I get paid for my work here.'

'It will be sad, though, letting your father's farm go.'

'Yes.' And yet I had hardly thought of the farm at all. The realization I had no feelings for my childhood home made me guilty. I had a sudden vision of my father's face. He looked sad, disap-pointed.

'Is that all that troubles you, Matthew?' Giles asked. 'That girl and Barak looked mighty worried when she called the other day. And you seem – strained.'

'Official matters, Giles,' I said with an apologetic smile.

He raised a hand. 'Well, if you feel you can talk of them at any time, I shall be glad to listen.' He opened the door. I looked out at the dark narrow street. Barak, waiting outside, bowed. Giles looked between him and me. 'Come over on Sunday, both of you, and I will show you round the Minster. I think you have not seen it yet?'

'No.' With all that had passed, I had forgotten my wish to see inside.

'Bring that comely wench of yours, young Barak. It does me good to see her.'

'Thank you, Master Wrenne.'

'Good, then that is settled. Goodnight, Matthew, till Sunday.'

'Goodnight, Giles.' We walked away. As ever when walking in the dark I tensed, my eyes alert for a shadow in a doorway, a stealthy footstep behind.

I told Barak Giles's nephew had practised in the same chambers as Bernard Locke. 'When we get back to London,' I said, 'I am going to go to Gray's Inn privately before taking Giles there, find out what the position is.'

'If we ever get out of York,' Barak answered gloomily.

✝

THE FOLLOWING DAY we had an unwelcome reminder of our meeting with Lady Rochford. I had spent the morning with Barak checking the orders made in the arbitration hearings before delivering them to Maleverer's office; that was my last task in connection with the petitions. I walked across to King's Manor with Barak and delivered the papers to a clerk; we had arranged to meet Tamasin outside and go to the refectory to lunch. As the three of us walked away from King's Manor, my heart sank at the sight of Lady Rochford approaching with a group of courtiers. Culpeper was not there, but Francis Dereham was with her. We bowed our heads and hurried by, hoping they would ignore us.

'Mistress Reedbourne!' Lady Rochford's sharp voice behind us made us halt and turn. Barak and I bowed, and Tamasin curtsied deeply, as Lady Rochford approached us.

'What are you doing away from the manor, mistress?' Lady Rochford asked sternly. Her eyes raked Barak's face and mine, too. The other courtiers looked on with interest.

'I am going to the refectory, my lady. Mistress Marlin gave me permission.'

Lady Rochford gave us a haughty look. 'Mistress Marlin allows her servants too much latitude. Still, I daresay it will do no harm.' She stared at me. 'You are lucky to have a gentleman for a patron to accompany you. Though I hear you had an encounter with an escaped bear, Master Shardlake. That would have been most sad, if it had got you. You would have had to take all your lawyer's secrets to the grave.' She gave a harsh, nervous laugh.

I eyed her narrowly. Was this some sort of threat? But I thought, no, it has been put about the bear escaped by accident. She is only reminding us she has her eye on us. And, of course, she believed I had a record of what Tamasin and Barak had seen. I had written nothing down, but the threat was enough. 'Be assured, my lady,' I said steadily, 'I take care to keep all my secrets where they are most safe.'

'Be sure you do,' she said, then turned away quickly. We walked on, but after a few yards I heard footsteps behind me. Before I could turn I felt a hand laid on my shoulder and was yanked round. Francis Dereham was glaring at me, a savage frown on the saturnine features above his black beard.

'You hunchback churl!' Dereham hissed at me. 'I heard your words. How dare you speak to Lady Rochford with such disrespect. God's death, you get above yourself for a lawyer. I should hammer you into the ground for your insolence.'

I did not reply. Fortunately, Dereham made no move to further violence; no doubt remembering that violence within the precincts of the royal court carried serious consequences.

'You annoy me, crookback,' he said. 'And for someone of your rank to annoy someone of mine is not wise. Now, crawl on your knees to Lady Rochford, and apologize.'

I breathed hard. All around the courtyard people had stopped to watch the scene. I looked at Lady Rochford. She stood at the front of the group of courtiers and for once looked uncertain what to do. Then she stepped forward and laid a hand on Dereham's arm.

'Leave him, Francis,' she said. 'He is not worth the trouble.'

Dereham turned to her, anger turning to puzzlement. Reasonableness, I imagined, was not a quality Lady Rochford often showed. 'Would you let him get away with answering you back?' he pressed.

'It does not matter!' She reddened.

'What is between you and these people?' Dereham asked.

'It is you who forgets your place now, Francis,' Lady Rochford said, her voice rising. 'Do not question me.'

'Fie!' Dereham released my shoulder and stalked off without a word. Lady Rochford gave me a savage look that showed what she would have liked to do had I not had a hold over her, and walked off with a swish of skirts. The others followed.

'They say Dereham suspects there is something the Queen is keeping from him,' Tamasin said in a low voice.

'Then let us hope for all our sakes he does not find out what it is,' I said. 'Or at least, our connection to it.'

†

By Sunday there was still no word of King James; we had been in York now thirteen days. After lunch I met Barak and Tamasin in the courtyard to go to Master Wrenne's. The sky was dark and there was a thin, biting wind; we had wrapped ourselves warmly in our coats.

'I am looking forward to this,' Tamasin said cheerfully.

'It will get us out of St Mary's for a while,' Barak agreed.

We walked down Petergate to the Minster. I looked at the great east window of the cathedral that dominated the view as we approached, one of the largest stained-glass windows in Christendom. Strange how I had got used to seeing it, how it had become merely part of the view. Services were over, the streets quiet, but there were many soldiers about and more standing before the gates to the precinct. As we approached two of them crossed their pikes to bar our way.

'The King is visiting the Minster. What business have you here?'

The three of us exchanged glances. I would have preferred to turn back there and then, but that would have been discourteous to Giles. I showed the guard my commission and explained we had an appointment to visit a lawyer who lived in the precinct. The guard allowed us to enter, but warned that if the King's train approached, we must stand well out of the way and keep our heads bowed till he passed. I wondered if it was just my imagination or whether the guard cast a look at my back as he let us through, whether he had heard about Fulford.

The precinct was quiet, though many more soldiers were posted around, wearing half-armour over their red tunics and plumed helmets, and carrying pikes. I hurried Barak and Tamasin over to Wrenne's house. Madge, who greeted me pleasantly these days, showed us into the solar where Master Wrenne stood before the fire, staring sadly at the falcon's perch.

'Ah, Matthew. And Master Barak, and Mistress Reedbourne.' He smiled at Tamasin. 'It is a long time since I have welcomed a pretty maid as my guest.'

'Where is your falcon, Giles?' I asked.

'Poor Octavia is dead. Madge came in this morning and found her lying on the floor. She was very old. Yes, I had promised myself we should go out hunting together again, to see her fly once more and feel the sun. How easy it is to leave things undone until they are too late.' He gave me a sudden look of intense sorrow. He must be thinking of his nephew, I thought.

He forced a smile. 'Come, have some wine. We will have to wait awhile before we can go into the Minster, the King is there. So common mortals must wait.' Giles walked over to the table with his slow steady gait, poured us wine and bade us sit. He asked Tamasin about her time on the Progress, and she told stories of the Queen's servants and attendants and their problems in keeping up cleanliness while camping in muddy fields in the rain. She avoided mention of Lady Rochford. Wrenne encouraged her stories, he clearly enjoyed having her there. At length we heard voices outside, and a guard shouting, 'Fall to!' Giles crossed to the window.

'The soldiers seem to be going, the King's visit must be over. I think we may make our way across to the Minster now.'

'I would have liked to see the King,' Tamasin said. 'I only glimpsed him for a moment when he came to York.'

'You do not see him in the course of your duties?' Giles asked.

'No. Only the Queen occasionally, and I have never spoken with her.'

'Well, seeing His Majesty once can be enough, eh, Matthew?'

'It can indeed,' I replied feelingly.

✞

WE MADE OUR WAY outside and walked up the little street to the Minster forecourt. But we had miscalculated; Henry had not gone. Soldiers still lined the walls and the King, who had just descended the Minster steps, was stumping heavily towards us on his stick. There was a retinue of courtiers behind him, and a white-haired old man in robes like Cranmer's walked at his side, who I realized must be Archbishop Lee of York. The King, dressed today in a heavy fur-lined robe open to show his jewelled doublet and thick gold chain, was berating the old man; his face was red with anger, redder than his beard. We stood by the wall, bowing our heads – I bowed mine as low as it would go, praying the King would not recognize me and stop for another of his merry jests.

'God's blood!' we heard Henry shout in his hoarse, squeaky voice. 'That shrine is large and rich enough to hold the bones of a monarch, not a long-dead archbishop! Remove all those offerings and have the whole thing down! God's death, Lee, I will have either it or you in pieces on a dunghill, do you hear? You would have kept me from seeing it!' His voice rose. 'I ordered the shrines closed and I will have every one in England down. I will have no authority in religion save mine!'

His voice faded as he passed by. I ventured to look up. The courtiers were following now and the King was walking on. I looked at the back of his fur-collared, rich velvet coat. Was he really the grandson of some commoner? I trembled a little, as though my thoughts could somehow reach him. I saw his limp was very bad; without his jewelled stick I doubted he could walk at all. The soldiers peeled away from the walls and followed behind their master as he went through the gates.

'Well, Tammy,' Barak said. 'You got to see the King close to after all.'

'I did not know he looked so *old*,' she said quietly. 'Pity the Queen.'

'Pity all of us,' Giles said. 'Come, let us go in.'

✝

THE INTERIOR OF THE Minster was a wonder, the nave larger than St Paul's and more brightly lit. I stared around me through a light haze of incense. From the inside the magnificence of the stained glass was even more apparent, the great east window dominating all. In side-chapels and little niches, chantry priests stood quietly murmuring their masses. Again I thought of the strangeness of the pattern reform had taken in England: the great monastic church at St Mary's had been turned into a stable and smithy, while the Minster stood intact.

Tamasin pointed to a strange object, the painted figure of a long-necked dragon that hung over the nave. 'What is that, Master Wrenne?'

'A lever for the lid of the great font. A touch of decorative humour. Out of fashion these days.'

I walked to where Barak stood a little way off, looking at a richly decorated side-chapel. A little group of clerics stood nearby. One of them was the man Wrenne had pointed out as the Dean. He was looking grimly pleased. 'So do it,' he said. 'Commission the workmen.' He stalked away, his footsteps echoing on the tiled floor.

'He's been ordering them to take down a great shrine in the quire,' Barak told me. 'The King was furious when he saw all the offerings laid before it.'

'Earwigging, were you?' I asked with a smile.

'Might as well.' He shrugged. 'Can't say these old churches interest me.'

'Tamasin seems enthralled.'

'That's women for you.'

'Any word from London? About who her father might be?'

'None. She's stopped talking about it. I lost my temper with her, in fact.' He looked shamefaced. 'Told her she should let it go, stop thinking about it all the time. Seems to have done the trick, she's hardly mentioned it since.'

We went over and joined Tamasin before the quire-screen. It was decorated with a series of life-size figures that I recognized as the kings of England, from William the Conqueror to Henry V. They were exquisitely done. I counted them. 'Eleven,' I said.

'Are they not marvellous?' Tamasin asked.

'Yes.'

She pointed to the statues. 'Why does the row stop with King Henry V?'

'Good question. Master Wrenne may know.' I looked around for the old man, but there was no sign of him.

'He went off through there,' Tamasin said, nodding to the door to the quire.

'I will go and look. No, stay here,' I added as they made to follow. I hoped he had not been taken ill again; if so, I did not want the others to see.

I walked into the quire, lined with rows of high, beautifully decorated wooden pews. To one side stood an enormous, ornate construction in dark wood, richly adorned with pillars and arches. A decorated sepulchre was set atop a bier ten feet high, with niches carved in the side where people could kneel and pray. Offerings were hung on the bier: rosaries and rings and necklaces. Giles knelt in a niche, praying intently, his lips moving silently. Hearing my footsteps, he turned. He stared blankly for a moment, his mind far away. Then he smiled and rose stiffly to his feet.

'Forgive me,' I said. 'I did not mean to interrupt.'

'No, no, it was discourteous of me to leave you.' He waved at the shrine. 'Well, behold the shrine of St William, that so angered the King.'

'Who was he?'

'An early archbishop of York. It is said the Ouse bridge collapsed when he was crossing it in procession, but by divine intervention none were killed. He is the patron saint of the city; many come to pray for his intercession, as you see.'

I nodded uncomfortably. To me tales of centuries-old miracles had no meaning; and the shrine struck me overelaborate, even ugly.

'It seems those who say the King's passion for reform died with Cromwell were wrong,' Giles said. 'As we heard from his own lips, St William's shrine will be destroyed. It offends his great vanity.'

'It seems so,' I said quietly.

'Would you approve?' He gave me a sharp look.

'I confess saints and shrines mean little to me. But perhaps it is a shame to destroy it if it means so much to the people.'

'Now this too is to be taken from York.' He sighed. 'Well, let us go.' With a last look at the shrine, he turned away. We returned to the nave, where Tamasin and Barak still stood before the statues of the kings.

'Master Wrenne?' Tamasin asked him. 'Why do the Kings stop at Henry V?'

'Ah. There used to be a figure of Henry VI there, the Lancastrian king who was defeated in the Wars of the Roses. Many believed him to be a saint, and people would come and make offerings beneath his statue. The Yorkist kings did not approve, so the statue was removed.' He turned to me and raised his eyebrows. 'So you see, kings as well as saints may be written out of history.'

Two clerks walked past us, going into the quire. 'Tomorrow?' I heard one say to the other.

'Ay. He's tired of waiting, they're packing up tonight and going on to Hull in the morning. The King's said to be furious, perhaps that's why the shrine angered him so.'

I turned to him. 'Pardon me, sir. Is the King leaving?'

The old man smiled. 'Ay sir. First thing tomorrow. He has given up on waiting for King James. They're packing everything up at the camp already.' He smiled, evidently pleased at the news.

I turned back to my companions. Our faces lit up with relief. 'At last,' Tamasin said. 'God be praised!'

Chapter Thirty-one

WHEN WE RETURNED TO St Mary's we found the scene already transformed. The royal tents were being taken down, men carefully wrapping the rich tapestries and furnishings and loading them on to carts.

An official posted in the yard stopped us. 'Sirs, mistress. A moment please. Have you horses stabled in the church?'

'Yes.'

'Be sure you fetch them early tomorrow morning. All must be present in the courtyard by six.'

'That early?'

'Yes. The Progress is to be at Howlme on Spalding Moor by nightfall The King wants to shake the dust of York from his feet.'

'Where will we sleep tomorrow?' Barak asked.

'In tents, of course, in the fields. Howlme Manor is big enough only for the royal household. Sir, excuse me.' The official grabbed the arm of another man who had come in, and Barak grinned at Tamasin. 'You'll have to sleep in the mud tomorrow, Tammy.'

She tossed her head. 'The Queen's servants always have good tents.' She made a face. 'Well, usually.' We laughed, our hearts lifted by the thought of moving on at last.

'I had best check what the arrangements are for Broderick,' I said to Barak. 'I will see you later.'

'D'you not want me to come with you?'

I hesitated. But surely I was safe in full daylight. 'No. I will be safe among the soldiery. I will see you at the refectory in an hour.'

I left them and headed off to the cell. I thought about Giles. He had said he would arrive at King's Manor at dawn; I hoped he would be able to find us in the melee there was bound to be tomorrow morning. He had returned home, to prepare for the journey that would end in London.

✝

SERGEANT LEACON WAS standing guard over Broderick's cell with a soldier. I greeted them.

'Well, sir,' the sergeant said. 'So we are to be off at last. I am not sorry.'

'Me neither. What is to happen with Broderick?'

'He is to be put in a carriage with Radwinter. Sir William came and told us. He is relieved Broderick is to be moved at last. He will be in the Tower soon.'

'Ay.' I thought the news that had brought such relief to me only brought Broderick nearer to torture and death.

'My men and I will ride alongside the carriage.' The sergeant looked at me seriously. 'It is to be close guarded, sealed from the rest of the Progress.'

'How is he?'

'Quiet, as usual. Radwinter is in with him now. He is back in charge.' His face twisted with distaste.

I looked through the barred window. Broderick was lying on his bed, Radwinter kneeling beside him talking quietly. A candle was set by the bed. Broderick's eyes glinted as he turned to look at me. Radwinter stood, frowned for a second, then came and unlocked the door. He gave me his mocking smile. 'Master Shardlake. We have been looking forward to your visit, Sir Edward and I tire of each other.'

I entered the cell. It smelled rankly. 'He fares well?'

'Ay. And has eaten his meals like a good fellow.' I looked at Broderick. He did not look well to me; his face had a yellow tinge.

'He should have some exercise,' I said.

Radwinter shook his head firmly. 'No, he is not to be seen abroad. He is to be kept close till we reach London. Though it makes the hours hang heavy. To help them pass I have been telling Sir Edward tales of the Lollards' Tower, some of the prisoners I have known.'

Broderick raised himself on one elbow. 'He seeks to frighten me with accounts of the burnings and disembowellings he has sent people to. It is a relief to see even your long face, Master Shardlake.' There was a hint of patrician disdain in his voice, reminding me he had once been a man of status.

'We move on tomorrow, Sir Edward,' I said. 'Have you been told?'

Radwinter answered. 'Ay. I've to rattle in a closed carriage with him all the way to Hull.'

'We stop at a place called Howlme tomorrow night.'

Broderick nodded. 'I know it well. The manor house used to belong to Sir Robert Constable, Robert Aske's deputy in the Pilgrimage of Grace. Constable's remains hang over the gates of Hull now, and the King stole his house at Howlme. 'Twas a fine mansion.'

I grunted, then nodded my head at the door. 'A word, sir,' I said to Radwinter. He followed me outside, telling the soldier to sit with Broderick. Clearly he was not to be left alone for a minute now.

Radwinter leaned against the wall and stared at me interrogatively. Sergeant Leacon stood looking on, leaning on his pike.

'I am worried by how pale Broderick is. And that cell stinks. He needs air.'

'He'll be in the carriage tomorrow.'

'I am not sure he is fit to travel.'

'What you think does not matter. Those are the rules.'

I met his gaze. 'I remember Cranmer said a man died under your care once. Were that to happen again, with this prisoner, I would not envy your position.'

I wondered if he would burst out in mocking anger, but he only nodded and smiled again. 'We are all allowed one mistake, Master Shardlake. The circumstances were quite different. Shall I tell you what happened?'

'Well?'

He shifted his position, making himself more comfortable. 'It was seven years ago, when the King had not long married Anne Boleyn. There was a Dominican monk from a house in Hertfordshire who had come to London and was preaching that the King's break with Rome meant he was condemned by God. He was brought before the Archbishop but would say nothing about who was feeding and sheltering him. Your old master Cromwell wanted him taken to the Tower so the information could be racked out of him, but the Archbishop decided a sojourn in the Lollards' Tower might be sufficient to cool him down and loosen his tongue. He was put under my care and I was told to deal with him strictly, and find out what I could.'

'And?'

'He was quite unrepentant. When I gave him an English book of prayers to read he threw it across the cell. So I decided to bring him to his senses by hanging him from the ceiling by his wrists, his toes just touching the floor. I am told the Scotch have a variant where they hang you by your thumbs, but of course the thumbs are wrenched out after a while and I wanted this Brother Frederick to suffer a good while.'

I gave him a look of disgust, which perhaps was what he had been waiting for.

He smiled again. 'That silenced the good old brother. It is hard to breathe in that position, as well as very painful. But I had not realized Brother Frederick had a weakness of the heart. Oh, I should have considered the possibility, I see that now; he was fat and had a high colour and wheezed when he was led up the stairs to the

Lollards' Tower. On the second day I found him hanging dead in his chains. The Archbishop was sore angry with me, I confess. He sent me on a visit to the Tower, where I learned from the experts how to judge how much a man may take.'

'Cranmer did that?'

'Yes.' Radwinter inclined his head. 'So now I have the skill to weigh a man's condition.'

'You are a vile creature,' I said.

'You feel sorry for that monk, crookback? Well, reflect that his death was easier than being drawn and quartered for treason. I did the churl a favour.'

I turned away, but he called me back.

'I hear you have been talking to Broderick while I was away. About who has the right to the throne. You mentioned the Queen may be pregnant.' I looked at him in surprise. 'Oh, the soldier outside listened to your converse, as I ordered him to. You had strict orders not to question him.'

'It was merely conversation,' I said dismissively.

'Was it?' Radwinter looked at me. 'Sometimes I wonder if you have some private agenda, Master Shardlake, whether your concern for the prisoner is more than soft stupid pity. If it is, beware.'

✝

I THOUGHT ANXIOUSLY on Radwinter's words as I ate with Barak in the refectory. It was full of people snatching a quick meal before making their preparations for leaving. There was much shouting and calling, a palpable air of relief that the Progress was on the move again, on its final leg before the return to London.

I went over what I had said to Broderick a few days before. Nothing incriminating or dangerous. I had been careful, although I had not thought Radwinter would go so far as to get one of the soldiers to eavesdrop on me. He had bribed the man, no doubt. I wondered whether to report it to Sergeant Leacon, but decided to leave it. I must not take any risks with Broderick again.

'How long do you think it will be before we reach London?' Barak asked.

'Three or four days to Hull perhaps, then maybe a week on the boat. Much will depend on the weather while we are at sea. Quicker than riding back, anyway.'

'There's been no trouble for a week,' he said thoughtfully. 'Do you think maybe whoever attacked you has given up?'

'I hope so. I'm not relaxing my guard.'

He smiled. 'Well, in a couple of weeks we may be safe, back working at Lincoln's Inn. Back to the grind.'

My heart lifted. 'You're definitely coming back to work in Chambers?'

'Looks like it.'

'When we get to Hull I will try to secure a place for Giles on the boat, and Tamasin too. Someone might have to be bribed but between us Giles and I could manage that.'

'Thank you,' he said quietly.

✝

I SLEPT UNEASILY, for the work of moving and loading went on through the night, with a constant shouting and rattling of carts. I rose at the first light of dawn and dressed, putting on my coat and donning my riding boots for the first time since we had arrived. Some of the clerks were awake already, standing round the fire while one tried to light it. I gave them a cold nod and went outside.

It was a cool, damp day, the sky covered with a canopy of high milky cloud. Barak was already up, standing in the doorway looking out at the courtyard. It had been stripped almost bare. The paddocks that had housed the animals were being dismantled.

'St Mary's last moment of glory over,' he said. 'I hear the King has ordered the last windows taken out of the church, and the roof taken off.'

I looked at the church, its spire lost in mist again, remembering poor Oldroyd.

After breakfasting we walked to the church to fetch the horses. The carpenters were at work dismantling the pavilions now. What a vast amount of money and labour had been wasted. Servants from the royal household were carefully wrapping up a huge tapestry, glinting with gold leaf, in a waterproof cover. It was forty feet long and it took four men to roll it up, with infinite care, soldiers standing guard around the precious thing. There was a tremendous bustle around the main doors of the church, which had been thrown wide open. People were leading their horses out and taking their places among the groups that were forming all around the yard. We went inside into a great crush as people jostled up and down the rows of stalls, peering round the high walls in search of their animals. Most had already been saddled. I saw Sergeant Leacon among the throng. 'Are you riding today?' I asked.

'Ay, if I can get to my horse.'

I felt myself pushed roughly against a stall, and turned angrily. 'Make way there. Queen's household.' Surrounded by a retinue of servants who shoved aside everyone in their path, a group of courtiers was leading their horses towards the doors. I recognized Francis Dereham. Seeing me, he gave an unpleasant smile. The courtiers passed, and Barak and I returned to the stalls.

'Take care, sir, take care!' A woman's voice I recognized, calling sharply. I saw Jennet Marlin just ahead. A young courtier was trying to calm his horse, which was tossing its head and neighing, upset by the crowd. It threatened to flatten Mistress Marlin against a stall. Barak stepped forward. 'Look out!' he called. 'There's a woman there.' He helped the man calm the horse, while I gave Mistress Marlin my arm and helped her away from the animal. She gave me a startled look.

'You? Oh – thank you.'

'Are you seeking your horse?'

'Yes, she is down here somewhere.'

Barak and I helped her find the stall containing her animal, a grey palfrey, ready saddled.

'Come with us,' I said. 'We'll just find our own.'

She coloured. 'No, I am all right now. Thank you. I am obliged.' She took her horse by the reins and led it away.

'Doesn't like to be seen as a poor weak woman,' Barak said.

'She certainly has her pride.' We made our way to the stalls where Sukey and Genesis stood, ready saddled like the others. We led them out, not without difficulty for both were nervous. Barak's Sukey had always been temperamental but I was surprised how skittish my normally calm Genesis was.

'What a melee,' I said. 'This hasn't been well organized. Someone could be trampled.'

✝

IT WAS A RELIEF to get out of the church again. Little groups of men had formed all round the churchyard now, some mounted, some standing holding their horses: the households of the various nobles and officials and, by the gates, the King and Queen's households. There was, too, a clutch of lawyers and clerks, grouped around the white-bearded Sir James Fealty. I saw him glance at us and cross a couple of names off a list he carried.

Among the Queen's household I saw Tamasin sitting on a grey palfrey, next to Jennet Marlin on her palfrey, still looking a little flustered. Nearby Lady Rochford was resplendent in a plum-coloured cloak and sitting on a big black mare, next to Sir Richard Rich on a big grey. Looking at the King's household I was disconcerted to see Maleverer among the brightly dressed throng. Was he to accompany the Progress? It was not a thought that pleased me. I sensed someone else looking at me and glanced round just in time to see Thomas Culpeper turn his handsome head away.

Master Craike sat nearby, on a strong-looking roan. Mounted as he was, he still had his portable desk round his neck. He was riffling through papers, but he too caught my eye. He hesitated and I guessed he would have preferred not to acknowledge me, but he smiled uncertainly. 'Good day, Master Shardlake.'

'Master Craike.' I made my voice cheerful. 'By Jesu, there is great confusion in that stable.'

'Ay. I fetched my horse early.'

'You will be busy now we are moving again.'

'Yes, I leave in a minute. I have to ride ahead to Howlme Manor and see all is ready for the King.'

'I gather we should wait with the other lawyers.'

'Yes, ' he said, 'though you may be waiting some time. The royal households will pass out first, with the King and Queen, then the officers of the royal households and the households of the nobles. The various officials come next. I am afraid the lawyers are at the back. After you will come all the servants from the camp and the wagons. Everything must be done in the correct sequence.'

'Of course.'

He looked over to the manor house. A servant stood pruning the roses set round the side, carefully setting the thorny branches in a cart, oblivious to the noise and bustle all round. The manor, I assumed, would revert to its original function as a headquarters for the Council of the North. 'The King is in a great fury that James of Scotland has let him down,' Craike said. 'He threatens fierce measures against the Scotch. I think they will pay for this.'

'That would be –' I sought a neutral word '– characteristic of him.'

'Ay.' There was a moment's awkward silence, then Craike smiled nervously. 'Well, sir, I shall be on the move constantly now. I may not see you again.'

'In that case, farewell.'

'Farewell,' he said, and then, quietly, 'thank you.' He turned his horse and rode away to the gate.

Barak looked after him thoughtfully. 'Poor old arsehole,' he said.

'Ay. Still, Genesis!' My horse had jumped to one side with a whinny.

'Let's not mount just yet,' Barak said. 'Give the horses time to calm themselves.'

'All right. Look, there's Giles. But where's his horse?'

The old man had come in at the gates. He was carrying a heavy pannier and seemed flustered. He stood looking round, overtopping by a head many of those who walked around his burly form. I waved him over and he walked slowly across to us.

'Ah, Matthew,' he said breathlessly. 'There you are, and Barak, good morning. I fear I have a problem. My horse got a sharp stone in her shoe last night, she cannot possibly ride out. I did not know what to do.'

'There will be spare horses,' Barak said.

'Yes,' I agreed. 'But they will be over at the camp, we cannot get one now.'

'Take Sukey,' Barak said. 'I'll walk beside you. Then later I'm sure we can find a horse for you.'

Giles looked at him with relief. 'Thank you, young Barak. Are you sure?'

'Ay, take Sukey.'

'Genesis would be better,' I said. 'Barak's mare might not like being ridden by a stranger. I can ride Sukey, she knows me. You take Genesis. He is a calm horse.'

'Thank you again, sir.' Giles laughed uneasily. 'I do not know what I would do without you.'

An official came up and compared notes with Fealty, who turned and addressed us. 'I want you all mounted now,' he called out.

'Here, let me help you.' Barak formed a stirrup of his hands for the old man to mount Genesis.

He heaved himself up and settled himself carefully in the saddle.

Then, so fast it startled me half out of my wits, Genesis reared up on his hind legs with a dreadful scream. Giles cried out and grabbed frantically at the reins but the horse bucked to unseat him and to my horror I saw the old man plunge head-first from the saddle. He would certainly have dashed his brains out on the stone flags of the courtyard had not Barak stepped forward. Giles fell heavily on top of him and they both crashed to the earth, Barak letting out a yell as he went down.

People turned to look. Some exclaimed, others laughed. Master Wrenne rolled off Barak's body and sprawled on the ground, shocked.

'Giles!' I cried. 'Are you all right?'

'Yes. I – I think so. But what. . .'

'Jack?' I turned to Barak. He too tried to sit up, but groaned and fell back. His face was ashen. 'Shit!' he said thickly. 'My fucking ankle.' He looked at his left foot, which was bent at an unnatural angle.

I looked up at the crowd that was quickly forming around us. 'A physician!' I cried out. 'There's a man hurt here!' I saw two of the clerks had grabbed Genesis' reins and were holding him with difficulty. My normally calm old horse was still agitated, twisting his body frantically as though in pain. Then a little figure shoved through the gathering crowd and knelt by Barak. It was Tamasin, her face distraught. 'Jack!' she cried. 'Jack!'

'It's all right, wench, I've hurt my leg, that's all.'

'I heard you cry out, I thought someone—'

'No, 'twas just an accident.' He looked round at the crowd with embarrassment. Sir James Fealty appeared, frowning angrily.

'What in Jesu's name is going on here?' he demanded angrily. 'Get up, woman!' he snapped at Tamasin. 'This is unseemly!'

'My clerk has hurt his leg!' I said with asperity.

'Yes.' Wrenne got shakily to his feet. 'He saved my life,' he added.

I was aware the crowd had suddenly gone quiet, and looking up I saw Lady Rochford standing above us. There was something frightened in her expression.

'What has happened?' she asked.

Wrenne bowed to her. 'An accident, my lady. This man has broken his leg.'

She looked at Barak, then at Tamasin and me. 'Nothing worse?'

'No, my lady,' I said.

She stalked away, the crowd parting to let her through. 'Come,

Tamasin,' I said quietly, lifting her to her feet. 'You should go too. I will see Jack is safe.'

She gulped and nodded, then looked at Genesis, still straining against the men who held him. 'Why did the horse buck like that?'

'I don't know.'

'It is as though he were trying to get rid of the saddle.' She caught her breath. 'Look, sir, there is blood!' My eyes widened as I saw a thin trickle of blood running from underneath the saddle, staining the horse's flank.

'Tamasin,' I said quietly. 'Help me get this off. Be careful, or he'll buck again.'

Watched by the curious group of lawyers, we lifted off the saddle. My eyes widened with horror. Underneath was a little thorny piece of branch from a rosebush, the thorns embedded now in my poor horse's flesh.

'It was put here so the horse would rear when someone sat on it,' I breathed. 'This was another attempt to kill me.'

Chapter Thirty-two

ALL THE LAWYERS HAD seen us find the branch under Genesis' saddle, and word went round the courtyard like wildfire. I waited with Barak until a doctor from the royal household appeared and examined him. His ankle was not broken, I was relieved to hear, but he had damaged his ligaments. The doctor bandaged up his foot and warned he would be unable to walk properly for some time. A crutch was improvised from the branch of a tree and a servant was sent for, to help him to one of the carts which were waiting in line at the camp. He would have to travel to Howlme in it. The King and Queen had already ridden out, and the vast train of courtiers and officials was starting to move, one group after another riding under the gate of St Mary's.

'Damn this,' Barak said as the servant offered his arm. 'I hate being laid up.'

'You must rest your foot,' Giles said. 'I want to see you fit again soon. Thank you once more.'

'I am glad I saved you, sir.' Barak looked round the emptying courtyard at the horsemen riding out, the men on ladders removing the roofs from the pavilions, the big silent church. 'I'll not be sorry to leave here.' He hopped away with the servant. As he did so I saw a large figure walking towards us. Maleverer. Beside him was Sir Richard Rich, resplendent in a black robe edged thickly with fur. They halted before us, and Maleverer put his hands on his hips.

'Well?' he barked. 'I hear you've had trouble again.'

'That man can never keep out of it,' Rich added waspishly.

'What happened?'

I nodded to where the servant was still pruning the roses by the house. 'Someone got hold of a pruning from a rosebush and put it under my horse's saddle.' I raised the twig, which I was still holding.

Maleverer whistled. 'God's death, that's bold.'

'Not really. There was such a melee in the church, no one would notice who was in a particular stall. With their high sides someone could stand with their back to the open end and slip something under the saddle without being noticed.' I thought, Dereham was in the stable. And Craike said he had been in there early. It could have been any one of hundreds.

'Pox on it,' Maleverer said. 'This is a clever opportunist. So he has not given up, and we are no nearer finding him.' He frowned, and I thought, yes, you are using me as bait.

'Are you coming with the Progress, Sir William?'

'I am coming all the way to London. I have business there.' He smiled. 'You are not rid of me yet.' He looked at Genesis. 'What about your horse?'

'He won't let anyone ride him today.'

'We'd better find you another. Yours can be led behind. This will delay everything. The carts can't start moving till the officials have taken their place at the head of the Progress.' He glared at me as though I had sabotaged the arrangements on purpose. 'Wait there.' He strode off.

Rich smiled at me. 'I hope nothing else happens to you, brother. What would they do without you at the Guildhall?' He turned and followed Maleverer. Giles looked at me. He was pale, his brow furrowed with concern.

'Someone has been trying to kill you?' he asked, aghast.

I sighed. 'For some time. This is their third attempt.'

'But – but why?'

'I do not know. It may be because they think I saw the papers in that damned casket we found at Oldroyd's house.'

'You think it is the thief?' He looked shocked.

'Yes. And the irony is, I saw hardly any of the papers. Not

enough to understand their import. Giles, I am sorry, I have put you in danger too.'

'No wonder you have looked so strained,' he said. 'I had no idea.'

A middle-aged soldier with an untidy brown beard appeared, leading a large grey horse. 'My name is Templeman,' he said. 'I've brought this horse for you, sir; I've been told to lead yours.'

'Thank you.' I suggested Wrenne take this animal while I mounted Sukey. The soldier took Genesis' reins and followed us to the gate. I gave St Mary's one last glance and rode out.

†

WE RODE SLOWLY through York, the King and Queen and their households in front, then the nobility, then the officials with us lawyers at the rear. Behind us rumbled the great train of carts. Lines of mounted soldiers rode two deep on either side of us. It felt strange to be part of the great concourse, like being washed along by a vast river. The Yorkers had got used to us – there were few faces at the windows today. Those that were there looked grimly pleased to see the Progress leave at last.

We took a road that headed east, travelling at little more than a walking pace, the sound of hooves all around and the rumble and creak of hundreds of carts behind. The countryside was flat and low-lying, with ponds and water meadows. A wind blew across the flatlands, ruffling the horses' manes and tails and making the banners the soldiers carried wave and snap. Occasionally a man on horseback would ride along the grass verge between the road and the field, carrying messages between different sections of the Progress.

Towards noon the great train slowed as it crossed a humpbacked bridge across a fast-flowing river. 'The Derwent,' Giles said. 'It is full after all the rains.'

'So I see.' I looked at him. He seemed to have rallied from his shock, there was colour in his cheeks again. We rode on through the afternoon, along roads commanding a wide view of the flat empty countryside. I studied the grey sky and the wide misty horizon, realizing only now how crowded and claustrophobic St Mary's had been. The country was scantily populated, with only a few poor villages through which we rode without stopping. The inhabitants gathered in their doorways to watch us pass; mothers holding children tightly to them, faces expressionless.

Towards noon the order to halt for lunch was given. Everyone stopped but remained in their places while a procession of cooks brought baskets of bread and cold meat up from the rear. We were all hungry and glad of the food. As we sat eating I heard hooves approaching from behind. Jennet Marlin on her little grey horse drew to a halt beside us, followed by Tamasin on her palfrey. 'There you are, sir,' Tamasin said. 'I rode back to see Jack.'

'Where is he?'

'A quarter of a mile back, in a cart full of waterproof coats. He says he feels a fool.' She looked at me seriously. 'Sir, please make sure he rests when we reach Howlme.'

'I will, I promise.'

Just then the cry of 'Fall to!' sounded again; the King, it seemed, was indeed keen to move on. Tamasin and Mistress Marlin fell into place beside us.

'I was shocked to hear what happened to you,' Jennet Marlin said. 'They are saying someone put that thorny branch under your horse's saddle so it would throw you. Why would anyone do such a terrible thing?'

'Someone thinks I know a secret, mistress.'

She turned in the saddle a moment and looked back over the great concourse. Then she turned back. 'This concourse is full of evil. Cannot you return straight to London?'

'No, I am not allowed.'

'I am sorry,' she said.

'Make way! Make way!' A messenger, riding forward with some message for one of the officials, came to a halt. Jennet Marlin pulled ahead to let him pass. Tamasin leaned in close to me. 'What did it mean?' she asked in a low voice. 'Lady Rochford coming over to us like that when Jack fell?'

'I do not know. She looked afraid.'

'And I have to go among them tonight. I hoped our troubles might end when we left York.'

'We must keep up our courage, Tamasin.'

Jennet Marlin looked over her shoulder. 'We had best return to the household.' She looked at me. 'Take care, sir.'

'Thank you.' They rode away towards the front of the Progress. I turned to find Giles looking at me quizzically.

'Who can be doing this to you?'

'I do not know. It would be better if I said no more.'

We rode on in silence. The road was raised above the level of the fields now, we looked down on soggy water meadows. After a while these gave way to uncultivated marshland, brown and dreary and spotted with dark reedy pools. The gloomy surroundings seemed to affect the Progress, the buzz of conversation dying away.

'A miserable setting,' I observed to Wrenne.

'Ay, Spalding Moor was ever a dreary and dangerous spot. But see ahead, our destination.' He smiled, then lifted a hand and pointed. Far ahead I saw a hill that rose, unexpectedly high, out of the marshland, crowned with an ancient church and thick with trees, their leaves red and gold. A straggle of houses lined the steep sides.

'There it is. Howlme.'

'You know it?'

He smiled for the first time since we had left York. 'Oh yes,' he said. 'I was born there.'

✝

I HAD WONDERED IF the Progress would try to mount the steep hill; getting all those carts up there would have been a mighty job. But we halted at the bottom, where a large mansion stood in the midst of fields carved out of the marshland. Everyone dismounted and stood waiting. Four huge carts containing the King's greyhounds in great cages rumbled past us, the animals barking and whining.

'What happens now?' I asked Templeman, who was holding Genesis by the reins.

'They'll come and tell us where we're billeted.' He looked at the meadow next to us. 'This is a damp place,' he added gloomily. 'I'll wager we'll wake in our tents with water seeping round our bedrolls. It won't be the first time.'

'I think I will walk up to the village,' Giles said. 'Pay a last visit to my childhood haunts.'

'Is it long since you were here?'

'Over fifty years. Since my mother died.' He dismounted, taking his stick from where he had tied it to the saddle, and looked up the steep hill. 'There will be none who remember me now, but I can visit my parents' grave.' He turned to the soldier. 'Would you mind my horse, fellow?'

'Yes, sir.'

'Look for me later, Matthew, in camp. We can eat together, though what food we will have in these fields I do not know.'

'Till later, then.' Giles walked away, weaving his way slowly among the crowd. I looked beyond the meadow to the mansion. There, in the distance, the royal household had gathered before the door, a shimmering parade of velvet and satin, steel and feathers. I glimpsed a figure around whom all seemed to be revolving, a man head and shoulders above the rest. The King. I turned away, in time to see a little man in a particoloured doublet of Tudor green and white shoving his way through the crowd towards me. He took off his cap and bowed.

'Have you come from Sir William Maleverer?' I asked.

'No, sir,' he said. 'Your presence is required elsewhere.'

'Where? By whom?' I asked sharply, suddenly conscious that I no longer had Barak beside me.

'I may not say, sir. But my orders come from a high authority.'

I frowned, but allowed the man to lead the way back through

the crowd. I had to walk quickly to keep up. At least he was leading me away from the manor house – for an awful second I thought this might be a summons from the King. I caught up with him. 'Who is it requires my presence?' I asked breathlessly.

He dodged as a huge cart laden with sides of beef trundled by. 'You will see in a moment, sir.'

He led me into a field where some large tents had been set up. A number of women were going in and out, from which I deduced this must be where members of the Queen's household were billeted. He went over to the largest tent, held the flap open a little and bowed for me to enter.

The interior was richly appointed. Rushmats had been placed on the floor and large beeswax candles gave the interior a warm yellow glow. To my astonishment Barak was there too, leaning on a wooden crutch someone had found for him. Beside him stood Tamasin, her face tense. Opposite stood Lady Rochford, her expression stern and haughty. And beside her a small plump figure I recognized, wearing a dress of silver satin and a black hood decorated with enormous pearls. At once I bowed low before Queen Catherine.

'Get up, please.' Her voice was soft, girlish. I stood and faced her, realizing I was shaking. The Queen looked at me. Close to she looked younger than ever, scarce more than a child, though even with the troubled expression I saw in her hazel eyes she had an aura of sexuality about her. Lady Rochford stepped forward.

'That surprised him, Your Majesty,' she said waspishly. 'He was very bold when I met him before.'

I said nothing, waiting for the Queen to speak. There was silence for a moment, then she said, 'Lady Rochford tells me Mistress Reedbourne and this man Barak are under your protection.'

'Yes, Your Majesty.'

'I saw you at Fulford,' Queen Catherine said. 'I was sorry for how you were treated there.'

'It is of no matter.'

She took a deep breath. 'I have been told there was an attempt on your life today.'

'Yes, Your Majesty. A thorn branch was placed under my horse's saddle. A friend was mounting the horse; he would have been killed had it not been for Master Barak's quick actions.'

The Queen looked at Lady Rochford. For a moment she seemed tongue-tied. But she rallied. 'Do you know why anyone would do such a thing, sir?'

I hesitated. 'No, Your Majesty. But it is not the first such attack.' I looked at Lady Rochford. 'Sir William Maleverer has the matter in hand.'

'See, Your Majesty!' Lady Rochford snapped. 'You saw how he looked at me. He thinks I had something to do with it.'

'Do you?' the Queen asked me, a tremble in her voice.

I hesitated again. Then: 'I do not know who may be responsible.'

She took a deep breath. 'I called you here, sir, to assure you it was nothing to do with my household.'

'Thank you, Your Majesty. I believe it has to do with — another matter than that which brought us into contact with Lady Rochford.'

A look of fear again. She glanced at Lady Rochford.

'What matter?' Lady Rochford snapped.

'It is to do with the conspiracy.'

She looked puzzled. 'I see.'

The Queen raised her hands. 'Do not tell me,' she said. 'They tell me nothing of politics and I do not wish to know.' I wondered if that was her survival strategy, keeping clear of factions. She looked at me again. 'As for what these people saw at St Mary's —' she glanced at Barak and Tamasin, who so far had said not a word — 'you have all given Lady Rochford your word you would keep silent. I — I rely on that.' She drew herself up, trying to seem like a queen instead of a frightened girl.

I bowed my head, for I could think of no reply.

'You *have* told no one what you saw?' Lady Rochford said sharply.

'No one, I swear.'

Her tone changed, became lighter. 'It was a mischance you saw Culpeper that night. The Queen only desired a little company of her own age, as I told you. There was nothing improper. I was with them all the time.'

'That is the truth,' Catherine Howard said quietly. 'Will you believe the word of your Queen?'

I looked at her. 'Yes, Your Majesty.' And I did believe her. I felt surer than ever that whatever meetings she and Culpeper had had under Lady Rochford's eye, it had gone no further than that. She would not dare. I felt sorry for her, married to King Henry and cast at her age and with little wit or intelligence among the pack of wolves that was the court.

She smiled. 'Then I thank you. You may be sure you will be rewarded when we return to London.'

'We seek no reward, Your Majesty.'

'Then I thank you again. And I hope whoever has been making trouble for you is caught and dealt with as they deserve.'

'Be sure you keep your word to us,' Lady Rochford said. 'I took risks in arranging this meeting. The Queen is due at Howlme Manor, we said she was coming here to change.'

The Queen turned away, and Lady Rochford waved a hand in dismissal. We bowed again and Tamasin took Barak's arm and helped him from the tent. We walked to the edge of the field and stopped.

'Fuck me,' Barak said.

'Jack,' Tamasin said reprovingly.

'When I answered that summons and found the Queen in there I nearly messed my pants.'

I looked at Tamasin. 'Well?' I asked. 'What did you think of that?'

'I think the Queen spoke the truth, sir.'

'Yes. So do I. They have nothing to do with this, I am more than ever certain.' I shook my head. 'The Queen is so young. . .'

'They say she was a saucy wench before the King's eyes lighted on her.'

'A silly flirt, perhaps. And Lady Rochford may get some perverse pleasure out of arranging secret meetings for her with young men, but she and the Queen are surely not so silly as to abandon all caution. They are frightened now.' I looked over to where the hundreds of carts were being driven into the fields 'Come, we have to find our billets.'

Barak nudged me. 'Look over there.'

I followed his gaze to where a little group of officials stood staring at us. Craike was there, and my heart sank as I saw Sir Richard Rich. He would have seen us come out of the Queen's tent. What would he have made of that?

Chapter Thirty-three

W E WALKED BACK TO where the soldier Templeman still stood with the horses on the grass verge by the road, eating an apple. Conical soldiers' tents were being set up in the field behind him. Barak found it hard to move among the barging, shoving crowd, and if Tamasin and I had not been there he might have fallen. I had relied on his strength and dexterity in many tight corners; it was disconcerting, now, to have to help him walk.

I went up to Genesis. He seemed more at ease now, though with those ugly punctures on his back it would be a little time before he could be ridden again. 'Do we know where we are berthed?' I asked the soldier.

'No, sir. They'll be along to tell us when they're ready. We'll have to wait.'

A cart lumbered by, so close we had to step up on the verge. Barak, leaning on the crutch, slithered and would have fallen had Tamasin not caught his arm.

'Damn it to Hell!' he exclaimed fiercely.

'You shouldn't be walking among these crowds,' I told him. 'Listen, you and Tamasin stay here with Templeman till we know where we are to be put.'

'What are you going to do?' he asked.

I felt an urgent need to get away from the roiling crowd. 'I am going to walk up to Howlme,' I said. 'I will find Master Wrenne, come back with him.'

'You should keep safe with us, sir,' Tamasin ventured. 'It will be dark soon.'

'I need to get away for a while. And I will be safer up there than in this tumult. Wrenne and I will find you later.' To stop further argument, I turned brusquely away and began walking up the road to the village.

✝

ALL AROUND people were driving carts into fields under the supervision of green-coated officers of the household, some carrying little portable desks like Craike's. One of the carts had tipped over in the road and some soldiers were trying to free the huge horses that lay on their sides in the traces, screaming and kicking out frantically. I saw that it contained weapons: swords and crossbows and guns lay scattered all over the road. Soldiers were picking them up and taking them into the neighbouring fields, shoving passers-by away from the deadly weapons. In the next field on I saw a carriage standing on its own, guarded by half a dozen soldiers. It was painted black and bore the royal arms. Recognizing Sergeant Leacon there I went over to him, my boots squelching on the muddy grass. The carriage was windowless, the door shut. The sergeant bowed.

'You had a safe journey?' I asked.

'Ay, 'twas uneventful.' He looked at me curiously. 'I heard about the thorns under your horse's saddle.'

'Does everyone on the Progress know?'

'It caused quite a stir.' He jerked his head at the carriage behind him. 'Is it something to do with Broderick?'

'I think not.' I sighed. 'I came for a walk, to get away from the crowds.'

He smiled. 'I too found that great pack of people on the Progress oppressive at first, when we left London. You get used to it.'

'I am not sure I ever could. I thought I would walk up to the village. A friend of mine has gone there. Perhaps you saw him pass? A tall old fellow with a stick, wearing a lawyer's robe?'

'Ay. He went up a short while ago.' He glanced at the carriage. 'Sir, I do not like the look of the prisoner. He has a yellow colour, he has seemed sickly ever since he was poisoned. He should be allowed some air; it cannot do him good to be locked up in there all the time with that man.'

'You are right.'

'It would pity any man's heart to see the poor fellow. Whatever he has done. He looks and moves like an old man, though I am told he is not yet thirty.'

'Yes.' I shook my head. 'And he will die horribly for his beliefs, like so many in these last years.'

Sergeant Leacon gave me a curious look. 'He was prepared to kill for those beliefs as well. If the north had risen this spring as they planned, there would have been much bloodshed.'

I nodded slowly. 'Yes, you are right, sergeant. There would. Perhaps I have become over-sympathetic to our prisoner. Yet I have to watch for his welfare. I will speak to Maleverer, see if some arrangement can be made for him to have exercise.' I looked at the black carriage. 'I cannot face seeing Radwinter just now. I will take my walk, and call in on my way back to see how Broderick does.'

'Be careful, sir, if you have enemies about.'

'I will.' I looked at the young soldier. 'Is there any more news of your parents' land case?'

'Only a letter from my uncle saying they are sore worried. He plans to bring them to London to see me when the Progress returns. I will be billeted at the Tower then.'

'Bring them to see me,' I said. 'I am sorry for my part in their trouble.'

'Can you help them, do you think?'

'I cannot say without seeing the papers in the case. But if I can, I shall. I promise.'

The sergeant gave me a long, searching look. 'I hope so, sir. If they are turned off their land they will have nothing.'

☦

FEELING GUILTY, I left the field and began to mount the hill. The path was wide, bordered by oak woods, covered thickly in fallen leaves so that I had to be careful not to slip. I felt a moment's nervousness at being thus alone, but reflected that if anyone else came up the hill I should see them.

A chill breeze blew. The village, when I reached it, was but a single street of poor houses straddling the upward path. A few chickens and pigs rooted about but apart from some children playing by a puddle I saw no one; most of the adults had probably been pressed into service to help settle the Progress for the night.

Beyond the village the hill grew steeper. At the summit the path came out on to a stretch of open ground in front of the square-towered Norman church, the ancient churchyard to its left extending back to woods behind. I halted in front of the lychgate to get my breath. There was a stiff breeze up here and the air felt clean. To my right I saw an enormous beacon, twenty feet high, made of planks secured in place by thick ropes. I went over to study it. It was one of the beacons Cromwell had ordered to be set on hills all over the country three years ago, when it looked as though the French and Spanish might invade England at the Pope's behest.

From up here I could see the camp as it spread itself out over the fields for the night. As when I first saw it approaching at Fulford, the Progress made me think of a great stain on the landscape. I looked across to the mansion where the King would have taken up residence now, a fine old building. Broderick said the King had stolen it from Robert Constable. He has stolen so much, I thought.

'On a clear day you can see York Minster.'

A voice at my elbow made me jump. I turned to see Giles beside me. 'Jesu, sir, you startled me.'

'I am sorry. I was over in the churchyard on my way to visit my parents' grave, and saw you coming. My footsteps made no sound on these wet leaves. You look sad, Matthew.'

'I needed to get away from the camp. I breathe easier up here.'

'Ay, 'tis all din and mess down there.' His eye went to the misty horizon. The sun was low behind the milky clouds, tinges of red showing through. He leaned heavily on his stick. 'You know, the day it was decided I would go to law I walked up here and looked over at the Minster. I thought, one day I shall work as a lawyer there.'

'As you did.'

'Ay.' He shook his head. 'So long ago. When man's relation to God seemed clear and settled.' He sighed. 'Since then the world has been turned upside down. And York and the north have ended on the bottom.'

'Perhaps things will settle now in the north, after the Progress.'

'I do not think the King has done much to assuage the bitterness up here. Oh, he has bought the gentry, secured their allegiance with oaths, but you only need to look at the faces of ordinary people to see what their true feelings are.'

I laughed uneasily. 'Giles, you sound like those who grudge all rich men and would pull them down.' I smiled sadly. 'Sometimes I wonder if they have not the right of it.'

'No, no.' Giles shook his leonine head. 'We must have kingship to have order. But — it is unfortunate that England has the King it does.'

'Yes. It is.' I looked out over the fields. They had been carved out of the boggy ground at the foot of the hill and ended abruptly at the marshland, which I saw stretched away for miles. I decided to change the subject, realizing anew how strained old loyalties I had once taken for granted had become.

'Where was your parents' farm, Giles?' I asked.

He pointed with his stick at a clutch of buildings. 'There. My father drained the land himself. Howlme marsh is quite trackless, you know. There is a hermitage some way off, where a couple of monks used to guide travellers who became lost. Gone now, of course, even their poor hovel taken by the King.'

'Were you happy as a child?' I asked him.

He smiled. 'Oh, yes.'

'Your father did not expect you to carry on the farm?'

'No. I enjoyed my schoolwork, you see. They saw my tastes lay with words and arguments rather than billhooks and drainage ditches, and they thought I might raise myself up in the world.'

'My tastes were bookish too. And I liked drawing – I used to paint for a pastime, though not recently. But I always knew my father would rather have had a strong son to carry on the farm than – well, than me.'

'He should have accepted you as you were, rejoiced that you had brains.'

'He tried, I think.' I hesitated. 'My mother died when I was ten.'

'No woman's softening influence on your father, then.'

'No, he was harder after that.' I was silent a moment.

'I was on my way to my parents' grave, and then the church. Would you like to see them?'

'Yes. I must consider a design for a headstone for my father.'

He led me into the churchyard. Most of the gravestones were sandstone, weathered with the years, but he took me to a prominent stone in white marble. The inscription was simple:

Edward Wrenne 1421–1486
and his wife Agnes 1439–1488
At rest

'They both died when I was a student,' he said. 'My mother was devoted to my father. She pined away and died eighteen months after him.'

'She was much younger.'

'Ay. My father had another wife before her, more his own age. They had no children. She died when they were in their forties and is buried with her family. Then my father married my mother. I was the child of his old age.'

'My father's family lived round Lichfield for generations. I think that was partly why he was sorry I did not carry on the farm. The line going out.'

'My father came to Howlme from beyond Wakefield when he was a young man. So there was less of a local tie.'

I nodded slowly. 'Well, it is a fine memorial. Marble, that is good. I shall provide a marble headstone for my father.'

'Leave me a moment, Matthew,' Giles said quietly. 'I will join you in the church in a minute. It is worth a visit.'

I turned and walked back to the church. I stopped. I had heard a branch crack, a loud pop. I stared at the trees that shadowed the graveyard but saw nothing. A deer, I thought, as I walked on to the little church.

The interior was lit dimly by candles. There were pretty little vaulted arches and a new roof whose beams were decorated with Tudor roses. In a large side-chapel a candle winked redly in a lamp set before an image of the Virgin. King Henry would not like that. I sat in a pew, thinking about my father as the light coming through the high stained-glass windows slowly faded. His face came into my mind: grizzled, unmoving, unsmiling. Yes, he had been hard. In truth that was why in adult life I had always been reluctant to go home.

The door opened and Giles came in, his stick tapping on the floor. He went to the side-chapel, crossed himself, then took a candle and lit it from the lamp. He came over, put the candle on the front of the pew and sat down heavily beside me.

'This is a pretty place, is it not? I was an altar boy once.' He laughed. 'We were naughty children. We used to catch the mice that came to nibble the candles, set them between the shafts of tiny carts we made and send them skittering down the aisles.'

I smiled. 'I was an altar boy too. I was obedient, though. I took it all seriously.'

He looked at me. 'Till you transferred your allegiance to reform.'

'Yes. I was hot-headed for reform once, believe it or not. Always questioning everything.'

'I think perhaps you still do that.'

'Perhaps. In a different way.'

Wrenne nodded at the side-chapel. 'That is the Constable chapel.'

'Sir Robert Constable's family?'

'Yes. They have been landowners here for centuries. A chantry priest still says a daily Mass for their souls. The priest of the church when I was a lad was a Constable.'

'Were they good landlords?'

'No. They were hard, grasping men, Robert Constable as much as any of them. Yet he died for his beliefs in the end.'

As I told Sergeant Leacon that Broderick would, I thought. 'I hear his bones still hang over the gates of Hull.'

'Yes. We shall see them.' He thought a moment. 'I sold the farm to the Constables after my father died. It made no sense to keep a farm so many miles from where I lived. No more than it makes sense for you. You should not feel guilty at selling your father's farm, Matthew.'

'No, you are right.'

He looked at me and shook his head. 'You have had much to bear. First your father, now these attacks on you. There have been others, you said?'

I took a deep breath. 'Three counting the thorn under Genesis' saddle. Not counting the time when I was struck down and that damned casket of papers stolen. A week ago someone tried to ram a spit through me at the camp.'

His eyes widened. 'Jesu.'

'And then a bear was let loose in my path.'

'Dear God.'

'I fear the person who is after me may think I learned more than I did from the papers inside that box. I only had time to glance at a few of them.' I paused. 'One of them was the *Titulus*.'

'Ah.'

'That was how I knew it was dangerous for you to have a copy.'

'I understand now. What others did you see?' he asked curiously. 'When he questioned me, Maleverer said you had had no time to look.'

'Nothing of note.'

'Maleverer must have been angry with you for that.'

'He and the Privy Council.'

'How have you borne it all?' he asked gently. 'That and what happened at Fulford as well?'

'One bears things because there is no alternative.' I looked at him. 'As you have cause to know, better than anyone.'

'Ay.' He nodded his head slowly. 'Ay. The Lord lays heavy burdens on us. Heavier than a man should have to bear, I think in dark moments.'

I shifted in the narrow pew, my neck was becoming uncomfortable again. 'I think we should go back now. It will be getting dark.'

'Allow me a few minutes more,' he said. 'I would like to say a prayer.'

'Of course. I will wait for you by the beacon.'

☦

I LEFT THE CHURCH. Outside the sun was below the horizon now, the churchyard dim. I walked through the gate. I looked out over the camp: torches and bonfires were alight across the fields, all the windows of the manor house were brightly lit. The King and Queen would be there now; Master Craike would have made sure all was ready for their comfort.

Giles was taking a long time at his prayers. I fingered the thick ropes holding the beacon upright, tied tightly to the top of an iron pole that protruded from the centre of the huge bonfire and secured to stakes in the ground at the bottom.

I was conscious of pressure on my bladder. I looked round the churchyard and the trees that bordered the open space to make sure no one was there. I unlaced my hose and sighed with relief as I let out a jet of piss against the beacon. I finished and laced myself up again. I turned, then stood stock still, rigid with shock. Jennet Marlin stood ten feet from me. She wore a dark coat with a hood and her mouth was set in its grimmest expression. She was holding a crossbow, and it was aimed at my heart.

I stared at her, my mouth open. She shifted the weight of the crossbow slightly on her shoulder. I flinched, waiting for the bolt to thud into me. But though her hand was on the trigger she did not fire.

'This time I have you,' she said, her voice sharp as a file.

I glanced over her shoulder at the church, a black shape against the evening sky, the light from the chapel outlining the windows in a dim red glow. She gave a rictus of a smile and shook her head. 'Do not look for help from the old man,' she said.

'What – what have you done to him?'

She looked at me with those large eyes. They were afire with gloating anger.

'I have secured the church door with a spar of wood through the handles. He is trapped, that is all. I do not take life unless it is necessary.'

'And mine?' I asked. 'Is it necessary to take mine?'

She did not answer. I saw the crossbow tremble in her arms a moment. She was at a great pitch of tension. I prayed her hand did not slip—

I knew I had to keep her talking as long as I could, keep her from pressing that trigger. 'It was you who tried to spit me at the camp? You who let the bear loose and put that thorn under my horse's saddle?'

'Yes. Seeing you in the camp that first time was a lucky chance – I was walking down by the river.' There was hatred in her look now. Why? What did she think I had done? 'As for the bear, I knew from Tamasin that you had gone into York and I waited by the outbuildings for your return. I thought there would be a chance in the dark. You came back and when you walked through the church I ran along the side and got behind the bear's cage. Oh, I have watched you for the last two weeks,' she added with intensity. 'From the windows of the manor, from the camp, from hidden places in the courtyard. When I saw you from the camp tonight, walking up the hill, I knew this was my best opportunity.'

'You got that crossbow from the overturned cart.'

'Yes.' She seemed steadier now, eyeing me along the length of the weapon.

'I thought someone was watching from the woods.' Keep her talking, I thought, keep her talking. 'You killed Oldroyd?' I asked her.

'Yes. Oldroyd had to die. He had that damned casket. He would not give it up to me even though I told him I came from Bernard.'

'You are on a mission from your fiancé? So Bernard Locke was a conspirator?'

'Yes, he was.'

'But I thought you were a reformer?'

'I am. Bernard regrets what he did. He wanted the contents of that box destroyed – they could endanger the throne, he told me. He has repented. Like me, he would save the King from treasonous conspiracies.'

I wondered whether Bernard Locke had truly repented. No, I thought – he has used this besotted woman as his catspaw.

Behind her, I saw a movement, a big dim shape edging towards her. It was Giles. He had got out of the church somehow and was approaching Jennet Marlin slowly, his stick raised in both hands, his expression intent as he tried to get closer to her without making a sound. I forced my eyes back to Jennet Marlin.

'Bernard told me the papers were in the possession of Master Oldroyd of York, kept in a secret place at his house. He told me I would have to kill the glazier and take his keys from his body to get hold of them. He would never give them up.'

'You toppled that defenceless man off his ladder, in cold blood.'

'I had no choice.' Her steely voice did not waver. 'And was he not a conspirator, deserving of a traitor's death? If it was not for his horse bolting when he fell, I would have had the keys to his house from his body, but that sounded the alarm.'

'You heard us coming and hid in the church?'

'Yes, you and that lout Barak nearly had me there. It was as well I had taken care to find keys. But then before I could get to Oldroyd's house, you appeared with that box. A jewel casket, just as Bernard had described to me.'

'And so you made friends with me, planning all the time to kill me. Because you thought I knew the contents of that box?'

Giles was right behind her now. He had lifted his stick high above her head with both arms but he hesitated – he must fear that if he struck her she would loose the bolt from the crossbow as she fell.

'Yes, to see what I could find out. As you pretended to be *my* friend, laughing in your sleeve all the time because you knew that some of those papers incriminated Bernard. It was harder to be civil than to try to kill you. Every time I saw your crooked form I wanted to be sick—'

Now I saw the reason for her anger. 'Mistress,' I said, 'I hardly saw the papers. I saw nothing about your fiancé.'

'Nonsense. You do not trust Maleverer with what you know, but when you get to London you will reveal all to your master Cranmer. You must know—'

She never finished her sentence, for at that moment Giles brought his stick down on her head with all the force of his arms. There was a horrible sharp crack. Jennet gave a little moan of surprise, then toppled to the ground. The crossbow clicked, and I threw myself to the right. There was a thud as the bolt buried itself in the wood next to me. I looked ahead again: Jennet Marlin lay face down on the ground, her head hidden by the hood of her coat. Giles stood behind her, swaying slightly, eyes wide.

I ran across to where she lay, the crossbow by her side. I grasped her arm. It felt floppy, lifeless. I turned her over. She was dead, her dark curls wet with blood, her wide eyes staring up lifelessly, like those of a fish, all that frantic emotion gone. I turned aside, bent over and was violently sick.

I felt an arm on my shoulder. I stood up. Giles's wide, staring eyes and a twitch in his cheek showed how shocked he was.

'I have killed her?' he asked in a whisper.

I nodded. 'You saved my life. You heard all?'

'Enough.' He looked down at her body. 'By God.' He took a long, deep breath.

'How did you get out?'

'I have known Howlme church since I was a boy. When I could not open the main door I got out another way. There is a side door.' He looked at Jennet Marlin's body. 'I was so afraid she would loose the bolt.'

I picked up the crossbow and took Giles's arm. 'Come,' I said quietly. 'We must go down to the camp. Maleverer has to know about this at once.'

Chapter Thirty-four

ON THE WAY BACK DOWN TO the camp I tried not to be impatient with Giles's slow pace; the old man walked carefully with his stick, feeling his way along the path for it was dark now. I had picked up the crossbow and it hung from my hand.

'Will Maleverer be at Howlme Manor?' Giles asked.

'I would think so. We should go there.'

'It is hard to credit that a woman could do what she did.'

'It can happen,' I replied. At the foot of the hill we turned right and headed for the manor house. Giles looked very tired now. I put a hand on his arm.

'Can you manage? Perhaps you should go back to the camp, find your tent and rest.'

'No, I will come with you. Maleverer will want to see both of us.'

We reached the high wall that enclosed the grounds. The manor house was approached though a large gateway where soldiers stood guard. They would not let us through, but I persuaded one of them to fetch Maleverer. Giles sank down on a knoll beside the gate, folded his hands over the top of his cane and lowered his head.

'Are you all right?' I asked.

'Yes, yes. I – I am in a little pain. Don't fuss,' he added with sudden asperity.

I looked at him with concern, remembering how he had collapsed at Fulford. There was a stir at the gate and Maleverer appeared. He loomed over us, frowning angrily.

'God's death, what is it now? The King is here.' He looked at my face, then said sharply, 'What's happened?'

'I have been attacked again, Sir William.' I held up the crossbow. 'With this. It was Jennet Marlin.'

'What? That woman?' He looked incredulous. 'Where is she?'

'Lying dead outside Howlme church.'

He gave me a long hard stare, then looked at Giles. 'What's this old fellow doing here?'

'Master Wrenne was with me. He saved me.'

Giles looked up. 'I had to strike her down,' he said. 'It was the only way.'

Maleverer held out a hand for the crossbow.

'She stole it when that cart overturned,' I told him.

'Come inside,' he snapped. 'Both of you.'

He led the way up the path and into the Great Hall. There was no sign of the King, thank goodness. Maleverer led us through to a downstairs room that had been converted into an office, and sat behind his desk. We stood before him. In the candlelight that filled the room, Wrenne's face looked white and pouchy.

'Might Master Wrenne sit, Sir William?' I asked. 'He has had a shock.' Maleverer looked at him and grunted assent. I pulled out a chair for the old man.

'Thank you.'

'Well? What happened?'

I told him what had taken place on the hill: Jennet Marlin's revelation that it had been her trying to kill me, her certainty I had seen papers in the casket that incriminated her fiancé. He leaned back, thinking, then turned to Giles who had sat silently throughout my narrative. He nodded at the stick he was holding between his knees.

'You brained her with that?'

'Yes.'

Giles looked down. He saw smears of blood on his hands and shuddered.

'How much of what she said did you hear, before you struck her?' I asked.

'Only the end. I did not mean to kill her. I have never killed another person—'

'Well, you did tonight.' Maleverer looked at him contemptuously. 'What's the matter with you? You look as though you're about to faint away. Seems you've a weak stomach for a lawyer.'

'He has – he is unwell,' I told Maleverer. He frowned anxiously at the old man.

'Then he should be got out of here. The King won't have illness in any house he is staying at. Guard!' he called. A soldier hurried in, and Maleverer gestured to Giles. 'Assist him to his tent. Find out where it is and take him there.'

The soldier helped Giles to his feet. He looked at me. 'I am sorry,' he said, then allowed himself to be helped out. There was a moment's silence. Maleverer ran his fingers along the edge of his black beard, a rapid flick, flick. Then he reached down and pulled something out of a drawer in his desk. It was the jewel casket. He set it on the desk. I looked again upon the painting of Diana the huntress, dressed in the style of a hundred years ago, aiming her bow at a stag.

'I've kept this by me since St Mary's. I've sat looking at it, pondering over who could be behind this.' He gave a bark of laughter. 'I've often wished it could speak, tell me what it contained.' He shook his head. 'I never thought of Mistress Marlin. I'll have them search her room. She may have those papers hidden there.'

'I did not suspect her either. But she was desperate to get her fiancé freed, it was all that mattered to her. And a desperate person can be more dangerous than the worst villain. You never know what they might do in their desperation, while a villain is always a villain.'

'She was clever, too. I expect she stole the keys of St Mary's church easily enough. Someone with a name as feared as Lady Rochford's behind her could go where she willed at King's Manor.'

'It was a cold cleverness. She pretended to be my friend.' I smiled sadly. 'It softened me towards her. I wanted her friendship.'

He looked at me interrogatively. 'Sweet on her, were you?'

I sighed. 'No, Sir William, I was not. I always distrusted that obsessive quality about her. I think that obsessiveness enabled her to justify to herself what she was doing. Desperate people can think up reasons to justify almost anything, be they stupid or clever.' I took a deep breath, then added, 'She thought you had been responsible for Master Locke being put in the Tower, said you coveted his lands and hoped to see him attainted for treason.'

I braced myself for a storm, but Maleverer only laughed. 'Insolent mare. I merely sent him south on the Privy Council's orders. Though if his lands are attainted, as they will be now, I might buy some of them.' A covetous look came into his eyes, and in the midst of our talk of traitors and murderers he gave a momentary smile at the thought of more profit. Perhaps soon he would have enough land to feel he had redeemed his name enough to marry.

He frowned at me. 'What's the matter with you? You still look worried.'

'Some things still puzzle me. Why was she so certain I had seen all the papers in the casket? When she knocked me down at St Mary's she must have seen I had only pulled out the topmost ones.'

He shrugged. 'Perhaps she thought you'd already looked at them, and put them back.'

'She believed I'd seen them all and was keeping my knowledge from you, perhaps to tell Cranmer.'

He looked at me hard. 'She wasn't right, was she?' He tapped the casket with a finger. 'We've only your word for how much you saw.'

'I spoke the truth, Sir William.'

He gave me another disdainful look. 'I'll have her quarters turned upside down, and if we don't find those papers hidden there I'll have everyone associated with her questioned. Young Miss Reedbourne. Lady Rochford.'

'Lady Rochford will not be pleased,' I said. 'And Tamasin will be terrified.'

'Pox on her.'

I thought, if soldiers appear at her quarters Lady Rochford, and Tamasin too, will think the Queen and Culpeper have been found out. As perhaps they will be if those papers still exist. If. I looked at Maleverer. 'Sir William, her aim was to destroy those papers. I think she may have done that long since, after she first took them at St Mary's.'

He nodded, running his finger along the edge of his beard again. 'If there is no trace of the papers we can assume that she got rid of them. She took them from Oldroyd and he was in with the conspirators.'

'Yes. Bernard Locke told her he had repented. She told herself she was helping scotch the conspirators' plans, as well as destroying evidence that would incriminate him. Though I think Locke's main concern may well have been to save his own skin.'

Maleverer nodded. 'Many held in the Tower come to see things that way. Especially if they've been shown the rack, and heard the screams.'

'Not Broderick.'

He grunted. 'He's not there yet. Well, if she has destroyed the papers, she did us a favour. Though the Privy Council would have preferred to see them.' He got up. 'Locke will have some stiff questioning now. I am going to start the search.' I could almost feel the nervous energy coming from his big frame. 'And I'd better have that bitch's body fetched down, before some villager stumbles over it. Until I come back, do not move from this room, do you understand?'

✝

HE LEFT THE ROOM, his robe whisking behind him. I sat down in the seat Wrenne had vacated. I thought, Maleverer is not the cleverest of men, he gets his way by bullying. He despises me but likes to pick my brain. I sighed and looked round the room. It might have been a study once. An old tapestry of a hunting scene hung behind Maleverer's desk. Had the executed Robert Constable sat gazing at it, as I did now? I turned away and looked out of the window at the dark night for some time, thinking.

I thought of Jennet Marlin. Even now I could not help but feel sorry for her. Her love for Bernard Locke must have been an obsession since childhood. She had not been unattractive, she could have made another match had she not fixed her heart so desperately on Locke. What manner of man was he, I wondered. A charismatic rogue perhaps, who could get women to do anything he asked. I had come across those in my career, usually when they had bled some woman of all her money and she was trying to recover it at law. Had Locke used that obsessive love of Jennet's to turn her into a murderess, to save him from execution? If so, he was worse than her. I shuddered as her face came to mind, her expression as she looked at me over the crossbow.

I looked at the box. Who did you originally belong to, I wondered. Someone rich. I leaned forward and opened it, looking into the empty interior. There was still a faint smell of old, musty papers. Had Jennet Marlin destroyed them all? If she had, anything there about the Queen and Culpeper was gone. How little I care about that, I thought; I have no loyalty left to Henry. Perhaps a false King. He will be relieved indeed if that was what the Blaybourne papers said.

I jumped violently as the door banged open and Maleverer reappeared. He shut the door and frowned down at me.

'What are you fiddling with that box for?' He threw himself down in his seat. 'There's no sign of the papers in her quarters. Just letters from Bernard Locke in the Tower, tied up with ribbon. They say nothing, they just say how much they love each other. Like turtle-doves.' He snorted. 'I'm having the ladies questioned to see if they remember anything that might help us, but I doubt they will. I think you were right, she destroyed those papers. Perhaps threw them on to one of the campfires in York. 'Go back to your tent now, I'll call you if need be. There's a soldier outside. He will take you back.'

'Very well, Sir William.' I rose, bowed and left the room. A soldier waiting outside led me out of Howlme Manor. It was a relief to be back in the open air.

'Is the King abed?' I asked the soldier, to make conversation.

'No, sir, he is playing chess with the gentlemen of the bedchamber. He will not sleep for many hours, I think.'

The soldier led me into the camp. The cooking fires were dying down now, the soldiers and servants fed. Men sat before their tents talking or playing cards.

'Is it far?' I asked. 'I am sore tired.'

'Not far. You have a tent by the fence. Your man and the old lawyer are next to you.'

He came to a halt where three small conical tents were set together in a corner of the field. There were others dotted around, some lit from within by flickering candlelight; the other lawyers, perhaps, whose status merited their own tent. I thanked the soldier, who walked away to the manor, and opened the flap of the only tent of the three that was lit from within.

Inside, Giles lay on a truckle bed which had been set on the bare grass. Barak sat on a box beside him, his injured leg up on another box and his crutch beside him, drinking beer.

'This is a homely scene,' I said quietly. 'How are you both?'

'Master Wrenne is asleep,' Barak answered. 'He told me what happened. Is Jennet Marlin truly dead?'

'Ay, she is. I have been with Maleverer; he has searched her belongings for the papers, but found nothing.'

'She destroyed them, then?'

'He thinks so. How is your leg?'

'All right so long as I don't put any weight on it. Tammy had to go back to her quarters.'

'Maleverer is going to question her about Jennet Marlin. And the other ladies. Lady Rochford too.'

'Tammy will be shocked,' he said seriously. 'She was fond of Mistress Marlin.' He sighed.

'Still no word from your friend in London? About her father?'

'Only a note to say he is following some leads.'

'Have you told her?'

'No. And if it's bad news in the end, as I suspect, I won't.'

I nodded, then went over and looked at Giles. He seemed deeply asleep.

'He saved my life,' I said. 'But I think it was all too much for him. He can only take so much. We must take care of him.'

'We will.' Barak looked at me. 'So. It is all over.'

'I hope so.'

'You're not sure?'

'There's something – but I am tired, I must go to my tent, sleep. I can't think straight now.' I laughed suddenly.

'What?'

'The soldier who brought me across told me the King is playing chess with his gentlemen. It struck me, this whole Progress is like a great chessboard, with a real king and queen trying to outmanoeuvre the people of the north.'

He looked at me seriously, eyes glinting in the candlelight. 'A real king?' he asked quietly. 'Or a cuckoo in the royal nest?'

'Either way we three are the humblest of pawns, easily dispensable.'

Chapter Thirty-five

W E WERE TRAVELLING DOWN a long stretch of road. I was still on the horse I had been given yesterday, for Genesis' cuts were not healed sufficiently for me to ride him. He was at the back of the Progress, with the spare horses. Alongside me, Barak sat wearily in Sukey's saddle; he had insisted on riding today, despite his leg. Giles was not with us; he had wakened feeling ill and weak, his face grey. I suspected he was in pain and had begged a place for him to travel in one of the carts. I too was feeling the effects of the previous night. Although I was thickly swathed in my coat, I felt cold.

We had an even longer ride today: to Leconfield Castle, five miles north of Hull. The country beyond Howlme was less flat, with low round hills capped with trees whose leaves glowed red and yellow this bright, cold autumn morning. It made a pretty picture. Away to the east I could see a line of hills I heard someone call the Yorkshire Wolds. All around us the Progress thundered and clattered. Behind, the procession of carts disappeared out of sight beyond a bend in the road. Ahead, the feathers in the caps of the officials bobbed up and down, while on either side the soldiers in their bright uniforms rode, with harnesses jangling, and the messengers ran up and down the verges.

The picture of Jennet Marlin with her head staved in kept coming into my mind. I guessed Giles's state of health this morning was at least partly a reaction to what he had had to do. I recalled his shocked expression and his words, 'I have never killed another person.'

'Penny for 'em,' Barak said.

'I was thinking of last night. Mistress Marlin lying dead on that hill.'

'I saw Tammy this morning, before we set off. She said Lady Rochford had looked terrified when Maleverer came to question her. He questioned Tammy too, but there was nothing she could tell him.' He glanced at me. 'She was sore upset to learn the truth about Mistress Marlin. She was in tears when I saw her.'

'Upset that her mistress was a murderess?'

'And that she was dead.'

'Lady Rochford must have been scared the Queen's foolery had been discovered.'

'Ay. But none of the ladies knew anything. Mistress Marlin had no friends apart from Tamasin. She used to go off for walks on her own sometimes, but no one knew where she went.'

'To spy on me,' I said.

Barak lowered his voice. 'You were right all along not to tell Maleverer about Culpeper. Cheer up, you are safe. It's over. And you can stop worrying about that family tree, and who Blaybourne was.' He grinned. 'Stop moithering, as the Yorkers say.'

'I wonder,' I said quietly.

'What do you mean?'

'Jennet Marlin never actually admitted to taking the papers.'

'What do you mean?'

'Surely she of all people would have made sure I was dead when I was struck down and the box stolen at King's Manor.'

'You mean she had a confederate?'

I shook my head. 'No, she worked alone on her mission.'

'Then who else can have taken them?' Barak sounded exasperated.

'I don't know. But why did she not kill me at once when she had the chance last night? She could have shot me in the back as I stood there pissing against that beacon. But she made me stand there.' I shuddered. 'I think if she had had the time she might have asked me if *I* knew where the papers were.'

'You can't know that.'

'No. But if she thought I had them it would explain why she was so sure I had seen the papers incriminating Bernard Locke.'

'But she didn't try to question you before. The bitch just tried to kill you.'

'She didn't have the opportunity before. If one of her earlier attempts had succeeded she might have somehow found the chance to go through my papers at the lodging house. Bribed a servant to do it, perhaps.'

Barak shook his head. 'I can't see it.'

'I've no proof. If it *was* someone else who struck me down at King's Manor, someone linked to the conspirators, the papers would probably have been despatched to them long ago.'

'So they're gone, whatever they were?'

'Long gone, I'd say.' I sighed. 'Maleverer said they would subject Bernard Locke to stiff questioning now. Perhaps they will learn more from him.'

Barak shrugged. 'I guess they'll rack him.'

'Yes.' I shuddered. 'And what will he say? I hope the name Martin Dakin does not come up. That would just about finish the old man.'

'There's no reason it should. Just because they share the same chambers.'

I nodded thoughtfully. 'There's an age difference, too. Giles said Dakin was over forty, and Locke must be about ten years younger if he was of an age with Jennet Marlin.'

'There you are. Barristers with that much difference in experience wouldn't normally mix much.'

'Unless they have other things in common.' I sighed again. 'I must visit Broderick when we arrive at Leconfield. I never went back to his carriage yesterday.'

Barak shifted his position to ease his leg. 'You should tell Maleverer what you have been thinking. That the papers might not have been destroyed.'

'I will. But he will probably only scoff. He will believe what he wants to believe, which is that it is all over.'

Barak looked round him at the crowds. 'Who could it have been?'

I followed his gaze. 'Anyone. Anyone at all.'

☦

WE PASSED THROUGH the little town of Market Weighton without stopping. The King and Queen were at the head of the Progress, far out of sight. People stood in the streets and watched the Progress as they had in the villages, with caps off but generally stony faces, though I heard some ragged cheers up ahead as the King and Queen went by.

Towards evening we came upon a wooded area where trees pressed upon the road, slowing our speed from the usual walking pace. As the sun was beginning to set we came to a halt in a grassy space before an enormous mansion, enclosed by a moat in the old fashion. We got down from our horses. Grooms made their way down the Progress, collecting the gentlemen's mounts.

'Do you know where we are billeted?' I asked the groom who took our horses.

'One of the steward's men will tell you, sir. You should wait here till then.'

I helped Barak; with his left leg useless he could not dismount unaided. He cursed and grumbled. Giles appeared; he looked better though he still leaned heavily on his stick. We sat on the grass and looked over the moat to the house and the procession of carts and people spreading out into the neighbouring fields. Already tents were starting to go up. My attention was drawn by a familiar black carriage, ringed by soldiers on horseback that had pulled into the next field. 'Broderick,' I said.

Giles looked at me curiously. 'Sir Edward Broderick of Hallington? I knew he was taken. Is he being brought south?'

'Ay.' It was inevitable, now the Progress was on the move again, that questions would be asked about that closed and guarded carriage. I looked at Giles. 'Did you know him?'

'Only by reputation. As a fine young man, a good landlord.' He smiled sadly.

'I am responsible for seeing he is properly looked after. At the request of Archbishop Cranmer.'

'On top of everything else?' Giles looked at me seriously. 'You carry a heavy load, Matthew.'

'Not for long, now we are on the move again. I had better go and see how he does. Excuse me.' I left the others sitting on the grass and walked across to the carriage.

Sergeant Leacon, who was brushing his horse, bowed to me. 'I was expecting to see you last night, sir,' he said.

'Something happened to detain me.' I looked at the closed carriage. 'How is the prisoner?'

'Listless.'

'And Radwinter?'

He spat on the ground. 'The same as usual.'

'I had best look in on them.'

'Sir William Maleverer was here last night, looking grim. He spent some time talking to the prisoner alone. Made Radwinter wait outside, which did not please him.'

I wondered if he had been trying to discover whether Broderick had any links with Jennet Marlin. 'Well, I will see how he does,' I said. I mounted the little step on the side of the carriage, and knocked on the door. It opened and Radwinter stared out at me. He appeared tired and a little unkempt, his hair untidy. He would be unable to keep up his usual standards in there.

'I thought you had forgotten us,' he said sourly.

He stood aside and I stepped into the dark airless carriage. It stank of sweat and unwashed bodies. The carriage seats had been knocked out and a couple of straw mattresses laid on the floor for prisoner and guard. Broderick lay on one of them, his wrists and ankles secured by heavy chains. Though it was hard to see in the gloom I thought he looked paler than ever.

'Well, Broderick,' I said.

He stared up at me with his bright angry eyes. I wondered what he might know of Jennet Marlin and her fiancé. But even if he did know something, Maleverer would have got nothing from him.

'Where are we now?' he asked.

'A place called Leconfield. We stay here tonight, and go on to Hull tomorrow, I believe.'

'Leconfield. Ah.' A look of sadness crossed his features.

'You know it?'

'Yes.' Broderick looked at the open door of the carriage. 'Are we at the castle?'

'Nearby. You can see it from here.'

'I would like to see it. Just through the door. If I may.'

'No,' said Radwinter.

'Yes,' I countered. I wanted to get a clearer look at the prisoner in the light. Radwinter shrugged angrily. Broderick tried to struggle to his feet but the heavy chains impeded him. I gave him my arm; he took it reluctantly. Through his dirty shirt his arm felt like skin and bone. He shuffled to the open door and looked out at the castle. Courtiers were riding across the drawbridge and a group of swans, disturbed by the noise, flew up from the still waters of the moat. The high brick walls shone red in the setting sun. All around, the trees in their bright autumn colours. I studied Broderick's face as he blinked in the unaccustomed light. He looked pitifully thin and pale.

'I came here many times as a boy,' he said, in softer tones than I had ever heard him use. 'This used to be the Yorkshire seat of the Percy family.' He looked at me. 'Once they were the greatest family in the north.'

'Who owns it now?' I asked.

'Who owns everything?' he answered. 'The King. He bullied the Earl of Northumberland into making him his heir, the King took everything when he died. And the earl's brother, Sir Thomas, who was the rightful heir, took part in the Pilgrimage of Grace and was executed.'

'Where do *his* bones hang?'

Broderick gave me a sharp look. 'Nowhere. The King had him

burned at Smithfield. He is naught but ashes on the wind now.'
Broderick looked back at Radwinter. 'I expect you saw it; you tell
me you go to all the burnings.'

Radwinter frowned. ''Tis everyone's duty to see the end of traitors.'

'For you it is entertainment. You are a fit servant for the
Mouldwarp.'

Radwinter laughed. 'I think you had best get back inside. Your
traitorous face is not to be seen by Christian people.' He took
Broderick's shoulder and shoved him back into the gloomy interior.
Broderick lowered himself clumsily on to the mattress, his chains
rattling.

'I could do with a little air myself,' Radwinter said. 'A word,
Master Shardlake?' He jumped lightly down on to the grass. I
clambered down beside him. He took a deep breath of the cold
evening air.

''Tis good to be outside. Do you know whether we move on to
Hull tomorrow?'

'I am not sure. I assume so.'

'I will be glad to be out of that carriage. It jolts constantly. But
at least it is safe. I hear someone tried to kill you,' he added in the
same light tone. 'And was herself killed. A woman.'

'Yes.'

'Maleverer told me when he came to question Broderick last
night. Broderick denied any knowledge of the woman or her
betrothed. Perhaps it was only someone you have annoyed with your
nosy priggish ways?'

'Very probably,' I replied flatly. I was not going to be provoked
into telling him more than the little Maleverer evidently had. 'Broderick looks ill and weak to me. Sergeant Leacon says you spend your
time telling him gruesome stories.'

'Fit subjects for a traitor. But there is a reason I talk to Broderick
thus.' His eyes narrowed. 'Tell me, Master Shardlake, do you frequent
the cockfight, or the bear-baiting? No, you would not, you are of a
weak nature.'

'What has this to do with anything?'

'When I was a boy I went to the bear pit as often as I could cozen a penny out of someone. And I would go to hangings with my father, and burnings, too, though there were fewer in those days. I learned there is a great difference between animals and people when they are led in to be killed for spectacle.'

I looked at him. Once I had been afraid of this man with his strange icy eyes, but increasingly when I encountered him now it was disgust I felt.

'The difference is *anticipation*. The dogs led into the pit do not think, Jesu, I am about to die in agony. They go in and they fight and they die. But the people *know*, will have known for days, what is coming to them. They anticipate the agony of slow strangling or having their flesh stripped from their bones by fire. For the condemned of course there is no release, but if a man may save himself by talking. . .' He raised his eyebrows. 'I have been telling Broderick of all that may come to him to try and frighten him. I have been forbidden to use physical methods but I have always found words may serve just as well.'

'Broderick will never talk,' I said impatiently. 'You know that.'

'Water wears away stone. I cannot believe he does not lie awake at night and think with terror of what is to come in the Tower.'

'Do you know, Radwinter,' I said, 'I think you are mad, and grow madder by the day.' And with that I turned and walked away.

✟

MY ENCOUNTER LEFT ME ill at ease. Radwinter always made me feel as though something unclean had been crawling over me. I walked off in the direction of the manor, frowning.

A number of officials were standing on the meadow in front of the moat, talking as they took the evening air. Among them I saw Master Craike standing on his own, checking papers on his little desk. I hesitated, for I knew my presence embarrassed him now, but crossed over. I wanted to talk to Tamasin and he might be able to tell me where she was billeted.

'Good evening, sir,' I greeted him. 'Still at work?'

'Yes. I am very busy, I fear.' He took a step away, and although I knew the reason for his reluctance to talk to me, nevertheless his brusqueness annoyed me.

'There is something I would ask you.' I made my voice as coldly formal as his. 'About the arrangements for tonight.'

'Very well. But I am busy. I have just learned we are to be here four nights.'

'Four?'

'Yes. We do not go on to Hull till the first of October.'

I set my lips. I wanted desperately to be on the boat to London, and here was more time lost. I turned back to Craike, remembering why I had sought him out. 'Do you know where the Queen's women-servants are camped?' I asked. He looked at me narrowly. 'Official business,' I said.

He pointed with his quill to a field where some tents were being set up a little away from the rest. 'Over there.'

'Thank you,' I said, then essayed a smile. 'I hope all goes smoothly with the arrangements.' But he had already turned his back. I shook my head and began walking towards the field. As I approached I saw Tamasin herself coming towards me from the tents, holding the hem of her skirts clear of the wet grass. As she approached I saw her eyes were red from crying.

'I came to find you,' I said. 'To tell you where we are.'

'And I was about to come looking for you, sir.' She gave me a watery smile and fell into step beside me. 'How is Jack?' she asked.

'All right so long as he does not put weight on that leg. Grumpy.'

'He will be.'

I looked at her. 'He told me Maleverer questioned you last night.'

She gave a sardonic smile that sat ill on her feminine features. 'So now *you* come to question me about it.'

'I need to know what he said.'

'He questioned all the Queen's servants. But neither they nor I could tell him anything. Jennet talked to me of little beyond our duties and her fiancé in the Tower. And her early life. It was very sad. She was an unwanted orphan, only Master Locke was ever kind to her. There was much to pity in her life, for all that she did.'

'Forgive me if I find it hard to sympathize.'

Tamasin did not reply.

'What about Lady Rochford? Jack said you told him that she seemed afraid when questioned?'

'I was not there. I only heard that she shouted at Maleverer and he shouted back.' She lowered her voice. 'I think she calmed when she realized it was nothing to do with the Queen and Culpeper. Culpeper has not been near for days.'

I looked at her. 'You have been crying. Were you afraid too?'

She met my gaze. 'I have been crying for Jennet. I cannot help it. She was kind to me, she treated me almost like a daughter.' She hesitated. 'What will happen to her body?'

'I have no idea. Left behind for burial at Howlme, probably. She tried to kill me, Tamasin.'

The girl gave a heartfelt sigh. 'I know. I do not understand any of it.'

'She acted at her fiancé's bidding, she admitted it herself. Her motive was love,' I added starkly. 'Love turned to obsession, excluding all other feelings.'

'Yes, she loved that man. It consumed her. What will happen to him now?'

'He will be questioned about this.'

'Harshly?'

'Yes.'

'That love could drive someone to do such evil, it is hard to believe.'

'It is what can happen when one gives oneself over entirely to feeling.'

She looked at me curiously. 'Is that what you believe?'

'Yes.'

'Then I am sorry for you, sir.'

I gave her a stern look. 'You know, Tamasin, some would say that trick you played with Jack the day we came to York was a sign of – not obsession, but – a lack of proportion.'

'We make our way in life by action, sir,' she said. 'Not endless talk.'

'Do we? Are you turned instructress now, to teach me?'

Tamasin turned her head away.

'So Jennet told you nothing that could help us fathom her plans?'

'No.' She kept her head averted.

'You must have talked with her about those stolen papers. After Maleverer questioned both of you at King's Manor?'

'We did not. She was not interested, or so it seemed.'

I looked at the side of her averted head. She was angry with me. I felt my old irritation against the girl rise again.

We reached the place where Giles and Barak were sitting on the grass. Barak heard us, looked up and waved at Tamasin. 'Jack,' she called eagerly, and ran towards him.

Chapter Thirty-six

WE STAYED AT LECONFIELD three days, in tents in the meadow beyond the moat. The King had business to conduct, we heard; the Scots were raiding the border villages, a sure sign James was not interested in a rapprochement with England. Perhaps the strengthening of the defences at Hull was no bad idea after all.

Those on the Progress were forbidden to wander beyond the fields that surrounded the camp but I did not go even that far; I stayed in my tent, resting. It did me good, and I felt myself relaxing, able to distance myself a little from my brush with death at Howlme. My only exercise was my daily visit to Broderick's carriage, which stood closely guarded in a neighbouring field. Broderick seemed to have retreated into himself, lying silently on his pallet and barely acknowledging my presence. Radwinter said little either; he was surly and there was none of his usual verbal sparring. Perhaps my accusation of madness had finally struck a nerve.

✝

ON MY FIRST MORNING at Leconfield I nerved myself to go and see Maleverer again. The guards directed me to an inner courtyard of the castle. As I entered my heart sank, for he was walking and talking with Richard Rich. They looked at me in surprise. I took off my cap and bowed.

'Master Shardlake again,' Rich said, a smile on his narrow face. I remembered he had seen me coming out of the Queen's tent at Howlme when Lady Rochford had summoned me, and wondered if he would refer to that, but he only said, 'I hear you have escaped assassination. By a woman. God's death, it would have made my life easier had she got you. I would not be put to the trouble of sorting out the Bealknap case.' He laughed, Maleverer joining in sycophantically.

I was so used to Rich's mockery that it made no impact on me now. I looked at Maleverer. 'It was about Mistress Marlin that I wished to speak to you, Sir William.'

Maleverer turned to Rich. 'He's a clever fellow, this. Sometimes he has good ideas. He delved out the truth about Broderick's poisoning.'

'He delves too much,' Rich growled. 'I will leave you, Sir William, we can talk about that piece of business later.' He walked away.

Maleverer gave me an irritated look. 'Well, Brother Shardlake?'

I told him I had been puzzling over Jennet Marlin's behaviour to me at the beacon. 'I have wondered whether it was she who attacked me at King's Manor. She never actually said so, and it is strange that I was left alive only to be hunted by her later.' I looked at him. 'Perhaps to keep from you, and show to Cranmer.'

He frowned and bit at one of his long yellow fingernails. 'That would mean those papers are in the hands of the conspirators after all.'

'Yes, Sir William, it would.'

'You have been thinking too much. If the conspirators had the papers they'd have used them by now.'

'They might be waiting for – for the right opportunity.'

He looked at me narrowly. 'Have you told anyone else about this notion of yours?'

'Only Barak.'

Maleverer grunted. 'And what does he say?'

I hesitated. 'He, too, thinks it is speculation.'

'There you are then. Forget about it. Do you hear, forget it.' He frowned mightily.

I thought, if he passed this on to the Privy Council and they thought the papers might be in the conspirators' hands after all, it would harm his reputation just when he thought all was mended.

'Very well, Sir William.' I bowed and turned to go. As I reached the gateway he called me back.

'Master Shardlake!'

'Yes, Sir William.'

His face was angry, troubled. 'Sir Richard Rich is right. You are a bothersome man.'

✝

OVER THE NEXT couple of days the weather remained fine, if a little colder each day. Leconfield was a pretty place, the castle and the surrounding meadows enclosed by woodland bright with autumn colour. Nonetheless the time passed slowly. Barak and Giles and I spent hours in my tent playing cards, swathed in coats. When we had lost all our money to Barak we switched to chess, and Giles and I taught him the game using chesspieces I drew on scraps of paper. We did not see Tamasin, for it would not have been proper for her to come to our tents. Barak met her most evenings, stumping round the camp with her; he had progressed to a stick now. Tamasin had been avoiding me since our quarrel in the field. She must have told Barak, for he had been a little uncomfortable with me since then.

On the morning of the third day I stood with Giles in front of my tent, looking at the woods in their autumn colours. I thought he seemed noticeably thinner now, less a solid oak of a man.

'How are you?' I asked.

'I have some pain,' he said quietly. 'But the cold in these tents is the worst thing. It saps my energy.' He looked at his big hands, adjusting his emerald ring. 'I am losing weight. This ring will fall off if I am not careful. I would be sorry to lose it; it was my father's.'

'Perhaps in Hull we will have brick walls around us again and a fire. 'Tis a large town, I believe.'

'I have already taken care of that.' He winked at me. 'Some gold has passed from me to one of Master Craike's underlings, it has secured me a room at an inn. You and Barak too.'

'That is generous, Giles.'

'No.' He smiled wryly. 'I might as well put my money to good use. Soon enough I will have no need of it. Jesu, but I miss my fire, and Madge to wait on me.' He looked at me. 'I have left her well provided for in my will, she will end her old age in comfort. And you will have my library.'

'Me?' I was taken aback.

'You are the only man I know who will appreciate it. But give those old lawbooks to Gray's Inn library. I should like my old Inn to have them.'

'But – your nephew...'

'Martin will have my house, and everything else. I made a new will before I left York. But I want to see him, to tell him.'

I put a hand on his arm. 'You will.'

For a moment he looked sad. Then we both jumped at the blast of a hunting horn. We saw, some way off, a procession of brightly robed riders heading for the woods, a huge pack of greyhounds loping along beside the horses.

'The King is going hunting,' Giles said. 'I hear he walks and rides so badly now he has to stand in a hide with his bow and arrow, and shoot at the stags as the hounds and keepers drive them by. He that was called the greatest athlete in Europe in his youth.'

The King. The true King, I wondered again.

✝

NEXT AFTERNOON we were told to make ready, we would be moving on to Hull the following day, the first of October. The new month came in with winds and heavy rain from the east, making it a miserable business getting the Progress together in the early morning, finding our horses and our place in the cavalcade. The fields had turned to mud, all the cart wheels and even the hems of the senior officials' robes were spattered with it. Barak was better able to ride now, the enforced rest had helped his leg. He probably wished he was back in his covered cart, though, as we rode slowly along with our heads bent against the driving rain.

Mercifully it stopped later that morning as we approached the town of Beverley. We passed through quickly, then went on through more flat countryside, white church steeples marking the occasional villages. The road began descending slowly, past fields of rich black soil, and late in the afternoon we saw a wide grey estuary in the distance, broader than the Thames at London and dotted with sails.

'Nearly there.' Giles, riding beside me, spoke with relief.

'Just the boat home now,' I said. My own heart lifted at the thought. 'That is the Humber, then? 'Tis wide.'

'It is. We will sail down there, past Spurn Head, and into the German Ocean.'

'Have you visited Hull before?'

'Once or twice, on legal business. The last time near twenty years ago. See, there are the walls.' I followed his pointing finger and saw, bounded by the grey estuary and a smaller river running into it at right angles, a walled town. It was smaller than I had expected, not half the size of York.

'The walls are an odd colour,' I said. 'Reddish.'

'They're brick,' Wrenne said. 'All the bricks in Yorkshire come through Hull.'

As we approached the city I saw a large group of dignitaries standing outside the walls, waiting to greet the King on this his second visit. The Progress drew to a halt and we sat waiting for some time as the royal party was welcomed in. Because of the press of people ahead I could not see them. I was glad, for even the sight of the assembled dignitaries had brought Fulford back to me, the thought of which still made me hot with shame and anger. I glimpsed Dereham and Culpeper, sitting on horseback among the courtiers.

At length officials began moving to and fro among us, directing people where they were to spend the night. I saw Master Craike among them, checking queries against papers on his portable desk. It was as well they were held down with a clip, for the wind was ruffling them. He came over to where we sat.

'Master Shardlake,' he said. 'You are to have accommodation at an inn. You and Master Wrenne and your man Barak. It seems someone has approved it.' He gave us a suspicious look and I wondered if he smelt bribery. Some of the other lawyers nearby, who would be sleeping in tents in the fields again, looked on enviously.

'I am to escort those with town lodgings into Hull now, if you would walk along. Your horses will be taken and stabled.'

So Giles and Barak and I walked into the city with Craike. We were among a fortunate group of officials, mostly far more senior than us, who had billets in Hull. As we approached the red-brick walls I saw another skeleton hanging in chains from the ramparts. Sir Robert Constable, I guessed, in whose mansion the King had stayed at Howlme. Wrenne averted his eyes, distaste clear on his face.

We walked under the gate and down a long main street Craike told me was named Lowgate. The buildings seemed in better repair than in York, the people a little more prosperous. They looked at us with a lack of interest as they stepped out of the way. This was the King's second visit; they had seen it all before.

'How long do we stay here?' I asked Craike.

'I do not know. The King wants to make plans for the new defences.'

'Where is he staying?'

Craike pointed to our left, where a clutch of tall chimneys overtopped the red-roofed houses. 'His manor house here. It used to belong to the de la Pole family.'

Yet another house he has taken, I thought. Craike seemed reluctant to converse, but I persisted. 'We have to get back to London by boat. Will many return that way?'

'No, after Hull the Progress will cross the river and ride to Lincoln. It breaks up there.'

'We have to return to London as soon as possible.'

Craike flattened his papers with a plump hand as the wind lifted them again. He looked up at the sky where grey clouds were scudding along. 'Then I hope the weather allows you to sail.' He stopped before the door of an inn. 'Well, here you are.'

Inside a number of gentlemen were already waiting. They looked down their noses at our lawyer's robes. Craike bowed to us. 'I must get back, my staff will doubtless have messed up the allocations. It is a nightmare.' He turned and left.

'Not the friendliest of men,' Wrenne observed.

Barak, leaning on his crutch, grinned wickedly. 'He has things on his mind.'

✝

BARAK AND I HAD a pleasant room at the back of the inn, Wrenne the one next to us. There was a fire, and a view over red-roofed houses sloping down to the muddy banks of the smaller river. The rain had started again, large drops streaking the little diamond-paned window. Barak sat down on the bed with relief. I looked at my panniers, unsure how much to unpack. Then I heard heavy footsteps on the stairs. The door opened without a knock and Maleverer strode in. He looked around the room.

'You've done well for yourself,' he said sardonically. 'I came to tell you Broderick is in Hull gaol. With Radwinter. One wing has been cleared of prisoners.' He ran his hand along the edge of his coal-black beard in that habitual gesture of his. 'I have new orders about him from the Privy Council. We don't know when we'll get back to London with this weather.'

'There may be delay?' I asked.

'There may. So the King has ordered that Broderick is to be groped here in Hull. There's a rack at Hull gaol. I'm supervising the racking myself.'

I had hoped, all this time, that somehow Broderick might escape what was coming to him. And now it would be done tomorrow.

'He is weak,' I said.

Maleverer shrugged. 'It has to be done. We don't think he knows exactly what was in that damned box of papers, but he may. And he may know the names of the London conspirators. We always knew there were London lawyers at the heart of the conspiracy, but we've not been able to lay them by the heels.' Maleverer cracked his fingers noisily. 'So, we'll see what can be got out of him tomorrow. And meanwhile they'll be getting information about Mistress Marlin's mission from Bernard Locke, in the Tower.'

I looked into his heavy, heartless face. For him it was just a task, another job. He gave me another quick, harsh smile, then left. Barak looked at the closed door. 'Jesu. He's a hard one. Hard as Lord Cromwell.'

☦

I SLEPT LITTLE that night. I lay awake thinking of what was coming to Broderick, remembering his mocking accusations that I was keeping him alive for the torturer. And for Bernard Locke it would have come already. Maleverer's heartlessness made me shudder. In the small hours I got up, quietly so as not to wake Barak who was snoring gently, and crossed to the window. The night was pitch dark, a high wind hammering raindrops against the panes. I wondered if Broderick was awake in his cell, perhaps trying to steel himself for the rack. A wet beech-leaf blew against the glass. Curled up on itself, it looked like an accusing finger.

☦

MALEVERER CAME TO the inn again after lunch. Once again Barak and Giles and I were playing cards. We were all in gloomy mood, for it was raining and blowing hard as ever, a real autumn gale. The innkeeper had said it was unusual for the wind to blow strongly from the southeast in October; but as long as it did, we could not set sail.

'Leave us,' he said curtly to the others. 'I would speak with Brother Shardlake alone.'

They went out. Maleverer threw himself into Barak's chair. It creaked loudly. He gave me that cold smile.

'You were right about Broderick,' he said without preliminaries.

'How?'

'He was in a weak state. I could see that when they brought him in. I had a room set up in the gaol, the rack in a corner and irons heating in the fire, so he could see what was coming.' He spoke as though he were describing preparations for a dinner. 'Radwinter brought him eagerly. Yet Broderick hardly looked at the implements, and when I said he'd feel their bite and singe unless he talked he only urged me to get it over. He's not short of courage.' Maleverer compressed his lips. 'So I did, I put him on the rack and because I couldn't trust any of the gaolers to hear what he might spill I sent them out, and Radwinter and I turned the wheels ourselves. Broderick was silent for a good minute, then he screamed and passed out, fainted clean away.' Maleverer shook his head. 'It took us several minutes to rouse him. I was worried, and Radwinter suddenly turned nervous, he said we should stop.'

'He had a prisoner die from his attentions once,' I said. 'Archbishop Cranmer was not pleased with him.'

'If Broderick died under my care before he talked, the King would have my balls.' Maleverer looked at me hard. 'What do you think is the matter with him?'

'Weakness and exhaustion. From his imprisonment, the poisoning, then being stuck in that carriage for days.'

He grunted. 'You were supposed to make sure he was in good health.'

'I did all I could.'

'Well, I'll take care of him myself now so he's in a better state when we get to the Tower. Feed him up. Radwinter won't dare defy *me*. Your job there is over.'

'Archbishop Cranmer—'

'My orders come from the Privy Council.'

'I see.' So that was it. My duties were over. I could wash my hands of Broderick. Like Pontius Pilate.

'Sir William,' I ventured. 'Do you know how long we will be in Hull?'

For answer he nodded at the window. 'There's a boat waiting, and as well as Broderick there's several officials who need to get back to London faster than they can ride. We must wait till the weather clears, though, for we'd be no faster on the roads in this rain, especially with Broderick in a carriage.' He glowered at the rain-spattered window.

'May I still go on the boat?' Now my escort duties were over there was no need for me to return to London quickly, but I desperately wanted to go home, and there were Giles and Barak to think of. I thought he would refuse, and was surprised when he nodded.

'Yes.'

'I wonder, sir, when we go, might Master Wrenne go with us?' I hesitated as I remembered an earlier promise. 'And Mistress Reedbourne?'

He shrugged. 'I care not. Talk to the Chamberlain's office if you want. There are places, but the officials will want paying.'

'Thank you.'

'Don't thank me till you're safe in London,' he said. There was something secret and mocking in his look as he went out. He left me feeling uneasy.

Chapter Thirty-seven

THE BAD WEATHER CONTINUED. Often it was raining hard and even when it was dry a strong wind blew, sending clouds scudding across the sky, always from the southeast. No boat could set out. We heard the King was visiting the mudflats on the other side of Hull river in pursuit of his idea of fortifying the city. He would be wet and windblown; he cannot command the weather after all, I thought sourly.

We became bored, for all that the inn was comfortable. It was worst for Barak. Still limited in how far he could walk, he was morose and irritable, only cheering up when Tamasin called. Then, from tact, I would leave the room and sit with Giles awhile. Since our talk in Leconfield Tamasin had been cold with me, and with Giles too; she seemed to blame us for Jennet Marlin's death, murderess though the woman had been. When Giles and I went to the Chamberlain's office, he had paid a great deal of money to secure places on the boat for Tamasin and Barak as well as ourselves, but although Barak had been effusively grateful, Tamasin had only thanked us in a cold voice.

Giles had taken to going for little walks around the town on the rare occasions when the weather was dry, and one evening as we sat in his room he told me what he had been doing. He had seemed well for some time now; the restful life here was good for him, for all it bored us.

'I have been getting to know some of the local lawyers,' he said. 'They live in a district down by the river. They even have a little library there.'

I looked up with interest. These last few days I had often wished I had something to read.

'It isn't up to much,' Giles continued. 'But they have a lot of old casebooks. I have been looking through them to pass the time. It is in one of the barrister's houses, other lawyers may use it for a small fee.'

'Even the barrister's opponents?'

'Ay. They must make such shift as they can up here, far from London. It is strange; I will never practise again and now I can read cases with interest and even amusement at the fumes and scratchings men make between each other.'

'It is hard,' I said gently. 'What you must face.'

He looked at me seriously. 'Not so hard now. I raged when I first realized what was wrong with me but I have had months to come to terms with what must be. I will be content so long as I can resolve matters in London. Mend that old quarrel with Martin. Ensure that when I die my name and family will not be forgotten, that I can leave a legacy to my kin.' Unconsciously he clenched a big fist, his emerald ring glinting.

'We will find Martin Dakin,' I said soothingly, although I was uncomfortably reminded of what Maleverer had said.

Giles nodded. 'Thank you.' He looked out of the window. 'The rain has stopped. Come, put on your lawyer's robe and I will take you to the library.'

'Jesu, I hope the weather will change soon. How I want to leave!'

He looked at me curiously. 'You will see that prisoner again on the boat? Broderick.'

'Ay.' I had told Giles that Maleverer had relieved me of my duties there. 'I hope he is not in too bad a state.'

'And then in London, he goes to the Tower.'

'Ay.'

'Well, let us not think of that.'

We went outside. It was a relief to smell fresh air. Many others from the Progress had taken advantage of the break in the endless bad weather to take a walk, and I saw a group of the lawyers' clerks coming towards us, including the fellow who had mocked me at the lodging house. I frowned and averted my face as they passed.

'Master Shardlake!' I jerked round at the sound of my name. If they dared to call after me in the street— But my brow cleared as I saw it was Sergeant Leacon who had addressed me. He was dressed in civilian clothes, a blue doublet and hose. With his blond hair and athletic frame he looked a handsome fellow.

'Sergeant. How are you? You remember Master Wrenne?'

'I do, sir.' He bowed to Giles.

'You are out of uniform, sergeant?'

'Ay, I am off duty. I have come out for a walk, since for once it is not pissing with rain.'

'We too. Walk with us,' I added, for I saw that he wished to speak to me. 'Any news on your parents' case?'

'Nothing good, sir. My uncle, that was helping my parents with their paperwork, he has had a stroke.'

'I am sorry to hear it.'

'Sir, will you still help us, when we return to London? If I can get my parents to come there?' There was a look of desperate appeal in his blue eyes.

'I will. Bring them to Lincoln's Inn.'

'They fret, for I do not know when we will get back. I have a place on the boat.'

'Have you?'

'Ay. To help guard Broderick. But heaven knows when it will leave.'

'Have you seen him?' I asked. 'How is he?'

Leacon shook his head. 'The castle gaolers have charge of him now. I know he was racked, but they had to stop because he was so weak. Perhaps Radwinter did him a good turn, keeping him locked up and in ill-health in that carriage all the way to Hull.'

'Ay, maybe.'

We had been walking through the narrow streets leading down

to the Hull River. It was tidal and seabirds foraged among the town rubbish on the mudflats, struggling to keep their balance in the wind.

'I had best get back,' Sergeant Leacon said.

'Tell your parents not to despair, I will help them if I can.' I watched as he turned a corner. 'I got them into this mess in the first place.' I said to Giles.

'How was that?'

I told him.

'Don't blame yourself,' he said. 'Blame the greedy men of spoil who descended on the monks' lands like vultures.'

'The monks could be hard landlords too.'

'Not up here.'

I did not reply.

'Come,' he said. 'The library is this way.'

He led me to a street of well-kept four-storey houses, and knocked at a door. A servant admitted us into a well-appointed hall, then to a large room filled with shelves where three or four black-robed lawyers sat reading casebooks and making notes at tables. One, a little middle-aged fellow, rose from his place and came to greet us.

'Brother Wrenne! Is this the lawyer from London tha told me of?'

'It is indeed. Brother Shardlake. Matthew, this is Brother Hal Davies, whose house this is and who had the splendid idea of turning this room into a library. And his fees to users are light, he makes no profit, it all goes to the upkeep.'

'I got a medal from the city for it,' Brother Davies said cheerfully. I liked his looks. He had an open face for a lawyer. 'You must come and visit the library while you are stuck here.'

'I would like to.'

'I fear you may be in Hull some while. This strong southeasterly is unusual in October. Even the Hanse merchants are wary of crossing the German Ocean just now.'

'How long do you think it might last?'

He inclined his head. 'It is hard to say with these autumn gales.

It could end tomorrow, or go on another fortnight. But divert yourselves here when you will. And for now, will you take a glass of wine with me?'

✝

WE PASSED A PLEASANT HOUR with Brother Davies. At the end of it Wrenne was looking tired, and readily agreed to my suggestion that we return to the inn. The rain had held off, and I wondered whether the weather might be about to change. Yet I had been disappointed in that hope many times these last few days.

As we turned into Lowgate I saw a group of young courtiers ambling along. They were walking down the middle of the street, making the locals step aside. My heart sank a little as I recognized Master Dereham and, a little behind him, Culpeper. Culpeper met my eye and then, without a word, left the group and vanished up a side-street. Dereham saw it, looked at me and frowned. I took Wrenne's arm and hurried him past the group, but a voice called after me. 'Hey there! You, the crookback lawyer!'

A couple of the courtiers laughed. I turned slowly. Master Dereham had left the group and was strolling towards me, hands on hips in an arrogant gesture. He stopped and waved me over. Reluctantly, I crossed to where he stood. He looked me over coldly.

'You again. I'm surprised you dare show your face about town after the arse you made of yourself at Fulford.'

'Have you business with me, sir?' I asked.

He spoke quietly. 'What have you done to Master Culpeper, lawyer, that he flees at the sight of you?'

'Who is Master Culpeper?' I asked calmly, though my heart was thudding fast.

He narrowed his eyes. 'And who was it coming out of the Queen's tent at Howlme? You, sir, and a young man and woman. Take care whom you meddle with, sir.'

I had not realized he had been there too. 'We had official business,' I said.

'Had you now?'

I stared back at him. He was naught but a young jackanapes for all his finery. He might be the Queen's secretary but she would not like him asking these questions of me. It worried me, though, the link he made between us: Culpeper, the Queen and I. He gave me a long stare, then turned away. I blew out my cheeks with relief as I stepped back to where Wrenne was.

'Come,' I said, then added, 'Oh, no,' beneath my breath; for now I saw Sir Richard Rich walking up the road, attended by a little gaggle of armed servants. He motioned me over with an imperious gesture. I felt suddenly angry at these people who could make me walk to and fro with a wave of their hands. What insults would Rich have for me in his turn?

He wore his cold little smile. 'Master Shardlake. The pies you have your fingers in. What business have you with the Queen's secretary?'

'Nothing of importance, Sir Richard. He just wanted to remind me of what happened at Fulford.'

Rich's smile broadened. 'Ah, yes, that.' Then his face went cold and hard. 'There is one pie I still want you to take your finger out of.'

'The Bealknap case.'

'Yes.' His cold grey eyes fixed mine. 'This will be my last civil request.'

'No, Sir Richard,' I told him.

He set his lips, took a deep breath. 'All right. I will give you fifty pounds to advise the London Guildhall to drop it. I know you are in need of money. Your father's estate.'

'No, Sir Richard.'

'Very well.' He nodded twice, then smiled again. 'In that case you may soon find that your life takes a nasty turn.'

'Do you threaten me with violence, sir?' I made myself speak boldly.

His cruel, knowing smile reminded me of the one Maleverer had given me. 'It is not violence I threaten. But there are other things I can do.'

'Persuade clients to leave me, as you did before?'

'Not that, no. Master Shardlake, you know what powers I have. I do not threaten lightly. Now. Will you drop the Bealknap case?'

'No, Sir Richard.'

'Very well.' He nodded, smiled again, and turned away.

✝

THAT EVENING WRENNE and I sat together over a glass of wine. Tamasin had come to visit Barak and I had made myself scarce. Faint moans and thuds came through the walls. Wrenne smiled. 'I suppose what they are doing should be called sinful, and you should tell Barak so as his employer.'

I laughed. 'Then I should hear his fine collection of oaths.' There was another thump. 'He'll do himself a mischief.'

Wrenne looked at me seriously. 'You risk mischief for yourself, Matthew.'

'What do you mean, Giles?'

'That case against this man Bealknap. I could not hear all Rich said to you, but I heard enough.'

I sighed. 'He tried to bribe me, then threatened me with nameless woes if I did not desist.'

'You don't have to accept his bribes, but why not drop it? You said yourself the case was weak.'

'To drop it under duress would be wrong.'

'Many lawyers would. You are obstinate, Matthew. And will you be doing your clients a service, advising them to pursue this case, if you cannot win? Because you dislike this man Bealknap and the corruption he stands for? The law has always been corrupt and always will be.'

I looked at him. 'But don't you see? Rich's desperation for me to drop the case means I *may* win. He has been unable to find a corrupt judge in Chancery. That must mean the judges think we do have a case, and they do not want to risk a ruling that is obviously corrupt.'

'Perhaps. But if the council win this case you know the King could just get Parliament to pass an Act reversing the law. He gets everything he wants, by fair means or foul, you know that.'

'If he does, he does.' I looked up at him. 'I shall go to that library tomorrow, look over some of the relevant case law again. After all this time away from the matter some new angle may strike me.'

He shook his head. 'Something *will* strike you, if you are not careful. That is what I fear.'

'I will *not* give into them,' I said. 'I will *not*.'

✝

A LITTLE LATER I left Giles to go to the jakes. As I stepped out I saw Tamasin walking up the hallway, perhaps from a visit to the same place. She looked at me coldly for a moment, then suddenly composed her features into a sweet smile. But I had seen the cold look.

'Master Shardlake,' she said, 'I have not thanked you properly for getting me a place on the boat. The sooner I am away from the Queen's household, the happier I shall be.'

'You should thank Master Wrenne,' I said. 'He paid for it.'

'Will you thank him for me?' she asked. She put a hand on the door of my and Barak's room.

Shameless creature, I thought. Her that thinks she might be of good birth. 'Yes,' I answered curtly.

She bit her lip. 'Do not be angry with me, sir,' she said in a small voice. 'I am sorry if I have been ill-mannered with you recently. Only Mistress Marlin's death was a blow. I could not quite believe she had done – what she did.'

'Well, she did. I am lucky to be here to tell the tale.'

'I see that now. I am sorry.'

'Very well,' I said, 'but now you must excuse me.'

I stepped past her quickly, making her move aside; more quickly than I had intended for she lost her balance, slipped and fell against the wall. Something fell from her dress to the floor.

'I am sorry,' I said quickly, for I had not meant to cause her to hurt herself. 'Let me.' I bent to pick up the object that had fallen on the floor. I looked at it, then held it up with a puzzled frown. It was a rosary, a cheap thing of wooden beads on a string, the beads smooth with long use. I looked up at her; her face had gone scarlet.

'You have found my secret, sir,' she said quietly.

I handed it to her. She quickly enclosed it in her little fist. She must have worn it on a belt round her underskirt, I thought, hidden.

I looked up and down the corridor. 'Does Barak know you are a papist?' I asked her quietly. 'He told me once you had no strong views on religion.'

She met my hard gaze. 'I am *not* a papist, sir. But my grandmother was brought up long before reform was heard of and she was always ticking at her beads. She said they calmed her when she was worried. It is a comfort to poor folk still.'

'A comfort that is disapproved of now. As you know, for you keep it hidden.'

Her voice rose defiantly. 'Saying the words in your head, sir, ticking the beads, what harm does it do? It calms me.' She looked at me and I saw the strain in her face. 'I am worried what we saw may come out. I am afraid. And I mourn Jennet.'

I looked at her fist closed round the rosary. I saw the nails were bitten to the quick. 'That is truly all the beads are, something to calm you?'

'Yes, that is all. I think I had better stop this habit,' she added bitterly. 'I will follow whatever forms of religion are required by the King, even though they change from year to year. It is a puzzle to me and perhaps a puzzle to God, but common folk must leave God and the King to resolve it between them, must they not?'

'That is wisest.'

She turned away then. She did not go back to our room where Barak waited but marched off down the corridor. Her footsteps sounded down the inn stairs. I followed more slowly. I wondered, had she told the truth about why she ticked the beads, or had she invented that tale about her grandmother with her usual quickness? I felt more than ever that I did not really know Tamasin, that she was a woman who kept much secret.

✝

THE NEXT MORNING found me at the little library once more, for all that it was raining again. As the servant took my wet coat in the hall, Brother Davies came clattering busily down the stairs, a leather bag under his arm.

'Brother Shardlake. Back so soon? I have to go now, a case before the City Council, but look at anything that interests you in the library.'

'Thank you. How much?'

He waved a hand. 'No fee for visitors. But a little word of warning.' He lowered his voice. 'Old Brother Swann is in this morning. He is over eighty, the oldest lawyer in Hull by many years. Long retired – he says he comes here to keep up to date with the law but really he comes to talk.'

'Ah. I see.'

'I looked in a moment ago, he is asleep before the fire. Do not wake him if you want to study.'

'Thank you.'

He nodded, took his coat from the servant and went out into the pelting rain. I opened the library door quietly. Within it was warm and peaceful, a good fire lit in the grate, the embossed lettering on the spines of the large old books glinting in the flames. The only occupant was an old man in a shiny lawyer's robe, fast asleep by the fire. His face was a mass of lines and wrinkles, the pink skull showing through sparse white hair. I tiptoed over to the shelves, took a couple of books containing cases relevant to the Bealknap case and sat down at a table. I found it hard to concentrate, though; I had been away from my books too long. I reflected on Giles's words. I had not liked that look Rich had given me as we parted. Yet every instinct told me Rich would not have gone to so much trouble unless he feared he might lose the case. I had to go on, I had to try to win. Fighting for my clients was my life's work; if I gave in, what was left for me?

I looked up to find the old man had woken and was looking at me with surprisingly bright blue eyes. He smiled, multiplying the wrinkles in his face.

'Not in the mood for work today, brother?'

I laughed. 'No, I fear not.'

'I do not think I have seen you before. Are you new to Hull?'

'I am here with the King's Progress.'

'Ah, yes, that.'

'My name is Matthew Shardlake.' I rose in my place and bowed.

'Forgive me if I do not rise. I am eighty-six. My name is Alan Swann. Barrister at law. Retired,' he added with a chuckle. 'So, then, the bad weather keeps you here.'

'I fear so.'

'I remember the great gale of 1460, the year of the Battle of Wakefield.'

'You remember that?' I asked in surprise.

'I recall the messenger coming to Hull saying the Duke of York was slain, his head set over the gates of York wearing a paper crown. My father cheered, for we all supported the House of Lancaster then. It was later the county went over to the Yorkists.'

'I know. I have a friend in York who has told me stories of the Striving between the Roses.'

'Hard times,' he said. 'Hard times.'

A thought struck me. 'You will remember Richard III's seizure of the throne after King Edward V died. The disappearance of the Princes in the Tower?'

He nodded. 'Ah, yes.'

'When Richard took the throne, rumours were put about that his brother Edward IV's marriage was invalid.' I hesitated. 'And was there not something about King Edward's own legitimacy?' I looked at Brother Swann keenly. Giles had been little more than a boy in 1483, but this ancient would already have been a man of almost thirty.

Brother Swann was silent, turning to look into the fire. The wind drew the yellow flames up the chimney with a faint roar. I wondered if he had forgotten me, but then he turned back to me with a smile.

'That is a matter no one has spoken of for many years. *Many* years.'

'I am something of an antiquarian. Like my friend from York. He was telling me about the rumours, about King Edward.' I felt guilty, lying to the old man, but I wanted to know what he remembered.

Brother Swann smiled. 'It was an interesting story. How much of it was true no one knows, nor ever will for the King's father suppressed all talk of it.'

'Yes, I heard.'

He looked at me. 'Edward's mother, Cecily Neville, she made the claim after Edward died. She said in public that Edward IV's father had not been the late Duke of York, her husband. She said Edward was illegitimate, the son of a liaison she had with an archer, when they were in France during the wars.'

My heart started beating fast.

'That made a mighty stir,' the old man said softly. He paused and wrapped his cloak around himself. 'There is a bitter draught from that window. This wind nearly blew me off my feet on my way here. I remember the gale of 1460. . .'

I controlled my impatience. 'Yes, you told me. But you were talking of Cecily Neville—'

'Ah, yes. Cecily Neville stood up outside St Paul's – I think it was St Paul's – and told the world that Edward IV was the offspring of a liaison between her and an archer. A lawyer came up here from London on a case shortly after, he told me all about it.'

'Do you remember the archer's name?'

'Blaybourne. Edward Blaybourne, a Kentish archer.'

The blood was thudding in my ears. 'What happened to him?'

'I think he must have been dead by the time of Richard III's usurpation. The liaison had been forty years before, after all.' He looked at me seriously. 'Perhaps he was done away with.'

'So there was no real evidence for the story?'

'Not that I know of. As I said, it was hushed up after the Tudors came to the throne. For Henry VII married Edward IV's daughter, the present King's mother. There was an Act of Richard's—'

'The *Titulus Regulus*.'

'You know of that?' He looked at me with sudden concern. 'I am not sure we should be talking of such things, even now. I have not thought of it for years.'

'You must be one of the few who remember it.'

'Yes. Not many reach eighty-six,' he said proudly. 'But it was only rumour, even then.'

I got up suddenly. 'Sir, I have just remembered something. I was so interested in our talk, I forgot I have an appointment.'

Brother Swann looked disappointed. 'Must you go so soon?'

'I fear so.'

'Well, perhaps I shall see you again. I am often here in the mornings, by Brother Davies's good fire.' He looked at me, sudden sadness in his eyes. 'He indulges me. I know I talk too much and distract people. But you see, sir, all my contemporaries are dead.'

I took his hand, thin and light as a bird's claw, and pressed it. 'You have a store of memories to be proud of, brother. Thank you.' And with that I went out. My head was in a mighty whirl.

Chapter Thirty-eight

I WALKED RAPIDLY BACK through Hull, my head down against the buffeting wind. My mind was racing, making calculations, connections.

So I had been right all along when I hazarded to Barak that Edward IV might have been illegitimate, and Blaybourne his father. But Blaybourne had not been done away with as old Brother Swann surmised; he had survived to write a confession on his deathbed. I remembered those few words I had read, in that rough uneducated hand: '*This is the true confession of me, Edward Blaybourne, that I make in contemplation of death, that the world may know of my great sin . . .*' He must have died before 1483, when old Cecily Neville made her announcement, or, as Brother Swann had said, surely she would have produced him as evidence of her claim.

And in the Tower, back in April after the conspiracy was discovered, someone had confessed on the rack to the existence of those papers, but had not known where they were nor who had them. The conspirators' policy of limiting information to those who needed to know had served them well. Bernard Locke, taken to the Tower, *did* know that Oldroyd had the papers, but ironically they had feared to torture him because he had connections and because the evidence against him was thin. Meanwhile they had arrested Broderick. My guess was that he did know something about the papers, but they had been unable to get him to talk in York and decided to bring him south.

And what of the other documents in that box? Probably more evidence about Blaybourne, to support his claim. Like the *Titulus*.

And that family tree was a sort of aide-memoire. I asked myself who knew about the Blaybourne story now. The King and the Privy Council would have known for months. When I told Maleverer that Oldroyd had spoken the name Blaybourne before he had died, he had taken it to the Duke of Suffolk. The Duke knew what that name meant. He would have told Maleverer then. That explained his saying that it all went back to Cecily Neville. I remembered the rest of Oldroyd's words: '*No child of Henry and Catherine Howard can ever be true heir. She knows.*' I stopped dead in the street. Of course. He meant no child of theirs could be true heir, not because a child of Catherine Howard's might be Culpeper's, but because Henry was the grandson of an archer. And when he said, 'She knows,' he had meant Jennet Marlin, who had just knocked him off his ladder. 'This is not about Catherine Howard at all,' I said aloud.

✞

IN OUR ROOM AT the inn Barak was stumping around; he had abandoned his stick, too soon in my opinion, and was limping around the chamber, wincing as he put his foot to the floor.

'Be careful,' I said.

'It's all right if I put only a little weight on it!' He took a step forward, winced again and sat down heavily on the bed. 'Fuck it!'

'Jack,' I said, sitting on my own bed next to his, 'I have found something out.'

'What?' There was irritation in his tone, but when I told him what Brother Swann had told me, and of what I had deduced on the way back, he whistled.

'Jesu.' He was silent a moment, letting it all sink in, then he looked at me. 'So it's true, the King is truly the grandson of a Kentish archer.'

'That's how it looks.'

His eyes were wide. 'And the King knows – he'll have known since the existence of these papers came out.'

'And will have been told I found the papers, and lost them. No wonder he wanted to hurt me at Fulford. And no wonder the rebels were desperate to get those documents, if Blaybourne's confession is in there.'

'Yet Bernard Locke wanted Jennet Marlin to destroy them, to save his skin.'

'Yes. It's an irony.'

'But how the hell did that confession get from Blaybourne in Kent, assuming that's where he went back to, into the hands of the Yorkshire rebels? And if it's – what – over sixty years old, why only use it now? Why not during the Pilgrimage of Grace five years ago?'

I stroked my chin. 'Robert Aske and the commons did not want to overthrow the King then, only Cromwell and Cranmer. And maybe they did not have the papers then.'

He looked at me keenly. 'So you think this has nothing to do with Catherine Howard and Culpeper at all?'

'No. The fact that Jennet Marlin killed him certainly puts a new light on Oldroyd's words. When he said, "She knows," I think he meant Jennet Marlin.'

He heaved a sigh of relief. 'Then we're in the clear. Tammy will be mightily relieved when I tell her.' He thought a moment. 'Will you tell Maleverer what the old lawyer said?'

'There's no point. He knows about Blaybourne already. No, there is no reason to do anything. We can forget about it, and about Catherine Howard, and go home.' I shook my head. 'Taking two dangerous secrets with us, about Blaybourne and the Queen. But we must keep our mouths shut.'

'I wonder if the conspirators have those papers now.'

'Who knows?' I waved a hand. 'If so, let them do what they will, let them print a thousand copies of Blaybourne's confession and post them round the streets of York and London. I do not care any more.'

'You could perhaps tell Cranmer what you suspect about Jennet Marlin never having the papers,' he mused. 'It might be of some help to them in unravelling the conspiracy.'

'I'll think about it.'

'You should do it.'

'I'll think on it,' I repeated irritably. I realized that despite the fact they were mostly papists, part of me was with the conspirators. 'Anyway, Jesu knows when we'll get back,' I added, nodding at the window. It had started raining again, a high wind blowing big drops against the pane.

'We'll get there eventually, I suppose. Back to Lincoln's Inn.'

I looked at him. 'You are still coming back to work with me? You haven't changed your mind?'

He nodded. 'I still want to come back. It's time to settle down. I shall be seeing Tammy,' he added, giving me a challenging look.

I hesitated. 'I know she still blames me in some way for that woman's death. Oh, she is making herself friendly again, it would not do to make an enemy of the man who employs you, but I can see she still blames me. It is not fair.'

Barak looked uncomfortable. 'Tammy finds it hard to accept Jennet Marlin is dead. She knows you are not to blame, but — women are illogical.'

I grunted. 'Tamasin can be clever enough when it suits her. Like faking that robbery. Like making up to me now, because she knows on which side her bread is buttered.' I wondered whether to tell him about the rosary, but thought, he will only believe the story that she has it because it was her grandmother's. True or not, he will take her side, for that is what people in love do.

He was frowning at me. 'Tammy has been in tears many nights since Jennet Marlin died. I wish she'd curse the woman as she deserved, but she won't. Between that and her worry over the Queen and Culpeper, she is finding things hard.'

'Well,' I said. 'It seems when we return to London I must get used to her ways.'

'Yes,' he answered boldly, then added quietly, 'You know what your trouble is?'

'What?'

'You don't understand women. *Normal* women, ordinary *feminine* women. when you do like a woman, it's some fierce malapert creature like Lady Honor last year—'

I stood up. 'I wonder how much *you* understand. Tamasin seems to have you wrapped round her little finger, which is a thing I thought I would never see.' I wished as soon as I said it that I had not spoken; apart from anything else, we were both fractious from being cooped up together.

Barak's eyes narrowed. 'You know what your *other* problem is? You're jealous. Jealous of what Tammy and I have. Perhaps you need to find another fine lady to moon over.'

I stood up. 'You have said enough!'

'Hit a nerve, have I?' he asked sardonically.

'I am going to see Master Wrenne.' I walked out, slamming the door like a silly child.

✝

RELATIONS BETWEEN BARAK and me remained strained over the following days. The weather continued windy with hard blustery showers, the wind still from the southeast so there was no question of setting sail. The innkeeper grumbled that if this went on, Hull would be ruined for lack of trade. Tamasin was cool with me again. Barak had probably told her of our quarrel; I wondered if she had told him about the rosary.

I was glad, though, that under this regime of enforced rest Giles's health had remained stable, though sometimes I sensed from his drawn expression that he was in pain. I spent much time with him, exchanging stories of our time in the law, and he told me much of life in York and the town's decline during his lifetime. I understood more and more how the north had been neglected and oppressed under the Tudors. I knew that, short as our acquaintance had been, when Giles died it would be like the loss of my father over again. But I would be with him at the end, I had decided, even if it meant coming back to York with him after he had visited London.

The Progress, meanwhile, had left Hull. On the fourth of October there had been a break in the weather; even some watery sunshine, the first we had seen in that place. Word went round that the Progress would be crossing the Humber next day, on the first leg of the long journey home. Giles and I walked down to the shore of the great estuary and watched as hundreds of boats ferried the vast retinue across the river to Barton on the Lincolnshire shore. It went on for hours. Boats must have been brought from all over Yorkshire, the water was thick with white sails.

As we walked back to the town it felt strange, empty. The Progress seemed to have been the centre of my life for so long that it was hard to realize that, so far as I was concerned, it was over. I felt a great relief, an uplifting of my heart, not least because every day that passed took King Henry and Queen Catherine another few miles further away. And Dereham and Culpeper and Lady Rochford too – I would never have to see any of them again. The Queen's secret would probably not be discovered now; she and Culpeper had had a nasty scare and I doubted she would see him again. That just left Rich to deal with in London, over the Bealknap case. And I was feeling more confident about that, almost looking forward to it.

✝

THE RAIN AND GALES returned the evening the Progress left, and the weather did not change for another ten days. Not until the fifteenth of October, when we had been there a fortnight, did I realize, walking back from Brother Davies's library, that there had been no wind or rain to speak of for two days. I had spent much of my time talking with, or rather listening to, old Brother Swann. Perhaps now at last we might set sail. I thought of Broderick. He had been two weeks in Hull gaol, and I wondered how he fared.

That night when I returned to the inn I found a message to go to the King's house, where Maleverer wished to see me. So he had not returned to York yet. Wondering anxiously what he wanted now, I went round at once. The old de la Pole family mansion was an enormous courtyard house, the finest building in the city. I was led to Maleverer's latest office at the back of the building. As always, his room was dominated by a large desk covered with documents; the image he set forth was ever that of the indispensable official.

He studied me with that heavy, stony look of his, twirling a quill in his big hand. 'Well, Master Shardlake,' he said abruptly. 'The waiting is over. We set sail tomorrow. The sea has been pronounced safe at last. The way things have turned out, we might have been better riding after all, but we never knew when the weather would end.'

'And you said you are going to London too, Sir William?'

'Yes. I have to account for what happened in York, as well as deal with certain property purchases.'

'I see.' And Rich blackmailed Craike so you could have them cheaply, I thought.

'Be at the dock tomorrow at ten. You and Barak, the Reedbourne girl and that old man who goes with you. Your little entourage.'

'We shall be there.'

'I may need to call you for questioning in London, about Mistress Marlin. Your horses will be taken back to London by road.'

So maybe it is not over yet, I thought.

'How long will the voyage take, Sir William?'

'Depends on the weather. Less than a week, if it holds. We will still be home before the King.'

'How is Broderick?' I asked hesitantly.

'Well enough. I've had some good fare taken to him and told him if he didn't eat he'd be fed forcibly with a tube down his throat. He's fattening up nicely, like a Christmas fowl.' He smiled, a slash of white in his black beard. 'By the way, I have had a letter by a fast rider from London. Bernard Locke has confessed. He confirmed Jennet Marlin was working on his instructions.'

'How did he get her to do it?' I asked quietly.

Maleverer shrugged his heavy shoulders. 'Apparently she was besotted with him. It was as she told you, he knew there was a box containing papers that could do damage to the King. He told her to find it, if need be kill anyone who stood in the way. He admitted he told her to get the box but to destroy it, not bring it back to London to give to a conspirator there, which is what Locke had been instructed to do if the northern rising failed. He told her he had repented, but he admitted in the Tower that it was to save his own skin.'

'I see,' I said neutrally.

'Apparently there was a letter among the papers authorizing Oldroyd to give them up to Locke if he called, giving a description of him. To Locke, not a woman. That was why Jennet Marlin had to kill Oldroyd to get the box, and that was why the box incrimi-nated Locke.'

'Did he . . .' The question stuck in my throat for a moment as I thought of how the answer would have been obtained. 'Did he give the names of any other conspirators?'

'No. That's where the bastards have been clever. I told you before how well they were organized: in cells, no one person knowing more names than he needed. And Locke wasn't told what else was in the box either, only that it contained important papers. His contact in London was one of the rebels who escaped — he's probably in Scotland now, helping King James plan trouble for us. Locke was supposed to have given the box to someone else, a fellow barrister who would make himself known to him.'

'From Gray's Inn?'

'He didn't know who. I believe him.' He set his mouth hard. 'But we'll find him, if we have to have every lawyer from the north brought to the Tower.' Wrenne's nephew, I thought with sudden alarm.

'How did Bernard Locke react when he learned Jennet Marlin was dead?' I asked quietly.

He shrugged. 'Didn't believe it, till the Tower warden waved his engagement ring, which I prised off her finger and sent down there, in his face.'

'Was he sorry?'

'I don't know. Who cares?' He walked across to me, standing close so that he looked down on me from his great height and I could smell his rank breath. 'You'll keep this quiet, you understand. You worked for Lord Cromwell. You know the value of a shut mouth and the penalties for opening it.'

'Yes, I will.' I thought, Martin Dakin is in trouble now if he wasn't before. They will have Garden Court inside out.

Maleverer was looking at me narrowly. He smiled, his cold knowing smile. 'Another acquaintance of yours will be on the boat, by the way. Sir Richard Rich.'

'He did not go back with the Progress?'

'No, he has a place on the boat. He wanted to return to London as soon as he could.' He smiled again. 'Have you given up that case against him?'

'No, Sir William.'

He smiled again. 'I hope you know what you are doing.'

✞

WE WERE AT the docks early. The first sunny day since we got to Hull, the water calm, seabirds wheeling and crying. Our ship dominated the harbour, a seventy-foot caravel, with big square sails adapted for speed. The huge stern rose twenty feet above the waterline. 'The Dauntless' was painted in white letters on its side. Blocked-off gunports showed it had once been a warship. I guessed the lower decks would have been partitioned into rooms and fitted out comfortably, for I could see by their expensive clothes that the half dozen or so officials waiting to go aboard, each attended by a servant, were senior people. Rich was among them, talking to Maleverer, but neither gave us a glance.

We stood in a little group, waiting to go aboard. Myself and Giles, leaning on his stick and eyeing the boat keenly; Barak and Tamasin next to Giles. I had still not told Giles his nephew might be in danger. I feared the shock it might be to him.

'Soon be off,' Giles said to Barak and Tamasin. Barak nodded and Tamasin smiled tightly. She stood by Barak's side, ready to give assistance should he fall, for he still limped heavily.

My attention was drawn by a carriage that trundled over the docks to the water's edge. Curious heads turned everywhere as the door opened and Sergeant Leacon stepped out, accompanied by two red-coated soldiers. They were followed by Radwinter, who stood on the dockside looking around him. Then the two soldiers helped Broderick from the carriage. A coat had been thrown over his shirt; he pulled it round him as he felt the keen wind from the sea. I saw he cradled his left arm in his right and winced with pain as he moved. Even a few minutes on the rack, I knew, could leave a man with a dislocated limb.

He looked at the little crowd on the dockside. His eyes fixed on my little group and he stared straight at us for a long moment, his face set hard. Then he nodded slowly, as though to say, here, see what has become of me. The soldiers nudged him towards the planks that led from the docks to the ship. I saw his feet were still shackled, the chains rattling as they guided him onto the boat, Radwinter following. They crossed the deck and went below.

'So that is Broderick,' Wrenne said quietly. He looked at me intently. 'He will die in London?'

'Yes,' I answered bleakly. 'If he survives his torture he will die a traitor's death, disembowelled at Tyburn.'

'I had not realized he was so young.'

The clerk in charge of the arrangements spoke to one of the courtiers. They began going aboard, several getting their servants to help them across the planks, looking down nervously at the water. Then the clerk came over to us. He was a plump, bustling fellow. He reminded me of Master Craike, well on his way back to London with the Progress by now. He had not said goodbye before he went.

'If you would go aboard, sirs.'

Giles stepped forward. I turned to Barak, essayed a smile. 'Well, here we go at last.'

'Ay. Goodbye to Yorkshire. And good riddance,' he added as Tamasin led him aboard by the hand.

Chapter Thirty-nine

THE FOUR OF US — me, Barak, Tamasin and Giles — each had
tiny cabins in the stern, no bigger than cupboards, with space
only for a narrow bunk nailed to the floor. Across the way I caught
a glimpse of a servant unpacking his master's bag in a larger cabin.
A little further down the two soldiers that had brought Broderick
aboard stood guard outside a heavy door; the ship's lock-up, no
doubt. I wondered if Radwinter was in there with the prisoner. We
four went back on deck. It was cold even with the sea calm and the
skies clear. I dreaded to think what would be like in rough weather.

The crew were busy with the sails, under the eye of the mate, a
stocky man with a weatherbeaten face. Satisfied, he marched off,
boots ringing on the planks. There was a bump, a creak and the
ship began moving away from the wharf. Giles, who was wearing a
cap, doffed it at the Yorkshire shore as we moved away.

'I should keep that off,' I said. 'Or you'll lose it in the wind.
You should really be below.'

'I'll manage.' But as he pulled his coat tightly round him I
noticed his face seemed drawn. He went to sit down on a bench
nailed to the deck, while Barak, Tamasin and I watched as Hull
faded slowly from view, a light swell in the Humber estuary making
the ship rise and fall. I felt a little sick, and recalling what someone
had told me once I fixed my eyes on the mudbanks on the horizon.

I heard a murmur behind me. 'That was him, at Fulford. The
King made him bare his back to the crowd.' I turned to see a pair
of clerks looking over their shoulders at me. I frowned at them and
they turned away. So the story of what had happened at Fulford

Cross was already growing in the telling, I thought bitterly, as stories do. Would I never be allowed to forget my humiliation by King Henry? I wondered what they would say if they knew he might be no more than a Kentish archer's grandson.

'Oh, God.' Barak lurched abruptly, then bent forward and vomited on the deck. He lost his balance, pitched forward and fell with a thud on the boards. There was a burst of laughter from the clerks, and the sailors working at the mast looked over and grinned. I helped him to his feet. Tamasin took his other arm and we led him to sit down next to Giles. The acid smell of vomit made my own stomach heave. Barak's face was white as paper. He put his head between his knees and groaned, then lifted it and looked at me.

'I hate being ill, and having only one fucking leg that works properly!' he burst out. 'I hate it!' He glared at the clerks. 'I'd make those arseholes laugh if I was fit!'

'You'll be back to normal soon.'

'You can rest when you get back to London, Jack,' Tamasin said. She looked at me appealingly behind Barak's back. 'Perhaps Master Shardlake will let you stay at his house for a while, so his housekeeper can look after you, speed your recovery.'

'Yes,' I said awkwardly. 'Yes, we can do that.'

'I don't want any favours. Oh, God.' He put his head between his knees again.

I walked to the rail to escape the smell of vomit. I felt annoyed at Tamasin's request; the calculating little piece had made it when I could least refuse. But she was right, he could not yet cope on his own; he would try to do too much and injure himself again.

After a few minutes I went back to where Barak still sat with his head between his knees, Tamasin's arm round him. On his other side Giles was slumped heavily on the bench. His stillness sent a momentary chill down my spine, until I touched him and his eyes opened.

'Giles?' I asked gently. 'Are you all right?' He winced with pain.

'I must have fallen asleep.'

'Barak has been sick, he fell over. Did you not hear?'

He looked tired, tired to death. He essayed a smile. 'Not a good sailor, eh? It is a long time since I was at sea, but fortunately I have never got sick.' He looked over to the mudbanks in the distance. 'We are still in sight of Yorkshire, then.'

'I gather it will be many hours before we are out of the estuary.'

'I wonder how Madge is coping, without me to fuss over.'

'When we get to London, Giles, my first task will be to help you find your nephew. Barak will help too.'

Giles lowered his voice. 'How are things between you and him?'

'Ah. You have noticed something was amiss.'

'It has been hard not to, these last days. Something to do with the girl?'

'In a roundabout way.' I looked at the coastline, a little further off now. 'But do not worry about that. We will be all right once all this is over, once we are back in our routine at Lincoln's Inn.' I smiled at him. 'And then we will find your nephew.'

He looked at me thoughtfully. 'How will you go about it? Finding Martin?'

'We can go to Garden Court, and if he is not there, the Inn Treasurer can tell us where he practises.'

He nodded. 'So it should be quite simple.'

'Yes.' I said, hoping to God it would be.

✞

FOR THE NEXT three days the weather stayed calm and bright, and though it was uncomfortable sitting around on deck or cramped in those tiny cabins, it could have been a great deal worse. We saw nothing of Rich or Maleverer; doubtless they were in comfortable quarters below decks. Giles too spent most of his time in his cabin, in his tiny bunk. He lay quietly, seeming withdrawn. I suspected he was in much pain, and worried about him.

Although the weather made life easier for the passengers, we heard the captain was unhappy, for in place of the gale there was now only the lightest of winds and the ship had to tack endlessly. On the fourth day the news went round that we would have to pull in at Great Yarmouth on the Norfolk coast, for we had not enough supplies left to complete the voyage. I saw Maleverer arguing fiercely with the captain, saying enough time had been lost, but the captain stood his ground.

We were at Great Yarmouth two days, taking on supplies. We learned the Progress had now dissolved at Lincoln. The King was hurrying south as fast as possible, for he had had word that Prince Edward was ill.

'The life on which the Tudor dynasty depends,' Giles said as we sat together on the deck, watching as the ship pulled away from Great Yarmouth. He had come up for some air, saying he felt better, though to me he still looked ill and frequently made those little winces of pain that cut me to the heart. Barak, who had found his sea-legs, was standing at the rail with Tamasin. We had spoken little in the last few days.

'Unless Queen Catherine becomes pregnant,' Giles ruminated. 'But they've been married over a year now, and nothing. Perhaps the King can father no more children.'

'Perhaps,' I said hesitantly. Knowing what I knew about the Queen, I did not want to get involved in a discussion along those lines.

'If the Prince dies,' Giles continued, 'who then will be heir to the throne? The Countess of Salisbury's family wiped out, both the King's daughters disinherited. What confusion King Henry would leave us then.' He gave a bitter little laugh.

I got up. 'I must stretch my legs, Giles, they are stiff.' He wrapped the rug he had brought up more tightly around his big frame. 'It will get cold now we are out at sea,' I told him. 'Perhaps you should go down again,' I added, hesitantly for I knew how he disliked being treated like an invalid. But he said, 'Yes, I will go below. Help me, would you?'

I saw him down to his cabin and returned to the deck. Tamasin and Barak were still talking at the rail, laughing. I felt excluded. I saw Barak incline his head to where a sailor was walking along the deck. To my astonishment, half a dozen rats swung by their tails from one hand, their long black bodies dripping blood on to the deck.

'The ship's ratcatcher,' Barak said to Tamasin with a grin. She screwed up her pretty face and turned her head away. He nudged her. 'D'you know what the main perk of his job is?'

'No. I don't want to.'

'He gets to eat the rats.'

'Sometimes you are disgusting,' she said.

'Better than the weevilly old biscuits they get.' He laughed.

Just then the two soldiers climbed out of the hatchway leading below deck. They waited as Broderick followed them up, his hands and feet chained, a scrawny pitiful figure beside the two big men. He was followed up by Sergeant Leacon, and then Radwinter.

The soldiers led Broderick across to the rail. He stood there, looking out to sea, a man on either side in case he thought to jump over the rail. Sergeant Leacon looked out over the deck, taking deep breaths of fresh air. Radwinter, seeing me, came over.

'Master Shardlake.'

His face had a tired, pinched look, and his hair and beard were longer, unkempt. He must have been below decks with Broderick nearly all the time since we left Hull. It struck me it was a long time since he had been as neat and dapper as when I first saw him at York Castle.

'Well, Radwinter,' I said. 'Not long now to London, let us hope.'

'No.' He looked up at the sails. 'I fancy there is more of a wind. I heard the captain say this was an unlucky voyage.'

'Superstition.'

'Yes. We will be in London in a few days.' He smiled, his old wicked smile. 'Then Sir Edward will have a merry time in the Tower.'

'Is he well?'

'Well enough. Do you know, he cried like a woman when I told him we had left Spurn Head behind. Said it was because he would never see Yorkshire again. I told him they may nail his quarters over the York gates once they are done with him.'

I shook my head. 'You have no pity for him, have you?'

Radwinter shrugged. 'In my work it does not do to have pity. You said I was mad once—' his eyes glinted and I saw that indeed he had not forgotten that – 'but to be a gaoler of traitors and heretics and be soft-hearted with them, that *would* be madness. Nor would it be God's will.'

'God's will is torture and bloodshed?'

'Where necessary to preserve true religion.' He looked at me with contemptuous pity. 'Have you not read your Testament, all the blood and battles? The world God made is full of violence and we must work in that world. The King knows that, he is not afraid of harshness.'

'Does it not say somewhere the meek shall inherit the earth?'

'Not until the strong have made it safe.'

'When will that be? When the quarters of the last papist are nailed above York's gates?'

'Perhaps. You have to be strong to do right in this world, Master Shardlake. You have to be ruthless, as ruthless as our enemies.'

I turned away. Sergeant Leacon was walking towards me. He gave Radwinter a look of distaste, then turned to me. 'Master Shardlake, good day.'

'Good day, sergeant. I called Radwinter mad once,' I said in a low voice. 'He seems more so every time I see him.'

Leacon nodded. 'I have been put over him now, by Sir William.' He looked at Radwinter, who had gone over to the rail and stood looking out to sea. 'I think Sir William has lost trust in him; he did not deal well with what happened in York.'

'No. It was outside his experience, I think.'

'He hates losing his authority. I see him looking at me sometimes and think he would like to kill me.'

'Not long now till we reach home, with luck. How is Broderick? Radwinter said he cried when he heard we were out of sight of Yorkshire.'

'Ay. He has been quiet since then.' He hesitated. 'When he saw you he asked to talk to you for a minute.'

I glanced to where Broderick stood, looking out to sea, ignoring the soldiers. I sighed. 'Very well. For a minute.'

Leacon looked over at his men. 'Move away there. And stand up straight, can't you?' He turned to me as they stepped away from Broderick. 'Maleverer gave me two of the surliest idiots in the troop to guard Broderick. I've already had to dock the pay of one for being drunk.'

Broderick turned to me as I approached. His thin face was drawn with pain above his yellow unkempt beard, which, like his long hair, glinted with spray. He looked more like a little old man than a young one. As he turned to me he winced as he moved his left arm.

'What ails your arm?'

'The rack.' He looked at me. The wildness had gone from his eyes, he seemed strangely calm. There had been some change in his state of mind since I saw him last.

'I hear you were nearly killed at Howlme,' he said quietly. 'By Bernard Locke's fiancée.'

'Yes.'

'I knew Locke a little. He is a man to get a woman to do his bidding. I wanted you to know it was nothing to do with me. Maleverer questioned me about it. He used forceful methods.'

'I am sorry for it. And I know Jennet Marlin acted alone.' I hesitated. 'We never found the papers she took. If it was she that took them.'

He did not answer.

'I wonder if it was someone else who stole them, whether perhaps they are in the hands of the conspirators now. Maleverer thinks I am a fool.'

He met my gaze evenly, but still said nothing.

'I am right, aren't I? You know?'

Again, no reply. I sighed and changed the subject.

'So, you are sorry Jennet Marlin tried to kill me?'

'Yes. I would not have you die. You have shown me kindness in your way.'

I looked at him. 'Yet if it served your purposes you would kill me, would you not?'

'Not with pleasure,' he said in an oddly matter-of-fact way. 'I view no one's death with pleasure. Even where it may be necessary. Nor would you, I think.'

'Mistress Marlin spoke of necessary deaths. I do not like the idea that anyone's death is necessary.'

'Mine is.' He gave his old sardonic smile. 'You accepted that, or you would not have taken the mission from Cranmer to look after my welfare.'

I sighed.

'Why did you do it? You do not belong with a company of brutes like Maleverer and Radwinter.'

'I let myself become obligated to the Archbishop.'

He nodded, then said, 'They will not make me talk in London.'

'They will, Broderick,' I answered quietly.

'No.' A faint smile, one that chilled me, the smile of one who has secret knowledge. He lowered his voice to a whisper. 'They will not. And remember, Master Shardlake, what I told you once. The time of the Mouldwarp is almost over.' He looked at me sadly. 'You know, I think you could have been one of us. You may be yet.'

I turned away. Sergeant Leacon was standing nearby.

'I have never seen him so calm,' I told him.

'He is in a strange mood. Did he say anything of importance?'

'He said they will not break him.'

'They will.'

'I know.'

I walked away to the hatch. Radwinter was still leaning over the rail, staring out to sea.

☦

THAT EVENING, after supper eaten from bowls on the deck, I sat on the bench as the sun sank below the horizon. The sea was quiet, only a little swell. A red sun, in a sky that had begun to fill with clouds. I hoped more bad weather was not coming. Tamasin had gone to her cabin and Barak was talking to a group of servants a little way off.

There was more of a wind now, enough to make some headway. I was glad, for I was increasingly worried about Giles, who still spent most of his time asleep in his cabin. All around dim forms, huddled against the evening cold, dozed or spoke quietly or played at cards or chess. The moon rose, a silvery line on the sea. A man swathed in furs came up the stair-ladder from below to take the air. Beneath a jewelled cap I recognized the thin features of Richard Rich. He walked down the deck, head sunk on his chin, thinking. The sailors working on deck moved quickly out of his way as he passed. Then he walked up the deck again. As he reached the bench where I sat his eyes held mine for a second. Then he gave his little smile, turned and walked away again. He descended the steps, his foot-steps fading away. When he had gone I rose. Barak came over to me.

'That arsehole.'

'Ay.' I was pleased by his concern.

'Did he say anything?'

'No, just gave me an evil look. I think I will go down.'

'Ay, it is getting cold.'

'I feel colder still for seeing Rich.'

Below decks all was quiet. As I passed Broderick's cell, though, I noticed with surprise that the two soldiers standing outside were drinking beer from a flagon they were passing between them. Seeing me, the one holding it tried to hide it behind his back. I frowned and went on to my room. As I was settling on to my bunk I heard raised voices outside. I rose and quickly opened the door. Other doors were opening, people looking out.

'What in God's name do you think you are doing?' It was Sergeant Leacon's voice, furious. The two soldiers stood red-faced, one holding the flagon at his side. The sergeant kicked it out of his hand and it crashed on the floor, the beer spilling out. The soldier staggered.

'God's wounds, you'll suffer for this. You'll both come with me to Maleverer, now.'

The soldiers paled. The door to the cell opened and Radwinter looked out. 'What in hell is going on?' he snapped.

Leacon turned to him, red-faced. 'These churls are drinking on duty. I'm taking them to Maleverer.' And with that he grabbed the two men by the collars and marched them away. Radwinter watched him go, smiling at his rival's discomfiture. I shut my door before he saw me.

⟨✝⟩

A ROUGH HAND, shaking me hard. I opened my eyes, blinking. Someone holding a lamp. My cabin door was open. Outside, voices were murmuring excitedly. I sat up, and found myself looking into Maleverer's grim face. In the shadows behind him I saw Barak in his shirt, his hair tousled.

'Wake up!' Maleverer snapped his fingers angrily in my face. 'Come on! Get up!'

I rose to my feet. In the doorway I saw Giles, clutching blankets around his big form and looking bemused, and Tamasin with Barak's coat draped round her. Maleverer turned and shouted at them and the other people who had wakened and come into the corridor.

'Get back to bed!' he bawled. 'I'll have the lot of you arrested!'

'What is this commotion?' Giles asked, a new querulousness in his voice.

'Come back to bed, Master Wrenne,' Tamasin said. She took

his arm and led him away. Other doors closed. Barak alone stayed in the doorway. Maleverer turned back to me.

'You spoke to Broderick yesterday,' he rasped. 'What did he say to you?'

My heart jumped as I remembered Broderick's words: you could have been one of us. I think you may be yet. 'I – nothing of note,' I said. 'I tried to question him about Jennet Marlin but he made no answer, as usual. What has happened?'

'I'll show you. Come with me.'

He shouldered his way out of the cabin. I got up; fortunately I had gone to bed in my shirt and hose. 'What is it?' I asked Barak.

'I don't know. I was woken up by voices and footsteps down there.' He nodded down the corridor to Broderick's cell. To my surprise the door was ajar. Radwinter sat slumped on the floor outside, his head in his hands, Sergeant Leacon standing over him.

'Here!' Maleverer called. I followed him reluctantly down the corridor. He threw open the door of Broderick's cell and stood aside. Barak had followed me; I felt warmed by the fact he was still loyal.

The cell was one of the larger rooms, a bunk against each wall and some space between. In that space Broderick hung from the ceiling. He was bare to the waist; his shirt had been twisted into a thick length of material and one end slung over a large beam. The other end had gone round his neck. He was dead, his body swinging in the light swell, the chains that bound his arms and legs making a slight rattle. His feet hung two or three inches above the floor. If he had been any taller he could not have done it in the low cabin. His eyes were closed and his head was bent over at a sickening angle. I looked away from his emaciated, lacerated chest. 'Dear God.' I looked at Maleverer. 'How—'

'The soldiers got drunk. Leacon brought them to me and I sent them to sleep it off. They'll suffer later. He and Radwinter were left alone to guard Broderick. Later Leacon came to me to discuss what was to be done with the soldiers. When he came back Radwinter was lying on the ground by the bench. Radwinter *says* someone knocked on the door. When he stepped out he saw no one there, then someone struck him from behind, knocked him out, stole his keys, then unlocked the chains and killed Broderick.' He stepped over to Radwinter, who looked up at him. He seemed stunned, confused. Ironically, that made him look normal, human, for the first time since I had known him.

'Couldn't he have killed himself?' I asked.

'No.' Maleverer almost snarled. He had lost his prisoner, this would go hard for him. 'Look at his wrists, they're manacled together behind him, there's only six inches of chain between them. Broderick was manacled if ever he was left alone, precisely so he could not harm himself. Someone helped him to this. They tied the rope to the rafter, helped Broderick to stand on the bed, got the rope round his neck. Then he jumped.'

I nodded. 'Yes.' I made myself look at the body again. 'And his helper pulled on his feet when he was dangling, to break his neck and stop him from strangling slowly. They were merciful. They helped him kill himself. He did it after all.' I looked at Broderick's face again. It was turned slightly away, his expression oddly peaceful. At last he had shut us all out, for ever.

'Radwinter's story doesn't add up, to me,' Maleverer said, glowering down at the gaoler. 'He *says* he was hit on the head from behind but I see no mark of a blow.' He addressed Radwinter. 'I am placing you under arrest for the murder of your prisoner. And by God, when we get to London we will find out why, one way or another.'

Radwinter stared up at him, then let out a terrible sound, somewhere between a screech and a moan. Maleverer nodded to Leacon. 'Lock him up, then take the body down. And by Jesu, you and your men will have to make answer too, for this mess.' Maleverer turned to me. 'So that's it,' he hissed. 'The last chance of finding out more about the conspirators. Gone!'

But it had not been Radwinter, I was sure. Maleverer merely

needed a culprit and he had found one. I realized something that set my heart hammering against my ribs. I had been right that it was not Jennet Marlin who had knocked me out at King's Manor. It was someone else. They were on this ship, and now they had helped Broderick die.

Chapter Forty

BAD WEATHER HIT US next morning, rain and wind and heavy seas that had the passengers retching all over the ship. After lunch the rain stopped, and I came up and sat alone on the bench on deck, looking out at the heaving grey wastes of the German Ocean. Mountainous seas heaved and rolled, giant waves capped with white foam, the sky only slightly less dark than the sea. I watched a herring gull swoop above the water. How did they survive out here, I wondered.

I had felt a need to be alone, to get away from the shocked, anxious atmosphere that Broderick's death and Radwinter's arrest had created below decks. I could not rid myself of the memory of Broderick's face, turned away as he swung gently. I wondered how God would judge him; suicide was a great sin but Broderick had only anticipated and eased his passage to death. And I had been, however reluctantly, an agent of those who had abused him so that killing himself with another's help was the only way left. I had come to admire him, for all that his intensity had sometimes frightened me.

I looked down the deck, beyond the billowing sails, to where the captain was running between the sailors, shouting and looking over the side. I wondered if something was wrong. I turned as the hatch to the lower decks banged open and Barak, swathed like me in a heavy coat, emerged and came over, grasping at the rails as the ship bucked and heaved. He sat beside me.

'How is Master Wrenne?' he asked.

'Still in bed. He says he's all right, but he looks weak to me. I worry this voyage may be too much for him.'

Barak sighed. 'He'll make it or he won't. There's not much we can do. Poor old arsehole.' We were silent a moment as he looked down the deck to where the captain was still pacing. 'There's a problem with the rudder. They think they've broken a pintail, it's some sort of a bolt.'

I looked at him. 'Serious?'

'It needs attending to. We're putting in at Ipswich now. We'll be later than ever, just when we've got a favourable wind. The sailors are even more convinced this voyage is cursed.'

'Sailors are a superstitious lot. What day is it? I lose track.'

'October twenty-third. We've been out seven days already. The sailor said Rich is furious, he's going to leave the ship at Ipswich and ride back to London.'

'The King will be back before us at this rate. Though with Broderick dead I suppose that matters little now.'

He nodded, screwing up his eyes against the spray as a large wave crashed over the side of the boat. I looked at him. 'Thank you for standing by last night,' I said.

'That's all right.'

I hesitated. 'How is Tamasin?'

'Fine.' He looked down a moment, then back at me. 'But I have told her she must stop mourning for Jennet Marlin. That however kind she was to Tamasin, the woman was a murderess. And she can't blame you for resenting her sorrow for her. Jesu, Jennet Marlin would have killed Tamasin if she had got in her way.'

'Yes. She would.'

He smiled sadly. 'Tamasin has so little security in her life, she cleaved to Jennet Marlin. As she cleaved to the idea of her father having good blood. If it turns out he hasn't, I'll say nothing.'

'Even if he has, he probably wouldn't want to know her.'

'No.' He looked at his feet for a moment. 'It's a pickle.' He looked up again. 'But I care for her. I am sorry, though, for what I said to you in Hull.'

'It is all right. We have been cooped up together too long.' I

thought of the rosary, but our reconciliation was too fragile to mention that now.

'I suppose Radwinter will go to the Tower when we land,'
Barak said.

'Yes. To be questioned.'

'The way Broderick would have been questioned?'

'Probably.' I shook my head. 'I do not believe Radwinter killed
him. Maleverer is wrong. He is so bull-headed, he sees only what is
straight ahead, like a blinkered horse.'

'Yet it all points to Radwinter. He was the only one with
Broderick at the time, he said he was knocked on the head but there
was no sign of a blow.'

'You know it is possible to knock someone out without leaving
a mark. Then there's motive. Why on earth would Radwinter do it?'

'Maleverer thinks he's gone mad, doesn't he?'

'Yes. That was partly my fault.' I sighed. Maleverer had questioned me after Broderick's body had been taken away, railing with
furious anger against Radwinter. Leacon had told him I had said
Radwinter was mad, and Maleverer had seized on that, believing the
erosion of his authority had sent the gaoler out of his wits until he
went berserk and killed Broderick. I had protested that I had not
meant I thought Radwinter would kill his prisoner, but Maleverer
had been in no mood to listen.

'Maleverer has more reason than just what you said to think
Radwinter mad,' Barak said. 'I'm told he's collapsed since he was
locked up in the cell, shrieking and crying and calling down plagues
on Maleverer. And who can tell what goes on in a man's mind
when it runs mad?'

'It still doesn't add up to me. How could he have done it alone?'

'Perhaps he knocked Broderick out, then hanged him.'

'I can't see him taking Broderick unawares.' I paused. 'You
know what I think happened?'

'Go on.'

'When I last saw him, Broderick seemed calm, almost resigned.

What if someone had already been to see him, to offer him this way out if he still wanted to kill himself?'

Barak whistled.

'Then when Leacon sent those drunken soldiers away and went to report to Maleverer, that someone was waiting in his cabin. You can hear what's going on outside. He knocked Radwinter out—'

'Took his keys, strung Broderick up, then pulled on his feet and broke his neck.'

'Yes.'

Barak looked out at the heaving, bitterly cold sea. 'It's an awful way to choose to die. Broderick must have had some courage.'

'We knew that.' I followed his gaze. Broderick's body was under those heaving waves now. The captain had refused to take a dead body back to London, fearing even more bad luck. He had said the burial service over the corpse and then it had been thrown overboard, tied in a sheet, landing with a splash among the grey waves then disappearing for ever.

'So someone here on board killed him?'

'Oh, I think so. Someone he knew already, I would guess.'

'The person who knocked you out at King's Manor?'

'Yes.' I told Barak what Broderick had said the day before. 'I am sure he knew who knocked me out at King's Manor and took the papers. If he hadn't, he would have denied it. He was different yesterday, quieter. No longer afraid of the Tower, which I think he always was before, however he tried to hide it. I think he had already made arrangements.'

'But how? He was guarded all the time.'

'That's the one thing I can't work out.'

'Have you told Maleverer what you suspect?'

'Ay. He dismissed it, and me too, with oaths. He believes he's got his man. He needs to, for he will be in disfavour now. First letting those papers be stolen, now letting Broderick be killed.' I smiled bitterly. 'I doubt he will have the great career he was looking for after this. Nor does he deserve it. He's all brute force, no time for thought, no subtlety.'

'Unlike Lord Cromwell.'

'Oh yes. He could see round corners.' I glanced at Barak. 'You think I'm wrong?'

'I don't know. If you are right, whoever helped Broderick die could be anyone on this ship. Even a crewman.'

'Yes.' I hesitated. 'Last night, before Broderick died, I was sitting here and Rich came up and walked the deck. He saw me, gave me one of his nasty smiles.'

'Why would Rich kill Broderick? Deprive his master the King of his pet prisoner?'

'I don't know.'

'Well, at least we can exclude Lady Rochford this time.'

'Yes.' I bit my lip. 'There is one other possibility. There is one person who had the perfect opportunity to plan with Broderick and then help him die. A man from Kent.'

'Sergeant Leacon?' Barak's voice was astonished.

'Perhaps there is more to him than meets the eye. Since I spoke to the old lawyer in Hull I have been wondering, what of the archer Blaybourne's family? Presumably he must have returned to them in Kent when he came back from France. How much did they know? The confession could have been made to a relative down in the south, kept in the family, brought to London and then up to York when the rebellion was planned.'

Barak shook his head. 'I can't see Sergeant Leacon as a killer.'

'He doesn't have to be. Whoever knocked me out at King's Manor might have meant not to kill me, only take the papers. And he didn't kill Broderick, he helped him kill himself. Leacon could have knocked out Radwinter and helped Broderick die before he went to make his report to Maleverer. He could even have given those soldiers access to drink.'

Barak blew out his cheeks. 'It fits. And yet . . .'

'I know. He seems so unlikely a candidate. I already feel bad about my part in his parents' problems. I have offered to try and help them.'

Barak pondered a moment. 'He's guarding Radwinter now, isn't he?'

'Yes.'

'Perhaps you ought to tell Maleverer.'

I shook my head. 'He wouldn't listen. There's no point.'

'You ought to.'

I sighed. 'One day I will provoke that man too far and I will be in trouble. But you are right.'

We looked round as another big wave hit the deck amidships, splashing water over the crewmen working the sails. There came a shout from the crow's nest high above us. 'Land!'

✝

WE WERE FOUR DAYS in Ipswich, a pretty little town. Getting the ship into dock and repairing the rudder was no easy task. It was simple enough to find an inn, though. Giles ceased to try and hide that he felt exhausted; he took to bed and lay there, his face drawn with pain, disinclined for conversation. I decided to follow Barak's advice, and went to seek out Maleverer. He had turned a room in the best inn in town into yet another office, got a table from somewhere and covered it with papers. He was sitting writing. He looked tired, his high colour turned to a greyish pallor. He greeted me, as usual, with a frown.

'I am busy, Master Shardlake. I have a long report to prepare for the council.'

'There was something that occurred to me, Sir William. About Broderick's death.'

He sighed, but put down his pen. 'Well?'

I told him my thoughts about Leacon. He looked at me impatiently.

'Leacon could have killed Broderick any time these past few weeks,' he answered.

'I doubt there was another time when there were no other soldiers around. This may have been the perfect opportunity.'

'He was careless, letting those men get drunk. That's in my report and he'll suffer for it. But why in God's name would he kill Broderick?'

'I don't know, Sir William. It was just he had the opportunity. And – well, he comes from Kent. You remember what I told you about Blaybourne.'

'For God's sake, don't mention that name! These walls are thin. Are you still ferreting about in your head over that?'

'I wondered about Blaybourne's family. Whether that confession I glimpsed had been passed down—'

'You love long shots, don't you?' He pointed his pen at me. 'Most of the soldiers with the Progress came from Kent, as you well know. Leacon has been with the Gentlemen Pensioners for five years, he's always been solid until this mistake.'

'Is that not itself a cause for concern? That he should be careless now, of all times?'

'You want to be careful. Those attempts on your life have made you willing to suspect anyone, blacken anyone's name on no good evidence.' He motioned me away. 'Get out. I don't want to see you again. Go.'

✝

AFTER WE LEFT IPSWICH, the ship's bad luck seemed to evaporate; a fair wind set in behind us and we reached the Thames in four days, on the first of November. I watched from the rail as the ship sailed up the broad estuary between the mudbanks. The water was calm and there were fingers of mist drifting along the shore. Like everyone else on board I was cold and exhausted. The first buildings began to appear and the boat tacked to the shore, heading for Billingsgate Dock. On the north bank the Tower of London loomed above us.

Barak and Tamasin appeared and stood beside me. Tamasin

gave me an uncertain look. I smiled at her; there was no point in an open quarrel.

'What are those for?' Barak asked. Everywhere in the city church bells were ringing loudly.

'Someone said it's for Queen Catherine,' Tamasin replied. 'The King has ordered services in all the churches, to express his thanks for having found such a good wife at last.'

'If he knew,' Barak said softly.

'Well, he doesn't,' I said quietly. 'And mustn't. We forget all about that now. Disappear back into London.'

Tamasin sighed. 'That sounds wonderful after these last six weeks.'

'Yes. I must go and fetch Master Wrenne,' I added awkwardly. 'Tell him we are nearly home.'

✝

I WENT BELOW DECKS to Giles's tiny cabin. All this last week he had lain in bed, sleeping mostly. He was awake when I entered, though, lying there looking sad.

'We are almost here,' I said.

'Yes. I heard the sailors calling.' He gave a little smile. 'So, I made it.'

'How are you?'

'Better.' He sighed. 'I must get up.'

'When we get to my house you must rest a few days. Barak and I can make enquiries at Gray's Inn.'

'Would you wait a few days before you do? Till I feel able to come with you.' He laughed awkwardly. 'I would like to meet my nephew standing on my feet, not have him brought to me in bed.'

'Very well, Giles. By all means wait a few days. I will get my friend Guy to come and see you. He is an apothecary, but a trained doctor too.'

'The old Spanish Moor you told me of?'

'Ay. At the least I am sure he can ease your pains. And you

will like my house. My housekeeper Joan is a good old body, she will take care of you.' My heart lifted at the thought of home. The first thing I would do was try to get the Bealknap case set down as soon as possible.

'You have been so good to me,' Giles said quietly. 'Like a son.'

I said nothing, only laid a hand on his arm. 'I will leave you to get ready. We will be on deck.'

When I returned the boat was pulling up to the dock. It bumped against the wharf. I saw half a dozen soldiers there, carrying pikes. The escort for Radwinter.

The boat tied up. Giles joined us, grasping the rail. 'London,' he said. 'It seems huge.'

'It is,' Barak said. 'A thousand more come each year, they say.'

'Jack will guide you round the town, sir,' Tamasin said.

'You too, I hope, mistress. It will be fine to walk the streets of London with a pretty girl.'

We watched as the courtiers got off, a bedraggled-looking crew now. Maleverer was there.

I saw Sergeant Leacon emerge with the two soldiers and, between them, Radwinter. The gaoler's once-neat clothes were crumpled, his face dirty and unshaven, hair and beard unkempt. His arms and legs were chained as Broderick's had been. There was no sign of violence about him now, his head hung low.

Leacon and the soldiers led him across the planks and over to the other waiting soldiers. A sailor waved to the remaining passengers and we descended the plank. When we reached the wharf I almost lost my balance, unused to dry land. Tamasin and Barak each gave me an arm.

'Careful, now,' Barak said. 'You'll have us all over. I'm unsteady too.'

Another hand was laid on my arm. I turned round, thinking someone else had come to my aid.

'I'm all right—' I broke off. The hand had gripped me tight, and now I saw it was Sergeant Leacon's. Three of the soldiers had come over and now they surrounded us, their pikes raised. Sergeant Leacon looked at me sternly.

'You are to come with the soldiers, Master Shardlake.'

I frowned at him. 'But what – what is this?'

'You are under arrest, sir. You are suspected of treason.'

Giles stepped forward. 'Treason?' There was a shocked quaver in his voice. 'What do you mean, there is some mistake—'

'No mistake, sir. The soldiers who came for Radwinter brought a warrant for Master Shardlake's arrest also.'

'Let me see!' Giles snapped authoritatively. 'I am a lawyer.' He held out a hand. Leacon produced a paper from his pocket and handed it to him. He studied it, eyes wide, then passed it to me with a trembling hand. It was a warrant for my arrest, signed by Archbishop Cranmer.

'What am I supposed to have done?' My lips felt thick, bruised, my heart was jumping wildly.

'You'll be told in the Tower.'

'No!' Barak thrust himself forward, grabbing at Leacon's arm. 'This is all wrong, it's a mistake. Archbishop Cranmer—'

A soldier reached out and grabbed his arm. Barak lost his balance and toppled over with a cry on the muddy cobbles. I was manhandled away.

'Find out what is happening, Jack!' I called out.

Tamasin was helping him to his feet. 'We will!' she called after me. Wrenne was standing watching, his face aghast. A little distance away I saw the courtiers watching me. Maleverer caught my eye. He inclined his head, raised his eyebrows and smiled. He had known.

Chapter Forty-one

THEY TOOK US TO a big rowing boat a little further down the dock. Sergeant Leacon did not accompany us, and oddly it affected me greatly that I was left entirely in strange hands. The soldiers made me climb down steps encrusted with green slime and I slipped; if one of them had not grasped me I would have fallen into the filthy Thames.

They sat me beside Radwinter and rowed out into the broad river. Looking back at the wharf I saw three receding figures watching, still as stones. Barak and Tamasin and Giles; helpless.

Other craft on the river pulled aside at the sight of the boat full of red uniforms. We passed close to a wherry; its passenger, a plump alderman, gave Radwinter and me a look in which fear was mixed with sympathy. I could imagine his thoughts. Taken to the Tower. *That could be me.* It was the fear that lurked in the back of every mind. And now, out of the blue, it had happened to me. Yet, I thought with terror, perhaps I should not be surprised. My head was full of forbidden knowledge, of Blaybourne and the King's legitimacy. Not that I had ever wanted any of it, but now they would have that knowledge out of my head, one way or another. Who was it that had informed against me? I furrowed my brow. Surely the old man Swann in Hull could not have done so. And other than him, only Barak knew the full extent of what I had discovered about Blaybourne. But he would have told Tamasin. Surely it could not be her? I swallowed; my throat was dry as paper. Beside me, Radwinter sat staring bleakly ahead, still no sign of the frantic madness Barak had described. It began to rain.

It was a short journey; suddenly the walls of the Tower were above us, wet with slime where they met the water for the tide was low. My heart began thumping frantically. We stopped at a portcullis gate that gave on to the river. The Watergate. I thought, Anne Boleyn came in here, Anne Boleyn, Anne Boleyn . . . I found myself repeating the name over and over in my mind. It was to stop my thoughts moving on to the end of that story, for I had been made by Cromwell to attend the Queen's execution, seen her head fly out from the block on Tower Green, that fine spring day five years before.

'Out!' The boat had bumped against stone stairs. The soldiers took our arms and hauled us up. I looked through a stone archway at the top of the steps and saw Tower Green where ravens pecked, the great square bulk of the White Tower beyond. The rain grew heavier.

'Let me go!' Beside me Radwinter had come to life. 'I've done nothing. I'm innocent.' He tried to struggle but the soldiers held him fast. They did not bother to reply. Innocent, I thought. So was Anne Boleyn, so was Margaret of Salisbury they had killed here last spring. Being innocent was no help in this place.

'Up you go!' The soldiers spoke to us only in clipped phrases. They led us up the steps and I almost slipped again for I had still not fully found my land legs.

'Wait here!'

We stood on a path. The soldiers surrounded us, pikes held straight, water bouncing off their breastplates and helmets. An official came along, head bent against the rain. He looked at us as he passed; a look of mild interest, as though thinking, who is it now? Here they would be used to it. I felt a terrible shame to have come to this; for a moment the shame was stronger than my fear. What if my father could see *this* from heaven?

A man walked towards us from the White Tower. He wore a fur robe and a wide cap and he came slowly, heedless of the rain. The soldiers saluted as he halted before us. He was in his late thirties, tall and thin with a neat sandy beard. A soldier handed him a couple of papers, the warrants no doubt. He studied Radwinter and me. His eyes were keen, calculating.

'Which is which?' he asked quietly.

The soldier inclined his head at me. 'This one is Shardlake, Sir Jacob. The other is Radwinter.'

Sir Jacob nodded. 'Bring them both.' He turned away. The soldiers surrounded us and we followed Sir Jacob across the green to the Tower. The ravens hopped away.

We were led up the main stairs of the White Tower, through the high vaulted inner hall where the men of the garrison sat playing cards and talking. They stopped to stare as we passed. Many of them would be newly returned from the Progress, perhaps some had even seen me at Fulford.

I had visited the Tower before, on official business, and my heart sank into my belly, with a lurch that made me feel sick, as I realized we were being led to the dungeons. Down a spiral staircase lit with torches, down and down, the walls glistening with damp as we passed below river level, to a door with a barred window at the bottom. I had come this way four years previously, on a mission to get information from a gaoler. I had had a glimpse then of what went on down here, yet had given it little attention for my mind had been on my mission. Sir Jacob banged on the door. There was a chink of keys, the door opened and we were led through. The door slammed behind us. Now I felt more helpless than ever, utterly cut off from the world above.

We were in a dimly lit space, stone walls and stone flags on the floor. It was cold and very damp. Heavy barred doors were set in the stone walls. In the centre of the floor, oddly domestic, was a desk with a fat beeswax candle on it, casting its yellow light over a strew of papers. The turnkey who had let us in, a fat man with short greasy hair, came and stood beside us. Sir Jacob took up a paper, studied it and nodded. 'Ah, *he's* ready, I see. Put Radwinter in number nine,' he said quietly. 'Chain him, then come back. Is Caffrey up there?'

'Yes, Sir Jacob.'

'Bring him back with you.' He nodded at the soldiers. 'You can go.'

They left, boots clattering noisily as they mounted the stairs. The turnkey let them out, then returned, took Radwinter's arm and led him away. He was unresisting, he seemed utterly shocked. They disappeared round a corner at the far end, the keys at the fat man's belt jingling. The official looked at me.

'I am Sir Jacob Rawling, deputy warden of the Tower. In charge of this side of things.' He gave a wintry smile as he waved his hand around.

'Yes, sir.' I shivered. The cold was eating through my soaked clothes into my bones.

'It is sad when someone of your rank comes to this.' There was something oddly schoolmasterly in the way he shook his head, as though I were a pupil about to be punished for some serious misdemeanour.

'I do not know why I am arrested, sir,' I ventured.

He studied me, pursing his lips, then said, 'The matter touches the Queen.' I blinked in surprise. So it was not about Blaybourne at all. But if so, why had I been taken, not Barak or Tamasin? I thought with horror, she's been discovered. They will say I have concealed evidence of her adultery with Culpeper. Maleverer must have known all along.

'Had you not enough to trouble you on the Progress?' Sir Jacob gave me another schoolmasterly smile, as though reluctantly amused by something in a pupil's misbehaviour, perhaps his stupidity in thinking he could get away with it. He studied me with interest. 'Your name has been heard in this place before, only a little time ago. When we racked Bernard Locke. They wanted to find out his role in attempts on your life.'

He said the word 'racked' not with pleasure as Radwinter would have, nor with cold determination like Maleverer, but without any emphasis at all. And suddenly I was very afraid of him.

'I know, sir.'

'I know you know. Sir William mentioned it in his report accusing you.'

'Then he is my accuser?'

'Yes. Of concealing certain matters between Francis Dereham and the Queen.'

'*Dereham?*' I stared at him in amazement.

He narrowed his eyes. 'Master Dereham is suspected of dalliance with Queen Catherine. It is believed you knew of this, and kept quiet.'

I remembered now. Rich had seen me come from the Queen's tent at Howlme, he had seen Dereham stop and question me in the street at Hull. Dereham must have been under suspicion, perhaps watched by Maleverer. Rich had told Maleverer and they had taken me. With all I knew, they had arrested me for something of which I knew nothing. 'Dereham?' I asked again.

'It would be better if you did not dissemble, Shardlake.' Sir Jacob spoke reasonably, the schoolmaster trying to persuade the obstinate pupil. 'I will show you what awaits you if you do.' But he made no move, just stood there looking at me. That unnerved me more than ever. I shivered again.

There was a jingling of keys. The fat turnkey had returned with a stocky young man in a stained leather jerkin. My eyes narrowed as I peered at it in the gloom. Were those stains blood?

Sir Jacob nodded at them. 'Search him.'

I flinched as the men seized me, ran rough hands over my clothes. They took my dagger, purse and Cranmer's seal, and laid them on the table. Sir Jacob picked up the seal, looked at it and grunted.

'Bring out Bernard Locke,' he told them. 'He's to be put in the execution cell.'

The pair opened the door of one of the cells and went in. I waited to see Jennet Marlin's fiancé step out, the man who had set her on her mission of murder.

They carried him out in a chair. He was unchained, and I

realized he had been racked so badly he could not walk, his legs hung uselessly down as did one arm, while the other twitched and shook as it held the seat of the chair to try and keep his balance. 'Here we go, matey,' the fat turnkey said pleasantly as they carried him across the central area. I tried to look at Locke's face but his head hung down, hidden by long rat's tails of hair. He was making little whines of pain.

Sir Jacob called out. 'One moment!' The sweating turnkeys stopped. The deputy warden went and lifted Locke's head by the hair. He whimpered. I saw the weeping sore of a burn running across his forehead. And I was surprised to see that he must always have been an ugly man: his features were heavy and lumpy, and his eyes, staring wildly round him now, were large and bulbous.

'Well, Master Locke,' Sir Jacob said. 'Here you are, almost at the end of your road. I thought you should see Master Shardlake. Another lawyer come to grief, the man your fiancée tried to kill. Have you aught to say to him?'

Bernard Locke looked at me for a moment. Turning his head made him wince. 'Nothing,' he whispered.

'Why did you do it?' I asked him. 'Why did you use that wretched woman so? Get her to take an innocent life, put her in such danger her own life was lost?'

Locke did not answer, only looked at me without interest as though he was already in another world.

'You betrayed the conspirators, you betrayed her.'

Still he did not respond.

'If you had succeeded, would you have married Jennet?' For some reason I had to know.

He ran a swollen tongue across cracked lips. 'Perhaps,' he said in a high, croaking voice. 'What does it matter now?'

Another question came into my mind. 'Do you know a barrister of Lincoln's Inn named Martin Dakin?' I knew the question could not place Dakin in danger. Anything incriminating Locke knew about anyone, he would have told his torturers already.

A flicker of interest in the hollow eyes. 'Ay. I knew Martin.' Already he was talking of himself in the past tense, as though he were already dead. His mouth twitched in a half-smile. 'He was not involved. He is safe.'

'Who is this Dakin?' Sir Jacob asked.

I sighed. 'Only the nephew of an old lawyer I know. A barrister of Gray's Inn. I was trying to help the old man find him.'

Sir Jacob frowned at me. 'You have other things to worry about now, Master Shardlake, believe me.' He nodded to the turnkeys and they bore Locke away, the fat one grunting with the effort. He had a hard time unlocking the door while trying to hold the chair, but he managed it and they carried Locke through. 'We'll have a job getting up these stairs,' the younger one said.

'Ay.' The fat man gasped. 'You're a nuisance, you are, matey,' he told Locke. They carried him upstairs; I heard him groan at the jolting of the chair. Sir Jacob inclined his head.

'Often by the end they're in such pain they can't think of anything beyond that. Well, he'll be out of it tomorrow, his head will be off.'

'There is to be no trial?'

Sir Jacob gave me a long sideways look, as though I had committed an impertinence. 'I think you need some time to reflect on where you are,' he said. 'Yes, that would be best. We shall talk again later.' He sat down at the desk and began writing notes on a paper, ignoring me again while he waited for the gaolers to return.

I stood there, my legs shaking, thinking frantically. Had the Queen had dalliance with Dereham as well as Culpeper? It seemed incredible, yet it was the only explanation for Cranmer's signature on the warrant. And they knew nothing about Culpeper. I could deny knowledge of Dereham truthfully. But would they believe me, would they try other means? And I knew that if they tortured me I would tell them anything to get them to stop, tell them about Culpeper or what I suspected of the King's ancestry, anything. I could bear less than Locke had, I knew that, less than Broderick would have. My head reeled with sudden terror and I hid my face in my hands and groaned.

With a puffing and blowing, the turnkeys came back down the stairs. I pulled my trembling hands from my face. Sir Jacob was looking at me with what seemed like quiet satisfaction. 'All right,' he said. 'I think the penny has dropped. Put him in with Radwinter.'

Chapter Forty-two

T HE FAT TURNKEY took me up a flight of stairs to a narrow
torchlit corridor lined with sturdy wooden doors. He opened
one and thrust me in with a twist of his arm so forceful I nearly fell.

The cell was a long chamber with a low roof. The bricks had
been whitewashed but were disfigured with patches of mould.
Through a small, high barred window at the other end of the room
I could see a patch of dark sky and hear the hiss of rain hitting the
river. We must be right by the water. The only furniture was a pair
of rickety truckle beds opposite each other by the door. On one of
them Radwinter sat, head in his hands. They were chained together,
as were his feet. He did not look up as the turnkey led me over to
the other bed.

'Sit down,' the fat man said. I collapsed rather than sat on a thin,
filthy mattress, stinking of damp. There was no blanket. 'Stretch out
your arms,' he ordered. 'Come on, I haven't got all day.' His tone
was still quiet but when I looked up his hard little eyes told me he
meant business. I reached out my arms. So quickly and dextrously
that I hardly had time to realize what he was doing, he took a chain
with a manacle on each end from under the bed and slipped the
manacles round my wrists. There was a double click and I was
pinioned. He bent down, pulled out another length of chain and
secured my feet. He stood back and inspected his handiwork with a
nod.

'There. That'll do.'

'Is this necessary?' I asked, my voice rising with fear.

'Is this nec-essary?' he repeated with a grin, imitating my educated tones. 'It's the rules, matey. This is the least of it, you'll see.' He glanced at Radwinter, who still sat with head bent, then left the cell. The key rattled in the lock.

I sat there, rigid with terror. The chains were long; I could move my arms and no doubt walk, but they were heavy and one of the gyves was tight, not enough to stop the blood but sufficient to scrape my wrist painfully when I moved it.

I looked up to see Radwinter staring at me. He was filthy, eyes wild and bloodshot in his dirty face. How different from the neat, confident figure who had greeted me at York Castle.

'What have you done?' he asked in a cracked, hoarse voice.

'Not what I am accused of.'

'You lie!' he shouted suddenly.

I did not reply. I thought, what if he leaps at me?

He went on, talking fast in bitter, intense tones. 'You were always a weakling, and weaklings are dangerous, can be prevailed upon by the sinful, like Broderick. Wrongdoers must be punished, that is right, my father said when he beat me that it was God's law and he was right, it is. It is!' he shouted, as though I had contradicted him. 'But I did not kill Broderick! I made mistakes but mistakes are not disloyalty, they should be punished but not with this!' His voice rose and he looked at me with frantic, glaring eyes.

'Perhaps they will only question you,' I said soothingly, 'then let you go when they realize you were not responsible for Broderick's death. I do not believe you killed him.'

What I said did not seem to register. 'Mistakes must be punished.' He frowned. 'But *not* so severely. It is deliberate wrongdoing that must be dealt with harshly. My father taught me. To forget my bedtime, only three strokes of the switch. To stay out playing *deliberately*, twelve. The scars remind me, that is why he put them there, to remind me.'

I did not reply. I did not need to, for his eyes were unfocused, looking inward; he was talking to himself rather than to me.

'Sometimes he would make me kneel and look at the switch for half an hour before he used it. It was part of the punishment. He told me that doesn't work with animals.' He looked up at me then. 'Do you remember,' he said with a smile, 'I told you that?'

'Yes.' I thought, Maleverer was right, his wits have gone, this has been too much for him. They have locked me in here with a madman.

'He told me about that when we went to the bull-baiting, when he held my hand so tight the blood stopped flowing. Waiting, it frightens a boy and I knew it would frighten a man too.' He smiled suddenly, a leer the like of which I hope to see on no man's face again. I moved down the bed in an involuntary effort to get further away from him. He seemed to come to himself and glared at me, the old icy stare.

'You will feel the switch, I mean the instruments, you will and I will not because I am innocent, I am righteous in God's eyes! The King who is God's representative on earth, he will not allow it!' He began to shout, suddenly full of mad fury. I cowered away. 'You weak bentbacked creature! The King gave you what you deserved at Fulford Cross!' He laughed, suddenly full of wicked glee like an evil imp in a morality play. He was in a world of his own, or perhaps he always had been. He stopped abruptly. 'Maleverer accuses me,' he said. 'Accuses me falsely. When I am out of here, *he* will feel the switch. I shall lay it on him.' He shook his head. 'No, I mean the irons, the fire. Why does my head fizz and burn, why can I hold nothing in it straight any more?' He gave me a look of desperate appeal.

'You should see a priest, Radwinter,' I said.

'They would send me a papist, a damned papist that should be burned . . .' His voice lowered and his muttering became incomprehensible, a mad babbling to himself. I stood up and crossed to the window. The chains clanked and rattled and made movement difficult. I thought again how this was the fear of everyone in London, to stand in a cell in the Tower, limbs chained, accused of treason, awaiting questioning by Jesu knew what terrible methods.

And I was cold, chilled to the bone. I closed my eyes and put my hands over my face, listening to Radwinter's demented whisperings and the hiss of the rain on the river outside. It sounded closer now, the tide must be rising. I had never been so afraid in my life.

I went back and lay on my bed, shivering with cold. Hours passed. Radwinter had lain down too and gone quiet. We both jumped up when a key turned in the lock but it was only the young turnkey bringing food, a thin pottage that smelt bad, little lumps of gristle floating on the scummy surface. He laid the bowls on the floor.

'If you want better,' he said, 'you'll have to pay.' He gave us a mercenary look. 'You're both gentlemen, will you be having visitors?'

'Are they allowed?' I asked.

He looked at me as though I were stupid. 'Ay, or how would you get money to pay for things? Will someone come?'

'I hope so,' I said with a sigh, realizing how desperate I was to see a friendly face.

'Archbishop Cranmer will come for *me*,' Radwinter said with sudden haughtiness. 'Then you and the Tower constable will be the ones that pay.'

'Will he bring the King with him?' The turnkey laughed and closed the door. Radwinter gave it a baleful look, then took up a bowl and began slurping at the pottage. I ate the filthy stuff too, adding more discomfort to my already churning stomach.

More hours passed. It began to get dark. Outside the hissing of the rain went on and on. Was this part of the plan, keeping us waiting, like Radwinter's father had, to anticipate all that might come? I lay down. Barak and Wrenne would help me, I told myself. They would come.

✝

As the hours passed the cold drove everything else from my mind. My clothes were wet from the rain on the river crossing. They would never dry in here. Still the rain pelted down outside. I heard the hissing grow louder and then quieter as the river rose and fell with the tide. In the end I lay on the bare planks of the bed, wrapping the filthy mattress round me as best I could to try and get a little warmth. It was a difficult task in the dark, chained as I was. The mattress stank of piss and old sweat and things crawled into my clothes, making me itch. There was no sound from Radwinter. I could just make out his form on the bed. I hoped he was asleep. I did not like the thought of him lying awake in the darkness, heaven knew what mad thoughts churning through his brain.

The mattress provided little warmth. I would doze for a while and wake shivering. I watched the sky lighten from black to grey, outlined by the thick bars on the window. Still the rain hissed down. After that I slept awhile, tormented by vivid, horrible dreams. In one I was led in my chains into the King's presence. He lay in an ornately decorated bed, in the room at the pavilion at King's Manor where we had met Lady Rochford. He wore a nightshirt which showed how truly fat he was, rolls of flesh heaving like the sea as he struggled to sit up. I saw he was nearly bald, only a fringe of reddish-grey hair above his ears. He glared at me. 'Look what you have done!' he said, and pulled aside his coverlet. On one of his tree-trunk legs was a great black patch and out of it a yellow fungus like the stuff Broderick had used to poison himself was growing. 'You will pay for this, Blaybourne,' he said, fixing me with those eyes that were so like Radwinter's.

'I am not Blaybourne!' I stretched out my arms in entreaty but the soldiers holding me pulled on the chains binding them. They rattled and the tight gyve cut into my wrist. I awoke with a gasp. The pain in my wrist was real. I had flung my arm outward and it was biting hard. The metallic rattle was real too, a key was turning in the door. Both turnkeys, the fat one and the young one, entered, without food and with set faces. My heart banged with fear and my bowels churned.

They gave me only a glance, though, before turning to Radwinter, who likewise had jumped up. From his groggy look he must have been sleeping after all. The fat turnkey heaved him to his feet. 'Right, matey, Sir Jacob wants you questioned.'

He tried to struggle. 'No! I have done nothing! It is Maleverer who should be here! I am Archbishop Cranmer's gaoler! Let me loose!' He began to struggle. The fat turnkey slapped his face, hard, then grabbed his head and looked into his eyes.

'Don't make trouble or we'll drag you along by your feet.'

Radwinter said nothing, shocked by the blow, and allowed himself to be manhandled from the cell. He recovered himself outside, though; I heard him screaming as he was dragged away, calling out to God for vengeance on Maleverer, yelling that he would have the turnkey in his own gaol. I sat down on the bed, my legs shaking. When would they come for me?

More hours passed.

The tide was rising once again, the hissing of the rain getting louder. I had heard of cells in the riverside gaols flooding at high tides, prisoners drowning. I half hoped that would happen, watched with a mixture of fear and anticipation for water to start lapping over the window. I started at the sound of the key in the lock again, whirling round with a gasp of fear. Was it my turn now?

Barak stood in the doorway, the young gaoler behind him. He looked exhausted. I jumped up and ran to him, grasping his arms, all reserve forgotten. 'Jack, Jack, thank God!'

He reddened with embarrassment at this unprecedented show of affection. He reddened further as he saw my chains. He took my arm gently. 'Come, sir, sit down.' He led me to my bed and turned to the gaoler. 'Half an hour, yes?'

'Ay. Half an hour for sixpence. Let me know if you're bringing anything in, and I'll tell you the tariff.' He went out, locking us in. Barak sat on Radwinter's bed. I knew from his weary anxious face that he had no good news for me.

'That's Radwinter's bed,' I said with a hysterical little laugh.

'Radwinter? They've kept him with you?'

'Ay. He is out of his wits, Jack, and I'll be out of mine if I'm here much longer. They've taken him away, Jesu knows what they are doing to him. I do not have the stomach for this.'

'What man has? God's wounds, you look rough. Is there anything I can bring you?'

'Blankets and dry clothes. I need them desperately.' My voice caught on the words and I felt tears welling up in my eyes. 'And some decent food. I'll pay you later.'

'I'll sort it out.'

'Thank you. Jesu, it is good to see you. Talk to me, help me remind myself there is still a world beyond here. Have you gone to my house?'

'Ay. I thought it best for us all to stay there. Tamasin is helping look after Master Wrenne.' He hesitated. 'Sir, he is not well at all, poor old fellow. He almost collapsed when we reached Chancery Lane. He had to be put to bed.'

'I feared he was in a bad way.' I looked at Barak. 'Is this the end for him?'

'I think he just needs rest. The voyage was too much for him.'

'Does Joan know where I am?'

'We thought it best not to tell her. We said you had business at Whitehall, had told us to stay at Chancery Lane and look after Master Wrenne till you returned.'

'Good.' We sat silent for a moment. 'Listen to that rain,' I said.

'Ay. Apparently the weather has been bad in London, hasn't stopped raining for a fortnight. You know the orchard behind your house, that the Inn authorities have pulled up for new building?'

'Yes.'

'Now the trees have gone it is a sea of mud. You know it slopes down towards the wall of your garden. Well, it's flooding, there's a little pond building up by the far wall. Hasn't come under the wall yet, but it could flood the garden. Joan showed me.'

I did not reply, I could not focus on what he was saying. He was silent for a moment then said, 'I spent yesterday and this morning trying to find out what this is about. I've been round my old contacts at Whitehall, but they don't know anything. The King's been back at Hampton Court some days, he's not been to London. They say there's something going on down there, something big. All the chief men are there, including Cranmer.'

'The Prince's illness?'

'No, he's better they say. I'm thinking of trying to get a pass to Hampton Court. What have they told you?'

I looked at the door, then leaned forward. 'Speak quiet now, I think they may listen at the door. It is about the Queen.' I told him what Sir Jacob had said about Dereham.

'*Dereham.* That makes no sense.'

I looked at him seriously. 'If they use harsh methods I don't think I can hold out, Jack. They've taken Radwinter for questioning. When I heard the key in the lock I thought it was my turn.' I groaned. 'I've even been tempted to call the turnkey and spill everything, about the Queen and Culpeper and about Blaybourne for good measure. But that means danger for you and Tamasin too.' I looked at him bleakly.

He nodded slowly, bit his lip. 'I don't understand this,' he said quietly. 'What do they think connects you to Dereham?'

I told him how Rich had seen us leave the Queen's tent, seen Dereham accost me later in Hull. 'This is Rich's doing, he and Maleverer.' I was thinking quickly now. 'There must have been some suspicion of Dereham already; maybe they've got the wrong man or maybe the Queen has been even more stupid than we thought.'

'Dereham too?'

'Yes. I think Rich got Maleverer to tell Cranmer, got me put here for questioning.'

'That's a strange way to proceed. Surely it would make more sense just to have you taken before Cranmer for questioning, especially as you're under his patronage.'

'I think they've told him some lie, said there's more against me than there is.' I pondered, my mind was growing rational again now

Barak was there. 'If I'm shut up in here with my reputation ruined, the Guildhall are more likely to drop the Bealknap case. I think that is what is behind all this – it fits with Rich's threats and Maleverer's sly grins.'

'Maybe.'

'Listen, go to the Guildhall and ask for Master Vervey, he is one of the Common Council attorneys and a good fellow. Find if there has been any approach made by Rich's men about the Bealknap case. If I am right and Rich is behind this, there will have been.'

'All right.'

'Then get that information to Cranmer. Get to Hampton Court. Bribe anyone you need to, you know where my money is kept. If Cranmer is being used he won't like it. Put in a word for Radwinter too, say he is out of his wits and I do not think he killed Broderick.'

Barak smiled and shook his head. 'You'd help that rogue?'

'I'll help anyone wrongly accused, even him.'

He essayed a joke. 'Without a fee?'

'Ay. Poor man's plea. *Pro bono*, for the common good.' I laughed again, bitterly.

'Who *did* kill Broderick?'

'Someone on that ship's manifest, who was at Howlme when Jennet Marlin died. Tell Cranmer that as well if you get the chance.'

'Do you still suspect Leacon? He came up to me after you were taken, said he was sorry to have to arrest you but he had his orders.'

'Perhaps. I wonder if that story of his parents' land was even true.' I paused, and when I spoke again my voice shook. 'Get me out of here, Jack, for pity's sake. They showed me what they did to Bernard Locke. He was broken.' I gave a shuddering sigh. 'He was executed this morning.'

Barak got up, looking resolute now he had a clear course of action. 'I'll go straight to the Common Council, then I'll cozen an entry into Hampton Court. There's a man at Whitehall owes me a favour from when I worked for Lord Cromwell. And I'll get Tamasin to fetch the things you need, she is waiting outside the

Tower Gates.' He hesitated. 'I didn't want her to see inside this place.'

'No. Of course not. That is good of her.'

'She sends her prayers.'

'Give her my thanks. You were right,' I continued, 'when you warned me not to take Rich's threats over the Bealknap case lightly. But – I thought I had gained the advantage, as a lawyer I could not drop it. And so he put me here.' I gave Barak a doleful smile. 'Will you say, I told you so?'

'No. Yours was the path of integrity.' He rose suddenly and took my hand in both of his. ''Tis unbearable to see you like this,' he burst out.

'Then we are truly friends again?'

'Ay.' He made an essay at another joke. 'Though you didn't need to go to these lengths to win me round.' He gripped my hand harder. I winced.

'Careful,' I said. 'That manacle is tight, the skin's rubbed raw.'

'Sorry.' He stepped away, looking at the gyve with distaste.

'You are still limping,' I said.

'I manage.'

I looked at him. 'Get to Hampton Court, Jack. For Jesu's sake, get to Cranmer. But be careful.'

Chapter Forty-three

ALL THE REST OF that long day I waited in the cell, hoping for further news, though I knew the tasks I had set Barak would take time. I remembered the bells we had heard along the river yesterday — was it only yesterday? — that Tamasin told me were ringing as part of special services the King had ordered to celebrate the happiness of his fifth marriage. He must not yet know the suspicions about Catherine. Cranmer would need strong evidence before he dared tell the King.

✝

RADWINTER RETURNED early in the afternoon. I was relieved to see that he did not seem to have been hurt. He was in a filthy temper though. He sat on his bed, muttering to himself so furiously that spittle gathered at the edges of his mouth. I shuddered at the sight. At one point he looked up, glared at me and said, 'The torture, they've promised me the torture tomorrow, though I've told them all. They can't see it's the truth. See, Father, they break the rules! You were wrong, the rules may be made by God but men put them into action, and they break them!' He stopped then and gave that strange impish giggle I had heard yesterday. 'You are not my father, I know that. You're the soft hunchback lawyer. You do not understand anything.' Then he turned his head away.

As the light began to fail our door was unlocked again and the young turnkey appeared. He carried three clean blankets and a neatly folded set of clothes, on top of which were some bread and cheese and fruit. He laid them down on the bed. 'A girl left these for you.' He gave me a lascivious grin. 'Tasty little blonde. She your doxy?'

'No.'

He looked at Radwinter, who had turned to stare at the wall when he saw the turnkey had not come for him. 'He is not well,' I said quietly. 'In his mind.'

'Ay, we've had a laugh with him, saying he'll fetch the King and Cranmer down on us. But when he sees what's in store for him tomorrow, that'll shock him back into his wits soon enough. Always does. Goodnight then, matey.' He slammed the door shut.

I tore a hunk off the bread and a lump of cheese. They tasted good. I had not realized how hungry I was. 'Radwinter,' I called. 'Do you want some?'

He turned round and I saw he had been weeping. 'No,' he said and looked at me. 'They still say I killed Broderick.'

'I believe you did not.'

'Who did then?'

'I do not know. But I do not think it was you.'

He looked at me hard. Something seemed to change in his eyes, the madness returning. 'Who cares what you think?' he spat out with renewed viciousness.

'No one.'

'Soft hunchback fool.' He turned away again.

'Dear Jesu,' I muttered under my breath, 'save us both from this.'

✠

A SECOND NIGHT in the cell, less cold under the blankets Tamasin had brought but no less full of terror. Radwinter muttered and cried out in his sleep. The rain stopped then began again, harder than ever, hissing like some furious animal. Another grey dawn took shape outside and I got up, wincing at the stiffness in my limbs, making the chains clank. I ate the last of the food. Where was Barak? Had he found anything out at the Guildhall? Had he made it to Hampton Court?

They came early that morning, their keys rattling in the lock. Both turnkeys. 'Come on,' the fat one said cheerfully to Radwinter. 'You're wanted.'

✝

THEY CAME BACK for me two hours later. 'Time to see Sir Jacob,' the fat one said. 'Now, *you're* not going to be any trouble, are you?' he coaxed ominously. 'It's just questions this time.'

I let them lead me out to the central area where the desk was. Beyond, I could see the barred door that led up to the White Tower. A soldier was waiting there. The young turnkey nodded to him. 'This one for the deputy warden,' he said. The soldier took my arm as the turnkey opened the door to the staircase. The soldier indicated I should walk ahead. I stumbled and clanked my way up the narrow staircase.

I heard a murmur of male voices ahead and felt shame and horror at the prospect of being marched past the soldiers in the Great Hall again, limping, in chains, unwashed. But the soldier led me past the entrance to the hall, up a further flight to another floor with large unbarred windows and fresh rushes on the floor. He stopped before a door and knocked. Sir Jacob's voice called, 'Come in.'

It was a light chamber, the walls painted yellow. Tables were covered with papers organized in neat piles. Maleverer's offices, I remembered, had always looked chaotic.

A window streaked with rain showed Tower Green, where people walked to and fro. Sir Jacob, wearing a black doublet and white shirt, sat behind a desk. He looked at me seriously.

'This is your one chance to answer my questions truthfully.' He spoke quietly. 'If you fail to satisfy me, what is being done to Radwinter now will be done to you. Do you understand?'

'Yes, Sir Jacob.' My heart was beating fast and again I suppressed the urge to blurt out everything I knew about the Queen. But I would not betray Barak and Tamasin, not while there was still a chance Barak could get to Cranmer, get me out of here.

'The Queen was placed under confinement yesterday,' Sir Jacob said, 'following information received by Archbishop Cranmer that before her marriage she had dalliance with Francis Dereham, whom she appointed her secretary in York. There may be a precontract of marriage between them, and as a lawyer you know what difficulties that may cause in her marriage to the King.'

I was silent for a moment, shocked. Then I said, 'I know nothing of this, sir. I scarce know Dereham. Sir, I believe I may know how this has come about.'

He nodded. I spoke rapidly, telling him of Rich's animus against me over the Bealknap case, how he had seen me leave the Queen's tent and, later, seen Dereham speak to me. I repeated the lie I had told Rich when he saw Dereham talking to me in Hull, that Dereham had seen me at Fulford and used our meeting in the street to make further mock of me. I hesitated before saying that and from a quick intense flicker of Sir Jacob's eyes I saw he had noticed. He was an experienced interrogator. He consulted a paper on his desk, then rapped, 'What was your business with the Queen at Howlme?'

It was as well I worked in a profession where you needed to think on your feet. 'It concerned one of her servants, Tamasin Reedbourne. She has a — a relationship with my assistant, Master Barak. She was in some trouble with Lady Rochford over it.'

He frowned, then laughed, again the schoolmaster who has caught out an errant pupil. 'The Queen was concerned with the morals of one of her servants?' he asked incredulously.

'Sir Jacob,' I said quickly, 'those are the only things Sir Richard Rich could have knowledge of. I cannot believe I have been brought here solely on those grounds.'

'This matter could not be more serious. I have a report from Sir William Maleverer that a senior official's servant overheard you in the refectory, telling Francis Dereham that if he could get into the Queen's drawers it would serve the King right for the way he treated you at Fulford.'

'That is a complete lie.' I almost shouted my denial. 'And I would guess the official who employs the servant is Sir Richard Rich.'

That knowing smile again. 'It is not. He is a clerk for Master Simon Craike of the Harbingers' Office.'

'Craike is in Rich's pay. Question the servant, sir. I beg you. Archbishop Cranmer has been fed false information by Rich.'

'I told you, the report was from Sir William Maleverer.'

'I believe he is in league with Rich. Please sir,' I begged. 'Please question this servant of Craike's.' How Craike had betrayed me. Rich must have put the pressure on.

Sir Jacob referred quickly to another paper. 'Master Barak and Mistress Reedbourne. They brought you food and clothes yesterday. The turnkey reports you and Barak spoke quietly, as though you did not wish to be overheard.'

'Would not you, sir, in my position?'

'I am hardly likely to be.'

'Sir, could you not enquire of the servant? It would take just a little time. I have already been here two days. Another day . . .'

Sir Jacob sat and thought, tapping a fingernail against his thin lips. I felt hope rising in my breast. Then he shook his head.

'No. I am not satisfied. You are keeping things back, I feel it.'

'Sir Jacob—'

'No!' He spoke sharply, waved an angry hand at me. 'You have had your chance. You will go back to your cell. There you will see what has happened to Radwinter, and perhaps tomorrow when you are taken to where he has been you will have the sense to speak the truth before they really start work.'

My jaw dropped in horror. 'Sir Jacob, please, a day—'

'No. When it comes to making a recalcitrant man spill the truth, there is no better means than the torture.'

✝

I WAS MARCHED DOWN the stairs again, past the hall where the soldiers talked and laughed and light spilled into the dark stairway, down again to the darkness and damp; through the barred door again and back into the hands of the young turnkey. The fat turnkey was there too. He smiled and shook his head.

'Down to the chamber tomorrow, is it? I see it in your face. My advice is to spill all you know as soon as you get in. Your pal Radwinter didn't, and he's in a sorry state.'

'See his mouth, Ted?' the young man said cheerily.

'Ay. They must have used the vice on his teeth. He won't be doing any chewing for a while.' The fat turnkey shook his head again. 'Come on, matey, back in the cell you go.' He grasped my arm.

'Has – has there been any word for me?' I asked. 'From my friend?'

'No, nothing.' He began leading me away. 'There's no point hoping,' he said as we approached the cell. 'Best just resolve to make a clean breast before they get properly started tomorrow.' He turned the key in the lock. 'Take my word for it, I've seen – oh fuck!' He yelled suddenly, letting go my arm.

I stared past him into the cell. At first I could make no sense of what I saw, it seemed that a gigantic pendulum had been brought to the cell and set swinging under the window. Then I saw it was Radwinter. He had taken the two beds and set them one on top of the other. He had removed his shirt and, like Broderick, had twisted it into a noose, tied one end to the window and the other round his neck. Then he had jumped from the bed. He had broken his neck, his head was bent at an unnatural angle. His face was hideous, his mouth open and smeared with blood, half his teeth gone. I fell back against the doorjamb, my legs gave way and I slid to the floor.

The fat turnkey had run across to the window. Now he ran back to the door. 'Billy!' he yelled. 'Billy!' Running feet, and a moment later the other turnkey joined him in the doorway.

'Oh, Hell!' he cried. 'We'll be in the shit for this.' He went over and looked at Radwinter, then turned back to the fat man. 'You know the beds should be fixed to the floor where there's a high window!'

'I've been trying to get the workmen in for months! How the fuck did he get the beds across with his hands in that state?' I saw Radwinter's hands, dangling at his side, were torn and bloody, his fingernails gone. I shuddered and looked away.

'They should have given him the rack,' young Billy said, 'instead of pissing about with his teeth. He couldn't have done it then. Fuck! He's still swinging, he can only just have jumped!' He grabbed one of Radwinter's legs, bringing the body to a halt.

'Why did he do it?' the fat man said in a tone of outrage.

'They were taking him back for another go tomorrow.'

'He did it for shame,' I said quietly. 'For him this would have been the ultimate shame. So much for torture bringing the truth.'

✝

THE DEPUTY WARDEN CAME, watched Radwinter cut down and his body taken away. 'And we got nothing out of him,' he muttered angrily. But then he had had nothing to give, I thought. He had not killed Broderick. Broderick, Jennet Marlin, Oldroyd, now Radwinter. What a harvest of lives that box of documents had reaped. And how many would Catherine Howard's dalliance cost?

I sat alone in the cell, through another day, another night. Outside the rain slashed down, hissing, dripping. When it grew dark I found myself looking nervously into corners, as though Radwinter's tormented spirit might appear there. But there was nothing, no sense of him. As the hours passed my hopes ebbed and flowed with the tide on the river outside, I thought, Barak will come, or there will be some message to give me hope. Surely he could have got to Hampton Court and back by now, on the river? If he did not come, what would they do to me tomorrow? My head swam as I thought of all the abominable things I had heard they used in the Tower: the rack, the vice, hot irons. I had been a fool to think for a moment I could lie to Sir Jacob. I thought of Radwinter's bloodied mouth. In a bleak moment at the darkest hour of the night I wondered wildly whether Barak and Tamasin might have fled to avoid questioning about the Queen. I cursed myself for such stupidity, Barak would not let me down. Then the dawn came again, light at the window from which a piece of Radwinter's shirt still hung.

✝

THE TURNKEYS CAME for me early in the afternoon. They watched me carefully lest I might struggle, but I knew there was no point and let them lead me away without resistance. I felt light-headed, as though my spirit might fly from my body.

They took me down a flight of stairs, then along a dark passage. They halted before a wide, solid door. The fat turnkey knocked. I looked at the dark old wood. My heart was thumping hard now, making me feel more faint than ever. The door was opened and they led me inside. The turnkeys released my arms and quickly stepped outside again.

It was a big, windowless room with smoke-blackened walls. A large brazier in an alcove put me momentarily in mind of a blacksmith's forge, as did the big bull of a man in a leather apron standing looking at me, hands on hips. A heavyset boy in his late teens was tending the brazier's coals. Then I saw the rack with its straps and wooden wheels in the corner, the row of instruments – pincers, pokers, knives – hanging on hooks, and I felt my head spin. Beside me was a big metal bin and on top, among the ashes of old coals, small white objects gleaming. I realized these were Radwinter's teeth, and my legs gave way.

The big man grabbed me as I fell, and sat me in a wooden chair. He sighed, as I might at the sight of a badly copied document. 'Take deep breaths,' he said. 'Just sit there and breathe slowly.'

I did as commanded, staring at him dumbly. His expression was frowning. I saw his apron was smeared with old blood. 'Got the thin knife heated, Tom?' he asked over his shoulder.

'Yes, Father. Coming along nicely.' Over the big man's shoulder the boy gave me a nasty smile.

'Got your breath back?' the big man asked.

'Yes. Listen, please, I—'

'Over here then, Tom.' And before I could react the big man pulled me up and held me while the boy tore off the new doublet Tamasin had brought and then my white shirt. The big man stepped away and studied me. There was no mockery at my shape, only a cold professional interest.

'All right,' he said. 'Chains.' And again before I had time to react they grabbed the irons holding my wrists together and hauled my arms up, looping the chain through a hook in the low ceiling. I was left dangling, my toes only just touching the floor. The gyves bit into my wrists, the one that had already rubbed my right wrist raw causing excruciating pain. I shouted out.

The big man stood looking at me. He had an impatient expression on his heavy features now. 'Right,' he said. 'We're not going to piss about, we want answers quickly. What do you know of relations between Francis Dereham and the Queen?'

'Nothing,' I shouted out. I thought, I could stop this if I mentioned Culpeper's name, tell what I knew of *him* and the Queen. Or could I? Might that just goad them on?'

'Come on,' the big man growled. 'You know better than that!'

'Torture is illegal in England!' I cried out. It made the torturer's face crack into a grin.

'Hear that, Tom?' he said. 'The soft-skinned fool thinks *this* is the torture! Oh no, that's just the hanging up to put you in position. Show him, Tom.'

The boy came forward. In one hand he held a thin knife, the point red-hot. In the other a tiny vice with a screw to turn it. He held them up for me to see. 'We'll have some teeth out with the vice,' his father said. 'Break them, mind, not pull 'em out by the roots. That's worse. Then we'll have that knife under your fingernails.'

My head was clear now, horribly clear, the earlier faintness gone, though it was hard to breathe with my arms stretched above me. 'Once more,' the torturer said in tones of heavy impatience. 'What do you know of the Queen and Francis Dereham?'

'Nothing. Please listen, I—'

I hadn't learned yet, I hadn't learned how speedily they moved. The big man grabbed my head between meaty hands and nodded to the boy. My mouth was forced open, I tasted the boy's sweaty hands, then felt metal in my mouth. There was a sharp crack and a terrible pain coursed through every nerve in my head. I felt blood seep onto my tongue. The pain went on and on, receding and returning in crashing waves. The boy held up the vice and I saw a gleam of white.

'Now,' the big man said again. 'Dereham, or it's the knife under the nails. We'll do nails and teeth turn about.'

'I – I—' I was gurgling, half mad with pain. 'I don't—'

The father nodded, and the son raised the knife to my pinioned hands.

Chapter Forty-four

H E STOPPED. A fraction of an inch away, the heat searing my finger. A high-pitched creak told me the door had opened and through waves of pain and terror I heard voices, recognized a harsh mutter, Sir Jacob Rawling's voice. The door closed again. I looked wildly round, groaning and spitting blood. The fat turnkey had come in and was standing by the torturer, looking at me with mild interest. The big man nodded to his son and the hot knife was pulled away. I felt myself lifted up and wondered if this was the start of some new horror, but they only pulled the chain holding my arms off the hook, then lowered me to the floor. I stood unsteadily. The big man looked at me, a faint smile on his meaty face.

'Your lucky day. We've to stop; you're to go back to your cell.'

I staggered and spat out blood and a fragment of tooth. The boy had broken off a big molar in the side of my lower jaw. The fat turnkey reached out a hand to steady me. 'Come on,' he said, 'let's get you back. Here's your shirt and doublet.' He helped me pull the torn clothes round my shoulders, then led me half-dazed from the chamber.

'What happened?' I asked as he walked me back. My voice sounded thick, my mouth was still bleeding. I had been proud of my teeth, I had had nearly a full set.

'You're to be taken to Archbishop Cranmer at Hampton Court. I don't know where he'll keep you, because he hasn't a gaoler any more, has he? Billy and I are in trouble about that,' he added lugubriously.

We turned the corner into the central area and there, standing by the desk with young Billy, I saw Barak. My heart leapt. His manner was quite different from the day before, he looked confident and energetic. At least, till he saw me. Then his jaw dropped.

'Jesu!' he shouted. 'What have you done to him? You fucking arseholes—'

'Now, none of that!' the fat turnkey admonished. 'He was taken to the torture on Sir Jacob's orders. My advice to you is to get him out of here before the Archbishop changes his mind.'

'There's a whole boatload of new captives coming in soon,' Billy told him.

'Just as well we'll have the cell, then.'

Barak took my arm. 'How many teeth did the arseholes pull?'

'Just one.'

'Let's get out. We've a long boat journey. It's raining, but I've got your coat and a blanket. And your things.' He took out my dagger and purse and Cranmer's seal that had been taken off me when I arrived. He handed them to me, then looked at the turnkeys. 'Can you get these irons off?'

'All right.' The fat man selected a key from his ring and, bending down, released my feet and left wrist. When he came to the manacle on my right wrist, though, the tight one, the key would not turn. 'Damn thing, it's stiff.'

'Try spitting on the key,' Barak said. The turnkey did as he suggested, but with no result.

'Looks like you'll have to keep it on, matey.'

Barak bent and studied the manacle. 'It's rusty. I could probably get that off with tools at home.' He turned to the gaoler. 'But he can't go before the Archbishop dragging a three-foot length of chain. Can you get the padlock off?'

The round gyve was connected to the chain by a stout little padlock. The gaoler grunted and went over to a bundle of little keys hanging from the wall. He opened the padlock, the chain falling to the floor. All the time I had been looking on dumbly, licking my cracked and swollen lips, but now I burst out weeping uncontrol‑

lably, my sobs echoing round that terrible chamber. Barak took my arm and led me gently through the barred door, up the stairs and through the Great Hall. I was past caring whether the soldiers saw my wretched state. I asked no questions; it was all I could do to stumble along.

We descended the steps of the White Tower, then I felt grass under my feet, rain on my head. We stopped walking at last and I looked up. We were by the Watergate again. A wherry stood there, a soldier and a boatman in Cranmer's livery sheltering under the arch. Beyond, the heavy rain made the Thames water hiss and boil.

'He's hurt, take care,' Barak told the boatman.

They helped me in and the boatman took the oars. Barak wrapped the blanket round me as we pulled out into the water. A hand to my throbbing jaw, I looked at the wide river. A large barge swept past us, sculling into the Watergate. Sitting inside was a cargo of bedraggled gentlemen and ladies, their fine clothes streaming water, surrounded by soldiers. My eyes widened as I saw Francis Dereham, no longer proud and arrogant but shrinking against the side of the boat, his face white as chalk. I also recognized some of the Queen's ladies, and then I saw Lady Rochford in the midst of them, staring at me with wide terrified eyes. Seeing my bloodied face, she began screaming and tried to stand up. Someone pulled her back down. The shrill sound faded away as the barge passed under the arch. I sat staring after it.

'Why is Lady Rochford there? Has she been arrested?'

'Looks like it. Perhaps they know about Culpeper.'

'If they don't now,' I said grimly, 'they will soon.'

'This means we're safe,' Barak said eagerly.

'Yes. Culpeper's doings will come out now anyway. What we know ceases to matter.'

'What will happen to the Queen?'

'The axe, I'd think. Poor silly girl.' The tears welled up again, and I wiped at my face with my sleeve, wincing as I brushed my damaged jaw.

Barak looked at me anxiously.

'Are you fit to go before Cranmer?'

'I must know what he wants.' I took a deep breath. 'You did it then, you got to him?'

He nodded, droplets flying from his soaking hair. 'I went to the Guildhall first and saw your friend Master Vervey. You were right: the day you were taken, one of Rich's men came and told the council you were under arrest, they'd be advised to drop the case and drop you. They were scared silly to hear their lawyer was in the Tower. They've agreed to drop the case against Bealknap on the basis each side pay their own costs. I'm sorry.'

'I'm past caring.' I sighed. 'You were right after all about that. I have paid for my obstinacy.'

'Then I went back to Whitehall, tried to get permission to visit Cranmer at Hampton Court. But there was no chance, the place is sealed off. My Whitehall contact told me the Queen's under arrest there, though that's not generally known yet. I don't think I could have got there but for an old friend of yours.'

'Who?'

He smiled. 'Master Simon Craike.'

'Craike?'

'I was hanging about the corridors, looking in an ill-humour no doubt, when he came up and asked what the matter was. I told him about your arrest. And what you suspected about Rich. He was horrified. He said he hated Rich and he owed you one, and wrote me out a letter to take to the Chamberlain's office at Hampton Court.'

'But the deputy warden told me a servant of Craike's said he'd overheard me telling Dereham to bed the Queen—'

Barak laughed. 'I can just see you saying that.'

'So Rich set that up without reference to Craike.'

'He's not such a bad old arsehole, even if he does like to have women beating him. He said to tell you how sorry he was for everything.'

'So Craike came right in the end. And you saw Cranmer?'

'His secretary. Jesu, things are buzzing at Hampton Court, I had soldiers with me all the time. I told him the story. He went in to see the Archbishop, then came back with an authority to fetch you from the Tower.' He looked at my face again. 'I worked as quick as I could, I had no sleep last night.'

'I will never forget this, Jack.' My voice shook. 'Thank you.'

✠

THE BOAT ROWED steadily on through the rain. I huddled inside my blankets as we passed Westminster and Lambeth Palace. I looked up at the Lollards' Tower. 'Radwinter is dead,' I said. 'He hanged himself yesterday, in the cell.'

'Good riddance,' Barak said bluntly.

'I felt sorry for him at the end.'

'You feel sorry for too many folk. That's your trouble.'

'Perhaps. How is Master Wrenne?'

'Better. I've had the old Moor up to see him.'

'Guy?' My face lightened at the thought of my old friend.

'He looked at my leg, says it's nearly mended. He says Master Wrenne was exhausted, but he should be up again in a few days with rest and good food.' His face became serious. 'I asked him how long Master Wrenne might have. He said, only months, and his pain and weariness will get worse.'

'I pray we find his nephew.'

'Why shouldn't we?'

'He's a northerner and a religious conservative. You remember I said they showed me Bernard Locke before they executed him?'

'Ay.'

'I asked him if he knew Martin Dakin and he said he did, and he was safe. There was something strange, mocking, in the way he said it.'

'I heard the Privy Council have had men around the Inns, questioning people. Mainly Gray's Inn.'

'Anyone arrested?'

'Not that I heard. I told the old Moor where you were, by the way. I had a job to stop him coming straight down to the Tower.'

'He is a good man.' I smiled.

'There's a bit of competition going on at your house, I am afraid. Joan does not approve of Tamasin very much.'

'You don't have her in your room, I hope?'

He shrugged. 'It's the competition for nursing old Wrenne Joan doesn't like. Two women in one house never works. But she is kind to him. She *is* kind.'

I suppressed a frown; I did not like the idea of Tamasin having the freedom of my house. 'She will domesticate *you* in the end,' I said.

He smiled. 'She can try. By the way, I'm going to see my old mate tomorrow. He has some news, I've had a message.'

'About Tamasin's father? What does he say?'

'Only that he's got a good lead.'

We rowed on in silence, my jaw throbbing painfully, the gyve cold against my wrist. At length the towers of Hampton Court appeared in the distance, and my heart began thumping again.

✝

THERE WERE SOLDIERS at the wharf, checking everyone's documents. Barak showed them Cranmer's letter, the one he had brought to the Tower. We were told to wait and escorted to a little wooden shelter with other arrivals, water dripping on to the boards. I put my torn shirt and doublet on properly, and pulled down the cuffs of my shirt to cover the damned manacle. I winced at the chafing, and the throbbing from my jaw. The soldier from the boat waited with us. I am still a prisoner, I thought.

A clerk arrived, the same soft-footed little fellow who had taken me to see Cranmer at that first meeting more than two months before. His eyes widened at the sight of my swollen, bloody face. The soldier following, he led us across the wide lawn, through a door at the back of the palace, then along dim back-corridors. Looking through a window into a courtyard I saw a familiar figure among the many soldiers posted at the doors. Sergeant Leacon, standing on his own in the yard, looking downcast.

The official halted before a little door. 'You are to wait here, Master Shardlake, till the Archbishop is free.' At least, I thought, I am 'Master' again. He turned to Barak. 'Come with me please, you shall wait elsewhere.'

'I'll see you soon, sir.' Barak followed the clerk reluctantly. The soldier opened the door and ushered me in. He closed the door behind me, and I guessed he would be standing guard outside. I looked around me. A room with tapestries of scenes of ancient Rome on the walls, distant views of pillared buildings. A fire in the grate. There was a heap of cushions by the fire and I sank gratefully on to them, not even bothering to remove my wet coat. My eyes closed instantly.

I woke feeling I was not alone. I opened my eyes. Archbishop Cranmer was standing above me, in his white robe and black stole. He was looking at me, an anxious expression on his austere tired face.

I scrambled to my feet. As I moved my head a fresh spasm shot through my jaw, making me groan. He put out a hand. 'Not so fast, Master Shardlake, you will faint. Here, take this chair.' He pulled a chair out from the card-table, and I sank heavily into it.

'What happened to your face?' he asked quietly. His cheeks had a grey look and there were bags of exhaustion under his eyes.

'I was taken to the torture, your grace, in the Tower. Barak did not arrive quite in time. They broke a tooth off.' I realized how muffled my voice sounded.

Cranmer frowned with distaste. 'I did not sanction that.' He hesitated. 'Sir Richard Rich came to see me, told me you knew the Queen was having a – a relationship with Dereham. He knew I was following up other information already, information that came to me while the Progress was away. An old servant of the Queen from before she was married, who said Catherine had had carnal relations with Dereham when she was younger, that there could be a precontract of marriage. They persuaded me to put you in the Tower, said you would be readier to confess if you were held in there.' He looked at me severely for a moment. 'I felt betrayed by you. That you had not told what you knew, but I did not sanction torture.'

'For Rich having me tortured was probably a matter of sport. I imagine the order to the warden came from him.'

'Maleverer brought me a deposition from a servant of Master Craike. That servant has now disappeared. And Craike came to see me this morning. He says Sir William Maleverer came to him, asked in Rich's name if he had a servant who would swear falsely for money. He told me he provided a man reluctantly. He did not know the victim of this deceit was to be you. When he heard you were in the Tower, he came to me.' Cranmer looked down at me. 'Craike told me, too, about the hold Rich has over him. He said he could bear it no more, realizing he had had a part in sending you falsely to the Tower.'

'Will he lose his position?'

'I fear so. These visits to the stews –' the Archbishop wrinkled his nose in distaste – 'are one thing, but he should not have let Rich blackmail him. That at least will stop. Maleverer is in Rich's pay. He seeks some of Robert Aske's lands.' Cranmer's lips set hard. 'He will lose his place on the Council of the North. I shall see to that.'

'Rich has won against me, your grace,' I said quietly. 'That case Barak told your secretary about – the Guildhall has dropped it.' I found I did care about that after all.

'Then I am sorry. But you must understand, Rich is too powerful, too useful for the King, for me to intervene against him.'

'So he has truly won.'

He looked at me seriously. 'You worked for Lord Cromwell, Master Shardlake. You know how much latitude the great men of the realm are allowed.'

I did not reply.

'So,' Cranmer went on quietly, 'you truly knew nothing of Dereham's relations with the Queen?'

'Nothing, my lord. I swear.'

He sighed. 'Dereham is in the Tower now. They will use harsh methods on him.' He bit his lip. 'But it must be.'

'I saw him brought in as we came out. And the Queen's ladies.'

'I have been set to question the Queen herself. There is more to come out, other men are mentioned already.' Culpeper, I thought. I looked at Cranmer, fearing more questions, but he only shook his head. 'That she could have behaved so . . .' He sighed again. 'The King will be exposed to public ridicule. He does not yet believe the Queen has deceived him. But he will. God help her then.'

I looked at him. 'If the Queen falls the Duke of Norfolk will be in dire straits. The head of the traditionalist faction. The Queen's uncle.'

Cranmer nodded. I thought, he cavils at the means but will use them for his ends. All the time the Progress was away he has been working towards this.

'This will be the end of the Howards,' he said neutrally. 'There are other families waiting in the wings, more favourable to reform, they will have the King's ear now. The Seymours, the Dudleys, the Parrs.' He nodded thoughtfully. 'Yes, the Parrs.'

'Will the Queen die?' I asked him.

He looked at me with those unreadable blue eyes. 'I think she must. But for now it is not to be spoken of outside Hampton Court. Do you understand?'

'Yes.'

I saw his eyes move to my wrist. My sleeve had ridden up, exposing the gyve and the raw skin. Cranmer gave an unhappy little sigh. 'I am sorry for what happened to you, Master Shardlake,' he said quietly. 'You will receive more pay than your strict due, I will see to that.'

'Broderick—' I said.

He waved a hand. 'I do not blame you for failing to save him. You were not to know Radwinter was mad.' He frowned.

'I think he was never quite normal in his mind.'

'I thought his – his cruelty – was in a way being used by God, harnessed in the service of truth, the destruction of heresy. I hope that may save his soul.' He looked out of the window at the teeming rain, the bare trees, and again I heard that unhappy sigh.

'Your grace,' I said. 'I do not think Radwinter killed Broderick. I think Maleverer was wrong.'

He looked at me in surprise. 'He seemed sure.'

'I knew Radwinter, your grace. In his mind, even at the end, to him such an act would have been wrong.' I met the Archbishop's gaze. 'He was loyal to you till the end.'

'Then who did kill Broderick?'

'I think someone helped him kill himself, as he had tried to do before. And I believe that person may also have stolen the papers in that casket.' Cranmer looked at me keenly as I told him of my suspicions. 'Sir William would not believe me,' I added.

Cranmer thought a moment. 'He seemed certain. If Maleverer ignored that possibility he is indeed a man of poor judgement. So someone stole the papers and stayed with the Progress, all the way to the ship. But who?'

I took a deep breath. 'The soldier who guarded Broderick on the boat: Sergeant Leacon. He was part of the guard at St Mary's too. A Kentishman. I saw him out in the yard just now.'

'Yes. I believe he has been dismissed.' He nodded slowly. 'It would do no harm to have him questioned.'

'But my lord, I am not sure,' I said. 'May I ask . . .'

'Yes?'

'That he be just questioned? Be put to no harsh measures. The evidence is only circumstantial as yet.'

'I will question him myself.' The archbishop frowned. 'If the conspirators have those papers it could make – difficulties. Some are still at large. Some of the papist sympathizers at Gray's Inn have already been questioned following Bernard Locke's confession, but we uncovered nothing about who his contact there was.'

'I saw Locke briefly, in the Tower. Before he was executed. He was in a grim state.'

'God receive his soul.' Cranmer gave another unhappy sigh. 'But he deserved to die, he was a traitor and conspirator to murder.' He waved a beringed hand. 'Go home now, Master Shardlake, rest. I will send word if we find new information.'

'Yes, your grace.' I thought, should I mention Blaybourne, the legend I discovered from the old lawyer in Hull? But he would know it, all those in power would know. And better they were left unaware that I knew too. I rose, wincing. 'Your grace?'

'Yes.'

'May I request that I be not asked to work in the service of politics again. Now, especially after what has befallen me, I desire only a peaceful life for such time as God allows me.' I reached for the seal and held it out to him. He looked at it, and then at me.

'You could be a useful man to me, Master Shardlake. Your old master Thomas Cromwell thought so.'

I did not reply. I continued holding out the seal. He looked at my ravaged face. 'Very well,' he said, and took it reluctantly. I rose painfully to my feet and bowed. I turned to the door but he called me back. 'Master Shardlake.'

'Your grace.'

'The harsh measures the King takes are necessary. Do not forget he is chosen by God, appointed by Him to guide England into the paths of wisdom and truth.'

I would have liked to tell him that was what Radwinter used to say, but I only nodded, bowed again and left the room. The soldier took me back down the corridors, across the lawn and down to the river stage. Barak was waiting there.

'The boatman will take you back to town, sir.' The soldier gave a quick bow and walked away. I watched him go, realizing that at last I was free. Barak touched my arm.

'Let's go home,' he said gently.

Chapter Forty-five

As we approached Westminster the rain eased and by the time the boat pulled in at Temple Stairs it had stopped completely. Barak helped me out. I stood looking at Temple Gardens and the familiar squat shape of the Templars' church.

'Can you manage the walk to Chancery Lane?' he asked.

'Ay. The thought of home draws me like a magnet.'

'The horses are back, by the way. Arrived two days ago, fresh as new paint.'

I laughed bitterly. 'Never doubt the ability of the King and his minions when it comes to organizing things. A Progress, a reception, an army. Torture and death.' I looked at him seriously. 'I got Cranmer to agree he will never call on my services again.'

'Suits me. I never want another few days like I've just had. What will happen to Rich and Maleverer?'

'To Rich, nothing. He stands too high. Maleverer will lose his position. Cranmer is worried about who Broderick's assassin might be. I suggested he question Sergeant Leacon.'

Barak shook his head. 'The sergeant? It can't be him. He's like old Wrenne, no concerns beyond his family and doing his work.'

'Then Cranmer will find that out. I just wanted to – to tie this up if I could. There's no one else I can think of that it could be.' And then I thought, but isn't there?

'Are you coming?' Barak asked.

'Yes, yes of course.' We began walking up the path, carefully, for it was carpeted with wet leaves.

'We'd better tell Joan something to explain your appearance,' he said. 'We could say you'd been set on and robbed.'

'Ay. I'll have to keep this gyve hidden. Damn the thing.'

'I'll get that off with my tools.'

I shook my head. 'Was it raining hard *all* the time I was in the Tower? It seemed like it.'

'Pretty much.'

I looked at the bare trees. 'When we started for York summer was not long past. Now we are come to winter.'

'Do you remember the great snow we had in November four years ago? Jesu, that was cold.'

'All too well. That was when I was sent to the monastery at Scarnsea. My first matter of state. My disillusion with the King and all his works started there.'

We trudged on, up to Fleet Bridge and then across to Chancery Lane. The red chimneys of my house came into view.

'Home!' I breathed. 'At last!' Tears pricked at the corners of my eyes.

✝

PETER THE KITCHEN BOY was in the hall as we entered, carrying a pail of slops. He stared wide-eyed at my appearance. I tucked my manacled hand into my coat pocket.

'Where is Joan?' Barak asked him sharply.

'Gone to market, sir. Mistress Reedbourne has just taken a bowl of broth to Master Wrenne.' He gave a saucy leer at Barak when he mentioned Tamasin's name.

'Is there a fire in the parlour?' I asked.

'Yes, sir.'

'Then bring us some beer.'

He went off. I followed Barak into the parlour and slumped down in my chair by the fire, massaging my wrist.

'I'll get my tools,' he said. I remembered the night he had picked the lock of the Wentworths' well for me, a year ago. I had been a little scandalized, then, by his lock-picking skills. Now I was past being scandalized by anything.

⸸

HE WORKED ON the gyve for half an hour, but without result. 'The damned lock's all rusted inside,' he said.

I looked at the cursed thing; already I hated that tight circle of iron more than any object in the world. 'Then how are we to get it off? It bites into my wrist.' I heard the edge of panic in my voice.

'I've a friend down Cheapside who can have any lock off,' he said. 'He's more skill and better tools than me.' Barak glared at the manacle, reluctant to admit defeat. 'I'll go and see if he's about.'

'You should rest.'

'No. I'll go now.' He finished his pot of beer and left. I heaved myself to my feet and slowly mounted the stairs.

Giles was sitting up in bed, in nightshirt and dressing gown. Tamasin sat at his side, sewing one of her dresses. She jumped up at my arrival. Both stared at my face.

'It looks worse than it is,' I said.

'You are free?' Giles asked.

'Yes. Thanks to Barak. I do not want to talk about it, not yet. How are you, Giles?'

He smiled. 'A little stronger every day. That voyage was too much for me. By Jesu, I am glad you are free. I have been sore worried.' I was moved by the concern in his face.

'He is not a good patient, sir,' Tamasin said. She smiled, but her eyes on me were watchful. She looked pale and tired.

'I hear you have been attending Master Wrenne well.'

'She has.' Giles smiled at her warmly.

'He will keep getting up, though your friend Master Guy says he should stay abed awhile yet.'

'Barak told me he came.'

'May I leave you for a while, sir?' Tamasin asked. 'I said I would do some shopping for Mistress Woode.'

'Ay. And thank you for bringing those things to the Tower.'

'I am pleased to see you out of that doleful place, sir. Jack was half mad with worry.' There was still something watchful, evaluating, in her look. Was that because she was uncertain of the treatment she might expect from me? She curtsied and went out. I took her chair by the bed.

'What did they do to you?' Giles asked quietly.

'Less than they might have, thanks to Jack.'

'Barak told me of the wicked plot Rich and Maleverer hatched against you.'

'Yes. Cranmer knows all now. Maleverer will be in trouble, though Cranmer says he cannot touch Rich.'

I saw Wrenne's eyes on my wrist. My wretched sleeve had ridden up again, exposing the gyve and the raw skin around it.

'That thing is like a symbol,' he said quietly. 'The whole nation fettered and bruised by the King. A piece of filth like Rich may have a man falsely imprisoned, even tortured, to get a legal case dropped. It is not justice, Matthew. This is not the country I once knew.'

'No. Giles,' I said, 'you said once that Maleverer's family were all strong Catholics, then he aligned with the reformers after 1536 in hope of gain.'

'That is right. He is a greedy man. But what—'

'What if he could satisfy his greed by standing with the reformers, yet secretly help the old cause?'

'How? What do you mean?'

'Nothing.'

Giles smiled at me. 'I am not sure he would have the brains.'

✝

I WENT TO BED and fell asleep at once. When I woke it was early morning, I had slept near twenty hours. I felt somewhat rested, though my shattered tooth hurt and my nerves were still so strung up the squeak of a mouse would have set me bounding. I got up and dressed, cursing the gyve again. I looked at my face in my steel mirror. I was startled by the staring apparition that looked back at me from sunken eyes, several days' stubble darkening the cheeks.

I went downstairs. Joan, hearing me, bustled out of the kitchen. She saw me and opened her mouth in horror. I raised a hand, frightened she would scream. 'It looks worse than it is.' I was getting used to that phrase.

'Oh sir, your poor mouth! The rogues! Is no one safe from vagabonds these days!' I stared at her in surprise, then remembered I was supposed to have been attacked by robbers. 'I will be all right, Joan. But I am very hungry, might I have some breakfast?'

'Of course, sir.' Her face working with concern, she hurried away to the kitchen. I took a seat in the parlour and looked out at my sopping garden, strewn with leaves. It was not raining, but the sky was heavy with dark clouds. My eye was drawn to the wall at the far end where the Lincoln's Inn authorities had grubbed up an old orchard for replanting, remembering what Barak had told me. I had warned them in the summer that without trees to absorb the groundwater the bottom of the slope could flood. I should go and take a look.

My thoughts went back to Maleverer. He had allowed Rich to involve him in a plot against me, no doubt in return for help to get rebels' lands, and that had been his downfall. But what if that had been a side issue, what if he had been playing a double game? He had refused to accept that Jennet Marlin might not have stolen those papers, had insisted Radwinter was guilty of Broderick's death, and had allowed a pair of drunks to be appointed as his guards. I had taken it all for stupidity and obstinacy, but what if it had been something else? Where was he now, in London or on his way back to York? I thought, if I knew who appointed those guards . . .

Joan returned with eggs, bread and cheese. 'I am sorry to land you with such a full household,' I told her. 'But I promised old Master Wrenne he could stay here till he is fit for some family business he has to deal with, and Barak hurt his leg. Where are they, by the way?'

She sniffed. 'Went out early. Master Jack had some private business, he said, and Tamasin was to go to Whitehall to see if she still had a place. There is some trouble in the Queen's household.'

'So I hear,' I replied neutrally. The household would be dissolved now. Tamasin could be out of a job.

She paused, then said, 'I don't mind Master Wrenne, sir, poor sick old gentleman, but that girl. It's not right her being in the house with Jack. And she's a pert way with her, in her fine ladylike clothes — she may say she only wants to help with the old man but I think she likes having her feet under a gentleman's table.'

'She'll be gone soon, Joan,' I said wearily. 'The four of us need a few days' rest.'

'She's no morals. They think I don't hear her scurrying across to Master Jack's room at dead of night, but I do.'

'All right, Joan. I am too tired to deal with that now.'

She curtsied and went out.

I ate heartily. The meal over, I prowled the room restlessly. I thought of Maleverer and Sergeant Leacon, and Broderick swinging in his cell aboard ship. I thought of Tamasin; Barak would probably see his friend today, what would he find out about her father? I thought of Martin Dakin, and half resolved to go to Lincoln's Inn, but I was still too tired to face the prospect of seeing familiar people, nosy lawyers who might have heard about Fulford. It could wait until tomorrow, when with luck the manacle would be off. Perhaps Bealknap would be there, and I wondered if that rogue knew what had been done to me to save that case for him.

I decided to go and look at the old orchard. Putting on my boots, I walked down the garden. Everything was drenched, and at the far wall, by the gate to the orchard, the ground was quite waterlogged. I unlocked the gate and went through.

The apple orchard had probably been there centuries; the trees had been gnarled and very old. The orchard walls bounded Chancery

Lane on one side, the Lincoln's Inn grounds on two, and my garden on the fourth. The ground sloped gently down to my wall. The orchard was, as Barak had said, a sea of mud, dotted with waterlogged holes where tree roots had been grubbed up. Without the trees to absorb any of the water from the rains, a pool the size of a small house had built up against my wall. I cursed; if there was much more rain my garden could be flooded. I resolved to visit the Inn Treasurer on the morrow.

The sight of the devastated orchard unsettled me. I went back into my garden and headed for the stables. There I found Genesis and Sukey in their stalls, munching hay. Both looked up and neighed in greeting. I went and stroked Genesis. Looking into his dark eyes I thought of what it must have been like for the horses, driven two hundred miles through unknown countryside by strangers. Did they wonder, as I had in the Tower, whether they would ever see home again? I had a sudden memory of Oldroyd's huge horse charging through the mist at Tamasin and me, that misty morning two months before. That was where it had all started.

As I left the stable I felt raindrops on my face. I walked quickly round to the front door. There was someone standing in the porch, his back to me, a tall figure in a black coat. He was looking at the door as though uncertain whether to knock. My hand went to the dagger at my belt. I had worn it since it was returned to me at the Tower.

'Can I help you?' I asked sharply.

He turned round. It was Sergeant Leacon, in civilian clothes, a cap on his head instead of a helmet. His boyish face looked careworn. I saw he wore a sword, then thought, so do most men in London. He doffed his cap and bowed.

'Master Shardlake—' He broke off as he saw my face.

'Yes,' I said grimly. 'I have had a hard time in the Tower.'

'I heard you were released, sir. I got your address from Lincoln's Inn. Sir, I am sorry I had to detain you at the wharf. Those were my orders—'

'What do you want?'

'A word, sir, if I may.'

He seemed tired and crestfallen. I took pity on him. 'Come in, then.' I walked past him, opened the door, and led him into the parlour.

'Would you take off your sword, sergeant? Only I am wary of sharp blades just now.'

'Of course, sir.' He reddened as he hastily unbuckled his scabbard. I took it and stood it against the door.

'Now, sergeant, what may I do for you?'

'I – I have been discharged, sir. I am plain George Leacon now. For letting those men get drunk, they said, providing Broderick's killer with an opportunity.' He hesitated. 'I was told Master Radwinter took his life. In the Tower.'

'Yes, he did.'

'I was questioned yesterday, by Archbishop Cranmer himself.' I studied his face but he looked only dejected and exhausted. So Cranmer had not told him I was his informant.

'Yes?'

'He asked me how it came the guards were drunk.'

'What did you say?'

'That they were a pair of sots, sir, and drunks can always find liquor. They smuggled it aboard.'

'Who chose those men?' I asked quietly.

'The guard captain suggested them to Sir William, I think to get them off his hands, save trouble on the journey back. When Sir William gave me the names of those two, said they were to come on the boat, I objected. I told him they were not good men to choose.'

I frowned. 'Then why did he pick them?'

Leacon shrugged. 'He did not want to be seen to do the bidding of a mere sergeant. I believe it was poor judgement on his part.'

That phrase again. 'Poor judgement. Yet it is you that pays the price. You are made the scapegoat.'

'That was ever the way of things, sir. Sir William has paid a price too, though. I hear he has been stripped of his place on the Council of the North.'

'Tell me, do you think Radwinter killed Broderick?'

He looked puzzled. 'Who else could it have been? Radwinter became stranger and stranger in his mind as time went on.'

'Perhaps.' I looked at him, then asked quickly, 'Does the name Blaybourne mean anything to you? Or Braybourne?'

'Braybourne is a place in Kent, sir, some way from where I come from. Have you another land case there?' He looked puzzled, and a little concerned, as though the dishevelled figure before him might also be wandering in his mind.

'It is not important,' I said with a smile. 'Now, Master Leacon, why have you come to see me?'

'Sir, you may think it an impertinence, after I arrested you, but—'

'Your parents' land case. Of course.' I had forgotten all about it.

'They are in London. And now I am dismissed, I have no money for a lawyer.'

'I will see them. A promise is a promise. But I have been away two months, I need a few days to straighten my affairs. Bring your parents to my chambers next Wednesday. Have they their papers with them?'

'Yes, sir.' His face relaxed with relief. 'Thank you, sir. I knew you were a gentleman.'

I smiled wryly. 'I shall have had a shave before then, I will look more presentable.'

'I am grateful to you, Master Shardlake.'

'Here is your sword.' I looked out of the window. The rain was teeming down again. 'I fear you will have a wet journey back.'

I watched him walk down my path from the little window by the front door. Dutiful soldier, I thought, dutiful son. Surely Leacon had nothing to do with any of what had happened. But what of Maleverer? Bad judgement? Or had he shut Broderick's mouth to stop him naming him as connected to the conspiracy? Did he have the papers? Yet Maleverer could not have struck me down at King's Manor – he had been away.

I climbed the stairs again to Giles's room. He was asleep but as I came in he stirred and opened his eyes.

'I am sorry,' I said. 'Did I wake you?'

'I sleep too much.' He heaved himself into a sitting position. 'I shall get up for supper this evening.'

'Guy said you should have a few more days in bed.'

He laughed. 'I shall take root here.' He looked at me. 'You still look tired yourself.'

'I am. I have just had a visitor. Young Leacon. He seeks my help on a legal matter.'

Wrenne raised his eyebrows. 'After arresting you on the wharf? I would have sent him off with a flea in his ear.'

I sighed. 'I promised him help in York. And as I told him, a promise is a promise.'

'That is true,' he said emphatically. 'There is nothing more important.' He looked at me. 'Unless you are the King, who breaks them all the time.'

'Ay,' I answered inattentively.

'You seem preoccupied, Matthew.'

'I am sorry. Only I still wonder who really attacked me at King's Manor, and helped Broderick die. Who is it who has been scurrying and slipping through our midst all this time? And if the person was on the boat, he is in London now.'

'Do you think you could be in danger?' Giles asked.

I shook my head. 'No. If I was, something would have happened long before now.' I gave him a wry smile. 'I should forget about it. I have told Cranmer I want only to live quietly as a lawyer from now on.'

''Tis a sensible policy these days.'

'For the rest of my life. Barak feels the same.'

'A lawyer's life is a good one,' Wrenne said. 'I found it so.' He sighed deeply. 'But that is over, now I must find my nephew, make my dispositions. I shall go to Gray's Inn, perhaps not tomorrow but the next day.' He leaned back on his pillow and his eyes closed. I thought, he is still weak, is he fit even to go up Chancery Lane to Gray's Inn?

I thought again about Bernard Locke's strange words to me in the Tower. He had said Martin Dakin was no conspirator, and he was safe. But if he was not a conspirator, what had Locke meant by safe? I decided I would go to Gray's Inn tomorrow, seek Martin Dakin out.

Chapter Forty-six

B ARAK AND TAMASIN returned in the afternoon. Barak came to my room where I was resting. He looked exhausted.

'I haven't been able to lay hold of my mate on Cheapside,' he said. 'He's on a job out of town. He won't be back till tomorrow.'

I put a hand to my sore jaw. I must visit Guy soon, have it looked at. 'Not breaking into a house, I hope.'

'No. He's a locksmith, as it happens. Fitting locks for a new house in the country. Why d'you always assume all my contacts are criminals?'

'I am sorry.' I pulled back my sleeve, displaying the rusty manacle. 'I've put some grease on it to ease the chafing, but it stinks and makes my shirt messy. I won't feel properly free of the Tower till this thing is off.'

'I'll try him again tomorrow. I was told he would be back then.'

'Thank you.' I looked at his tired face, his wet hair. Outside it was still raining. 'Did Tamasin go to Whitehall?'

'Yes. She was told there were to be rearrangements in the Queen's household, she should go back in a few days.' He looked at me seriously. 'She is afraid to return, given that questions are being asked of the Queen's ladies.'

'Not the servants, like Tamasin?'

'No, but she fears it may come to that, considers it better just to melt away into the background. I think she's right.'

'But she will lose the chance of getting a job in the household. The best-paid work in the land for a servant.'

He shrugged. 'She's afraid, especially after seeing what they did to you. She'll find something else. And she still has a little of her grandmother's money left, she says.'

'That has lasted her well.'

'Ay.' He sighed. 'I spoke with my old mate.'

'Any luck?'

He frowned. 'Seems there's a possible candidate. I've got to go back tomorrow.'

'Who?'

'He wouldn't say. But I was told he is a professional man, whatever that might mean.' He broke off at a knock on the door. Tamasin came in.

'I am sorry you have lost your place, Tamasin,' I said gently.

'Yes.' She stood there, looking exhausted.

'Stay a few days longer,' I said. 'Both of you. Until – well, until things are clearer. Perhaps you may find work at court again.'

'When the Queen is dead?' She spoke in a bitter tone I had never heard. 'Perhaps to be a servant in the household of a new Queen, watching to see how long she will last, what secrets I may accidentally hear that could get me into trouble?' She shook her head emphatically. 'No, I will never go back to work there, whatever they pay.'

'All right, Tammy,' Barak said, but she went on.

'They say at Whitehall Lady Rochford has gone mad in the Tower, screams and raves and can make no sensible answer. The poor Queen is held at Hampton Court, Jesu knows what state she is in. Still, a woman must smile and be cheerful, must she not?' She twisted her face into a parody of a girlish smile, then turned and ran from the room.

†

THAT EVENING Giles and I dined quietly in the parlour, listening to the rain buffeting down outside. Barak had been with Tamasin in her room all afternoon. Joan's face had been sour but I was past caring.

It was Giles's first meal out of bed and he seemed better. I told him about the state of the orchard and he agreed I ought to go to the

Inn Treasurer the next day. 'Otherwise they will say you did not give them proper notice if your garden does flood.' He smiled. 'You know what lawyers are like.'

'You are right. I want them to dig a trench halfway down that slope, to catch the water. It should be done now, this rain seems never-ending.' I sighed. 'And it is time I showed my face.'

✝

NEXT MORNING I rose early and, after breakfast, made ready to walk to Lincoln's Inn. Tamasin and Barak had gone out together, Tamasin to look for a room, Barak to find the lockpicker – and to find out about Tamasin's father. It had stopped raining for now but there were pools of water everywhere in Chancery Lane, and slippery clumps of wet leaves in the muddy roadway. I picked my way along carefully. There was a cold wind too; winter was truly begun. There was a barber in Chancery Lane and I decided to take advantage of his services first, to make myself look presentable. I sat in his chair, conscious of that damned manacle still on my wrist, which I did my best to hide under my sleeve. His conversation was of the strange doings at Hampton Court. Rumours were flying around now, that the Queen had been arrested, that she had been found to be a spy, or in bed with everyone from a scullery boy to Cranmer himself. The barber retold these gems of gossip with relish. ''Tis like the days of Anne Bullen again,' he said cheerfully. I told him I was sure it was all untrue, then went on to Lincoln's Inn.

It felt strange to pass under the Great Gate again, to see the solid red-brick buildings of Gatehouse Court, the barristers passing to and fro. Acquaintances nodded to me as I made my way to the Treasurer's office, but I was eager to press on and conclude my business. As the Treasurer disclaimed all responsibility for the flood at first, I sharply reminded him of the laws of nuisance and before I left I had the promise that a trench would be dug on the morrow. I returned to my chambers feeling slightly more cheerful.

Two solicitors were passing by; they paused and eyed me

curiously. I frowned; my hand was in the pocket of my robe, the manacle well hidden.

My clerk Skelly was busy at his desk. He greeted me with a genuine enthusiasm that disarmed me, his eyes shining behind his glasses. 'I have prayed for you, sir,' he said. 'Out among those wild heathens. And now you are returned to us. But your face is swollen, sir.'

'A bad tooth,' I said. And indeed it was throbbing again. So at least rumours about my imprisonment had not reached Lincoln's Inn. They would soon enough, though. 'How is the work?' I asked. I had parcelled my cases out among barristers I knew and trusted to deal with while I was away.

'No real problems, sir. Brother Hennessy won in *Re. Cropper* last week.'

'Did he? Good.' I paused. 'I have heard there have been officials from the Privy Council at the Inns, making enquiries to do with the spring conspiracy.'

'Not here, sir.' He wrinkled his nose. 'Maybe up at Gray's Inn.'

☩

IT WAS EARLY AFTERNOON before I brought myself up to date. Yes, I thought, there is enough business here for me to pick up and be quite busy. And the payment Cranmer had promised would mean I could clear the debt on my father's estate. There was a letter waiting from the mortgagee asking when he would be paid, and I wrote a terse reply saying he would not have to wait long. Then I went over to the dining hall for lunch.

I had decided I would walk up to Gray's Inn that afternoon, and over my meal I thought more about Martin Dakin. What if he spurned the idea of mending his quarrel with Giles, as he might, given what family quarrels can be like. Again I wondered if my concern for the old man was linked to my guilty feeling that I had let my father down. But no, I thought, this is the only right thing to do.

As I walked to the gate I saw Bealknap approaching from his chambers. I wondered if he had seen me from his window. 'Brother Shardlake!' He greeted me cheerfully. 'I hear you have had some adventures since we last met – some trouble with His Majesty at York, was it not? And a sojourn in the Tower.' His eyes went to my right hand, where the damned manacle had slipped down and was visible. 'Goodness me,' he said mildly.

'My time in the Tower is not generally known about yet. Richard Rich told you, no doubt. He had me put there.'

'Your face is swollen, Master Shardlake,' Bealknap said with fake concern. I had a sudden memory of the torture chamber, the crack as the tooth was broken off, the terror. I blinked, then glared at my opponent. His eyes slid away from meeting mine.

'You know the Guildhall have settled your case,' he said with that gentle smile of his. 'Each side pays their own costs. Doubtless you will have a large bill for the Guildhall. Mine is being defrayed by the Court of Augmentations.'

'By Rich.'

'By the court. Because of their interest in the case. Well, it has been an interesting result.' He removed his cap, made a mocking, exaggerated bow and walked on.

'Next time it will be a fair fight,' I shouted after him. 'And I will beat you! I will best you yet, Bealknap!' He did not turn.

✟

I WALKED UP Chancery Lane to Gray's Inn, just the other side of Holborn. The rain still held off although the sky was grey and heavy. I asked for Garden Court at the porter's lodge and was directed to a building on the other side of the courtyard. As I walked across, looking at the barristers going to and fro, I thought that Bernard Locke's contact, the one he was to give the papers to, could be here – unless he had been taken. I went through the door and found myself in an outer office, where a plump little clerk looked up from his desk.

'Good afternoon,' I said. 'Matthew Shardlake, from Lincoln's Inn. I am seeking a brother who works in Garden Chambers. Martin Dakin.'

The clerk sat upright. 'Oh,' he said. He looked surprised, then flustered.

'You know the name?'

'Yes, sir, but . . .' He got up slowly, his eyes still on my face. 'If you would wait a moment, perhaps you should speak to Brother Philips. Excuse me.'

He went across to a door, knocked and went in. I stood waiting. Anxiety clawed at me. The clerk had looked startled, concerned. Has Dakin been taken in for questioning, I wondered. I looked around the room, its tables piled with papers tied up in pink ribbon. This was where Bernard Locke had practised too. I remembered that last sight of him in the Tower, his broken limbs and burned face, and shivered.

The clerk reappeared in the doorway. 'Brother Philips would like a word, sir.' He stood aside to let me enter, looking relieved to be passing me on.

Inside a room very like my own, a plump middle-aged barrister had risen from behind a desk. He looked exhausted, dark circles under his eyes. He bowed, then looked at me with an expression of concern.

'Brother Ralph Philips,' he said. His accent revealed him as a man of the north.

'Brother Matthew Shardlake, of Lincoln's Inn.'

'You are seeking Brother Martin Dakin?'

'Yes.'

'Do not think me impertinent, sir, but – might I ask your connection?'

'I am a friend of his uncle, Brother Giles Wrenne of York. He fell out with his nephew years ago, and has come to London to put things right. I have been with the Progress in York. Brother Wrenne came back with me, he is at my house in Chancery Lane.' I paused. 'He is aged, and not well.'

'Ah.' Brother Philips sighed heavily.

'What has happened?' I asked, more sharply than I should. 'Has he been taken for questioning about the northern conspiracy? I know there have been enquiries among the lawyers.'

He gave me a keen look. 'Yes, they have been here. We have all been questioned.' He sighed again. 'But no one has anything to hide, and certainly not Brother Dakin.' He smiled, a strange sad smile.

'Then what?'

'Martin Dakin is dead, sir. He died the winter before last, from a congestion of the lungs.'

'Oh no,' I breathed. 'Oh no, that is too hard.' All Giles's efforts, all his hopes, the journey that had taken such a toll on him. All for nothing.

'Are you all right, sir?' Brother Philips came round his desk, looking concerned.

'Yes. Forgive me. It was a shock. I had not expected . . .' So that was what Locke had meant, in the Tower. Martin Dakin was safe because he was dead. And he had been using the past tense to refer to Dakin, not himself. I stifled a groan. Then a ray of hope struck me. 'Had he a wife, any children?'

'I fear not.' Brother Philips shook his head. 'He had no relatives I knew of, and I never heard mention of an uncle.'

'They had fallen out.' I looked at him. 'So he had no one.'

'Not that I know of. The Inn Treasurer took charge of his belongings when he died.' He hesitated. 'I should say, sir, Brother Dakin and I were not close.'

'No.'

Brother Philips hesitated. 'He was a very strong reformer, brother, and not many in these chambers are.'

'But I thought he was an arch-conservative.'

'He was once. But he was won over by the evangelical preaching at a local church.' Brother Philips smiled sadly again. 'Many who were hot for one side have turned and became equally hot for the other. It has happened much these last few years.'

'Yes, it has.'

'But Brother Dakin was a good lawyer, and an honest man.'

I nodded dumbly.

'The Inn Treasurer would have made enquiries, seen to the disposition of his estate. If you enquire there . . .'

'Yes. Yes, perhaps I should.'

'Can I offer you some wine before you go, brother?' He still looked concerned. 'I see you have had a shock, perhaps you should sit down.'

'No. No, I will go to the Treasurer. Thank you, brother, thank you for your help.' I bowed and took my leave.

What an irony, I thought. A reformer, the last person to want any connections to the northern conspiracy.

†

THERE WAS A BENCH under a tree nearby. The wood was wet but I sat there nonetheless. Poor Wrenne, this would be a dreadful blow for him. I was glad, though, that I had come to Gray's Inn; at least I could break the news gently to him, at home. I looked up as a big man in a lawyer's robe passed by. Black beard, black hair. Surely it was Maleverer. Then the man's features settled into those of a different, older man. He gave me a puzzled look and hurried inside.

A drop of water landing on my hand brought me back to myself. The rain again. I got up. The wretched manacle was chafing at my wrist still. I rubbed it and checked to make sure the thing was out of sight, then enquired of a passing clerk where the Treasurer's rooms might be found. I made my way across to them, doused yet again by pelting rain.

The Treasurer was a tall, stooped man, suspicious of a barrister from another chambers come making enquiries. When I explained my mission, though, he became sympathetic and invited me into his comfortable rooms.

'I am wary of all enquiries about members of the Inn these days,' he told me.

'Ah yes. The enquiries about the conspirators.'

'Many barristers have been questioned in recent days. Robert Aske practised here, you know. God rot him and all these malcontents. Inns are for practising law, not conspiring against the King.'

He led me through into an office where an elderly man sat working through papers. 'Brother Gibbs would have dealt with the matter. He is retired from practice, but helps me out.'

The old fellow rose and bowed, peering at me from behind thick-lensed spectacles. He looked almost as ancient as Brother Swann from Hull.

'Brother Shardlake here is trying to trace relatives of a Brother Martin Dakin,' the Treasurer told him. 'He died the winter before last. He had no wife or children.'

The old man nodded sagely. 'Ah yes, I remember. The Inn administered the estate. Yes, it is sad when a brother dies without family. But he *did* have a relative, as I recall.'

'He did?' I said eagerly. I thought, even some bastard child would be better than nothing.

The old man put a finger to his chin. 'Yes, yes he had. I think so.'

I controlled my impatience as Brother Gibbs began ferreting through a pile of papers on a shelf.

'I will leave you, sir,' the Treasurer said.

'Yes, yes, thank you. I am obliged.'

I turned to find Brother Gibbs holding up a packet of papers and smiling. 'Here it is.' He pulled out a will. 'Martin Dakin, died the tenth of January 1540. At his request all his possessions were sold, and the proceeds, together with his savings – a goodly sum, I see –' he scanned the will – 'yes, he left fifty pounds to St Giles' church in Cripplegate.' He looked at me over his spectacles, disapproval on his face. 'A *very* reforming church. Some say heretical.'

'Yes, yes. And the rest?'

'All to a single legatee.'

'Who?'

'See for yourself, sir.'

The old man handed me the will. I read the name of the legatee. My mouth fell open with shock.

'This legatee claimed the property?'

'Oh yes.' The old man frowned. 'All was done properly.'

'I am sure it was.'

And now I knew, I knew it all. Who had knocked me out at St Mary's, who had helped Broderick to die. And the identity of the one who now held the documents that could topple the throne.

Chapter Forty-seven

THE RAIN WAS LASHING down harder than ever, and I had to bend my head to stop the water running from my cap into my eyes as I walked back up Chancery Lane. When I left the Treasurer's office I had returned to Lincoln's Inn and gone to the library. I had sat there for hours, thinking, puzzling, while the short November afternoon deepened to dusk and lamps were lit along the tables. In the end I believed I had worked it all out. And then there was nothing left but to go home.

It was quite dark as I walked down Chancery Lane with a heavy heart. Flickering squares of candlelight from house windows were reflected in puddles whose surfaces danced with raindrops. I pulled my coat tight about me, the wretched manacle digging into the raw wet skin of my wrist.

I stumbled through my front door, dripping onto the rush matting. Joan was crossing the hall; she turned to look at me, shading her lamp. 'Master Shardlake! You are soaked, sir! What rain, I fear what may be happening out in that orchard. Let me find you some clean clothes—'

'No,' I said, pulling off my sodden cap. I leaned against the door for a moment, breathing hard. 'I am all right. Are Jack and Mistress Reedbourne in?'

'Not yet, sir.' She sniffed. 'They said they would be back before dark, but I'll warrant she's made him find some warm tavern to cuddle in.'

'Oh.' I was taken aback; I had assumed they would have

returned by now, that they would be here. I had been preparing what I would say.

'Master Wrenne came down a little while ago,' Joan said. 'He asked for some food. I've taken him a pottage in the parlour.'

I hesitated. The sensible thing to do would be to go upstairs and change. Then I shivered, suddenly and violently.

'Are you all right?' Joan asked, her face full of concern.

'Just – tired.'

'There is a good fire lit in the parlour.'

'I can dry myself there.' I forced a smile. 'And I am hungry. Thank you, Joan.'

She looked at me doubtfully a moment longer, then went upstairs. I locked the front door; Barak had his own key and could let himself back in. I crossed to the parlour. I paused there, overcome with a weariness that seemed to drain what little energy I had left. Then I took a deep breath and opened the door.

Giles was sitting at the table, supping Joan's good pottage. A large bowl steamed on the table. In the candlelight his face looked tired, seamed with deeper lines as his face grew slowly thinner. He looked up at me with concern.

'Matthew! You look half drowned. You will catch an ague.'

'The rain has come on heavy again.'

'I know. Will it never end?' He gestured to the black squares of the window, against which we could hear it pattering. 'I think Barak and young Tamasin are still out in it.'

I went and stood with my back to the roaring fire, feeling it warm my legs.

'Did you speak to them at Lincoln's Inn?' he asked. 'Will they dig the trench?'

'Yes, it took some argument but they promised.'

'There is steam rising from your clothes. You should change. You look exhausted, you will catch a fever.'

'I must eat before I do anything else.'

'Here, have some pottage.'

I took a plate from the buffet, filled it from the bowl and sat opposite him. But after all I did not feel like eating. 'Are you feeling better?' I asked.

'Yes.' He smiled, that sad heavy smile. 'It comes and goes, just as with my father. For now I feel almost my old self, except for . . .' He patted the place where his lump grew, and grimaced. I nodded. 'Is there any more news about the Queen?' he asked.

'She is taken.'

He shook his big head sadly. I looked at him. I needed Barak and Tamasin back, Barak at least, before I spoke. Yet somehow I could not hold back. 'I took it on myself to walk to Gray's Inn, Giles. I wanted to seek out Martin Dakin.'

Giles stopped with the spoon halfway to his mouth. 'You should not have done that,' he said slowly. 'Without my permission.'

'It was to help you.'

'Did you find him?'

'I found he died near two years ago.'

He laid down his spoon. 'Dead?' he whispered. He sat back in his chair. His shoulders slumped and his face sagged. 'Martin is dead?'

And then I said quietly, 'I think you know he is. I think you knew before I came to York. I remember you saying once a good lawyer needs to be a good actor. I think you have been acting since the day we met.'

He frowned, then looked outraged. 'How can you say such a thing, Matthew? How——'

'I will tell you. I went to Dakin's old chambers. They told me he died from an illness two winters ago. Wifeless and childless. They said I should go to the Treasurer, who dealt with his estate. So I did, and found he had left everything to you. His money was sent to you in York, and you signed a receipt for it in March of 1540, eighteen months ago. I saw it.'

'Some imposter——'

'No. I saw the signature. It was yours; I saw it enough times when we were dealing with the petitions. Come, Giles,' I added impatiently. 'I have been a lawyer near twenty years. Do you think I would not know a forged hand?'

He stared at me, a fierce look in his eyes I had never seen before. 'Matthew,' he said, a tremor in his voice, 'you are my good friend but you wound me. It is the strain of your time in the Tower. This is some imposter, someone got hold of the Inns' letter and pretended to be me. I remember, I had a clerk then I had to dismiss for dishonesty. From a distance of two hundred miles it is easy to pretend to be someone you are not.'

'To hide your true identity. Yes, you would know.'

He did not reply then, only sat very still, looking at me intently. He started to play with the big emerald ring on his finger. A drop of water ran down my neck, making me shiver. He was right, I risked a fever. The crackling of the fire and the hissing of the rain against the window seemed unnaturally loud. I thought I heard the outside door open, but it was only a creak somewhere in the house. Where were Barak and Tamasin?

'I went from the Treasurer's office to the Lincoln's Inn library,' I continued. 'I have been there hours. Working it out.'

Still he did not speak.

'You invented the story of wishing to reconcile with Martin Dakin to get me to help you to London. Was there ever a quarrel between you? There must have been,' I answered myself, 'for old Madge knew of it, though not that Martin had died and left you his estate.'

'We were never reconciled,' he said quietly then. 'What I told you about our quarrel was true. Despite it he left me everything when he died. I was his only living relative, you see. Family. How important it is.' He sighed, a sigh that seemed to come from the depths of his big frame. 'I did not tell Madge that Martin had died and left me everything, nor anyone else in York. I was too ashamed.' He looked at me. 'And yet that served me well; I could tell you he was still alive, no one else knew otherwise.'

I said, still speaking slowly and quietly, 'The question puzzling me was, why did you want to come to London, now when you knew you were dying? It had to be something very important. Then I remembered when it was you first mentioned coming here. It was after I was knocked out at King's Manor. It was you who knocked me out, was it not? You took the papers. To bring to your fellow conspirators in London.'

Still he said nothing, only continued staring at me. I had had a strange notion that when I confronted him Giles's face would change, take on some monstrous aspect, but it was still my friend's lined strong old face that looked back at me; only more watchful and somehow more vulnerable than I had ever seen it before.

'That day you rescued Barak and me from the mob outside Oldroyd's house, had you come to fetch the box?' I laughed bitterly. 'It must have been a shock when it fell out from under my robe. You hid that well, as you have hidden so much since.'

He spoke then. 'I did rescue you. Do not forget that as you judge me.'

'And meanwhile, Mistress Jennet Marlin was on a mission of her own, from Bernard Locke, that you had not known about. So when you found that out at Howlme beacon, you killed her before she could reveal that it was not she who had taken the papers.'

'I saved you from her too.'

'For your own ends. You always had the papers she sought, no doubt you have them still. In my house.'

Giles sighed then, a sigh that seemed to shake his big body from head to toe. 'I always saw you as a friend, Matthew,' he said quietly. 'It grieved me to lie to you and I would never have hurt you. I never intended to kill you at King's Manor, only knock you out, and I never harmed you afterwards, though I could have, many times. I took a gamble that you spoke true when you said you had not read the papers. I – it wasn't—'

'It wasn't personal, is that it? The using me, all the lies. Not personal, just political, as you said the King's mockery of me was?'

'I have hated it all, I hated killing that woman.' He shuddered slightly. 'I spoke true when I said I never killed anyone in my life.'

'And Broderick, what about him?'

'I helped Sir Edward Broderick kill himself because he wanted to die. He would have died a far worse death in the Tower, as we both know. No, that I do not regret. I knew him from the conspiracy, of which I was an important part. Do you remember when he was led out to the wharf in Hull, in chains? He looked towards us and nodded. You thought he was nodding at you, but it was me he recognized. That nod was enough. I knew he had tried to kill himself at York and I decided then I would help him. I waited night after night for an opportunity on that ship, and when it came I took it. I knocked Radwinter out, took his keys and helped Broderick hang himself. It was a terrible thing to do, but he was resolute.' He straightened his shoulders. 'He was a fine man, a brave man.'

'Yes, he was,' I said, then frowned. 'But you were ill on the boat, all the time.'

He smiled sadly. 'You know my condition comes and goes. I pretended to appear frailer than I actually felt on the journey.'

'Jesu, how you have deceived me,' I said quietly.

'I owed Sir Edward my help. He held out under terrible torture, to keep secret certain matters that affected me.'

'So he knew all along.' I paused. 'The secret of your true identity.'

There was silence for a long moment. The rain drove violently against the window. Come on, Barak, I thought.

'So what do you know about me, Matthew?' Giles asked at length.

'What I managed to work out this afternoon, as I tried to puzzle out what made you lie to me, assault me and betray me. The key to everything has always been Edward Blaybourne's confession. Did you meet old Brother Swann, in the library in Hull? He told me of the old legend that Blaybourne was the real father of King Edward IV.'

His eyes widened. 'I thought all who remembered the old rumours must be dead by now.'

'He was very old indeed. I did not tell you, for I feared it would be dangerous for you to know.' I laughed bitterly. 'But of course you knew already, better than anyone.'

Giles sat up, and now I saw something fierce spark in his blue eyes. 'The truth is dangerous for *you* to know, Matthew. Believe me, and ask no more questions. Stop while you can. Let me walk out of your house, now. You will never see me again.'

'It is too late for that.'

He sat back, his mouth tightening as I went on.

'I remembered Howlme, your parents' grave. I am blessed with a good memory, Giles, blessed or cursed. The name of your father, whom you told me you resemble, was Edward. Born in 1421, from his gravestone. Near fifty when you were born, you said you were the child of his old age. He would have been old enough to sire a son in 1442, when King Edward IV was born. I think Edward Blaybourne was your father.'

Giles answered simply. 'Yes, he was. King Edward IV was my much older half-brother. Henry VIII is my great-nephew. When I saw him at Fulford, saw the evil in his face, smelt his foul smell, I knew he was the Mouldwarp and it made me sick to think that creature was of my blood. This false King, whose grandsire was the son of an archer.'

'When did you first know?'

'I will tell you, Matthew.' He still spoke quietly, though his eyes burned. 'Perhaps then you will understand and forgive my abuse of your friendship. Understand that what I have done was right.'

'Tell me, then.' My voice came cold and sharp.

'My childhood was happy, as I told you that evening by Howlme church. I knew my father had come to the district many years before

I was born. I imagine then he was a man much like young Leacon. Tall and strong, fair and comely. He would never say where he came from, only that it was far beyond Yorkshire. I never gave thought to the possibility that our name, Wrenne, might have been assumed.'

'That is easy to do, take a new name in a new place.'

'Shortly after he came to Howlme and bought the farm, my father married a local woman. They were childless and when they were in their forties she died of consumption. There is much of it in those marshes. A year later he married my mother. I was their only child.' He took a bread roll and began kneading it between his big fingers. 'When I was sixteen I went to London to study law. At Christmas of the following year I came home to visit. That was in 1485. Four months previously the future father of King Henry VIII had beaten Richard III at Bosworth and taken the throne as Henry VII.

'I found my father on his deathbed.' For a second his voice faltered. 'He told me he had first felt a lump in his side the year before, and had gradually become iller and weaker.' His hand went, unconsciously, to his own side. 'He had been to a physician who told him there was nothing to do but prepare for death. I wished he had told me earlier but I think, like your father, he did not want to disturb my new life far away in London.

'I remember the night he called me to his sickbed. He was near the end then, his big strong body half melted away. The road I am following him down now.' He looked at the remains of the little loaf, almost crumbled away. 'It was a still night, snow thick on the ground, everything silent. He told me he had a secret, a secret he had kept hidden over forty years. He wanted to dictate a confession. Shall I tell you what it says?' As he spoke Wrenne's hand went to his doublet, touching his pocket. I made out something there. He saw my glance and his expression hardened.

'Yes,' I said. 'Tell me.'

'It relates he was born Edward Blaybourne, the son of a poor family of Braybourne in Kent. Like many such boys he went into the King's service as an archer. Those were the last years of the French wars, Joan of Arc had been burned and all France had risen against us. My father was sent to garrison duty in the town of Rouen in the year 1441. The Duke of York, who was leading the campaign, was away fighting, and my father joined the guard in attendance upon the duchess.'

'Cecily Neville.'

'Yes. The duchess was young, lonely, afraid in a strange and hostile country. She befriended him and one night he ended in her bed. One night, that was all it was, but enough for her to fall pregnant. When she found out she decided to say the child was her husband's; she would pretend it had been conceived before the duke went away and when it was born she would say it was overdue. The duchess could have had him killed but instead she sent him away, with enough money to start a new life, coins in a decorated jewelbox—'

'The box—'

'Yes. And an emerald ring she used to wear.' He raised his hand. 'My father always kept it and he gave it to me that night. I have worn it ever since.'

He paused. I heard the rain hammering down, harder than ever, as though it would force a way through the walls. 'Why did Cecily Neville not produce your father as evidence when she confessed to what else she had done in 1483?'

'She had no idea where he was. My father did not hear the news until months later.' He sighed again. 'That winter night my father was in an agony of soul. All his life he had felt he had committed a terrible sin, been responsible for a man taking the throne who had no right to be King. He hid his feelings well under a hearty veneer, as I have learned to do. But when his son King Edward died and Richard III seized the throne he was overjoyed, for Richard was the true son of Cecily Neville and Richard Duke of York, entitled to the succession by virtue of the blood royal. But then Richard was overthrown and Henry Tudor seized the throne. He had only the thinnest stream of royal blood and he married Edward IV's daughter to strengthen it. You remember the family tree?'

'Yes. Elizabeth of York that married Henry VII, and is the mother of Henry VIII, was in truth the granddaughter of Edward Blaybourne.'

'My niece. And the Princes in the Tower were my nephews, not King Richard's. So by an irony of fate Henry VII had not strengthened his family's claim, but weakened it beyond measure. That sore afflicted my father. He felt his dreadful illness was a punishment by God.' Wrenne took a deep breath. 'He made me swear that night, on the Holy Bible, that if ever a right time came to use his confession to bring the true line back to the throne, I would use it.'

'Yet you have waited fifty years.'

'Yes!' He spoke with sudden passion, leaning forward. 'Yes, I did nothing, I watched as the Tudors ruined Yorkshire. Watched as the present King, the Mouldwarp as he truly is, stole the lands and positions of the old Yorkshire families, replacing them with common rogues like Maleverer. Watched as he destroyed the monasteries, perverted our faith, stood by as the enclosers took the people's land. Stood by, in the early years at least, because *I did not believe my father's story*!'

He spoke with fierce passion and I saw that he felt a guilt about his father far worse than anything I felt about mine.

'I could not believe so fantastic a tale at first. But I set myself to seek out the truth, to trawl in old and forbidden papers to find if it *could* be true. It took me years, years of ferreting out old books, manuscripts, pictures. Some of them forbidden.'

'So that was how you became an antiquary and built that astonishing library.'

'Yes, and found I loved the work for its own sake so that in the end it became a pastime rather than what should have been, a mission. It was hard, the Tudors hid traces of the Yorkist legacy well.'

'They knew all along, though, didn't they? The King knows he has no right to the throne.'

'Oh, yes. The King and his father have always known that. But no doubt they convinced themselves they were each entitled to keep it. Those who have power do not give it up readily. And *such* power this King has.' He was silent for a moment, then resumed in a quieter tone.

'Years I worked away at it, years. I went to Braybourne, visited the grave of my grandparents, heard the local people speak in the same accent as my father. But it was a decade before I found a copy of the *Titulus*, in a chest of discarded papers at York Minster. Then I found a painting of Cecily Neville, in one of Lord Percy's houses. I bought it, though it cost a year's fees. It is hidden in my library. It shows her sitting at a table, with the jewelbox before her, the jewelbox my father kept to the end of his days and that Maleverer has now. And wearing this ring.' He held up his hand, the emerald glinting. 'Then I began making visits to London. I found, as you did in Hull, people who remembered Cecily Neville declaiming after Edward IV died that he was the son of an archer and that Richard III, not King Edward's young son, was the true King. I had to be very careful, it was nearer in time to the event then, but gold loosens tongues and eventually I had a number of depositions written down.' His hand went unconsciously to his doublet again. 'In time I had enough evidence. Perhaps it is as well my wife and I had no children, or I would not have been able to afford my bribes, my purchases of papers and pictures.'

'Yet you have left me your library. Or was that another falsehood to secure my friendship?'

He winced. 'No, I have left it to you and it is out of affection. Others will have removed the dangerous things before it comes to you.'

'Before it comes to me. I will still be alive, then. I thought perhaps you plan to kill me now.'

His eyes bored into mine. 'I want you on our side, Matthew. I feel you are on our side already. I have seen that you know the King for what he is, feel for the cruel things he has done to the north, to all England.'

'Why did you wait so long, Giles?'

He sighed. 'Yes, many more years went by and I did nothing, content with my life. But those were the quiet years, before the King married the witch Anne Boleyn and prohibited religion itself while we were taxed and oppressed more each year. Public opinion loved the King before then. To reveal what I knew would have brought punishment and death, not popular support. And I wondered, had I the right to threaten the throne when England was at peace? I did not want bloodshed. My father had said to act if a right time came, and this was not it.' His face clouded. 'Or was I just lazy, content in my prosperous middle age? Perhaps I needed to be looking my own death in the face before I found my courage.'

'Then the north rose in rebellion. The Pilgrimage of Grace.'

'Yes. And still I did nothing. To my shame. I thought the rebels would win, you see. I thought the King's power would be broken and I could reveal the truth afterwards, when it would be safe. Back in 1536, as you know, the King promised negotiation. But then he broke his word, and sent an army to the north with fire and sword. You saw yourself what he did to Robert Aske. Cromwell's informers and servants came to run the Council of the North and supervise the destruction of our monasteries, selling their lands to London merchants who take the rents to the capital, leaving Yorkshire to starve. It was then I decided to act at last, reveal my knowledge to others. When my illness began, and I had nothing to lose. I screwed up my courage, my resolution.'

'So you joined the conspirators.'

'Yes. I made certain contacts in York, told them my secret, showed them the papers. They were ready at last to overthrow the King. Royal spies were everywhere and it was agreed I would keep silent until Yorkshire had risen and was ready with the Scots to march south. Then the truth of King Henry's ancestry would be cast in his face to confound him. The papers were handed over to Master Oldroyd, to keep them safe and to bind me irrevocably to the conspirators.'

'But the conspiracy was betrayed.'

'There was an informer, yes. We do not know who. And after the leaders were taken someone must have been tortured into revealing that a cache of papers proving Edward Blaybourne was Edward IV's father existed. But whoever talked did not know my identity. And why should anyone suspect a respectable old lawyer? But Broderick knew. It was he who came to me and told me to bring the papers to London, try to make contact with sympathizers there. He didn't have names, but I had to look at Gray's Inn.'

'Now he is dead.'

'There are others in London. I will find them before I die. *That* is my final task.'

'You must have lived in constant fear that Broderick would talk.'

'I knew what manner of man he was. Far braver than me. I knew it would take the utmost torture to make him talk. It was my duty to help him die. I am not ashamed; you should be more ashamed of helping keep him alive against his will. I was deeply shocked when you told me Cranmer gave you that task.'

'Perhaps you were right to be,' I said slowly.

Wrenne's keen eyes narrowed. He leaned back in his chair. 'That is my tale, Matthew. I regret nothing. Believe me, though, when I say I never meant to kill you at King's Manor. Only knock you out, as I did Radwinter. Sometimes one must do unpalatable deeds for a higher end. I hated deceiving you. Sometimes it brought me to tears.'

Another shiver ran through me, followed by a hot flush. I felt sweat on my brow. I was catching a fever.

'But it was for a higher end,' I repeated. 'The overthrow of the King.'

'You have seen him. You have seen Yorkshire. You know he is the Mouldwarp, the Great Tyrant, cruelty and darkness personified.'

A heavy splash of rain from outside, as a gutter flooded over, made me start.

'Yes,' I agreed. 'He is a monster.' I rubbed at my wrist, where the manacle was chafing again.

'And no rightful King, a pretender to the throne as his father was. He does not have the royal blood that God ordains for Kings.'

'A few drops from the Tudor side. But none from the House of York, no. There too you are right.'

He patted his pocket. 'I have the papers here. Tomorrow I take them into town. I will find the men I seek. I will have those papers printed and posted all over London. With the arrest of the Queen there will be more discontent. What better time could there be to start a new rebellion?'

'Your last chance.'

'Come with me, Matthew, be a part of it. A part of the new dawn.'

'No,' I said quietly.

'Remember how he mocked you at Fulford. A casual piece of cruelty that people will gossip about behind their hands for the rest of your life.'

'There is far more than my feelings at stake. Whom would you make King in Henry's place?' I asked quietly. 'The only Clarence left, if she still lives, is a female child. And the law is not even clear a female can inherit. The people will not rally to a little girl.'

'We shall offer a regency to the next living Clarence. Cardinal Pole.'

'A papist bishop?'

'The Pope would let him renounce his office to take the throne. Come with me, Matthew,' he said intently. 'Let us destroy these brutes and vultures.'

'And Cranmer?'

'The fire,' he said with certainty.

'No,' I told him again.

For a moment he looked deflated, then a calculating look came into his eyes. I thought, what will he do? This was why I had wanted Barak back; to provide force if it was needed to keep Giles Wrenne here.

'You are still a reformist at heart?' he asked. 'You oppose the restoration of true religion?'

'No. I am beyond allegiance to either side, I have seen too much of both. I oppose you because your belief in the rightness of your cause blinds you to the reality of what would happen. I doubt your rebellion would succeed but whether or not it did there would be bloodshed, anarchy, protestant south against papist north. Women left widows, children orphans, lands laid waste. The Striving of the Roses come again.' I shook my head. 'Papists and reformers, you are so alike. You think you have a holy truth and that if the state is run by its principles all men will become happy and good. It is a delusion. It is always men like Maleverer who benefit from such upheavals while poor men still cry out to heaven for justice.'

'We shall have true faith back again,' he said with a sudden cold fierceness. 'True faith and a rightful monarch.'

'And the fire for Cranmer. And how many more? Even if you win you will create a mirror-image of the world we have, perhaps a worse one.'

'I should have realized.' Wrenne sighed deeply. 'You are not a man of faith. But knowing the King is not of royal blood, does that count for nothing with you?' His tone was almost pleading.

'Not enough to countenance drowning England in fire and blood, no. Not enough for that.'

'Then let me go quietly. I will not trouble you again. I will leave you to your peaceful life.' There was angry bitterness in his voice now.

'If you give me the papers,' I said, 'I will let you walk free.'

He leaned back in his seat, casting his eyes down. He seemed to be reflecting. But I knew he would never give up the documents, not having come so far.

He looked at me again, his eyes still fierce though his voice was quiet. 'Do not make me do this, Matthew. I cannot give you the papers. It has taken me so long—'

'I will not join you.'

Then in a movement I had been half-expecting, but more speedily than I could have imagined him capable of, Wrenne leaped up, grasped the bowl of pottage and threw it in my face. A terrible growling noise came from his throat, fury and sorrow somehow mixed together. I cried out, jumping up. Half-blind, I grabbed at Giles but he twisted away and tumbled out of the door. I heard his heavy footsteps as he went out to the hall in a sort of shambling run, then a curse as he hauled uselessly at the locked front door. He turned again, gasping as he ran for the door to the garden. I felt a gust of cold air as it was thrown open.

I stepped into the hall. The garden door yawned wide, giving on to a blackness through which a curtain of rain fell. Apart from the rain there was silence. Joan must be asleep in her room at the front of the house. I stared out into the darkness and the hammering rain.

Chapter Forty-eight

L ITTLE WAS VISIBLE beyond the doorway, the light from the parlour window showing only the rain, still falling hard and straight as ever, and the dim shapes of bushes and trees. My face smarted, but the pottage had not really scalded me. It had been standing for some time and had cooled. My hand went to my dagger. I pulled it from my belt. I shivered again, violently.

'Giles!' I called out. 'You are trapped! There is no way out of the garden except the gate to the orchard, and the door from the orchard to Lincoln's Inn is locked at night! Surrender yourself, it is all you can do.' There was no reply, only the relentless sound of the lashing water.

'For pity's sake, man,' I called. 'Come out of the rain!'

I could wait, here in the doorway, till Barak returned. But what if Wrenne managed to climb the orchard wall? He was old and ill but he was also desperate. If he got away with those papers – I stepped outside.

It was hard to see. I kept to those parts of the garden where there was some illumination from the windows and the open door, watching lest he run at me out of the darkness. The rain appeared to be lessening at last but it was still hard to see and I stumbled and nearly fell against a bench. I walked to the back of the garden, feeling my boots squelch into mud as I approached the orchard gate – the water was now seeping under the wall, as I had feared. I saw the gate was open; large footprints in the mud showed that Giles had gone through. I saw the key was in the lock and pulled it out. Passing through, I locked the gate behind me, put the key in my pocket and stood with my back against it, inside the orchard. I began to shiver again.

Looking up, I caught a faint white glow of moonlight through the still-roiling clouds. Even so, I could see little in the orchard beyond a vista of black mud.

'Giles!' I called again. 'Giles! I am armed! You cannot escape!' I looked at the high walls separating the orchard from Lincoln's Inn. No, Wrenne could not scale those. He was in here with me, somewhere.

The clouds parted and the full moon appeared, showing a sea of undulating mud broken by the water-filled holes where the trees had been. Up against my wall there was now a pond thirty feet across, little ripples dancing in the moonlight. I squinted and stared out across the mud.

Then I thought I saw something move slightly. I leaned forward, staring at a dim shape in the mud by the pool. Holding the knife firmly, I began moving carefully towards it. My boots sank deep into the mud, making squelching sucking sounds. The shape did not move again. Had Wrenne collapsed here, the strain too much for him? I reached the figure and bent carefully, ready for a sudden spring. If I had to I would stab him. Then I gritted my teeth as I saw a surface of uneven bark and realized I was staring at a log half-buried in the mud.

He struck from somewhere behind me, his weight sending me tumbling to the ground and making me drop the dagger. I gasped as I hit the mud, the breath knocked from my body. A knee crunched into my back, then I felt Giles lean over to one side to grab the dagger. So he would kill me. I bucked and heaved to throw him off balance, and he toppled sideways. As I hauled myself to my feet I saw his bulky shape rising too, slowly, the knife gleaming in his hand. I could not see the expression on his face because it was black with mud, no more than a dark circle with two glinting eyes.

'For pity's sake, Giles,' I gasped, 'surrender the papers. We cannot end like this.'

'We must.' He stepped forward, his arms held wide, the knife glinting in his right hand. 'Unless you let me go. Please, Matthew, let me go.'

He thrust at me suddenly. I jumped aside and hit out with my manacled wrist. The iron caught him hard on the side of the head; he gasped and dropped the knife. I must have half stunned him for he reeled away, staggered into the margin of the pool and fell over with a splash. He hauled himself up and sat, a dark shape up to its waist in water. Then the moon vanished, leaving us once more in darkness, and the rain began pelting down again.

I threw myself at him before he had time to rise, gasping at the impact of the cold water. And now it was Giles who struggled and bucked underneath me, and he was starting to weaken, his resistance feeble as I put both hands round his neck and forced his head under the water. I knew only one of us could come out of that cursed swamp alive. I kept his head under, ignoring the horrible gasps and gurglings he made.

Giles's struggles ceased, he went limp. A ghastly sucking sound came as he breathed water into his lungs, a sound I still hear in dreams; there was a last frantic spasm and then he went limp as a rag doll. But I did not move; I realized I was weeping, warm water mingling with the cold on my cheeks. For minutes more I knelt there holding him fast, sobbing in the darkness as the rain lashed relentlessly down on me.

I do not know how long it was before I got shakily to my feet. I was trembling from head to toe, but I made myself bend down and turn Giles over so he lay face down. Then I put my hands under the water, lifted his sodden robe, and felt through his pockets. I found a purse, and a thick pack of papers wrapped in oilskin. I took them and staggered away, without looking back.

✝

BARAK AND TAMASIN returned an hour later, dripping wet for it was still raining. Tamasin looked upset, as though she had been crying. I was sitting by the fire in the parlour; I had banked it up with logs and sat stirring it with the poker, trembling and sweating for the fever had come on me properly now. They stared at me in horror, covered from head to foot in mud as I was, steam rising from my sodden clothes. They ran over to me.

'Sir!' Barak exclaimed. 'In God's name, what has happened?'

'Giles Wrenne is dead,' I said quietly. 'We were eating and he seemed to lose his senses, he ran outside calling for his nephew.' I looked directly into Tamasin's blue eyes; I had thought this story through carefully and the lie was to protect them as well as me. 'He ran into the orchard. I followed. I found him in that pool of water, almost a lake it is now. He must have collapsed and drowned.'

Tamasin's hand flew to her mouth. 'His mind gone too?'

'It must have been his illness, affecting his brain. I had to give him bad news this afternoon. His nephew Martin Dakin died two years ago.'

'The poor old man,' Tamasin whispered. How full of compassion she had always been, I realized – for Wrenne, for Jennet Marlin, for me under the copper beech in York.

'Where is he?' Barak asked.

'Still out there. He was too heavy to bring back, and I – I think I am unwell.' I heard my voice break.

'I'll go and look,' Barak told Tamasin. 'Wait here.'

She knelt by me, put a cool hand to my brow. 'You are burning up, sir. You must go to bed.'

'I will now. I am sorry, Tamasin.'

'What for?'

'How I have treated you sometimes.'

She smiled weakly. 'I deserved it by starting with that foolish trick.'

'Perhaps. I lost a friend tonight,' I added quietly.

She laid her other hand on mine, my manacled hand. 'It took us a long time to find Jack's locksmith. But he will come tomorrow morning with his tools, have you released from that horrible fetter.'

'Good. Good. Thank you.'

'Is Mistress Woode asleep?'

'Ay, Joan slept through it all. There is no need to disturb her.' I looked at her. 'You have been crying.'

'Jack has found my father, sir. He is a professional man, as Jack said. He is a cook in the royal kitchens. A man with a fine opinion of himself, Jack says. He does not want to know me.' She took a sobbing breath and bit her lip, but held back her tears.

'I am sorry, Tamasin.'

'It was a childish fantasy. It is better to know the truth.'

'Yes.' I thought of Giles. 'But lonely.'

We sat in silence a few minutes longer. Then Barak returned, shaking water from his hair. The look he gave me held calculation as well as concern.

'Can you leave us, Tammy?' he asked quietly.

She nodded and rose. 'Goodnight, sir,' she said quietly, and left the room. I looked at Barak. He drew my dagger from beneath his doublet and laid it on the table.

'I found this outside, by the pool.'

'It must have fallen from my belt.'

'The mud round where he lay was all churned up, as though there had been a struggle.' He knows, I thought; he has guessed it was no accident.

'His face was terrible, a wild desperate look on it.'

I was glad I had not seen that. I met Barak's gaze. 'We must tell the coroner of his death first thing tomorrow. There will be no doubt of the finding. He drowned.'

Barak looked at me, took a deep breath, and nodded slowly. The matter was closed.

'Tamasin says you found her father?'

'Ay. A cook. When I went to see him he railed at me, said he would deny all. He thought Tamasin was after his money.' He laughed grimly. 'A fine professional gentleman.'

'Poor Tamasin.'

'Ay. But I decided to tell her. Best to know the truth, is it not?'

I glanced at the dagger. 'Perhaps.'

'She will get over it. She's tough. That's one of the things I admire about her.'

'Families and claims of rank, by Jesu they cause much trouble, do they not?' I laughed bitterly, then shivered violently. Barak looked at me.

'You should come to bed. You look a sight.'

'All right. Help me up.'

As he stepped towards me I took the poker and stirred the fire, where a last fragment of paper had failed to burn. The flames took them, and the name of Edward Blaybourne disappeared for ever.

Epilogue

I STOOD AT the window of my room in the little inn, watching the sun rise. A hard frost had held the countryside in its grip for a week and as the blood-red orb appeared it turned the landscape first pink then white; the grass and the trees and the roof of the little church opposite all outlined in frost.

I wondered if Queen Catherine had watched the icy dawn from the Tower three days before, the morning of her beheading. Thomas Culpeper and Francis Dereham had been executed back in December but legal necessities had kept the Queen alive for two more months. They said in London she had been too weak with fear to mount the scaffold unaided; they had had to half carry her up the steps. Poor little creature, she must have been so cold, there on Tower Green with her head and neck bare, exposed for the executioner. Lady Rochford had followed her to the block; she had gone quite mad when she was arrested and the King had passed a law allowing insane persons to be executed. Yet the balladeers said that at the end Jane Rochford had composed herself and made a speech confessing a lifetime of faults and sins, standing bravely before the block from which the Queen's blood still dripped. It had been a long speech and the crowd had grown bored. I remembered her at York, that strange mixture of arrogance and fear. Poor woman, I thought. What drove her to weave those endless meshes of deceit which in the end could only trap her too? I hoped they had found peace now, she and the Queen.

✝

Barak and I had left London the day after the executions. It was a cold ride to Kent but fortunately the frost kept the roads dry and we reached Ashford by evening. We had spent the next day nosing through various archives, and I had been pleased to find evidence to back Sergeant Leacon's claim that his parents' land was indeed held under a valid freehold grant. I suspected the landlord had falsified a document somewhere, and I was looking forward to meeting the landlord's lawyer tomorrow in Ashford, along with young Leacon and his parents. That left a free day, which I had told Barak I needed for some private business. I had left him in Ashford the previous afternoon and ridden the ten miles to the village. A small, poor place like a hundred such hamlets in England; a few houses straggling along one street, an inn and a church.

I stepped quietly outside, pulling my coat around me tightly, or at least as tightly as I could for it was loose now; I had lost weight in the fever I had caught in November. I had spent three weeks in bed, delirious at first. When the fever subsided it had amused and touched me to see how Joan and Tamasin argued over who should bring my food.

It was bitterly cold. My breath steamed in front of me as I crossed to the little church and stepped round the side to the graveyard. My feet crunched in the frozen grass as I walked among the headstones, searching.

It was a small, poor stone, hidden right at the back and shaded by trees from a little wood behind. I bent and studied the faded, lichened inscription:

In memory of Giles Blaybourne

1390–1446

his wife Elizabeth

1395–1444

and their son Edward

died in the King's service in France, 1441

I stood there, lost in thought. I did not hear the light footsteps approaching, and jumped violently at the sound of a voice.

'So Edward Blaybourne gave his son his father's name. Giles.'

I turned to find Barak grinning at me.

'God's death,' I demanded, 'What are you doing here?'

'I guessed where you must have been going. It wasn't that difficult. Somewhere less than a day's ride from Ashford. It had to be Braybourne village. I left before sun-up this morning and rode down. Sukey is tied up behind the church.'

'You nearly gave me a seizure.'

'Sorry.' He looked around him. 'Not much of a place, is it?'

'No.' I looked at the gravestone. 'Poor Blaybourne's parents, they did not live long after their son disappeared. Cecily Neville must have had him declared dead.' The import of his words earlier suddenly struck me. 'Wait – you said – you know Giles Wrenne was Blaybourne's son?'

'I guessed. And there were some things you said, when you were delirious.'

My eyes widened. 'What things?'

'Once you shouted out that Wrenne was England's true King, and should be set on a great throne. Then you wept. Another time Tamasin said you were shouting out about papers that burned in Hell. I remembered you sitting poking at the fire when Tamasin and I came in that night, and put two and two together.'

I looked at him seriously. 'You know how dangerous that knowledge is.'

He shrugged. 'Without those papers, who can prove anything? You burned them all, didn't you?'

'Yes. I did not want to tell you, it is better no one else knows the truth.'

He nodded slowly, then looked at me again. 'You killed him, didn't you? Wrenne?'

I bit my lip and sighed deeply. 'It will haunt me till I die.'

'It was self-defence. There was no alternative.'

'No.' I sighed again. 'I held his head under the water until he drowned. Then I turned the body over so he lay face down and it would look as though he had fallen in and drowned himself. That was how you found him, Jack. With the great lump they found inside him, it was enough for the coroner.'

'Who was Wrenne going to give the papers to?'

'He was going to look for supporters of the conspiracy in London. Ironically his original contact was Bernard Locke.'

'I suppose there still are some conspirators in London.'

I shrugged. 'I suppose so. Perhaps the King in his foolishness and tyranny will create another opportunity for them to gain support. Perhaps not. Either way I want nothing to do with it.'

We stood looking in silence at the old gravestone. Then Barak asked, 'Why come here? Curiosity?'

I laughed sadly. 'When I recovered from my fever and learned Wrenne had been buried in London with none but you and Tamasin and Joan at his funeral, I had a crazed idea of having the body exhumed and burying him again down here. Guilt, I suppose.' I pointed at the gravestone. 'They were his grandparents, after all. And King Edward IV's,' I added.

'You owe him nothing,' Barak said.

'It was a crazed notion, as I said; perhaps I was still a little delirious.'

'You should feel no guilt over him.' Barak paused. 'Nor over your father.'

I nodded slowly. 'No. You are right. I have paid my father's mortgage, put a fine marble headstone over his grave. I shall visit it soon. But I see now that we were always distant, always apart. That was the way it was and there is no point in regretting it now.'

'No.'

'But I wanted to come here. To see. I still cannot quite come to terms with how Giles lied to me, tried to kill me at the end. But that is foolish, people betray each other all the time and for far lesser causes than he believed he had.'

'What will you do with his library?'

'I do not know.' We had found Wrenne's will with his possessions. No mention of his dead nephew, of course. He had bequeathed everything to Madge except the library, which he had left to me as he had promised. 'I do not want it. But there are certain things – a picture, perhaps some other items – that should be destroyed.' I looked at him. 'Will you do that? Go to York again for me, now the winter is ending? Madge plans to keep living in the house, her attorney's letter said.'

He made a face. 'Visit the damp demesne of York again? Eat her pottage? Only if I must.'

'After you have done that I think I will get in touch with Master Leland the antiquarian, see if there is anything he wants. I suppose you had better bring back the old lawbooks. Gray's Inn library could use those.' I smiled mirthlessly. 'There may be some old forgotten cases there that I can quote in court.'

'I might see Maleverer there. Now he has lost his place on the Council of the North I can thumb my nose at the arsehole.'

I laughed. 'That he would not like. I suspected him for a while, you know. But you were right, he was too stupid to plot anything. There was nothing behind that bluster of his, he was an empty vessel. Yes, thumb your nose if you see him.'

Barak looked at me. 'There is something I have been meaning to tell you. Now might be a good time.'

'Oh, yes?'

'I have asked Tamasin to marry me.'

'It did not take her too long to bring you round, then.'

'No.' He laughed. 'She has agreed.' He looked down, nudging a loose stone with his boot. 'And we were careless. It seems I may have a son myself before long.' He laughed again, embarrassed. 'Perhaps one day someone will make him king. He could start another reformation, bring England back to the faith of my Jewish ancestors.'

'That would be something.' I looked at him. 'You are sure it is what you want, this marriage?'

'Yes,' he said decidedly.

'You will suit each other well. Perhaps she will make you tidier in your habits when she is mistress of your home, and we shall have a neater office.'

'She can try.'

'Thank you for all you did,' I said quietly. 'At York and afterwards. You stayed steadfast and loyal, while I was unfair to Tamasin.'

''S all right.' He smiled. ''Tis time to settle down at last. Unless you grub up more adventures.'

'Never,' I said. 'Never again so long as I live. But I have grubbed up something else.'

'Oh?'

'Cranmer has written to me. I think he feels guilty for my time in the Tower, perhaps for cozening me into that job in York in the first place. He is a complicated man. I think the things he feels he must do bring him disquiet, in a way they never did to Thomas Cromwell. There is a vacancy for an advocate in the Court of Requests, and he has put my name forward. Things are changing again. The Duke of Norfolk has lost his place now Queen Catherine has fallen. His whole family are in disgrace. The reformers like Cranmer have access to patronage again. The pay could be better, but anyway it will suffice now I have paid off that damned mortgage on my father's farm. I will be working for common folk, ordinary people. I think I would like that.'

He smiled. 'No more arse-licking to rich clients.'

I laughed. 'No.'

'Then I'd like it too.'

I rubbed my hands together. 'Then shall we start with Sergeant Leacon, get his family their lands back?'

'Yes.' Barak extended his hand, and I shook it. Not all men betray, I thought. We turned away, leaving the true ancestors of our false King to their eternal rest.

HISTORICAL NOTE

The major political significance of Henry VIII's great Progress to the North of 1541 has been largely overlooked by historians, perhaps distracted by the wholly unexpected exposure just afterwards of Catherine Howard's liaison with Thomas Culpeper. In *Sovereign* I have followed David Starkey's interpretation of their relationship (*Six Wives*, 2003), that it probably went no further than flirtation. Cranmer was the key figure in Catherine's interrogation, and her downfall was a setback for the religious conservatives at Henry's court, especially her uncle the Duke of Norfolk. Henry's sixth wife, Catherine Parr, whom he married a year later, was a strong reformist.

I have made one alteration to historical fact: Thomas Howard Duke of Norfolk was in fact co-organizer of the Progress along with the Duke of Suffolk and was present in York. However, as he featured so prominently in the last Shardlake novel, *Dark Fire*, I thought it would overcomplicate the plot if I brought him back in a minor role here. While Henry VIII did seek petitions for justice along the route, I have invented the arbitrations in York.

The Progress was indeed beset by cold weather and unremitting rain in July, and calling it off was discussed. I have, however, invented the stormy weather of October 1541.

The north of England had never been fully reconciled to Tudor rule. Under pressure of changing trade patterns, falling wages and the enclosure movement, discontent grew in the early sixteenth century until the religious changes of the 1530s brought the commons of the doctrinally conservative region to rebel in October 1536. Within weeks, an army of perhaps 30,000 armed northerners was camped on the river Don, prepared to march south, collect support and remove Cromwell, Cranmer and Rich from the council.

Henry broke his promises to meet some of the rebels' demands if they disbanded, and ruthlessly suppressed fresh outbreaks of rebellion in 1537. Robert Aske and the other leaders of the Pilgrimage of Grace were executed. There are conflicting accounts on whether Robert Aske was hanged in chains and left to die at York Castle, or whether he was granted a speedier death. I think he was hanged in chains; for Henry VIII to keep his promise that Aske would be dead ere his head was struck off in such a macabre way seems to me exactly in tune with the King's character.

After 1536, the dissolution of the larger monasteries, which meant the seizure of their resources by the Crown and the remittance of rents and profits to London, together with the effects of heavy taxation in 1540–1, caused further economic distress and religious discontent. Anger can only have festered deeper in 1537–41, for all that things seemed quiet. The revived Council of the North in York, set up to maintain royal control there, would almost certainly have operated a network of informers. Sir William Maleverer is a fictional character, but I think he was probably not untypical. And in early 1541 a conspiracy was uncovered. It was planned by a group of gentry and ex-religious and was to start with a rising at Pontefract Fair in April. The limited evidence indicates that the 1541 rebels were prepared to go further than those of 1536 – the French ambassador Marillac reported to Philip V that they called the King a tyrant; surely this indicated they intended to dethrone him. Even more surprising and dangerous, Marillac reported that they were prepared to make an alliance with the still Catholic Scots. Northern English people looked on the Scots as uncivilized, dangerous barbarians (exactly the way the southern English looked on the northern English), and the conspirators' anger must have been desperate indeed to consider allying with the ancient enemy. There was no evidence of a link to conservative Gray's Inn lawyers in 1541, though there may have been one in 1536; I have revived this aspect for my plot.

The prospect of another army of northern rebels marching towards London, this time perhaps accompanied by the Scots, and perhaps even the Scots' allies the French, must have been the ultimate nightmare for the Henrician state. Foreign ambassadors reported in 1541 that the English rulers were even more alarmed than they had been in 1536. After the Pilgrimage of Grace, a Royal Progress to the North had been mooted, but the idea was shelved. Now it was quickly revived, and Henry's anxiety is indicated by the extraordinary speed with which the gigantic Progress was organized – it set out three months after the conspiracy was exposed. This was a remarkable feat, for not only was it at least three times the size of a normal Progress, not only did it travel much further than a royal Progress had since the 1480s, but it was an armed Progress, with a thousand soldiers accompanying the King and England's artillery shipped to Hull. Meanwhile, the heir of the alternative (and Catholic) royal line, the Countess of Salisbury, was butchered in the Tower without trial.

For details of how the Progress looked, sounded and smelt I have had to rely on the books cited below, and on my imagination, to flesh out the limited information provided by the French ambassador Marillac's reports and other records in the *Letters and Papers of the Reign of Henry VIII*. The portrayal of the supplication of the City of York at Fulford Cross is based on the official account in the York civic records.

What struck me forcefully, reading the state papers, were the many indications that the King and his advisers were frightened they might meet with hostility and even violence in the north. The organizers made certain that the gentry and city councillors who came to submit themselves along the way, both in the towns and in rural stopping-places, came in numbers limited by them. Henry's soldiers were always there.

This most political of Progresses was brilliantly choreographed. The local ruling classes would meet Henry and Queen Catherine along the way, make gifts to them, and those who had rebelled in 1536 would read long submissions begging forgiveness before taking fresh oaths of loyalty. Oaths were vitally important in Tudor times; those who swore knew for sure they had the King's forgiveness for the past, but equally that if they broke their oaths their fate would be terrible. And no doubt favours and positions were handed out behind the scenes. The attempt to bring James IV of Scotland into an English alliance failed, however; the following year a decade of aggressive warfare against Scotland began.

The ordinary people who had created the great army of 1536, and could have formed another in 1541, played no part other than as spectators. The whole strategy was based on the belief that if Henry could decisively win the loyalty of the northern elites, he would be safe. It worked; there were no more rebellions in Yorkshire in Tudor times. In 1541, however, given the prevailing mood in the north, I think there must have been some hostility to the Progress among the commons, and this is the mood I have portrayed in York; a sullen populace who, as the city records show, drove the council to their wits' end by refusing to lay sand and ashes before their doors to ease the King's passage through the streets.

The Blaybourne story, remarkable as it may seem, is founded on fact. There is evidence that Cecily Neville, mother of the Yorkist kings Edward IV and Richard III, claimed that Edward IV was not fathered by the Duke of York, and rumours at the French court identified the father as an English archer named Blaybourne. Michael K. Jones' *Bosworth 1485* (Tempus Publishing, 2002) relates the story, which was also told in a Channel 4 documentary, *Britain's Real Monarch* (2004). They traced the man who would be the rightful King today if Cecily spoke true, an amiable Australian sheep farmer (and republican) who would be King Michael I. I am not entirely convinced that Cecily Neville spoke the truth; I think there are flaws in some of Dr Jones' lines of argument, particularly on possible dates of conception for Edward IV. But it might be true. Certainly the story was known to Thomas Cromwell; the Spanish ambassador Chapuys asked him about it in 1535, perhaps to annoy him.

What is still true – astonishingly, in the twenty-first century – is that Queen Elizabeth II retains the title Henry VIII took for himself: Supreme Head of the Church of England, Defender of the Faith and – in theory at least – God's chosen representative in England.

ACKNOWLEDGEMENTS

I am very grateful to the staff of the libraries of York City Council, East Yorkshire and Lincolnshire County Councils, and the Universities of Sussex and London, for their help in locating research materials about the Progress of 1541. The Richard III Society, American Branch, enabled me to download the *Titulus Regulus* from their website. The highlights of a research trip to York were the remarkable re-creation of a late-fifteenth-century house at Barley Hall in the city centre, and the excellent and imaginative exhibition on St Mary's Abbey at the Yorkshire Museum. I am most grateful to Warwick Burton of York Walks for a very informative tour of King's Manor and for his help with subsequent queries, to Robert Edwards for driving me across the route of the Progress from York to Hull, to Rev. Nigel Stafford for showing me round the lovely old church at Howlme-on-Spalding Moor, and to Mrs Ann Los for sharing her information on Leconfield Castle. Andrew Belshaw kindly found Arnold Kellett's *The Yorkshire Dictionary* (Smith Settle, 2002) for me, which was very helpful on matters of dialect. Thanks also to Jeanette Howlett for taking me on a visit to the Sussex Working Horse Trust, where I learned much about the type of horses that moved the Progress across England; to Dr Jeremy Bending who kindly advised me about Wrenne's cancer, and to Mike Holmes who corrected my wildly inaccurate notions about what the sea journey would have been like. Needless to say, any errors in interpreting the wealth of helpful information I was given are my own.

More thanks – once again – to Roz Brody, Jan King, Mike Holmes and William Shaw for reading the book in draft, and to my indefatigable agent Antony Topping for his help and comments – and for the title. Thanks again to my editor Maria Rejt and to Mari Roberts for her copyediting; and to Frankie Lawrence for a mammoth bout of typing.

Select Bibliography

The only study of the 1541 conspiracy I have found is an article written by Geoffrey Dickens as long ago as 1938: A.G. Dickens, 'Sedition and Conspiracy in Yorkshire' (*Yorkshire Archaeological Journal*, vol. xxxiv, 1938–39). Michael K. Jones's book, cited above, was fascinating and thought-provoking on the Blaybourne legend. For the Catherine Howard story, Lacey Baldwin Smith's *A Tudor Tragedy* (Alden Press, 1961) remains the fullest account, with David Starkey's *Six Wives: The Queens of Henry VIII* (Vintage, 2004) giving an interesting modern perspective.

R.W. Hoyle and J.B. Ramsdale's article 'The Royal Progress of 1541, the North of England, and Anglo-Scottish Relations, 1534–42', in *Northern History*, XLI:2 (September 2004) is useful on the politics of the Progress, though I think it seriously underestimates the centrality of the conspiracy in Henry's journey north. For details of what the Tudor court on Progress might have been like I am indebted to Simon Thurley's *The Royal Palaces of Tudor England* (Yale University Press, 1993) and David Loades's *The Tudor Court* (Barnes & Noble, 1987). Dairmaid Mac-Culloch's *Thomas Cranmer: A Life* (Yale University Press, 1996) helped in my attempts to get the measure of that most complex of men. For both the conspiracy and the Progress the ambassadorial reports in the *Letters and Papers, Foreign and Domestic, of the Reign of Henry VIII*, vol. XVI provide material that is fascinating but frustratingly limited.

R.W. Hoyle's *The Pilgrimage of Grace and the Politics of the 1530s* (OUP, 2001) and Geoffrey Moorcock's *The Pilgrimage of Grace* (Weidenfeld & Nicholson, 2002) were both very useful. Moorcock tells the story of the Mouldwarp legend.

D.M. Palliser's *Tudor York* (OUP, 2002) was a mine of information on the city. Christopher Wilson & Janet Burton's well-illustrated *St Mary's Abbey* (Yorkshire Museum, 1988) was very helpful on the layout of the monastic precinct. There is still debate in York about whether Henry stayed at King's Manor when he was there. I think he did; it makes obvious logistic sense. The idea that the hundreds of workmen known to be present and building tents and pavilions were building a scaled-down version of those used at the Field of the Cloth of Gold is mine, but it fits with the limited evidence in the *Letters and Papers*. And there was no time to build anything more substantial; they had less than two months to get there and complete everything.

The song welcoming the King to York in Chapter 16 will not be found in any book on Tudor music; I made it up. I hope it has an authentic ring.

DISCOVER MORE OUTSTANDING BOOKS
BY C. J. SANSOM

Available from Viking

Winter in Madrid
A Novel

In September 1940, the Spanish Civil War is over and Madrid lies in ruins while the Germans continue their march through Europe. Into this uncertain world comes Harry Brett, a privileged young man recently traumatized by his experience in Dunkirk and now a reluctant spy for the British Secret Service. Sent to gain the confidence of an old school friend turned shadowy businessman, Brett finds himself involved in a dangerous game . . .

"A compelling tale . . . If you like Sebastian Faulks and Carlos Ruiz Zafón, you'll love this." —*Daily Express*
ISBN 978-0-670-01848-2

The Matthew Shardlake Mystery Series—Available from Penguin

Dissolution

Exciting and elegantly written, *Dissolution* is an utterly compelling debut novel and a riveting portrayal of Tudor England. The year is 1537, and the country is divided between those faithful to the Catholic Church and those loyal to Henry VIII and the newly established Church of England. When a royal commissioner is brutally murdered in a monastery on the south coast of England, the formidable vicar general Thomas Cromwell summons lawyer Matthew Shardlake to lead the inquiry. Shardlake and his young protégé uncover evidence of sexual misconduct, embezzlement, and treason, and when two other murders are committed, they must move quickly to prevent the killer from striking again. ISBN 978-0-14-200430-2

Dark Fire

In the second novel in the series, hunchback lawyer Matthew Shardlake is asked to help a young girl accused of murder. She refuses to speak in her defense even when threatened with torture. But just when the case seems lost, Thomas Cromwell, Henry VIII's feared vicar general, offers Shardlake two more weeks to prove his client's innocence. In exchange, Shardlake must find a lost cache of "Dark Fire," a legendary weapon of mass destruction. What ensues is a page-turning adventure, filled with period detail and history. ISBN 978-0-14-303643-2